Henry James

Henry James OM (15 April 1843 – 28 February 1916) was an American-British author regarded as a key transitional figure between literary realism and literary modernism, and is considered by many to be among the greatest novelists in the English language. He was the son of Henry James Sr. and the brother of renowned philosopher and psychologist William James and diarist Alice James.

He is best known for a number of novels dealing with the social and marital interplay between émigré Americans, English people, and continental Europeans. Examples of such novels include The Portrait of a Lady, The Ambassadors, and The Wings of the Dove. His later works were increasingly experimental. In describing the internal states of mind and social dynamics of his characters, James often made use of a style in which ambiguous or contradictory motives and impressions were overlaid or juxtaposed in the discussion of a character's psyche.(Source: Wikipedia)

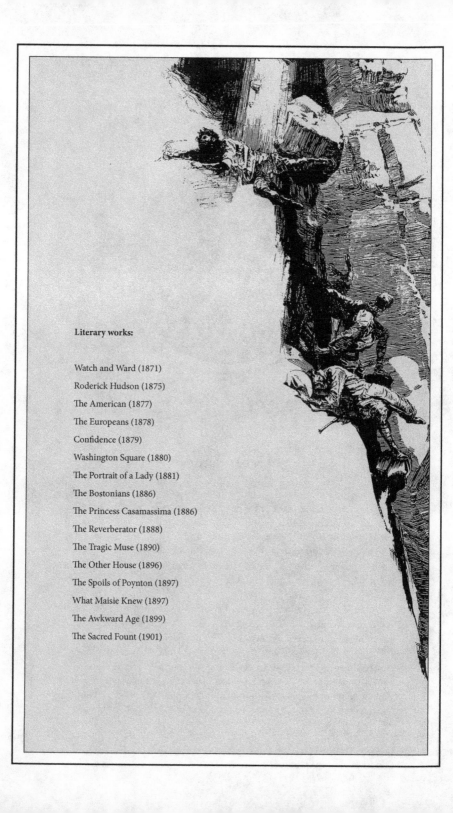

Literary works:

Watch and Ward (1871)

Roderick Hudson (1875)

The American (1877)

The Europeans (1878)

Confidence (1879)

Washington Square (1880)

The Portrait of a Lady (1881)

The Bostonians (1886)

The Princess Casamassima (1886)

The Reverberator (1888)

The Tragic Muse (1890)

The Other House (1896)

The Spoils of Poynton (1897)

What Maisie Knew (1897)

The Awkward Age (1899)

The Sacred Fount (1901)

THE
WORKS
OF
HENRY JAMES

VOL. 33 (OF 36)

THE TRAGIC MUSE
THE TURN OF THE SCREW

An Imprint of Moon Classics LLC

A Wholly Owned Subsidiary of Queenior LLC

A Melodragon Company

First Printing: 2020

ISBN 978-1-6627-1612-6 (Paperback)

ISBN 978-1-6627-1613-3 (Hardcover)

Published by Moon Classics

www.moonclassics.com

Contents

THE
WORKS
OF
HENRY JAMES
VOL. 33 (OF 36)

THE TRAGIC MUSE

PREFACE

I profess a certain vagueness of remembrance in respect to the origin and growth of *The Tragic Muse*, which appeared in the *Atlantic Monthly* again, beginning January 1889 and running on, inordinately, several months beyond its proper twelve. If it be ever of interest and profit to put one's finger on the productive germ of a work of art, and if in fact a lucid account of any such work involves that prime identification, I can but look on the present fiction as a poor fatherless and motherless, a sort of unregistered and unacknowledged birth. I fail to recover my precious first moment of consciousness of the idea to which it was to give form; to recognise in it—as I like to do in general—the effect of some particular sharp impression or concussion. I call such remembered glimmers always precious, because without them comes no clear vision of what one may have intended, and without that vision no straight measure of what one may have succeeded in doing. What I make out from furthest back is that I must have had from still further back, must in fact practically have always had, the happy thought of some dramatic picture of the "artist-life" and of the difficult terms on which it is at the best secured and enjoyed, the general question of its having to be not altogether easily paid for. To "do something about art"—art, that is, as a human complication and a social stumbling-block—must have been for me early a good deal of a nursed intention, the conflict between art and "the world" striking me thus betimes as one of the half-dozen great primary motives. I remember even having taken for granted with this fond inveteracy that no one of these pregnant themes was likely to prove under the test more full of matter. This being the case, meanwhile, what would all experience have done but enrich one's conviction?—since if, on the one hand, I had gained a more and more intimate view of the nature of art and the conditions therewith imposed, so the world was a conception that clearly required, and that would for ever continue to take, any amount of filling-in. The happy and fruitful truth, at all events, was that there was opposition—why there *should* be was another matter—and that the opposition would beget an infinity of situations. What had doubtless occurred in fact, moreover, was that just this question of the essence and the reasons of the opposition had shown itself to demand the light of experience; so that to the growth of experience, truly, the treatment of the subject had yielded. It had waited for that advantage.

Yet I continue to see experience giving me its jog mainly in the form of an invitation from the gentle editor of the *Atlantic*, the late Thomas Bailey Aldrich, to contribute to his pages a serial that should run through the year. That friendly appeal becomes thus the most definite statement I can make of the "genesis" of the book; though from the moment of its reaching me everything else in the matter seems to live again. What lives not least, to be quite candid, is the fact that I was to see this production make a virtual end, for the time, as by its sinister effect—though for reasons still obscure to me—of the pleasant old custom of the "running" of the novel. Not for many years was I to feel the practice, for my benefit, confidingly revive. The influence of *The Tragic Muse* was thus exactly other than what I had all earnestly (if of course privately enough) invoked for it, and I remember well the particular chill, at last, of the sense of my having launched it in a great grey void from which no echo or message whatever would come back. None, in the event, ever came, and as I now read the book over I find the circumstance make, in its name, for a special tenderness of charity; even for that finer consideration hanging in the parental breast about the maimed or slighted, the disfigured or defeated, the unlucky or unlikely child—with this hapless small mortal thought of further as somehow "compromising." I am thus able to take the thing as having quite wittingly and undisturbedly existed for itself alone, and to liken it to some aromatic bag of gathered herbs of which the string has never been loosed; or, better still, to some jar of potpourri, shaped and overfigured and polished, but of which the lid, never lifted, has provided for the intense accumulation of the fragrance within. The consistent, the sustained, preserved *tone* of *The Tragic Muse*, its constant and doubtless rather fine-drawn truth to its particular sought pitch and accent, are, critically speaking, its principal merit—the inner harmony that I perhaps presumptuously permit myself to compare to an unevaporated scent.

After which indeed I may well be summoned to say what I mean, in such a business, by an appreciable "tone" and how I can justify my claim to it—a demonstration that will await us later. Suffice it just here that I find the latent historic clue in my hand again with the easy recall of my prompt grasp of such a chance to make a story about art. *There* was my subject this time—all mature with having long waited, and with the blest dignity that my original perception of its value was quite lost in the mists of youth. I must long have carried in my head the notion of a young man who should amid difficulty— the difficulties being the story—have abandoned "public life" for the zealous pursuit of some supposedly minor craft; just as, evidently, there had hovered before me some possible picture (but all comic and ironic) of one of the most salient London "social" passions, the unappeasable curiosity for the things of the theatre; for every one of them, that is, except the drama itself, and for the "personality" of the performer (almost any performer quite sufficiently serving) in particular. This latter, verily, had struck me as an aspect appealing mainly to satiric treatment; the only adequate or effective treatment, I had again and again felt, for most of the distinctively social aspects of London: the general artlessly histrionised air of things caused so many examples to spring from behind any hedge. What came up, however, at once, for my own stretched canvas, was that it would have to be ample, give me really space to turn round, and that a single illustrative case might easily be meagre fare. The young man who should "chuck" admired politics, and of course some other admired object with them, would be all very well; but he wouldn't be enough—therefore what should one say to some other young man who would chuck something and somebody else, admired in their way too?

There need never, at the worst, be any difficulty about the things advantageously chuckable for art; the question is all but of choosing them in the heap. Yet were I to represent a struggle—an interesting one, indispensably—with the passions of the theatre (as a profession, or at least as an absorption) I should have to place the theatre in another light than the satiric. This, however, would by good luck be perfectly possible too— without a sacrifice of truth; and I should doubtless even be able to make my theatric case as important as I might desire it. It seemed clear that I needed big cases—small ones would practically give my central idea away; and I make out now my still labouring under the illusion that the case of the sacrifice for art *can* ever be, with truth, with taste, with discretion involved, apparently and showily "big." I daresay it glimmered upon me even then that the very sharpest difficulty of the victim of the conflict I should seek to represent, and the very highest interest of his predicament, dwell deep in the fact that his repudiation of the great obvious, great moral or functional or useful character, shall just have to consent to resemble a surrender for absolutely nothing. Those characters are all large and expansive, seated and established and endowed; whereas the most charming truth about the preference for art is that to parade abroad so thoroughly inward and so naturally embarrassed a matter is to falsify and vulgarise it; that as a preference attended with the honours of publicity it is indeed nowhere; that in fact, under the rule of its sincerity, its only honours are those of contradiction, concentration and a seemingly deplorable indifference to everything but itself. Nothing can well figure as less "big," in an honest thesis, than a marked instance of somebody's willingness to pass mainly for an ass. Of these things I must, I say, have been in strictness aware; what I perhaps failed of was to note that if a certain romantic glamour (even that of mere eccentricity or of a fine perversity) may be flung over the act of exchange of a "career" for the esthetic life in general, the prose and the modesty of the matter yet come in with any exhibition of the particular branch of esthetics selected. Then it is that the attitude of hero or heroine may look too much—for the romantic effect—like a low crouching over proved trifles. Art indeed has in our day taken on so many honours and emoluments that the recognition of its importance is more than a custom, has become on occasion almost a fury: the line is drawn—especially in the English world—only at the importance of heeding what it may mean.

The more I turn my pieces over, at any rate, the more I now see I must have found in them, and I remember how, once well in presence of my three typical examples, my fear of too ample a canvas quite dropped. The only question was that if I had marked my political case, from so far back, for "a story by itself," and then marked my theatrical case for another, the joining together of these interests, originally seen as separate, might, all disgracefully, betray the seam, show for mechanical and superficial. A story was a story, a picture a picture, and I had a mortal horror of two stories, two pictures, in one. The reason of this was the clearest—my subject was immediately, under that disadvantage, so cheated of its indispensable centre as to become of no more use for expressing a main intention than a wheel without a hub is of use for moving a cart. It was a fact, apparently, that one *had* on occasion seen two pictures in one; were there not for instance certain sublime Tintorettos at Venice, a measureless Crucifixion in especial, which showed without loss of authority half-a-dozen actions separately taking place? Yes, that might be, but there had surely been nevertheless a mighty pictorial fusion, so that the virtue of composition had somehow thereby come all mysteriously to its own. Of course the affair would be simple enough if composition could be kept out of the question; yet by what art or process, what bars and bolts, what unmuzzled dogs and pointed guns, perform that feat? I had to know myself utterly inapt for any such valour and recognise that, to make it possible, sundry things should have begun for me much further back than I had felt them even in their dawn. A picture without composition slights its most precious chance for beauty, and is, moreover, not composed at all unless the painter knows *how* that principle of health and safety, working as an absolutely premeditated art, has prevailed. There may in its absence be life, incontestably, as *The Newcomes* has life, as *Les Trois Mousquetaires*, as Tolstoi's *Peace and War*, have it; but what do such large, loose, baggy monsters, with their queer elements of the accidental and the arbitrary, artistically *mean*? We have heard it maintained, we well remember, that such things are "superior to art"; but we understand least of all what *that* may mean, and we look in vain for the artist, the divine explanatory genius, who will come to our aid and tell us. There is life and life, and as waste is only life sacrificed and thereby prevented from "counting," I delight in a deep-breathing economy and an organic form. My business was accordingly to "go in" for complete pictorial fusion, some such common interest between my two first notions as would, in spite of their birth under quite different stars, do them no violence at all.

I recall with this confirmed infatuation of retrospect that through the mild perceptions I here glance at there struck for *The Tragic Muse* the first hour of a season of no small subjective felicity; lighted mainly, I seem to see, by a wide west window that, high aloft, looked over near and far London sunsets, a half-grey, half-flushed expanse of London life. The production of the thing, which yet took a good many months, lives for me again all contemporaneously in that full projection, upon my very table, of the good fog-filtered Kensington mornings; which had a way indeed of seeing the sunset in and which at the very last are merged to memory in a different and a sharper pressure, that of an hotel bedroom in Paris during the autumn of 1889, with the Exposition du Centenaire about to end—and my long story, through the usual difficulties, as well. The usual difficulties—and I fairly cherish the record as some adventurer in another line may hug the sense of his inveterate habit of just saving in time the neck he ever undiscourageably risks—were those bequeathed as a particular vice of the artistic spirit, against which vigilance had been destined from the first to exert itself in vain, and the effect of which was that again and again, perversely, incurably, the centre of my structure would insist on placing itself *not*, so to speak, in the middle. It mattered little that the reader with the idea or the suspicion of a structural centre is the rarest of friends and of critics—a bird, it would seem, as merely fabled as the phoenix: the terminational terror was none the less certain to break in and my work threaten to masquerade for me as an active figure condemned to the disgrace of legs too short, ever so much too short, for its body. I urge myself to the candid confession that in very few of my productions, to my eye, *has* the organic centre succeeded in getting into proper position.

Time after time, then, has the precious waistband or girdle, studded and buckled and placed for brave outward show, practically worked itself, and in spite of desperate remonstrance, or in other words essential counterplotting, to a point perilously near the knees—perilously I mean for the freedom of these parts. In several of my compositions this displacement has so succeeded, at the crisis, in defying and resisting me, has appeared so fraught with probable dishonour, that I still turn upon them, in spite of the greater or less success of final dissimulation, a rueful and wondering eye. These productions have in fact, if I may be so bold about it, specious and spurious centres altogether, to make up for the failure of the true. As to which in my list they are, however, that is another business, not on any terms to be made known. Such at least would seem my resolution so far as I have thus proceeded. Of any attention ever arrested by the pages forming the object of this reference that rigour of discrimination has wholly and consistently failed, I gather, to constitute a part. In which fact there is perhaps after all a rough justice—since the infirmity I speak of, for example, has been always but the direct and immediate fruit of a positive excess of foresight, the overdone desire to provide for future need and lay up heavenly treasure against the demands of my climax. If the art of the drama, as a great French master of it has said, is above all the art of preparations, that is true only to a less extent of the art of the novel, and true exactly in the degree in which the art of the particular novel comes near that of the drama. The first half of a fiction insists ever on figuring to me as the stage or theatre for the second half, and I have in general given so much space to making the theatre propitious that my halves have too often proved strangely unequal. Thereby has arisen with grim regularity the question of artfully, of consummately masking the fault and conferring on the false quantity the brave appearance of the true.

But I am far from pretending that these desperations of ingenuity have not—as through seeming *most* of the very essence of the problem—their exasperated charm; so far from it that my particular supreme predicament in the Paris hotel, after an undue primary leakage of time, no doubt, over at the great river-spanning museum of the Champ de Mars and the Trocadero, fairly takes on to me now the tender grace of a day that is dead. Re-reading the last chapters of *The Tragic Muse* I catch again the very odour of Paris, which comes up in the rich rumble of the Rue de la Paix—with which my room itself, for that matter, seems impregnated—and which hangs for reminiscence about the embarrassed effort to "finish," not ignobly, within my already exceeded limits; an effort prolonged each day to those late afternoon hours during which the tone of the terrible city seemed to deepen about one to an effect strangely composed at once of the auspicious and the fatal. The "plot" of Paris thickened at such hours beyond any other plot in the world, I think; but there one sat meanwhile with another, on one's hands, absolutely requiring precedence. Not the least imperative of one's conditions was thus that one should have really, should have finely and (given one's scale) concisely treated one's subject, in spite of there being so much of the confounded irreducible quantity still to treat. If I spoke just now, however, of the "exasperated" charm of supreme difficulty, that is because the challenge of economic representation so easily becomes, in any of the arts, intensely interesting to meet. To put all that is possible of one's idea into a form and compass that will contain and express it only by delicate adjustments and an exquisite chemistry, so that there will at the end be neither a drop of one's liquor left nor a hair's breadth of the rim of one's glass to spare—every artist will remember how often that sort of necessity has carried with it its particular inspiration. Therein lies the secret of the appeal, to his mind, of the successfully *foreshortened* thing, where representation is arrived at, as I have already elsewhere had occasion to urge, not by the addition of items (a light that has for its attendant shadow a possible dryness) but by the art of figuring synthetically, a compactness into which the imagination may cut thick, as into the rich density of wedding-cake. The moral of all which indeed, I fear, is, perhaps too trivially, but that the "thick," the false, the dissembling second half of the work before me, associated throughout with the effort to weight my dramatic values as heavily as might be, since they had to be so few, presents that effort as at the very last a quite convulsive, yet in its way highly agreeable, spasm. Of such mild prodigies is the "history" of any specific creative effort composed!

But I have got too much out of the "old" Kensington light of twenty years ago—a lingering oblique ray of which, to-day surely quite extinct, played for a benediction over my canvas. From the moment I made out, at my high-perched west window, my lucky title, that is from the moment Miriam Rooth herself had given it me, so this young woman had given me with it her own position in the book, and so that in turn had given me my precious unity, to which no more than Miriam was either Nick Dormer or Peter Sherringham to be sacrificed. Much of the interest of the matter was immediately, therefore, in working out the detail of that unity and—always entrancing range of questions—the order, the reason, the relation, of presented aspects. With three *general* aspects, that of Miriam's case, that of Nick's and that of Sherringham's, there was work in plenty cut out; since happy as it might be to say, "My several actions beautifully become one," the point of the affair would be in *showing* them beautifully become so—without which showing foul failure hovered and pounced. Well, the pleasure of handling an action (or, otherwise expressed, of a "story") is at the worst, for a storyteller, immense, and the interest of such a question as for example keeping Nick Dormer's story his and yet making it also and all effectively in a large part Peter Sherringham's, of keeping Sherringham's his and yet making it in its high degree his kinsman's too, and Miriam Rooth's into the bargain; just as Miriam Rooth's is by the same token quite operatively his and Nick's, and just as that of each of the young men, by an equal logic, is very contributively hers—the interest of such a question, I say, is ever so considerably the interest of the system on which the whole thing is done. I see to-day that it was but half a system to say, "Oh Miriam, a case herself, is the *link* between the two other cases"; that device was to ask for as much help as it gave and to require a good deal more application than it announced on the surface. The sense of a system saves the painter from the baseness of the *arbitrary* stroke, the touch without its reason, but as payment for that service the process insists on being kept impeccably the right one.

These are intimate truths indeed, of which the charm mainly comes out but on experiment and in practice; yet I like to have it well before me here that, after all, *The Tragic Muse* makes it not easy to say which of the situations concerned in it predominates and rules. What has become in that imperfect order, accordingly, of the famous centre of one's subject? It is surely not in Nick's consciousness—since why, if it be, are we treated to such an intolerable dose of Sherringham's? It can't be in Sherringham's—we have for that altogether an excess of Nick's. How, on the other hand, can it be in Miriam's, given that we have no direct exhibition of hers whatever, that we get at it all inferentially and inductively, seeing it only through a more or less bewildered interpretation of it by others. The emphasis is all on an absolutely objective Miriam, and, this affirmed, how—with such an amount of exposed subjectivity all round her—can so dense a medium be a centre? Such questions as those go straight—thanks to which they are, I profess, delightful; going straight they are of the sort that makes answers possible. Miriam *is* central then to analysis, in spite of being objective; central in virtue of the fact that the whole thing has visibly, from the first, to get itself done in dramatic, or at least in scenic conditions—though scenic conditions which are as near an approach to the dramatic as the novel may permit itself and which have this in common with the latter, that they move in the light of *alternation*. This imposes a consistency other than that of the novel at its loosest, and, for one's subject, a different view and a different placing of the centre. The charm of the scenic consistency, the consistency of the multiplication of *aspects*, that of making them amusingly various, had haunted the author of *The Tragic Muse* from far back, and he was in due course to yield to it all luxuriously, too luxuriously perhaps, in *The Awkward Age*, as will doubtless with the extension of these remarks be complacently shown.

To put himself at any rate as much as possible under the protection of it had been ever his practice (he had notably done so in *The Princess Casamassima*, so frankly panoramic and processional); and in what case could this protection have had more price than in the one before us? No character in a play (any play not a mere monologue) has, for the right expression of the thing, a *usurping* consciousness; the consciousness of others is exhibited exactly in the same way as that of the "hero"; the prodigious consciousness of Hamlet, the most capacious and most crowded, the moral presence the most asserted, in the whole range of fiction, only takes its turn with that of the other agents of the story, no matter how occasional these may be. It is left, in other words, to answer for itself equally with theirs: wherefore (by a parity of reasoning if not of example) Miriam's might without inconsequence be placed on the same footing; and all in spite of the fact that the "moral presence" of each of the men most importantly concerned with her—or with the second of whom she at least is importantly concerned—*is* independently answered for. The idea of the book being, as I have said, a picture of some of the personal consequences of the art-appetite raised to intensity, swollen to voracity, the heavy emphasis falls where the symbol of some of the complications so begotten might be made (as I judged, heaven forgive me!) most "amusing": amusing I mean in the best very modern sense. I never "go behind" Miriam; only poor Sherringham goes, a great deal, and Nick Dormer goes a little, and the author, while they so waste wonderment, goes behind *them*: but none the less she is as thoroughly symbolic, as functional, for illustration of the idea, as either of them, while her image had seemed susceptible of a livelier and "prettier" concretion. I had desired for her, I remember, all manageable vividness—so ineluctable had it long appeared to "do the actress," to touch the theatre, to meet that connexion somehow or other, in any free plunge of the speculative fork into the contemporary social salad.

The late R. L. Stevenson was to write to me, I recall—and precisely on the occasion of *The Tragic Muse*—that he was at a loss to conceive how one could find an interest in anything so vulgar or pretend to gather fruit in so scrubby an orchard; but the view of a creature of the stage, the view of the "histrionic temperament," as suggestive much less, verily, in respect to the poor stage *per se* than in respect to "art" at large, affected me in spite of that as justly tenable. An objection of a more pointed order was forced upon me by an acute friend later on and in another connexion: the challenge of one's right, in any pretended show of social realities, to attach to the image of a "public character," a supposed particular celebrity, a range of interest, of intrinsic distinction, greater than any such display of importance on the part of eminent members of the class as we see them about us. There *was* a nice point if one would—yet only nice enough, after all, to be easily amusing. We shall deal with it later on, however, in a more urgent connexion. What would have worried me much more had it dawned earlier is the light lately thrown by that admirable writer M. Anatole France on the question of any animated view of the histrionic temperament—a light that may well dazzle to distress any ingenuous worker in the same field. In those parts of his brief but inimitable *Histoire Comique* on which he is most to be congratulated—for there are some that prompt to reserves—he has "done the actress," as well as the actor, done above all the mountebank, the mummer and the *cabotin*, and mixed them up with the queer theatric air, in a manner that practically warns all other hands off the material for ever. At the same time I think I saw Miriam, and without a sacrifice of truth, that is of the particular glow of verisimilitude I wished her most to benefit by, in a complexity of relations finer than any that appear possible for the gentry of M. Anatole France.

Her relation to Nick Dormer, for instance, was intended as a superior interest—that of being (while perfectly sincere, sincere for *her*, and therefore perfectly consonant with her impulse perpetually to perform and with her success in performing) the result of a touched imagination, a touched pride for "art," as well as of the charm cast on other sensibilities still. Dormer's relation to herself is a different matter, of which more presently; but the sympathy she, poor young woman, very generously and intelligently offers him where most people have so stinted it, is disclosed largely at the cost of her egotism and her personal pretensions, even though in fact determined by her sense of their together, Nick and she, postponing the "world" to their conception of other and finer decencies. Nick can't on the whole see—for I have represented him as in his day quite sufficiently troubled and anxious—why he should condemn to ugly feebleness his most prized faculty (most prized, at least, by himself) even in order to keep his seat in Parliament, to inherit Mr. Carteret's blessing and money, to gratify his mother and carry out the mission of his father, to marry Julia Dallow in fine, a beautiful imperative woman with a great many thousands a year. It all comes back in the last analysis to the individual vision of decency, the critical as well as the passionate judgement of it under sharp stress; and Nick's vision and judgement, all on the esthetic ground, have beautifully coincided, to Miriam's imagination, with a now fully marked, an inspired and impenitent, choice of her own: so that, other considerations powerfully aiding indeed, she is ready to see their interest all splendidly as one. She is in the uplifted state to which sacrifices and submissions loom large, but loom so just because they must write sympathy, write passion, large. Her measure of what she would be capable of for him—capable, that is, of *not* asking of him—will depend on what he shall ask of *her*, but she has no fear of not being able to satisfy him, even to the point of "chucking" for him, if need be, that artistic identity of her own which she has begun to build up. It will all be to the glory, therefore, of their common infatuation with "art": she will doubtless be no less willing to serve his than she was eager to serve her own, purged now of the too great shrillness.

This puts her quite on a different level from that of the vivid monsters of M. France, whose artistic identity is the last thing *they* wish to chuck—their only dismissal is of all material and social over-draping. Nick Dormer in point of fact asks of Miriam nothing but that she shall remain "awfully interesting to paint"; but that is *his* relation, which, as I say, is quite a matter by itself. He at any rate, luckily for both of them it may be, doesn't put her to the test: he is so busy with his own case, busy with testing himself and feeling his reality. He has seen himself as giving up precious things for an object, and that object has somehow not been the young woman in question, nor anything very nearly like her. She, on the other hand, has asked everything of Peter Sherringham, who has asked everything of *her*; and it is in so doing that she has really most testified for art and invited him to testify. With his professed interest in the theatre—one of those deep subjections that, in men of "taste," the Comédie Française used in old days to conspire for and some such odd and affecting examples of which were to be noted—he yet offers her his hand and an introduction to the very best society if she will leave the stage. The power—and her having the sense of the power—to "shine" in the world is his highest measure of her, the test applied by him to her beautiful human value; just as the manner in which she turns on him is the application of her own standard and touchstone. She is perfectly sure of her own; for— if there were nothing else, and there is much—she has tasted blood, so to speak, in the form of her so prompt and auspicious success with the public, leaving all probations behind (the whole of which, as the book gives it, is too rapid and sudden, though inevitably so: processes, periods, intervals, stages, degrees, connexions, may be easily enough and barely enough named, may be unconvincingly stated, in fiction, to the deep discredit of the writer, but it remains the very deuce to *represent* them, especially represent them under strong compression and in brief and subordinate terms; and this even though the novelist who doesn't represent, and represent "all the time," is lost, exactly as much lost as the painter who, at his work and given his intention, doesn't paint "all the time").

Turn upon her friend at any rate Miriam does; and one of my main points is missed if it fails to appear that she does so with absolute sincerity and with the cold passion of the high critic who knows, on sight of them together, the more or less dazzling false from the comparatively grey-coloured true. Sherringham's whole profession has been that he rejoices in her as she is, and that the theatre, the organised theatre, will be, as Matthew Arnold was in those very days pronouncing it, irresistible; and it is the promptness with which he sheds his pretended faith as soon as it feels in the air the breath of reality, as soon as it asks of him a proof or a sacrifice, it is this that excites her doubtless sufficiently arrogant scorn. Where is the virtue of his high interest if it has verily never *been* an interest to speak of and if all it has suddenly to suggest is that, in face of a serious call, it shall be unblushingly relinquished? If he and she together, and her great field and future, and the whole cause they had armed and declared for, have not been serious things they have been base make-believes and trivialities—which is what in fact the homage of society to art always turns out so soon as art presumes not to be vulgar and futile. It is immensely the fashion and immensely edifying to listen to, this homage, while it confines its attention to vanities and frauds; but it knows only terror, feels only horror, the moment that, instead of making all the concessions, art proceeds to ask for a few. Miriam is nothing if not strenuous, and evidently nothing if not "cheeky," where Sherringham is concerned at least: these, in the all-egotistical exhibition to which she is condemned, are the very elements of her figure and the very colours of her portrait. But she is mild and inconsequent for Nick Dormer (who demands of her so little); as if gravely and pityingly embracing the truth that *his* sacrifice, on the right side, is probably to have very little of her sort of recompense. I must have had it well before me that she was all aware of the small strain a great sacrifice to Nick would cost her—by reason of the strong effect on her of his own superior logic, in which the very intensity of concentration was so to find its account.

If the man, however, who holds her personally dear yet holds her extremely personal message to the world cheap, so the man capable of a consistency and, as she regards the matter, of an honesty so much higher than Sherringham's, virtually cares, "really" cares, no straw for his fellow-struggler. If Nick Dormer attracts and all-indifferently holds her it is because, like herself and unlike Peter, he puts "art" first; but the most he thus does for her in the event is to let her see how she may enjoy, in intimacy, the rigour it has taught him and which he cultivates at her expense. This is the situation in which we leave her, though there would be more still to be said about the difference for her of the two relations—that to each of the men—could I fondly suppose as much of the interest of the book "left over" for the reader as for myself. Sherringham, for instance, offers Miriam marriage, ever so "handsomely"; but if nothing might lead me on further than the question of what it would have been open to us—us novelists, especially in the old days—to show, "serially," a young man in Nick Dormer's quite different position as offering or a young woman in Miriam's as taking, so for that very reason such an excursion is forbidden me. The trade of the stage-player, and above all of the actress, must have so many detestable sides for the person exercising it that we scarce imagine a full surrender to it without a full surrender, not less, to every immediate compensation, to every freedom and the largest ease within reach: which presentment of the possible case for Miriam would yet have been condemned—and on grounds both various and interesting to trace—to remain very imperfect.

I feel, moreover, that I might still, with space, abound in remarks about Nick's character and Nick's crisis suggested to my present more reflective vision. It strikes me, alas, that he is not quite so interesting as he was fondly intended to be, and this in spite of the multiplication, within the picture, of his pains and penalties; so that while I turn this slight anomaly over I come upon a reason that affects me as singularly charming and touching and at which indeed I have already glanced. Any presentation of the artist *in triumph* must be flat in proportion as it really sticks to its subject—it can only smuggle in relief and variety. For, to put the matter in an image, all we then—in his triumph—see of the charm-compeller is the back he turns to us as he bends over his work. "His" triumph, decently, is but the triumph of what he produces, and that is another affair. His romance is the romance he himself projects; he eats the cake of the very rarest privilege, the most luscious baked in the oven of the gods—therefore he mayn't "have" it, in the form of the privilege of the hero, at the same time. The privilege of the hero—that is, of the martyr or of the interesting and appealing and comparatively floundering *person*—places him in quite a different category, belongs to him only as to the artist deluded, diverted, frustrated or vanquished; when the "amateur" in him gains, for our admiration or compassion or whatever, all that the expert has to do without. Therefore I strove in vain, I feel, to embroil and adorn this young man on whom a hundred ingenious touches are thus lavished: he has insisted in the event on looking as simple and flat as some mere brass check or engraved number, the symbol and guarantee of a stored treasure. The better part of him is locked too much away from us, and the part we see has to pass for—well, what it passes for, so lamentedly, among his friends and relatives. No, accordingly, Nick Dormer isn't "the best thing in the book," as I judge I imagined he would be, and it contains nothing better, I make out, than that preserved and achieved unity and quality of tone, a value in itself, which I referred to at the beginning of these remarks. What I mean by this is that the interest created, and the expression of that interest, are things kept, as to kind, genuine and true to themselves. The appeal, the fidelity to the prime motive, is, with no little art, strained clear (even as silver is polished) in a degree answering—at least by intention—to the air of beauty. There is an awkwardness again in having thus belatedly to point such features out; but in that wrought appearance of animation and harmony, that effect of free movement and yet of recurrent and insistent reference, *The Tragic Muse* has struck me again as conscious of a bright advantage.

HENRY JAMES.

BOOK FIRST

I

The people of France have made it no secret that those of England, as a general thing, are to their perception an inexpressive and speechless race, perpendicular and unsociable, unaddicted to enriching any bareness of contact with verbal or other embroidery. This view might have derived encouragement, a few years ago, in Paris, from the manner in which four persons sat together in silence, one fine day about noon, in the garden, as it is called, of the Palais de l'Industrie—the central court of the great glazed bazaar where, among plants and parterres, gravelled walks and thin fountains, are ranged the figures and groups, the monuments and busts, which form in the annual exhibition of the Salon the department of statuary. The spirit of observation is naturally high at the Salon, quickened by a thousand artful or artless appeals, but it need have put forth no great intensity to take in the characters I mention. As a solicitation of the eye on definite grounds these visitors too constituted a successful plastic fact; and even the most superficial observer would have marked them as products of an insular neighbourhood, representatives of that tweed-and-waterproof class with which, on the recurrent occasions when the English turn out for a holiday—Christmas and Easter, Whitsuntide and the autumn—Paris besprinkles itself at a night's notice. They had about them the indefinable professional look of the British traveller abroad; the air of preparation for exposure, material and moral, which is so oddly combined with the serene revelation of security and of persistence, and which excites, according to individual susceptibility, the ire or the admiration of foreign communities. They were the more unmistakable as they presented mainly the happier aspects of the energetic race to which they had the honour to belong. The fresh diffused light of the Salon made them clear and important; they were finished creations, in their way, and, ranged there motionless on their green bench, were almost as much on exhibition as if they had been hung on the line.

Three ladies and a young man, they were obviously a family—a mother, two daughters and a son; a circumstance which had the effect at once of making each member of the group doubly typical and of helping to account for their fine taciturnity. They were not, with each other, on terms of ceremony, and also were probably fatigued with their course among the pictures, the rooms on the upper floor. Their attitude, on the part of visitors who had superior features even if they might appear to some passers-by to have neglected a fine opportunity for completing these features with an expression, was after all a kind of tribute to the state of exhaustion, of bewilderment, to which the genius of France is still capable of reducing the proud.

"En v'là des abrutis!" more than one of their fellow-gazers might have been heard to exclaim; and certain it is that there was something depressed and discouraged in this interesting group, who sat looking vaguely before them, not noticing the life of the place, somewhat as if each had a private anxiety. It might have been finely guessed, however, that though on many questions they were closely united this present anxiety was not the same for each. If they looked grave, moreover, this was doubtless partly the result of their all being dressed in such mourning as told of a recent bereavement. The eldest of the three ladies had indeed a face of a fine austere mould which would have been moved to gaiety only by some force more insidious than any she was likely to recognise in Paris. Cold, still, and considerably worn, it was neither stupid nor hard—it was firm, narrow and sharp. This competent matron, acquainted evidently with grief but not weakened by it, had a high forehead to which the quality of the skin gave a singular polish—it glittered even when seen at a distance; a nose which achieved a high free curve; and a tendency to throw back her head and carry it well above her, as if to disengage it from the possible entanglements of the rest of her person. If you had seen her walk you would have felt her to tread the earth after a fashion suggesting that in a world where she had long since discovered that one couldn't have one's own way one could never tell what annoying aggression might take place, so that it was well, from hour to hour, to save what one could. Lady Agnes saved her head, her white triangular forehead, over which her close-crinkled flaxen hair, reproduced in different shades in her children, made a looped silken canopy like the marquee at a garden-party. Her daughters were as tall as herself—that was visible even as they sat there—and one of them, the younger evidently, altogether pretty; a straight, slender, grey-eyed English girl of the sort who show "good" figures and fresh complexions. The sister, who was not pretty, was also straight and slender and grey-eyed. But the grey in this case was not so pure, nor were the straightness and the slenderness so maidenly. The brother of these young ladies had taken off his hat as if he felt the air of the summer day heavy in the great pavilion. He was a lean, strong, clear-faced youth, with a formed nose and thick light-brown hair which lay continuously and profusely back from his forehead, so that to smooth it from the brow to the neck but a single movement of the hand was required. I cannot describe him better than by saying that he was the sort of young Englishman who looks particularly well in strange lands and whose general aspect—his inches, his limbs, his friendly eyes, the modulation of his voice, the cleanness of his flesh-tints and the fashion of his garments—excites on the part of those who encounter him in far countries on the ground of a common speech a delightful sympathy of race. This sympathy may sometimes be qualified by the seen limits of his apprehension, but it almost revels as such horizons recede. We shall see quickly enough how accurate a measure it might have taken of Nicholas Dormer. There was food for suspicion perhaps in the wandering blankness that sat at moments in his eyes, as if he had no attention at all, not the least in the world, at his command; but it is no more than just to add without delay that this discouraging symptom was known among those who liked him by the indulgent name of dreaminess. By his mother and sisters, for instance, his dreaminess was constantly noted. He is the more welcome to the benefit of such an interpretation as there is always held to be something engaging in the combination of the muscular and the musing, the mildness of strength.

After some time, an interval during which these good people might have appeared to have come, individually, to the Palais de l'Industrie much less to see the works of art than to think over their domestic affairs, the young man, rousing himself from his reverie, addressed one of the girls.

"I say, Biddy, why should we sit moping here all day? Come and take a turn about with me."

His younger sister, while he got up, leaned forward a little, looking round her, but she gave for the moment no further sign of complying with his invitation.

"Where shall we find you, then, if Peter comes?" asked the other Miss Dormer, making no movement at all.

"I daresay Peter won't come. He'll leave us here to cool our heels."

"Oh Nick dear!" Biddy exclaimed in a small sweet voice of protest. It was plainly her theory that Peter would come, and even a little her fond fear that she might miss him should she quit that spot.

"We shall come back in a quarter of an hour. Really I must look at these things," Nick declared, turning his face to a marble group which stood near them on the right—a man with the skin of a beast round his loins, tussling with a naked woman in some primitive effort of courtship or capture.

Lady Agnes followed the direction of her son's eyes and then observed: "Everything seems very dreadful. I should think Biddy had better sit still. Hasn't she seen enough horrors up above?"

"I daresay that if Peter comes Julia'll be with him," the elder girl remarked irrelevantly.

"Well then he can take Julia about. That will be more proper," said Lady Agnes.

"Mother dear, she doesn't care a rap about art. It's a fearful bore looking at fine things with Julia," Nick returned.

"Won't you go with him, Grace?"—and Biddy appealed to her sister.

"I think she has awfully good taste!" Grace exclaimed, not answering this inquiry.

"*Don't* say nasty things about her!" Lady Agnes broke out solemnly to her son after resting her eyes on him a moment with an air of reluctant reprobation.

34

"I say nothing but what she'd say herself," the young man urged. "About some things she has very good taste, but about this kind of thing she has no taste at all."

"That's better, I think," said Lady Agnes, turning her eyes again to the "kind of thing" her son appeared to designate.

"She's awfully clever—awfully!" Grace went on with decision.

"Awfully, awfully!" her brother repeated, standing in front of her and smiling down at her.

"You are nasty, Nick. You know you are," said the young lady, but more in sorrow than in anger.

Biddy got up at this, as if the accusatory tone prompted her to place herself generously at his side. "Mightn't you go and order lunch—in that place, you know?" she asked of her mother. "Then we'd come back when it was ready."

"My dear child, I can't order lunch," Lady Agnes replied with a cold impatience which seemed to intimate that she had problems far more important than those of victualling to contend with.

"Then perhaps Peter will if he comes. I'm sure he's up in everything of that sort."

"Oh hang Peter!" Nick exclaimed. "Leave him out of account, and *do* order lunch, mother; but not cold beef and pickles."

"I must say—about *him*—you're not nice," Biddy ventured to remark to her brother, hesitating and even blushing a little.

"You make up for it, my dear," the young man answered, giving her chin—a very charming, rotund, little chin—a friendly whisk with his forefinger.

"I can't imagine what you've got against him," her ladyship said gravely.

"Dear mother, it's disappointed fondness," Nick argued. "They won't answer one's notes; they won't let one know where they are nor what to expect. 'Hell has no fury like a woman scorned'; nor like a man either."

"Peter has such a tremendous lot to do—it's a very busy time at the embassy; there are sure to be reasons," Biddy explained with her pretty eyes.

"Reasons enough, no doubt!" said Lady Agnes—who accompanied these words with an ambiguous sigh, however, as if in Paris even the best reasons would naturally be bad ones.

"Doesn't Julia write to you, doesn't she answer you the very day?" Grace asked, looking at Nick as if she were the bold one.

He waited, returning her glance with a certain severity. "What do you know about my correspondence? No doubt I ask too much," he went on; "I'm so attached to them. Dear old Peter, dear old Julia!"

"She's younger than you, my dear!" cried the elder girl, still resolute.

"Yes, nineteen days."

"I'm glad you know her birthday."

"She knows yours; she always gives you something," Lady Agnes reminded her son.

"Her taste is good *then*, isn't it, Nick?" Grace Dormer continued.

"She makes charming presents; but, dear mother, it isn't *her* taste. It's her husband's."

"How her husband's?"

"The beautiful objects of which she disposes so freely are the things he collected for years laboriously, devotedly, poor man!"

"She disposes of them to you, but not to others," said Lady Agnes. "But that's all right," she added, as if this might have been taken for a complaint of the limitations of Julia's bounty. "She has to select among so many, and that's a proof of taste," her ladyship pursued.

"You can't say she doesn't choose lovely ones," Grace remarked to her brother in a tone of some triumph.

"My dear, they're all lovely. George Dallow's judgement was so sure, he was incapable of making a mistake," Nicholas Dormer returned.

"I don't see how you can talk of him, he was dreadful," said Lady Agnes.

"My dear, if he was good enough for Julia to marry he's good enough for us to talk of."

"She did him a very great honour."

"I daresay, but he was not unworthy of it. No such enlightened collection of beautiful objects has been made in England in our time."

"You think too much of beautiful objects!" Lady Agnes sighed.

"I thought you were just now lamenting that I think too little."

"It's very nice—his having left Julia so well off," Biddy interposed soothingly, as if she foresaw a tangle.

"He treated her *en grand seigneur*, absolutely," Nick went on.

"He used to look greasy, all the same"—Grace bore on it with a dull weight. "His name ought to have been Tallow."

"You're not saying what Julia would like, if that's what you are trying to say," her brother observed.

"Don't be vulgar, Grace," said Lady Agnes.

"I know Peter Sherringham's birthday!" Biddy broke out innocently, as a pacific diversion. She had passed her hand into Nick's arm, to signify her readiness to go with him, while she scanned the remoter reaches of the garden as if it had occurred to her that to direct their steps in some such sense might after all be the shorter way to get at Peter.

"He's too much older than you, my dear," Grace answered without encouragement.

37

"That's why I've noticed it—he's thirty-four. Do you call that too old? I don't care for slobbering infants!" Biddy cried.

"Don't be vulgar," Lady Agnes enjoined again.

"Come, Bid, we'll go and be vulgar together; for that's what we are, I'm afraid," her brother said to her. "We'll go and look at all these low works of art."

"Do you really think it's necessary to the child's development?" Lady Agnes demanded as the pair turned away. And then while her son, struck as by a challenge, paused, lingering a moment with his little sister on his arm: "What we've been through this morning in this place, and what you've paraded before our eyes—the murders, the tortures, all kinds of disease and indecency!"

Nick looked at his mother as if this sudden protest surprised him, but as if also there were lurking explanations of it which he quickly guessed. Her resentment had the effect not so much of animating her cold face as of making it colder, less expressive, though visibly prouder. "Ah dear mother, don't do the British matron!" he replied good-humouredly.

"British matron's soon said! I don't know what they're coming to."

"How odd that you should have been struck only with the disagreeable things when, for myself, I've felt it to be most interesting, the most suggestive morning I've passed for ever so many months!"

"Oh Nick, Nick!" Lady Agnes cried with a strange depth of feeling.

"I like them better in London—they're much less unpleasant," said Grace Dormer.

"They're things you can look at," her ladyship went on. "We certainly make the better show."

"The subject doesn't matter, it's the treatment, the treatment!" Biddy protested in a voice like the tinkle of a silver bell.

"Poor little Bid!"—her brother broke into a laugh.

"How can I learn to model, mamma dear, if I don't look at things and if I don't study them?" the girl continued.

This question passed unheeded, and Nicholas Dormer said to his mother, more seriously, but with a certain kind explicitness, as if he could make a particular allowance: "This place is an immense stimulus to me; it refreshes me, excites me—it's such an exhibition of artistic life. It's full of ideas, full of refinements; it gives one such an impression of artistic experience. They try everything, they feel everything. While you were looking at the murders, apparently, I observed an immense deal of curious and interesting work. There are too many of them, poor devils; so many who must make their way, who must attract attention. Some of them can only *taper fort*, stand on their heads, turn somersaults or commit deeds of violence, to make people notice them. After that, no doubt, a good many will be quieter. But I don't know; to-day I'm in an appreciative mood—I feel indulgent even to them: they give me an impression of intelligence, of eager observation. All art is one—remember that, Biddy dear," the young man continued, smiling down from his height. "It's the same great many-headed effort, and any ground that's gained by an individual, any spark that's struck in any province, is of use and of suggestion to all the others. We're all in the same boat."

"'We,' do you say, my dear? Are you really setting up for an artist?" Lady Agnes asked.

Nick just hesitated. "I was speaking for Biddy."

"But you *are* one, Nick—you are!" the girl cried.

Lady Agnes looked for an instant as if she were going to say once more "Don't be vulgar!" But she suppressed these words, had she intended them, and uttered sounds, few in number and not completely articulate, to the effect that she hated talking about art. While her son spoke she had watched him as if failing to follow; yet something in the tone of her exclamation hinted that she had understood him but too well.

"We're all in the same boat," Biddy repeated with cheerful zeal.

"Not me, if you please!" Lady Agnes replied. "It's horrid messy work, your modelling."

"Ah but look at the results!" said the girl eagerly—glancing about at the monuments in the garden as if in regard even to them she were, through that unity of art her brother had just proclaimed, in some degree an effective cause.

"There's a great deal being done here—a real vitality," Nicholas Dormer went on to his mother in the same reasonable informing way. "Some of these fellows go very far."

"They do indeed!" said Lady Agnes.

"I'm fond of young schools—like this movement in sculpture," Nick insisted with his slightly provoking serenity.

"They're old enough to know better!"

"Mayn't I look, mamma? It *is* necessary to my development," Biddy declared.

"You may do as you like," said Lady Agnes with dignity.

"She ought to see good work, you know," the young man went on.

"I leave it to your sense of responsibility." This statement was somewhat majestic, and for a moment evidently it tempted Nick, almost provoked him, or at any rate suggested to him an occasion for some pronouncement he had had on his mind. Apparently, however, he judged the time on the whole not quite right, and his sister Grace interposed with the inquiry—

"Please, mamma, are we never going to lunch?"

"Ah mother, mother!" the young man murmured in a troubled way, looking down at her with a deep fold in his forehead.

For Lady Agnes also, as she returned his look, it seemed an occasion; but with this difference that she had no hesitation in taking advantage of it. She was encouraged by his slight embarrassment, for ordinarily Nick was not embarrassed. "You used to have so *much* sense of responsibility," she pursued; "but sometimes I don't know what has become of it—it seems all, *all* gone!"

"Ah mother, mother!" he exclaimed again—as if there were so many things to say that it was impossible to choose. But now he stepped closer, bent over her and in spite of the publicity of their situation gave her a quick expressive kiss. The foreign observer whom I took for granted in beginning to sketch this scene would have had to admit that the rigid English family had after all a capacity for emotion. Grace Dormer indeed looked round her to see if at this moment they were noticed. She judged with satisfaction that they had escaped.

II

Nick Dormer walked away with Biddy, but he had not gone far before he stopped in front of a clever bust, where his mother, in the distance, saw him playing in the air with his hand, carrying out by this gesture, which presumably was applausive, some critical remark he had made to his sister. Lady Agnes raised her glass to her eyes by the long handle to which rather a clanking chain was attached, perceiving that the bust represented an ugly old man with a bald head; at which her ladyship indefinitely sighed, though it was not apparent in what way such an object could be detrimental to her daughter. Nick passed on and quickly paused again; this time, his mother discerned, before the marble image of a strange grimacing woman. Presently she lost sight of him; he wandered behind things, looking at them all round.

"I ought to get plenty of ideas for my modelling, oughtn't I, Nick?" his sister put to him after a moment.

"Ah my poor child, what shall I say?"

"Don't you think I've any capacity for ideas?" the girl continued ruefully.

"Lots of them, no doubt. But the capacity for applying them, for putting them into practice—how much of that have you?"

"How can I tell till I try?"

"What do you mean by trying, Biddy dear?"

41

"Why you know—you've seen me."

"Do you call that trying?" her brother amusedly demanded.

"Ah Nick!" she said with sensibility. But then with more spirit: "And please what do you call it?"

"Well, this for instance is a good case." And her companion pointed to another bust—a head of a young man in terra-cotta, at which they had just arrived; a modern young man to whom, with his thick neck, his little cap and his wide ring of dense curls, the artist had given the air of some sturdy Florentine of the time of Lorenzo.

Biddy looked at the image a moment. "Ah that's not trying; that's succeeding."

"Not altogether; it's only trying seriously."

"Well, why shouldn't I be serious?"

"Mother wouldn't like it. She has inherited the fine old superstition that art's pardonable only so long as it's bad—so long as it's done at odd hours, for a little distraction, like a game of tennis or of whist. The only thing that can justify it, the effort to carry it as far as one can (which you can't do without time and singleness of purpose), she regards as just the dangerous, the criminal element. It's the oddest hind-part-before view, the drollest immorality."

"She doesn't want one to be professional," Biddy returned as if she could do justice to every system.

"Better leave it alone then. There are always duffers enough."

"I don't want to be a duffer," Biddy said. "But I thought you encouraged me."

"So I did, my poor child. It was only to encourage myself."

"With your own work—your painting?"

"With my futile, my ill-starred endeavours. Union is strength—so that we might present a wider front, a larger surface of resistance."

Biddy for a while said nothing and they continued their tour of observation. She noticed how he passed over some things quickly, his first glance sufficing to show him if they were worth another, and then recognised in a moment the figures that made some appeal. His tone puzzled but his certainty of eye impressed her, and she felt what a difference there was yet between them—how much longer in every case she would have taken to discriminate. She was aware of how little she could judge of the value of a thing till she had looked at it ten minutes; indeed modest little Biddy was compelled privately to add "And often not even then." She was mystified, as I say—Nick was often mystifying, it was his only fault—but one thing was definite: her brother had high ability. It was the consciousness of this that made her bring out at last: "I don't so much care whether or no I please mamma, if I please you."

"Oh don't lean on me. I'm a wretched broken reed—I'm no use *really*!" he promptly admonished her.

"Do you mean you're a duffer?" Biddy asked in alarm.

"Frightful, frightful!"

"So that you intend to give up your work—to let it alone, as you advise *me*?"

"It has never been my work, all that business, Biddy. If it had it would be different. I should stick to it."

"And you *won't* stick to it?" the girl said, standing before him open-eyed.

Her brother looked into her eyes a moment, and she had a compunction; she feared she was indiscreet and was worrying him. "Your questions are much simpler than the elements out of which my answer should come."

"A great talent—what's simpler than that?"

"One excellent thing, dear Biddy: no talent at all!"

"Well, yours is so real you can't help it."

"We shall see, we shall see," said Nick Dormer. "Let us go look at that big group."

43

"We shall see if your talent's real?" Biddy went on as she accompanied him.

"No; we shall see if, as you say, I can't help it. What nonsense Paris makes one talk!" the young man added as they stopped in front of the composition. This was true perhaps, but not in a sense he could find himself tempted to deplore. The present was far from his first visit to the French capital: he had often quitted England and usually made a point of "putting in," as he called it, a few days there on the outward journey to the Continent or on the return; but at present the feelings, for the most part agreeable, attendant upon a change of air and of scene had been more punctual and more acute than for a long time before, and stronger the sense of novelty, refreshment, amusement, of the hundred appeals from that quarter of thought to which on the whole his attention was apt most frequently, though not most confessedly, to stray. He was fonder of Paris than most of his countrymen, though not so fond perhaps as some other captivated aliens: the place had always had the virtue of quickening in him sensibly the life of reflexion and observation. It was a good while since his impressions had been so favourable to the city by the Seine; a good while at all events since they had ministered so to excitement, to exhilaration, to ambition, even to a restlessness that was not prevented from being agreeable by the excess of agitation in it. Nick could have given the reason of this unwonted glow, but his preference was very much to keep it to himself. Certainly to persons not deeply knowing, or at any rate not deeply curious, in relation to the young man's history the explanation might have seemed to beg the question, consisting as it did of the simple formula that he had at last come to a crisis. Why a crisis—what was it and why had he not come to it before? The reader shall learn these things in time if he cares enough for them.

Our young man had not in any recent year failed to see the Salon, which the general voice this season pronounced not particularly good. None the less it was the present exhibition that, for some cause connected with his "crisis," made him think fast, produced that effect he had spoken of to his mother as a sense of artistic life. The precinct of the marbles and bronzes spoke to him especially to-day; the glazed garden, not florally rich, with its new productions alternating with perfunctory plants and its queer, damp smell, partly the odour of plastic clay, of the studios of sculptors, put forth the voice of old associations, of other visits, of companionships now ended— an insinuating eloquence which was at the same time somehow identical with the general sharp contagion of Paris. There was youth in the air, and a multitudinous newness, for ever reviving, and the diffusion of a hundred talents, ingenuities, experiments. The summer clouds made shadows on the roof of the great building; the white images, hard in their crudity, spotted the place with provocations; the rattle of plates at the restaurant sounded sociable in the distance, and our young man congratulated himself more than ever that he had not missed his chance. He felt how it would help him to settle something. At the moment he made this reflexion his eye fell upon a person who appeared—just in the first glimpse—to carry out the idea of help. He uttered a lively ejaculation, which, however, in its want of finish, Biddy failed to understand; so pertinent, so relevant and congruous, was the other party to this encounter.

The girl's attention followed her brother's, resting with it on a young man who faced them without seeing them, engaged as he was in imparting to two companions his ideas about one of the works exposed to view. What Biddy remarked was that this young man was fair and fat and of the middle stature; he had a round face and a short beard and on his crown a mere reminiscence of hair, as the fact that he carried his hat in his hand permitted to be observed. Bridget Dormer, who was quick, placed him immediately as a gentleman, but as a gentleman unlike any other gentleman she had ever seen. She would have taken him for very foreign but that the words proceeding from his mouth reached her ear and imposed themselves as a rare variety of English. It was not that a foreigner might not have spoken smoothly enough, nor yet that the speech of this young man was not smooth. It had in truth a conspicuous and aggressive perfection, and Biddy was sure no mere learner would have ventured to play such tricks with the tongue. He seemed to draw rich effects and wandering airs from it—to modulate and manipulate it as he would have done a musical instrument. Her view of the gentleman's companions was less operative, save for her soon making the reflexion that they were people whom in any country, from China to Peru, you would immediately have taken for natives. One of them was an old lady with a shawl; that was the most salient way in which she presented herself. The shawl was an ancient much-used fabric of embroidered cashmere, such as many ladies wore forty years ago in their walks abroad and such as no lady wears to-day. It had fallen half off the back of the wearer, but at the moment Biddy permitted herself to consider her she gave it a violent jerk and brought it up to her shoulders again, where she continued to arrange and settle it, with a good deal of jauntiness and elegance, while she listened to the talk of the gentleman. Biddy guessed that this little transaction took place very frequently, and was not unaware of its giving the old lady a droll, factitious, faded appearance, as if she were singularly out of step with the age. The other person was very much younger—she might have been a daughter—and had a pale face, a low forehead, and thick dark hair. What she chiefly had, however, Biddy rapidly discovered, was a pair of largely-gazing eyes. Our young friend was helped to the discovery by the accident of their resting at this moment for a time—it struck Biddy as very long—on her own. Both these ladies were clad in light, thin, scant gowns, giving an impression of flowered figures and odd transparencies, and in low shoes which showed a great deal of stocking and were ornamented with large rosettes. Biddy's slightly agitated perception travelled directly to their shoes: they suggested to her vaguely that the wearers were dancers—connected possibly with the old-fashioned exhibition of the shawl-dance. By the time she had taken in so much as this the mellifluous young man had perceived and addressed himself to her brother. He came on with an offered hand. Nick greeted him and said it was a happy chance—he was uncommonly glad to see him.

"I never come across you—I don't know why," Nick added while the two, smiling, looked each other up and down like men reunited after a long interval.

"Oh it seems to me there's reason enough: our paths in life are so different." Nick's friend had a great deal of manner, as was evinced by his fashion of saluting Biddy without knowing her.

"Different, yes, but not so different as that. Don't we both live in London, after all, and in the nineteenth century?"

"Ah my dear Dormer, excuse me: I don't live in the nineteenth century. *Jamais de la vie!*" the gentleman declared.

"Nor in London either?"

"Yes—when I'm not at Samarcand! But surely we've diverged since the old days. I adore what you burn, you burn what I adore." While the stranger spoke he looked cheerfully, hospitably, at Biddy; not because it was she, she easily guessed, but because it was in his nature to desire a second auditor—a kind of sympathetic gallery. Her life was somehow filled with shy people, and she immediately knew she had never encountered any one who seemed so to know his part and recognise his cues.

"How do you know what I adore?" Nicholas Dormer asked.

"I know well enough what you used to."

"That's more than I do myself. There were so many things."

"Yes, there are many things—many, many: that's what makes life so amusing."

"Do you find it amusing?"

"My dear fellow, *c'est à se tordre.* Don't you think so? Ah it was high time I should meet you—I see. I've an idea you need me."

"Upon my word I think I do!" Nick said in a tone which struck his sister and made her wonder still more why, if the gentleman was so important as that, he didn't introduce him.

"There are many gods and this is one of their temples," the mysterious personage went on. "It's a house of strange idols—isn't it?—and of some strange and unnatural sacrifices."

To Biddy as much as to her brother this remark might have been offered; but the girl's eyes turned back to the ladies who for the moment had lost their companion. She felt irresponsive and feared she should pass with this easy cosmopolite for a stiff, scared, English girl, which was not the type she aimed at; but wasn't even ocular commerce overbold so long as she hadn't a sign from Nick? The elder of the strange women had turned her back and was looking at some bronze figure, losing her shawl again as she did so; but the other stood where their escort had quitted her, giving all her attention to his sudden sociability with others. Her arms hung at her sides, her head was bent, her face lowered, so that she had an odd appearance of raising her eyes from under her brows; and in this attitude she was striking, though her air was so unconciliatory as almost to seem dangerous. Did it express resentment at having been abandoned for another girl? Biddy, who began to be frightened—there was a moment when the neglected creature resembled a tigress about to spring—was tempted to cry out that she had no wish whatever to appropriate the gentleman. Then she made the discovery that the young lady too had a manner, almost as much as her clever guide, and the rapid induction that it perhaps meant no more than his. She only looked at Biddy from beneath her eyebrows, which were wonderfully arched, but there was ever so much of a manner in the way she did it. Biddy had a momentary sense of being a figure in a ballet, a dramatic ballet—a subordinate motionless figure, to be dashed at to music or strangely capered up to. It would be a very dramatic ballet indeed if this young person were the heroine. She had magnificent hair, the girl reflected; and at the same moment heard Nick say to his interlocutor: "You're not in London—one can't meet you there?"

"I rove, drift, float," was the answer; "my feelings direct me—if such a life as mine may be said to have a direction. Where there's anything to feel I try to be there!" the young man continued with his confiding laugh.

"I should like to get hold of you," Nick returned.

"Well, in that case there would be no doubt the intellectual adventure. Those are the currents—any sort of personal relation—that govern my career."

"I don't want to lose you this time," Nick continued in a tone that excited Biddy's surprise. A moment before, when his friend had said that he tried to be where there was anything to feel, she had wondered how he could endure him.

"Don't lose me, don't lose me!" cried the stranger after a fashion which affected the girl as the highest expression of irresponsibility she had ever seen.

"After all why should you? Let us remain together unless I interfere"—and he looked, smiling and interrogative, at Biddy, who still remained blank, only noting again that Nick forbore to make them acquainted. This was an anomaly, since he prized the gentleman so. Still, there could be no anomaly of Nick's that wouldn't impose itself on his younger sister.

"Certainly, I keep you," he said, "unless on my side I deprive those ladies—!"

"Charming women, but it's not an indissoluble union. We meet, we communicate, we part! They're going—I'm seeing them to the door. I shall come back." With this Nick's friend rejoined his companions, who moved away with him, the strange fine eyes of the girl lingering on Biddy's brother as well as on Biddy herself as they receded.

"Who *is* he—who *are* they?" Biddy instantly asked.

"He's a gentleman," Nick made answer—insufficiently, she thought, and even with a shade of hesitation. He spoke as if she might have supposed he was not one, and if he was really one why didn't he introduce him? But Biddy wouldn't for the world have put this question, and he now moved to the nearest bench and dropped upon it as to await the other's return. No sooner, however, had his sister seated herself than he said: "See here, my dear, do you think you had better stay?"

"Do you want me to go back to mother?" the girl asked with a lengthening visage.

"Well, what do you think?" He asked it indeed gaily enough.

"Is your conversation to be about—about private affairs?"

"No, I can't say that. But I doubt if mother would think it the sort of thing that's 'necessary to your development.'"

This assertion appeared to inspire her with the eagerness with which she again broke out: "But who are they—who are they?"

"I know nothing of the ladies. I never saw them before. The man's a fellow I knew very well at Oxford. He was thought immense fun there. We've diverged, as he says, and I had almost lost sight of him, but not so much as he thinks, because I've read him—read him with interest. He has written a very clever book."

"What kind of a book?"

"A sort of novel."

"What sort of novel?"

"Well, I don't know—with a lot of good writing." Biddy listened to this so receptively that she thought it perverse her brother should add: "I daresay Peter will have come if you return to mother."

"I don't care if he has. Peter's nothing to me. But I'll go if you wish it."

Nick smiled upon her again and then said: "It doesn't signify. We'll all go."

"All?" she echoed.

"He won't hurt us. On the contrary he'll do us good."

This was possible, the girl reflected in silence, but none the less the idea struck her as courageous, of their taking the odd young man back to breakfast with them and with the others, especially if Peter should be there. If Peter was nothing to her it was singular she should have attached such importance to this contingency. The odd young man reappeared, and now that she saw him without his queer female appendages he seemed personally less weird. He struck her moreover, as generally a good deal accounted for by the literary character, especially if it were responsible for a lot of good writing. As he took his place on the bench Nick said to him, indicating her, "My sister Bridget," and then mentioned his name, "Mr. Gabriel Nash."

"You enjoy Paris—you're happy here?" Mr. Nash inquired, leaning over his friend to speak to the girl.

Though his words belonged to the situation it struck her that his tone didn't, and this made her answer him more dryly than she usually spoke. "Oh yes, it's very nice."

"And French art interests you? You find things here that please?"

"Oh yes, I like some of them."

Mr. Nash considered her kindly. "I hoped you'd say you like the Academy better."

"She would if she didn't think you expected it," said Nicholas Dormer.

"Oh Nick!" Biddy protested.

"Miss Dormer's herself an English picture," their visitor pronounced in the tone of a man whose urbanity was a general solvent.

"That's a compliment if you don't like them!" Biddy exclaimed.

"Ah some of them, some of them; there's a certain sort of thing!" Mr. Nash continued. "We must feel everything, everything that we can. We're here for that."

"You do like English art then?" Nick demanded with a slight accent of surprise.

Mr. Nash indulged his wonder. "My dear Dormer, do you remember the old complaint I used to make of you? You had formulas that were like walking in one's hat. One may see something in a case and one may not."

"Upon my word," said Nick, "I don't know any one who was fonder of a generalisation than you. You turned them off as the man at the street-corner distributes hand-bills."

"They were my wild oats. I've sown them all."

"We shall see that!"

"Oh there's nothing of them now: a tame, scanty, homely growth. My only good generalisations are my actions."

"We shall see *them* then."

"Ah pardon me. You can't see them with the naked eye. Moreover, mine are principally negative. People's actions, I know, are for the most part the things they do—but mine are all the things I *don't* do. There are so many of those, so many, but they don't produce any effect. And then all the rest are shades—extremely fine shades."

"Shades of behaviour?" Nick inquired with an interest which surprised his sister, Mr. Nash's discourse striking her mainly as the twaddle of the under-world.

"Shades of impression, of appreciation," said the young man with his explanatory smile. "All my behaviour consists of my feelings."

"Well, don't you show your feelings? You used to!"

"Wasn't it mainly those of disgust?" Nash asked. "Those operate no longer. I've closed that window."

"Do you mean you like everything?"

"Dear me, no! But I look only at what I do like."

"Do you mean that you've lost the noble faculty of disgust?"

"I haven't the least idea. I never try it. My dear fellow," said Gabriel Nash, "we've only one life that we know anything about: fancy taking it up with disagreeable impressions! When then shall we go in for the agreeable?"

"What do you mean by the agreeable?" Nick demanded.

"Oh the happy moments of our consciousness—the multiplication of those moments. We must save as many as possible from the dark gulf."

Nick had excited surprise on the part of his sister, but it was now Biddy's turn to make him open his eyes a little. She raised her sweet voice in appeal to the stranger.

"Don't you think there are any wrongs in the world—any abuses and sufferings?"

"Oh so many, so many! That's why one must choose."

"Choose to stop them, to reform them—isn't that the choice?" Biddy asked. "That's Nick's," she added, blushing and looking at this personage.

"Ah our divergence—yes!" Mr. Nash sighed. "There are all kinds of machinery for that—very complicated and ingenious. Your formulas, my dear Dormer, your formulas!"

"Hang 'em, I haven't got any!" Nick now bravely declared.

"To me personally the simplest ways are those that appeal most," Mr. Nash went on. "We pay too much attention to the ugly; we notice it, we magnify it. The great thing is to leave it alone and encourage the beautiful."

"You must be very sure you get hold of the beautiful," said Nick.

"Ah precisely, and that's just the importance of the faculty of appreciation. We must train our special sense. It's capable of extraordinary extension. Life's none too long for that."

"But what's the good of the extraordinary extension if there is no affirmation of it, if it all goes to the negative, as you say? Where are the fine consequences?" Dormer asked.

"In one's own spirit. One is one's self a fine consequence. That's the most important one we have to do with. *I* am a fine consequence," said Gabriel Nash.

Biddy rose from the bench at this and stepped away a little as to look at a piece of statuary. But she had not gone far before, pausing and turning, she bent her eyes on the speaker with a heightened colour, an air of desperation and the question, after a moment: "Are you then an æsthete?"

"Ah there's one of the formulas! That's walking in one's hat! I've *no* profession, my dear young lady. I've no *état civil*. These things are a part of the complicated ingenious machinery. As I say, I keep to the simplest way. I find that gives one enough to do. Merely to be is such a *métier*; to live such an art; to feel such a career!"

53

Bridget Dormer turned her back and examined her statue, and her brother said to his old friend: "And to write?"

"To write? Oh I shall never do it again!"

"You've done it almost well enough to be inconsistent. That book of yours is anything but negative; it's complicated and ingenious."

"My dear fellow, I'm extremely ashamed of that book," said Gabriel Nash.

"Ah call yourself a bloated Buddhist and have done with it!" his companion exclaimed.

"Have done with it? I haven't the least desire to have done with it. And why should one call one's self anything? One only deprives other people of their dearest occupation. Let me add that you don't *begin* to have an insight into the art of life till it ceases to be of the smallest consequence to you what you may be called. That's rudimentary."

"But if you go in for shades you must also go in for names. You must distinguish," Nick objected. "The observer's nothing without his categories, his types and varieties."

"Ah trust him to distinguish!" said Gabriel Nash sweetly. "That's for his own convenience; he has, privately, a terminology to meet it. That's one's style. But from the moment it's for the convenience of others the signs have to be grosser, the shades begin to go. That's a deplorable hour! Literature, you see, is for the convenience of others. It requires the most abject concessions. It plays such mischief with one's style that really I've had to give it up."

"And politics?" Nick asked.

"Well, what about them?" was Mr. Nash's reply with a special cadence as he watched his friend's sister, who was still examining her statue. Biddy was divided between irritation and curiosity. She had interposed space, but she had not gone beyond ear-shot. Nick's question made her curiosity throb as a rejoinder to his friend's words.

"That, no doubt you'll say, is still far more for the convenience of others—is still worse for one's style."

Biddy turned round in time to hear Mr. Nash answer: "It has simply nothing in life to do with shades! I can't say worse for it than that."

Biddy stepped nearer at this and drew still further on her courage. "Won't mamma be waiting? Oughtn't we to go to luncheon?"

Both the young men looked up at her and Mr. Nash broke out: "You ought to protest! You ought to save him!"

"To save him?" Biddy echoed.

"He had a style, upon my word he had! But I've seen it go. I've read his speeches."

"You were capable of that?" Nick laughed.

"For you, yes. But it was like listening to a nightingale in a brass band."

"I think they were beautiful," Biddy declared.

Her brother got up at this tribute, and Mr. Nash, rising too, said with his bright colloquial air: "But, Miss Dormer, he had eyes. He was made to see—to see all over, to see everything. There are so few like that."

"I think he still sees," Biddy returned, wondering a little why Nick didn't defend himself.

"He sees his 'side,' his dreadful 'side,' dear young lady. Poor man, fancy your having a 'side'—you, you—and spending your days and your nights looking at it! I'd as soon pass my life looking at an advertisement on a hoarding."

"You don't see me some day a great statesman?" said Nick.

"My dear fellow, it's exactly what I've a terror of."

"Mercy! don't you admire them?" Biddy cried.

"It's a trade like another and a method of making one's way which society certainly condones. But when one can be something better—!"

"Why what in the world is better?" Biddy asked.

The young man gasped and Nick, replying for him, said: "Gabriel Nash is better! You must come and lunch with us. I must keep you—I must!" he added.

"We shall save him yet," Mr. Nash kept on easily to Biddy while they went and the girl wondered still more what her mother would make of him.

III

After her companions left her Lady Agnes rested for five minutes in silence with her elder daughter, at the end of which time she observed: "I suppose one must have food at any rate," and, getting up, quitted the place where they had been sitting. "And where are we to go? I hate eating out of doors," she went on.

"Dear me, when one comes to Paris—!" Grace returned in a tone apparently implying that in so rash an adventure one must be prepared for compromises and concessions. The two ladies wandered to where they saw a large sign of "Buffet" suspended in the air, entering a precinct reserved for little white-clothed tables, straw-covered chairs and long-aproned waiters. One of these functionaries approached them with eagerness and with a *"Mesdames sont seules?"* receiving in return from her ladyship the slightly snappish announcement *"Non; nous sommes beaucoup!"* He introduced them to a table larger than most of the others, and under his protection they took their places at it and began rather languidly and vaguely to consider the question of the repast. The waiter had placed a *carte* in Lady Agnes's hands and she studied it, through her eye-glass, with a failure of interest, while he enumerated with professional fluency the resources of the establishment and Grace watched the people at the other tables. She was hungry and had already broken a morsel from a long glazed roll.

"Not cold beef and pickles, you know," she observed to her mother. Lady Agnes gave no heed to this profane remark, but dropped her eye-glass and laid down the greasy document. "What does it signify? I daresay it's all nasty," Grace continued; and she added inconsequently: "If Peter comes he's sure to be particular."

"Let him first be particular to come!" her ladyship exclaimed, turning a cold eye upon the waiter.

"Poulet chasseur, filets mignons sauce bearnaise," the man suggested.

"You'll give us what I tell you," said Lady Agnes; and she mentioned with distinctness and authority the dishes of which she desired that the meal should be composed. He interjected three or four more suggestions, but as they produced absolutely no impression on her he became silent and submissive, doing justice apparently to her ideas. For Lady Agnes had ideas, and, though it had suited her humour ten minutes before to profess herself helpless in such a case, the manner in which she imposed them on the waiter as original, practical, and economical, showed the high executive woman, the mother of children, the daughter of earls, the consort of an official, the dispenser of hospitality, looking back upon a lifetime of luncheons. She carried many cares, and the feeding of multitudes—she was honourably conscious of having fed them decently, as she had always done everything—had ever been one of them. "Everything's absurdly dear," she remarked to her daughter as the waiter went away. To this remark Grace made no answer. She had been used for a long time back to hearing that everything was very dear; it was what one always expected. So she found the case herself, but she was silent and inventive about it, and nothing further passed, in the way of conversation with her mother, while they waited for the latter's orders to be executed, till Lady Agnes reflected audibly: "He makes me unhappy, the way he talks about Julia."

"Sometimes I think he does it to torment one. One can't mention her!" Grace responded.

"It's better not to mention her, but to leave it alone."

"Yet he never mentions her of himself."

"In some cases that's supposed to show that people like people—though of course something more's required to prove it," Lady Agnes continued to meditate. "Sometimes I think he's thinking of her, then at others I can't fancy *what* he's thinking of."

"It would be awfully suitable," said Grace, biting her roll.

Her companion had a pause, as if looking for some higher ground to put it upon. Then she appeared to find this loftier level in the observation: "Of course he must like her—he has known her always."

"Nothing can be plainer than that she likes him," Grace opined.

"Poor Julia!" Lady Agnes almost wailed; and her tone suggested that she knew more about that than she was ready to state.

"It isn't as if she wasn't clever and well read," her daughter went on. "If there were nothing else there would be a reason in her being so interested in politics, in everything that he is."

"Ah what Nick is—that's what I sometimes wonder!"

Grace eyed her parent in some despair: "Why, mother, isn't he going to be like papa?" She waited for an answer that didn't come; after which she pursued: "I thought you thought him so like him already."

"Well, I don't," said Lady Agnes quietly.

"Who is then? Certainly Percy isn't."

Lady Agnes was silent a space. "There's no one like your father."

"Dear papa!" Grace handsomely concurred. Then with a rapid transition: "It would be so jolly for all of us—she'd be so nice to us."

"She's that already—in her way," said Lady Agnes conscientiously, having followed the return, quick as it was. "Much good does it do her!" And she reproduced the note of her bitterness of a moment before.

"It does her some good that one should look out for her. I do, and I think she knows it," Grace declared. "One can at any rate keep other women off."

"Don't meddle—you're very clumsy," was her mother's not particularly sympathetic rejoinder. "There are other women who are beautiful, and there are others who are clever and rich."

"Yes, but not all in one: that's what's so nice in Julia. Her fortune would be thrown in; he wouldn't appear to have married her for it."

"If he does he won't," said Lady Agnes a trifle obscurely.

"Yes, that's what's so charming. And he could do anything then, couldn't he?"

"Well, your father had no fortune to speak of."

"Yes, but didn't Uncle Percy help him?"

"His wife helped him," said Lady Agnes.

"Dear mamma!"—the girl was prompt. "There's one thing," she added: "that Mr. Carteret will always help Nick."

"What do you mean by 'always'?"

"Why whether he marries Julia or not."

"Things aren't so easy," Lady Agnes judged. "It will all depend on Nick's behaviour. He can stop it to-morrow."

Grace Dormer stared; she evidently thought Mr. Carteret's beneficence a part of the scheme of nature. "How could he stop it?"

"By not being serious. It isn't so hard to prevent people giving you money."

"Serious?" Grace repeated. "Does he want him to be a prig like Lord Egbert?"

"Yes—that's exactly what he wants. And what he'll do for him he'll do for him only if he marries Julia."

"Has he told you?" Grace inquired. And then, before her mother could answer, "I'm delighted at that!" she cried.

"He hasn't told me, but that's the way things happen." Lady Agnes was less optimistic than her daughter, and such optimism as she cultivated was a thin tissue with the sense of things as they are showing through. "If Nick becomes rich Charles Carteret will make him more so. If he doesn't he won't give him a shilling."

"Oh mamma!" Grace demurred.

"It's all very well to say that in public life money isn't as necessary as it used to be," her ladyship went on broodingly. "Those who say so don't know anything about it. It's always intensely necessary."

Her daughter, visibly affected by the gloom of her manner, felt impelled to evoke as a corrective a more cheerful idea. "I daresay; but there's the fact—isn't there?—that poor papa had so little."

"Yes, and there's the fact that it killed him!"

These words came out with a strange, quick, little flare of passion. They startled Grace Dormer, who jumped in her place and gasped, "Oh mother!" The next instant, however, she added in a different voice, "Oh Peter!" for, with an air of eagerness, a gentleman was walking up to them.

"How d'ye do, Cousin Agnes? How d'ye do, little Grace?" Peter Sherringham laughed and shook hands with them, and three minutes later was settled in his chair at their table, on which the first elements of the meal had been placed. Explanations, on one side and the other, were demanded and produced; from which it appeared that the two parties had been in some degree at cross-purposes. The day before Lady Agnes and her companions travelled to Paris Sherringham had gone to London for forty-eight hours on private business of the ambassador's, arriving, on his return by the night-train, only early that morning. There had accordingly been a delay in his receiving Nick Dormer's two notes. If Nick had come to the embassy in person—he might have done him the honour to call—he would have learned that the second secretary was absent. Lady Agnes was not altogether successful in assigning a motive to her son's neglect of this courteous form; she could but say: "I expected him, I wanted him to go; and indeed, not hearing from you, he would have gone immediately—an hour or two hence, on leaving this place. But we're here so quietly—not to go out, not to seem to appeal to the ambassador. Nick put it so—'Oh mother, we'll keep out of it; a friendly note will do.' I don't know definitely what he wanted to keep out of, unless anything like gaiety. The embassy isn't gay, I know. But I'm sure his note was friendly, wasn't it? I daresay you'll see for yourself. He's different directly he gets abroad; he doesn't seem to care." Lady Agnes paused a moment, not carrying out this particular elucidation; then she resumed: "He said you'd have seen Julia and that you'd understand everything from her. And when I asked how she'd know he said, 'Oh she knows everything!'"

"He never said a word to me about Julia," Peter Sherringham returned. Lady Agnes and her daughter exchanged a glance at this: the latter had already asked three times where Julia was, and her ladyship dropped that they had been hoping she would be able to come with Peter. The young man set forth that she was at the moment at an hotel in the Rue de la Paix, but had only been there since that morning; he had seen her before proceeding to the Champs Elysées. She had come up to Paris by an early train—— she had been staying at Versailles, of all places in the world. She had been a week in Paris on her return from Cannes—her stay there had been of nearly a month: fancy!—and then had gone out to Versailles to see Mrs. Billinghurst. Perhaps they'd remember her, poor Dallow's sister. She was staying there to teach her daughters French—she had a dozen or two!—and Julia had spent three days with her. She was to return to England about the twenty-fifth. It would make seven weeks she must have been away from town—a rare thing for her; she usually stuck to it so in summer.

"Three days with Mrs. Billinghurst—how very good-natured of her!" Lady Agnes commented.

"Oh they're very nice to her," Sherringham said.

"Well, I hope so!" Grace Dormer exhaled. "Why didn't you make her come here?"

"I proposed it, but she wouldn't." Another eye-beam, at this, passed between the two ladies and Peter went on: "She said you must come and see her at the Hôtel de Hollande."

"Of course we'll do that," Lady Agnes declared. "Nick went to ask about her at the Westminster."

"She gave that up; they wouldn't give her the rooms she wanted, her usual set."

"She's delightfully particular!" Grace said complacently. Then she added: "She *does* like pictures, doesn't she?"

Peter Sherringham stared. "Oh I daresay. But that's not what she has in her head this morning. She has some news from London—she's immensely excited."

"What has she in her head?" Lady Agnes asked.

"What's her news from London?" Grace added.

"She wants Nick to stand."

"Nick to stand?" both ladies cried.

"She undertakes to bring him in for Harsh. Mr. Pinks is dead—the fellow, you know, who got the seat at the general election. He dropped down in London—disease of the heart or something of that sort. Julia has her telegram, but I see it was in last night's papers."

"Imagine—Nick never mentioned it!" said Lady Agnes.

"Don't you know, mother?—abroad he only reads foreign papers."

"Oh I know. I've no patience with him," her ladyship continued. "Dear Julia!"

"It's a nasty little place, and Pinks had a tight squeeze—107 or something of that sort; but if it returned a Liberal a year ago very likely it will do so again. Julia at any rate believes it can be made to—if the man's Nick—and is ready to take the order to put him in."

"I'm sure if she can do it she will," Grace pronounced.

"Dear, dear Julia! And Nick can do something for himself," said the mother of this candidate.

"I've no doubt he can do anything," Peter Sherringham returned good-naturedly. Then, "Do you mean in expenses?" he inquired.

"Ah I'm afraid he can't do much in expenses, poor dear boy! And it's dreadful how little we can look to Percy."

"Well, I daresay you may look to Julia. I think that's her idea."

"Delightful Julia!" Lady Agnes broke out. "If poor Sir Nicholas could have known! Of course he must go straight home," she added.

"He won't like that," said Grace.

"Then he'll have to go without liking it."

"It will rather spoil *your* little excursion, if you've only just come," Peter suggested; "to say nothing of the great Biddy's, if she's enjoying Paris."

"We may stay perhaps—with Julia to protect us," said Lady Agnes.

"Ah she won't stay; she'll go over for her man."

"Her man——?"

"The fellow who stands, whoever he is—especially if he's Nick." These last words caused the eyes of Peter Sherringham's companions to meet again, and he went on: "She'll go straight down to Harsh."

"Wonderful Julia!" Lady Agnes panted. "Of course Nick must go straight there too."

"Well, I suppose he must see first if they'll have him."

"If they'll have him? Why how can he tell till he tries?"

"I mean the people at headquarters, the fellows who arrange it."

Lady Agnes coloured a little. "My dear Peter, do you suppose there will be the least doubt of their 'having' the son of his father?"

"Of course it's a great name, Cousin Agnes—a very great name."

"One of the greatest, simply," Lady Agnes smiled.

"It's the best name in the world!" said Grace more emphatically.

"All the same it didn't prevent his losing his seat."

"By half-a-dozen votes: it was too odious!" her ladyship cried.

"I remember—I remember. And in such a case as that why didn't they immediately put him in somewhere else?"

"How one sees you live abroad, dear Peter! There happens to have been the most extraordinary lack of openings—I never saw anything like it—for a year. They've had their hand on him, keeping him all ready. I daresay they've telegraphed him."

"And he hasn't told you?"

Lady Agnes faltered. "He's so very odd when he's abroad!"

"At home too he lets things go," Grace interposed. "He does so little—takes no trouble." Her mother suffered this statement to pass unchallenged, and she pursued philosophically: "I suppose it's because he knows he's so clever."

"So he is, dear old man. But what does he do, what has he been doing, in a positive way?"

"He has been painting."

"Ah not seriously!" Lady Agnes protested.

"That's the worst way," said Peter Sherringham. "Good things?"

Neither of the ladies made a direct response to this, but Lady Agnes said: "He has spoken repeatedly. They're always calling on him."

"He speaks magnificently," Grace attested.

"That's another of the things I lose, living in far countries. And he's doing the Salon now with the great Biddy?"

"Just the things in this part. I can't think what keeps them so long," Lady Agnes groaned. "Did you ever see such a dreadful place?"

Sherringham stared. "Aren't the things good? I had an idea——!"

"Good?" cried Lady Agnes. "They're too odious, too wicked."

"Ah," laughed Peter, "that's what people fall into if they live abroad. The French oughtn't to live abroad!"

"Here they come," Grace announced at this point; "but they've got a strange man with them."

"That's a bore when we want to talk!" Lady Agnes sighed.

Peter got up in the spirit of welcome and stood a moment watching the others approach. "There will be no difficulty in talking, to judge by the gentleman," he dropped; and while he remains so conspicuous our eyes may briefly rest on him. He was middling high and was visibly a representative of the nervous rather than of the phlegmatic branch of his race. He had an oval face, fine firm features, and a complexion that tended to the brown. Brown were his eyes, and women thought them soft; dark brown his hair, in which the same critics sometimes regretted the absence of a little undulation. It was perhaps to conceal this plainness that he wore it very short. His teeth were white, his moustache was pointed, and so was the small beard that adorned the extremity of his chin. His face expressed intelligence and was very much alive; it had the further distinction that it often struck superficial observers with a certain foreignness of cast. The deeper sort, however, usually felt it latently English enough. There was an idea that, having taken up the diplomatic career and gone to live in strange lands, he cultivated the mask of an alien, an Italian or a Spaniard; of an alien in time even—one of the wonderful ubiquitous diplomatic agents of the sixteenth century. In fact, none the less, it would have been impossible to be more modern than Peter Sherringham—more of one's class and one's country. But this didn't prevent several stray persons—Bridget Dormer for instance—from admiring the hue of his cheek for its olive richness and his moustache and beard for their resemblance to those of Charles I. At the same time—she rather jumbled her comparisons—she thought he recalled a Titian.

IV

Peter's meeting with Nick was of the friendliest on both sides, involving a great many "dear fellows" and "old boys," and his salutation to the younger of the Miss Dormers consisted of the frankest "Delighted to see you, my dear Bid!" There was no kissing, but there was cousinship in the air, of a conscious, living kind, as Gabriel Nash doubtless quickly noted, hovering for a moment outside the group. Biddy said nothing to Peter Sherringham, but there was no flatness in a silence which heaved, as it were, with the fairest physiognomic portents. Nick introduced Gabriel Nash to his mother and to the other two as "a delightful old friend" whom he had just come across, and Sherringham acknowledged the act by saying to Mr. Nash, but as if rather less for his sake than for that of the presenter: "I've seen you very often before."

"Ah repetition—recurrence: we haven't yet, in the study of how to live, abolished that clumsiness, have we?" Mr. Nash genially inquired. "It's a poverty in the supernumeraries of our stage that we don't pass once for all, but come round and cross again like a procession or an army at the theatre. It's a sordid economy that ought to have been managed better. The right thing would be just *one* appearance, and the procession, regardless of expense, for ever and for ever different." The company was occupied in placing itself at table, so that the only disengaged attention for the moment was Grace's, to whom, as her eyes rested on him, the young man addressed these last words with a smile. "Alas, it's a very shabby idea, isn't it? The world isn't got up regardless of expense!"

Grace looked quickly away from him and said to her brother: "Nick, Mr. Pinks is dead."

"Mr. Pinks?" asked Gabriel Nash, appearing to wonder where he should sit.

"The member for Harsh; and Julia wants you to stand," the girl went on.

"Mr. Pinks, the member for Harsh? What names to be sure!" Gabriel mused cheerfully, still unseated.

66

"Julia wants me? I'm much obliged to her!" Nick absently said. "Nash, please sit by my mother, with Peter on her other side."

"My dear, it isn't Julia"—Lady Agnes spoke earnestly. "Every one wants you. Haven't you heard from your people? Didn't you know the seat was vacant?"

Nick was looking round the table to see what was on it. "Upon my word I don't remember. What else have you ordered, mother?"

"There's some *bœuf braisé*, my dear, and afterwards some galantine. Here's a dish of eggs with asparagus-tips."

"I advise you to go in for it, Nick," said Peter Sherringham, to whom the preparation in question was presented.

"Into the eggs with asparagus-tips? *Donnez m'en s'il vous plaît.* My dear fellow, how can I stand? how can I sit? Where's the money to come from?"

"The money? Why from Jul——!" Grace began, but immediately caught her mother's eye.

"Poor Julia, how you do work her!" Nick exclaimed. "Nash, I recommend you the asparagus-tips. Mother, he's my best friend—do look after him."

"I've an impression I've breakfasted—I'm not sure," Nash smiled.

"With those beautiful ladies? Try again—you'll find out."

"The money can be managed; the expenses are very small and the seat's certain," Lady Agnes pursued, not apparently heeding her son's injunction in respect to Nash.

"Rather—if Julia goes down!" her elder daughter exclaimed.

"Perhaps Julia won't go down!" Nick answered humorously.

Biddy was seated next to Mr. Nash, so that she could take occasion to ask, "Who are the beautiful ladies?" as if she failed to recognise her brother's allusion. In reality this was an innocent trick: she was more curious than she could have given a suitable reason for about the odd women from whom her neighbour had lately separated.

"Deluded, misguided, infatuated persons!" Mr. Nash replied, understanding that she had asked for a description. "Strange eccentric, almost romantic, types. Predestined victims, simple-minded sacrificial lambs!"

This was copious, yet it was vague, so that Biddy could only respond: "Oh all that?" But meanwhile Peter Sherringham said to Nick: "Julia's here, you know. You must go and see her."

Nick looked at him an instant rather hard, as if to say: "You too?" But Peter's eyes appeared to answer, "No, no, not I"; upon which his cousin rejoined: "Of course I'll go and see her. I'll go immediately. Please to thank her for thinking of me."

"Thinking of you? There are plenty to think of you!" Lady Agnes said. "There are sure to be telegrams at home. We must go back—we must go back!"

"We must go back to England?" Nick Dormer asked; and as his mother made no answer he continued: "Do you mean I must go to Harsh?"

Her ladyship evaded this question, inquiring of Mr. Nash if he would have a morsel of fish; but her gain was small, for this gentleman, struck again by the unhappy name of the bereaved constituency, only broke out: "Ah what a place to represent! How can you—how can you?"

"It's an excellent place," said Lady Agnes coldly. "I imagine you've never been there. It's a very good place indeed. It belongs very largely to my cousin, Mrs. Dallow."

Gabriel partook of the fish, listening with interest. "But I thought we had no more pocket-boroughs."

"It's pockets we rather lack, so many of us. There are plenty of Harshes," Nick Dormer observed.

"I don't know what you mean," Lady Agnes said to Nash with considerable majesty.

Peter Sherringham also addressed him with an "Oh it's all right; they come down on you like a shot!" and the young man continued ingenuously:

"Do you mean to say you've to pay money to get into that awful place—that it's not *you* who are paid?"

"Into that awful place?" Lady Agnes repeated blankly.

"Into the House of Commons. That you don't get a high salary?"

"My dear Nash, you're delightful: don't leave me—don't leave me!" Nick cried; while his mother looked at him with an eye that demanded: "Who in the world's this extraordinary person?"

"What then did you think pocket-boroughs were?" Peter Sherringham asked.

Mr. Nash's facial radiance rested on him. "Why, boroughs that filled your pocket. To do that sort of thing without a bribe—*c'est trop fort!*"

"He lives at Samarcand," Nick Dormer explained to his mother, who flushed perceptibly. "What do you advise me? I'll do whatever you say," he went on to his old acquaintance.

"My dear, my dear——!" Lady Agnes pleaded.

"See Julia first, with all respect to Mr. Nash. She's of excellent counsel," said Peter Sherringham.

Mr. Nash smiled across the table at his host. "The lady first—the lady first! I've not a word to suggest as against any idea of hers."

"We mustn't sit here too long, there'll be so much to do," said Lady Agnes anxiously, perceiving a certain slowness in the service of the *bœuf braisé*.

Biddy had been up to this moment mainly occupied in looking, covertly and in snatches, at Peter Sherringham; as was perfectly lawful in a young lady with a handsome cousin whom she had not seen for more than a year. But her sweet voice now took license to throw in the words: "We know what Mr. Nash thinks of politics: he told us just now he thinks them dreadful."

"No, not dreadful—only inferior," the personage impugned protested. "Everything's relative."

"Inferior to what?" Lady Agnes demanded.

Mr. Nash appeared to consider a moment. "To anything else that may be in question."

"Nothing else is in question!" said her ladyship in a tone that would have been triumphant if it had not been so dry.

"Ah then!" And her neighbour shook his head sadly. He turned after this to Biddy. "The ladies whom I was with just now and in whom you were so good as to express an interest?" Biddy gave a sign of assent and he went on: "They're persons theatrical. The younger one's trying to go upon the stage."

"And are you assisting her?" Biddy inquired, pleased she had guessed so nearly right.

"Not in the least—I'm rather choking her off. I consider it the lowest of the arts."

"Lower than politics?" asked Peter Sherringham, who was listening to this.

"Dear no, I won't say that. I think the Théâtre Français a greater institution than the House of Commons."

"I agree with you there!" laughed Sherringham; "all the more that I don't consider the dramatic art a low one. It seems to me on the contrary to include all the others."

"Yes—that's a view. I think it's the view of my friends."

"Of your friends?"

"Two ladies—old acquaintances—whom I met in Paris a week ago and whom I've just been spending an hour with in this place."

"You should have seen them; they struck me very much," Biddy said to her cousin.

"I should like to see them if they really have anything to say to the theatre."

"It can easily be managed. Do you believe in the theatre?" asked Gabriel Nash.

"Passionately," Sherringham confessed. "Don't you?"

Before Nash had had time to answer Biddy had interposed with a sigh. "How I wish I could go—but in Paris I can't!"

"I'll take you, Biddy—I vow I'll take you."

"But the plays, Peter," the girl objected. "Mamma says they're worse than the pictures."

"Oh, we'll arrange that: they shall do one at the Français on purpose for a delightful little yearning English girl."

"Can you make them?"

"I can make them do anything I choose."

"Ah then it's the theatre that believes in *you*," said Mr. Nash.

"It would be ungrateful if it didn't after all I've done for it!" Sherringham gaily opined.

Lady Agnes had withdrawn herself from between him and her other guest and, to signify that she at least had finished eating, had gone to sit by her son, whom she held, with some importunity, in conversation. But hearing the theatre talked of she threw across an impersonal challenge to the paradoxical young man. "Pray should you think it better for a gentleman to be an actor?"

"Better than being a politician? Ah, comedian for comedian, isn't the actor more honest?"

Lady Agnes turned to her son and brought forth with spirit: "Think of your great father, Nicholas!"

"He was an honest man," said Nicholas. "That's perhaps why he couldn't stand it."

Peter Sherringham judged the colloquy to have taken an uncomfortable twist, though not wholly, as it seemed to him, by the act of Nick's queer comrade. To draw it back to safer ground he said to this personage: "May I ask if the ladies you just spoke of are English—Mrs. and Miss Rooth: isn't that the rather odd name?"

"The very same. Only the daughter, according to her kind, desires to be known by some *nom de guerre* before she has even been able to enlist."

"And what does she call herself?" Bridget Dormer asked.

"Maud Vavasour, or Edith Temple, or Gladys Vane—some rubbish of that sort."

"What then is her own name?"

"Miriam—Miriam Rooth. It would do very well and would give her the benefit of the prepossessing fact that—to the best of my belief at least—she's more than half a Jewess."

"It is as good as Rachel Felix," Sherringham said.

"The name's as good, but not the talent. The girl's splendidly stupid."

"And more than half a Jewess? Don't you believe it!" Sherringham laughed.

"Don't believe she's a Jewess?" Biddy asked, still more interested in Miriam Rooth.

"No, no—that she's stupid, really. If she is she'll be the first."

"Ah you may judge for yourself," Nash rejoined, "if you'll come to-morrow afternoon to Madame Carré, Rue de Constantinople, *à l'entresol.*"

"Madame Carré? Why, I've already a note from her—I found it this morning on my return to Paris—asking me to look in at five o'clock and listen to a *jeune Anglaise.*"

"That's my arrangement—I obtained the favour. The ladies want an opinion, and dear old Carré has consented to see them and to give one. Maud Vavasour will recite, and the venerable artist will pass judgement."

Sherringham remembered he had his note in his pocket and took it out to look it over. "She wishes to make her a little audience—she says she'll do better with that—and she asks me because I'm English. I shall make a point of going."

"And bring Dormer if you can: the audience will be better. Will you come, Dormer?" Mr. Nash continued, appealing to his friend—"will you come with me to hear an English amateur recite and an old French actress pitch into her?"

Nick looked round from his talk with his mother and Grace. "I'll go anywhere with you so that, as I've told you, I mayn't lose sight of you—may keep hold of you."

"Poor Mr. Nash, why is he so useful?" Lady Agnes took a cold freedom to inquire.

"He steadies me, mother."

"Oh I wish you'd take *me*, Peter," Biddy broke out wistfully to her cousin.

"To spend an hour with an old French actress? Do *you* want to go upon the stage?" the young man asked.

"No, but I want to see something—to know something."

"Madame Carré's wonderful in her way, but she's hardly company for a little English girl."

"I'm not little, I'm only too big; and *she* goes, the person you speak of."

"For a professional purpose and with her good mother," smiled Mr. Nash. "I think Lady Agnes would hardly venture——!"

"Oh I've seen her good mother!" said Biddy as if she had her impression of what the worth of that protection might be.

"Yes, but you haven't heard her. It's then that you measure her."

Biddy was wistful still. "Is it the famous Honorine Carré, the great celebrity?"

"Honorine in person: the incomparable, the perfect!" said Peter Sherringham. "The first artist of our time, taking her altogether. She and I are old pals; she has been so good as to come and 'say' things—which she does sometimes still *dans le monde* as no one else *can*—- in my rooms."

"Make her come then. We can go *there*!"

"One of these days!"

"And the young lady—Miriam, Maud, Gladys—make her come too."

Sherringham looked at Nash and the latter was bland. "Oh you'll have no difficulty. She'll jump at it!"

"Very good. I'll give a little artistic tea—with Julia too of course. And you must come, Mr. Nash." This gentleman promised with an inclination, and Peter continued: "But if, as you say, you're not for helping the young lady, how came you to arrange this interview with the great model?"

"Precisely to stop her short. The great model will find her very bad. Her judgements, as you probably know, are Rhadamanthine."

"Unfortunate creature!" said Biddy. "I think you're cruel."

"Never mind—I'll look after them," Sherringham laughed.

"And how can Madame Carré judge if the girl recites English?"

"She's so intelligent that she could judge if she recited Chinese," Peter declared.

"That's true, but the *jeune Anglaise* recites also in French," said Gabriel Nash.

"Then she isn't stupid."

"And in Italian, and in several more tongues, for aught I know."

Sherringham was visibly interested. "Very good—we'll put her through them all."

"She must be *most* clever," Biddy went on yearningly.

74

"She has spent her life on the Continent; she has wandered about with her mother; she has picked up things."

"And is she a lady?" Biddy asked.

"Oh tremendous! The great ones of the earth on the mother's side. On the father's, on the other hand, I imagine, only a Jew stockbroker in the City."

"Then they're rich—or ought to be," Sherringham suggested.

"Ought to be—ah there's the bitterness! The stockbroker had too short a go—he was carried off in his flower. However, he left his wife a certain property, which she appears to have muddled away, not having the safeguard of being herself a Hebrew. This is what she has lived on till to-day—this and another resource. Her husband, as she has often told me, had the artistic temperament: that's common, as you know, among *ces messieurs*. He made the most of his little opportunities and collected various pictures, tapestries, enamels, porcelains, and similar gewgaws. He parted with them also, I gather, at a profit; in short he carried on a neat little business as a *brocanteur*. It was nipped in the bud, but Mrs. Rooth was left with a certain number of these articles in her hands; indeed they must have formed her only capital. She was not a woman of business; she turned them, no doubt, to indifferent account; but she sold them piece by piece, and they kept her going while her daughter grew up. It was to this precarious traffic, conducted with extraordinary mystery and delicacy, that, five years ago, in Florence, I was indebted for my acquaintance with her. In those days I used to collect—heaven help me!—I used to pick up rubbish which I could ill afford. It was a little phase—we have our little phases, haven't we?" Mr. Nash asked with childlike trust—"and I've come out on the other side. Mrs. Rooth had an old green pot and I heard of her old green pot. To hear of it was to long for it, so that I went to see it under cover of night. I bought it and a couple of years ago I overturned and smashed it. It was the last of the little phase. It was not, however, as you've seen, the last of Mrs. Rooth. I met her afterwards in London, and I found her a year or two ago in Venice. She appears to be a great wanderer. She had other old pots, of other colours, red, yellow, black, or blue—she could produce them of any complexion you liked. I don't know whether she carried them about with her or whether she had little secret stores in the principal cities of Europe. To-day at any rate they seem all gone. On the other hand she has her daughter, who has grown up and who's a precious vase of another kind—less fragile I hope than the rest. May she not be overturned and smashed!"

Peter Sherringham and Biddy Dormer listened with attention to this history, and the girl testified to the interest with which she had followed it by saying when Mr. Nash had ceased speaking: "A Jewish stockbroker, a dealer in curiosities: what an odd person to marry—for a person who was well born! I daresay he was a German."

"His name must have been simply Roth, and the poor lady, to smarten it up, has put in another *o*," Sherringham ingeniously suggested.

"You're both very clever," said Gabriel, "and Rudolf Roth, as I happen to know, was indeed the designation of Maud Vavasour's papa. But so far as the question of derogation goes one might as well drown as starve—for what connexion is *not* a misalliance when one happens to have the unaccommodating, the crushing honour of being a Neville-Nugent of Castle Nugent? That's the high lineage of Maud's mamma. I seem to have heard it mentioned that Rudolf Roth was very versatile and, like most of his species, not unacquainted with the practice of music. He had been employed to teach the harmonium to Miss Neville-Nugent and she had profited by his lessons. If his daughter's like him—and she's not like her mother—he was darkly and dangerously handsome. So I venture rapidly to reconstruct the situation."

A silence, for the moment, had fallen on Lady Agnes and her other two children, so that Mr. Nash, with his universal urbanity, practically addressed these last remarks to them as well as to his other auditors. Lady Agnes looked as if she wondered whom he was talking about, and having caught the name of a noble residence she inquired: "Castle Nugent—where in the world's that?"

"It's a domain of immeasurable extent and almost inconceivable splendour, but I fear not to be found in any prosaic earthly geography!" Lady Agnes rested her eyes on the tablecloth as if she weren't sure a liberty had not been taken with her, or at least with her "order," and while Mr. Nash continued to abound in descriptive suppositions—"It must be on the banks of the Manzanares or the Guadalquivir"—Peter Sherringham, whose imagination had seemingly been kindled by the sketch of Miriam Rooth, took up the argument and reminded him that he had a short time before assigned a low place to the dramatic art and had not yet answered the question as to whether he believed in the theatre. Which gave the speaker a further chance. "I don't know that I understand your question; there are different ways of taking it. Do I think it's important? Is that what you mean? Important certainly to managers and stage-carpenters who want to make money, to ladies and gentlemen who want to produce themselves in public by limelight, and to other ladies and gentlemen who are bored and stupid and don't know what to do with their evening. It's a commercial and social convenience which may be infinitely worked. But important artistically, intellectually? How *can* it be— so poor, so limited a form?"

"Upon my honour it strikes me as rich and various! Do *you* think it's a poor and limited form, Nick?" Sherringham added, appealing to his kinsman.

"I think whatever Nash thinks. I've no opinion to-day but his."

This answer of the hope of the Dormers drew the eyes of his mother and sisters to him and caused his friend to exclaim that he wasn't used to such responsibilities—so few people had ever tested his presence of mind by agreeing with him. "Oh I used to be of your way of feeling," Nash went on to Sherringham. "I understand you perfectly. It's a phase like another. I've been through it—*j'ai été comme ça.*"

"And you went then very often to the Théâtre Français, and it was there I saw you. I place you now."

"I'm afraid I noticed none of the other spectators," Nash explained. "I had no attention but for the great Carré—she was still on the stage. Judge of my infatuation, and how I can allow for yours, when I tell you that I sought her acquaintance, that I couldn't rest till I had told her how I hung upon her lips."

"That's just what *I* told her," Sherringham returned.

"She was very kind to me. She said: '*Vous me rendez des forces.*'"

"That's just what she said to me!"

"And we've remained very good friends."

"So have we!" laughed Sherringham. "And such perfect art as hers—do you mean to say you don't consider *that* important, such a rare dramatic intelligence?"

"I'm afraid you read the *feuilletons*. You catch their phrases"—Nash spoke with pity. "Dramatic intelligence is never rare; nothing's more common."

"Then why have we so many shocking actors?"

"Have we? I thought they were mostly good; succeeding more easily and more completely in that business than in anything else. What could they do—those people generally—if they didn't do that poor thing? And reflect that the poor thing enables them to succeed! Of course, always, there are numbers of people on the stage who are no actors at all, for it's even easier to our poor humanity to be ineffectively stupid and vulgar than to bring down the house."

"It's not easy, by what I can see, to produce, completely, any artistic effect," Sherringham declared; "and those the actor produces are among the most momentous we know. You'll not persuade me that to watch such an actress as Madame Carré wasn't an education of the taste, an enlargement of one's knowledge."

"She did what she could, poor woman, but in what belittling, coarsening conditions! She had to interpret a character in a play, and a character in a play—not to say the whole piece: I speak more particularly of modern pieces—is such a wretchedly small peg to hang anything on! The dramatist shows us so little, is so hampered by his audience, is restricted to so poor an analysis."

"I know the complaint. It's all the fashion now. The *raffinés* despise the theatre," said Peter Sherringham in the manner of a man abreast with the culture of his age and not to be captured by a surprise. "*Connu, connu!*"

"It will be known better yet, won't it? when the essentially brutal nature of the modern audience is still more perceived, when it has been properly analysed: the *omnium gatherum* of the population of a big commercial city at the hour of the day when their taste is at its lowest, flocking out of hideous hotels and restaurants, gorged with food, stultified with buying and selling and with all the other sordid preoccupations of the age, squeezed together in a sweltering mass, disappointed in their seats, timing the author, timing the actor, wishing to get their money back on the spot—all before eleven o'clock. Fancy putting the exquisite before such a tribunal as that! There's not even a question of it. The dramatist wouldn't if he could, and in nine cases out of ten he couldn't if he would. He has to make the basest concessions. One of his principal canons is that he must enable his spectators to catch the suburban trains, which stop at 11.30. What would you think of any other artist—the painter or the novelist—whose governing forces should be the dinner and the suburban trains? The old dramatists didn't defer to them—not so much at least—and that's why they're less and less actable. If they're touched— the large loose men—it's only to be mutilated and trivialised. Besides, they had a simpler civilisation to represent—societies in which the life of man was in action, in passion, in immediate and violent expression. Those things could be put upon the playhouse boards with comparatively little sacrifice of their completeness and their truth. To-day we're so infinitely more reflective and complicated and diffuse that it makes all the difference. What can you do with a character, with an idea, with a feeling, between dinner and the suburban trains? You can give a gross, rough sketch of them, but how little you touch them, how bald you leave them! What crudity compared with what the novelist does!"

"Do you write novels, Mr. Nash?" Peter candidly asked.

"No, but I read them when they're extraordinarily good, and I don't go to plays. I read Balzac for instance—I encounter the admirable portrait of Valérie Marneffe in *La Cousine Bette*."

"And you contrast it with the poverty of Emile Augier's Séraphine in *Les Lionnes Pauvres*? I was awaiting you there. That's the *cheval de bataille* of you fellows."

"What an extraordinary discussion! What dreadful authors!" Lady Agnes murmured to her son. But he was listening so attentively to the other young men that he made no response, and Peter Sherringham went on:

"I've seen Madame Carré in things of the modern repertory, which she has made as vivid to me, caused to abide as ineffaceably in my memory, as Valérie Marneffe. She's the Balzac, as one may say, of actresses."

"The miniaturist, as it were, of whitewashers!" Nash offered as a substitute.

It might have been guessed that Sherringham resented his damned freedom, yet could but emulate his easy form. "You'd be magnanimous if you thought the young lady you've introduced to our old friend would be important."

Mr. Nash lightly weighed it. "She might be much more so than she ever will be."

Lady Agnes, however, got up to terminate the scene and even to signify that enough had been said about people and questions she had never so much as heard of. Every one else rose, the waiter brought Nicholas the receipt of the bill, and Sherringham went on, to his interlocutor: "Perhaps she'll be more so than you think."

"Perhaps—if you take an interest in her!"

"A mystic voice seems to exhort me to do so, to whisper that though I've never seen her I shall find something in her." On which Peter appealed. "What do you say, Biddy—shall I take an interest in her?"

The girl faltered, coloured a little, felt a certain embarrassment in being publicly treated as an oracle. "If she's not nice I don't advise it."

"And if she *is* nice?"

"You advise it still less!" her brother exclaimed, laughing and putting his arm round her.

Lady Agnes looked sombre—she might have been saying to herself: "Heaven help us, what chance has a girl of mine with a man who's so agog about actresses?" She was disconcerted and distressed; a multitude of incongruous things, all the morning, had been forced upon her attention— displeasing pictures and still more displeasing theories about them, vague portents of perversity on Nick's part and a strange eagerness on Peter's, learned apparently in Paris, to discuss, with a person who had a tone she never had been exposed to, topics irrelevant and uninteresting, almost disgusting, the practical effect of which was to make light of her presence. "Let us leave this—let us leave this!" she grimly said. The party moved together toward the door of departure, and her ruffled spirit was not soothed by hearing her son remark to his terrible friend: "You know you don't escape me; I stick to you!"

At this Lady Agnes broke out and interposed. "Pardon my reminding you that you're going to call on Julia."

"Well, can't Nash also come to call on Julia? That's just what I want— that she should see him."

Peter Sherringham came humanely to his kinswoman's assistance. "A better way perhaps will be for them to meet under my auspices at my 'dramatic tea.' This will enable me to return one favour for another. If Mr. Nash is so good as to introduce me to this aspirant for honours we estimate so differently, I'll introduce him to my sister, a much more positive quantity."

"It's easy to see who'll have the best of it!" Grace Dormer declared; while Nash stood there serenely, impartially, in a graceful detached way which seemed characteristic of him, assenting to any decision that relieved him of the grossness of choice and generally confident that things would turn out well for him. He was cheerfully helpless and sociably indifferent; ready to preside with a smile even at a discussion of his own admissibility.

"Nick will bring you. I've a little corner at the embassy," Sherringham continued.

"You're very kind. You must bring *him* then to-morrow—Rue de Constantinople."

"At five o'clock—don't be afraid."

"Oh dear!" Biddy wailed as they went on again and Lady Agnes, seizing his arm, marched off more quickly with her son. When they came out into the Champs Elysées Nick Dormer, looking round, saw his friend had disappeared. Biddy had attached herself to Peter, and Grace couldn't have encouraged Mr. Nash.

V

Lady Agnes's idea had been that her son should go straight from the Palais de l'Industrie to the Hôtel de Hollande, with or without his mother and his sisters as his humour should seem to recommend. Much as she desired to see their valued Julia, and as she knew her daughters desired it, she was quite ready to put off their visit if this sacrifice should contribute to a speedy confrontation for Nick. She was anxious he should talk with Mrs. Dallow, and anxious he should be anxious himself; but it presently appeared that he was conscious of no pressure of eagerness. His view was that she and the girls should go to their cousin without delay and should, if they liked, spend the rest of the day in her society. He would go later; he would go in the evening. There were lots of things he wanted to do meanwhile.

This question was discussed with some intensity, though not at length, while the little party stood on the edge of the Place de la Concorde, to which they had proceeded on foot; and Lady Agnes noticed that the "lots of things" to which he proposed to give precedence over an urgent duty, a conference with a person who held out full hands to him, were implied somehow in the friendly glance with which he covered the great square, the opposite bank of the Seine, the steep blue roofs of the quay, the bright immensity of Paris. What in the world could be more important than making sure of his seat?—so quickly did the good lady's imagination travel. And now that idea appealed to him less than a ramble in search of old books and prints—since she was sure this was what he had in his head. Julia would be flattered should she know it, but of course she mustn't know it. Lady Agnes was already thinking of the least injurious account she could give of the young man's want of precipitation. She would have liked to represent him as tremendously occupied, in his room at their own hotel, in getting off political letters to every one it should concern, and particularly in drawing up his address to the electors of Harsh. Fortunately she was a woman of innumerable discretions, and a part of the worn look that sat in her face came from her having schooled herself for years, in commerce with her husband and her sons, not to insist unduly. She would have liked to insist, nature had formed her to insist, and the self-control had told in more ways than one. Even now it was powerless to prevent her suggesting that before doing anything else Nick should at least repair to the inn and see if there weren't some telegrams.

He freely consented to do as much as this, and, having called a cab that she might go her way with the girls, kissed her again as he had done at the exhibition. This was an attention that could never displease her, but somehow when he kissed her she was really the more worried: she had come to recognise it as a sign that he was slipping away from her, and she wished she might frankly take it as his clutch at her to save him. She drove off with a vague sense that at any rate she and the girls might do something toward keeping the place warm for him. She had been a little vexed that Peter had not administered more of a push toward the Hôtel de Hollande, clear as it had become to her now that there was a foreignness in Peter which was not to be counted on and which made him speak of English affairs and even of English domestic politics as local and even "funny." They were very grandly local, and if one recalled, in public life, an occasional droll incident wasn't that, liberally viewed, just the warm human comfort of them? As she left the two young men standing together in the middle of the Place de la Concorde, the grand composition of which Nick, as she looked back, appeared to have paused to admire—as if he hadn't seen it a thousand times!—she wished she might have thought of Peter's influence with her son as exerted a little more in favour of localism. She had a fear he wouldn't abbreviate the boy's ill-timed *flânerie*. However, he had been very nice: he had invited them all to dine with him that evening at a convenient café, promising to bring Julia and one of his colleagues. So much as this he had been willing to do to make sure Nick and his sister should meet. His want of localism, moreover, was not so great as that if it should turn out that there *was* anything beneath his manner toward Biddy—! The upshot of this reflexion might have been represented by the circumstance of her ladyship's remarking after a minute to her younger daughter, who sat opposite her in the *voiture de place*, that it would do no harm if she should get a new hat and that the search might be instituted that afternoon.

"A French hat, mamma?" said Grace. "Oh do wait till she gets home!"

"I think they're really prettier here, you know," Biddy opined; and Lady Agnes said simply: "I daresay they're cheaper." What was in her mind in fact was: "I daresay Peter thinks them becoming." It will be seen she had plenty of inward occupation, the sum of which was not lessened by her learning when she reached the top of the Rue de la Paix that Mrs. Dallow had gone out half an hour before and had left no message. She was more disconcerted by this incident than she could have explained or than she thought was right, as she had taken for granted Julia would be in a manner waiting for them. How could she be sure Nick wasn't coming? When people were in Paris a few days they didn't mope in the house, but she might have waited a little longer or have left an explanation. Was she then not so much in earnest about Nick's standing? Didn't she recognise the importance of being there to see him about it? Lady Agnes wondered if her behaviour were a sign of her being already tired of the way this young gentleman treated her. Perhaps she had gone out because an instinct told her that the great propriety of their meeting early would make no difference with him—told her he wouldn't after all come. His mother's heart sank as she glanced at this possibility that their precious friend was already tired, she having on her side an intuition that there were still harder things in store. She had disliked having to tell Mrs. Dallow that Nick wouldn't see her till the evening, but now she disliked still more her not being there to hear it. She even resented a little her kinswoman's not having reasoned that she and the girls would come in any event, and not thought them worth staying in for. It came up indeed that she would perhaps have gone to their hotel, which was a good way up the Rue de Rivoli, near the Palais Royal—on which the cabman was directed to drive to that establishment.

As he jogged along she took in some degree the measure of what that might mean, Julia's seeking a little to avoid them. Was she growing to dislike them? Did she think they kept too sharp an eye on her, so that the idea of their standing in a still closer relation wouldn't be enticing? Her conduct up to this time had not worn such an appearance, unless perhaps a little, just a very little, in the matter of her ways with poor Grace. Lady Agnes knew she wasn't particularly fond of poor Grace, and could even sufficiently guess the reason—the manner in which Grace betrayed most how they wanted to make sure of her. She remembered how long the girl had stayed the last time she had been at Harsh—going for an acceptable week and dragging out her visit to a month. She took a private heroic vow that Grace shouldn't go near the place again for a year; not, that is, unless Nick and Julia were married within the time. If that were to happen she shouldn't care. She recognised that it wasn't absolutely everything Julia should be in love with Nick; it was also better she should dislike his mother and sisters after a probable pursuit of him than before. Lady Agnes did justice to the natural rule in virtue of which it usually comes to pass that a woman doesn't get on with her husband's female belongings, and was even willing to be sacrificed to it in her disciplined degree. But she desired not to be sacrificed for nothing: if she was to be objected to as a mother-in-law she wished to be the mother-in-law first.

At the hotel in the Rue de Rivoli she had the disappointment of finding that Mrs. Dallow had not called, and also that no telegrams had come. She went in with the girls for half an hour and then straggled out with them again. She was undetermined and dissatisfied and the afternoon was rather a problem; of the kind, moreover, that she disliked most and was least accustomed to: not a choice between different things to do—her life had been full of that—but a want of anything to do at all. Nick had said to her before they separated: "You can knock about with the girls, you know; everything's amusing here." That was easily said while he sauntered and gossiped with Peter Sherringham and perhaps went to see more pictures like those in the Salon. He was usually, on such occasions, very good-natured about spending his time with them; but this episode had taken altogether a perverse, profane form. She had no desire whatever to knock about and was far from finding everything in Paris amusing. She had no aptitude for aimlessness, and moreover thought it vulgar. If she had found Julia's card at the hotel—the sign of a hope of catching them just as they came back from the Salon—she would have made a second attempt to see her before the evening; but now certainly they would leave her alone. Lady Agnes wandered joylessly with the girls in the Palais Royal and the Rue de Richelieu, and emerged upon the Boulevard, where they continued their frugal prowl, as Biddy rather irritatingly called it. They went into five shops to buy a hat for Biddy, and her ladyship's presumptions of cheapness were woefully belied.

"Who in the world's your comic friend?" Peter Sherringham was meanwhile asking of his kinsman as they walked together.

"Ah there's something else you lost by going to Cambridge—you lost Gabriel Nash!"

"He sounds like an Elizabethan dramatist," Sherringham said. "But I haven't lost him, since it appears now I shan't be able to have you without him."

"Oh, as for that, wait a little. I'm going to try him again, but I don't know how he wears. What I mean is that you've probably lost his freshness, which was the great thing. I rather fear he's becoming conventional, or at any rate serious."

"Bless me, do you call that serious?"

"He used to be so gay. He had a real genius for playing with ideas. He was a wonderful talker."

"It seems to me he does very well now," said Peter Sherringham.

"Oh this is nothing. He had great flights of old, very great flights; one saw him rise and rise and turn somersaults in the blue—one wondered how far he could go. He's very intelligent, and I should think it might be interesting to find out what it is that prevents the whole man from being as good as his parts. I mean in case he isn't so good."

"I see you more than suspect that. Mayn't it be simply that he's too great an ass?"

"That would be the whole—I shall see in time—but it certainly isn't one of the parts. It may be the effect, but it isn't the cause, and it's for the cause I claim an interest. Do you think him an ass for what he said about the theatre—his pronouncing it a coarse art?"

"To differ from you about him that reason would do," said Sherringham. "The only bad one would be one that shouldn't preserve our difference. You needn't tell me you agree with him, for frankly I don't care."

"Then your passion still burns?" Nick Dormer asked.

"My passion—?"

"I don't mean for any individual exponent of the equivocal art: mark the guilty conscience, mark the rising blush, mark the confusion of mind! I mean the old sign one knew you best by; your permanent stall at the Français, your inveterate attendance at *premières*, the way you 'follow' the young talents and the old."

"Yes, it's still my little hobby, my little folly if you like," Sherringham said. "I don't find I get tired of it. What will you have? Strong predilections are rather a blessing; they're simplifying. I'm fond of representation—the representation of life: I like it better, I think, than the real thing. You like it too, you'd be ready in other conditions to go in for it, in your way—so you've no right to cast the stone. You like it best done by one vehicle and I by another; and our preference on either side has a deep root in us. There's a fascination to me in the way the actor does it, when his talent—ah he must have that!—has been highly trained. Ah it must *be* that! The things he can do in this effort at representation, with the dramatist to back him, seem to me innumerable—he can carry it to a point!—and I take great pleasure in observing them, in recognising and comparing them. It's an amusement like another—I don't pretend to call it by any exalted name, but in this vale of friction it will serve. One can lose one's self in it, and it has the recommendation—in common, I suppose, with the study of the other arts—that the further you go in it the more you find. So I go rather far, if you will. But is it the principal sign one knows me by?" Peter abruptly asked.

"Don't be ashamed of it," Nick returned—"else it will be ashamed of you. I ought to discriminate. You're distinguished among my friends and relations by your character of rising young diplomatist; but you know I always want the final touch to the picture, the last fruit of analysis. Therefore I make out that you're conspicuous among rising young diplomatists for the infatuation you describe in such pretty terms."

"You evidently believe it will prevent my ever rising very high. But pastime for pastime is it any idler than yours?"

"Than mine?"

"Why you've half-a-dozen while I only allow myself the luxury of one. For the theatre's my sole vice, really. Is this more wanton, say, than to devote weeks to the consideration of the particular way in which your friend Mr. Nash may be most intensely a twaddler and a bore? That's not my ideal of choice recreation, but I'd undertake to satisfy you about him sooner. You're a young statesman—who happens to be an *en disponibilité* for the moment—but you spend not a little of your time in besmearing canvas with bright-coloured pigments. The idea of representation fascinates you, but in your case it's representation in oils—or do you practise water-colours and pastel too? You even go much further than I, for I study my art of predilection only in the works of others. I don't aspire to leave works of my own. You're a painter, possibly a great one; but I'm not an actor." Nick Dormer declared he would certainly become one—he was so well on the way to it; and Sherringham, without heeding this charge, went on: "Let me add that, considering you *are* a painter, your portrait of the complicated Nash is lamentably dim."

"He's not at all complicated; he's only too simple to give an account of. Most people have a lot of attributes and appendages that dress them up and superscribe them, and what I like Gabriel for is that he hasn't any at all. It makes him, it keeps him, so refreshingly cool."

"By Jove, you match him there! Isn't it an appendage and an attribute to escape kicking? How does he manage that?" Sherringham asked.

"I haven't the least idea—I don't know that he doesn't rouse the kicking impulse. Besides, he can kick back and I don't think any one has ever seen him duck or dodge. His means, his profession, his belongings have never anything to do with the question. He doesn't shade off into other people; he's as neat as an outline cut out of paper with scissors. I like him, therefore, because in dealing with him you know what you've got hold of. With most men you don't: to pick the flower you must break off the whole dusty, thorny, worldly branch; you find you're taking up in your grasp all sorts of other people and things, dangling accidents and conditions. Poor Nash has none of those encumbrances: he's the solitary-fragrant blossom."

"My dear fellow, you'd be better for a little of the same pruning!" Sherringham retorted; and the young men continued their walk and their gossip, jerking each other this way and that, punching each other here and there, with an amicable roughness consequent on their having, been boys together. Intimacy had reigned of old between the little Sherringhams and the little Dormers, united in the country by ease of neighbouring and by the fact that there was first cousinship, not neglected, among the parents, Lady Agnes standing in this plastic relation to Lady Windrush, the mother of Peter and Julia as well as of other daughters and of a maturer youth who was to inherit, and who since then had inherited, the ancient barony. Many things had altered later on, but not the good reasons for not explaining. One of our young men had gone to Eton and the other to Harrow—the scattered school on the hill was the tradition of the Dormers—and the divergence had rather taken its course in university years. Bricket, however, had remained accessible to Windrush, and Windrush to Bricket, to which estate Percival Dormer had now succeeded, terminating the interchange a trifle rudely by letting out that pleasant white house in the midlands—its expropriated inhabitants, Lady Agnes and her daughters, adored it—to an American reputed rich, who in the first flush of his sense of contrasts considered that for twelve hundred a year he got it at a bargain. Bricket had come to the late Sir Nicholas from his elder brother, dying wifeless and childless. The new baronet, so different from his father—though recalling at some points the uncle after whom he had been named—that Nick had to make it up by cultivating conformity, roamed about the world, taking shots which excited the enthusiasm of society, when society heard of them, at the few legitimate creatures of the chase the British rifle had up to that time spared. Lady Agnes meanwhile settled with her girls in a gabled, latticed house in a mentionable quarter, though it still required a little explaining, of the temperate zone of London. It was not into her lap, poor woman, that the revenues of Bricket were poured. There was no dower-house attached to that moderate property, and the allowance with which the estate was charged on her ladyship's behalf was not an incitement to grandeur.

Nick had a room under his mother's roof, which he mainly used to dress for dinner when dining in Calcutta Gardens, and he had "kept on" his chambers in the Temple; for to a young man in public life an independent address was indispensable. Moreover, he was suspected of having a studio in an out-of-the-way district, the indistinguishable parts of South Kensington, incongruous as such a retreat might seem in the case of a member of Parliament. It was an absurd place to see his constituents unless he wanted to paint their portraits, a kind of "representation" with which they would scarce have been satisfied; and in fact the only question of portraiture had been when the wives and daughters of several of them expressed a wish for the picture of their handsome young member. Nick had not offered to paint it himself, and the studio was taken for granted rather than much looked into by the ladies in Calcutta Gardens. Too express a disposition to regard whims of this sort as extravagance pure and simple was known by them to be open to correction; for they were not oblivious that Mr. Carteret had humours which weighed against them in the shape of convenient cheques nestling between the inside pages of legible letters of advice. Mr. Carteret was Nick's providence, just as Nick was looked to, in a general way, to be that of his mother and sisters, especially since it had become so plain that Percy, who was not subtly selfish, would operate, mainly with a "six-bore," quite out of that sphere. It was not for studios certainly that Mr. Carteret sent cheques; but they were an expression of general confidence in Nick, and a little expansion was natural to a young man enjoying such a luxury as that. It was sufficiently felt in Calcutta Gardens that he could be looked to not to betray such confidence; for Mr. Carteret's behaviour could have no name at all unless one were prepared to call it encouraging. He had never promised anything, but he was one of the delightful persons with whom the redemption precedes or dispenses with the vow. He had been an early and lifelong friend of the late right honourable gentleman, a political follower, a devoted admirer, a stanch supporter in difficult hours. He had never married, espousing nothing more reproductive than Sir Nicholas's views—he used to write letters to the *Times* in favour of them—and had, so far as was known, neither chick nor child; nothing but an amiable little family of eccentricities, the flower of which was his odd taste for living in a small, steep, clean country town, all green gardens and red walls with a girdle of hedge-rows, all clustered about an immense brown old abbey. When Lady Agnes's imagination rested upon the future of her second son she liked to remember that Mr. Carteret had nothing to "keep up": the inference seemed so direct that he would keep up Nick.

The most important event in the life of this young man had been incomparably his success, under his father's eyes, more than two years before, in the sharp contest for Crockhurst—a victory which his consecrated name, his extreme youth, his ardour in the fray, the marked personal sympathy of the party, and the attention excited by the fresh cleverness of his speeches, tinted with young idealism and yet sticking sufficiently to the question—the burning question which has since burned out—had made quite splendid. There had been leaders in the newspapers about it, half in compliment to her husband, who was known to be failing so prematurely—he was almost as young to die, and to die famous, for Lady Agnes regarded it as famous, as his son had been to stand—tributes the boy's mother religiously preserved, cut out and tied together with a ribbon, in the innermost drawer of a favourite cabinet. But it had been a barren, or almost a barren triumph, for in the order of importance in Nick's history another incident had run it, as the phrase is, very close: nothing less than the quick dissolution of the Parliament in which he was so manifestly destined to give symptoms of a future. He had not recovered his seat at the general election, for the second contest was even sharper than the first and the Tories had put forward a loud, vulgar, rattling, bullying, money-spending man. It was to a certain extent a comfort that poor Sir Nicholas, who had been witness of the bright hour, should have passed away before the darkness. He died with all his hopes on his second son's head, unconscious of near disappointment, handing on the torch and the tradition, after a long, supreme interview with Nick at which Lady Agnes had not been present, but which she knew to have been a thorough paternal dedication, an august communication of ideas on the highest national questions (she had reason to believe he had touched on those of external as well as of domestic and of colonial policy) leaving on the boy's nature and manner from that moment the most unmistakable traces. If his tendency to reverie increased it was because he had so much to think over in what his pale father had said to him in the hushed dim chamber, laying on him the great mission that death had cut short, breathing into him with unforgettable solemnity the very accents—Sir Nicholas's voice had been wonderful for richness—that he was to sound again. It was work cut out for a lifetime, and that "co-ordinating power in relation to detail" which was one of the great characteristics of the lamented statesman's high distinction—the most analytic of the weekly papers was always talking about it—had enabled him to rescue the prospect from any shade of vagueness or of ambiguity.

Five years before Nick Dormer went up to be questioned by the electors of Crockhurst Peter Sherringham had appeared before a board of examiners who let him off much less easily, though there were also some flattering prejudices in his favour; such influences being a part of the copious, light, unembarrassing baggage with which each of the young men began life. Peter passed, however, passed high, and had his reward in prompt assignment to small, subordinate, diplomatic duties in Germany. Since then he had had his professional adventures, which need not arrest us, inasmuch as they had all paled in the light of his appointment, nearly three years previous to the moment of our making his acquaintance, to a secretaryship of embassy in Paris. He had done well and had gone fast and for the present could draw his breath at ease. It pleased him better to remain in Paris as a subordinate than to go to Honduras as a principal, and Nick Dormer had not put a false colour on the matter in speaking of his stall at the Théâtre Français as a sedative to his ambition. Nick's inferiority in age to his cousin sat on him more lightly than when they had been in their teens; and indeed no one can very well be much older than a young man who has figured for a year, however imperceptibly, in the House of Commons. Separation and diversity had made them reciprocally strange enough to give a price to what they shared; they were friends without being particular friends; that further degree could always hang before them as a suitable but not oppressive contingency, and they were both conscious that it was in their interest to keep certain differences to "chaff" each other about—so possible was it that they might have quarrelled if they had had everything in common. Peter, as being wide-minded, was a little irritated to find his cousin always so intensely British, while Nick Dormer made him the object of the same compassionate criticism, recognised in him a rare knack with foreign tongues, but reflected, and even with extravagance declared, that it was a pity to have gone so far from home only to remain so homely. Moreover, Nick had his ideas about the diplomatic mind, finding in it, for his own sympathy, always the wrong turn. Dry, narrow, barren, poor he pronounced it in familiar conversation with the clever secretary; wanting in imagination, in generosity, in the finest perceptions and the highest courage. This served as well as anything else to keep the peace between them; it was a necessity of their friendly intercourse that they should scuffle a little, and it scarcely mattered what they scuffled about. Nick Dormer's express enjoyment of Paris, the shop-windows on the quays, the old books on the parapet, the gaiety of the river, the grandeur of the Louvre, every fine feature of that prodigious face, struck his companion as a sign of insularity; the appreciation of such things having become with Sherringham an unconscious habit, a contented assimilation. If poor Nick, for the hour, was demonstrative and lyrical, it was because he had no other way of sounding the note of farewell to the independent life of which the term seemed now definitely in sight—the sense so pressed upon him that these were the last moments of his freedom. He would waste time till half-past seven, because half-past seven meant dinner, and dinner meant his mother solemnly attended by the strenuous shade of his father and re-enforced by Julia.

VI

When he arrived with the three members of his family at the restaurant of their choice Peter Sherringham was already seated there by one of the immaculate tables, but Mrs. Dallow was not yet on the scene, and they had time for a sociable settlement—time to take their places and unfold their napkins, crunch their rolls, breathe the savoury air, and watch the door, before the usual raising of heads and suspension of forks, the sort of stir that accompanied most of this lady's movements, announced her entrance. The *dame de comptoir* ducked and re-ducked, the people looked round, Peter and Nick got up, there was a shuffling of chairs—Julia had come. Peter was relating how he had stopped at her hotel to bring her with him and had found her, according to her custom, by no means ready; on which, fearing his guests would arrive first at the rendezvous and find no proper welcome, he had come off without her, leaving her to follow. He had not brought a friend, as he intended, having divined that Julia would prefer a pure family party if she wanted to talk about her candidate. Now she stood looking down at the table and her expectant kinsfolk, drawing off her gloves, letting her brother draw off her jacket, lifting her hands for some rearrangement of her hat. She looked at Nick last, smiling, but only for a moment. She said to Peter: "Are we going to dine here? Oh dear, why didn't you have a private room?"

Nick had not seen her at all for several weeks and had seen her but little for a year, but her off-hand cursory manner had not altered in the interval. She spoke remarkably fast, as if speech were not in itself a pleasure—to have it over as soon as possible; and her *brusquerie* was of the dark shade friendly critics account for by pleading shyness. Shyness had never appeared to him an ultimate quality or a real explanation of anything; it only explained an effect by another effect, neither with a cause to boast of. What he suspected in Julia was that her mind was less pleasing than her person; an ugly, a really blighting idea, which as yet he had but half accepted. It was a case in which she was entitled to the benefit of every doubt and oughtn't to be judged without a complete trial. Nick meanwhile was afraid of the trial—this was partly why he had been of late to see her so little—because he was afraid of the sentence, afraid of anything that might work to lessen the charm it was actually in the power of her beauty to shed. There were people who thought her rude, and he hated rude women. If he should fasten on that view, or rather if that view should fasten on him, what could still please and what he admired in her would lose too much of its sweetness. If it be thought odd that he had not yet been able to read the character of a woman he had known since childhood the answer is that this character had grown faster than Nick's observation. The growth was constant, whereas the observation was but occasional, though it had begun early. If he had attempted inwardly to phrase the matter, as he probably had not, he might have pronounced the effect she produced upon him too much a compulsion; not the coercion of design, of importunity, nor the vulgar pressure of family expectation, a betrayed desire he should like her enough to marry her, but a mixture of divers urgent things; of the sense that she was imperious and generous—probably more the former than the latter—and of a certain prevision of doom, the influence of the idea that he should come to it, that he was predestined.

This had made him shrink from knowing the worst about her; not the wish to get used to it in time, but what was more characteristic of him, the wish to interpose a temporary illusion. Illusions and realities and hopes and fears, however, fell into confusion whenever he met her after a separation. The separation, so far as seeing her alone or as continuous talk was concerned, had now been tolerably long; had lasted really ever since his failure to regain his seat. An impression had come to him that she judged that failure rather stiffly, had thought, and had somewhat sharply said, that he ought to have done better. This was a part of her imperious way, and a part not *all* to be overlooked on a mere present basis. If he were to marry her he should come to an understanding with her: he should give her his own measure as well as take hers. But the understanding might in the actual case suggest too much that he *was* to marry her. You could quarrel with your wife because there were compensations—for her; but you mightn't be prepared to offer these compensations as prepayment for the luxury of quarrelling.

It was not that such a luxury wouldn't be considerable, our young man none the less thought as Julia Dallow's fine head poised itself before him again; a high spirit was of course better than a mawkish to be mismated with, any day in the year. She had much the same colour as her brother, but as nothing else in her face was the same the resemblance was not striking. Her hair was of so dark a brown that it was commonly regarded as black, and so abundant that a plain arrangement was required to keep it in natural relation to the rest of her person. Her eyes were of a grey sometimes pronounced too light, and were not sunken in her face, but placed well on the surface. Her nose was perfect, but her mouth was too small; and Nick Dormer, and doubtless other persons as well, had sometimes wondered how with such a mouth her face could have expressed decision. Her figure helped it, for she appeared tall—being extremely slender—yet was not; and her head took turns and positions which, though a matter of but half an inch out of the common this way or that, somehow contributed to the air of resolution and temper. If it had not been for her extreme delicacy of line and surface she might have been called bold; but as it was she looked refined and quiet—refined by tradition and quiet for a purpose. And altogether she was beautiful, with the gravity of her elegant head, her hair like the depths of darkness, her eyes like its earlier clearing, her mouth like a rare pink flower.

Peter said he had not taken a private room because he knew Biddy's tastes; she liked to see the world—she had told him so—the curious people, the coming and going of Paris. "Oh anything for Biddy!" Julia replied, smiling at the girl and taking her place. Lady Agnes and her elder daughter exchanged one of their looks, and Nick exclaimed jocosely that he didn't see why the whole party should be sacrificed to a presumptuous child. The presumptuous child blushingly protested she had never expressed any such wish to Peter, upon which Nick, with broader humour, revealed that Peter had served them so out of stinginess: he had pitchforked them together in the public room because he wouldn't go to the expense of a *cabinet*. He had brought no guest, no foreigner of distinction nor diplomatic swell, to honour them, and now they would see what a paltry dinner he would give them. Peter stabbed him indignantly with a long roll, and Lady Agnes, who seemed to be waiting for some manifestation on Mrs. Dallow's part which didn't come, concluded, with a certain coldness, that they quite sufficed to themselves for privacy as well as for society. Nick called attention to this fine phrase of his mother's and said it was awfully neat, while Grace and Biddy looked harmoniously at Julia's clothes. Nick felt nervous and joked a good deal to carry it off—a levity that didn't prevent Julia's saying to him after a moment: "You might have come to see me to-day, you know. Didn't you get my message from Peter?"

"Scold him, Julia—scold him well. I begged him to go," said Lady Agnes; and to this Grace added her voice with an "Oh Julia, do give it to him!" These words, however, had not the effect they suggested, since Mrs. Dallow only threw off for answer, in her quick curt way, that that would be making far too much of him. It was one of the things in her that Nick mentally pronounced ungraceful, the perversity of pride or of shyness that always made her disappoint you a little if she saw you expected a thing. She snubbed effusiveness in a way that yet gave no interesting hint of any wish to keep it herself in reserve. Effusiveness, however, certainly, was the last thing of which Lady Agnes would have consented to be accused; and Nick, while he replied to Julia that he was sure he shouldn't have found her, was not unable to perceive the operation on his mother of that shade of manner. "He ought to have gone; he owed you that," she went on; "but it's very true he would have had the same luck as we. I went with the girls directly after luncheon. I suppose you got our card."

"He might have come after I came in," said Mrs. Dallow.

"Dear Julia, I'm going to see you to-night. I've been waiting for that," Nick returned.

"Of course *we* had no idea when you'd come in," said Lady Agnes.

"I'm so sorry. You must come to-morrow. I hate calls at night," Julia serenely added.

"Well then, will you roam with me? Will you wander through Paris on my arm?" Nick asked, smiling. "Will you take a drive with me?"

"Oh that would be perfection!" cried Grace.

"I thought we were all going somewhere—to the Hippodrome, Peter," Biddy said.

"Oh not all; just you and me!" laughed Peter.

"I'm going home to my bed. I've earned my rest," Lady Agnes sighed.

"Can't Peter take *us*?" demanded Grace. "Nick can take you home, mamma, if Julia won't receive him, and I can look perfectly after Peter and Biddy."

"Take them to something amusing; please take them," Mrs. Dallow said to her brother. Her voice was kind, but had the expectation of assent in it, and Nick observed both the good nature and the pressure. "You're tired, poor dear," she continued to Lady Agnes. "Fancy your being dragged about so! What did you come over for?"

"My mother came because I brought her," Nick said. "It's I who have dragged her about. I brought her for a little change. I thought it would do her good. I wanted to see the Salon."

"It isn't a bad time. I've a carriage and you must use it; you must use nothing else. It shall take you everywhere. I'll drive you about to-morrow." Julia dropped these words with all her air of being able rather than of wanting; but Nick had already noted, and he noted now afresh and with pleasure, that her lack of unction interfered not a bit with her always acting. It was quite sufficiently manifest to him that for the rest of the time she might be near his mother she would do for her numberless good turns. She would give things to the girls—he had a private adumbration of that; expensive Parisian, perhaps not perfectly useful, things.

Lady Agnes was a woman who measured outlays and returns, but she was both too acute and too just not to recognise the scantest offer from which an advantage could proceed. "Dear Julia!" she exclaimed responsively; and her tone made this brevity of acknowledgment adequate. Julia's own few words were all she wanted. "It's so interesting about Harsh," she added. "We're immensely excited."

"Yes, Nick looks it. *Merci, pas de vin.* It's just the thing for you, you know," Julia said to him.

"To be sure he knows it. He's immensely grateful. It's really very kind of you."

"You do me a very great honour, Julia," Nick hastened to add.

"Don't be tiresome, please," that lady returned.

"We'll talk about it later. Of course there are lots of points," Nick pursued. "At present let's be purely convivial. Somehow Harsh is such a false note here. *Nous causerons de ça.*"

"My dear fellow, you've caught exactly the tone of Mr. Gabriel Nash," Peter Sherringham declared on this.

"Who's Mr. Gabriel Nash?" Mrs. Dallow asked.

"Nick, is he a gentleman? Biddy says so," Grace Dormer interposed before this inquiry was answered.

"It's to be supposed that any one Nick brings to lunch with us—!" Lady Agnes rather coldly sighed.

"Ah Grace, with your tremendous standard!" her son said; while Peter Sherringham explained to his sister that Mr. Nash was Nick's new Mentor or oracle—whom, moreover, she should see if she would come and have tea with him.

"I haven't the least desire to see him," Julia made answer, "any more than I have to talk about Harsh and bore poor Peter."

"Oh certainly, dear, you'd bore me," her brother rang out.

"One thing at a time then. Let us by all means be convivial. Only you must show me how," Mrs. Dallow went on to Nick. "What does he mean, Cousin Agnes? Does he want us to drain the wine-cup, to flash with repartee?"

"You'll do very well," said Nick. "You're thoroughly charming to-night."

"Do go to Peter's, Julia, if you want something exciting. You'll see a wonderful girl," Biddy broke in with her smile on Peter.

"Wonderful for what?"

"For thinking she can act when she can't," said the roguish Biddy.

"Dear me, what people you all know! I hate Peter's theatrical people."

"And aren't you going home, Julia?" Lady Agnes inquired.

"Home to the hotel?"

"Dear, no, to Harsh—to see about everything."

"I'm in the midst of telegrams. I don't know yet."

"I suppose there's no doubt they'll have him," Lady Agnes decided to pursue.

"Who'll have whom?"

"Why, the local people and the party managers. I'm speaking of the question of my son's standing."

"They'll have the person I want them to have, I daresay. There are so many people in it, in one way or another—it's dreadful. I like the way you sit there," Julia went on to Nick.

"So do I," he smiled back at her; and he thought she *was* charming now, because she was gay and easy and willing really, though she might plead incompetence, to understand how jocose a dinner in a pothouse in a foreign town might be. She was in good humour or was going to be, and not grand nor stiff nor indifferent nor haughty nor any of the things people who disliked her usually found her and sometimes even a little made him believe her. The spirit of mirth in some cold natures manifests itself not altogether happily, their effort of recreation resembles too much the bath of the hippopotamus; but when Mrs. Dallow put her elbows on the table one felt she could be trusted to get them safely off again.

For a family in mourning the dinner was lively; the more so that before it was half over Julia had arranged that her brother, eschewing the inferior spectacle, should take the girls to the Théâtre Français. It was her idea, and Nick had a chance to observe how an idea was apt to be not successfully controverted when it was Julia's. Even the programme appeared to have been prearranged to suit it, just the thing for the cheek of the young person—*Il ne*

Faut Jurer de Rien and *Mademoiselle de la Seiglière*. Peter was all willingness, but it was Julia who settled it, even to sending for the newspaper—he was by a rare accident unconscious of the evening's bill—and to reassuring Biddy, who was happy but anxious, on the article of their being too late for good places. Peter could always get good places: a word from him and the best box was at his disposal. She made him write the word on a card and saw a messenger despatched with it to the Rue de Richelieu; and all this without loudness or insistence, parenthetically and authoritatively. The box was bespoken and the carriage, as soon as they had had their coffee, found to be in attendance. Peter drove off in it with the girls, understanding that he was to send it back, and Nick waited for it over the finished repast with the two ladies. After this his mother was escorted to it and conveyed to her apartments, and all the while it had been Julia who governed the succession of events. "Do be nice to her," Lady Agnes breathed to him as he placed her in the vehicle at the door of the café; and he guessed it gave her a comfort to have left him sitting there with Mrs. Dallow.

He had every disposition to be nice to his charming cousin; if things went as she liked them it was the proof of a certain fine force in her—the force of assuming they would. Julia had her differences—some of them were much for the better; and when she was in a mood like this evening's, liberally dominant, he was ready to encourage most of what she took for granted. While they waited for the return of the carriage, which had rolled away with his mother, she sat opposite him with her elbows on the table, playing first with one and then with another of the objects that encumbered it; after five minutes of which she exclaimed, "Oh I say, well go!" and got up abruptly, asking for her jacket. He said something about the carriage and its order to come back for them, and she replied, "Well, it can go away again. I don't want a carriage," she added: "I want to walk"—and in a moment she was out of the place, with the people at the tables turning round again and the *caissière* swaying in her high seat. On the pavement of the boulevard she looked up and down; there were people at little tables by the door; there were people all over the broad expanse of the asphalt; there was a profusion of light and a pervasion of sound; and everywhere, though the establishment at which they had been dining was not in the thick of the fray, the tokens of a great traffic of pleasure, that night-aspect of Paris which represents it as a huge market for sensations. Beyond the Boulevard des Capucines it flared through the warm evening like a vast bazaar, and opposite the Café Durand the Madeleine rose theatrical, a high artful *décor* before the footlights of the Rue Royale. "Where shall we go, what shall we do?" Mrs. Dallow asked, looking at her companion and somewhat to his surprise, as he had supposed she wanted but to go home.

"Anywhere you like. It's so warm we might drive instead of going indoors. We might go to the Bois. That would be agreeable."

"Yes, but it wouldn't be walking. However, that doesn't matter. It's mild enough for anything—for sitting out like all these people. And I've never walked in Paris at night. It would amuse me."

Nick hesitated. "So it might, but it isn't particularly recommended to ladies."

"I don't care for that if it happens to suit me."

"Very well then, we'll walk to the Bastille if you like."

Julia hesitated, on her side, still looking about. "It's too far; I'm tired; we'll sit here." And she dropped beside an empty table on the "terrace" of M. Durand. "This will do; it's amusing enough and we can look at the Madeleine—that's respectable. If we must have something we'll have a *madère*—is that respectable? Not particularly? So much the better. What are those people having? *Bocks*? Couldn't we have *bocks*? Are they very low? Then I shall have one. I've been so wonderfully good—I've been staying at Versailles: *je me dois bien cela.*"

She insisted, but pronounced the thin liquid in the tall glass very disgusting when it was brought. Nick was amazed, reflecting that it was not for such a discussion as this that his mother had left him with hands in his pockets. He had been looking out, but as his eloquence flowed faster he turned to his friend, who had dropped upon a sofa with her face to the window. She had given her jacket and gloves to her maid, but had kept on her hat; and she leaned forward a little as she sat, clasping her hands together in her lap and keeping her eyes on him. The lamp, in a corner, was so thickly veiled that the room was in tempered obscurity, lighted almost equally from the street and the brilliant shop-fronts opposite. "Therefore why be sapient and solemn about it, like an editorial in a newspaper?" Nick added with a smile.

She continued to look at him after he had spoken, then she said: "If you don't want to stand you've only to say so. You needn't give your reasons."

"It's too kind of you to let me off that! And then I'm a tremendous fellow for reasons; that's my strong point, don't you know? I've a lot more besides those I've mentioned, done up and ready for delivery. The odd thing is that they don't always govern my behaviour. I rather think I do want to stand."

"Then what you said just now was a speech," Julia declared.

"A speech?"

"The 'rot,' the humbug of the hustings."

"No, those great truths remain, and a good many others. But an inner voice tells me I'm in for it. And it will be much more graceful to embrace this opportunity, accepting your co-operation, than to wait for some other and forfeit that advantage."

"I shall be very glad to help you anywhere," she went on.

"Thanks awfully," he returned, still standing there with his hands in his pockets. "You'd do it best in your own place, and I've no right to deny myself such a help."

Julia calmly considered. "I don't do it badly."

"Ah you're so political!"

"Of course I am; it's the only decent thing to be. But I can only help you if you'll help yourself. I can do a good deal, but I can't do everything. If you'll work I'll work with you; but if you're going into it with your hands in your pockets I'll have nothing to do with you." Nick instantly changed the position of these members and sank into a seat with his elbows on his knees. "You're very clever, but you must really take a little trouble. Things don't drop into people's mouths."

"I'll try—I'll try. I've a great incentive," he admitted.

"Of course you have."

"My mother, my poor mother." Julia breathed some vague sound and he went on: "And of course always my father, dear good man. My mother's even more political than you."

"I daresay she is, and quite right!" said Mrs. Dallow.

"And she can't tell me a bit more than you can what she thinks, what she believes, what she wants."

"Pardon me, I can tell you perfectly. There's one thing I always immensely want—to keep out a Tory."

"I see. That's a great philosophy."

"It will do very well. And I desire the good of the country. I'm not ashamed of that."

"And can you give me an idea of what it is—the good of the country?"

"I know perfectly what it isn't. It isn't what the Tories want to do."

"What do they want to do?"

"Oh it would take me long to tell you. All sorts of trash."

"It would take you long, and it would take them longer! All they want to do is to prevent *us* from doing. On our side we want to prevent them from preventing us. That's about as clearly as we all see it. So on both sides it's a beautiful, lucid, inspiring programme."

"I don't believe in you," Mrs. Dallow replied to this, leaning back on her sofa.

"I hope not, Julia, indeed!" He paused a moment, still with his face toward her and his elbows on his knees; then he pursued: "You're a very accomplished woman and a very zealous one; but you haven't an idea, you know—not to call an idea. What you mainly want is to be at the head of a political salon; to start one, to keep it up, to make it a success."

"Much you know me!" Julia protested; but he could see, through the dimness, that her face spoke differently.

"You'll have it in time, but I won't come to it," Nick went on.

"You can't come less than you do."

"When I say you'll have it I mean you've already got it. That's why I don't come."

"I don't think you know what you mean," said Mrs. Dallow. "I've an idea that's as good as any of yours, any of those you've treated me to this evening, it seems to me—the simple idea that one ought to do something or other for one's country."

"'Something or other' certainly covers all the ground. There's one thing one can always do for one's country, which is not to be afraid."

"Afraid of what?"

Nick Dormer waited a little, as if his idea amused him, but he presently said, "I'll tell you another time. It's very well to talk so glibly of standing," he added; "but it isn't absolutely foreign to the question that I haven't got the cash."

"What did you do before?" she asked.

"The first time my father paid."

"And the other time?"

"Oh Mr. Carteret."

"Your expenses won't be at all large; on the contrary," said Julia.

"They shan't be; I shall look out sharp for that. I shall have the great Hutchby."

"Of course; but you know I want you to do it well." She paused an instant and then: "Of course you can send the bill to me."

"Thanks awfully; you're tremendously kind. I shouldn't think of that." Nick Dormer got up as he spoke, and walked to the window again, his companion's eyes resting on him while he stood with his back to her. "I shall manage it somehow," he wound up.

"Mr. Carteret will be delighted," said Julia.

"I daresay, but I hate taking people's money."

"That's nonsense—when it's for the country. Isn't it for *them*?"

"When they get it back!" Nick replied, turning round and looking for his hat. "It's startlingly late; you must be tired." Mrs. Dallow made no response to this, and he pursued his quest, successful only when he reached a duskier corner of the room, to which the hat had been relegated by his cousin's maid. "Mr. Carteret will expect so much if he pays. And so would you."

"Yes, I'm bound to say I should! I should expect a great deal—everything." And Mrs. Dallow emphasised this assertion by the way she rose erect. "If you're riding for a fall, if you're only going in to miss it, you had better stay out."

"How can I miss it with *you*?" the young man smiled. She uttered a word, impatiently but indistinguishably, and he continued: "And even if I do it will have been immense fun."

"It is immense fun," said Julia. "But the best fun is to win. If you don't——!"

"If I don't?" he repeated as she dropped.

"I'll never speak to you again."

"How much you expect even when you don't pay!"

Mrs. Dallow's rejoinder was a justification of this remark, expressing as it did the fact that should they receive on the morrow information on which she believed herself entitled to count, information tending to show how hard the Conservatives meant to fight, she should look to him to be in the field as early as herself. Sunday was a lost day; she should leave Paris on Monday.

"Oh they'll fight it hard; they'll put up Kingsbury," said Nick, smoothing his hat. "They'll all come down—all that can get away. And Kingsbury has a very handsome wife."

"She's not so handsome as your cousin," Julia smiled.

"Oh dear, no—a cousin sooner than a wife any day!" Nick laughed as soon as he had said this, as if the speech had an awkward side; but the reparation perhaps scarcely mended it, the exaggerated mock-meekness with which he added: "I'll do any blessed thing you tell me."

"Come here to-morrow then—as early as ten." She turned round, moving to the door with him; but before they reached it she brought out: "Pray isn't a gentleman to do anything, to be anything?"

"To be anything——?"

"If he doesn't aspire to serve the State."

"Aspire to make his political fortune, do you mean? Oh bless me, yes, there are other things."

"What other things that can compare with that?"

"Well, I for instance, I'm very fond of the arts."

"Of the arts?" she echoed.

"Did you never hear of them? I'm awfully fond of painting."

At this Julia stopped short, and her fine grey eyes had for a moment the air of being set further forward in her head. "Don't be odious! Good-night," she said, turning away and leaving him to go.

BOOK SECOND

VII

Peter Sherringham reminded Nick the next day that he had promised to be present at Madame Carré's interview with the ladies introduced to her by Gabriel Nash; and in the afternoon, conformably to this arrangement, the two men took their way to the Rue de Constantinople. They found Mr. Nash and his friends in the small beflounced drawing-room of the old actress, who, as they learned, had sent in a request for ten minutes' grace, having been detained at a lesson—a rehearsal of the *comédie de salon* about to be given for a charity by a fine lady, at which she had consented to be present as an adviser. Mrs. Rooth sat on a black satin sofa with her daughter beside her while Gabriel Nash, wandering about the room, looked at the votive offerings which converted the little panelled box, decorated in sallow white and gold, into a theatrical museum: the presents, the portraits, the wreaths, the diadems, the letters, framed and glazed, the trophies and tributes and relics collected by Madame Carré during half a century of renown. The profusion of this testimony was hardly more striking than the confession of something missed, something hushed, which seemed to rise from it all and make it melancholy, like a reference to clappings which, in the nature of things, could now only be present as a silence: so that if the place was full of history it was the form without the fact, or at the most a redundancy of the one to a pinch of the other—the history of a mask, of a squeak, of a series of vain gestures.

Some of the objects exhibited by the distinguished artist, her early portraits, in lithograph or miniature, represented the costume and embodied the manner of a period so remote that Nick Dormer, as he glanced at them, felt a quickened curiosity to look at the woman who reconciled being alive to-day with having been alive so long ago. Peter Sherringham already knew how she managed this miracle, but every visit he paid her added to his amused, charmed sense that it *was* a miracle and that his extraordinary old friend had seen things he should never, never see. Those were just the things he wanted to see most, and her duration, her survival, cheated him agreeably and helped him a little to guess them. His appreciation of the actor's art was so systematic that it had an antiquarian side, and at the risk of representing him as attached to an absurd futility it must be said that he had as yet hardly known a keener regret for anything than for the loss of that antecedent world, and in particular for his having belatedly missed the great *comédienne*, the light of the French stage in the early years of the century, of whose example and instruction Madame Carré had had the inestimable benefit. She had often described to him her rare predecessor, straight from whose hands she had received her most celebrated parts and of whom her own manner was often a religious imitation; but her descriptions troubled him more than they consoled, only confirming his theory, to which so much of his observation had already ministered, that the actor's art in general was going down and down, descending a slope with abysses of vulgarity at its foot, after having reached its perfection, more than fifty years ago, in the talent of the lady in question. He would have liked to dwell for an hour beneath the meridian.

Gabriel Nash introduced the new-comers to his companions; but the younger of the two ladies gave no sign of lending herself to this transaction. The girl was very white; she huddled there, silent and rigid, frightened to death, staring, expressionless. If Bridget Dormer had seen her at this moment she might have felt avenged for the discomfiture of her own spirit suffered at the Salon, the day before, under the challenging eyes of Maud Vavasour. It was plain at the present hour that Miss Vavasour would have run away had she not regarded the persons present as so many guards and keepers. Her appearance made Nick feel as if the little temple of art in which they were collected had been the waiting-room of a dentist. Sherringham had seen a great many nervous girls tremble before the same ordeal, and he liked to be kind to them, to say things that would help them to do themselves justice. The probability in a given case was almost overwhelmingly in favour of their having any other talent one could think of in a higher degree than the dramatic; but he could rarely refrain from some care that the occasion shouldn't be, even as against his conscience, too cruel. There were occasions indeed that could scarce be too cruel to punish properly certain examples of presumptuous ineptitude. He remembered what Mr. Nash had said about this blighted maiden, and perceived that though she might be inept she was now anything but presumptuous. Gabriel fell to talking with Nick Dormer while Peter addressed himself to Mrs. Rooth. There was no use as yet for any direct word to the girl, who was too scared even to hear. Mrs. Rooth, with her shawl fluttering about her, nestled against her daughter, putting out her hand to take one of Miriam's soothingly. She had pretty, silly, near-sighted eyes, a long thin nose, and an upper lip which projected over the under as an ornamental cornice rests on its support. "So much depends—really everything!" she said in answer to some sociable observation of Sherringham's. "It's either this," and she rolled her eyes expressively about the room, "or it's—I don't know what!"

"Perhaps we're too many," Peter hazarded to her daughter. "But really you'll find, after you fairly begin, that you'll do better with four or five."

Before she answered she turned her head and lifted her fine eyes. The next instant he saw they were full of tears. The words she spoke, however, though uttered as if she had tapped a silver gong, had not the note of sensibility: "Oh, I don't care for *you!*" He laughed at this, declared it was very well said and that if she could give Madame Carré such a specimen as that——! The actress came in before he had finished his phrase, and he observed the way the girl ruefully rose to the encounter, hanging her head a little and looking out from under her brows. There was no sentiment in her face—only a vacancy of awe and anguish which had not even the merit of being fine of its kind, for it spoke of no spring of reaction. Yet the head was good, he noted at the same moment; it was strong and salient and made to tell at a distance. Madame Carré scarcely heeded her at first, greeting her only in her order among the others and pointing to seats, composing the circle with smiles and gestures, as if they were all before the prompter's box. The old actress presented herself to a casual glance as a red-faced, raddled woman in a wig, with beady eyes, a hooked nose, and pretty hands; but Nick Dormer, who had a sense for the over-scored human surface, soon observed that these comparatively gross marks included a great deal of delicate detail—an eyebrow, a nostril, a flitting of expressions, as if a multitude of little facial wires were pulled from within.

This accomplished artist had in particular a mouth which was visibly a rare instrument, a pair of lips whose curves and fine corners spoke of a lifetime of "points" unerringly made and verses exquisitely spoken, helping to explain the purity of the sound that issued from them. Her whole countenance had the look of long service—of a thing infinitely worn and used, drawn and stretched to excess, with its elasticity overdone and its springs relaxed, yet religiously preserved and kept in repair, even as some valuable old timepiece which might have quivered and rumbled but could be trusted to strike the hour. At the first words she spoke Gabriel Nash exclaimed endearingly: *"Ah la voix de Célimène!"* Célimène, who wore a big red flower on the summit of her dense wig, had a very grand air, a toss of the head, and sundry little majesties of manner; in addition to which she was strange, almost grotesque, and to some people would have been even terrifying, capable of reappearing, with her hard eyes, as a queer vision of the darkness. She excused herself for having made the company wait, and mouthed and mimicked in the drollest way, with intonations as fine as a flute, the performance and the pretensions of the *belles dames* to whom she had just been endeavouring to communicate a few of the rudiments. *"Mais celles-là, c'est une plaisanterie,"* she went on to Mrs. Rooth; "whereas you and your daughter, *chère madame*—I'm sure you are quite another matter."

The girl had got rid of her tears, and was gazing at her, and Mrs. Rooth leaned forward and said portentously: "She knows four languages."

Madame Carré gave one of her histrionic stares, throwing back her head. "That's three too many. The thing's to do something proper with one."

"We're very much in earnest," continued Mrs. Rooth, who spoke excellent French.

"I'm glad to hear it—*il n'y a que ça. La tête est bien*—the head's very good," she said as she looked at the girl. "But let us see, my dear child, what you've got in it!" The young lady was still powerless to speak; she opened her lips, but nothing came. With the failure of this effort she turned her deep sombre eyes to the three men. *"Un beau regard*—it carries well." Madame Carré further commented. But even as she spoke Miss Rooth's fine gaze was suffused again and the next moment she had definitely begun to weep. Nick Dormer sprung up; he felt embarrassed and intrusive—there was such an indelicacy in sitting there to watch a poor working-girl's struggle with timidity. There was a momentary confusion; Mrs. Rooth's tears were seen also to flow; Mr. Nash took it gaily, addressing, however, at the same time, the friendliest, most familiar encouragement to his companions, and Peter Sherringham offered to retire with Nick on the spot, should their presence incommode the young lady. But the agitation was over in a minute; Madame Carré motioned Mrs. Rooth out of her seat and took her place beside the girl, and Nash explained judiciously to the other men that she'd be worse should they leave her. Her mother begged them to remain, "so that there should be at least some English"; she spoke as if the old actress were an army of Frenchwomen. The young heroine of the occasion quickly came round, and Madame Carré, on the sofa beside her, held her hand and emitted a perfect music of reassurance. "The nerves, the nerves—they're half our affair. Have as many as you like, if you've got something else too. *Voyons*—do you know anything?"

"I know some pieces."

"Some pieces of the *répertoire*?"

Miriam Rooth stared as if she didn't understand. "I know some poetry."

"English, French, Italian, German," said her mother.

Madame Carré gave Mrs. Rooth a look which expressed irritation at the recurrence of this announcement. "Does she wish to act in all those tongues? The phrase-book isn't the comedy!"

"It's only to show you how she has been educated."

"Ah, *chère madame*, there's no education that matters! I mean save the right one. Your daughter must have a particular form of speech, like me, like *ces messieurs*."

"You see if I can speak French," said the girl, smiling dimly at her hostess. She appeared now almost to have collected herself.

"You speak it in perfection."

"And English just as well," said Miss Rooth.

"You oughtn't to be an actress—you ought to be a governess."

"Oh don't tell us that: it's to escape from that!" pleaded Mrs. Rooth.

"I'm very sure your daughter will escape from that," Peter Sherringham was moved to interpose.

"Oh if *you* could help her!" said the lady with a world of longing.

"She has certainly all the qualities that strike the eye," Peter returned.

"You're *most* kind, sir!" Mrs. Rooth declared, elegantly draping herself.

"She knows Célimène; I've heard her do Célimène," Gabriel Nash said to Madame Carré".

"And she knows Juliet, she knows Lady Macbeth and Cleopatra," added Mrs. Rooth.

"*Voyons*, my dear child, do you wish to work for the French stage or for the English?" the old actress demanded.

"Ours would have sore need of you, Miss Rooth," Sherringham gallantly threw off.

"Could you speak to any one in London—could you introduce her?" her mother eagerly asked.

"Dear madam, I must hear her first, and hear what Madame Carré says."

"She has a voice of rare beauty, and I understand voices," said Mrs. Rooth.

"Ah then if she has intelligence she has every gift."

"She has a most poetic mind," the old lady went on.

"I should like to paint her portrait; she's made for that," Nick Dormer ventured to observe to Mrs. Rooth; partly because struck with the girl's suitability for sitting, partly to mitigate the crudity of inexpressive spectatorship.

"So all the artists say. I've had three or four heads of her, if you would like to see them: she has been done in several styles. If you were to do her I'm sure it would make her celebrated."

"And me too," Nick easily laughed.

"It would indeed—a member of Parliament!" Nash declared.

"Ah, I have the honour——?" murmured Mrs. Rooth, looking gratified and mystified.

Nick explained that she had no honour at all, and meanwhile Madame Carré had been questioning the girl "*Chère madame*, I can do nothing with your daughter: she knows too much!" she broke out. "It's a pity, because I like to catch them wild."

"Oh she's wild enough, if that's all! And that's the very point, the question of where to try," Mrs. Rooth went on. "Into what do I launch her—upon what dangerous stormy sea? I've thought of it so anxiously."

"Try here—try the French public: they're so much the most serious," said Gabriel Nash.

"Ah no, try the English: there's such a rare opening!" Sherringham urged in quick opposition.

"Oh it isn't the public, dear gentlemen. It's the private side, the other people—it's the life, it's the moral atmosphere."

"*Je ne connais qu'une scène,—la nôtre*," Madame Carré declared. "I'm assured by every one who knows that there's no other."

"Very correctly assured," said Mr. Nash. "The theatre in our countries is puerile and barbarous."

"There's something to be done for it, and perhaps mademoiselle's the person to do it," Sherringham contentiously suggested.

"Ah but, *en attendant,* what can it do for her?" Madame Carré asked.

"Well, anything I can help to bring about," said Peter Sherringham, more and more struck with the girl's rich type. Miriam Rooth sat in silence while this discussion went on, looking from one speaker to the other with a strange dependent candour.

"Ah, if your part's marked out I congratulate you, mademoiselle!"—and the old actress underlined the words as she had often underlined others on the stage. She smiled with large permissiveness on the young aspirant, who appeared not to understand her. Her tone penetrated, however, to certain depths in the mother's nature, adding another stir to agitated waters.

"I feel the responsibility of what she shall find in the life, the standards, of the theatre," Mrs. Rooth explained. "Where is the purest tone—where are the highest standards? That's what I ask," the good lady continued with a misguided intensity which elicited a peal of unceremonious but sociable laughter from Gabriel Nash.

"The purest tone—*qu'est-ce que c'est que ça?*" Madame Carré demanded in the finest manner of modern comedy.

"We're very, *very* respectable," Mrs. Rooth went on, but now smiling and achieving lightness too.

"What I want is to place my daughter where the conduct—and the picture of conduct in which she should take part—wouldn't be quite absolutely dreadful. Now, *chère madame,* how about all that; how about *conduct* in the French theatre—all the things she should see, the things she should hear, the things she should learn?"

Her hostess took it, as Sherringham felt, *de très-haut.* "I don't think I know what you're talking about. They're the things she may see and hear and learn everywhere; only they're better done, they're better said, above all they're better taught. The only conduct that concerns an, actress, it seems to me, is her own, and the only way for her to behave herself is not to be a helpless stick. I know no other conduct."

"But there are characters, there are situations, which I don't think I should like to see *her* undertake."

"There are many, no doubt, which she would do well to leave alone!" laughed the Frenchwoman.

"I shouldn't like to see her represent a very bad woman—a *really* bad one," Mrs. Rooth serenely pursued.

"Ah in England then, and in your theatre, every one's immaculately good? Your plays must be even more ingenious than I supposed!"

"We haven't any plays," said Gabriel Nash.

"People will write them for Miss Rooth—it will be a new era," Sherringham threw in with wanton, or at least with combative, optimism.

"Will *you*, sir—will you do something? A sketch of one of our grand English ideals?" the old lady asked engagingly.

"Oh I know what you do with our pieces—to show your superior virtue!" Madame Carré cried before he had time to reply that he wrote nothing but diplomatic memoranda. "Bad women? *Je n'ai joué que ça, madame.* 'Really' bad? I tried to make them real!"

"I can say 'L'Aventurière,'" Miriam interrupted in a cold voice which seemed to hint at a want of participation in the maternal solicitudes.

"Allow us the pleasure of hearing you then. Madame Carré will give you the *réplique*," said Peter Sherringham.

"Certainly, my child; I can say it without the book," Madame Carré responded. "Put yourself there—move that chair a little away." She patted her young visitor, encouraging her to rise, settling with her the scene they should take, while the three men sprang up to arrange a place for the performance. Miriam left her seat and looked vaguely about her; then having taken off her hat and given it to her mother she stood on the designated spot with her eyes to the ground. Abruptly, however, instead of beginning the scene, Madame Carré turned to the elder lady with an air which showed that a rejoinder to this visitor's remarks of a moment before had been gathering force in her breast.

"You mix things up, *chère madame*, and I have it on my heart to tell you so. I believe it's rather the case with you other English, and I've never been able to learn that either your morality or your talent is the gainer by it. To be too respectable to go where things are done best is in my opinion to be very vicious indeed; and to do them badly in order to preserve your virtue is to fall into a grossness more shocking than any other. To do them well is virtue enough, and not to make a mess of it the only respectability. That's hard enough to merit Paradise. Everything else is base humbug! *Voilà, chère madame*, the answer I have for your scruples!"

"It's admirable—admirable; and I am glad my friend Dormer here has had the great advantage of hearing you utter it!" Nash exclaimed with a free designation of Nick.

That young man thought it in effect a speech denoting an intelligence of the question, yet he rather resented the idea that Gabriel should assume it would strike him as a revelation; and to show his familiarity with the line of thought it indicated, as well as to play his part appreciatively in the little circle, he observed to Mrs. Rooth, as if they might take many things for granted: "In other words, your daughter must find her safeguard in the artistic conscience." But he had no sooner spoken than he was struck with the oddity of their discussing so publicly, and under the poor girl's handsome nose, the conditions which Miss Rooth might find the best for the preservation of her personal integrity. However, the anomaly was light and unoppressive— the echoes of a public discussion of delicate questions seemed to linger so familiarly in the egotistical little room. Moreover, the heroine of the occasion evidently was losing her embarrassment; she was the priestess on the tripod, awaiting the afflatus and thinking only of that. Her bared head, of which she had changed the position, holding it erect, while her arms hung at her sides, was admirable; her eyes gazed straight out of the window and at the houses on the opposite side of the Rue de Constantinople.

Mrs. Rooth had listened to Madame Carré with startled, respectful attention, but Nick, considering her, was very sure she hadn't at all taken in the great artist's little lesson. Yet this didn't prevent her from exclaiming in answer to himself: "Oh a fine artistic life—what indeed is more beautiful?"

Peter Sherringham had said nothing; he was watching Miriam and her attitude. She wore a black dress which fell in straight folds; her face, under her level brows, was pale and regular—it had a strange, strong, tragic beauty. "I don't know what's in her," he said to himself; "nothing, it would seem, from her persistent vacancy. But such a face as that, such a head, is a fortune!" Madame Carré brought her to book, giving her the first line of the speech of Clorinde: "*Vous ne me fuyez pas, mon enfant, aujourd'hui.*" But still the girl hesitated, and for an instant appeared to make a vain, convulsive effort. In this convulsion she frowned portentously; her low forehead overhung her eyes; the eyes themselves, in shadow, stared, splendid and cold, and her hands clinched themselves at her sides. She looked austere and terrible and was during this moment an incarnation the vividness of which drew from Sherringham a stifled cry. "*Elle est bien belle—ah ça*," murmured the old actress; and in the pause which still preceded the issue of sound from the girl's lips Peter turned to his kinsman and said in a low tone: "You must paint her just like that."

"Like that?"

"As the Tragic Muse."

She began to speak; a long, strong, colourless voice quavered in her young throat. She delivered the lines of Clorinde in the admired interview with Célie, the gem of the third act, with a rude monotony, and then, gaining confidence, with an effort at modulation which was not altogether successful and which evidently she felt not to be so. Madame Carré sent back the ball without raising her hand, repeating the speeches of Célie, which her memory possessed from their having so often been addressed to her, and uttering the verses with soft, communicative art. So they went on through the scene, which, when it was over, had not precisely been a triumph for Miriam Rooth. Sherringham forbore to look at Gabriel Nash, and Madame Carré said: "I think you've a voice, *ma fille*, somewhere or other. We must try and put our hand on it." Then she asked her what instruction she had had, and the girl, lifting her eyebrows, looked at her mother while her mother prompted her.

"Mrs. Delamere in London; she was once an ornament of the English stage. She gives lessons just to a very few; it's a great favour. Such a very nice person! But above all, Signor Ruggieri—I think he taught us most." Mrs. Rooth explained that this gentleman was an Italian tragedian, in Rome, who instructed Miriam in the proper manner of pronouncing his language and also in the art of declaiming and gesticulating.

"Gesticulating I'll warrant!" declared their hostess. "They mimic as for the deaf, they emphasise as for the blind. Mrs. Delamere is doubtless an epitome of all the virtues, but I never heard of her. You travel too much," Madame Carré went on; "that's very amusing, but the way to study is to stay at home, to shut yourself up and hammer at your scales." Mrs. Rooth complained that they had no home to stay at; in reply to which the old actress exclaimed: "Oh you English, you're *d'une légèreté à faire frémir*. If you haven't a home you must make, or at least for decency pretend to, one. In our profession it's the first requisite."

"But where? That's what I ask!" said Mrs. Rooth.

"Why not here?" Sherringham threw out.

"Oh here!" And the good lady shook her head with a world of sad significance.

"Come and live in London and then I shall be able to paint your daughter," Nick Dormer interposed.

"Is that all it will take, my dear fellow?" asked Gabriel Nash.

"Ah, London's full of memories," Mrs. Rooth went on. "My father had a great house there—we always came up. But all that's over."

"Study here and then go to London to appear," said Peter, feeling frivolous even as he spoke.

"To appear in French?"

"No, in the language of Shakespeare."

"But we can't study that here."

"Mr. Sherringham means that he will give you lessons," Madame Carré explained. "Let me not fail to say it—he's an excellent critic."

"How do you know that—you who're beyond criticism and perfect?" asked Sherringham: an inquiry to which the answer was forestalled by the girl's rousing herself to make it public that she could recite the "Nights" of Alfred de Musset.

"Diable!" said the actress: "that's more than I can! By all means give us a specimen."

The girl again placed herself in position and rolled out a fragment of one of the splendid conversations of Musset's poet with his muse—rolled it loudly and proudly, tossed it and tumbled it about the room. Madame Carré watched her at first, but after a few moments she shut her eyes, though the best part of the business was to take in her young candidate's beauty. Sherringham had supposed Miriam rather abashed by the flatness of her first performance, but he now saw how little she could have been aware of this: she was rather uplifted and emboldened. She made a mush of the divine verses, which in spite of certain sonorities and cadences, an evident effort to imitate a celebrated actress, a comrade of Madame Carré, whom she had heard declaim them, she produced as if she had been dashing blindfold at some playfellow she was to "catch." When she had finished Madame Carré passed no judgement, only dropping: "Perhaps you had better say something English." She suggested some little piece of verse—some fable if there were fables in English. She appeared but scantily surprised to hear that there were not—it was a language of which one expected so little. Mrs. Rooth said: "She knows her Tennyson by heart. I think he's much deeper than La Fontaine"; and after some deliberation and delay Miriam broke into "The Lotus-Eaters," from which she passed directly, almost breathlessly, to "Edward Gray." Sherringham had by this time heard her make four different attempts, and the only generalisation very present to him was that she uttered these dissimilar compositions in exactly the same tone—a solemn, droning, dragging measure suggestive of an exhortation from the pulpit and adopted evidently with the "affecting" intention and from a crude idea of "style." It was all funereal, yet was artlessly rough. Sherringham thought her English performance less futile than her French, but he could see that Madame Carré listened to it even with less pleasure. In the way the girl wailed forth some of her Tennysonian lines he detected a faint gleam as of something pearly in deep water. But the further she went the more violently she acted on the nerves of Mr. Gabriel Nash: that also he could discover from the way this gentleman ended by slipping discreetly to the window and leaning there with his head out and his back to the exhibition. He had the art of mute expression; his attitude said as clearly as possible: "No, no, you can't call me either ill-mannered or ill-natured. I'm the showman of the occasion, moreover, and I avert myself, leaving you to judge. If there's a thing in life I hate it's this idiotic new fashion of the drawing-room recitation and of the insufferable creatures who practise it, who prevent conversation, and whom, as they're beneath it, you can't punish by criticism. Therefore what I'm doing's only too magnanimous— bringing these benighted women here, paying with my person, stifling my just repugnance."

While Sherringham judged privately that the manner in which Miss Rooth had acquitted herself offered no element of interest, he yet remained aware that something surmounted and survived her failure, something that would perhaps be worth his curiosity. It was the element of outline and attitude, the way she stood, the way she turned her eyes, her head, and moved her limbs. These things held the attention; they had a natural authority and, in spite of their suggesting too much the school-girl in the *tableau-vivant*, a "plastic" grandeur. Her face, moreover, grew as he watched it; something delicate dawned in it, a dim promise of variety and a touching plea for patience, as if it were conscious of being able to show in time more shades than the simple and striking gloom which had as yet mainly graced it. These rather rude physical felicities formed in short her only mark of a vocation. He almost hated to have to recognise them; he had seen them so often when they meant nothing at all that he had come at last to regard them as almost a guarantee of incompetence. He knew Madame Carré valued them singly so little that she counted them out in measuring an histrionic nature; when deprived of the escort of other properties which helped and completed them she almost held them a positive hindrance to success—success of the only kind she esteemed. Far oftener than himself she had sat in judgement on young women for whom hair and eyebrows and a disposition for the statuesque would have worked the miracle of sanctifying their stupidity if the miracle were workable. But that particular miracle never was. The qualities she rated highest were not the gifts but the conquests, the effects the actor had worked hard for, had dug out of the mine by unwearied study. Sherringham remembered to have had in the early part of their acquaintance a friendly dispute with her on this subject, he having been moved at that time to defend doubtless to excess the cause of the gifts. She had gone so far as to say that a serious comedian ought to be ashamed of them—ashamed of resting his case on them; and when Sherringham had cited the great Rachel as a player whose natural endowment was rich and who had owed her highest triumphs to it, she had declared that Rachel was the very instance that proved her point;—a talent assisted by one or two primary aids, a voice and a portentous brow, but essentially formed by work, unremitting and ferocious work. "I don't care a straw for your handsome girls," she said; "but bring me one who's ready to drudge the tenth part of the way Rachel drudged, and I'll forgive her her beauty. Of course, *notez bien*, Rachel wasn't a *grosse bête*: that's a gift if you like!"

Mrs. Rooth, who was evidently very proud of the figure her daughter had made—her daughter who for all one could tell affected their hostess precisely as a *grosse bête*—appealed to Madame Carré rashly and serenely for a verdict; but fortunately this lady's voluble *bonne* came rattling in at the same moment with the tea-tray. The old actress busied herself in dispensing this refreshment, an hospitable attention to her English visitors, and under cover of the diversion thus obtained, while the others talked together, Sherringham put her the question: "Well, is there anything in my young friend?"

"Nothing I can see. She's loud and coarse."

"She's very much afraid. You must allow for that."

"Afraid of me, immensely, but not a bit afraid of her authors—nor of you!" Madame Carré smiled.

"Aren't you prejudiced by what that fellow Nash has told you?"

"Why prejudiced? He only told me she was very handsome."

"And don't you think her so?"

"Admirable. But I'm not a photographer nor a dressmaker nor a coiffeur. I can't do anything with 'back hair' nor with a mere big stare."

"The head's very noble," said Peter Sherringham. "And the voice, when she spoke English, had some sweet tones."

"Ah your English—possibly! All I can say is that I listened to her conscientiously, and I didn't perceive in what she did a single *nuance*, a single inflexion or intention. But not one, *mon cher*. I don't think she's intelligent."

"But don't they often seem stupid at first?"

"Say always!"

"Then don't some succeed—even when they're handsome?"

"When they're handsome they always succeed—in one way or another."

"You don't understand us English," said Peter Sherringham.

Madame Carré drank her tea; then she replied: "Marry her, my son, and give her diamonds. Make her an ambassadress; she'll look very well."

"She interests you so little that you don't care to do anything for her?"

"To do anything?"

"To give her a few lessons."

The old actress looked at him a moment; after which, rising from her place near the table on which the tea had been served, she said to Miriam Rooth: "My dear child, I give my voice for the *scène anglaise*. You did the English things best."

123

"Did I do them well?" asked the girl.

"You've a great deal to learn; but you've rude force. The main things *sont encore a dégager*, but they'll come. You must work."

"I think she has ideas," said Mrs. Rooth.

"She gets them from you," Madame Carré replied.

"I must say that if it's to be *our* theatre I'm relieved. I do think ours safer," the good lady continued.

"Ours is dangerous, no doubt."

"You mean you're more severe," said the girl.

"Your mother's right," the actress smiled; "you have ideas."

"But what shall we do then—how shall we proceed?" Mrs. Rooth made this appeal, plaintively and vaguely, to the three gentlemen; but they had collected a few steps off and were so occupied in talk that it failed to reach them.

"Work—work—work!" exclaimed the actress.

"In English I can play Shakespeare. I want to play Shakespeare," Miriam made known.

"That's fortunate, as in English you haven't any one else to play."

"But he's so great—and he's so pure!" said Mrs. Rooth.

"That indeed seems the saving of you," Madame Carré returned.

"You think me actually pretty bad, don't you?" the girl demanded with her serious face.

"*Mon Dieu, que vous dirai-je?* Of course you're rough; but so was I at your age. And if you find your voice it may carry you far. Besides, what does it matter what I think? How can I judge for your English public?"

"How shall I find my voice?" asked Miriam Rooth.

"By trying. *Il n'y a que ça.* Work like a horse, night and day. Besides, Mr. Sherringham, as he says, will help you."

That gentleman, hearing his name, turned round and the girl appealed to him. "Will you help me really?"

"To find her voice," said Madame Carré.

"The voice, when it's worth anything, comes from the heart; so I suppose that's where to look for it," Gabriel Nash suggested.

"Much you know; you haven't got any!" Miriam retorted with the first scintillation of gaiety she had shown on this occasion.

"Any voice, my child?" Mr. Nash inquired.

"Any heart—or any manners!"

Peter Sherringham made the secret reflexion that he liked her better lugubrious, as the note of pertness was not totally absent from her mode of emitting these few words. He was irritated, moreover, for in the brief conference he had just had with the young lady's introducer he had had to meet the rather difficult call of speaking of her hopefully. Mr. Nash had said with his bland smile, "And what impression does my young friend make?"—in respect to which Peter's optimism felt engaged by an awkward logic. He answered that he recognised promise, though he did nothing of the sort;—at the same time that the poor girl, both with the exaggerated "points" of her person and the vanity of her attempt at expression, constituted a kind of challenge, struck him as a subject for inquiry, a problem, an explorable tract. She was too bad to jump at and yet too "taking"—perhaps after all only vulgarly—to overlook, especially when resting her tragic eyes on him with the trust of her deep "Really?" This note affected him as addressed directly to his honour, giving him a chance to brave verisimilitude, to brave ridicule even a little, in order to show in a special case what he had always maintained in general, that the direction of a young person's studies for the stage may be an interest of as high an order as any other artistic appeal.

"Mr. Nash has rendered us the great service of introducing us to Madame Carré, and I'm sure we're immensely indebted to him," Mrs. Rooth said to her daughter with an air affectionately corrective.

"But what good does that do us?" the girl asked, smiling at the actress and gently laying her finger-tips upon her hand. "Madame Carré listens to me with adorable patience, and then sends me about my business—ah in the prettiest way in the world."

"Mademoiselle, you're not so rough; the tone of that's very *juste. A la bonne heure*; work—work!" the actress cried. "There was an inflexion there—or very nearly. Practise it till you've got it."

"Come and practise it to *me*, if your mother will be so kind as to bring you," said Peter Sherringham.

"Do you give lessons—do you understand?" Miriam asked.

"I'm an old play-goer and I've an unbounded belief in my own judgement."

"'Old,' sir, is too much to say," Mrs. Rooth remonstrated. "My daughter knows your high position, but she's very direct. You'll always find her so. Perhaps you'll say there are less honourable faults. We'll come to see you with pleasure. Oh I've been at the embassy when I was her age. Therefore why shouldn't she go to-day? That was in Lord Davenant's time."

"A few people are coming to tea with me to-morrow. Perhaps you'll come then at five o'clock."

"It will remind me of the dear old times," said Mrs. Rooth.

"Thank you; I'll try and do better to-morrow," Miriam professed very sweetly.

"You do better every minute!" Sherringham returned—and he looked at their hostess in support of this declaration.

"She's finding her voice," Madame Carré acknowledged.

"She's finding a friend!" Mrs. Rooth threw in.

"And don't forget, when you come to London, my hope that you'll come and see *me*," Nick Dormer said to the girl. "To try and paint you—that would do me good!"

"She's finding even two," said Madame Carré.

"It's to make up for one I've lost!" And Miriam looked with very good stage-scorn at Gabriel Nash. "It's he who thinks I'm bad."

"You say that to make me drive you home; you know it will," Nash returned.

"We'll all take you home; why not?" Sherringham asked.

Madame Carré looked at the handsome girl, handsomer than ever at this moment, and at the three young men who had taken their hats and stood ready to accompany her. A deeper expression came for an instant into her hard, bright eyes. "*Ah la jeunesse!*" she sighed. "You'd always have that, my child, if you were the greatest goose on earth!"

VIII

At Peter Sherringham's the next day Miriam had so evidently come with the expectation of "saying" something that it was impossible such a patron of the drama should forbear to invite her, little as the exhibition at Madame Carré's could have contributed to render the invitation prompt. His curiosity had been more appeased than stimulated, but he felt none the less that he had "taken up" the dark-browed girl and her reminiscential mother and must face the immediate consequences of the act. This responsibility weighed upon him during the twenty-four hours that followed the ultimate dispersal of the little party at the door of the Hôtel de la Garonne.

On quitting Madame Carré the two ladies had definitely declined Mr. Nash's offered cab and had taken their way homeward on foot and with the gentlemen in attendance. The streets of Paris at that hour were bright and episodical, and Sherringham trod them good-humouredly enough and not too fast, leaning a little to talk with Miriam as he went. Their pace was regulated by her mother's, who advanced on the arm of Gabriel Nash (Nick Dormer was on her other side) in refined deprecation. Her sloping back was before them, exempt from retentive stillness in spite of her rigid principles, with the little drama of her lost and recovered shawl perpetually going on.

Sherringham said nothing to the girl about her performance or her powers; their talk was only of her manner of life with her mother—their travels, their *pensions*, their economies, their want of a home, the many cities she knew well, the foreign tongues and the wide view of the world she had acquired. He guessed easily enough the dolorous type of exile of the two ladies, wanderers in search of Continental cheapness, inured to queer contacts and compromises, "remarkably well connected" in England, but going out for their meals. The girl was but indirectly communicative; though seemingly less from any plan of secrecy than from the habit of associating with people whom she didn't honour with her confidence. She was fragmentary and abrupt, as well as not in the least shy, subdued to dread of Madame Carré as she had been for the time. She gave Sherringham a reason for this fear, and he thought her reason innocently pretentious. "She admired a great artist more than anything in the world; and in the presence of art, of *great* art, her heart beat so fast." Her manners were not perfect, and the friction of a varied experience had rather roughened than smoothed her. She said nothing that proved her intelligent, even though he guessed this to be the design of two or three of her remarks; but he parted from her with the suspicion that she was, according to the contemporary French phrase, a "nature."

The Hôtel de la Garonne was in a small unrenovated street in which the cobble-stones of old Paris still flourished, lying between the Avenue de l'Opéra and the Place de la Bourse. Sherringham had occasionally traversed the high dimness, but had never noticed the tall, stale *maison meublée*, the aspect of which, that of a third-rate provincial inn, was an illustration of Mrs. Rooth's shrunken standard. "We would ask you to come up, but it's quite at the top and we haven't a sitting-room," the poor lady bravely explained. "We had to receive Mr. Nash at a café."

Nick Dormer declared that he liked cafés, and Miriam, looking at his cousin, dropped with a flash of passion the demand: "Do you wonder I should want to do something—so that we can stop living like pigs?"

Peter recognised the next day that though it might be boring to listen to her it was better to make her recite than to let her do nothing, so effectually did the presence of his sister and that of Lady Agnes, and even of Grace and Biddy, appear, by a strange tacit opposition, to deprive hers, ornamental as it was, of a reason. He had only to see them all together to perceive that she couldn't pass for having come to "meet" them—even her mother's insinuating gentility failed to put the occasion on that footing—and that she must therefore be assumed to have been brought to show them something. She was not subdued, not colourless enough to sit there for nothing, or even for conversation—the sort of conversation that was likely to come off—so that it was inevitable to treat her position as connected with the principal place on the carpet, with silence and attention and the pulling together of chairs. Even when so established it struck him at first as precarious, in the light, or the darkness, of the inexpressive faces of the other ladies, seated in couples and rows on sofas—there were several in addition to Julia and the Dormers; mainly the wives, with their husbands, of Sherringham's fellow-secretaries— scarcely one of whom he felt he might count upon for a modicum of gush when the girl should have finished.

Miss Rooth gave a representation of Juliet drinking the potion, according to the system, as her mother explained, of the famous Signor Ruggieri—a scene of high fierce sound, of many cries and contortions: she shook her hair (which proved magnificent) half-down before the performance was over. Then she declaimed several short poems by Victor Hugo, selected among many hundred by Mrs. Rooth, as the good lady was careful to make known. After this she jumped to the American lyre, regaling the company with specimens, both familiar and fresh, of Longfellow, Lowell, Whittier, Holmes, and of two or three poetesses now revealed to Sherringham for the first time. She flowed so copiously, keeping the floor and rejoicing visibly in her luck, that her host was mainly occupied with wondering how he could make her leave off. He was surprised at the extent of her repertory, which, in view of

the circumstance that she could never have received much encouragement—
it must have come mainly from her mother, and he didn't believe in Signor
Ruggieri—denoted a very stiff ambition and a blundering energy. It was her
mother who checked her at last, and he found himself suspecting that Gabriel
Nash had intimated to the old woman that interference was necessary. For
himself he was chiefly glad Madame Carré hadn't come. It was present to him
that she would have judged the exhibition, with its badness, its impudence,
the absence of criticism, wholly indecent.

His only new impression of the heroine of the scene was that of this
same high assurance—her coolness, her complacency, her eagerness to go on.
She had been deadly afraid of the old actress but was not a bit afraid of a
cluster of *femmes du monde*, of Julia, of Lady Agnes, of the smart women
of the embassy. It was positively these personages who were rather in fear;
there was certainly a moment when even Julia was scared for the first time
he had ever remarked it. The space was too small, the cries, the convulsions
and rushes of the dishevelled girl were too near. Lady Agnes wore much of
the time the countenance she might have shown at the theatre during a play
in which pistols were fired; and indeed the manner of the young reciter had
become more spasmodic and more explosive. It appeared, however, that the
company in general thought her very clever and successful; which showed, to
Sherringham's sense, how little they understood the matter. Poor Biddy was
immensely struck; she grew flushed and absorbed in proportion as Miriam,
at her best moments, became pale and fatal. It was she who spoke to her first,
after it was agreed that they had better not fatigue her any more; she advanced
a few steps, happening to be nearest—she murmured: "Oh thank you so
much. I never saw anything so beautiful, so grand."

She looked very red and very pretty as she said this, and Peter Sherringham
liked her enough to notice her more and like her better when she looked
prettier than usual. As he turned away he heard Miriam make answer with
no great air of appreciation of her tribute: "I've seen you before—two days
ago at the Salon with Mr. Dormer. Yes, I know he's your brother. I've made
his acquaintance since. He wants to paint my portrait. Do you think he'll
do it well?" He was afraid the girl was something of a brute—also somewhat

grossly vain. This impression would perhaps have been confirmed if a part of the rest of the short conversation of the two young women had reached his ear. Biddy ventured to observe that she herself had studied modelling a little and that she could understand how any artist would think Miss Rooth a splendid subject. If indeed *she* could attempt her head, that would be a chance indeed.

"Thank you," said Miriam with a laugh as of high comedy. "I think I had rather not *passer par toute la famille*!" Then she added: "If your brother's an artist I don't understand how he's in Parliament."

"Oh he isn't in Parliament now—we only hope he will be."

"Ah I see."

"And he isn't an artist either," Biddy felt herself conscientiously bound to state.

"Then he isn't anything," said Miss Rooth.

"Well—he's immensely clever."

"Ah I see," Miss Rooth again replied. "Mr. Nash has puffed him up so."

"I don't know Mr. Nash," said Biddy, guilty of a little dryness as well as of a little misrepresentation, and feeling rather snubbed.

"Well, you needn't wish to."

Biddy stood with her a moment longer, still looking at her and not knowing what to say next, but not finding her any less handsome because she had such odd manners. Biddy had an ingenious little mind, which always tried as much as possible to keep different things separate. It was pervaded now by the reflexion, attended with some relief, that if the girl spoke to her with such unexpected familiarity of Nick she said nothing at all about Peter. Two gentlemen came up, two of Peter's friends, and made speeches to Miss Rooth of the kind Biddy supposed people learned to make in Paris. It was also doubtless in Paris, the girl privately reasoned, that they learned to listen to them as this striking performer listened. She received their advances very

131

differently from the way she had received Biddy's. Sherringham noticed his young kinswoman turn away, still very red, to go and sit near her mother again, leaving Miriam engaged with the two men. It appeared to have come over her that for a moment she had been strangely spontaneous and bold, and that she had paid a little of the penalty. The seat next her mother was occupied by Mrs. Rooth, toward whom Lady Agnes's head had inclined itself with a preoccupied tolerance. He had the conviction Mrs. Rooth was telling her about the Neville-Nugents of Castle Nugent and that Lady Agnes was thinking it odd she never had heard of them. He said to himself that Biddy was generous. She had urged Julia to come in order that they might see how bad the strange young woman would be, but now that the event had proved dazzling she forgot this calculation and rejoiced in what she innocently supposed to be the performer's triumph. She kept away from Julia, however; she didn't even look at her to invite her also to confess that, in vulgar parlance, they had been sold. He himself spoke to his sister, who was leaning back with a detached air in the corner of a sofa, saying something which led her to remark in reply: "Ah I daresay it's extremely fine, but I don't care for tragedy when it treads on one's toes. She's like a cow who has kicked over the milking-pail. She ought to be tied up."

"My poor Julia, it isn't extremely fine; it isn't fine at all," Sherringham returned with some irritation.

"Pardon me then. I thought that was why you invited us."

"I imagined she was different," Peter said a little foolishly.

"Ah if you don't care for her so much the better. It has always seemed to me you make too awfully much of those people."

"Oh I do care for her too—rather. She's interesting." His sister gave him a momentary, mystified glance and he added: "And she's dreadful." He felt stupidly annoyed and was ashamed of his annoyance, as he could have assigned no reason for it. It didn't grow less for the moment from his seeing Gabriel Nash approach Julia, introduced by Nick Dormer. He gave place to the two young men with some alacrity, for he had a sense of being put in the wrong in respect to their specimen by Nash's very presence. He remembered how it had been a part of their bargain, as it were, that he should present that gentleman to his sister. He was not sorry to be relieved of the office by Nick, and he even tacitly and ironically wished his kinsman's friend joy of a colloquy with Mrs. Dallow. Sherringham's life was spent with people, he was used to people, and both as host and as guest he carried the social burden in general lightly. He could observe, especially in the former capacity, without uneasiness and take the temperature without anxiety. But at present his company oppressed him; he felt worried and that he showed it—which was the thing in the world he had ever held least an honour to a gentleman dedicated to diplomacy. He was vexed with the levity that had made him call his roomful together on so poor a pretext, and yet was vexed with the stupidity that made the witnesses so evidently find the pretext sufficient. He inwardly groaned at the delusion under which he had saddled himself with the Tragic Muse—a tragic muse who was strident and pert—and yet wished his visitors would go away and leave him alone with her.

Nick Dormer said to Mrs. Dallow that he wanted her to know an old friend of his, one of the cleverest men he knew; and he added the hope that she would be gentle and encouraging with him; he was so timid and so easily disconcerted. Mr. Nash hereupon dropped into a chair by the arm of her sofa, their companion went away, and Mrs. Dallow turned her glance upon her new acquaintance without a perceptible change of position. Then she emitted with rapidity the remark: "It's very awkward when people are told one's clever."

"It's only awkward if one isn't," Gabriel smiled.

"Yes, but so few people are—enough to be talked about."

"Isn't that just the reason why such a matter, such an exception, ought to be mentioned to them?" he asked. "They mightn't find it out for themselves. Of course, however, as you say, there ought to be a certainty; then they're surer to know it. Dormer's a dear fellow, but he's rash and superficial."

Mrs. Dallow, at this incitement, turned her glance a second time on her visitor; but during the rest of the conversation she rarely repeated the movement. If she liked Nick Dormer extremely—and it may without more delay be communicated to the reader that she did—her liking was of a kind that opposed no difficulty whatever to her not liking, in case of such a complication, a person attached or otherwise belonging to him. It was not in her nature to "put up" with others for the sake of an individual she loved: the putting up was usually consumed in the loving, and with nothing left over. If the affection that isolates and simplifies its object may be distinguished from the affection that seeks communications and contracts for it, Julia Dallow's was quite of the encircling, not to say the narrowing sort. She was not so much jealous as essentially exclusive. She desired no experience for the familiar and yet partly unsounded kinsman in whom she took an interest that she wouldn't have desired for herself; and indeed the cause of her interest in him was partly the vision of his helping her to the particular extensions she did desire—the taste and thrill of great affairs and of public action. To have such ambitions for him appeared to her the highest honour she could do him; her conscience was in it as well as her inclination, and her scheme, to her sense, was noble enough to varnish over any disdain she might feel for forces drawing him another way. She had a prejudice, in general, against his existing connexions, a suspicion of them, and a supply of off-hand contempt in waiting. It was a singular circumstance that she was sceptical even when, knowing her as well as he did, he thought them worth recommending to her: the recommendation indeed mostly confirmed the suspicion.

This was a law from which Gabriel Nash was condemned to suffer, if suffering could on any occasion be predicated of Gabriel Nash. His pretension was in truth that he had purged his life of such possibilities of waste, though probably he would have admitted that if that fair vessel should spring a leak the wound in its side would have been dealt by a woman's hand. In dining two evenings before with her brother and with the Dormers Mrs. Dallow had been moved to exclaim that Peter and Nick knew the most extraordinary people. As regards Peter the attitudinising girl and her mother now pointed that moral with sufficient vividness; so that there was little arrogance in taking a similar quality for granted of the conceited man at her elbow, who sat there as if he might be capable from one moment to another of leaning over the arm of her sofa. She had not the slightest wish to talk with him about himself, and was afraid for an instant that he was on the point of passing from the chapter of his cleverness to that of his timidity. It was a false alarm, however, for he only animadverted on the pleasures of the elegant extract hurled—literally *hurlé* in general—from the centre of the room at one's defenceless head. He intimated that in his opinion these pleasures were all for the performers. The auditors had at any rate given Miss Rooth a charming afternoon; that of course was what Mrs. Dallow's kind brother had mainly intended in arranging the little party. (Julia hated to hear him call her brother "kind": the term seemed offensively patronising.) But he himself, he related, was now constantly employed in the same beneficence, listening two-thirds of his time to "intonations" and shrieks. She had doubtless observed it herself, how the great current of the age, the adoration of the mime, was almost too strong for any individual; how it swept one along and dashed one against the rocks. As she made no response to this proposition Gabriel Nash asked her if she hadn't been struck with the main sign of the time, the preponderance of the mountebank, the glory and renown, the personal favour, he enjoyed. Hadn't she noticed what an immense part of the public attention he held in London at least? For in Paris society was not so pervaded with him, and the women of the profession, in particular, were not in every drawing-room.

"I don't know what you mean," Mrs. Dallow said. "I know nothing of any such people."

"Aren't they under your feet wherever you turn—their performances, their portraits, their speeches, their autobiographies, their names, their manners, their ugly mugs, as the people say, and their idiotic pretensions?"

"I daresay it depends on the places one goes to. If they're everywhere"— and she paused a moment—"I don't go everywhere."

"I don't go anywhere, but they mount on my back at home like the Old Man of the Sea. Just observe a little when you return to London," Mr. Nash went on with friendly instructiveness. Julia got up at this—she didn't like receiving directions; but no other corner of the room appeared to offer her any particular reason for crossing to it: she never did such a thing without a great inducement. So she remained standing there as if she were quitting the place in a moment, which indeed she now determined to do; and her interlocutor, rising also, lingered beside her unencouraged but unperturbed. He proceeded to remark that Mr. Sherringham was quite right to offer Miss Rooth an afternoon's sport; she deserved it as a fine, brave, amiable girl. She was highly educated, knew a dozen languages, was of illustrious lineage, and was immensely particular.

"Immensely particular?" Mrs. Dallow repeated.

"Perhaps I should say rather that her mother's so on her behalf. Particular about the sort of people they meet—the tone, the standard. I'm bound to say they're like *you*: they don't go everywhere. That spirit's not so common in the mob calling itself good society as not to deserve mention."

She said nothing for a moment; she looked vaguely round the room, but not at Miriam Rooth. Nevertheless she presently dropped as in forced reference to her an impatient shake. "She's dreadfully vulgar."

"Ah don't say that to my friend Dormer!" Mr. Nash laughed.

"Are you and he such great friends?" Mrs. Dallow asked, meeting his eyes.

"Great enough to make me hope we shall be greater."

Again for a little she said nothing, but then went on: "Why shouldn't I say to him that she's vulgar?"

"Because he admires her so much. He wants to paint her."

"To paint her?"

"To paint her portrait."

"Oh I see. I daresay she'd do for that."

Mr. Nash showed further amusement. "If that's your opinion of her you're not very complimentary to the art he aspires to practise."

"He aspires to practise?" she echoed afresh.

"Haven't you talked with him about it? Ah you must keep him up to it!"

Julia Dallow was conscious for a moment of looking uncomfortable; but it relieved her to be able to demand of her neighbour with a certain manner: "Are you an artist?"

"I try to be," Nash smiled, "but I work in such difficult material."

He spoke this with such a clever suggestion of mysterious things that she was to hear herself once more pay him the attention of taking him up. "Difficult material?"

"I work in life!"

At this she turned away, leaving him the impression that she probably misunderstood his speech, thinking he meant that he drew from the living model or some such platitude: as if there could have been any likelihood he would have dealings with the dead. This indeed would not fully have explained the abruptness with which she dropped their conversation. Gabriel, however, was used to sudden collapses and even to sudden ruptures on the part of those addressed by him, and no man had more the secret of remaining gracefully with his conversational wares on his hands. He saw Mrs. Dallow approach Nick Dormer, who was talking with one of the ladies of the embassy, and apparently signify that she wished to speak to him. He got up and they had a minute's talk, after which he turned and took leave of his fellow-visitors. She said a word to her brother, Nick joined her, and they then came together to the door. In this movement they had to pass near Nash, and it gave her an opportunity to nod good-bye to him, which he was by no means sure she would have done if Nick hadn't been with her. The young man just stopped; he said to Nash: "I should like to see you this evening late. You must meet me somewhere."

"We'll take a walk—I should like that," Nash replied. "I shall smoke a cigar at the café on the corner of the Place de l'Opéra—you'll find me there." He prepared to compass his own departure, but before doing so he addressed himself to the duty of a few civil words to Lady Agnes. This effort proved vain, for on one side she was defended by the wall of the room and on the other rendered inaccessible by Miriam's mother, who clung to her with a quickly-rooted fidelity, showing no symptom of desistance. Nash declined perforce upon her daughter Grace, who said to him: "You were talking with my cousin Mrs. Dallow."

"To her rather than with her," he smiled.

"Ah she's very charming," Grace said.

"She's very beautiful."

"And very clever," the girl continued.

"Very, very intelligent." His conversation with Miss Dormer went little beyond this, and he presently took leave of Peter Sherringham, remarking to him as they shook hands that he was very sorry for him. But he had courted his fate.

"What do you mean by my fate?" Sherringham asked.

"You've got them for life."

"Why for life, when I now clearly and courageously recognise that she isn't good?"

"Ah but she'll become so," said Gabriel Nash.

"Do you think that?" Sherringham brought out with a candour that made his visitor laugh.

"*You* will—that's more to the purpose!" the latter declared as he went away.

Ten minutes later Lady Agnes substituted a general, vague assent for all further particular ones, drawing off from Mrs. Rooth and from the rest of the company with her daughters. Peter had had very little talk with Biddy, but the girl kept her disappointment out of her pretty eyes and said to him: "You told us she didn't know how—but she does!" There was no suggestion of disappointment in this.

Sherringham held her hand a moment. "Ah it's you who know how, dear Biddy!" he answered; and he was conscious that if the occasion had been more private he would have all lawfully kissed her.

Presently three more of his guests took leave, and Mr. Nash's assurance that he had them for life recurred to him as he observed that Mrs. Rooth and her damsel quite failed to profit by so many examples. The Lovicks remained—a colleague and his sociable wife—and Peter gave them a hint that they were not to plant him there only with the two ladies. Miriam quitted Mrs. Lovick, who had attempted, with no great subtlety, to engage her, and came up to her host as if she suspected him of a design of stealing from the room and had the idea of preventing it.

"I want some more tea: will you give me some more? I feel quite faint. You don't seem to suspect how this sort of thing takes it out of one."

Peter apologised extravagantly for not having seen to it that she had proper refreshment, and took her to the round table, in a corner, on which the little collation had been served. He poured out tea for her and pressed bread and butter on her and *petits fours*, of all which she profusely and methodically partook. It was late; the afternoon had faded and a lamp been brought in, the wide shade of which shed a fair glow on the tea-service and the plates of pretty food. The Lovicks sat with Mrs. Rooth at the other end of the room, and the girl stood at the table, drinking her tea and eating her bread and butter. She consumed these articles so freely that he wondered if she had been truly in want of a meal—if they were so poor as to have to count with that sort of privation. This supposition was softening, but still not so much so as to make him ask her to sit down. She appeared indeed to prefer to stand: she looked better so, as if the freedom, the conspicuity of being on her feet and treading a stage were agreeable to her. While Sherringham lingered near her all vaguely, his hands in his pockets and his mind now void of everything but a planned evasion of the theatrical question—there were moments when he was so plentifully tired of it—she broke out abruptly: "Confess you think me intolerably bad!"

"Intolerably—no."

"Only tolerably! I find that worse."

"Every now and then you do something very right," Sherringham said.

"How many such things did I do to-day?"

"Oh three or four. I don't know that I counted very carefully."

She raised her cup to her lips, looking at him over the rim of it—a proceeding that gave her eyes a strange expression. "It bores you and you think it disagreeable," she then said—"I mean a girl always talking about herself." He protested she could never bore him and she added: "Oh I don't want compliments—I want the hard, the precious truth. An actress has to talk about herself. What else can she talk about, poor vain thing?"

"She can talk sometimes about other actresses."

"That comes to the same thing. You won't be serious. I'm awfully serious." There was something that caught his attention in the note of this—a longing half hopeless, half argumentative to be believed in. "If one really wants to do anything one must worry it out; of course everything doesn't come the first day," she kept on. "I can't see everything at once; but I can see a little more—step by step—as I go; can't I?"

"That's the way—that's the way," he gently enough returned. "When you see the things to do the art of doing them will come—if you hammer away. The great point's to see them."

"Yes; and you don't think me clever enough for that."

"Why do you say so when I've asked you to come here on purpose?"

"You've asked me to come, but I've had no success."

"On the contrary; every one thought you wonderful."

"Oh but they don't know!" said Miriam Rooth. "You've not said a word to me. I don't mind your not having praised me; that would be too banal. But if I'm bad—and I know I'm dreadful—I wish you'd talk to me about it."

"It's delightful to talk to you," Peter found himself saying.

"No, it isn't, but it's kind"; and she looked away from him.

Her voice had with this a quality which made him exclaim: "Every now and then you 'say' something—!"

She turned her eyes back to him and her face had a light. "I don't want it to come by accident." Then she added: "If there's any good to be got from trying, from showing one's self, how can it come unless one hears the simple truth, the truth that turns one inside out? It's all for that—to know what one is, if one's a stick!"

"You've great courage, you've rare qualities," Sherringham risked. She had begun to touch him, to seem different: he was glad she had not gone.

But for a little she made no answer, putting down her empty cup and yearning over the table as for something more to eat. Suddenly she raised her head and broke out with vehemence: "I will, I will, I will!"

"You'll do what you want, evidently."

"I *will* succeed—I *will* be great. Of course I know too little, I've seen too little. But I've always liked it; I've never liked anything else. I used to learn things and do scenes and rant about the room when I was but five years old." She went on, communicative, persuasive, familiar, egotistical (as was necessary), and slightly common, or perhaps only natural; with reminiscences, reasons, and anecdotes, an unexpected profusion, and with an air of comradeship, of freedom in any relation, which seemed to plead that she was capable at least of embracing that side of the profession she desired to adopt. He noted that if she had seen very little, as she said, she had also seen a great deal; but both her experience and her innocence had been accidental and irregular. She had seen very little acting—the theatre was always too expensive. If she could only go often—in Paris for instance every night for six months—to see the best, the worst, everything, she would make things out, would observe and learn what to do, what not to do: it would be a school of schools. But she couldn't without selling the clothes off her back. It was vile and disgusting to be poor, and if ever she were to know the bliss of having a few francs in her pocket she would make up for it—that she could promise! She had never been acquainted with any one who could tell her anything—if it was good or bad or right or wrong—except Mrs. Delamere and poor Ruggieri. She supposed they had told her a great deal, but perhaps they hadn't, and she was perfectly willing to give it up if it was bad. Evidently

Madame Carré thought so; she thought it was horrid. Wasn't it perfectly divine, the way the old woman had said those verses, those speeches of Célie? If she would only let her come and listen to her once in a while like that it was all she would ask. She had got lots of ideas just from that half-hour; she had practised them over, over, and over again, the moment she got home. He might ask her mother—he might ask the people next door. If Madame Carré didn't think she could work, she might have heard, could she have listened at the door, something that would show her. But she didn't think her even good enough to criticise—since that wasn't criticism, telling her her head was good. Of course her head was good—she needn't travel up to the *quartiers excentriques* to find that out. It was her mother, the way she talked, who gave the idea that she wanted to be elegant and moral and a *femme du monde* and all that sort of trash. Of course that put people off, when they were only thinking of the real right way. Didn't she know, Miriam herself, that this was the one thing to think of? But any one would be kind to her mother who knew what a dear she was. "She doesn't know when any thing's right or wrong, but she's a perfect saint," said the girl, obscuring considerably her vindication. "She doesn't mind when I say things over by the hour, dinning them into her ears while she sits there and reads. She's a tremendous reader; she's awfully up in literature. She taught me everything herself. I mean all that sort of thing. Of course I'm not so fond of reading; I go in for the book of life." Sherringham wondered if her mother had not at any rate taught her that phrase—he thought it highly probable. "It would give on *my* nerves, the life I lead her," Miriam continued; "but she's really a delicious woman."

The oddity of this epithet made Peter laugh, and altogether, in a few minutes, which is perhaps a sign that he abused his right to be a man of moods, the young lady had produced in him a revolution of curiosity, set his sympathy in motion. Her mixture, as it spread itself before him, was an appeal and a challenge: she was sensitive and dense, she was underbred and fine. Certainly she was very various, and that was rare; quite not at this moment the heavy-eyed, frightened creature who had pulled herself together with such an effort at Madame Carré's, nor the elated "phenomenon" who had just been declaiming, nor the rather affected and contradictious young person with whom he had walked home from the Rue de Constantinople. Was this succession of phases a sign she was really a case of the celebrated artistic temperament, the nature that made people provoking and interesting? That Sherringham himself was of this shifting complexion is perhaps proved by his odd capacity for being of two different minds very nearly at the same time. Miriam was pretty now, with felicities and graces, with charming, unusual eyes. Yes, there were things he could do for her; he had already forgotten the chill of Mr. Nash's irony, of his prophecy. He was even scarce conscious how little in general he liked hints, insinuations, favours asked obliquely and plaintively: that was doubtless also because the girl was suddenly so taking and so fraternising. Perhaps indeed it was unjust to qualify as roundabout the manner in which Miss Rooth conveyed that it was open to him not only to pay for her lessons, but to meet the expense of her nightly attendance with her mother at instructive exhibitions of theatrical art. It was a large order, sending the pair to all the plays; but what Peter now found himself thinking of was not so much its largeness as the possible interest of going with them sometimes and pointing the moral—the technical one—of showing her the things he liked, the things he disapproved. She repeated her declaration that she recognised the fallacy of her mother's view of heroines impossibly virtuous and of the importance of her looking out for such tremendously proper people. "One must let her talk, but of course it creates a prejudice," she said with her eyes on Mr. and Mrs. Lovick, who had got up, terminating their communion with Mrs. Rooth. "It's a great muddle, I know, but she can't bear anything coarse or nasty—and quite right too. I shouldn't either if I didn't have to. But I don't care a sou where I go if I can get to act, or who they are if they'll help me. I want to act—that's what I want to do; I don't want to meddle in people's affairs. I can look out for myself—I'm all right!" the girl exclaimed roundly, frankly, with a ring of honesty which made her crude and pure. "As for doing the bad ones I'm not afraid of that."

"The bad ones?"

"The bad women in the plays—like Madame Carré. I'll do any vile creature."

"I think you'll do best what you are"—and Sherringham laughed for the interest of it. "You're a strange girl."

"*Je crois bien*! Doesn't one have to be, to want to go and exhibit one's self to a loathsome crowd, on a platform, with trumpets and a big drum, for money—to parade one's body and one's soul?"

He looked at her a moment: her face changed constantly; now it had a fine flush and a noble delicacy. "Give it up. You're too good for it," he found himself pleading. "I doubt if you've an idea of what girls have to go through."

"Never, never—never till I'm pelted!" she cried.

"Then stay on here a bit. I'll take you to the theatres."

"Oh you dear!" Miriam delightedly exclaimed. Mr. and Mrs. Lovick, accompanied by Mrs. Rooth, now crossed the room to them, and the girl went on in the same tone: "Mamma dear, he's the best friend we've ever had—he's a great deal nicer than I thought."

"So are you, mademoiselle," said Peter Sherringham.

"Oh, I trust Mr. Sherringham—I trust him infinitely," Mrs. Rooth returned, covering him with her mild, respectable, wheedling eyes. "The kindness of every one has been beyond everything. Mr. and Mrs. Lovick can't say enough. They make the most obliging offers. They want you to know their brother."

"Oh I say, he's no brother of mine," Mr. Lovick protested good-naturedly.

"They think he'll be so suggestive, he'll put us up to the right things," Mrs. Rooth went on.

"It's just a little brother of mine—such a dear, amusing, clever boy," Mrs. Lovick explained.

"Do you know she has got nine? Upon my honour she has!" said her husband. "This one is the sixth. Fancy if I had to take them all over!"

"Yes, it makes it rather awkward," Mrs. Lovick amiably conceded. "He has gone on the stage, poor darling—but he acts rather well."

"He tried for the diplomatic service, but he didn't precisely dazzle his examiners," Mr. Lovick further mentioned.

"Edmund's very nasty about him. There are lots of gentlemen on the stage—he's not the first."

"It's such a comfort to hear that," said Mrs. Rooth.

"I'm much obliged to you. Has he got a theatre?" Miriam asked.

"My dear young lady, he hasn't even got an engagement," replied the young man's terrible brother-in-law.

"He hasn't been at it very long, but I'm sure he'll get on. He's immensely in earnest and very good-looking. I just said that if he should come over to see us you might rather like to meet him. He might give you some tips, as my husband says."

"I don't care for his looks, but I should like his tips," Miriam liberally smiled.

"And is he coming over to see you?" asked Sherringham, to whom, while this exchange of remarks, which he had not lost, was going on, Mrs. Rooth had in lowered accents addressed herself.

"Not if I can help it I think!" But Mr. Lovick was so gaily rude that it wasn't embarrassing.

"Oh sir, I'm sure you're fond of him," Mrs. Rooth remonstrated as the party passed together into the antechamber.

"No, really, I like some of the others—four or five of them; but I don't like Arty."

"We'll make it up to him, then; *we*'ll like him," Miriam answered with spirit; and her voice rang in the staircase—Sherringham attended them a little way—with a charm which her host had rather missed in her loudness of the day before.

IX

Nick Dormer found his friend Nash that evening at the place of their tryst—smoking a cigar, in the warm bright night, on the terrace of the café forming one of the angles of the Place de l'Opéra. He sat down with him, but at the end of five minutes uttered a protest against the crush and confusion, the publicity and vulgarity of the place, the shuffling procession of the crowd, the jostle of fellow-customers, the perpetual brush of waiters. "Come away; I want to talk to you and I can't talk here. I don't care where we go. It will be pleasant to walk; we'll stroll away to the *quartiers sérieux.* Each time I come to Paris I at the end of three days take the Boulevard, with its conventional grimace, into greater aversion. I hate even to cross it—I go half a mile round to avoid it."

The young men took their course together down the Rue de la Paix to the Rue de Rivoli, which they crossed, passing beside the gilded rails of the Tuileries. The beauty of the night—the only defect of which was that the immense illumination of Paris kept it from being quite night enough, made it a sort of bedizened, rejuvenated day—gave a charm to the quieter streets, drew our friends away to the right, to the river and the bridges, the older, duskier city. The pale ghost of the palace that had perished by fire hung over them a while, and, by the passage now open at all times across the garden of the Tuileries, they came out upon the Seine. They kept on and on, moving slowly, smoking, talking, pausing, stopping to look, to emphasise, to compare. They fell into discussion, into confidence, into inquiry, sympathetic or satiric, and into explanations which needed in turn to be explained. The balmy night, the time for talk, the amusement of Paris, the memory of younger passages, gave a lift to the occasion. Nick had already forgotten his little brush with Julia on his leaving Peter's tea-party at her side, and that he had been almost disconcerted by the asperity with which she denounced the odious man he had taken it into his head to force upon her. Impertinent and fatuous she had called him; and when Nick began to plead that he was really neither of these things, though he could imagine his manner might sometimes suggest them, she had declared that she didn't wish to argue about him or ever to hear of him again. Nick hadn't counted on her liking Gabriel Nash, but had thought her not liking him wouldn't perceptibly matter. He had given himself the diversion, not cruel surely to any one concerned, of seeing what she would make of a type she had never before met. She had made even less than he expected, and her intimation that he had played her a trick had been irritating enough to prevent his reflecting that the offence might have been in some degree with Nash. But he had recovered from his resentment sufficiently to ask this personage, with every possible circumstance of implied consideration for the lady, what had been the impression made by his charming cousin.

"Upon my word, my dear fellow, I don't regard that as a fair question," Gabriel said. "Besides, if you think Mrs. Dallow charming what on earth need it matter to you what I think? The superiority of one man's opinion over another's is never so great as when the opinion's about a woman."

"It was to help me to find out what I think of yourself," Nick returned.

"Oh, that you'll never do. I shall bewilder you to the end. The lady with whom you were so good as to make me acquainted is a beautiful specimen of the English garden-flower, the product of high cultivation and much tending; a tall, delicate stem with the head set upon it in a manner which, as a thing seen and remembered, should doubtless count for us as a gift of the gods. She's the perfect type of the object *raised* or bred, and everything about her hangs together and conduces to the effect, from the angle of her elbow to the way she drops that vague, conventional, dry little 'Oh!' which dispenses with all further performance. That degree of completeness is always satisfying. But I didn't satisfy her, and she didn't understand me. I don't think they usually understand."

"She's no worse than I then."

"Ah she didn't try."

"No, she doesn't try. But she probably thought you a monster of conceit, and she would think so still more if she were to hear you talk about her trying."

147

"Very likely—very likely," said Gabriel Nash. "I've an idea a good many people think that. It strikes me as comic. I suppose it's a result of my little system."

"What little system?"

"Oh nothing more wonderful than the idea of being just the same to every one. People have so bemuddled themselves that the last thing they can conceive is that one should be simple."

"Lord, do you call yourself simple?" Nick ejaculated.

"Absolutely; in the sense of having no interest of my own to push, no nostrum to advertise, no power to conciliate, no axe to grind. I'm not a savage—ah far from it!—but I really think I'm perfectly independent."

"Well, that's always provoking!" Nick knowingly returned.

"So it would appear, to the great majority of one's fellow-mortals; and I well remember the pang with which I originally made that discovery. It darkened my spirit at a time when I had no thought of evil. What we like, when we're unregenerate, is that a new-comer should give us a password, come over to our side, join our little camp or religion, get into our little boat, in short, whatever it is, and help us to row it. It's natural enough; we're mostly in different tubs and cockles, paddling for life. Our opinions, our convictions and doctrines and standards, are simply the particular thing that will make the boat go—*our boat*, naturally, for they may very often be just the thing that will sink another. If you won't get in people generally hate you."

"Your metaphor's very lame," said Nick. "It's the overcrowded boat that goes to the bottom."

"Oh I'll give it another leg or two! Boats can be big, in the infinite of space, and a doctrine's a raft that floats the better the more passengers it carries. A passenger jumps over from time to time, not so much from fear of sinking as from a want of interest in the course or the company. He swims, he plunges, he dives, he dips down and visits the fishes and the mermaids and the submarine caves; he goes from craft to craft and splashes about, on his own account, in the blue, cool water. The regenerate, as I call them, are the passengers who jump over in search of better fun. I jumped over long ago."

"And now of course you're at the head of the regenerate; for, in your turn"—Nick found the figure delightful—"you all form a select school of porpoises."

"Not a bit, and I know nothing about heads—in the sense you mean. I've grown a tail if you will; I'm the merman wandering free. It's the jolliest of trades!"

Before they had gone many steps further Nick Dormer stopped short with a question. "I say, my dear fellow, do you mind mentioning to me whether you're the greatest humbug and charlatan on earth, or a genuine intelligence, one that has sifted things for itself?"

"I do lead your poor British wit a dance—I'm so sorry," Nash replied benignly. "But I'm very sincere. And I *have* tried to straighten out things a bit for myself."

"Then why do you give people such a handle?"

"Such a handle?"

"For thinking you're an—for thinking you're a mere *farceur*."

"I daresay it's my manner: they're so unused to any sort of candour."

"Well then why don't you try another?" Nick asked.

"One has the manner that one can, and mine moreover's a part of my little system."

"Ah if you make so much of your little system you're no better than any one else," Nick returned as they went on.

"I don't pretend to be better, for we're all miserable sinners; I only pretend to be bad in a pleasanter, brighter way—by what I can see. It's the simplest thing in the world; just take for granted our right to be happy and brave. What's essentially kinder and more helpful than that, what's more beneficent? But the tradition of dreariness, of stodginess, of dull, dense, literal prose, has so sealed people's eyes that they've ended by thinking the most natural of all things the most perverse. Why so keep up the dreariness, in our poor little day? No one can tell me why, and almost every one calls me names for simply asking the question. But I go on, for I believe one can do a little good by it. I want so much to do a little good," Gabriel Nash continued, taking his companion's arm. "My persistence is systematic: don't you see what I mean? I won't be dreary—no, no, no; and I won't recognise the necessity, or even, if there be any way out of it, the accident, of dreariness in the life that surrounds me. That's enough to make people stare: they're so damned stupid!"

"They think you so damned impudent," Nick freely explained.

At this Nash stopped him short with a small cry, and, turning his eyes, Nick saw under the lamps of the quay that he had brought a flush of pain into his friend's face. "I don't strike you that way?"

"Oh 'me!' Wasn't it just admitted that I don't in the least make you out?"

"That's the last thing!" Nash declared, as if he were thinking the idea over, with an air of genuine distress. "But with a little patience we'll clear it up together—if you care enough about it," he added more cheerfully. Letting his companion proceed again he continued: "Heaven help us all, what do people mean by impudence? There are many, I think, who don't understand its nature or its limits; and upon my word I've literally seen mere quickness of intelligence or of perception, the jump of a step or two, a little whirr of the wings of talk, mistaken for it. Yes, I've encountered men and women who thought you impudent if you weren't simply so stupid as they. The only impudence is unprovoked, or even mere dull, aggression, and I indignantly protest that I'm never guilty of *that* clumsiness. Ah for what do they take one, with *their* beastly presumption? Even to defend myself sometimes I've to make believe to myself that I care. I always feel as if I didn't successfully make others think so. Perhaps they see impudence in that. But I daresay the offence is in the things that I take, as I say, for granted; for if one tries to be pleased one passes perhaps inevitably for being pleased above all with one's self. That's really not my case—I find my capacity for pleasure deplorably below the mark I've set. This is why, as I've told you, I cultivate it, I try to bring it up. And I'm actuated by positive benevolence; I've that impudent pretension. That's what I mean by being the same to every one, by having only one manner. If one's conscious and ingenious to that end what's the harm—when one's motives are so pure? By never, *never* making the concession, one may end by becoming a perceptible force for good."

"What concession are you talking about, in God's name?" Nick demanded.

"Why, that we're here all for dreariness. It's impossible to grant it sometimes if you wish to deny it ever."

"And what do you mean then by dreariness? That's modern slang and terribly vague. Many good things are dreary—virtue and decency and charity, and perseverance and courage and honour."

"Say at once that life's dreary, my dear fellow!" Gabriel Nash exclaimed.

"That's on the whole my besetting impression."

"*Cest là que je vous attends!* I'm precisely engaged in trying what can be done in taking it the other way. It's my little personal experiment. Life consists of the personal experiments of each of us, and the point of an experiment is that it shall succeed. What we contribute is our treatment of the material, our rendering of the text, our style. A sense of the qualities of a style is so rare that many persons should doubtless be forgiven for not being able to read, or at all events to enjoy, us; but is that a reason for giving it up—for not being, in this other sphere, if one possibly can, an Addison, a Ruskin, a Renan? Ah we must write our best; it's the great thing we can do in the world, on the right side. One has one's form, *que diable*, and a mighty good thing that one has. I'm not afraid of putting all life into mine, and without unduly squeezing it. I'm not afraid of putting in honour and courage and charity—without spoiling them: on the contrary I shall only do them good. People may not read you at sight, may not like you, but there's a chance they'll come round; and the only way to court the chance is to keep it up—always to keep it up. That's what I

151

do, my dear man—if you don't think I've perseverance. If some one's touched here and there, if you give a little impression of truth and charm, that's your reward; besides of course the pleasure for yourself."

"Don't you think your style's a trifle affected?" Nick asked for further amusement.

"That's always the charge against a personal manner: if you've any at all people think you've too much. Perhaps, perhaps—who can say? The lurking unexpressed is infinite, and affectation must have begun, long ago, with the first act of reflective expression—the substitution of the few placed articulate words for the cry or the thump or the hug. Of course one isn't perfect; but that's the delightful thing about art, that there's always more to learn and more to do; it grows bigger the more one uses it and meets more questions the more they come up. No doubt I'm rough still, but I'm in the right direction: I make it my business to testify for the fine."

"Ah the fine—there it stands, over there!" said Nick Dormer. "I'm not so sure about yours—I don't know what I've got hold of. But Notre Dame *is* truth; Notre Dame *is* charm; on Notre Dame the distracted mind can rest. Come over with me and look at her!"

They had come abreast of the low island from which the great cathedral, disengaged to-day from her old contacts and adhesions, rises high and fair, with her front of beauty and her majestic mass, darkened at that hour, or at least simplified, under the stars, but only more serene and sublime for her happy union far aloft with the cool distance and the night. Our young men, fantasticating as freely as I leave the reader to estimate, crossed the wide, short bridge which made them face toward the monuments of old Paris—the Palais de Justice, the Conciergerie, the holy chapel of Saint Louis. They came out before the church, which looks down on a square where the past, once so thick in the very heart of Paris, has been made rather a blank, pervaded however by the everlasting freshness of the vast cathedral-face. It greeted Nick Dormer and Gabriel Nash with a kindness the long centuries had done nothing to dim. The lamplight of the old city washed its foundations, but the towers and buttresses, the arches, the galleries, the statues, the vast rose-window, the large full composition, seemed to grow clearer while they climbed higher, as if they had a conscious benevolent answer for the upward gaze of men.

"How it straightens things out and blows away one's vapours—anything that's *done*!" said Nick; while his companion exclaimed blandly and affectionately:

"The dear old thing!"

"The great point's to do something, instead of muddling and questioning; and, by Jove, it makes me want to!"

"Want to build a cathedral?" Nash inquired.

"Yes, just that."

"It's you who puzzle *me* then, my dear fellow. You can't build them out of words."

"What is it the great poets do?" asked Nick.

"*Their* words are ideas—their words are images, enchanting collocations and unforgettable signs. But the verbiage of parliamentary speeches—!"

"Well," said Nick with a candid, reflective sigh, "you can rear a great structure of many things—not only of stones and timbers and painted glass." They walked round this example of one, pausing, criticising, admiring, and discussing; mingling the grave with the gay and paradox with contemplation. Behind and at the sides the huge, dusky vessel of the church seemed to dip into the Seine or rise out of it, floating expansively—a ship of stone with its flying buttresses thrown forth like an array of mighty oars. Nick Dormer lingered near it in joy, in soothing content, as if it had been the temple of a faith so dear to him that there was peace and security in its precinct. And there was comfort too and consolation of the same sort in the company at this moment of Nash's equal appreciation, of his response, by his own signs, to the great effect. He took it all in so and then so gave it all out that Nick was reminded of the radiance his boyish admiration had found in him of old, the easy grasp of everything of that kind. "Everything of that kind" was to Nick's sense the description of a wide and bright domain.

They crossed to the farther side of the river, where the influence of the Gothic monument threw a distinction even over the Parisian smartnesses—the municipal rule and measure, the importunate symmetries, the "handsomeness" of everything, the extravagance of gaslight, the perpetual click on the neat bridges. In front of a quiet little café on the left bank Gabriel Nash said, "Let's sit down"—he was always ready to sit down. It was a friendly establishment and an unfashionable quarter, far away from the caravan-series; there were the usual little tables and chairs on the quay, the muslin curtains behind the glazed front, the general sense of sawdust and of drippings of watery beer. The place was subdued to stillness, but not extinguished, by the lateness of the hour; no vehicles passed, only now and then a light Parisian foot. Beyond the parapet they could hear the flow of the Seine. Nick Dormer said it made him think of the old Paris, of the great Revolution, of Madame Roland, *quoi*! Gabriel said they could have watery beer but were not obliged to drink it. They sat a long time; they talked a great deal, and the more they said the more the unsaid came up. Presently Nash found occasion to throw out: "I go about my business like any good citizen—that's all."

"And what is your business?"

"The spectacle of the world."

Nick laughed out. "And what do you do with that?"

"What does any one do with spectacles? I look at it. I see."

"You're full of contradictions and inconsistencies," Nick however objected. "You described yourself to me half an hour ago as an apostle of beauty."

"Where's the inconsistency? I do it in the broad light of day, whatever I do: that's virtually what I meant. If I look at the spectacle of the world I look in preference at what's charming in it. Sometimes I've to go far to find it—very likely; but that's just what I do. I go far—as far as my means permit me. Last year I heard of such a delightful little spot; a place where a wild fig-tree grows in the south wall, the outer side, of an old Spanish city. I was told it was a deliciously brown corner—the sun making it warm in winter. As soon as I could I went there."

"And what did you do?"

"I lay on the first green grass—I liked it."

"If that sort of thing's all you accomplish you're not encouraging."

"I accomplish my happiness—it seems to me that's something. I have feelings, I have sensations: let me tell you that's not so common. It's rare to have them, and if you chance to have them it's rare not to be ashamed of them. I go after them—when I judge they won't hurt any one."

"You're lucky to have money for your travelling expenses," said Nick.

"No doubt, no doubt; but I do it very cheap. I take my stand on my nature, on my fortunate character. I'm not ashamed of it, I don't think it's so horrible, my character. But we've so befogged and befouled the whole question of liberty, of spontaneity, of good humour and inclination and enjoyment, that there's nothing that makes people stare so as to see one natural."

"You're always thinking too much of 'people.'"

"They say I think too little," Gabriel smiled.

"Well, I've agreed to stand for Harsh," said Nick with a roundabout transition.

"It's you then who are lucky to have money."

"I haven't," Nick explained. "My expenses are to be paid."

"Then you too must think of 'people.'"

Nick made no answer to this, but after a moment said: "I wish very much you had more to show for it."

"To show for what?"

"Your little system—the æsthetic life."

Nash hesitated, tolerantly, gaily, as he often did, with an air of being embarrassed to choose between several answers, any one of which would be so right. "Oh having something to show's such a poor business. It's a kind of confession of failure."

"Yes, you're more affected than anything else," said Nick impatiently.

"No, my dear boy, I'm more good-natured: don't I prove it? I'm rather disappointed to find you not more accessible to esoteric doctrine. But there is, I confess, another plane of intelligence, honourable, and very honourable, in its way, from which it may legitimately appear important to have something to show. If you must confine yourself to that plane I won't refuse you my sympathy. After all that's what I have to show! But the degree of my sympathy must of course depend on the nature of the demonstration you wish to make."

"You know it very well—you've guessed it," Nick returned, looking before him in a conscious, modest way which would have been called sheepish had he been a few years younger.

"Ah you've broken the scent with telling me you're going back to the House of Commons," said Nash.

"No wonder you don't make it out! My situation's certainly absurd enough. What I really hanker for is to be a painter; and of portraits, on the whole, I think. That's the abject, crude, ridiculous fact. In this out-of-the-way corner, at the dead of night, in lowered tones, I venture to disclose it to you. Isn't that the æsthetic life?"

"Do you know how to paint?" asked Nash.

"Not in the least. No element of burlesque is therefore wanting to my position."

"That makes no difference. I'm so glad."

"So glad I don't know how?"

"So glad of it all. Yes, that only makes it better. You're a delightful case, and I like delightful cases. We must see it through. I rejoice I met you again."

"Do you think I can do anything?" Nick inquired.

"Paint good pictures? How can I tell without seeing some of your work? Doesn't it come back to me that at Oxford you used to sketch very prettily? But that's the last thing that matters."

"What does matter then?" Nick asked with his eyes on his companion.

"To be on the right side—on the side of the 'fine.'"

"There'll be precious little of the 'fine' if I produce nothing but daubs."

"Ah you cling to the old false measure of success! I must cure you of that. There'll be the beauty of having been disinterested and independent; of having taken the world in the free, brave, personal way."

"I shall nevertheless paint decently if I can," Nick presently said.

"I'm almost sorry! It will make your case less clear, your example less grand."

"My example will be grand enough, with the fight I shall have to make."

"The fight? With whom?"

"With myself first of all. I'm awfully against it."

"Ah but you'll have me on the other side," Nash smiled.

"Well, you'll have more than a handful to meet—everything, every one that belongs to me, that touches me near or far; my family, my blood, my heredity, my traditions, my promises, my circumstances, my prejudices; my little past—such as it is; my great future—such as it has been supposed it may be."

"I see, I see. It's splendid!" Nash exclaimed. "And Mrs. Dallow into the bargain," he added.

"Yes, Mrs. Dallow if you like."

"Are you in love with her?"

"Not in the least."

"Well, she is with you—so I understood."

"Don't say that," said Nick Dormer with sudden sternness.

"Ah you are, you are!" his companion pronounced, judging apparently from this accent.

"I don't know *what* I am—heaven help me!" Nick broke out, tossing his hat down on his little tin table with vehemence. "I'm a freak of nature and a sport of the mocking gods. Why should they go out of their way to worry me? Why should they do everything so inconsequent, so improbable, so preposterous? It's the vulgarest practical joke. There has never been anything of the sort among us; we're all Philistines to the core, with about as much esthetic sense as that hat. It's excellent soil—I don't complain of it—but not a soil to grow that flower. From where the devil then has the seed been dropped? I look back from generation to generation; I scour our annals without finding the least little sketching grandmother, any sign of a building or versifying or collecting or even tulip-raising ancestor. They were all as blind as bats, and none the less happy for that. I'm a wanton variation, an unaccountable monster. My dear father, rest his soul, went through life without a suspicion that there's anything in it that can't be boiled into blue-books, and became in that conviction a very distinguished person. He brought me up in the same simplicity and in the hope of the same eminence. It would have been better if I had remained so. I think it's partly your fault that I haven't," Nick went on. "At Oxford you were very bad company for me—my evil genius: you opened my eyes, you communicated the poison. Since then, little by little, it has been working within me; vaguely, covertly, insensibly at first, but during the last year or two with violence, pertinacity, cruelty. I've resorted to every antidote in life; but it's no use—I'm stricken. *C'est Vénus toute entière à sa proie attachée*—putting Venus for 'art.' It tears me to pieces as I may say."

"I see, I follow you," said Nash, who had listened to this recital with radiant interest and curiosity. "And that's why you are going to stand."

"Precisely—it's an antidote. And at present you're another."

"Another?"

"That's why I jumped at you. A bigger dose of you may disagree with me to that extent that I shall either die or get better."

"I shall control the dilution," said Nash. "Poor fellow—if you're elected!" he added.

"Poor fellow either way. You don't know the atmosphere in which I live, the horror, the scandal my apostasy would provoke, the injury and suffering it would inflict. I believe it would really kill my mother. She thinks my father's watching me from the skies."

"Jolly to make him jump!" Nash suggested.

"He'd jump indeed—come straight down on top of me. And then the grotesqueness of it—to *begin* all of a sudden at my age."

"It's perfect indeed, it's too lovely a case," Nash raved.

"Think how it sounds—a paragraph in the London papers: 'Mr. Nicholas Dormer, M. P. for Harsh and son of the late Right Honourable and so forth and so forth, is about to give up his seat and withdraw from public life in order to devote himself to the practice of portrait-painting—and with the more commendable perseverance by reason of all the dreadful time he has lost. Orders, in view of this, respectfully solicited.'"

"The nineteenth century's a sweeter time than I thought," said Nash. "It's the portrait then that haunts your dreams?"

"I wish you could see. You must of course come immediately to my place in London."

"Perfidious wretch, you're capable of having talent—which of course will spoil everything!" Gabriel wailed.

"No, I'm too old and was too early perverted. It's too late to go through the mill."

"You make *me* young! Don't miss your election at your peril. Think of the edification."

"The edification—?"

"Of your throwing it all up the next moment."

"That would be pleasant for Mr. Carteret," Nick brooded.

"Mr. Carteret—?"

"A dear old family friend who'll wish to pay my agent's bill."

"Serve him right for such depraved tastes."

"You do me good," said Nick as he rose and turned away.

"Don't call me useless then."

"Ah but not in the way you mean. It's only if I don't get in that I shall perhaps console myself with the brush," Nick returned with humorous, edifying elegance while they retraced their steps.

"For the sake of all the muses then don't stand. For you *will* get in."

"Very likely. At any rate I've promised."

"You've promised Mrs. Dallow?"

"It's her place—she'll *put* me in," Nick said.

"Baleful woman! But I'll pull you out!" cried Gabriel Nash.

X

For several days Peter Sherringham had business in hand which left him neither time nor freedom of mind to occupy himself actively with the ladies of the Hôtel de la Garonne. There were moments when they brushed across his memory, but their passage was rapid and not lighted with complacent attention; for he shrank from bringing to the proof the question of whether Miriam would be an interest or only a bore. She had left him after their second meeting with a quickened sympathy, but in the course of a few hours that flame had burned dim. Like most other men he was a mixture of impulse and reflexion, but was peculiar in this, that thinking things over almost always made him think less conveniently. He found illusions necessary, so that in order to keep an adequate number going he often forbade himself any excess of that exercise. Mrs. Rooth and her daughter were there and could certainly be trusted to make themselves felt. He was conscious of their anxiety and their calculations as of a frequent oppression, and knew that whatever results might ensue he should have to do the costly thing for them. An idea of tenacity, of worrying feminine duration, associated itself with their presence; he would have assented with a silent nod to the proposition—enunciated by Gabriel Nash—that he was saddled with them. Remedies hovered before him, but these figured also at the same time as complications; ranging vaguely from the expenditure of money to the discovery that he was in love. This latter accident would be particularly tedious; he had a full perception of the arts by which the girl's mother might succeed in making it so. It wouldn't be a compensation for trouble, but a trouble which in itself would require compensations. Would that balm spring from the spectacle of the young lady's genius? The genius would have to be very great to justify a rising young diplomatist in making a fool of himself.

With the excuse of pressing work he put off Miss Rooth from day to day, and from day to day he expected to hear her knock at his door. It would be time enough when they ran him to earth again; and he was unable to see how after all he could serve them even then. He had proposed impetuously a course of the theatres; but that would be a considerable personal effort now that the summer was about to begin—a free bid for bad air, stale pieces, and tired actors. When, however, more than a week had elapsed without a reminder of his neglected promise it came over him that he must himself in honour give a sign. There was a delicacy in such unexpected and such difficult discretion—he was touched by being let alone. The flurry of work at the embassy was over and he had time to ask himself what in especial he should do. He wanted something definite to suggest before communicating with the Hôtel de la Garonne.

As a consequence of this speculation he went back to Madame Carré to ask her to reconsider her stern judgement and give the young English lady—to oblige him—a dozen lessons of the sort she knew so well how to give. He was aware that this request scarcely stood on its feet; for in the first place Madame Carré never reconsidered when once she had got her impression, and in the second never wasted herself on subjects whom nature had not formed to do her honour. He knew his asking her to strain a point to please him would give her a false idea—save that for that matter she had it already—of his relations, actual or prospective, with the girl; but he decided he needn't care for this, since Miriam herself probably wouldn't care. What he had mainly in mind was to say to the old actress that she had been mistaken—the *jeune Anglaise* wasn't such a *grue*. This would take some courage, but it would also add to the amusement of his visit.

He found her at home, but as soon as he had expressed his conviction she began: "Oh, your *jeune Anglaise*, I know a great deal more about her than you! She has been back to see me twice; she doesn't go the longest way round. She charges me like a grenadier and asks me to give her—guess a little what!—private recitations all to herself. If she doesn't succeed it won't be for want of knowing how to thump at doors. The other day when I came in she was waiting for me; she had been there two hours. My private recitations—have you an idea what people pay for them?"

"Between artists, you know, there are easier conditions," Sherringham laughed.

"How do I know if she's an artist? She won't open her mouth to me; what she wants is to make me say things to *her*. She does make me—I don't know how—and she sits there gaping at me with her big eyes. They look like open pockets!"

"I daresay she'll profit by it," said Sherringham.

"I daresay *you* will! Her face is stupid while she watches me, and when she has tired me out she simply walks away. However, as she comes back—!"

Madame Carré paused a moment, listened and then cried: "Didn't I tell you?"

Sherringham heard a parley of voices in the little antechamber, and the next moment the door was pushed open and Miriam Rooth bounded into the room. She was flushed and breathless, without a smile, very direct.

"Will you hear me to-day? I know four things," she immediately broke out. Then seeing Sherringham she added in the same brisk, earnest tone, as if the matter were of the highest importance: "Oh how d'ye do? I'm very glad you're here." She said nothing else to him than this, appealed to him in no way, made no allusion to his having neglected her, but addressed herself to Madame Carré as if he had not been there; making no excuses and using no flattery; taking rather a tone of equal authority—all as if the famous artist had an obvious duty toward her. This was another variation Peter thought; it differed from each of the attitudes in which he had previously seen her. It came over him suddenly that so far from there being any question of her having the histrionic nature she simply had it in such perfection that she was always acting; that her existence was a series of parts assumed for the moment, each changed for the next, before the perpetual mirror of some curiosity or admiration or wonder—some spectatorship that she perceived or imagined in the people about her. Interested as he had ever been in the profession of which she was potentially an ornament, this idea startled him by its novelty and even lent, on the spot, a formidable, a really appalling character to Miriam Rooth. It struck him abruptly that a woman whose only being was to "make believe," to make believe she had any and every being you might like and that would serve a purpose and produce a certain effect, and whose identity resided in the continuity of her personations, so that she had no moral privacy, as he phrased it to himself, but lived in a high wind of exhibition, of figuration— such a woman was a kind of monster in whom of necessity there would be nothing to "be fond" of, because there would be nothing to take hold of. He felt for a moment how simple he had been not to have achieved before this analysis of the actress. The girl's very face made it vivid to him now— the discovery that she positively had no countenance of her own, but only the countenance of the occasion, a sequence, a variety—capable possibly of becoming immense—of representative movements. She was always trying them, practising them, for her amusement or profit, jumping from one to the other and extending her range; and this would doubtless be her occupation more and more as she acquired ease and confidence. The expression that came nearest belonging to her, as it were, was the one that came nearest being a blank—an air of inanity when she forgot herself in some act of sincere attention. Then her eye was heavy and her mouth betrayed a commonness; though it was perhaps just at such a moment that the fine line of her head told most. She had looked slightly *bête* even when Sherringham, on their first meeting at Madame Carré's, said to Nick Dormer that she was the image of the Tragic Muse.

Now, at any rate, he seemed to see that she might do what she liked with her face. It was an elastic substance, an element of gutta-percha, like the flexibility of the gymnast, the lady at the music-hall who is shot from the mouth of a cannon. He winced a little at this coarser view of the actress; he had somehow always looked more poetically at that priestess of art. Yet what was she, the priestess, when one came to think of it, but a female gymnast, a mountebank at higher wages? She didn't literally hang by her heels from a trapeze and hold a fat man in her teeth, but she made the same use of her tongue, of her eyes, of the imitative trick, that her muscular sister made of leg and jaw. It was an odd circumstance that Miss Rooth's face seemed to him to-day a finer instrument than old Madame Carré's. It was doubtless that the girl's was fresh and strong and had a future in it, while poor Madame Carré's was worn and weary and had only a past.

The old woman said something, half in jest, half in real resentment, about the brutality of youth while Miriam went to a mirror and quickly took off her hat, patting and arranging her hair as a preliminary to making herself heard. Sherringham saw with surprise and amusement that the keen Frenchwoman, who had in her long life exhausted every adroitness, was in a manner helpless and coerced, obliging all in spite of herself. Her young friend had taken but a few days and a couple of visits to become a successful force; she had imposed herself, and Madame Carré, while she laughed—yet looked terrible too, with such high artifices of eye and gesture—was reduced to the last line of defence; that of pronouncing her coarse and clumsy, saying she might knock her down, but that this proved nothing. She spoke jestingly enough not to offend, but her manner betrayed the irritation of an intelligent woman who at an advanced age found herself for the first time failing to understand. What she didn't understand was the kind of social product thus presented to her by Gabriel Nash; and this suggested to Sherringham that the *jeune Anglaise* was perhaps indeed rare, a new type, as Madame Carré must have seen innumerable varieties. He saw the girl was perfectly prepared to be abused and that her indifference to what might be thought of her discretion was a proof of life, health, and spirit, the insolence of conscious resources.

When she had given herself a touch at the glass she turned round, with a rapid "*Ecoutez maintenant*!" and stood leaning a moment—slightly lowered and inclined backward, her hands behind her and supporting her—on the *console* before the mirror. She waited an instant, turning her eyes from one of her companions to the other as to take possession of them—an eminently conscious, intentional proceeding, which made Sherringham ask himself what had become of her former terror and if that and her tears had all been a comedy: after which, abruptly straightening herself, she began to repeat a short French poem, an ingenious thing of the day, that she had induced Madame Carré to say over to her. She had learned it, practised it, rehearsed it to her mother, and had now been childishly eager to show what she could do with it. What she mainly did was to reproduce with a crude fidelity, but in extraordinary detail, the intonations, the personal quavers and cadences of her model.

"How bad you make me seem to myself and if I were you how much better I should say it!" was Madame Carré's first criticism.

Miriam allowed her, however, little time to develop it, for she broke out, at the shortest intervals, with the several other specimens of verse to which the old actress had handed her the key. They were all fine lyrics, of tender or ironic intention, by contemporary poets, but depending for effect on taste and art, a mastery of the rare shade and the right touch, in the interpreter. Miriam had gobbled them up, and she gave them forth in the same way as the first, with close, rude, audacious mimicry. There was a moment for Sherringham when it might have been feared their hostess would see in the performance a designed burlesque of her manner, her airs and graces, her celebrated simpers and grimaces, so extravagant did it all cause these refinements to appear. When it was over the old woman said, "Should you like now to hear how *you* do?" and, without waiting for an answer, phrased and trilled the last of the pieces, from beginning to end, exactly as her visitor had done, making this imitation of an imitation the drollest thing conceivable. If she had suffered from the sound of the girl's echo it was a perfect revenge. Miriam had dropped on a sofa, exhausted, and she stared at first, flushed and wild; then she frankly gave way to pleasure, to interest and large laughter. She said afterwards, to defend herself, that the verses in question, and indeed all those she had recited, were of the most difficult sort: you had to do them; they didn't do themselves— they were things in which the *gros moyens* were of no avail.

"Ah my poor child, your means are all *gros moyens*; you appear to have no others," Madame Carré replied. "You do what you can, but there are people like that; it's the way they're made. They can never come nearer to fine truth, to the just indication; shades don't exist for them, they don't see certain differences. It was to show you a difference that I repeated that thing as you repeat it, as you represent my doing it. If you're struck with the little the two ways have in common so much the better. But you seem to me terribly to *alourdir* everything you touch."

Peter read into this judgement a deep irritation—Miriam clearly set the teeth of her instructress on edge. She acted on her nerves, was made up of roughnesses and thicknesses unknown hitherto to her fine, free-playing finger-tips. This exasperation, however, was a degree of flattery; it was neither indifference nor simple contempt; it acknowledged a mystifying reality in the *jeune Anglaise* and even a shade of importance. The latter remarked, serenely enough, that the things she wanted most to do were just those that were not for the *gros moyens*, the vulgar obvious dodges, the starts and shouts that any one could think of and that the *gros public* liked. She wanted to do what was most difficult, and to plunge into it from the first; and she explained as if it were a discovery of her own that there were two kinds of scenes and speeches: those which acted themselves, of which the treatment was plain, the only way, so that you had just to take it; and those open to interpretation, with which you had to fight every step, rendering, arranging, doing the thing according to your idea. Some of the most effective passages and the most celebrated and admired, like the frenzy of Juliet with her potion, were of the former sort; but it was the others she liked best.

Madame Carré received this revelation good-naturedly enough, considering its want of freshness, and only laughed at the young lady for looking so nobly patronising while she gave it. Her laughter appeared partly addressed to the good faith with which Miriam described herself as preponderantly interested in the subtler problems of her art. Sherringham was charmed with the girl's pluck—if it was pluck and not mere density; the stout patience with which she submitted, for a purpose, to the old woman's rough usage. He wanted to take her away, to give her a friendly caution, to advise her not to become a bore, not to expose herself. But she held up her beautiful head as to show how little she cared at present for any exposure, and that (it was half coarseness—Madame Carré was so far right—and half fortitude) she had no intention of coming away so long as; there was anything to be picked up. She sat and still she sat, challenging her hostess with every sort of question—some reasonable, some ingenious, some strangely futile and some highly indiscreet; but all with the effect that, contrary to Peter's expectation, their distinguished friend warmed to the work of answering and explaining, became interested, was content to keep her and to talk. Yes, she took her ease; she relieved herself, with the rare cynicism of the artist—all the crudity, the irony and intensity of a discussion of esoteric things—of personal mysteries, of methods and secrets. It was the oddest hour our young man had ever spent, even in the course of investigations which had often led him into the *cuisine*, the distillery or back shop, of the admired profession. He got up several times to come away; then he remained, partly in order not to leave Miriam alone with her terrible initiatress, partly because he was both amused and edified, and partly because Madame Carré held him by the appeal of her sharp, confidential, old eyes, addressing her talk to himself, with Miriam but a pretext and subject, a vile illustration. She undressed this young lady, as it were, from head to foot, turned her inside out, weighed and measured and sounded her: it was all, for Sherringham, a new revelation of the point to which, in her profession and nation, an intelligence of the business, a ferocious analysis, had been carried and a special vocabulary developed. What struck him above all was the way she knew her grounds and reasons, so that everything was sharp and clear in her mind and lay under her hand. If she had rare perceptions she had traced them to their source; she could give an account of what she did; she knew perfectly why, could explain it, defend it, amplify it, fight for it: all of which was an intellectual joy to her, allowing her a chance to abound and insist and discriminate. There was a kind of cruelty or at least of hardness in it all, to poor Peter's shy English sense, that sense which can never really reconcile itself to any question of method and form, and has extraneous sentiments to "square," to pacify with compromises and superficialities, the general plea for innocence in everything and often the flagrant proof of it. In theory there was nothing he valued more than just such a logical passion as Madame Carré's, but it was apt in fact, when he found himself at close quarters with it, to appear an ado about nothing.

If the old woman was hard it was not that many of her present conclusions about the *jeune Anglaise* were not indulgent, but that she had a vision of the great manner, of right and wrong, of the just and the false, so high and religious that the individual was nothing before it—a prompt and easy sacrifice. It made our friend uncomfortable, as he had been made uncomfortable by certain *feuilletons*, reviews of the theatres in the Paris newspapers, which he was committed to thinking important but of which, when they were very good, he was rather ashamed. When they were very good, that is when they were very thorough, they were very personal, as was inevitable in dealing with the most personal of the arts: they went into details; they put the dots on the *i*'s; they discussed impartially the qualities of appearance, the physical gifts of the poor aspirant, finding them in some cases reprehensibly inadequate Peter could never rid himself of a dislike to these pronouncements; in the case of the actresses especially they struck him as brutal and offensive—unmanly as launched by an ensconced, moustachioed critic over a cigar. At the same time he was aware of the dilemma (he hated it; it made him blush still more) in which his objection lodged him. If one was right in caring for the actor's art one ought to have been interested in every honest judgement of it, which, given the peculiar conditions, would be useful in proportion as it should be free. If the criticism that recognised frankly these conditions seemed an inferior or an unholy thing, then what was to be said for the art itself? What an implication, if the criticism was tolerable only so long as it was worthless—so long as it remained vague and timid! This was a knot Peter had never straightened out: he contented himself with feeling that there was no reason a theatrical critic shouldn't be a gentleman, at the same time that he often dubbed it an odious trade, which no gentleman could possibly follow. The best of the fraternity, so conspicuous in Paris, were those who didn't follow it—those who, while pretending to write about the stage, wrote about everything else.

It was as if Madame Carré, in pursuance of her inflamed sense that the art was everything and the individual nothing save as he happened to serve it, had said: "Well, if she *will* have it she shall; she shall know what she's in for, what I went through, battered and broken in as we all have been—all who are worthy, who have had the honour. She shall know the real point of view." It was as if she were still beset with Mrs. Rooth's twaddle and muddle, her hypocrisy, her idiotic scruples—something she felt all need to belabour, to trample on. Miriam took it all as a bath, a baptism, with shuddering joy and gleeful splashes; staring, wondering, sometimes blushing and failing to follow, but not shrinking nor wounded; laughing, when convicted, at her own expense and feeling evidently that this at last was the high cold air of art, an initiation, a discipline that nothing could undo. Sherringham said he would see her home—he wanted to talk to her and she must walk away with him. "And it's understood then she may come back," he added to Madame Carré. "It's *my* affair of course. You'll take an interest in her for a month or two; she'll sit at your feet."

The old actress had an admirable shrug. "Oh I'll knock her about—she seems stout enough!"

XI

When they had descended to the street Miriam mentioned to Peter that she was thirsty, dying to drink something: upon which he asked her if she should have an objection to going with him to a café.

"Objection? I've spent my life in cafés! They're warm in winter and you get your lamplight for nothing," she explained. "Mamma and I have sat in them for hours, many a time, with a *consommation* of three sous, to save fire and candles at home. We've lived in places we couldn't sit in, if you want to know—where there was only really room if we were in bed. Mamma's money's sent out from England and sometimes it usedn't to come. Once it didn't come for months—for months and months. I don't know how we lived. There wasn't any to come; there wasn't any to get home. That isn't amusing when you're away in a foreign town without any friends. Mamma used to borrow, but people wouldn't always lend. You needn't be afraid—she won't borrow of *you*. We're rather better now—something has been done in England; I don't understand what. It's only fivepence a year, but it has been settled; it comes regularly; it used to come only when we had written and begged and waited. But it made no difference—mamma was always up to her ears in books. They served her for food and drink. When she had nothing to eat she began a novel in ten volumes—the old-fashioned ones; they lasted longest. She knows every *cabinet de lecture* in every town; the little, cheap, shabby ones, I mean, in the back streets, where they have odd volumes and only ask a sou and the books are so old that they smell like close rooms. She takes them to the cafés—the little, cheap, shabby cafés too—and she reads there all the evening. That's very well for her, but it doesn't feed me. I don't like a diet of dirty old novels. I sit there beside her with nothing to do, not even a stocking to mend; she doesn't think that *comme il faut*. I don't know what the people take me for. However, we've never been spoken to: any one can see mamma's a great lady. As for me I daresay I might be anything dreadful. If you're going to be an actress you must get used to being looked at. There were people in England who used to ask us to stay; some of them were our cousins—or mamma says they were. I've never been very clear about our cousins and I don't think they were at all clear about us. Some of them are dead; the others don't ask us any more. You should hear mamma on the subject of our visits in England. It's very convenient when your cousins are dead—that explains everything. Mamma has delightful phrases: 'My family is almost extinct.' Then your family may have been anything you like. Ours of course was magnificent. We did stay in a place once where there was a deer-park, and also private theatricals. I played in them; I was only fifteen years old, but I was very big and I thought I was in heaven. I'll go anywhere you like; you needn't be afraid; we've been in places! I've learned a great deal that way—sitting beside mamma and watching people, their faces, their types, their movements. There's a great deal goes on in cafés: people come to them to talk things over, their private affairs, their complications; they have important meetings. Oh I've observed scenes between men and women—very quiet, terribly quiet, but awful, pathetic, tragic! Once I saw a woman do something that I'm going to do some day when I'm great—if I can get the situation. I'll tell you what it is sometime—I'll do it for you. Oh it is the book of life!"

So Miriam discoursed, familiarly, disconnectedly, as the pair went their way down the Rue de Constantinople; and she continued to abound in anecdote and remark after they were seated face to face at a little marble table in an establishment Peter had selected carefully and where he had caused her, at her request, to be accommodated with *sirop d'orgeat*. "I know what it will come to: Madame Carré will want to keep me." This was one of the felicities she presently threw off.

"To keep you?"

"For the French stage. She won't want to let you have me." She said things of that kind, astounding in self-complacency, the assumption of quick success. She was in earnest, evidently prepared to work, but her imagination flew over preliminaries and probations, took no account of the steps in the process, especially the first tiresome ones, the hard test of honesty. He had done nothing for her as yet, given no substantial pledge of interest; yet she was already talking as if his protection were assured and jealous. Certainly, however, she seemed to belong to him very much indeed as she sat facing him at the Paris café in her youth, her beauty, and her talkative confidence. This degree of possession was highly agreeable to him and he asked nothing more than to make it last and go further. The impulse to draw her out was irresistible, to encourage her to show herself all the way; for if he was really destined to take her career in hand he counted on some good equivalent—such for instance as that she should at least amuse him.

"It's very singular; I know nothing like it," he said—"your equal mastery of two languages."

"Say of half-a-dozen," Miriam smiled.

"Oh I don't believe in the others to the same degree. I don't imagine that, with all deference to your undeniable facility, you'd be judged fit to address a German or an Italian audience in their own tongue. But you might a French, perfectly, and they're the most particular of all; for their idiom's supersensitive and they're incapable of enduring the *baragouinage* of foreigners, to which we listen with such complacency. In fact your French is better than your English—it's more conventional; there are little queernesses and impurities in your English, as if you had lived abroad too much. Ah you must work that."

"I'll work it with *you*. I like the way you speak."

"You must speak beautifully; you must do something for the standard."

"For the standard?"

"Well, there isn't any after all." Peter had a drop. "It has gone to the dogs."

"Oh I'll bring it back. I know what you mean."

"No one knows, no one cares; the sense is gone—it isn't in the public," he continued, ventilating a grievance he was rarely able to forget, the vision of which now suddenly made a mission full of possible sanctity for his companion. "Purity of speech, on our stage, doesn't exist. Every one speaks as he likes and audiences never notice; it's the last thing they think of. The place is given up to abominable dialects and individual tricks, any vulgarity flourishes, and on top of it all the Americans, with every conceivable crudity, come in to make confusion worse confounded. And when one laments it people stare; they don't know what one means."

"Do you mean the grand manner, certain pompous pronunciations, the style of the Kembles?"

"I mean any style that *is* a style, that's a system, a consistency, an art, that contributes a positive beauty to utterance. When I pay ten shillings to hear you speak I want you to know how, *que diable*! Say that to people and they're mostly lost in stupor; only a few, the very intelligent, exclaim: 'Then you want actors to be affected?'"

"And do you?" asked Miriam full of interest.

"My poor child, what else under the sun should they be? Isn't their whole art the affectation *par excellence*? The public won't stand that to-day, so one hears it said. If that be true it simply means that the theatre, as I care for it, that is as a personal art, is at an end."

"Never, never, never!" the girl cried in a voice that made a dozen people look round.

"I sometimes think it—that the personal art is at an end and that henceforth we shall have only the arts, capable no doubt of immense development in their way—indeed they've already reached it—of the stage-carpenter and the costumer. In London the drama is already smothered in scenery; the interpretation scrambles off as it can. To get the old personal impression, which used to be everything, you must go to the poor countries, and most of all to Italy."

"Oh I've had it; it's very personal!" said Miriam knowingly.

"You've seen the nudity of the stage, the poor, painted, tattered screen behind, and before that void the histrionic figure, doing everything it knows how, in complete possession. The personality isn't our English personality and it may not always carry us with it; but the direction's right, and it has the superiority that it's a human exhibition, not a mechanical one."

"I can act just like an Italian," Miriam eagerly proclaimed.

"I'd rather you acted like an Englishwoman if an Englishwoman would only act."

"Oh, I'll show you!"

"But you're not English," said Peter sociably, his arms on the table.

"I beg your pardon. You should hear mamma about our 'race.'"

"You're a Jewess—I'm sure of that," he went on.

173

She jumped at this, as he was destined to see later she would ever jump at anything that might make her more interesting or striking; even at things that grotesquely contradicted or excluded each other. "That's always possible if one's clever. I'm very willing, because I want to be the English Rachel."

"Then you must leave Madame Carré as soon as you've got from her what she can give."

"Oh, you needn't fear; you shan't lose me," the girl replied with charming gross fatuity. "My name's Jewish," she went on, "but it was that of my grandmother, my father's mother. She was a baroness in Germany. That is, she was the daughter of a baron."

Peter accepted this statement with reservations, but he replied: "Put all that together and it makes you very sufficiently of Rachel's tribe."

"I don't care if I'm of her tribe artistically. I'm of the family of the artists—*je me fiche* of any other! I'm in the same style as that woman—I know it."

"You speak as if you had seen her," he said, amused at the way she talked of "that woman." "Oh I know all about her—I know all about all the great actors. But that won't prevent me from speaking divine English."

"You must learn lots of verse; you must repeat it to me," Sherringham went on. "You must break yourself in till you can say anything. You must learn passages of Milton, passages of Wordsworth."

"Did *they* write plays?"

"Oh it isn't only a matter of plays! You can't speak a part properly till you can speak everything else, anything that comes up, especially in proportion as it's difficult. That gives you authority."

"Oh yes, I'm going in for authority. There's more chance in English," the girl added in the next breath. "There are not so many others—the terrible competition. There are so many here—not that I'm afraid," she chattered on. "But we've got America and they haven't. America's a great place."

"You talk like a theatrical agent. They're lucky not to have it as we have it. Some of them do go, and it ruins them."

"Why, it fills their pockets!" Miriam cried.

"Yes, but see what they pay. It's the death of an actor to play to big populations that don't understand his language. It's nothing then but the *gros moyens*; all his delicacy perishes. However, they'll understand *you*."

"Perhaps I shall be too affected," she said.

"You won't be more so than Garrick or Mrs. Siddons or John Kemble or Edmund Kean. They understood Edmund Kean. All reflexion is affectation, and all acting's reflexion."

"I don't know—mine's instinct," Miriam contended.

"My dear young lady, you talk of 'yours'; but don't be offended if I tell you that yours doesn't exist. Some day it will—if the thing comes off. Madame Carré's does, because she has reflected. The talent, the desire, the energy are an instinct; but by the time these things become a performance they're an instinct put in its place."

"Madame Carré's very philosophic. I shall never be like her."

"Of course you won't—you'll be original. But you'll have your own ideas."

"I daresay I shall have a good many of yours"—and she smiled at him across the table.

They sat a moment looking at each other. "Don't go in for coquetry," Peter then said. "It's a waste of time."

"Well, that's civil!" the girl cried.

"Oh I don't mean for me, I mean for yourself I want you to be such good faith. I'm bound to give you stiff advice. You don't strike me as flirtatious and that sort of thing, and it's much in your favour."

"In my favour?"

"It does save time."

"Perhaps it saves too much. Don't you think the artist ought to have passions?"

Peter had a pause; he thought an examination of this issue premature. "Flirtations are not passions," he replied. "No, you're simple—at least I suspect you are; for of course with a woman one would be clever to know."

She asked why he pronounced her simple, but he judged it best and more consonant with fair play to defer even a treatment of this branch of the question; so that to change the subject he said: "Be sure you don't betray me to your friend Mr. Nash."

"Betray you? Do you mean about your recommending affectation?"

"Dear me, no; he recommends it himself. That is, he practises it, and on a scale!"

"But he makes one hate it."

"He proves what I mean," said Sherringham: "that the great comedian's the one who raises it to a science. If we paid ten shillings to listen to Mr. Nash we should think him very fine. But we want to know what it's supposed to be."

"It's too odious, the way he talks about us!" Miriam cried assentingly.

"About 'us'?"

"Us poor actors."

"It's the competition he dislikes," Peter laughed.

"However, he's very good-natured; he lent mamma thirty pounds," the girl added honestly. Our young man, at this information, was not able to repress a certain small twinge noted by his companion and of which she appeared to mistake the meaning. "Of course he'll get it back," she went on while he looked at her in silence a little. Fortune had not supplied him profusely with money, but his emotion was caused by no foresight of his probably having also to put his hand in his pocket for Mrs. Rooth. It was simply the instinctive recoil of a fastidious nature from the idea of familiar intimacy with people who lived from hand to mouth, together with a sense that this intimacy would have to be defined if it was to go much further. He would wish to know what it was supposed to be, like Nash's histrionics. Miriam after a moment mistook his thought still more completely, and in doing so flashed a portent of the way it was in her to strike from time to time a note exasperatingly, almost consciously vulgar, which one would hate for the reason, along with others, that by that time one would be in love with her. "Well then, he won't—if you don't believe it!" she easily laughed. He was saying to himself that the only possible form was that they should borrow only from him. "You're a funny man. I make you blush," she persisted.

"I must reply with the *tu quoque*, though I've not that effect on you."

"I don't understand," said the girl.

"You're an extraordinary young lady."

"You mean I'm horrid. Well, I daresay I am. But I'm better when you know me."

He made no direct rejoinder to this, but after a moment went on: "Your mother must repay that money. I'll give it her."

"You had better give it *him*!" cried Miriam. "If once mamma has it—!" She interrupted herself and with another and a softer tone, one of her professional transitions, remarked: "I suppose you've never known any one that was poor."

"I'm poor myself. That is, I'm very far from rich. But why receive favours—?" And here he in turn checked himself with the sense that he was indeed taking a great deal on his back if he pretended already—he had not seen the pair three times—to regulate their intercourse with the rest of the world. But the girl instantly carried out his thought and more than his thought.

"Favours from Mr. Nash? Oh he doesn't count!"

The way she dropped these words—they would have been admirable on the stage—made him reply with prompt ease: "What I meant just now was that you're not to tell him, after all my swagger, that I consider that you and I are really required to save our theatre."

"Oh if we can save it he shall know it!" She added that she must positively get home; her mother would be in a state: she had really scarce ever been out alone. He mightn't think it, but so it was. Her mother's ideas, those awfully proper ones, were not all talk. She *did* keep her! Sherringham accepted this—he had an adequate and indeed an analytic vision of Mrs. Rooth's conservatism; but he observed at the same time that his companion made no motion to rise. He made none either; he only said:

"We're very frivolous, the way we chatter. What you want to do to get your foot in the stirrup is supremely difficult. There's everything to overcome. You've neither an engagement nor the prospect of an engagement."

"Oh you'll get me one!" Her manner presented this as so certain that it wasn't worth dilating on; so instead of dilating she inquired abruptly a second time: "Why do you think I'm so simple?"

"I don't then. Didn't I tell you just now that you were extraordinary? That's the term, moreover, that you applied to yourself when you came to see me—when you said a girl had to be a kind of monster to wish to go on the stage. It remains the right term and your simplicity doesn't mitigate it. What's rare in you is that you have—as I suspect at least—no nature of your own." Miriam listened to this as if preparing to argue with it or not, only as it should strike her as a sufficiently brave picture; but as yet, naturally, she failed to understand. "You're always at concert pitch or on your horse; there are no intervals. It's the absence of intervals, of a *fond* or background, that I don't comprehend. You're an embroidery without a canvas."

"Yes—perhaps," the girl replied, her head on one side as if she were looking at the pattern of this rarity. "But I'm very honest."

"You can't be everything, both a consummate actress and a flower of the field. You've got to choose."

She looked at him a moment. "I'm glad you think I'm so wonderful."

"Your feigning may be honest in the sense that your only feeling is your feigned one," Peter pursued. "That's what I mean by the absence of a ground or of intervals. It's a kind of thing that's a labyrinth!"

"I know what I am," she said sententiously.

But her companion continued, following his own train. "Were you really so frightened the first day you went to Madame Carré's?"

She stared, then with a flush threw back her head. "Do you think I was pretending?"

"I think you always are. However, your vanity—if you had any!—would be natural."

"I've plenty of that. I'm not a bit ashamed to own it."

"You'd be capable of trying to 'do' the human peacock. But excuse the audacity and the crudity of my speculations—it only proves my interest. What is it that you know you are?"

"Why, an artist. Isn't that a canvas?"

"Yes, an intellectual, but not a moral."

"Ah it's everything! And I'm a good girl too—won't that do?"

"It remains to be seen," Sherringham laughed. "A creature who's absolutely *all* an artist—I'm curious to see that."

"Surely it has been seen—in lots of painters, lots of musicians."

"Yes, but those arts are not personal like yours. I mean not so much so. There's something left for—what shall I call it?—for character."

She stared again with her tragic light. "And do you think I haven't a character?" As he hesitated she pushed back her chair, rising rapidly.

He looked up at her an instant—she seemed so "plastic"; and then rising too answered: "Delightful being, you've a hundred!"

179

XII

The summer arrived and the dense air of the Paris theatres became in fact a still more complicated mixture; yet the occasions were not few on which Sherringham, having placed a box near the stage (most often a stuffy, dusky *baignoire*) at the disposal of Mrs. Rooth and her daughter, found time just to look in, as he said, to spend a part of the evening with them and point the moral of the performance. The pieces, the successes of the winter, had entered the automatic phase: they went on by the force of the impetus acquired, deriving little fresh life from the interpretation, and in ordinary conditions their strong points, as rendered by the actors, would have been as wearisome to this student as an importunate repetition of a good story. But it was not long before he became aware that the conditions couldn't be taken for ordinary. There was a new infusion in his consciousness—an element in his life which altered the relations of things. He was not easy till he had found the right name for it—a name the more satisfactory that it was simple, comprehensive, and plausible. A new "distraction," in the French sense, was what he flattered himself he had discovered; he could recognise that as freely as possible without being obliged to classify the agreeable resource as a new entanglement. He was neither too much nor too little diverted; he had all his usual attention to give to his work: he had only an employment for his odd hours which, without being imperative, had over various others the advantage of a certain continuity.

And yet, I hasten to add, he was not so well pleased with it but that among his friends he maintained for the present a rich reserve about it. He had no irresistible impulse to describe generally how he had disinterred a strange, handsome girl whom he was bringing up for the theatre. She had been seen by several of his associates at his rooms, but was not soon to be seen there again. His reserve might by the ill-natured have been termed dissimulation, inasmuch as when asked by the ladies of the embassy what had become of the young person who had amused them that day so cleverly he gave it out that her whereabouts was uncertain and her destiny probably obscure; he let it be supposed in a word that his benevolence had scarcely survived an accidental, a charitable occasion. As he went about his customary business, and perhaps even put a little more conscience into the transaction of it, there was nothing to suggest to others that he was engaged in a private speculation of an absorbing kind. It was perhaps his weakness that he carried the apprehension of ridicule too far; but his excuse may have dwelt in his holding it unpardonable for a man publicly enrolled in the service of his country to be markedly ridiculous. It was of course not out of all order that such functionaries, their private situation permitting, should enjoy a personal acquaintance with stars of the dramatic, the lyric, or even the choregraphic stage: high diplomatists had indeed not rarely, and not invisibly, cultivated this privilege without its proving the sepulchre of their reputation. That a gentleman who was not a fool should consent a little to become one for the sake of a celebrated actress or singer—*cela s'était vu*, though it was not perhaps to be recommended. It was not a tendency that was encouraged at headquarters, where even the most rising young men were not incited to believe they could never fall. Still, it might pass if kept in its place; and there were ancient worthies yet in the profession—though not those whom the tradition had helped to go furthest—who held that something of the sort was a graceful ornament of the diplomatic character. Sherringham was aware he was very "rising"; but Miriam Rooth was not yet a celebrated actress. She was only a young artist in conscientious process of formation and encumbered with a mother still more conscientious than herself. She was a *jeune Anglaise*—a "lady" withal—very earnest about artistic, about remunerative problems. He had accepted the office of a formative influence; and that was precisely what might provoke derision. He was a ministering angel—his patience and good nature really entitled him to the epithet and his rewards would doubtless some day define themselves; but meanwhile other promotions were in precarious prospect, for the failure of which these would not even in their abundance, be a compensation. He kept an unembarrassed eye on Downing Street, and while it may frankly be said for him that he was neither a pedant nor a prig he remembered that the last impression he ought to wish to produce there was that of a futile estheticism.

He felt the case sufficiently important, however, when he sat behind Miriam at the play and looked over her shoulder at the stage; her observation being so keen and her comments so unexpected in their vivacity that his curiosity was refreshed and his attention stretched beyond its wont. If the exhibition before the footlights had now lost much of its annual brilliancy the fashion in which she followed it was perhaps exhibition enough. The attendance of the little party was, moreover, in most cases at the Théâtre Français; and it has been sufficiently indicated that our friend, though the child of a sceptical age and the votary of a cynical science, was still candid enough to take the serious, the religious view of that establishment the view of M. Sarcey and of the unregenerate provincial mind. "In the trade I follow we see things too much in the hard light of reason, of calculation," he once remarked to his young charge; "but it's good for the mind to keep up a superstition or two; it leaves a margin—like having a second horse to your brougham for night-work. The arts, the amusements, the esthetic part of life, are night-work, if I may say so without suggesting that they're illicit. At any rate you want your second horse—your superstition that stays at home when the sun's high—to go your rounds with. The Français is my second horse."

Miriam's appetite for this interest showed him vividly enough how rarely in the past it had been within her reach; and she pleased him at first by liking everything, seeing almost no differences and taking her deep draught undiluted. She leaned on the edge of the box with bright voracity; tasting to the core, yet relishing the surface, watching each movement of each actor, attending to the way each thing was said or done as if it were the most important thing, and emitting from time to time applausive or restrictive sounds. It was a charming show of the critical spirit in ecstasy. Sherringham had his wonder about it, as a part of the attraction exerted by this young lady was that she caused him to have his wonder about everything she did. Was it in fact a conscious show, a line taken for effect, so that at the Comédie her own display should be the most successful of all? That question danced attendance on the liberal intercourse of these young people and fortunately as yet did little to embitter Sherringham's share of it. His general sense that she was personating had its especial moments of suspense and perplexity, and added variety and even occasionally a degree of excitement to their commerce.

At the theatre, for the most part, she was really flushed with eagerness; and with the spectators who turned an admiring eye into the dim compartment of which she pervaded the front she might have passed for a romantic or at least an insatiable young woman from the country.

Mrs. Rooth took a more general view, but attended immensely to the story, in respect to which she manifested a patient good faith which had its surprises and its comicalities for her daughter's patron. She found no play too tedious, no *entr'acte* too long, no *baignoire* too hot, no tissue of incidents too complicated, no situation too unnatural and no sentiments too sublime. She gave him the measure of her power to sit and sit—an accomplishment to which she owed in the struggle for existence such superiority as she might be said to have achieved. She could out-sit everybody and everything; looking as if she had acquired the practice in repeated years of small frugality combined with large leisure—periods when she had nothing but hours and days and years to spend and had learned to calculate in any situation how long she could stay. "Staying" was so often a saving—a saving of candles, of fire and even (as it sometimes implied a scheme for stray refection) of food. Peter saw soon enough how bravely her shreds and patches of gentility and equanimity hung together, with the aid of whatever casual pins and other makeshifts, and if he had been addicted to studying the human mixture in its different combinations would have found in her an interesting compendium of some of the infatuations that survive a hard discipline. He made indeed without difficulty the reflexion that her life might have taught her something of the real, at the same time that he could scarce help thinking it clever of her to have so persistently declined the lesson. She appeared to have put it by with a deprecating, ladylike smile—a plea of being too soft and bland for experience.

She took the refined, sentimental, tender view of the universe, beginning with her own history and feelings. She believed in everything high and pure, disinterested and orthodox, and even at the Hôtel de la Garonne was unconscious of the shabby or the ugly side of the world. She never despaired: otherwise what would have been the use of being a Neville-Nugent? Only not to have been one—that would have been discouraging. She delighted in novels, poems, perversions, misrepresentations, and evasions, and had a capacity for smooth, superfluous falsification which made our young man think her sometimes an amusing and sometimes a tedious inventor. But she wasn't dangerous even if you believed her; she wasn't even a warning if you didn't. It was harsh to call her a hypocrite, since you never could have resolved her back into her character, there being no reverse at all to her blazonry. She built in the air and was not less amiable than she pretended, only that was a pretension too. She moved altogether in a world of elegant fable and fancy, and Sherringham had to live there with her for Miriam's sake, live there in sociable, vulgar assent and despite his feeling it rather a low neighbourhood. He was at a loss how to take what she said—she talked sweetly and discursively of so many things—till he simply noted that he could only take it always for untrue. When Miriam laughed at her he was rather disagreeably affected: "dear mamma's fine stories" was a sufficiently cynical reference to the immemorial infirmity of a parent. But when the girl backed her up, as he phrased it to himself, he liked that even less.

Mrs. Rooth was very fond of a moral and had never lost her taste for edification. She delighted in a beautiful character and was gratified to find so many more than she had supposed represented in the contemporary French drama. She never failed to direct Miriam's attention to them and to remind her that there is nothing in life so grand as a sublime act, above all when sublimely explained. Peter made much of the difference between the mother and the daughter, thinking it singularly marked—the way one took everything for the sense, or behaved as if she did, caring only for the plot and the romance, the triumph or defeat of virtue and the moral comfort of it all, and the way the other was alive but to the manner and the art of it, the intensity of truth to appearances. Mrs. Rooth abounded in impressive evocations, and yet he saw no link between her facile genius and that of which Miriam gave symptoms. The poor lady never could have been accused of successful deceit, whereas the triumph of fraud was exactly what her clever child achieved. She made even the true seem fictive, while Miriam's effort was to make the fictive true. Sherringham thought it an odd unpromising stock (that of the Neville-Nugents) for a dramatic talent to have sprung from, till he reflected that the evolution was after all natural: the figurative impulse in the mother had become conscious, and therefore higher, through finding an aim, which was beauty, in the daughter. Likely enough the Hebraic Mr. Rooth, with his love of old pots and Christian altar-cloths, had supplied in the girl's composition the esthetic element, the sense of colour and form. In their visits to the theatre there was nothing Mrs. Rooth more insisted on than the unprofitableness of deceit, as shown by the most distinguished authors—the folly and degradation, the corrosive effect on the spirit, of tortuous ways. Their companion soon gave up the futile task of piecing together her incongruous references to her early life and her family in England. He renounced even the doctrine that there was a residuum of truth in her claim of great relationships, since, existent or not, he cared equally little for her ramifications. The principle of this indifference was at bottom a certain desire to disconnect and isolate Miriam; for it was disagreeable not to be independent in dealing with her, and he could be fully so only if she herself were.

The early weeks of that summer—they went on indeed into August— were destined to establish themselves in his memory as a season of pleasant things. The ambassador went away and Peter had to wait for his own holiday, which he did during the hot days contentedly enough—waited in spacious halls and a vast, dim, bird-haunted garden. The official world and most other worlds withdrew from Paris, and the Place de la Concorde, a larger, whiter desert than ever, became by a reversal of custom explorable with safety. The Champs Elysées were dusty and rural, with little creaking booths and exhibitions that made a noise like grasshoppers; the Arc de Triomphe threw its cool, thick shadow for a mile; the Palais de l'Industrie glittered in the light of the long days; the cabmen, in their red waistcoats, dozed inside their boxes, while Sherringham permitted himself a "pot" hat and rarely met a friend. Thus was Miriam as islanded as the chained Andromeda, and thus was it possible to deal with her, even Perseus-like, in deep detachment. The theatres on the boulevard closed for the most part, but the great temple of the Rue de Richelieu, with an esthetic responsibility, continued imperturbably to dispense examples of style. Madame Carré was going to Vichy, but had not yet taken flight, which was a great advantage for Miriam, who could now solicit her attention with the consciousness that she had no engagements *en ville.*

"I make her listen to me—I make her tell me," said the ardent girl, who was always climbing the slope of the Rue de Constantinople on the shady side, where of July mornings a smell of violets came from the moist flower-stands of fat, white-capped *bouquetières* in the angles of doorways. Miriam liked the Paris of the summer mornings, the clever freshness of all the little trades and the open-air life, the cries, the talk from door to door, which reminded her of the south, where, in the multiplicity of her habitations, she had lived; and most of all, the great amusement, or nearly, of her walk, the enviable baskets of the laundress piled up with frilled and fluted whiteness—the certain luxury, she felt while she passed with quick prevision, of her own dawn of glory. The greatest amusement perhaps was to recognise the pretty sentiment of earliness, the particular congruity with the hour, in the studied, selected dress of the little tripping women who were taking the day, for important advantages, while it was tender. At any rate she mostly brought with her from her passage through the town good humour enough—with the penny bunch of violets she always stuck in the front of her dress—for whatever awaited her at Madame Carré's. She declared to her friend that her dear mistress was terribly severe, giving her the most difficult, the most exhausting exercises, showing a kind of rage for breaking her in.

"So much the better," Sherringham duly answered; but he asked no questions and was glad to let the preceptress and the pupil fight it out together. He wanted for the moment to know as little as possible about their ways together: he had been over-dosed with that knowledge while attending at their second interview. He would send Madame Carré her money—she was really most obliging—and in the meantime was certain Miriam could take care of herself. Sometimes he remarked to her that she needn't always talk "shop" to him: there were times when he was mortally tired of shop—of hers. Moreover, he frankly admitted that he was tired of his own, so that the restriction was not brutal. When she replied, staring, "Why, I thought you considered it as such a beautiful, interesting art!" he had no rejoinder more philosophic than "Well, I do; but there are moments when I'm quite sick of it all the same," At other times he put it: "Oh yes, the results, the finished thing, the dish perfectly seasoned and served: not the mess of preparation—at least not always—not the experiments that spoil the material."

"I supposed you to feel just these questions of study, of the artistic education, as you've called it to me, so fascinating," the girl persisted. She was sometimes so flatly lucid.

"Well, after all, I'm not an actor myself," he could but impatiently sigh.

"You might be one if you were serious," she would imperturbably say. To this her friend replied that Mr. Gabriel Nash ought to hear this; which made her promise with a certain grimness that she would settle *him* and his theories some day. Not to seem too inconsistent—for it was cruel to bewilder her when he had taken her up to enlighten—Peter repeated over that for a man like himself the interest of the whole thing depended on its being considered in a large, liberal way and with an intelligence that lifted it out of the question of the little tricks of the trade, gave it beauty and elevation. But she hereupon let him know that Madame Carré held there were no *little* tricks, that everything had its importance as a means to a great end, and that if you were not willing to try to *approfondir* the reason why, in a given situation, you should scratch your nose with your left hand rather than with your right, you were not worthy to tread any stage that respected itself.

"That's very well, but if I must go into details read me a little Shelley," groaned the young man in the spirit of a high *raffiné*.

"You're worse than Madame Carré; you don't know what to invent; between you you'll kill me!" the girl declared. "I think there's a secret league between you to spoil my voice, or at least to weaken my *souffle*, before I get it. But *à la guerre comme à la guerre*! How can I read Shelley, however, when I don't understand him?"

"That's just what I want to make you do. It's a part of your general training. You may do without that of course—without culture and taste and perception; but in that case you'll be nothing but a vulgar *cabotine*, and nothing will be of any consequence." He had a theory that the great lyric poets—he induced her to read, and recite as well, long passages of Wordsworth and Swinburne—would teach her many of the secrets of the large utterance, the mysteries of rhythm, the communicableness of style, the latent music of the language and the art of "composing" copious speeches and of retaining her stores of free breath. He held in perfect sincerity that there was a general sense of things, things of the mind, which would be of the highest importance to her and to which it was by good fortune just in his power to contribute. She would do better in proportion as she had more knowledge—even knowledge that might superficially show but a remote connexion with her business. The actor's talent was essentially a gift, a thing by itself, implanted, instinctive, accidental, equally unconnected with intellect and with virtue— Sherringham was completely of that opinion; but it struck him as no *bêtise* to believe at the same time that intellect—leaving virtue for the moment out of the question—might be brought into fruitful relation with it. It would be a bigger thing if a better mind were projected upon it—projected without sacrificing the mind. So he lent his young friend books she never read—she was on almost irreconcilable terms with the printed page save for spouting it—and in the long summer days, when he had leisure, took her to the Louvre to admire the great works of painting and sculpture. Here, as on all occasions, he was struck with the queer jumble of her taste, her mixture of intelligence and puerility. He saw she never read what he gave her, though she sometimes would shamelessly have liked him to suppose so; but in the presence of famous pictures and statues she had remarkable flashes of perception. She felt these things, she liked them, though it was always because she had an idea she could use them. The belief was often presumptuous, but it showed what an eye she had to her business. "I could look just like that if I tried." "That's the dress I mean to wear when I do Portia." Such were the observations apt to drop from her under the suggestion of antique marbles or when she stood before a Titian or a Bronzino.

When she uttered them, and many others besides, the effect was sometimes irritating to her adviser, who had to bethink himself a little that she was no more egotistical than the histrionic conscience required. He wondered if there were necessarily something vulgar in the histrionic conscience— something condemned only to feel the tricky, personal question. Wasn't it better to be perfectly stupid than to have only one eye open and wear for ever in the great face of the world the expression of a knowing wink? At the theatre, on the numerous July evenings when the Comédie Française exhibited the repertory by the aid of exponents determined the more sparse and provincial audience should have a taste of the tradition, her appreciation was tremendously technical and showed it was not for nothing she was now in and out of Madame Carré's innermost counsels. But there were moments when even her very acuteness seemed to him to drag the matter down, to see it in a small and superficial sense. What he flattered himself he was trying to do for her—and through her for the stage of his time, since she was the instrument, and incontestably a fine one, that had come to his hand—was precisely to lift it up, make it rare, keep it in the region of distinction and breadth. However, she was doubtless right and he was wrong, he eventually reasoned: you could afford to be vague only if you hadn't a responsibility. He had fine ideas, but she was to act them out, that is to apply them, and not he; and application was of necessity a vulgarisation, a smaller thing than theory. If she should some day put forth the great art it wasn't purely fanciful to forecast for her, the matter would doubtless be by that fact sufficiently transfigured and it wouldn't signify that some of the onward steps should have been lame.

This was clear to him on several occasions when she recited or motioned or even merely looked something for him better than usual; then she quite carried him away, making him wish to ask no more questions, but only let her disembroil herself in her own strong fashion. In these hours she gave him forcibly if fitfully that impression of beauty which was to be her justification. It was too soon for any general estimate of her progress; Madame Carré had at last given her a fine understanding as well as a sore, personal, an almost physical, sense of how bad she was. She had therefore begun on a new basis, had returned to the alphabet and the drill. It was a phase of awkwardness, the splashing of a young swimmer, but buoyancy would certainly come out of it. For the present there was mainly no great alteration of the fact that when she did things according to her own idea they were not, as yet and seriously judged, worth the devil, as Madame Carré said, and when she did them according to that of her instructress were too apt to be a gross parody of that lady's intention. None the less she gave glimpses, and her glimpses made him feel not only that she was not a fool—this was small relief—but that he himself was not.

He made her stick to her English and read Shakespeare aloud to him. Mrs. Rooth had recognised the importance of apartments in which they should be able to receive so beneficent a visitor, and was now mistress of a small salon with a balcony and a rickety flower-stand—to say nothing of a view of many roofs and chimneys—a very uneven waxed floor, an empire clock, an *armoire à glace*, highly convenient for Miriam's posturings, and several cupboard doors covered over, allowing for treacherous gaps, with the faded magenta paper of the wall. The thing had been easily done, for Sherringham had said: "Oh we must have a sitting-room for our studies, you know, and I'll settle it with the landlady," Mrs. Rooth had liked his "we"—indeed she liked everything about him—and he saw in this way that she heaved with no violence under pecuniary obligations so long as they were distinctly understood to be temporary. That he should have his money back with interest as soon as Miriam was launched was a comfort so deeply implied that it only added to intimacy. The window stood open on the little balcony, and when the sun had left it Peter and Miriam could linger there, leaning on the rail and talking above the great hum of Paris, with nothing but the neighbouring tiles and tall tubes to take account of. Mrs. Rooth, in limp garments much ungirdled, was on the sofa with a novel, making good her frequent assertion that she could put up with any life that would yield her these two conveniences. There were romantic works Peter had never read and as to which he had vaguely wondered to what class they were addressed—the earlier productions of M. Eugène Sue, the once-fashionable compositions of Madame Sophie Gay—with which Mrs. Rooth was familiar and which she was ready to enjoy once more if she could get nothing fresher. She had always a greasy volume tucked under her while her nose was bent upon the pages in hand. She scarcely looked up even when Miriam lifted her voice to show their benefactor what she could do. These tragic or pathetic notes all went out of the window and mingled with the undecipherable concert of Paris, so that no neighbour was disturbed by them. The girl shrieked and wailed when the occasion required it, and Mrs. Rooth only turned her page, showing in this way a great esthetic as well as a great personal trust.

She rather annoyed their visitor by the serenity of her confidence—for a reason he fully understood only later—save when Miriam caught an effect or a tone so well that she made him in the pleasure of it forget her parent's contiguity. He continued to object to the girl's English, with its foreign patches that might pass in prose but were offensive in the recitation of verse, and he wanted to know why she couldn't speak like her mother. He had justly to acknowledge the charm of Mrs. Rooth's voice and tone, which gave a richness even to the foolish things she said. They were of an excellent insular tradition, full both of natural and of cultivated sweetness, and they puzzled him when other indications seemed to betray her—to refer her to more common air. They were like the reverberation of some far-off tutored circle.

The connexion between the development of Miriam's genius and the necessity of an occasional excursion to the country—the charming country that lies in so many directions beyond the Parisian *banlieue*—would not have been immediately apparent to a superficial observer; but a day, and then another, at Versailles, a day at Fontainebleau and a trip, particularly harmonious and happy, to Rambouillet, took their places in our young man's plan as a part of the indirect but contributive culture, an agency in the formation of taste. Intimations of the grand manner for instance would proceed in abundance from the symmetrical palace and gardens of Louis XIV. Peter "adored" Versailles and wandered there more than once with the ladies of the Hôtel de la Garonne. They chose quiet hours, when the fountains were dry; and Mrs. Rooth took an armful of novels and sat on a bench in the park, flanked by clipped hedges and old statues, while her young companions strolled away, walked to the Trianon, explored the long, straight vistas of the woods. Rambouillet was vague and vivid and sweet; they felt that they found a hundred wise voices there; and indeed there was an old white chateau which contained nothing but ghostly sounds. They found at any rate a long luncheon, and in the landscape the very spirit of silvery summer and of the French pictorial brush.

I have said that in these days Sherringham wondered about many things, and by the time his leave of absence came this practice had produced a particular speculation. He was surprised that he shouldn't be in love with Miriam Rooth and considered at moments of leisure the causes of his exemption. He had felt from the first that she was a "nature," and each time she met his eyes it seemed to come to him straighter that her beauty was rare. You had to get the good view of her face, but when you did so it was a splendid mobile mask. And the wearer of this high ornament had frankness and courage and variety—no end of the unusual and the unexpected. She had qualities that seldom went together—impulses and shynesses, audacities and lapses, something coarse, popular, and strong all intermingled with disdains and languors and nerves. And then above all she was *there*, was accessible, almost belonged to him. He reflected ingeniously that he owed his escape to a peculiar cause—to the fact that they had together a positive outside object. Objective, as it were, was all their communion; not personal and selfish, but a matter of art and business and discussion. Discussion had saved him and would save him further, for they would always have something to quarrel about. Sherringham, who was not a diplomatist for nothing, who had his reasons for steering straight and wished neither to deprive the British public of a rising star nor to exchange his actual situation for that of a yoked *impresario*, blessed the beneficence, the salubrity, the pure exorcism of art. At the same time, rather inconsistently and feeling that he had a completer vision than before of that oddest of animals the artist who happens to have been born a woman, he felt warned against a serious connexion—he made a great point of the "serious"—with so slippery and ticklish a creature. The two ladies had only to stay in Paris, save their candle-ends and, as Madame Carré had enjoined, practise their scales: there were apparently no autumn visits to English country-houses in prospect for Mrs. Rooth. Peter parted with them on the understanding that in London he would look as thoroughly as possible into the question of an engagement. The day before he began his holiday he went to see Madame Carré, who said to him, "*Vous devriez bien nous la laisser.*"

"She *has* something then——?"

"She has most things. She'll go far. It's the first time in my life of my beginning with a mistake. But don't tell her so. I don't flatter her. She'll be too puffed up."

"Is she very conceited?" Sherringham asked.

"*Mauvais sujet!*" said Madame Carré.

It was on the journey to London that he indulged in some of those questionings of his state that I have mentioned; but I must add that by the time he reached Charing Cross—he smoked a cigar deferred till after the Channel in a compartment by himself—it had suddenly come over him that they were futile. Now that he had left the girl a subversive, unpremeditated heart-beat told him—it made him hold his breath a minute in the carriage— that he had after all not escaped. He *was* in love with her: he had been in love with her from the first hour.

BOOK THIRD

XIII

The drive from Harsh to the Place, as it was called thereabouts, could be achieved by swift horses in less than ten minutes; and if Mrs. Dallow's ponies were capital trotters the general high pitch of the occasion made it all congruous they should show their speed. The occasion was the polling-day an hour after the battle. The ponies had kept pace with other driven forces for the week before, passing and repassing the neat windows of the flat little town— Mrs. Dallow had the complacent belief that there was none in the kingdom in which the flower-stands looked more respectable between the stiff muslin curtains—with their mistress behind them on her all but silver wheels. Very often she was accompanied by the Liberal candidate, but even when she was not the equipage seemed scarce less to represent his easy, friendly confidence. It moved in a radiance of ribbons and hand-bills and hand-shakes and smiles; of quickened commerce and sudden intimacy; of sympathy which assumed without presuming and gratitude which promised without soliciting. But under Julia's guidance the ponies pattered now, with no indication of a loss of freshness, along the firm, wide avenue which wound and curved, to make up in large effect for not undulating, from the gates opening straight on the town to the Palladian mansion, high, square, grey, and clean, which stood among terraces and fountains in the centre of the park. A generous steed had been sacrificed to bring the good news from Ghent to Aix, but no such extravagance was after all necessary for communicating with Lady Agnes.

She had remained at the house, not going to the Wheatsheaf, the Liberal inn, with the others; preferring to await in privacy and indeed in solitude the momentous result of the poll. She had come down to Harsh with the two girls in the course of the proceedings. Julia hadn't thought they would do much good, but she was expansive and indulgent now and had generously asked them. Lady Agnes had not a nice canvassing manner, effective as she might have been in the character of the high, benignant, affable mother—looking sweet participation but not interfering—of the young and handsome, the shining, convincing, wonderfully clever and certainly irresistible aspirant. Grace Dormer had zeal without art, and Lady Agnes, who during her husband's lifetime had seen their affairs follow the satisfactory principle of a tendency to defer to supreme merit, had never really learned the lesson that voting goes by favour. However, she could pray God if, she couldn't make love to the cheesemonger, and Nick felt she had stayed at home to pray for him. I must add that Julia Dallow was too happy now, flicking her whip in the bright summer air, to say anything so ungracious even to herself as that her companion had been returned in spite of his nearest female relatives. Besides, Biddy *had* been a rosy help: she had looked persuasively pretty, in white and blue, on platforms and in recurrent carriages, out of which she had tossed, blushing and making people feel they would remember her eyes, several words that were telling for their very simplicity.

Mrs. Dallow was really too glad for any definite reflexion, even for personal exultation, the vanity of recognising her own large share of the work. Nick was in and was now beside her, tired, silent, vague, beflowered and beribboned, and he had been splendid from beginning to end, beautifully good-humoured and at the same time beautifully clever—still cleverer than she had supposed he could be. The sense of her having quickened his cleverness and been repaid by it or by his gratitude—it came to the same thing—in a way she appreciated was not assertive and jealous: it was lost for the present in the general happy break of the long tension. So nothing passed between them in their progress to the house; there was no sound in the park but the pleasant rustle of summer—it seemed an applausive murmur—and the swift roll of the vehicle.

Lady Agnes already knew, for as soon as the result was declared Nick had despatched a mounted man to her, carrying the figures on a scrawled card. He himself had been far from getting away at once, having to respond to the hubbub of acclamation, to speak yet again, to thank his electors individually and collectively, to chaff the Tories without cheap elation, to be carried hither and yon, and above all to pretend that the interest of the business was now greater for him than ever. If he had said never a word after putting himself in Julia's hands to go home it was partly perhaps because the consciousness had begun to glimmer within him, on the contrary, of some sudden shrinkage of that interest. He wanted to see his mother because he knew she wanted to fold him close in her arms. They had been open there for this purpose the last half-hour, and her expectancy, now no longer an ache of suspense, was the reason of Julia's round pace. Yet this very impatience in her somehow made Nick wince a little. Meeting his mother was like being elected over again.

The others had not yet come back, and Lady Agnes was alone in the large, bright drawing-room. When Nick went in with Julia he saw her at the further end; she had evidently been walking up and down the whole length of it, and her tall, upright, black figure seemed in possession of the fair vastness after the manner of an exclamation-point at the bottom of a blank page. The room, rich and simple, was a place of perfection as well as of splendour in delicate tints, with precious specimens of French furniture of the last century ranged against walls of pale brocade, and here and there a small, almost priceless picture. George Dallow had made it, caring for these things and liking to talk about them—scarce ever about anything else; so that it appeared to represent him still, what was best in his kindly, limited nature, his friendly, competent, tiresome insistence on harmony—on identity of "period." Nick could hear him yet, and could see him, too fat and with a congenital thickness in his speech, lounging there in loose clothes with his eternal cigarette. "Now my dear fellow, *that*'s what I call form: I don't know what you call it"—that was the way he used to begin. All round were flowers in rare vases, but it looked a place of which the beauty would have smelt sweet even without them.

Lady Agnes had taken a white rose from one of the clusters and was holding it to her face, which was turned to the door as Nick crossed the threshold. The expression of her figure instantly told him—he saw the creased card he had sent her lying on one of the beautiful bare tables—how she had been sailing up and down in a majesty of satisfaction. The inflation of her long plain dress and the brightened dimness of her proud face were still in the air.

In a moment he had kissed her and was being kissed, not in quick repetition, but in tender prolongation, with which the perfume of the white rose was mixed. But there was something else too—her sweet smothered words in his ear: "Oh my boy, my boy—oh your father, your father!" Neither the sense of pleasure nor that of pain, with Lady Agnes—as indeed with most of the persons with whom this history is concerned—was a liberation of chatter; so that for a minute all she said again was, "I think of Sir Nicholas and wish he were here"; addressing the words to Julia, who had wandered forward without looking at the mother and son.

"Poor Sir Nicholas!" said Mrs. Dallow vaguely.

"Did you make another speech?" Lady Agnes asked.

"I don't know. Did I?" Nick appealed.

"I don't know!"—and Julia spoke with her back turned, doing something to her hat before the glass.

"Oh of course the confusion, the bewilderment!" said Lady Agnes in a tone rich in political reminiscence.

"It was really immense fun," Mrs. Dallow went so far as to drop.

"Dearest Julia!" Lady Agnes deeply breathed. Then she added: "It was you who made it sure."

"There are a lot of people coming to dinner," said Julia.

"Perhaps you'll have to speak again," Lady Agnes smiled at her son.

"Thank you; I like the way you talk about it!" cried Nick. "I'm like Iago: 'from this time forth I never will speak word!'"

"Don't say that, Nick," said his mother gravely.

"Don't be afraid—he'll jabber like a magpie!" And Julia went out of the room.

Nick had flung himself on a sofa with an air of weariness, though not of completely extinct cheer; and Lady Agnes stood fingering her rose and looking down at him. His eyes kept away from her; they seemed fixed on something she couldn't see. "I hope you've thanked Julia handsomely," she presently remarked.

"Why of course, mother."

"She has done as much as if you hadn't been sure."

"I wasn't in the least sure—and she has done everything."

"She has been too good—but *we*'ve done something. I hope you don't leave out your father," Lady Agnes amplified as Nick's glance appeared for a moment to question her "we."

"Never, never!" Nick uttered these words perhaps a little mechanically, but the next minute he added as if suddenly moved to think what he could say that would give his mother most pleasure: "Of course his name has worked for me. Gone as he is he's still a living force." He felt a good deal of a hypocrite, but one didn't win such a seat every day in the year. Probably indeed he should never win another.

"He hears you, he watches you, he rejoices in you," Lady Agnes opined.

This idea was oppressive to Nick—that of the rejoicing almost as much as of the watching. He had made his concession, but, with a certain impulse to divert his mother from following up her advantage, he broke out: "Julia's a tremendously effective woman."

"Of course she is!" said Lady Agnes knowingly.

"Her charming appearance is half the battle"—Nick explained a little coldly what he meant. But he felt his coldness an inadequate protection to him when he heard his companion observe with something of the same sapience:

"A woman's always effective when she likes a person so much."

It discomposed him to be described as a person liked, and so much, and by a woman; and he simply said abruptly: "When are you going away?"

"The first moment that's civil—to-morrow morning. *You*'ll stay on I hope."

"Stay on? What shall I stay on for?"

"Why you might stay to express your appreciation."

Nick considered. "I've everything to do."

"I thought everything was done," said Lady Agnes.

"Well, that's just why," her son replied, not very lucidly. "I want to do other things—quite other things. I should like to take the next train," And he looked at his watch.

"When there are people coming to dinner to meet you?"

"They'll meet *you*—that's better."

"I'm sorry any one's coming," Lady Agnes said in a tone unencouraging to a deviation from the reality of things. "I wish we were alone—just as a family. It would please Julia to-day to feel that we *are* one. Do stay with her to-morrow."

"How will that do—when she's alone?"

"She won't be alone, with Mrs. Gresham."

"Mrs. Gresham doesn't count."

"That's precisely why I want you to stop. And her cousin, almost her brother: what an idea that it won't do! Haven't you stayed here before when there has been no one?"

"I've never stayed much, and there have always been people. At any rate it's now different."

"It's just because it's different. Besides, it isn't different and it never was," said Lady Agnes, more incoherent in her earnestness than it often happened to her to be. "She always liked you and she likes you now more than ever— if you call *that* different!" Nick got up at this and, without meeting her eyes, walked to one of the windows, where he stood with his back turned and looked out on the great greenness. She watched him a moment and she might well have been wishing, while he appeared to gaze with intentness, that it would come to him with the same force as it had come to herself—very often before, but during these last days more than ever—that the level lands of Harsh, stretching away before the window, the French garden with its symmetry, its screens and its statues, and a great many more things of which these were the superficial token, were Julia's very own to do with exactly as she liked. No word of appreciation or envy, however, dropped from the young man's lips, and his mother presently went on: "What could be more natural than that after your triumphant contest you and she should have lots to settle and to talk about—no end of practical questions, no end of urgent business? Aren't you her member, and can't her member pass a day with her, and she a great proprietor?"

Nick turned round at this with an odd expression. "*Her* member—am I hers?"

Lady Agnes had a pause—she had need of all her tact. "Well, if the place is hers and you represent the place—!" she began. But she went no further, for Nick had interrupted her with a laugh.

"What a droll thing to 'represent,' when one thinks of it! And what does *it* represent, poor stupid little borough with its strong, though I admit clean, smell of meal and its curiously fat-faced inhabitants? Did you ever see such a collection of fat faces turned up at the hustings? They looked like an enormous sofa, with the cheeks for the gathers and the eyes for the buttons."

"Oh well, the next time you shall have a great town," Lady Agnes returned, smiling and feeling that she *was* tactful.

"It will only be a bigger sofa! I'm joking, of course!" Nick pursued, "and I ought to be ashamed of myself. They've done me the honour to elect me and I shall never say a word that's not civil about them, poor dears. But even a new member may blaspheme to his mother."

"I wish you'd be serious to your mother"—and she went nearer him.

"The difficulty is that I'm two men; it's the strangest thing that ever was," Nick professed with his bright face on her. "I'm two quite distinct human beings, who have scarcely a point in common; not even the memory, on the part of one, of the achievements or the adventures of the other. One man wins the seat but it's the other fellow who sits in it."

"Oh Nick, don't spoil your victory by your perversity!" she cried as she clasped her hands to him.

"I went through it with great glee—I won't deny that: it excited me, interested me, amused me. When once I was in it I liked it. But now that I'm out of it again——!"

"Out of it?" His mother stared. "Isn't the whole point that you're in?"

"Ah *now* I'm only in the House of Commons."

For an instant she seemed not to understand and to be on the point of laying her finger quickly to her lips with a "Hush!"—as if the late Sir Nicholas might have heard the "only." Then while a comprehension of the young man's words promptly superseded that impulse she replied with force: "You'll be in the Lords the day you determine to get there."

This futile remark made Nick laugh afresh, and not only laugh, but kiss her, which was always an intenser form of mystification for poor Lady Agnes and apparently the one he liked best to inflict; after which he said: "The odd thing is, you know, that Harsh has no wants. At least it's not sharply, not articulately conscious of them. We all pretended to talk them over together, and I promised to carry them in my heart of hearts. But upon my honour I can't remember one of them. Julia says the wants of Harsh are simply the national wants—rather a pretty phrase for Julia. She means *she* does everything for the place; *she's* really their member and this house in which we stand their legislative chamber. Therefore the *lacunae* I've undertaken to fill out are the national wants. It will be rather a job to rectify some of them, won't it? I don't represent the appetites of Harsh—Harsh is gorged. I represent the ideas of my party. That's what Julia says."

201

"Oh never mind what Julia says!" Lady Agnes broke out impatiently. This impatience made it singular that the very next word she uttered should be: "My dearest son, I wish to heaven you'd marry her. It would be so fitting now!" she added.

"Why now?" Nick frowned.

"She has shown you such sympathy, such devotion."

"Is it for that she has shown it?"

"Ah you might *feel*—I can't tell you!" said Lady Agnes reproachfully.

He blushed at this, as if what he did feel was the reproach. "Must I marry her because you like her?"

"I? Why we're *all* as fond of her as we can be."

"Dear mother, I hope that any woman I ever may marry will be a person agreeable not only to you, but also, since you make a point of it, to Grace and Biddy. But I must tell you this—that I shall marry no woman I'm not unmistakably in love with."

"And why are you not in love with Julia—charming, clever, generous as she is?" Lady Agnes laid her hands on him—she held him tight. "Dearest Nick, if you care anything in the world to make me happy you'll stay over here to-morrow and be nice to her."

He waited an instant. "Do you mean propose to her?"

"With a single word, with the glance of an eye, the movement of your little finger"—and she paused, looking intensely, imploringly up into his face—"in less time than it takes me to say what I say now, you may have it all." As he made no answer, only meeting her eyes, she added insistently: "You know she's a fine creature—you know she is!"

"Dearest mother, what I seem to know better than anything else in the world is that I love my freedom. I set it far above everything."

"Your freedom? What freedom is there in being poor?" Lady Agnes fiercely demanded. "Talk of that when Julia puts everything she possesses at your feet!"

"I can't talk of it, mother—it's too terrible an idea. And I can't talk of *her*, nor of what I think of her. You must leave that to me. I do her perfect justice."

"You don't or you'd marry her to-morrow," she passionately argued. "You'd feel the opportunity so beautifully rare, with everything in the world to make it perfect. Your father would have valued it for you beyond everything. Think a little what would have given *him* pleasure. That's what I meant when I spoke just now of us all. It wasn't of Grace and Biddy I was thinking—fancy!—it was of him. He's with you always; he takes with you, at your side, every step you take yourself. He'd bless devoutly your marriage to Julia; he'd feel what it would be for you and for us all. I ask for no sacrifice and he'd ask for none. We only ask that you don't commit the crime——!"

Nick Dormer stopped her with another kiss; he murmured "Mother, mother, mother!" as he bent over her. He wished her not to go on, to let him off; but the deep deprecation in his voice didn't prevent her saying:

"You know it—you know it perfectly. All and more than all that I can tell you you know." He drew her closer, kissed her again, held her as he would have held a child in a paroxysm, soothing her silently till it could abate. Her vehemence had brought with it tears; she dried them as she disengaged herself. The next moment, however, she resumed, attacking him again: "For a public man she'd be the perfect companion. She's made for public life—she's made to shine, to be concerned in great things, to occupy a high position and to help him on. She'd back you up in everything as she has backed you in this. Together there's nothing you couldn't do. You can have the first house in England—yes, the very first! What freedom *is* there in being poor? How can you do anything without money, and what money can you make for yourself—what money will ever come to you? That's the crime—to throw away such an instrument of power, such a blessed instrument of good."

203

"It isn't everything to be rich, mother," said Nick, looking at the floor with a particular patience—that is with a provisional docility and his hands in his pockets. "And it isn't so fearful to be poor."

"It's vile—it's abject. Don't I know?"

"Are you in such acute want?" he smiled.

"Ah don't make me explain what you've only to look at to see!" his mother returned as if with a richness of allusion to dark elements in her fate.

"Besides," he easily went on, "there's other money in the world than Julia's. I might come by some of that."

"Do you mean Mr. Carteret's?" The question made him laugh as her feeble reference five minutes before to the House of Lords had done. But she pursued, too full of her idea to take account of such a poor substitute for an answer: "Let me tell you one thing, for I've known Charles Carteret much longer than you and I understand him better. There's nothing you could do that would do you more good with him than to marry Julia. I know the way he looks at things and I know exactly how that would strike him. It would please him, it would charm him; it would be the thing that would most prove to him that you're in earnest. You need, you know, to do something of that sort," she said as for plain speaking.

"Haven't I come in for Harsh?" asked Nick.

"Oh he's very canny. He likes to see people rich. *Then* he believes in them—then he's likely to believe more. He's kind to you because you're your father's son; but I'm sure your being poor takes just so much off."

"He can remedy that so easily," said Nick, smiling still. "Is my being kept by Julia what you call my making an effort for myself?"

Lady Agnes hesitated; then "You needn't insult Julia!" she replied.

"Moreover, if I've *her* money I shan't want his," Nick unheedingly remarked.

Again his mother waited before answering; after which she produced: "And pray wouldn't you wish to be independent?"

"You're delightful, dear mother—you're very delightful! I particularly like your conception of independence. Doesn't it occur to you that at a pinch I might improve my fortune by some other means than by making a mercenary marriage or by currying favour with a rich old gentleman? Doesn't it occur to you that I might work?"

"Work at politics? How does that make money, honourably?"

"I don't mean at politics."

"What do you mean then?"—and she seemed to challenge him to phrase it if he dared. This demonstration of her face and voice might have affected him, for he remained silent and she continued: "Are you elected or not?"

"It seems a dream," he rather flatly returned.

"If you are, act accordingly and don't mix up things that are as wide asunder as the poles!" She spoke with sternness and his silence appeared again to represent an admission that her sternness counted for him. Possibly she was touched by it; after a few moments, at any rate, during which nothing more passed between them, she appealed to him in a gentler and more anxious key, which had this virtue to touch him that he knew it was absolutely the first time in her life she had really begged for anything. She had never been obliged to beg; she had got on without it and most things had come to her. He might judge therefore in what a light she regarded this boon for which in her bereft old age she humbled herself to be a suitor. There was such a pride in her that he could feel what it cost her to go on her knees even to her son. He did judge how it was in his power to gratify her; and as he was generous and imaginative he was stirred and shaken as it came over him in a wave of figurative suggestion that he might make up to her for many things. He scarcely needed to hear her ask with a pleading wail that was almost tragic: "Don't you see how things have turned out for us? Don't you know how unhappy I am, don't you know what a bitterness——?" She stopped with a sob in her voice and he recognised vividly this last tribulation, the unhealed wound of her change of life and her lapse from eminence to flatness. "You know what Percival is and the comfort I have of him. You know the property and what he's doing with it and what comfort I get from *that*! Everything's

205

dreary but what you can do for us. Everything's odious, down to living in a hole with one's girls who don't marry. Grace is impossible—I don't know what's the matter with her; no one will look at her, and she's so conceited with it—sometimes I feel as if I could beat her! And Biddy will never marry, and we're three dismal women in a filthy house, and what are three dismal women, more or less, in London?"

So with an unexpected rage of self-exposure she poured out her disappointments and troubles, tore away the veil from her sadness and soreness. It almost scared him to see how she hated her life, though at another time it might have been amusing to note how she despised her gardenless house. Of course it wasn't a country-house, and she couldn't get used to that. Better than he could do—for it was the sort of thing into which in any case a woman enters more than a man—she felt what a lift into brighter air, what a regilding of his sisters' possibilities, his marriage to Julia would effect for them. He couldn't trace the difference, but his mother saw it all as a shining picture. She hung the bright vision before him now—she stood there like a poor woman crying for a kindness. What was filial in him, all the piety he owed, especially to the revived spirit of his father, more than ever present on a day of such public pledges, became from one moment to the other as the very handle to the door of the chamber of concessions. He had the impulse, so embarrassing when it is a question of consistent action, to see in a touching, an interesting light any forcibly presented side of the life of another: such things effected a union with something in *his* life, and in the recognition of them was no soreness of sacrifice and no consciousness of merit.

Rapidly, at present, this change of scene took place before his spiritual eye. He found himself believing, because his mother communicated the belief, that it depended but on his own conduct richly to alter the social outlook of the three women who clung to him and who declared themselves forlorn. This was not the highest kind of motive, but it contained a spring, it touched into life again old injunctions and appeals. Julia's wide kingdom opened out round him and seemed somehow to wear the face of his own possible future. His mother and sisters floated in the rosy element as if he had breathed it about them. "The first house in England" she had called it; but it might be the first house in Europe, the first in the world, by the fine air and the high humanities that should fill it. Everything beautiful in his actual, his material view seemed to proclaim its value as never before; the house rose over his head as a museum of exquisite rewards, and the image of poor George Dallow hovered there obsequious, expressing that he had only been the modest, tasteful organiser, or even upholsterer, appointed to set it all in order and punctually retire. Lady Agnes's tone in fine penetrated further than it had done yet when she brought out with intensity: "Don't desert us—don't desert us."

"Don't desert you——?"

"Be great—be great. I'm old, I've lived, I've seen. Go in for a great material position. That will simplify everything else."

"I'll do what I can for you—anything, everything I can. Trust me—leave me alone," Nick went on.

"And you'll stay over—you'll spend the day with her?"

"I'll stay till she turns me out!"

His mother had hold of his hand again now: she raised it to her lips and kissed it. "My dearest son, my only joy!" Then: "I don't see how you can resist her," she added.

"No more do I!"

She looked about—there was so much to look at—with a deep exhalation. "If you're so fond of art, what art is equal to all this? The joy of living in the midst of it—of seeing the finest works every day! You'll have everything the world can give."

"That's exactly what was just passing in my own mind. It's too much," Nick reasoned.

"Don't be selfish!"

"Selfish?" he echoed.

207

"Unselfish then. You'll share it with us."

"And with Julia a little, I hope," he said.

"God bless you!" cried his mother, looking up at him. Her eyes were detained by the sudden sense of something in his own that was not clear to her; but before she could challenge it he asked abruptly:

"Why do you talk so of poor Biddy? Why won't she marry?"

"You had better ask Peter Sherringham," said Lady Agnes.

"What has he to do with it?"

"How odd of you not to know—when it's so plain how she thinks of him that it's a matter of common gossip."

"Yes, if you will—we've made it so, and she takes it as an angel. But Peter likes her."

"Does he? Then it's the more shame to him to behave as he does. He had better leave his wretched actresses alone. That's the love of art too!" mocked Lady Agnes.

But Nick glossed it all over. "Biddy's so charming she'll easily marry some one else."

"Never, if she loves him. However, Julia will bring it about—Julia will help her," his mother pursued more cheerfully. "That's what you'll do for us—that *she'll* do everything!"

"Why then more than now?" he asked.

"Because we shall be yours."

"You're mine already."

"Yes, but she isn't. However, she's as good!" Lady Agnes exulted.

"She'll turn me out of the house," said Nick.

"Come and tell me when she does! But there she is—go to her!" And she gave him a push toward one of the windows that stood open to the terrace. Their hostess had become visible outside; she passed slowly along the terrace with her long shadow. "Go to her," his mother repeated—"she's waiting for you."

Nick went out with the air of a man as ready to pass that way as another, and at the same moment his two sisters, still flushed with participation, appeared in a different quarter.

"We go home to-morrow, but Nick will stay a day or two," Lady Agnes said to them.

"Dear old Nick!" Grace ejaculated looking at her with intensity.

"He's going to speak," she went on. "But don't mention it."

"Don't mention it?" Biddy asked with a milder stare. "Hasn't he spoken enough, poor fellow?"

"I mean to Julia," Lady Agnes replied.

"Don't you understand, you goose?"—and Grace turned on her sister

XIV

The next morning brought the young man many letters and telegrams, and his coffee was placed beside him in his room, where he remained until noon answering these communications. When he came out he learned that his mother and sisters had left the house. This information was given him by Mrs. Gresham, whom he found dealing with her own voluminous budget at one of the tables in the library. She was a lady who received thirty letters a day, the subject-matter of which, as well as of her punctual answers in a hand that would have been "ladylike" in a manageress, was a puzzle to those who observed her.

209

She told Nick that Lady Agnes had not been willing to disturb him at his work to say good-bye, knowing she should see him in a day or two in town. He was amused at the way his mother had stolen off—as if she feared further conversation might weaken the spell she believed herself to have wrought. The place was cleared, moreover, of its other visitors, so that, as Mrs. Gresham said, the fun was at an end. This lady expressed the idea that the fun was after all rather a bore. At any rate now they could rest, Mrs. Dallow and Nick and she, and she was glad Nick was going to stay for a little quiet. She liked Harsh best when it was not *en fête*: then one could see what a sympathetic old place it was. She hoped Nick was not dreadfully fagged—she feared Julia was completely done up. Julia, however, had transported her exhaustion to the grounds—she was wandering about somewhere. She thought more people would be coming to the house, people from the town, people from the country, and had gone out so as not to have to see them. She had not gone far—Nick could easily find her. Nick intimated that he himself was not eager for more people, whereupon Mrs. Gresham rather archly smiled. "And of course you hate *me* for being here." He made some protest and she added: "But I'm almost part of the house, you know—I'm one of the chairs or tables." Nick declared that he had never seen a house so well furnished, and Mrs. Gresham said: "I believe there *are* to be some people to dinner; rather an interference, isn't it? Julia lives so in public. But it's all for you." And after a moment she added: "It's a wonderful constitution." Nick at first failed to seize her allusion—he thought it a retarded political reference, a sudden tribute to the great unwritten instrument by which they were all governed and under the happy operation of which his fight had been so successful. He was on the point of saying, "The British? Wonderful!" when he gathered that the intention of his companion had been simply to praise Mrs. Dallow's fine robustness. "The surface so delicate, the action so easy, yet the frame of steel."

He left Mrs. Gresham to her correspondence and went out of the house; wondering as he walked if she wanted him to do the same thing his mother wanted, so that her words had been intended for a prick—whether even the two ladies had talked over their desire together. Mrs. Gresham was a married woman who was usually taken for a widow, mainly because she was perpetually "sent for" by her friends, who in no event sent for Mr. Gresham.

She came in every case, with her air of being *répandue* at the expense of dingier belongings. Her figure was admired—that is it was sometimes mentioned—and she dressed as if it was expected of her to be smart, like a young woman in a shop or a servant much in view. She slipped in and out, accompanied at the piano, talked to the neglected visitors, walked in the rain, and after the arrival of the post usually had conferences with her hostess, during which she stroked her chin and looked familiarly responsible. It was her peculiarity that people were always saying things to her in a lowered voice. She had all sorts of acquaintances and in small establishments sometimes wrote the *menus*. Great ones, on the other hand, had no terrors for her—she had seen too many. No one had ever discovered whether any one else paid her. People only knew what *they* did.

If Lady Agnes had in the minor key discussed with her the propriety of a union between the mistress of Harsh and the hope of the Dormers this last personage could take the circumstance for granted without irritation and even with cursory indulgence; for he was got unhappy now and his spirit was light and clear. The summer day was splendid and the world, as he looked at it from the terrace, offered no more worrying ambiguity than a vault of airy blue arching over a lap of solid green. The wide, still trees in the park appeared to be waiting for some daily inspection, and the rich fields, with their official frill of hedges, to rejoice in the light that smiled upon them as named and numbered acres. Nick felt himself catch the smile and all the reasons of it: they made up a charm to which he had perhaps not hitherto done justice—something of the impression he had received when younger from showy "views" of fine country-seats that had pressed and patted nature, as by the fat hands of "benches" of magistrates and landlords, into supreme respectability and comfort. There were a couple of peacocks on the terrace, and his eye was caught by the gleam of the swans on a distant lake, where was also a little temple on an island; and these objects fell in with his humour, which at another time might have been ruffled by them as aggressive triumphs of the conventional.

It was certainly a proof of youth and health on his part that his spirits had risen as the plot thickened and that after he had taken his jump into the turbid waters of a contested election he had been able to tumble and splash not only without a sense of awkwardness but with a considerable capacity for the frolic. Tepid as we saw him in Paris he had found his relation to his opportunity surprisingly altered by his little journey across the Channel, had seen things in a new perspective and breathed an air that set him and kept him in motion. There had been something in it that went to his head—an element that his mother and his sisters, his father from beyond the grave, Julia Dallow, the Liberal party and a hundred friends, were both secretly and overtly occupied in pumping into it. If he but half-believed in victory he at least liked the wind of the onset in his ears, and he had a general sense that when one was "stuck" there was always the nearest thing at which one must pull. The embarrassment, that is the revival of scepticism, which might produce an inconsistency shameful to exhibit and yet difficult to conceal, was safe enough to come later. Indeed at the risk of presenting our young man as too whimsical a personage I may hint that some such sickly glow had even now begun to tinge one quarter of his inward horizon.

I am afraid, moreover, that I have no better excuse for him than the one he had touched on in that momentous conversation with his mother which I have thought it useful to reproduce in full. He was conscious of a double nature; there were two men in him, quite separate, whose leading features had little in common and each of whom insisted on having an independent turn at life. Meanwhile then, if he was adequately aware that the bed of his moral existence would need a good deal of making over if he was to lie upon it without unseemly tossing, he was also alive to the propriety of not parading his inconsistencies, not letting his unregulated passions become a spectacle to the vulgar. He had none of that wish to appear deep which is at the bottom of most forms of fatuity; he was perfectly willing to pass for decently superficial; he only aspired to be decently continuous. When you were not suitably shallow this presented difficulties; but he would have assented to the proposition that you must be as subtle as you can and that a high use of subtlety is in consuming the smoke of your inner fire. The fire was the great thing, not the chimney. He had no view of life that counted out the need of learning; it was teaching rather as to which he was conscious of no particular mission. He enjoyed life, enjoyed it immensely, and was ready to pursue it with patience through as many channels as possible. He was on his guard, however, against making an ass of himself, that is against not thinking out his experiments before trying them in public. It was because, as yet, he liked life in general better than it was clear to him he liked particular possibilities that, on the occasion of a constituency's holding out a cordial hand to him while it extended another in a different direction, a certain bloom of boyhood that was on him had not paled at the idea of a match.

He had risen to the fray as he had risen to matches at school, for his boyishness could still take a pleasure in an inconsiderate show of agility. He could meet electors and conciliate bores and compliment women and answer questions and roll off speeches and chaff adversaries—he could do these things because it was amusing and slightly dangerous, like playing football or ascending an Alp, pastimes for which nature had conferred on him an aptitude not so very different in kind from a due volubility on platforms. There were two voices to admonish him that all this was not really action at all, but only a pusillanimous imitation of it: one of them fitfully audible in the depths of his own spirit and the other speaking, in the equivocal accents of a very crabbed hand, from a letter of four pages by Gabriel Nash. However, Nick carried the imitation as far as possible, and the flood of sound floated him. What more could a working faith have done? He had not broken with the axiom that in a case of doubt one should hold off, for this applied to choice, and he had not at present the slightest pretension to choosing. He knew he was lifted along, that what he was doing was not first-rate, that nothing was settled by it and that if there was a hard knot in his life it would only grow harder with keeping. Doing one's sum to-morrow instead of to-day doesn't make the sum easier, but at least makes to-day so.

Sometimes in the course of the following fortnight it seemed to him he had gone in for Harsh because he was sure he should lose; sometimes he foresaw that he should win precisely to punish him for having tried and for his want of candour; and when presently he did win he was almost scared at his success. Then it appeared to him he had done something even worse than not choose—he had let others choose for him. The beauty of it was that they had chosen with only their own object in their eye, for what did they know about his strange alternative? He was rattled about so for a fortnight—Julia taking care of this—that he had no time to think save when he tried to remember a quotation or an American story, and all his life became an overflow of verbiage. Thought couldn't hear itself for the noise, which had to be pleasant and persuasive, had to hang more or less together, without its aid. Nick was surprised at the airs he could play, and often when, the last thing at night, he shut the door of his room, found himself privately exclaiming that he had had no idea he was such a mountebank.

I must add that if this reflexion didn't occupy him long, and if no meditation, after his return from Paris, held him for many moments, there was a reason better even than that he was tired, that he was busy, that he appreciated the coincidence of the hit and the hurrah, the hurrah and the hit. That reason was simply Mrs. Dallow, who had suddenly become a still larger fact in his consciousness than his having turned actively political. She *was* indeed his being so—in the sense that if the politics were his, how little soever, the activity was hers. She had better ways of showing she was clever than merely saying clever things—which in general only prove at the most that one would be clever if one could. The accomplished fact itself was almost always the demonstration that Mrs. Dallow could; and when Nick came to his senses after the proclamation of the victor and the drop of the uproar her figure was, of the whole violent dance of shadows, the only thing that came back, that stayed. She had been there at each of the moments, passing, repassing, returning, before him, beside him, behind him. She had made the business infinitely prettier than it would have been without her, added music and flowers and ices, a finer charm, converting it into a kind of heroic "function," the form of sport most dangerous. It had been a garden-party, say, with one's life at stake from pressure of the crowd. The concluded affair had bequeathed him thus not only a seat in the House of Commons, but a perception of what may come of women in high embodiments and an abyss of intimacy with one woman in particular.

She had wrapped him up in something, he didn't know what—a sense of facility, an overpowering fragrance—and they had moved together in an immense fraternity. There had been no love-making, no contact that was only personal, no vulgarity of flirtation: the hurry of the days and the sharpness with which they both tended to an outside object had made all that irrelevant. It was as if she had been too near for him to see her separate from himself; but none the less, when he now drew breath and looked back, what had happened met his eyes as a composed picture—a picture of which the subject was inveterately Julia and her ponies: Julia wonderfully fair and fine, waving her whip, cleaving the crowd, holding her head as if it had been a banner, smiling up into second-storey windows, carrying him beside her, carrying him to his doom. He had not reckoned at the time, in the few days, how much he had driven about with her; but the image of it was there, in his consulted conscience, as well as in a personal glow not yet chilled: it looked large as it rose before him. The things his mother had said to him made a rich enough frame for it all, and the whole impression had that night kept him much awake.

XV

While, after leaving Mrs. Gresham, he was hesitating which way to go and was on the point of hailing a gardener to ask if Mrs. Dallow had been seen, he noticed, as a spot of colour in an expanse of shrubbery, a far-away parasol moving in the direction of the lake. He took his course toward it across the park, and as the bearer of the parasol strolled slowly it was not five minutes before he had joined her. He went to her soundlessly, on the grass—he had been whistling at first, but as he got nearer stopped—and it was not till he was at hand that she looked round. He had watched her go as if she were turning things over in her mind, while she brushed the smooth walks and the clean turf with her dress, slowly made her parasol revolve on her shoulder and carried in the other hand a book which he perceived to be a monthly review.

"I came out to get away," she said when he had begun to walk with her.

"Away from me?"

"Ah that's impossible." Then she added: "The day's so very nice."

"Lovely weather," Nick dropped. "You want to get away from Mrs. Gresham, I suppose."

She had a pause. "From everything!"

"Well, I want to get away too."

"It has been such a racket. Listen to the dear birds."

"Yes, our noise isn't so good as theirs," said Nick. "I feel as if I had been married and had shoes and rice thrown after me," he went on. "But not to you, Julia—nothing so good as that."

Julia made no reply; she only turned her eyes on the ornamental water stretching away at their right. In a moment she exclaimed, "How nasty the lake looks!" and Nick recognised in her tone a sign of that odd shyness—a perverse stiffness at a moment when she probably but wanted to be soft—which, taken in combination with her other qualities, was so far from being displeasing to him that it represented her nearest approach to extreme charm. *He* was not shy now, for he considered this morning that he saw things very straight and in a sense altogether superior and delightful. This enabled him to be generously sorry for his companion—if he were the reason of her being in any degree uncomfortable, and yet left him to enjoy some of the motions, not in themselves without grace, by which her discomfort was revealed. He wouldn't insist on anything yet: so he observed that her standard in lakes was too high, and then talked a little about his mother and the girls, their having gone home, his not having seen them that morning, Lady Agnes's deep satisfaction in his victory, and the fact that she would be obliged to "do something" for the autumn—take a house or something or other.

"I'll lend her a house," said Mrs. Dallow.

"Oh Julia, Julia!" Nick half groaned.

But she paid no attention to his sound; she only held up her review and said: "See what I've brought with me to read—Mr. Hoppus's article."

"That's right; then *I* shan't have to. You'll tell me about it." He uttered this without believing she had meant or wished to read the article, which was entitled "The Revision of the British Constitution," in spite of her having encumbered herself with the stiff, fresh magazine. He was deeply aware she was not in want of such inward occupation as periodical literature could supply. They walked along and he added: "But is that what we're in for, reading Mr. Hoppus? Is it the sort of thing constituents expect? Or, even worse, pretending to have read him when one hasn't? Oh what a tangled web we weave!"

"People are talking about it. One has to know. It's the article of the month."

Nick looked at her askance. "You say things every now and then for which I could really kill you. 'The article of the month,' for instance: I could kill you for that."

"Well, kill me!" Mrs. Dallow returned.

"Let me carry your book," he went on irrelevantly. The hand in which she held it was on the side of her on which he was walking, and he put out his own hand to take it. But for a couple of minutes she forbore to give it up, so that they held it together, swinging it a little. Before she surrendered it he asked where she was going.

"To the island," she answered.

"Well, I'll go with you—and I'll kill you there."

"The things I say are the right things," Julia declared.

"It's just the right things that are wrong. It's because you're so political," Nick too lightly explained. "It's your horrible ambition. The woman who has a salon should have read the article of the month. See how one dreadful thing leads to another."

"There are some things that lead to nothing," said Mrs. Dallow.

"No doubt—no doubt. And how are you going to get over to your island?"

"I don't know."

"Isn't there a boat?"

"I don't know."

Nick had paused to look round for the boat, but his hostess walked on without turning her head. "Can you row?" he then asked.

"Don't you know I can do everything?"

"Yes, to be sure. That's why I want to kill you. There's the boat."

"Shall you drown me?" she asked.

"Oh let me perish with you!" Nick answered with a sigh. The boat had been hidden from them by the bole of a great tree which rose from the grass at the water's edge. It was moored to a small place of embarkation and was large enough to hold as many persons as were likely to wish to visit at once the little temple in the middle of the lake, which Nick liked because it was absurd and which Mrs. Dallow had never had a particular esteem for. The lake, fed by a natural spring, was a liberal sheet of water, measured by the scale of park scenery; and though its principal merit was that, taken at a distance, it gave a gleam of abstraction to the concrete verdure, doing the office of an open eye in a dull face, it could also be approached without derision on a sweet summer morning when it made a lapping sound and reflected candidly various things that were probably finer than itself—the sky, the great trees, the flight of birds. A man of taste, coming back from Rome a hundred years before, had caused a small ornamental structure to be raised, from artificial foundations, on its bosom, and had endeavoured to make this architectural pleasantry as nearly as possible a reminiscence of the small ruined rotunda which stands on the bank of the Tiber and is pronounced by *ciceroni* once sacred to Vesta. It was circular, roofed with old tiles, surrounded by white columns and considerably dilapidated. George Dallow had taken an interest in it—it reminded him not in the least of Rome, but of other things he liked—and had amused himself with restoring it. "Give me your hand—sit there and I'll ferry you," Nick said.

Julia complied, placing herself opposite him in the boat; but as he took up the paddles she declared that she preferred to remain on the water—there was too much malice prepense in the temple. He asked her what she meant by that, and she said it was ridiculous to withdraw to an island a few feet square on purpose to meditate. She had nothing to meditate about that required so much scenery and attitude.

"On the contrary, it would be just to change the scene and the *pose*. It's what we have been doing for a week that's attitude; and to be for half an hour where nobody's looking and one hasn't to keep it up is just what I wanted to put in an idle irresponsible day for. I'm not keeping it up now—I suppose you've noticed," Nick went on as they floated and he scarcely dipped the oars.

"I don't understand you"—and Julia leaned back in the boat.

He gave no further explanation than to ask in a minute: "Have you people to dinner to-night?"

"I believe there are three or four, but I'll put them off if you like."

"Must you *always* live in public, Julia?" he continued.

She looked at him a moment and he could see how she coloured. "We'll go home—I'll put them off."

"Ah no, don't go home; it's too jolly here. Let them come, let them come, poor wretches!"

"How little you know me," Julia presently broke out, "when, ever so many times, I've lived here for months without a creature!"

"Except Mrs. Gresham, I suppose."

"I have had to have the house going, I admit."

"You're perfect, you're admirable, and I don't criticise you."

"I don't understand you!" she tossed back.

"That only adds to the generosity of what you've done for me," Nick returned, beginning to pull faster. He bent over the oars and sent the boat

219

forward, keeping this up for a succession of minutes during which they both remained silent. His companion, in her place, motionless, reclining—the seat in the stern was most comfortable—looked only at the water, the sky, the trees. At last he headed for the little temple, saying first, however, "Shan't we visit the ruin?"

"If you like. I don't mind seeing how they keep it."

They reached the white steps leading up to it. He held the boat and his companion got out; then, when he had made it fast, they mounted together to the open door. "They keep the place very well," Nick said, looking round. "It's a capital place to give up everything in."

"It might do at least for you to explain what you mean." And Julia sat down.

"I mean to pretend for half an hour that I don't represent the burgesses of Harsh. It's charming—it's very delicate work. Surely it has been retouched."

The interior of the pavilion, lighted by windows which the circle of columns was supposed outside and at a distance to conceal, had a vaulted ceiling and was occupied by a few pieces of last-century furniture, spare and faded, of which the colours matched with the decoration of the walls. These and the ceiling, tinted and not exempt from indications of damp, were covered with fine mouldings and medallions. It all made a very elegant little tea-house, the mistress of which sat on the edge of a sofa rolling her parasol and remarking, "You ought to read Mr. Hoppus's article to me."

"Why, is *this* your salon?" Nick smiled.

"What makes you always talk of that? My salon's an invention of your own."

"But isn't it the idea you're most working for?"

Suddenly, nervously, she put up her parasol and sat under it as if not quite sensible of what she was doing. "How much you know me! I'm not 'working' for anything—that you'll ever guess."

Nick wandered about the room and looked at various things it contained—the odd volumes on the tables, the bits of quaint china on the shelves. "They do keep it very well. You've got charming things."

"They're supposed to come over every day and look after them."

"They must come over in force."

"Oh no one knows."

"It's spick and span. How well you have everything done!"

"I think you've some reason to say so," said Mrs. Dallow. Her parasol was now down and she was again rolling it tight.

"But you're right about my not knowing you. Why were you so ready to do so much for me?"

He stopped in front of her and she looked up at him. Her eyes rested long on his own; then she broke out: "Why do you hate me so?"

"Was it because you like me personally?" Nick pursued as if he hadn't heard her. "You may think that an odd or positively an odious question; but isn't it natural, my wanting to know?"

"Oh if you don't know!" Julia quite desperately sighed.

"It's a question of being sure."

"Well then if you're not sure——!"

"Was it done for me as a friend, as a man?"

"You're not a man—you're a child," his hostess declared with a face that was cold, though she had been smiling the moment before.

"After all I was a good candidate," Nick went on.

"What do I care for candidates?"

"You're the most delightful woman, Julia," he said as he sat down beside her, "and I can't imagine what you mean by my hating you."

221

"If you haven't discovered that I like you, you might as well."

"Might as well discover it?"

She was grave—he had never seen her so pale and never so beautiful. She had stopped rolling her parasol; her hands were folded in her lap and her eyes bent on them. Nick sat looking at them as well—a trifle awkwardly. "Might as well have hated me," she said.

"We've got on so beautifully together all these days: why shouldn't we get on as well for ever and ever?" he brought out. She made no answer, and suddenly he said: "Ah Julia, I don't know what you've done to me, but you've done it. You've done it by strange ways, but it will serve. Yes, I hate you," he added in a different tone and with his face all nearer.

"Dear Nick, dear Nick——!" she began. But she stopped, feeling his nearness and its intensity, a nearness now so great that his arm was round her, that he was really in possession of her. She closed her eyes but heard him ask again, "Why shouldn't it be for ever, for ever?" in a voice that had for her ear a vibration none had ever had.

"You've done it, you've done it," Nick repeated.

"What do you want of me?" she appealed.

"To stay with me—this way—always."

"Ah not this way," she answered softly, but as if in pain and making an effort, with a certain force, to detach herself.

"This way then—or this!" He took such pressing advantage of her that he had kissed her with repetition. She rose while he insisted, but he held her yet, and as he did so his tenderness turned to beautiful words. "If you'll marry me, why shouldn't it be so simple, so right and good?" He drew her closer again, too close for her to answer. But her struggle ceased and she rested on him a minute; she buried her face in his breast.

"You're hard, and it's cruel!" she then exclaimed, shaking herself free.

"Hard—cruel?"

"You do it with so little!" And with this, unexpectedly to Nick, Julia burst straight into tears. Before he could stop her she was at the door of the pavilion as if she wished to get immediately away. There, however, he stayed her, bending over her while she sobbed, unspeakably gentle with her.

"So little? It's with everything—with everything I have."

"I've done it, you say? What do you accuse me of doing?" Her tears were already over.

"Of making me yours; of being so precious, Julia, so exactly what a man wants, as it seems to me. I didn't know you could," he went on, smiling down at her. "I didn't—no, I didn't."

"It's what I say—that you've always hated me."

"I'll make it up to you!" he laughed.

She leaned on the doorway with her forehead against the lintel. "You don't even deny it."

"Contradict you *now*? I'll admit it, though it's rubbish, on purpose to live it down."

"It doesn't matter," she said slowly; "for however much you might have liked me you'd never have done so half as much as I've cared for you."

"Oh I'm so poor!" Nick murmured cheerfully.

With her eyes looking at him as in a new light she slowly shook her head. Then she declared: "You never can live it down."

"I like that! Haven't I asked you to marry me? When did you ever ask me?"

"Every day of my life! As I say, it's hard—for a proud woman."

"Yes, you're too proud even to answer me."

"We must think of it, we must talk of it."

"Think of it? I've thought of it ever so much."

"I mean together. There are many things in such a question."

"The principal thing is beautifully to give me your word."

She looked at him afresh all strangely; then she threw off: "I wish I didn't adore you!" She went straight down the steps.

"You don't adore me at all, you know, if you leave me now. Why do you go? It's so charming here and we're so delightfully alone."

"Untie the boat; we'll go on the water," Julia said.

Nick was at the top of the steps, looking down at her. "Ah stay a little—*do* stay!" he pleaded.

"I'll get in myself, I'll pull off," she simply answered.

At this he came down and bent a little to undo the rope. He was close to her and as he raised his head he felt it caught; she had seized it in her hands and she pressed her lips, as he had never felt lips pressed, to the first place they encountered. The next instant she was in the boat.

This time he dipped the oars very slowly indeed; and, while for a period that was longer than it seemed to them they floated vaguely, they mainly sat and glowed at each other as if everything had been settled. There were reasons enough why Nick should be happy; but it is a singular fact that the leading one was the sense of his having escaped a great and ugly mistake. The final result of his mother's appeal to him the day before had been the idea that he must act with unimpeachable honour. He was capable of taking it as an assurance that Julia had placed him under an obligation a gentleman could regard but in one way. If she herself had understood it so, putting the vision, or at any rate the appreciation, of a closer tie into everything she had done for him, the case was conspicuously simple and his course unmistakably plain. That is why he had been gay when he came out of the house to look for her: he could be gay when his course was plain. He could be all the gayer, naturally, I must add, that, in turning things over as he had done half the night, what he had turned up oftenest was the recognition that Julia now had a new personal power with him. It was not for nothing that she had thrown herself personally into his life. She had by her act made him live twice as intensely, and such an office, such a service, if a man had accepted and deeply tasted it, was certainly a thing to put him on his honour. He took it as distinct that there was nothing he could do in preference that wouldn't be spoiled for him by any deflexion from that point. His mother had made him uncomfortable by bringing it so heavily up that Julia was in love with him— he didn't like in general to be told such things; but the responsibility seemed easier to carry and he was less shy about it when once he was away from other eyes, with only Julia's own to express that truth and with indifferent nature all about. Besides, what discovery had he made this morning but that he also was in love?

"You've got to be a very great man, you know," she said to him in the middle of the lake. "I don't know what you mean about my salon, but I *am* ambitious."

"We must look at life in a large, bold way," he concurred while he rested his oars.

"That's what I mean. If I didn't think you could I wouldn't look at you."

"I could what?"

"Do everything you ought—everything I imagine, I dream of. You *are* clever: you can never make me believe the contrary after your speech on Tuesday, Don't speak to me! I've seen, I've heard, and I know what's in you. I shall hold you to it. You're everything you pretend not to be."

Nick looked at the water while she talked. "Will it always be so amusing?" he asked.

"Will what always be?"

"Why my career."

"Shan't I make it so?"

"Then it will be yours—it won't be mine," said Nick.

"Ah don't say that—don't make me out that sort of woman! If they should say it's me I'd drown myself."

"If they should say what's you?"

"Why your getting on. If they should say I push you and do things for you. Things I mean that you can't do yourself."

"Well, won't you do them? It's just what I count on."

"Don't be dreadful," Julia said. "It would be loathsome if I were thought the cleverest. That's not the sort of man I want to marry."

"Oh I shall make you work, my dear!"

"Ah *that*——!" she sounded in a tone that might come back to a man after years.

"You'll do the great thing, you'll make my life the best life," Nick brought out as if he had been touched to deep conviction. "I daresay that will keep me in heart."

"In heart? Why shouldn't you be in heart?" And her eyes, lingering on him, searching him, seemed to question him still more than her lips.

"Oh it will be all right!" he made answer.

"You'll like success as well as any one else. Don't tell me—you're not so ethereal!"

"Yes, I shall like success."

"So shall I! And of course I'm glad you'll now be able to do things," Julia went on. "I'm glad you'll have things. I'm glad I'm not poor."

"Ah don't speak of that," Nick murmured. "Only be nice to my mother. We shall make her supremely happy."

"It wouldn't be for your mother I'd do it—yet I'm glad I like your people," Mrs. Dallow rectified. "Leave them to me!"

"You're generous—you're noble," he stammered.

"Your mother must live at Broadwood; she must have it for life. It's not at all bad."

"Ah Julia," her companion replied, "it's well I love you!"

"Why shouldn't you?" she laughed; and after this no more was said between them till the boat touched shore. When she had got out she recalled that it was time for luncheon; but they took no action in consequence, strolling in a direction which was not that of the house. There was a vista that drew them on, a grassy path skirting the foundations of scattered beeches and leading to a stile from which the charmed wanderer might drop into another division of Mrs. Dallow's property. She said something about their going as far as the stile, then the next instant exclaimed: "How stupid of you—you've forgotten Mr. Hoppus!"

Nick wondered. "We left him in the temple of Vesta. Darling, I had other things to think of there."

"I'll send for him," said Julia.

"Lord, can you think of him now?" he asked.

"Of course I can—more than ever."

"Shall we go back for him?"—and he pulled up.

She made no direct answer, but continued to walk, saying they would go as far as the stile. "Of course I know you're fearfully vague," she presently resumed.

"I wasn't vague at all. But you were in such a hurry to get away."

"It doesn't signify. I've another at home."

"Another summer-house?" he more lightly suggested.

"A copy of Mr. Hoppus."

"Mercy, how you go in for him! Fancy having two!"

"He sent me the number of the magazine, and the other's the one that comes every month."

"Every month; I see"—but his manner justified considerably her charge of vagueness. They had reached the stile and he leaned over it, looking at a great mild meadow and at the browsing beasts in the distance.

"Did you suppose they come every day?" Julia went on.

"Dear no, thank God!" They remained there a little; he continued to look at the animals and before long added: "Delightful English pastoral scene. Why do they say it won't paint?"

"Who says it won't?"

"I don't know—some of them. It will in France; but somehow it won't here."

"What are you talking about?" Mrs. Dallow demanded.

He appeared unable to satisfy her on this point; instead of answering her directly he at any rate said: "Is Broadwood very charming?"

"Have you never been there? It shows how you've treated me. We used to go there in August. George had ideas about it," she added. She had never affected not to speak of her late husband, especially with Nick, whose kinsman he had in a manner been and who had liked him better than some others did.

"George had ideas about a great many things."

Yet she appeared conscious it would be rather odd on such an occasion to take this up. It was even odd in Nick to have said it. "Broadwood's just right," she returned at last. "It's neither too small nor too big, and it takes care of itself. There's nothing to be done: you can't spend a penny."

"And don't you want to use it?"

"We can go and stay with *them*," said Julia.

"They'll think I bring them an angel." And Nick covered her white hand, which was resting on the stile, with his own large one.

"As they regard you yourself as an angel they'll take it as natural of you to associate with your kind."

"Oh *my* kind!" he quite wailed, looking at the cows.

But his very extravagance perhaps saved it, and she turned away from him as if starting homeward, while he began to retrace his steps with her. Suddenly she said: "What did you mean that night in Paris?"

"That night——?"

"When you came to the hotel with me after we had all dined at that place with Peter."

"What did I mean——?"

"About your caring so much for the fine arts. You seemed to want to frighten me."

"Why should you have been frightened? I can't imagine what I had in my head: not now."

"You *are* vague," said Julia with a little flush.

"Not about the great thing."

"The great thing?"

"That I owe you everything an honest man has to offer. How can I care about the fine arts now?"

She stopped with lighted eyes on him. "Is it because you think you *owe* it——" and she paused, still with the heightened colour in her cheek, then went on—"that you've spoken to me as you did there?" She tossed her head toward the lake.

"I think I spoke to you because I couldn't help it."

"You *are* vague!" And she walked on again.

"You affect me differently from any other woman."

"Oh other women——! Why shouldn't you care about the fine arts now?" she added.

"There'll be no time. All my days and my years will be none too much for what you expect of me."

"I don't expect you to give up anything. I only expect you to do more."

"To do more I must do less. I've no talent."

"No talent?"

"I mean for painting."

Julia pulled up again. "That's odious! You *have*—you must."

He burst out laughing. "You're altogether delightful. But how little you know about it—about the honourable practice of any art!"

"What do you call practice? You'll have all our things—you'll live in the midst of them."

"Certainly I shall enjoy looking at them, being so near them."

"Don't say I've taken you away then."

"Taken me away——?"

"From the love of art. I like them myself now, poor George's treasures. I didn't of old so much, because it seemed to me he made too much of them—he was always talking."

"Well, I won't always talk," said Nick.

"You may do as you like—they're yours."

"Give them to the nation," Nick went on.

"I like that! When we've done with them."

"We shall have done with them when your Vandykes and Moronis have cured me of the delusion that I may be of *their* family. Surely that won't take long."

"You shall paint *me*," said Julia.

"Never, never, never!" He spoke in a tone that made his companion stare—then seemed slightly embarrassed at this result of his emphasis. To relieve himself he said, as they had come back to the place beside the lake where the boat was moored, "Shan't we really go and fetch Mr. Hoppus?"

She hesitated. "You may go; I won't, please."

"That's not what I want."

"Oblige me by going. I'll wait here." With which she sat down on the bench attached to the little landing.

Nick, at this, got into the boat and put off; he smiled at her as she sat there watching him. He made his short journey, disembarked and went into the pavilion; but when he came out with the object of his errand he saw she had quitted her station, had returned to the house without him. He rowed back quickly, sprang ashore and followed her with long steps. Apparently she had gone fast; she had almost reached the door when he overtook her.

"Why did you basely desert me?" he asked, tenderly stopping her there.

"I don't know. Because I'm so happy."

"May I tell mother then?"

"You may tell her she shall have Broadwood."

XVI

He lost no time in going down to see Mr. Carteret, to whom he had written immediately after the election and who had answered him in twelve revised pages of historical parallel. He used often to envy Mr. Carteret's leisure, a sense of which came to him now afresh, in the summer evening, as he walked up the hill toward the quiet house where enjoyment had ever been mingled for him with a vague oppression. He was a little boy again, under Mr. Carteret's roof—a little boy on whom it had been duly impressed that in the wide, plain, peaceful rooms he was not to "touch." When he paid a visit to his father's old friend there were in fact many things—many topics—from which he instinctively kept his hands. Even Mr. Chayter, the immemorial blank butler, who was so like his master that he might have been a twin brother, helped to remind him that he must be good. Mr. Carteret seemed to Nick a very grave person, but he had the sense that Chayter thought him rather frivolous.

Our young man always came on foot from the station, leaving his portmanteau to be carried: the direct way was steep and he liked the slow approach, which gave him a chance to look about the place and smell the new-mown hay. At this season the air was full of it—the fields were so near that it was in the clean, still streets. Nick would never have thought of rattling up to Mr. Carteret's door, which had on an old brass plate the proprietor's name, as if he had been the principal surgeon. The house was in the high part, and the neat roofs of other houses, lower down the hill, made an immediate prospect for it, scarcely counting, however, since the green country was just below these, familiar and interpenetrating, in the shape of small but thick-tufted gardens. Free garden-growths flourished in all the intervals, but the only disorder of the place was that there were sometimes oats on the pavements. A crooked lane, with postern doors and cobble-stones, opened near Mr. Carteret's house and wandered toward the old abbey; for the abbey was the secondary fact of Beauclere—it came after Mr. Carteret. Mr. Carteret sometimes went away and the abbey never did; yet somehow what was most of the essence of the place was that it could boast of the resident in the squarest of the square red houses, the one with the finest of the arched hall-windows, in three divisions, over the widest of the last-century doorways. You saw the great church from the doorstep, beyond gardens of course, and in the stillness you could hear the flutter of the birds that circled round its huge short towers. The towers had been finished only as time finishes things, by lending assurances to their lapses. There is something right in old monuments that have been wrong for centuries: some such moral as that was usually in Nick's mind as an emanation of Beauclere when he saw the grand line of the roof ride the sky and draw out its length.

When the door with the brass plate was opened and Mr. Chayter appeared in the middle distance—he always advanced just to the same spot, as a prime minister receives an ambassador—Nick felt anew that he would be wonderfully like Mr. Carteret if he had had an expression. He denied himself this freedom, never giving a sign of recognition, often as the young man had been at the house. He was most attentive to the visitor's wants, but apparently feared that if he allowed a familiarity it might go too far. There was always the same question to be asked—had Mr. Carteret finished his nap? He usually had not finished it, and this left Nick what he liked—time to smoke a cigarette in the garden or even to take before dinner a turn about the place. He observed now, every time he came, that Mr. Carteret's nap lasted a little longer. There was each year a little more strength to be gathered for the ceremony of dinner: this was the principal symptom—almost the only one—that the clear-cheeked old gentleman gave of not being so fresh as of yore. He was still wonderful for his age. To-day he was particularly careful: Chayter went so far as to mention to Nick that four gentlemen were expected to dinner—an exuberance perhaps partly explained by the circumstance that Lord Bottomley was one of them.

The prospect of Lord Bottomley was somehow not stirring; it only made the young man say to himself with a quick, thin sigh, "This time I *am* in for it!" And he immediately had the unpolitical sense again that there was nothing so pleasant as the way the quiet bachelor house had its best rooms on the big garden, which seemed to advance into them through their wide windows and ruralise their dulness.

"I expect it will be a lateish eight, sir," said Mr. Chayter, superintending in the library the production of tea on a large scale. Everything at Mr. Carteret's seemed to Nick on a larger scale than anywhere else—the tea-cups, the knives and forks, the door-handles, the chair-backs, the legs of mutton, the candles, and the lumps of coal: they represented and apparently exhausted the master's sense of pleasing effect, for the house was not otherwise decorated. Nick thought it really hideous, but he was capable at any time of extracting a degree of amusement from anything strongly characteristic, and Mr. Carteret's interior expressed a whole view of life. Our young man was generous enough

233

to find in it a hundred instructive intimations even while it came over him—as it always did at Beauclere—that this was the view he himself was expected to take. Nowhere were the boiled eggs at breakfast so big or in such big receptacles; his own shoes, arranged in his room, looked to him vaster there than at home. He went out into the garden and remembered what enormous strawberries they should have for dinner. In the house was a great deal of Landseer, of oilcloth, of woodwork painted and "grained."

Finding there would be time before the evening meal or before Mr. Carteret was likely to see him he quitted the house and took a stroll toward the abbey. It covered acres of ground on the summit of the hill, and there were aspects in which its vast bulk reminded him of the ark left high and dry upon Ararat. It was the image at least of a great wreck, of the indestructible vessel of a faith, washed up there by a storm centuries before. The injury of time added to this appearance—the infirmities round which, as he knew, the battle of restoration had begun to be fought. The cry had been raised to save the splendid pile, and the counter-cry by the purists, the sentimentalists, whatever they were, to save it from being saved. They were all exchanging compliments in the morning papers.

Nick sauntered about the church—it took a good while; he leaned against low things and looked up at it while he smoked another cigarette. It struck him as a great pity such a pile should be touched: so much of the past was buried there that it was like desecrating, like digging up a grave. Since the years were letting it down so gently why jostle the elbow of slow-fingering time? The fading afternoon was exquisitely pure; the place was empty; he heard nothing but the cries of several children, which sounded sweet, who were playing on the flatness of the very old tombs. He knew this would inevitably be one of the topics at dinner, the restoration of the abbey; it would give rise to a considerable deal of orderly debate. Lord Bottomley, oddly enough, would probably oppose the expensive project, but on grounds that would be characteristic of him even if the attitude were not. Nick's nerves always knew on this spot what it was to be soothed; but he shifted his position with a slight impatience as the vision came over him of Lord Bottomley's treating a question of esthetics. It was enough to make one want to take the other side, the idea of having the same taste as his lordship: one would have it for such different reasons.

Dear Mr. Carteret would be deliberate and fair all round and would, like his noble friend, exhibit much more architectural knowledge than he, Nick, possessed: which would not make it a whit less droll to our young man that an artistic idea, so little really assimilated, should be broached at that table and in that air. It would remain so outside of their minds and their minds would remain so outside of it. It would be dropped at last, however, after half an hour's gentle worrying, and the conversation would incline itself to public affairs. Mr. Carteret would find his natural level—the production of anecdote in regard to the formation of early ministries. He knew more than any one else about the personages of whom certain cabinets would have consisted if they had not consisted of others. His favourite exercise was to illustrate how different everything might have been from what it was, and how the reason of the difference had always been somebody's inability to "see his way" to accept the view of somebody else—a view usually at the time discussed in strict confidence with Mr. Carteret, who surrounded his actual violation of that confidence thirty years later with many precautions against scandal. In this retrospective vein, at the head of his table, the old gentleman enjoyed a hearing, or at any rate commanded a silence, often intense. Every one left it to some one else to ask another question; and when by chance some one else did so every one was struck with admiration at any one's being able to say anything. Nick knew the moment when he himself would take a glass of a particular port and, surreptitiously looking at his watch, perceive it was ten o'clock. That timepiece might as well mark 1830.

All this would be a part of the suggestion of leisure that invariably descended upon him at Beauclere—the image of a sloping shore where the tide of time broke with a ripple too faint to be a warning. But there was another admonition almost equally sure to descend upon his spirit during a stroll in a summer hour about the grand abbey; to sink into it as the light lingered on the rough red walls and the local accent of the children sounded soft in the churchyard. It was simply the sense of England—a sort of apprehended revelation of his country. The dim annals of the place were sensibly, heavily in the air—foundations bafflingly early, a great monastic life, wars of the Roses, with battles and blood in the streets, and then the long quietude of the respectable centuries, all corn-fields and magistrates and vicars—and these things were connected with an emotion that arose from the green country, the rich land so infinitely lived in, and laid on him a hand that was too ghostly to press and yet somehow too urgent to be light. It produced a throb he couldn't have spoken of, it was so deep, and that was half imagination and half responsibility. These impressions melted together and made a general appeal, of which, with his new honours as a legislator, he was the sentient subject. If he had a love for that particular scene of life mightn't it have a love for him and expect something of him? What fate could be so high as to grow old in a national affection? What a fine sort of reciprocity, making mere soreness of all the balms of indifference!

The great church was still open and he turned into it and wandered a little in the twilight that had gathered earlier there. The whole structure, with its immensity of height and distance, seemed to rest on tremendous facts—facts of achievement and endurance—and the huge Norman pillars to loom through the dimness like the ghosts of heroes. Nick was more struck with its thick earthly than with its fine spiritual reference, and he felt the oppression of his conscience as he walked slowly about. It was in his mind that nothing in life was really clear, all things were mingled and charged, and that patriotism might be an uplifting passion even if it had to allow for Lord Bottomley and for Mr. Carteret's blindness on certain sides. He presently noticed that half-past seven was about to strike, and as he went back to his old friend's he couldn't have said if he walked in gladness or in gloom.

"Mr. Carteret will be in the drawing-room at a quarter to eight, sir," Chayter mentioned, and Nick as he went to dress asked himself what was the use of being a member of Parliament if one was still sensitive to an intimation on the part of such a functionary that one ought already to have begun that business. Chayter's words but meant that Mr. Carteret would expect to have a little comfortable conversation with him before dinner. Nick's usual rapidity in dressing was, however, quite adequate to the occasion, so that his host had not appeared when he went down. There were flowers in the unfeminine saloon, which contained several paintings in addition to the engravings of pictures of animals; but nothing could prevent its reminding Nick of a comfortable committee-room.

Mr. Carteret presently came in with his gold-headed stick, a laugh like a series of little warning coughs and the air of embarrassment that our young man always perceived in him at first. He was almost eighty but was still shy—he laughed a great deal, faintly and vaguely, at nothing, as if to make up for the seriousness with which he took some jokes. He always began by looking away from his interlocutor, and it was only little by little that his eyes came round; after which their limpid and benevolent blue made you wonder why they should ever be circumspect. He was clean-shaven and had a long upper lip. When he had seated himself he talked of "majorities" and showed a disposition to converse on the general subject of the fluctuation of Liberal gains. He had an extraordinary memory for facts of this sort, and could mention the figures relating to the returns from innumerable places in particular years. To many of these facts he attached great importance, in his simple, kindly, presupposing way; correcting himself five minutes later if he had said that in 1857 some one had had 6014 instead of 6004.

Nick always felt a great hypocrite as he listened to him, in spite of the old man's courtesy—a thing so charming in itself that it would have been grossness to speak of him as a bore. The difficulty was that he took for granted all kinds of positive assent, and Nick, in such company, found himself steeped in an element of tacit pledges which constituted the very medium of intercourse and yet made him draw his breath a little in pain when for a moment he measured them. There would have been no hypocrisy at all if he could have regarded Mr. Carteret as a mere sweet spectacle, the last or almost the last illustration of a departing tradition of manners. But he represented something more than manners; he represented what he believed to be morals and ideas, ideas as regards which he took your personal deference—not discovering how natural that was—for participation. Nick liked to think that his father, though ten years younger, had found it congruous to make his best friend of the owner of so nice a nature: it gave a softness to his feeling for that memory to be reminded that Sir Nicholas had been of the same general type—a type so pure, so disinterested, so concerned for the public good. Just so it endeared Mr. Carteret to him to perceive that he considered his father had done a definite work, prematurely interrupted, which had been an absolute benefit to the people of England. The oddity was, however, that though both Mr. Carteret's aspect and his appreciation were still so fresh this relation of his to his late distinguished friend made the latter appear to Nick even more irrecoverably dead. The good old man had almost a vocabulary of his own, made up of old-fashioned political phrases and quite untainted with the new terms, mostly borrowed from America; indeed his language and his tone made those of almost any one who might be talking with him sound by contrast rather American. He was, at least nowadays, never severe nor denunciatory; but sometimes in telling an anecdote he dropped such an expression as "the rascal said to me" or such an epithet as "the vulgar dog."

Nick was always struck with the rare simplicity—it came out in his countenance—of one who had lived so long and seen so much of affairs that draw forth the passions and perversities of men. It often made him say to himself that Mr. Carteret must have had many odd parts to have been able to achieve with his means so many things requiring cleverness. It was as if experience, though coming to him in abundance, had dealt with him so clean-handedly as to leave no stain, and had moreover never provoked him to any general reflexion. He had never proceeded in any ironic way from the particular to the general; certainly he had never made a reflexion upon anything so unparliamentary as Life. He would have questioned the taste of such an extravagance and if he had encountered it on the part of another have regarded it as an imported foreign toy with the uses of which he was unacquainted. Life, for him, was a purely practical function, not a question of more or less showy phrasing. It must be added that he had to Nick's perception his variations—his back windows opening into grounds more private. That was visible from the way his eye grew cold and his whole polite face rather austere when he listened to something he didn't agree with or perhaps even understand; as if his modesty didn't in strictness forbid the suspicion that a thing he didn't understand would have a probability against it. At such times there was something rather deadly in the silence in which he simply waited with a lapse in his face, not helping his interlocutor out. Nick would have been very sorry to attempt to communicate to him a matter he wouldn't be likely to understand. This cut off of course a multitude of subjects.

The evening passed exactly as he had foreseen, even to the markedly prompt dispersal of the guests, two of whom were "local" men, earnest and distinct, though not particularly distinguished. The third was a young, slim, uninitiated gentleman whom Lord Bottomley brought with him and concerning whom Nick was informed beforehand that he was engaged to be married to the Honourable Jane, his lordship's second daughter. There were recurrent allusions to Nick's victory, as to which he had the fear that he might appear to exhibit less interest in it than the company did. He took energetic precautions against this and felt repeatedly a little spent with them, for the subject always came up once more. Yet it was not as his but as theirs that they liked the triumph. Mr. Carteret took leave of him for the night directly after the other guests had gone, using at this moment the words he had often used before:

"You may sit up to any hour you like. I only ask that you don't read in bed."

XVII

Nick's little visit was to terminate immediately after luncheon the following day: much as the old man enjoyed his being there he wouldn't have dreamed of asking for more of his time now that it had such great public uses. He liked infinitely better that his young friend should be occupied with parliamentary work than only occupied in talking it over with him. Talking it over, however, was the next best thing, as on the morrow, after breakfast, Mr. Carteret showed Nick he considered. They sat in the garden, the morning being warm, and the old man had a table beside him covered with the letters and newspapers the post had poured forth. He was proud of his correspondence, which was altogether on public affairs, and proud in a manner of the fact that he now dictated almost everything. That had more in it of the statesman in retirement, a character indeed not consciously assumed by Mr. Carteret, but always tacitly attributed to him by Nick, who took it rather from the pictorial point of view—remembering on each occasion only afterwards that though he was in retirement he had not exactly been a statesman. A young man, a very sharp, handy young man, came every morning at ten o'clock and wrote for him till luncheon. The young man had a holiday to-day in honour of Nick's visit—a fact the mention of which led Nick to make some not particularly sincere speech about *his* being ready to write anything if Mr. Carteret were at all pressed.

"Ah but your own budget—what will become of that?" the old gentleman objected, glancing at Nick's pockets as if rather surprised not to see them stuffed out with documents in split envelopes. His visitor had to confess that he had not directed his letters to meet him at Beauclere: he should find them in town that afternoon. This led to a little homily from Mr. Carteret which made him feel quite guilty; there was such an implication of neglected duty in the way the old man said, "You won't do them justice—you won't do them justice." He talked for ten minutes, in his rich, simple, urbane way, about the fatal consequences of getting behind. It was his favourite doctrine that one should always be a little before, and his own eminently regular respiration seemed to illustrate the idea. A man was certainly before who had so much in his rear.

This led to the bestowal of a good deal of general advice on the mistakes to avoid at the beginning of a parliamentary career—as to which Mr. Carteret spoke with the experience of one who had sat for fifty years in the House of Commons. Nick was amused, but also mystified and even a little irritated, by his talk: it was founded on the idea of observation and yet our young man couldn't at all regard him as an observer. "He doesn't observe *me*," he said to himself; "if he did he would see, he wouldn't think——!" The end of this private cogitation was a vague impatience of all the things his venerable host took for granted. He didn't see any of the things Nick saw. Some of these latter were the light touches the summer morning scattered through the sweet old garden. The time passed there a good deal as if it were sitting still with a plaid under its feet while Mr. Carteret distilled a little more of the wisdom he had laid up in his fifty years. This immense term had something fabulous and monstrous for Nick, who wondered whether it were the sort of thing his companion supposed *he* had gone in for. It was not strange Mr.

Carteret should be different; he might originally have been more—well, to himself Nick was not obliged to phrase it: what our young man meant was more of what it was perceptible to him that his old friend was not. Should even he, Nick, be like that at the end of fifty years? What Mr. Carteret was so good as to expect for him was that he should be much more distinguished; and wouldn't this exactly mean much more like that? Of course Nick heard some things he had heard before; as for instance the circumstances that had originally led the old man to settle at Beauclere. He had been returned for that borough—it was his second seat—in years far remote, and had come to live there because he then had a conscientious conviction, modified indeed by later experience, that a member should be constantly resident. He spoke of this now, smiling rosily, as he might have spoken of some wild aberration of his youth; yet he called Nick's attention to the fact that he still so far clung to his conviction as to hold—though of what might be urged on the other side he was perfectly aware—that a representative should at least be as resident as possible. This gave Nick an opening for something that had been on and off his lips all the morning.

"According to that I ought to take up my abode at Harsh."

"In the measure of the convenient I shouldn't be sorry to see you do it."

"It ought to be rather convenient," Nick largely smiled. "I've got a piece of news for you which I've kept, as one keeps that sort of thing—for it's very good—till the last." He waited a little to see if Mr. Carteret would guess, and at first thought nothing would come of this. But after resting his young-looking eyes on him for a moment the old man said:

"I should indeed be very happy to hear that you've arranged to take a wife."

"Mrs. Dallow has been so good as to say she'll marry me," Nick returned.

"That's very suitable. I should think it would answer."

"It's very jolly," said Nick. It was well Mr. Carteret was not what his guest called observant, or he might have found a lower pitch in the sound of this sentence than in the sense.

241

"Your dear father would have liked it."

"So my mother says."

"And *she* must be delighted."

"Mrs. Dallow, do you mean?" Nick asked.

"I was thinking of your mother. But I don't exclude the charming lady. I remember her as a little girl. I must have seen her at Windrush. Now I understand the fine spirit with which she threw herself into your canvass."

"It was her they elected," said Nick.

"I don't know," his host went on, "that I've ever been an enthusiast for political women, but there's no doubt that in approaching the mass of electors a graceful, affable manner, the manner of the real English lady, is a force not to be despised."

"Julia's a real English lady and at the same time a very political woman," Nick remarked.

"Isn't it rather in the family? I remember once going to see her mother in town and finding the leaders of both parties sitting with her."

"My principal friend, of the others, is her brother Peter. I don't think he troubles himself much about that sort of thing," said Nick.

"What does he trouble himself about?" Mr. Carteret asked with a certain gravity.

"He's in the diplomatic service; he's a secretary in Paris."

"That may be serious," said the old man.

"He takes a great interest in the theatre. I suppose you'll say that may be serious too," Nick laughed.

"Oh!"—and Mr. Carteret looked as if he scarcely understood. Then he continued; "Well, it can't hurt you."

"It can't hurt me?"

"If Mrs. Dallow takes an interest in your interests."

"When a man's in my situation he feels as if nothing could hurt him."

"I'm very glad you're happy," said Mr. Carteret. He rested his mild eyes on our young man, who had a sense of seeing in them for a moment the faint ghost of an old story, the last strange flicker, as from cold ashes, of a flame that had become the memory of a memory. This glimmer of wonder and envy, the revelation of a life intensely celibate, was for an instant infinitely touching. Nick had harboured a theory, suggested by a vague allusion from his father, who had been discreet, that their benevolent friend had had in his youth an unhappy love-affair which had led him to forswear for ever the commerce of woman. What remained in him of conscious renunciation gave a throb as he looked at his bright companion, who proposed to take the matter so much the other way. "It's good to marry and I think it's right. I've not done right, I know that. If she's a good woman it's the best thing," Mr. Carteret went on. "It's what I've been hoping for you. Sometimes I've thought of speaking to you."

"She's a very good woman," said Nick.

"And I hope she's not poor." Mr. Carteret spoke exactly with the same blandness.

"No indeed, she's rich. Her husband, whom I knew and liked, left her a large fortune."

"And on what terms does she enjoy it?"

"I haven't the least idea," said Nick.

Mr. Carteret considered. "I see. It doesn't concern you. It needn't concern you," he added in a moment.

Nick thought of his mother at this, but he returned: "I daresay she can do what she likes with her money."

"So can I, my dear young friend," said Mr. Carteret.

Nick tried not to look conscious, for he felt a significance in the old man's face. He turned his own everywhere but toward it, thinking again of his mother. "That must be very pleasant, if one has any."

"I wish you had a little more."

"I don't particularly care," said Nick.

"Your marriage will assist you; you can't help that," Mr. Carteret declared. "But I should like you to be under obligations not quite so heavy."

"Oh I'm so obliged to her for caring for me——!"

"That the rest doesn't count? Certainly it's nice of her to like you. But why shouldn't she? Other people do."

"Some of them make me feel as if I abused it," said Nick, looking at his host. "That is, they don't make me, but I feel it," he corrected.

"I've no son "—and Mr. Carteret spoke as if his companion mightn't have been sure. "Shan't you be very kind to her?" he pursued. "You'll gratify her ambition."

"Oh she thinks me cleverer than I am."

"That's because she's in love," the old gentleman hinted as if this were very subtle. "However, you must be as clever as we think you. If you don't prove so——!" And he paused with his folded hands.

"Well, if I don't?" asked Nick.

"Oh it won't do—it won't do," said Mr. Carteret in a tone his companion was destined to remember afterwards. "I say I've no son," he continued; "but if I had had one he should have risen high."

"It's well for me such a person doesn't exist. I shouldn't easily have found a wife."

"He would have gone to the altar with a little money in his pocket."

"That would have been the least of his advantages, sir," Nick declared.

"When are you to be married?" Mr. Carteret asked.

"Ah that's the question. Julia won't yet say."

"Well," said the old man without the least flourish, "you may consider that when it comes off I'll make you a settlement."

"I feel your kindness more than I can express," Nick replied; "but that will probably be the moment when I shall be least conscious of wanting anything."

"You'll appreciate it later—you'll appreciate it very soon. I shall like you to appreciate it," Mr. Carteret went on as if he had a just vision of the way a young man of a proper spirit should feel. Then he added; "Your father would have liked you to appreciate it."

"Poor father!" Nick exclaimed vaguely, rather embarrassed, reflecting on the oddity of a position in which the ground for holding up his head as the husband of a rich woman would be that he had accepted a present of money from another source. It was plain he was not fated to go in for independence; the most that he could treat himself to would be dependence that was duly grateful "How much do you expect of me?" he inquired with a grave face.

"Well, Nicholas, only what your father did. He so often spoke of you, I remember, at the last, just after you had been with him alone—you know I saw him then. He was greatly moved by his interview with you, and so was I by what he told me of it. He said he should live on in you—he should work in you. It has always given me a special feeling, if I may use the expression, about you."

"The feelings are indeed not usual, dear Mr. Carteret, which take so munificent a form. But you do—oh you do—expect too much," Nick brought himself to say.

"I expect you to repay me!" the old man returned gaily. "As for the form, I have it in my mind."

"The form of repayment?"

"The form of repayment!"

"Ah don't talk of that now," said Nick, "for, you see, nothing else is settled. No one has been told except my mother. She has only consented to my telling you."

"Lady Agnes, do you mean?"

"Ah no; dear mother would like to publish it on the house-tops. She's so glad—she wants us to have it over to-morrow. But Julia herself," Nick explained, "wishes to wait. Therefore kindly mention it for the present to no one."

"My dear boy, there's at this rate nothing to mention! What does Julia want to wait for?"

"Till I like her better—that's what she says."

"It's the way to make you like her worse," Mr. Carteret knowingly declared. "Hasn't she your affection?"

"So much so that her delay makes me exceedingly unhappy."

Mr. Carteret looked at his young friend as if he didn't strike him as quite wretched; but he put the question: "Then what more does she want?" Nick laughed out at this, though perceiving his host hadn't meant it as an epigram; while the latter resumed: "I don't understand. You're engaged or you're not engaged."

"She is, but I'm not. That's what she says about it. The trouble is she doesn't believe in me."

Mr. Carteret shone with his candour. "Doesn't she love you then?"

"That's what I ask her. Her answer is that she loves me only too well. She's so afraid of being a burden to me that she gives me my freedom till I've taken another year to think."

"I like the way you talk about other years!" Mr. Carteret cried. "You had better do it while I'm here to bless you."

"She thinks I proposed to her because she got me in for Harsh," said Nick.

"Well, I'm sure it would be a very pretty return."

"Ah she doesn't believe in me," the young man repeated.

"Then I don't believe in *her*."

"Don't say that—don't say that. She's a very rare creature. But she's proud, shy, suspicious."

"Suspicious of what?"

"Of everything. She thinks I'm not persistent."

"Oh, oh!"—Nick's host deprecated such freedom.

"She can't believe I shall arrive at true eminence."

"A good wife should believe what her husband believes," said Mr. Carteret.

"Ah unfortunately"—and Nick took the words at a run—"I don't believe it either."

Mr. Carteret, who might have been watching an odd physical rush, spoke with a certain dryness. "Your dear father did."

"I think of that—I think of that," Nick replied.

"Certainly it will help me. If I say we're engaged," he went on, "it's because I consider it so. She gives me my liberty, but I don't take it."

"Does she expect you to take back your word?"

"That's what I ask her. *She* never will. Therefore we're as good as tied."

"I don't like it," said Mr. Carteret after a moment. "I don't like ambiguous, uncertain situations. They please me much better when they're definite and clear." The retreat of expression had been sounded in his face—the aspect it wore when he wished not to be encouraging. But after an instant he added in a tone more personal: "Don't disappoint me, dear boy."

"Ah not willingly!" his visitor protested.

"I've told you what I should like to do for you. See that the conditions come about promptly in which I *may*, do it. Are you sure you do everything to satisfy Mrs. Dallow?" Mr. Carteret continued.

"I think I'm very nice to her," Nick declared. "But she's so ambitious. Frankly speaking, it's a pity for her that she likes me."

"She can't help that!" the old man charmingly said.

"Possibly. But isn't it a reason for taking me as I am? What she wants to do is to take me as I may be a year hence."

"I don't understand—since you tell me that even then she won't take back her word," said Mr. Carteret.

"If she doesn't marry me I think she'll never marry again at all."

"What then does she gain by delay?"

"Simply this, as I make it out," said Nick—"that she'll feel she has been very magnanimous. She won't have to reproach herself with not having given me a chance to change."

"To change? What does she think you liable to do?"

Nick had a pause. "I don't know!" he then said—not at all candidly.

"Everything has altered: young people in my day looked at these questions more naturally," Mr. Carteret observed. "A woman in love has no need to be magnanimous. If she plays too fair she isn't in love," he added shrewdly.

"Oh, Julia's safe—she's safe," Nick smiled.

"If it were a question between you and another gentleman one might comprehend. But what does it mean, between you and nothing?"

"I'm much obliged to you, sir," Nick returned. "The trouble is that she doesn't know what she has got hold of."

"Ah, if you can't make it clear to her!"—and his friend showed the note of impatience.

"I'm such a humbug," said the young man. And while his companion stared he continued: "I deceive people without in the least intending it."

"What on earth do you mean? Are you deceiving me?"

"I don't know—it depends on what you think."

"I think you're flighty," said Mr. Carteret, with the nearest approach to sternness Nick had ever observed in him. "I never thought so before."

"Forgive me; it's all right. I'm not frivolous; that I promise you I'm not."

"You *have* deceived me if you are."

"It's all right," Nick stammered with a blush.

"Remember your name—carry it high."

"I will—as high as possible."

"You've no excuse. Don't tell me, after your speeches at Harsh!" Nick was on the point of declaring again that he was a humbug, so vivid was his inner sense of what he thought of his factitious public utterances, which had the cursed property of creating dreadful responsibilities and importunate credulities for him. If *he* was "clever" (ah the idiotic "clever"!) what fools many other people were! He repressed his impulse and Mr. Carteret pursued. "If, as you express it, Mrs. Dallow doesn't know what she has got hold of, won't it clear the matter up a little by informing her that the day before your marriage is definitely settled to take place you'll come into something comfortable?"

A quick vision of what Mr. Carteret would be likely to regard as something comfortable flitted before Nick, but it didn't prevent his replying: "Oh I'm afraid that won't do any good. It would make her like you better, but it wouldn't make her like me. I'm afraid she won't care for any benefit that comes to me from another hand than hers. Her affection's a very jealous sentiment."

"It's a very peculiar one!" sighed Mr. Carteret. "Mine's a jealous sentiment too. However, if she takes it that way don't tell her."

"I'll let you know as soon as she comes round," said Nick.

"And you'll tell your mother," Mr. Carteret returned. "I shall like *her* to know."

"It will be delightful news to her. But she's keen enough already."

"I know that. I may mention now that she has written to me," the old man added.

"So I suspected."

"We've—a—corresponded on the subject," Mr. Carteret continued to confess. "My view of the advantageous character of such an alliance has entirely coincided with hers."

"It was very good-natured of you then to leave me to speak first," said Nick.

"I should have been disappointed if you hadn't. I don't like all you've told me. But don't disappoint me now."

"Dear Mr. Carteret!" Nick vaguely and richly sounded.

"I won't disappoint *you*," that gentleman went on with a finer point while he looked at his big old-fashioned watch.

BOOK FOURTH

XVIII

At first Peter Sherringham thought of asking to be transferred to another post and went so far, in London, as to take what he believed good advice on the subject. The advice, perhaps struck him as the better for consisting of a strong recommendation to do nothing so foolish. Two or three reasons were mentioned to him why such a request would not, in the particular circumstances, raise him in the esteem of his superiors, and he promptly recognised their force. He next became aware that it might help him—not with his superiors but with himself—to apply for an extension of leave, and then on further reflexion made out that, though there are some dangers before which it is perfectly consistent with honour to flee, it was better for every one concerned that he should fight this especial battle on the spot. During his holiday his plan of campaign gave him plenty of occupation. He refurbished his arms, rubbed up his strategy, laid down his lines of defence.

There was only one thing in life his mind had been much made up to, but on this question he had never wavered: he would get on, to the utmost, in his profession. That was a point on which it was perfectly lawful to be unamiable to others—to be vigilant, eager, suspicious, selfish. He had not in fact been unamiable to others, for his affairs had not required it: he had got on well enough without hardening his heart. Fortune had been kind to him and he had passed so many competitors on the way that he could forswear jealousy and be generous. But he had always flattered himself his hand wouldn't falter on the day he should find it necessary to drop bitterness into his cup. This day would be sure to dawn, since no career could be all clear water to the end; and then the sacrifice would find him ready. His mind was familiar with the thought of a sacrifice: it is true that no great plainness invested beforehand the occasion, the object or the victim. All that particularly stood out was that the propitiatory offering would have to be some cherished enjoyment. Very likely indeed this enjoyment would be associated with the charms of another person—a probability pregnant with the idea that such charms would have to be dashed out of sight. At any rate it never had occurred to Sherringham that he himself might be the sacrifice. You had to pay to get on, but at least you borrowed from others to do it. When you couldn't borrow you didn't get on, for what was the situation in life in which you met the whole requisition yourself?

Least of all had it occurred to our friend that the wrench might come through his interest in that branch of art on which Nick Dormer had rallied him. The beauty of a love of the theatre was precisely in its being a passion exercised on the easiest terms. This was not the region of responsibility. It was sniffed at, to its discredit, by the austere; but if it was not, as such people said, a serious field, was not the compensation just that you couldn't be seriously entangled in it? Sherringham's great advantage, as he regarded the matter, was that he had always kept his taste for the drama quite in its place. His facetious cousin was free to pretend that it sprawled through his life; but this was nonsense, as any unprejudiced observer of that life would unhesitatingly attest. There had not been the least sprawling, and his interest in the art of Garrick had never, he was sure, made him in any degree ridiculous. It had never drawn down from above anything approaching a reprimand, a remonstrance, a remark. Sherringham was positively proud of his discretion, for he was not a little proud of what he did know about the stage. Trifling for trifling, there were plenty of his fellows who had in their lives infatuations less edifying and less confessable. Hadn't he known men who collected old invitation-cards and were ready to commit *bassesses* for those of the eighteenth century? hadn't he known others who had a secret passion for shuffleboard? His little weaknesses were intellectual—they were a part of the life of the mind. All the same, on the day they showed a symptom of interfering they should be plucked off with a turn of the wrist.

Sherringham scented interference now, and interference in rather an invidious form. It might be a bore, from the point of view of the profession, to find one's self, as a critic of the stage, in love with a *coquine*; but it was a much greater bore to find one's self in love with a young woman whose character remained to be estimated. Miriam Rooth was neither fish nor flesh: one had with her neither the guarantees of one's own class nor the immunities of hers. What *was* hers if one came to that? A rare ambiguity on this point was part of the fascination she had ended by throwing over him. Poor Peter's scheme for getting on had contained no proviso against his falling in love, but it had embodied an important clause on the subject of surprises. It was always a surprise to fall in love, especially if one was looking out for it; so this contingency had not been worth official paper. But it became a man who respected the service he had undertaken for the State to be on his guard against predicaments from which the only issue was the rigour of matrimony. Ambition, in the career, was probably consistent with marrying—but only with opening one's eyes very wide to do it. That was the fatal surprise—to be led to the altar in a dream. Sherringham's view of the proprieties attached to such a step was high and strict; and if he held that a man in his position was, above all as the position improved, essentially a representative of the greatness of his country, he considered that the wife of such a personage would exercise in her degree—for instance at a foreign court—a function no less symbolic. She would in short always be a very important quantity, and the scene was strewn with illustrations of this general truth. She might be such a help and might be such a blight that common prudence required some test of her in advance. Sherringham had seen women in the career, who were stupid or vulgar, make such a mess of things as would wring your heart. Then he had his positive idea of the perfect ambassadress, the full-blown lily of the future; and with this idea Miriam Rooth presented no analogy whatever.

The girl had described herself with characteristic directness as "all right"; and so she might be, so she assuredly was: only all right for what? He had made out she was not sentimental—that whatever capacity she might have for responding to a devotion or for desiring it was at any rate not in the direction of vague philandering. With him certainly she had no disposition to philander. Sherringham almost feared to dwell on this, lest it should beget in him a rage convertible mainly into caring for her more. Rage or no rage it would be charming to be in love with her if there were no complications; but the complications were just what was clearest in the prospect. He was perhaps cold-blooded to think of them, but it must be remembered that they were the particular thing his training had equipped him for dealing with. He was at all events not too cold-blooded to have, for the two months of his holiday, very little inner vision of anything more abstract than Miriam's face. The desire to see it again was as pressing as thirst, but he tried to practise the endurance of the traveller in the desert. He kept the Channel between them, but his spirit consumed every day an inch of the interval, until—and it was not long—there were no more inches left. The last thing he expected the future ambassadress to have been was *fille de théâtre*. The answer to this objection was of course that Miriam was not yet so much of one but that he could easily, by a handsome "worldly" offer, arrest her development. Then came worrying retorts to that, chief among which was the sense that to his artistic conscience arresting her development would be a plan combining on his part fatuity, not to say imbecility, with baseness. It was exactly to her development the poor girl had the greatest right, and he shouldn't really alter anything by depriving her of it. Wasn't she the artist to the tips of her tresses—the ambassadress never in the world—and wouldn't she take it out in something else if one were to make her deviate? So certain was that demonic gift to insist ever on its own.

Besides, *could* one make her deviate? If she had no disposition to philander what was his warrant for supposing she could be corrupted into respectability? How could the career—his career—speak to a nature that had glimpses as vivid as they were crude of such a different range and for which success meant quite another sauce to the dish? Would the brilliancy of marrying Peter Sherringham be such a bribe to relinquishment? How could he think so without pretensions of the sort he pretended exactly not to flaunt?— how could he put himself forward as so high a prize? Relinquishment of the opportunity to exercise a rare talent was not, in the nature of things, an easy effort to a young lady who was herself presumptuous as well as ambitious. Besides, she might eat her cake and have it—might make her fortune both on the stage and in the world. Successful actresses had ended by marrying dukes, and was not that better than remaining obscure and marrying a commoner? There were moments when he tried to pronounce the girl's "gift" not a force to reckon with; there was so little to show for it as yet that the caprice of believing in it would perhaps suddenly leave him. But his conviction that it was real was too uneasy to make such an experiment peaceful, and he came back, moreover, to his deepest impression—that of her being of the inward mould for which the only consistency is the play of genius. Hadn't Madame Carré declared at the last that she could "do anything"? It was true that if Madame Carré had been mistaken in the first place she might also be mistaken in the second. But in this latter case she would be mistaken with him—and such an error would be too like a truth.

How, further, shall we exactly measure for him—Sherringham felt the discomfort of the advantage Miriam had of him—the advantage of her presenting herself in a light that rendered any passion he might entertain an implication of duty as well as of pleasure? Why there should have been this implication was more than he could say; sometimes he held himself rather abject, or at least absurdly superstitious, for seeing it. He didn't know, he could scarcely conceive, of another case of the same general type in which he would have recognised it. In foreign countries there were very few ladies of Miss Rooth's intended profession who would not have regarded it as too strong an order that, to console them for not being admitted into drawing-rooms, they should have no offset but the exercise of a virtue in which no one would believe. This was because in foreign countries actresses were not admitted into drawing-rooms: that was a pure English drollery, ministering equally little to real histrionics and to the higher tone of these resorts. Did the oppressive sanctity which made it a burden to have to reckon with his young friend come then from her being English? Peter could recall cases in which that privilege operated as little as possible as a restriction. It came a great deal from Mrs. Rooth, in whom he apprehended depths of calculation as to what she might achieve for her daughter by "working" the idea of a life blameless amid dire obsessions. Her romantic turn of mind wouldn't in the least prevent her regarding that idea as a substantial capital, to be laid out to the best worldly advantage. Miriam's essential irreverence was capable, on a pretext, of making mince-meat of it—that he was sure of; for the only capital she recognised was the talent which some day managers and agents would outbid each other in paying for. Yet as a creature easy at so many points she was fond of her mother, would do anything to oblige—that might work in all sorts of ways—and would probably like the loose slippers of blamelessness quite as well as having to meet some of the queer high standards of the opposite camp.

Sherringham, I may add, had no desire that she should indulge a different preference: it was distasteful to him to compute the probabilities of a young lady's misbehaving for his advantage—that seemed to him definitely base—and he would have thought himself a blackguard if, even when a prey to his desire, he had not wished the thing that was best for the object of it. The thing best for Miriam might be to become the wife of the man to whose suit she should incline her ear. That this would be the best thing for the gentleman in question by no means, however, equally followed, and Sherringham's final conviction was that it would never do for him to act the part of that hypothetic personage. He asked for no removal and no extension of leave, and he proved to himself how well he knew what he was about by never addressing a line, during his absence, to the Hôtel de la Garonne. He would simply go straight, inflicting as little injury on Peter Sherringham as on any one else. He remained away to the last hour of his privilege and continued to act lucidly in having nothing to do with the mother and daughter for several days after his return to Paris.

It was when this discipline came to an end one afternoon after a week had passed that he felt most the force of the reference we have just made to Mrs. Rooth's private calculations. He found her at home, alone, writing a letter under the lamp, and as soon as he came in she cried out that he was the very person to whom the letter was addressed. She could bear it no longer; she had permitted herself to reproach him with his terrible silence—to ask why he had quite forsaken them. It was an illustration of the way in which her visitor had come to regard her that he put rather less than more faith into this description of the crumpled papers lying on the table. He was not even sure he quite believed Miriam to have just gone out. He told her mother how busy he had been all the while he was away and how much time above all he had had to give in London to seeing on her daughter's behalf the people connected with the theatres.

"Ah if you pity me tell me you've got her an engagement!" Mrs. Rooth cried while she clasped her hands.

"I took a great deal of trouble; I wrote ever so many notes, sought introductions, talked with people—such impossible people some of them. In short I knocked at every door, I went into the question exhaustively." And he enumerated the things he had done, reported on some of the knowledge he had gathered. The difficulties were immense, and even with the influence he could command, such as it was, there was very little to be achieved in face of them. Still he had gained ground: two or three approachable fellows, men with inferior theatres, had listened to him better than the others, and there was one in particular whom he had a hope he really might have interested. From him he had extracted benevolent assurances: this person would see Miriam, would listen to her, would do for her what he could. The trouble was that no one would lift a finger for a girl unless she were known, and yet that she never could become known till innumerable fingers had been lifted. You couldn't go into the water unless you could swim, and you couldn't swim until you had been in the water.

"But new performers appear; they get theatres, they get audiences, they get notices in the newspapers," Mrs. Rooth objected. "I know of these things only what Miriam tells me. It's no knowledge that I was born to."

"It's perfectly true. It's all done with money."

"And how do they come by money?" Mrs. Rooth candidly asked.

"When they're women people give it to them."

"Well, what people now?"

"People who believe in them."

"As you believe in Miriam?"

Peter had a pause. "No, rather differently. A poor man doesn't believe in anything the same way that a rich man does."

"Ah don't call yourself poor!" groaned Mrs. Rooth.

"What good would it do me to be rich?"

"Why you could take a theatre. You could do it all yourself."

"And what good would that do me?"

"Ah don't you delight in her genius?" demanded Mrs. Rooth.

"I delight in her mother. You think me more disinterested than I am," Sherringham added with a certain soreness of irritation.

"I know why you didn't write!" Mrs. Rooth declared archly.

"You must go to London," Peter said without heeding this remark.

"Ah if we could only get there it would be a relief. I should draw a long breath. There at least I know where I am and what people are. But here one lives on hollow ground!"

"The sooner you get away the better," our young man went on.

"I know why you say that."

"It's just what I'm explaining."

"I couldn't have held out if I hadn't been so sure of Miriam," said Mrs. Rooth.

"Well, you needn't hold out any longer."

"Don't *you* trust her?" asked Sherringham's hostess.

"Trust her?"

"You don't trust yourself. That's why you were silent, why we might have thought you were dead, why we might have perished ourselves."

"I don't think I understand you; I don't know what you're talking about," Peter returned. "But it doesn't matter."

"Doesn't it? Let yourself go. Why should you struggle?" the old woman agreeably inquired.

Her unexpected insistence annoyed her visitor, and he was silent again, meeting her eyes with reserve and on the point of telling her that he didn't like her tone. But he had his tongue under such control that he was able presently to say instead of this—and it was a relief to him to give audible voice to the reflexion—"It's a great mistake, either way, for a man to be in love with an actress. Either it means nothing serious, and what's the use of that? or it means everything, and that's still more delusive."

"Delusive?"

"Idle, unprofitable."

"Surely a pure affection is its own beautiful reward," Mrs. Rooth pleaded with soft reasonableness.

"In such a case how can it be pure?"

"I thought you were talking of an English gentleman," she replied.

"Call the poor fellow whatever you like: a man with his life to lead, his way to make, his work, his duties, his career to attend to. If it means nothing, as I say, the thing it means least of all is marriage."

"Oh my own Miriam!" Mrs. Rooth wailed.

"Fancy, on the other hand, the complication when such a man marries a woman who's on the stage."

Mrs. Rooth looked as if she were trying to follow. "Miriam isn't on the stage yet."

"Go to London and she soon will be."

"Yes, and then you'll have your excuse."

"My excuse?"

"For deserting us altogether."

He broke into laughter at this, the logic was so droll. Then he went on: "Show me some good acting and I won't desert you."

"Good acting? Ah what's the best acting compared with the position of a true English lady? If you'll take her as she is you may have her," Mrs. Rooth suddenly added.

"As she is, with all her ambitions unassuaged?"

"To marry *you*—might not that be an ambition?"

"A very paltry one. Don't answer for her, don't attempt that," said Peter. "You can do much better."

"Do you think *you* can?" smiled Mrs. Rooth.

"I don't want to; I only want to let it alone. She's an artist; you must give her her head," the young man pursued. "You must always give an artist his head."

"But I've known great ladies who were artists. In English society there's always a field."

"Don't talk to me of English society! Thank goodness, in the first place, I don't live in it. Do you want her to give up her genius?" he demanded.

"I thought you didn't care for it."

"She'd say, 'No I thank you, dear mamma.'"

"My wonderful child!" Mrs. Rooth almost comprehendingly murmured.

"Have you ever proposed it to her?"

"Proposed it?"

"That she should give up trying."

Mrs. Rooth hesitated, looking down. "Not for the reason you mean. We don't talk about love," she simpered.

"Then it's so much less time wasted. Don't stretch out your hand to the worse when it may some day grasp the better," Peter continued. Mrs. Rooth raised her eyes at him as if recognising the force there might be in that, and he added: "Let her blaze out, let her look about her. Then you may talk to me if you like."

"It's very puzzling!" the old woman artlessly sighed.

He laughed again and then said: "Now don't tell me I'm not a good friend."

"You are indeed—you're a very noble gentleman. That's just why a quiet life with you——"

"It wouldn't be quiet for *me!*" he broke in. "And that's not what Miriam was made for."

"*Don't say that* for my precious one!" Mrs. Rooth quavered.

"Go to London—go to London," her visitor repeated.

Thoughtfully, after an instant, she extended her hand and took from the table the letter on the composition of which he had found her engaged. Then with a quick movement she tore it up. "That's what Mr. Dashwood says."

"Mr. Dashwood?"

"I forgot you don't know him. He's the brother of that lady we met the day you were so good as to receive us; the one who was so kind to us—Mrs. Lovick."

"I never heard of him."

"Don't you remember how she spoke of him and that Mr. Lovick didn't seem very nice about him? She told us that if he were to meet us—and she was so good as to intimate that it would be a pleasure to him to do so—he might give us, as she said, a tip."

Peter achieved the effort to recollect. "Yes he comes back to me. He's an actor."

"He's a gentleman too," said Mrs. Rooth.

"And you've met him, and he *has* given you a tip?"

"As I say, he wants us to go to London."

"I see, but even I can tell you that."

"Oh yes," said Mrs. Rooth; "but *he* says he can help us."

"Keep hold of him then, if he's in the business," Peter was all for that.

"He's a perfect gentleman," said Mrs. Rooth. "He's immensely struck with Miriam."

"Better and better. Keep hold of him."

"Well, I'm glad you don't object," she grimaced.

"Why should I object?"

"You don't regard us as *all* your own?"

"My own? Why, I regard you as the public's—the world's."

She gave a little shudder. "There's a sort of chill in that. It's grand, but it's cold. However, I needn't hesitate then to tell you that it's with Mr. Dashwood Miriam has gone out."

"Why hesitate, gracious heaven?" But in the next breath Sherringham asked: "Where have they gone?"

"You don't like it!" his hostess laughed.

"Why should it be a thing to be enthusiastic about?"

"Well, he's charming and *I* trust him."

"So do I," said Sherringham.

"They've gone to see Madame Carré."

"She has come back then?"

"She was expected back last week. Miriam wants to show her how she has improved."

"And *has* she improved?"

"How can I tell—with my mother's heart?" asked Mrs. Rooth. "I don't judge; I only wait and pray. But Mr. Dashwood thinks she's wonderful."

"That's a blessing. And when did he turn up?"

"About a fortnight ago. We met Mrs. Lovick at the English church, and she was so good as to recognise us and speak to us. She said she had been away with her children—otherwise she'd have come to see us. She had just returned to Paris."

"Yes, I've not yet seen her. I see Lovick," Peter added, "but he doesn't talk of his brother-in-law."

"I didn't, that day, like his tone about him," Mrs. Rooth observed. "We walked a little way with Mrs. Lovick after church and she asked Miriam about her prospects and if she were working. Miriam said she had no prospects."

"That wasn't very nice to me," Sherringham commented.

"But when you had left us in black darkness what *were* our prospects?"

"I see. It's all right. Go on."

"Then Mrs. Lovick said her brother was to be in Paris a few days and she would tell him to come and see us. He arrived, she told him and he came. *Voilà!*" said Mrs. Rooth.

"So that now—so far as *he* is concerned—Miss Rooth has prospects?"

"He isn't a manager unfortunately," she qualified.

"Where does he act?"

"He isn't acting just now; he has been abroad. He has been to Italy, I believe, and is just stopping here on his way to London."

"I see; he *is* a perfect gentleman," said Sherringham.

"Ah you're jealous of him!"

"No, but you're trying to make me so. The more competitors there are for the glory of bringing her out the better for her."

"Mr. Dashwood wants to take a theatre," said Mrs. Rooth.

"Then perhaps he's our man."

"Oh if you'd help him!" she richly cried.

"Help him?"

"Help him to help us."

"We'll all work together; it will be very jolly," said Sherringham gaily. "It's a sacred cause, the love of art, and we shall be a happy band. Dashwood's his name?" he added in a moment. "Mrs. Lovick wasn't a Dashwood."

"It's his *nom de théâtre*—Basil Dashwood. Do you like it?" Mrs. Rooth wonderfully inquired.

"You say that as Miriam might. Her talent's catching!"

"She's always practising—always saying things over and over to seize the tone. I've her voice in my ears. He wants *her* not to have any."

"Not to have any what?"

"Any *nom de théâtre*. He wants her to use her own; he likes it so much. He says it will do so well—you can't better it."

"He's a capital adviser," said Sherringham, getting up. "I'll come back to-morrow."

"I won't ask you to wait for them—they may be so long," his hostess returned.

"Will he come back with her?" Peter asked while he smoothed his hat.

"I hope so, at this hour. With my child in the streets I tremble. We don't live in cabs, as you may easily suppose."

"Did they go on foot?" Sherringham continued.

"Oh yes; they started in high spirits."

"And is Mr. Basil Dashwood acquainted with Madame Carré?"

"Ah no, but he longed to be introduced to her; he persuaded Miriam to take him. Naturally she wishes to oblige him. She's very nice to him—if he can do anything."

"Quite right; that's the way!" Peter cheerfully rang out.

"And she also wanted him to see what she can do for the great critic," Mrs. Rooth added—"that terrible old woman in the red wig."

"That's what I should like to see too," Peter permitted himself to acknowledge.

"Oh she has gone ahead; she's pleased with herself. 'Work, work, work,' said Madame Carré. Well, she has worked, worked, worked. That's what Mr. Dashwood is pleased with even more than with other things."

"What do you mean by other things?"

"Oh her genius and her fine appearance."

"He approves of her fine appearance? I ask because you think he knows what will take."

"I know why you ask!" Mrs. Rooth bravely mocked. "He says it will be worth hundreds of thousands to her."

"That's the sort of thing I like to hear," Peter returned. "I'll come in to-morrow," he repeated.

"And shall you mind if Mr. Dash wood's here?"

"Does he come every day?"

"Oh they're always at it."

"At it——?" He was vague.

"Why she acts to him—every sort of thing—and he says if it will do."

"How many days has he been here then?"

Mrs. Rooth reflected. "Oh I don't know! Since he turned up they've passed so quickly."

"So far from 'minding' it I'm eager to see him," Sherringham declared; "and I can imagine nothing better than what you describe—if he isn't an awful ass."

"Dear me, if he isn't clever you must tell us: we can't afford to be deceived!" Mrs. Rooth innocently wailed. "What do we know—how can we judge?" she appealed.

He had a pause, his hand on the latch. "Oh, I'll tell you frankly what I think of him!"

XIX

When he got into the street he looked about him for a cab, but was obliged to walk some distance before encountering one. In this little interval he saw no reason to modify the determination he had formed in descending the steep staircase of the Hôtel de la Garonne; indeed the desire prompting it only quickened his pace. He had an hour to spare and would also go to see Madame Carré. If Miriam and her companion had proceeded to the Rue de Constantinople on foot he would probably reach the house as soon as they. It was all quite logical: he was eager to see Miriam—that was natural enough; and he had admitted to Mrs. Rooth that he was keen on the subject of Mrs. Lovick's theatrical brother, in whom such effective aid might perhaps reside. To catch Miriam really revealing herself to the old actress after the jump she believed herself to have taken—since that was her errand—would be a very happy stroke, the thought of which made her benefactor impatient. He presently found his cab and, as he bounded in, bade the coachman drive fast. He learned from Madame Carré's portress that her illustrious *locataire* was at home and that a lady and a gentleman had gone up some time before.

In the little antechamber, after his admission, he heard a high voice come from the salon and, stopping a moment to listen, noted that Miriam was already launched in a recitation. He was able to make out the words, all the more that before he could prevent the movement the maid-servant who had led him in had already opened the door of the room—one of the leaves of it, there being, as in most French doors, two of these—before which, within, a heavy curtain was suspended. Miriam was in the act of rolling out some speech from the English poetic drama—

"For I am sick and capable of fears,

Oppressed with wrongs and therefore full of fears."

He recognised one of the great tirades of Shakespeare's Constance and saw she had just begun the magnificent scene at the beginning of the third act of *King John*, in which the passionate, injured mother and widow sweeps in wild organ-tones the entire scale of her irony and wrath. The curtain concealed him and he lurked three minutes after he had motioned to the *femme de chambre* to retire on tiptoe. The trio in the salon, absorbed in the performance, had apparently not heard his entrance or the opening of the door, which was covered by the girl's splendid declamation. Peter listened intently, arrested by the spirit with which she attacked her formidable verses. He had needed to hear her set afloat but a dozen of them to measure the long stride she had taken in his absence; they assured him she had leaped into possession of her means. He remained where he was till she arrived at

"Then speak again; not all thy former tale,

But this one word, whether thy tale be true."

This apostrophe, briefly responded to in another voice, gave him time quickly to raise the curtain and show himself, passing into the room with a "Go on, go on!" and a gesture earnestly deprecating a stop.

Miriam, in the full swing of her part, paused but for an instant and let herself ring out again, while Peter sank into the nearest chair and she fixed him with her illumined eyes, that is, with those of the raving Constance. Madame Carré, buried in a chair, kissed her hand to him, and a young man who, near the girl, stood giving the cue, stared at him over the top of a little book. "Admirable, magnificent, go on," Sherringham repeated—"go on to

267

the end of the scene, do it all!" Miriam's colour rose, yet he as quickly felt that she had no personal emotion in seeing him again; the cold passion of art had perched on her banner and she listened to herself with an ear as vigilant as if she had been a Paganini drawing a fiddle-bow. This effect deepened as she went on, rising and rising to the great occasion, moving with extraordinary ease and in the largest, clearest style at the dizzy height of her idea. That she had an idea was visible enough, and that the whole thing was very different from all Sherringham had hitherto heard her attempt. It belonged quite to another class of effort; she was now the finished statue lifted from the ground to its pedestal. It was as if the sun of her talent had risen above the hills and she knew she was moving and would always move in its guiding light. This conviction was the one artless thing that glimmered like a young joy through the tragic mask of Constance, and Sherringham's heart beat faster as he caught it in her face. It only showed her as more intelligent, and yet there had been a time when he thought her stupid! Masterful the whole spirit in which she carried the scene, making him cry to himself from point to point, "How she feels it, sees it and really 'renders' it!"

He looked now and again at Madame Carré and saw she had in her lap an open book, apparently a French prose version, brought by her visitors, of the play; but she never either glanced at him or at the volume: she only sat screwing into the girl her hard, bright eyes, polished by experience like fine old brasses. The young man uttering the lines of the other speakers was attentive in another degree; he followed Miriam, in his own copy, to keep sure of the cue; but he was elated and expressive, was evidently even surprised; he coloured and smiled, and when he extended his hand to assist Constance to rise, after the performer, acting out her text, had seated herself grandly on "the huge firm earth," he bowed over her as obsequiously as if she had been his veritable sovereign. He was a good-looking young man, tall, well-proportioned, straight-featured and fair, of whom manifestly the first thing to be said on any occasion was that he had remarkably the stamp of a gentleman. He earned this appearance, which proved inveterate and importunate, to a point that was almost a denial of its spirit: so prompt the question of whether it could be in good taste to wear any character, even that particular one, so much on one's sleeve. It was literally on his sleeve that this young man partly wore his own; for it resided considerably in his garments, and in especial in a certain close-fitting dark blue frock-coat, a miracle of a fit, which moulded his juvenility just enough and not too much, and constituted, as Sherringham was destined to perceive later, his perpetual uniform or badge. It was not till afterwards that Peter began to feel exasperated by Basil Dashwood's "type"—the young stranger was of course Basil Dashwood—and even by his blue frock-coat, the recurrent, unvarying, imperturbable good form of his aspect. This unprofessional air ended by striking the observer as the very profession he had adopted, and was indeed, so far as had as yet been indicated, his mimetic capital, his main qualification for the stage.

The ample and powerful manner in which Miriam handled her scene produced its full impression, the art with which she surmounted its difficulties, the liberality with which she met its great demand upon the voice, and the variety of expression that she threw into a torrent of objurgation. It was a real composition, studded with passages that called a suppressed tribute to the lips and seeming to show that a talent capable of such an exhibition was capable of anything.

> "But thou art fair, and at thy birth, dear boy,
>
> Nature and Fortune join'd to make thee great:
>
> Of Nature's gifts thou mayst with lilies boast,
>
> And with the half-blown rose."

As the girl turned to her imagined child with this exquisite apostrophe—she addressed Mr. Dashwood as if he were playing Arthur, and he lowered his book, dropped his head and his eyes and looked handsome and ingenuous—she opened at a stroke to Sherringham's vision a prospect that they would yet see her express tenderness better even than anything else. Her voice was enchanting in these lines, and the beauty of her performance was that though she uttered the full fury of the part she missed none of its poetry.

"Where did she get hold of that—where did she get hold of that?" Peter wondered while his whole sense vibrated. "She hadn't got hold of it when I went away." And the assurance flowed over him again that she had found the key to her box of treasures. In the summer, during their weeks of frequent meeting, she had only fumbled with the lock. One October day, while he was away, the key had slipped in, had fitted, or her finger at last had touched the right spring and the capricious casket had flown open.

It was during the present solemnity that, excited by the way she came out and with a hundred stirred ideas about her wheeling through his mind, he was for the first time and most vividly visited by a perception that ended by becoming frequent with him—that of the perfect presence of mind, unconfused, unhurried by emotion, that any artistic performance requires and that all, whatever the instrument, require in exactly the same degree: the application, in other words, clear and calculated, crystal-firm as it were, of the idea conceived in the glow of experience, of suffering, of joy. He was afterwards often to talk of this with Miriam, who, however, was never to be able to present him with a neat theory of the subject. She had no knowledge that it was publicly discussed; she only ranged herself in practice on the side of those who hold that at the moment of production the artist can't too much have his wits about him. When Peter named to her the opinion of those maintaining that at such a crisis the office of attention ceases to be filled she stared with surprise and then broke out: "Ah the poor idiots!" She eventually became, in her judgements, in impatience and the expression of contempt, very free and absolutely irreverent.

"What a splendid scolding!" the new visitor exclaimed when, on the entrance of the Pope's legate, her companion closed the book on the scene. Peter pressed his lips to Madame Carré's finger-tips; the old actress got up and held out her arms to Miriam. The girl never took her eyes off Sherringham while she passed into that lady's embrace and remained there. They were full of their usual sombre fire, and it was always the case that they expressed too much anything they could express at all; but they were not defiant nor even triumphant now—they were only deeply explicative. They seemed to say, "That's the sort of thing I meant; that's what I had in mind when I asked you to try to do something for me." Madame Carré folded her pupil to her bosom, holding her there as the old marquise in a *comédie de mœurs* might in the last scene have held her god-daughter the *ingénue*.

"Have you got me an engagement?"—the young woman then appealed eagerly to her friend. "Yes, he has done something splendid for me," she went on to Madame Carré, resting her hand caressingly on one of the actress's while the old woman discoursed with Mr. Dashwood, who was telling her in very pretty French that he was tremendously excited about Miss Rooth. Madame Carré looked at him as if she wondered how he appeared when he was calm and how, as a dramatic artist, he expressed that condition.

"Yes, yes, something splendid, for a beginning," Peter answered radiantly, recklessly; feeling now only that he would say anything and do anything to please her. He spent on the spot, in imagination, his last penny.

"It's such a pity you couldn't follow it; you'd have liked it so much better," Mr. Dashwood observed to their hostess.

"Couldn't follow it? Do you take me for *une sotte?*" the celebrated artist cried. "I suspect I followed it *de plus près que vous, monsieur!*"

"Ah you see the language is so awfully fine," Basil Dashwood replied, looking at his shoes.

"The language? Why she rails like a fish-wife. Is that what you call language? Ours is another business."

"If you understood, if you understood, you'd see all the greatness of it," Miriam declared. And then in another tone: "Such delicious expressions!"

"*On dit que c'est très-fort.* But who can tell if you really say it?" Madame Carré demanded.

"Ah, *par exemple*, I can!" Sherringham answered.

"Oh you—you're a Frenchman."

"Couldn't he make it out if he weren't?" asked Basil Dashwood.

The old woman shrugged her shoulders. "He wouldn't know."

"That's flattering to me."

"Oh you—don't you pretend to complain," Madame Carré said. "I prefer *our* imprecations—those of Camille," she went on. "They have the beauty *des plus belles choses*."

"I can say them too," Miriam broke in.

"*Insolente!*" smiled Madame Carré. "Camille doesn't squat down on the floor in the middle of them.

> "For grief is proud and makes his owner stoop.
>
> To me and to the state of my great grief
>
> Let kings assemble,"

Miriam quickly declaimed. "Ah if you don't feel the way she makes a throne of it!"

"It's really tremendously fine, *chère madame*," Sherringham said. "There's nothing like it."

"*Vous êtes insupportables*," the old woman answered. "Stay with us. I'll teach you Phèdre."

"Ah Phædra, Phædra!" Basil Dashwood vaguely ejaculated, looking more gentlemanly than ever.

"You've learned all I've taught you, but where the devil have you learned what I haven't?" Madame Carré went on.

"I've worked—I have; you'd call it work—all through the bright, late summer, all through the hot, dull, empty days. I've battered down the door—I did hear it crash one day. But I'm not so very good yet. I'm only in the right direction."

"*Malicieuse!*" growled Madame Carré.

"Oh I can beat that," the girl went on.

"Did you wake up one morning and find you had grown a pair of wings?" Peter asked. "Because that's what the difference amounts to—you really soar. Moreover, you're an angel," he added, charmed with her unexpectedness, the good nature of her forbearance to reproach him for not having written to her. And it seemed to him privately that she *was* angelic when in answer to this she said ever so blandly:

"You know you read *King John* with me before you went away. I thought over immensely what you said. I didn't understand it much at the time—I was so stupid. But it all came to me later."

"I wish you could see yourself," Peter returned.

"My dear fellow, I do. What sort of a dunce do you take me for? I didn't miss a vibration of my voice, a fold of my robe."

"Well, I didn't see you troubling about it," Peter handsomely insisted.

"No one ever will. Do you think I'd ever show it?"

"*Ars celare artem*," Basil Dashwood jocosely dropped.

"You must first have the art to hide," said Sherringham, wondering a little why Miriam didn't introduce her young friend to him. She was, however, both then and later perfectly neglectful of such cares, never thinking, never minding how other people got on together. When she found they didn't get on she jeered at them: that was the nearest she came to arranging for them. Our young man noted in her from the moment she felt her strength an immense increase of this good-humoured inattention to detail—all detail save that of her work, to which she was ready to sacrifice holocausts of feelings when the feelings were other people's. This conferred on her a large profanity, an absence of ceremony as to her social relations, which was both amusing because it suggested that she would take what she gave, and formidable because it was inconvenient and you mightn't care to give what she would take.

"If you haven't any art it's not quite the same as if you didn't hide it, is it?" Basil Dashwood ingeniously threw out.

"That's right—say one of your clever things!" Miriam sweetly responded.

"You're always acting," he declared in English and with a simple-minded laugh, while Sherringham remained struck with his expressing just what he himself had felt weeks before.

"And when you've shown them your fish-wife, to your public *de là-bas*, what will you do next?" asked Madame Carré.

"I'll do Juliet—I'll do Cleopatra."

"Rather a big bill, isn't it?" Mr. Dashwood volunteered to Sherringham in a friendly but discriminating manner.

"Constance and Juliet—take care you don't mix them," said Sherringham.

"I want to be various. You once told me I had a hundred characters," Miriam returned.

"Ah, *vous en êtes là?*" cried the old actress. "You may have a hundred characters, but you've only three plays. I'm told that's all there are in English."

Miriam, admirably indifferent to this charge, appealed to Peter. "What arrangements have you made? What do the people want?"

"The people at the theatre?"

"I'm afraid they don't want *King John*, and I don't believe they hunger for *Antony and Cleopatra*," Basil Dashwood suggested. "Ships and sieges and armies and pyramids, you know: we mustn't be too heavy."

"Oh I hate scenery!" the girl sighed.

"*Elle est superbe*," said Madame Carré. "You must put those pieces on the stage: how will you do it?"

"Oh we know how to get up a play in London, Madame Carré"—Mr. Dashwood was all geniality. "They put money on it, you know."

274

"On it? But what do they put *in* it? Who'll interpret them? Who'll manage a style like that—the style of which the rhapsodies she has just repeated are a specimen? Whom have you got that one has ever heard of?"

"Oh you'll hear of a good deal when once she gets started," Dashwood cheerfully contended.

Madame Carré looked at him a moment; then, "I feel that you'll become very bad," she said to Miriam. "I'm glad I shan't see it."

"People will do things for me—I'll make them," the girl declared. "I'll stir them up so that they'll have ideas."

"What people, pray?"

"Ah terrible woman!" Peter theatrically groaned.

"We translate your pieces—there will be plenty of parts," Basil Dashwood said.

"Why then go out of the door to come in at the window?—especially if you smash it! An English arrangement of a French piece is a pretty woman with her back turned."

"Do you really want to keep her?" Sherringham asked of Madame Carré—quite as if thinking for a moment that this after all might be possible.

She bent her strange eyes on him. "No, you're all too queer together. We couldn't be bothered with you and you're not worth it."

"I'm glad it's 'together' that we're queer then—we can console each other."

"If you only would; but you don't seem to! In short I don't understand you—I give you up. But it doesn't matter," said the old woman wearily, "for the theatre's dead and even you, *ma toute-belle*, won't bring it to life. Everything's going from bad to worse, and I don't care what becomes of you. You wouldn't understand us here and they won't understand you there, and everything's impossible, and no one's a whit the wiser, and it's not of the least consequence. Only when you raise your arms lift them just a little higher," Madame Carré added.

"My mother will be happier *chez nous*" said Miriam, throwing her arms straight up and giving them a noble tragic movement.

"You won't be in the least in the right path till your mother's in despair."

"Well, perhaps we can bring that about even in London," Sherringham patiently laughed.

"Dear Mrs. Rooth—she's great fun," Mr. Dashwood as imperturbably dropped.

Miriam transferred the dark weight of her gaze to him as if she were practising. "*You* won't upset her, at any rate." Then she stood with her beautiful and fatal mask before her hostess. "I want to do the modern too. I want to do *le drame*, with intense realistic effects."

"And do you want to look like the portico of the Madeleine when it's draped for a funeral?" her instructress mocked. "Never, never. I don't believe you're various: that's not the way I see you. You're pure tragedy, with *de grands éclats de voix* in the great style, or you're nothing."

"Be beautiful—be only that," Peter urged with high interest. "Be only what you can be so well—something that one may turn to for a glimpse of perfection, to lift one out of all the vulgarities of the day."

Thus apostrophised the girl broke out with one of the speeches of Racine's Phædra, hushing her companions on the instant. "You'll be the English Rachel," said Basil Dashwood when she stopped.

"Acting in French!" Madame Carré amended. "I don't believe in an English Rachel."

"I shall have to work it out, what I shall be," Miriam concluded with a rich pensive effect.

"You're in wonderfully good form to-day," Sherringham said to her; his appreciation revealing a personal subjection he was unable to conceal from his companions, much as he wished it.

"I really mean to do everything."

276

"Very well; after all Garrick did."

"Then I shall be the Garrick of my sex."

"There's a very clever author doing something for me; I should like you to see it," said Basil Dashwood, addressing himself equally to Miriam and to her diplomatic friend.

"Ah if you've very clever authors——!" And Madame Carré spun the sound to the finest satiric thread.

"I shall be very happy to see it," Peter returned.

This response was so benevolent that Basil Dashwood presently began: "May I ask you at what theatre you've made arrangements?"

Sherringham looked at him a moment. "Come and see me at the embassy and I'll tell you." Then he added: "I know your sister, Mrs. Lovick."

"So I supposed: that's why I took the liberty of asking such a question."

"It's no liberty, but Mr. Sherringham doesn't appear to be able to tell you," said Miriam.

"Well, you know, it's a very curious world, all those theatrical people over there," Peter conceded.

"Ah don't say anything against them when I'm one of them," Basil Dashwood laughed.

"I might plead the absence of information," Peter returned, "as Miss Rooth has neglected to make us acquainted."

Miriam vaguely smiled. "I know you both so little." But she presented them with a great stately air to each other, and the two men shook hands while Madame Carré observed them.

"*Tiens*! you gentlemen meet here for the first time? You do right to become friends—that's the best thing. Live together in peace and mutual confidence. *C'est de beaucoup le plus sage.*"

277

"Certainly, for yoke-fellows," said Sherringham.

He began the next moment to repeat to his new acquaintance some of the things he had been told in London; but their hostess stopped him off, waving the talk away with charming overdone stage horror and the young hands of the heroines of Marivaux. "Ah wait till you go—for that! Do you suppose I care for news of your mountebanks' booths?"

XX

As many people know, there are not, in the famous Théâtre Français, more than a dozen good seats accessible to ladies.[*] The stalls are forbidden them, the boxes are a quarter of a mile from the stage and the balcony is a delusion save for a few chairs at either end of its vast horseshoe. But there are two excellent *baignoires d'avant-scène*, which indeed are by no means always to be had. It was, however, into one of them that, immediately after his return to Paris, Sherringham ushered Mrs. Rooth and her daughter, with the further escort of Basil Dashwood. He had chosen the evening of the reappearance of the celebrated Mademoiselle Voisin—she had been enjoying a *congé* of three months—an actress whom Miriam had seen several times before and for whose method she professed a high though somewhat critical esteem. It was only for the return of this charming performer that Peter had been waiting to respond to Miriam's most ardent wish—that of spending an hour in the *foyer des artistes* of the great theatre. She was the person whom he knew best in the house of Molière; he could count on her to do them the honours some night when she was in the "bill," and to make the occasion sociable. Miriam had been impatient for it—she was so convinced that her eyes would be opened in the holy of holies; but wishing as particularly as he did to participate in her impression he had made her promise she wouldn't taste of this experience without him—not let Madame Carré, for instance, take her in his absence. There were questions the girl wished to put to Mademoiselle Voisin—questions which, having admired her from the balcony, she felt she was exactly the person to answer. She was more "in it" now, after all, than

Madame Carré, in spite of her slenderer talent: she was younger, fresher, more modern and—Miriam found the word—less academic. She was in fine less "*vieux jeu*." Peter perfectly foresaw the day when his young friend would make indulgent allowances for poor Madame Carré, patronising her as an old woman of good intentions.

[*: 1890]

The play to-night was six months old, a large, serious, successful comedy by the most distinguished of authors, with a thesis, a chorus embodied in one character, a *scène à faire* and a part full of opportunities for Mademoiselle Voisin. There were things to be said about this artist, strictures to be dropped as to the general quality of her art, and Miriam leaned back now, making her comments as if they cost her less, but the actress had knowledge and distinction and pathos, and our young lady repeated several times: "How quiet she is, how wonderfully quiet! Scarcely anything moves but her face and her voice. *Le geste rare*, but really expressive when it comes. I like that economy; it's the only way to make the gesture significant."

"I don't admire the way she holds her arms," Basil Dash wood said: "like a *demoiselle de magasin* trying on a jacket."

"Well, she holds them at any rate. I daresay it's more than you do with yours."

"Oh yes, she holds them; there's no mistake about that. 'I hold them, I hope, *hein*?' she seems to say to all the house." The young English professional laughed good-humouredly, and Sherringham was struck with the pleasant familiarity he had established with their brave companion. He was knowing and ready and he said in the first *entr'acte*—they were waiting for the second to go behind—amusing perceptive things. "They teach them to be ladylike and Voisin's always trying to show that. 'See how I walk, see how I sit, see how quiet I am and how I have *le geste rare*. Now can you say I ain't a lady?' She does it all as if she had a class."

"Well, to-night I'm her class," said Miriam.

"Oh I don't mean of actresses, but of *femmes du monde*. She shows them how to act in society."

"You had better take a few lessons," Miriam retorted.

"Ah you should see Voisin in society," Peter interposed.

"Does she go into it?" Mrs. Rooth demanded with interest.

Her friend hesitated. "She receives a great many people."

"Why shouldn't they when they're nice?" Mrs. Rooth frankly wanted to know.

"When the people are nice?" Miriam asked.

"Now don't tell me she's not what one would wish," said Mrs. Rooth to Sherringham.

"It depends on what that is," he darkly smiled.

"What I should wish if she were my daughter," the old woman rejoined blandly.

"Ah wish your daughter to act as well as that and you'll do the handsome thing for her!"

"Well, she *seems* to feel what she says," Mrs. Rooth piously risked.

"She has some stiff things to say. I mean about her past," Basil Dashwood remarked. "The past—the dreadful past—on the stage!"

"Wait till the end, to see how she comes out. We must all be merciful!" sighed Mrs. Rooth.

"We've seen it before; you know what happens," Miriam observed to her mother.

"I've seen so many I get them mixed."

"Yes, they're all in queer predicaments. Poor old mother—what we show you!" laughed the girl.

"Ah it will be what *you* show me—something noble and wise!"

"I want to do this; it's a magnificent part," said Miriam.

"You couldn't put it on in London—they wouldn't swallow it," Basil Dashwood declared.

"Aren't there things they do there to get over the difficulties?" the girl inquired.

"You can't get over what *she did*!"—her companion had a rueful grimace.

"Yes, we must pay, we must expiate!" Mrs. Rooth moaned as the curtain rose again.

When the second act was over our friends passed out of their *baignoire* into those corridors of tribulation where the bristling *ouvreuse*, like a pawnbroker driving a roaring trade, mounts guard upon piles of heterogeneous clothing, and, gaining the top of the fine staircase which forms the state entrance and connects the statued vestibule of the basement with the grand tier of boxes, opened an ambiguous door composed of little mirrors and found themselves in the society of the initiated. The janitors were courteous folk who greeted Sherringham as an acquaintance, and he had no difficulty in marshalling his little troop toward the foyer. They traversed a low, curving lobby, hung with pictures and furnished with velvet-covered benches where several unrecognised persons of both sexes looked at them without hostility, and arrived at an opening, on the right, from which, by a short flight of steps, there was a descent to one of the wings of the stage. Here Miriam paused, in silent excitement, like a young warrior arrested by a glimpse of the battle-field. Her vision was carried off through a lane of light to the point of vantage from which the actor held the house; but there was a hushed guard over the place and curiosity could only glance and pass.

Then she came with her companions to a sort of parlour with a polished floor, not large and rather vacant, where her attention flew delightedly to a coat-tree, in a corner, from which three or four dresses were suspended—dresses she immediately perceived to be costumes in that night's play—accompanied by a saucer of something and a much-worn powder-puff casually left on a sofa. This was a familiar note in the general impression of high decorum which had begun at the threshold—a sense of majesty in the place. Miriam rushed at the powder-puff—there was no one in the room—

snatched it up and gazed at it with droll veneration, then stood rapt a moment before the charming petticoats ("That's Dunoyer's first underskirt," she said to her mother) while Sherringham explained that in this apartment an actress traditionally changed her gown when the transaction was simple enough to save the long ascent to her *loge*. He felt himself a cicerone showing a church to a party of provincials; and indeed there was a grave hospitality in the air, mingled with something academic and important, the tone of an institution, a temple, which made them all, out of respect and delicacy, hold their breath a little and tread the shining floors with discretion.

These precautions increased—Mrs. Rooth crept about like a friendly but undomesticated cat—after they entered the foyer itself, a square, spacious saloon covered with pictures and relics and draped in official green velvet, where the *genius loci* holds a reception every night in the year. The effect was freshly charming to Peter; he was fond of the place, always saw it again with pleasure, enjoyed its honourable look and the way, among the portraits and scrolls, the records of a splendid history, the green velvet and the waxed floors, the *genius loci* seemed to be "at home" in the quiet lamplight. At the end of the room, in an ample chimney, blazed a fire of logs. Miriam said nothing; they looked about, noting that most of the portraits and pictures were "old-fashioned," and Basil Dashwood expressed disappointment at the absence of all the people they wanted most to see. Three or four gentlemen in evening dress circulated slowly, looking, like themselves, at the pictures, and another gentleman stood before a lady, with whom he was in conversation, seated against the wall. The foyer resembled in these conditions a ball-room, cleared for the dance, before the guests or the music had arrived.

"Oh it's enough to see *this*; it makes my heart beat," said Miriam. "It's full of the vanished past, it makes me cry. I feel them here, all, the great artists I shall never see. Think of Rachel—look at her grand portrait there!—and how she stood on these very boards and trailed over them the robes of Hermione and Phèdre." The girl broke out theatrically, as on the spot was right, not a bit afraid of her voice as soon as it rolled through the room; appealing to her companions as they stood under the chandelier and making the other persons present, who had already given her some attention, turn round to stare at so unusual a specimen of the English miss. She laughed, musically, when she noticed this, and her mother, scandalised, begged her to lower her tone. "It's all right. I produce an effect," said Miriam: "it shan't be said that I too haven't had my little success in the maison de Molière." And Sherringham repeated that it was all right—the place was familiar with mirth and passion, there was often wonderful talk there, and it was only the setting that was still and solemn. It happened that this evening—there was no knowing in advance—the scene was not characteristically brilliant; but to confirm his assertion, at the moment he spoke, Mademoiselle Dunoyer, who was also in the play, came into the room attended by a pair of gentlemen.

She was the celebrated, the perpetual, the necessary *ingénue*, who with all her talent couldn't have represented a woman of her actual age. She had the gliding, hopping movement of a small bird, the same air of having nothing to do with time, and the clear, sure, piercing note, a miracle of exact vocalisation. She chaffed her companions, she chaffed the room; she might have been a very clever little girl trying to personate a more innocent big one. She scattered her amiability about—showing Miriam how the children of Molière took their ease—and it quickly placed her in the friendliest communication with Peter Sherringham, who already enjoyed her acquaintance and who now extended it to his companions, and in particular to the young lady *sur le point d'entrer au théâtre.*

"You deserve a happier lot," said the actress, looking up at Miriam brightly, as if to a great height, and taking her in; upon which Sherringham left them together a little and led Mrs. Rooth and young Dashwood to consider further some of the pictures.

"Most delightful, most curious," the old woman murmured about everything; while Basil Dashwood exclaimed in the presence of most of the portraits: "But their ugliness—their ugliness: did you ever see such a collection of hideous people? And those who were supposed to be good-looking—the beauties of the past—they're worse than the others. Ah you may say what you will, *nous sommes mieux que ça!*" Sherringham suspected him of irritation, of not liking the theatre of the great rival nation to be thrust down his throat. They returned to Miriam and Mademoiselle Dunoyer, and

Peter asked the actress a question about one of the portraits to which there was no name attached. She replied, like a child who had only played about the room, that she was *toute honteuse* not to be able to tell him the original: she had forgotten, she had never asked—"*Vous allez me trouver bien légère!*" She appealed to the other persons present, who formed a gallery for her, and laughed in delightful ripples at their suggestions, which she covered with ridicule. She bestirred herself; she declared she would ascertain, she shouldn't be happy till she did, and swam out of the room, with the prettiest paddles, to obtain the information, leaving behind her a perfume of delicate kindness and gaiety. She seemed above all things obliging, and Peter pronounced her almost as natural off the stage as on. She didn't come back.

XXI

Whether he had prearranged it is more than I can say, but Mademoiselle Voisin delayed so long to show herself that Mrs. Rooth, who wished to see the rest of the play, though she had sat it out on another occasion, expressed a returning relish for her corner of the *baignoire* and gave her conductor the best pretext he could have desired for asking Basil Dashwood to be so good as to escort her back. When the young actor, of whose personal preference Peter was quite aware, had led Mrs. Rooth away with an absence of moroseness which showed that his striking resemblance to a gentleman was not kept for the footlights, the two others sat on a divan in the part of the room furthest from the entrance, so that it gave them a degree of privacy, and Miriam watched the coming and going of their fellow-visitors and the indefinite people, attached to the theatre, hanging about, while her companion gave a name to some of the figures, Parisian celebrities.

"Fancy poor Dashwood cooped up there with mamma!" the girl exclaimed whimsically.

"You're awfully cruel to him; but that's of course," said Sherringham.

"It seems to me I'm as kind as you; you sent him off."

"That was for your mother; she was tired."

"Oh gammon! And why, if I *were* cruel, should it be of course?"

"Because you must destroy and torment and wear out—that's your nature. But you can't help your type, can you?"

"My type?" she echoed.

"It's bad, perverse, dangerous. It's essentially insolent."

"And pray what's yours when you talk like that? Would you say such things if you didn't know the depths of my good nature?"

"Your good nature all comes back to that," said Sherringham. "It's an abyss of ruin—for others. You've no respect. I'm speaking of the artistic character—in the direction and in the plentitude in which you have it. It's unscrupulous, nervous, capricious, wanton."

"I don't know about respect. One can be good," Miriam mused and reasoned.

"It doesn't matter so long as one's powerful," he returned. "We can't have everything, and surely we ought to understand that we must pay for things. A splendid organisation for a special end, like yours, is so rare and rich and fine that we oughtn't to grudge it its conditions."

"What do you call its conditions?" Miriam asked as she turned and looked at him.

"Oh the need to take its ease, to take up space, to make itself at home in the world, to square its elbows and knock, others about. That's large and free; it's the good nature you speak of. You must forage and ravage and leave a track behind you; you must live upon the country you traverse. And you give such delight that, after all, you're welcome—you're infinitely welcome!"

"I don't know what you mean. I only care for the idea," the girl said.

"That's exactly what I pretend—and we must all help you to it. You use us, you push us about, you break us up. We're your tables and chair, the simple furniture of your life."

"Whom do you mean by 'we'?"

Peter gave an ironic laugh. "Oh don't be afraid—there will be plenty of others!"

She made no return to this, but after a moment broke out again. "Poor Dashwood immured with mamma—he's like a lame chair that one has put into the corner."

"Don't break him up before he has served. I really believe something will come out of him," her companion went on. "However, you'll break me up first," he added, "and him probably never at all."

"And why shall I honour you so much more?"

"Because I'm a better article and you'll feel that."

"You've the superiority of modesty—I see."

"I'm better than a young mountebank—I've vanity enough to say that."

She turned on him with a flush in her cheek and a splendid dramatic face. "How you hate us! Yes, at bottom, below your little cold taste, you *hate* us!" she repeated.

He coloured too, met her eyes, looked into them a minute, seemed to accept the imputation and then said quickly: "Give it up: come away with me."

"Come away with you?"

"Leave this place. Give it up."

"You brought me here, you insisted it should be only you, and now you must stay," she declared with a head-shake and a high manner. "You should know what you want, dear Mr. Sherringham."

"I do—I know now. Come away before you see her."

"Before——?" she seemed to wonder.

"She's success, this wonderful Voisin, she's triumph, she's full accomplishment: the hard, brilliant realisation of what I want to avert for you." Miriam looked at him in silence, the cold light still in her face, and he repeated: "Give it up—give it up."

Her eyes softened after a little; she smiled and then said: "Yes, you're better than poor Dashwood."

"Give it up and we'll live for ourselves, in ourselves, in something that can have a sanctity."

"All the same you do hate us," the girl went on.

"I don't want to be conceited, but I mean that I'm sufficiently fine and complicated to tempt you. I'm an expensive modern watch with a wonderful escapement—therefore you'll smash me if you can."

"Never—never!" she said as she got up. "You tell me the hour too well." She quitted her companion and stood looking at Gérôme's fine portrait of the pale Rachel invested with the antique attributes of tragedy. The rise of the curtain had drawn away most of the company. Peter, from his bench, watched his friend a little, turning his eyes from her to the vivid image of the dead actress and thinking how little she suffered by the juxtaposition. Presently he came over and joined her again and she resumed: "I wonder if that's what your cousin had in his mind."

"My cousin——?"

"What was his name? Mr. Dormer; that first day at Madame Carré's. He offered to paint my portrait."

"I remember. I put him up to it."

"Was he thinking of this?"

"I doubt if he has ever seen it. I daresay I was."

"Well, when we go to London he must do it," said Miriam.

"Oh there's no hurry," Peter was moved to reply.

287

"Don't you want my picture?" asked the girl with one of her successful touches.

"I'm not sure I want it from *him*. I don't know quite what he'd make of you."

"He looked so clever—I liked him. I saw him again at your party."

"He's a jolly good fellow; but what's one to say," Peter put to her, "of a painter who goes for his inspiration to the House of Commons?"

"To the House of Commons?" she echoed.

"He has lately got himself elected."

"Dear me, what a pity! I wanted to sit for him. But perhaps he won't have me—as I'm not a member of Parliament."

"It's my sister, rather, who has got him in."

"Your sister who was at your house that day? What has she to do with it?" Miriam asked.

"Why she's his cousin just as I am. And in addition," Sherringham went on, "she's to be married to him."

"Married—really?" She had a pause, but she continued. "So he paints *her*, I suppose?"

"Not much, probably. His talent in that line isn't what she esteems in him most."

"It isn't great, then?"

"I haven't the least idea."

"And in the political line?" the girl persisted.

"I scarcely can tell. He's very clever."

"He does paint decently, then?"

"I daresay."

Miriam looked once more at Gérôme's picture. "Fancy his going into the House of Commons! And your sister put him there?"

"She worked, she canvassed."

"Ah you're a queer family!" she sighed, turning round at the sound of a step.

"We're lost—here's Mademoiselle Voisin," said Sherringham.

This celebrity presented herself smiling and addressing Miriam. "I acted for *you* to-night—I did my best."

"What a pleasure to speak to you, to thank you!" the girl murmured admiringly. She was startled and dazzled.

"I couldn't come to you before, but now I've got a rest—for half an hour," the actress went on. Gracious and passive, as if a little spent, she let Sherringham, without looking at him, take her hand and raise it to his lips. "I'm sorry I make you lose the others—they're so good in this act," she added.

"We've seen them before and there's nothing so good as you," Miriam promptly returned.

"I like my part," said Mademoiselle Voisin gently, smiling still at our young lady with clear, charming eyes. "One's always better in that case."

"She's so bad sometimes, you know!" Peter jested to Miriam; leading the actress thus to glance at him, kindly and vaguely, in a short silence which you couldn't call on her part embarrassment, but which was still less affectation.

"And it's so interesting to be here—so interesting!" Miriam protested.

"Ah you like our old house? Yes, we're very proud of it." And Mademoiselle Voisin smiled again at Sherringham all good-humouredly, but as if to say: "Well, here I am, and what do you want of me? Don't ask me to invent it myself, but if you'll tell me I'll do it." Miriam admired the note of discreet interrogation in her voice—the slight suggestion of surprise at their "old house" being liked. This performer was an astonishment from her seeming still more perfect on a nearer view—which was not, the girl had an idea, what performers usually did. This was very encouraging to her—it widened the programme of a young lady about to embrace the scenic career. To have so much to show before the footlights and yet to have so much left when you came off—that was really wonderful. Mademoiselle Voisin's eyes, as one looked into them, were still more agreeable than the distant spectator would have supposed; and there was in her appearance an extreme finish which instantly suggested to Miriam that she herself, in comparison, was big and rough and coarse.

"You're lovely to-night—you're particularly lovely," Sherringham said very frankly, translating Miriam's own impression and at the same time giving her an illustration of the way that, in Paris at least, gentlemen expressed themselves to the stars of the drama. She thought she knew her companion very well and had been witness of the degree to which, in such general conditions, his familiarity could increase; but his address to the slim, distinguished, harmonious woman before them had a different quality, the note of a special usage. If Miriam had had an apprehension that such directness might be taken as excessive it was removed by the manner in which Mademoiselle Voisin returned:

"Oh one's always well enough when one's made up; one's always exactly the same." That served as an example of the good taste with which a star of the drama could receive homage that was wanting in originality. Miriam determined on the spot that this should be the way *she* would ever receive it. The grace of her new acquaintance was the greater as the becoming bloom to which she alluded as artificial was the result of a science so consummate that it had none of the grossness of a mask. The perception of all this was exciting to our young aspirant, and her excitement relieved itself in the inquiry, which struck her as rude as soon as she had uttered it:

"You acted for 'me'? How did you know? What am I to you?"

"Monsieur Sherringham has told me about you. He says we're nothing beside you—that you're to be the great star of the future. I'm proud that you've seen me."

"That of course is what I tell every one," Peter acknowledged a trifle awkwardly to Miriam.

"I can believe it when I see you. *Je vous ai bien observée,*" the actress continued in her sweet conciliatory tone.

Miriam looked from one of her interlocutors to the other as if there were joy for her in this report of Sherringham's remarks—joy accompanied and partly mitigated, however, by a quicker vision of what might have passed between a secretary of embassy and a creature so exquisite as Mademoiselle Voisin. "Ah you're wonderful people—a most interesting impression!" she yearningly sighed.

"I was looking for you; he had prepared me. We're such old friends!" said the actress in a tone courteously exempt from intention: upon which Sherringham, again taking her hand, raised it to his lips with a tenderness which her whole appearance seemed to bespeak for her, a sort of practical consideration and carefulness of touch, as if she were an object precious and frail, an instrument for producing rare sounds, to be handled, like a legendary violin, with a recognition of its value.

"Your dressing-room is so pretty—show her your dressing-room," he went on.

"Willingly, if she'll come up. *Vous savez que c'est une montée.*"

"It's a shame to inflict it on *you,*" Miriam objected.

"*Comment donc?* If it will interest you in the least!" They exchanged civilities, almost caresses, trying which could have the nicest manner to the other. It was the actress's manner that struck Miriam most; it denoted such a training, so much taste, expressed such a ripe conception of urbanity.

"No wonder she acts well when she has that tact—feels, perceives, is so remarkable, *mon Dieu, mon Dieu!*" the girl said to herself as they followed their conductress into another corridor and up a wide, plain staircase. The staircase was spacious and long and this part of the establishment sombre and still, with the gravity of a college or a convent. They reached another passage lined with little doors, on each of which the name of a comedian was painted, and here the aspect became still more monastic, like that of a row of solitary cells. Mademoiselle Voisin led the way to her own door all obligingly and as if wishing to be hospitable; she dropped little subdued, friendly attempts at explanation on the way. At her threshold the monasticism stopped—Miriam found herself in a wonderfully upholstered nook, a nest of lamplight and delicate cretonne. Save for its pair of long glasses it might have been a tiny boudoir, with a water-colour drawing of value in each of its panels of stretched stuff, with its crackling fire and its charming order. It was intensely bright and extremely hot, singularly pretty and exempt from litter. Nothing lay about, but a small draped doorway led into an inner sanctuary. To Miriam it seemed royal; it immediately made the art of the comedian the most distinguished thing in the world. It was just such a place as they *should* have for their intervals if they were expected to be great artists. It was a result of the same evolution as Mademoiselle Voisin herself—not that our young lady found this particular term at hand to express her idea. But her mind was flooded with an impression of style, of refinement, of the long continuity of a tradition. The actress said, *"Voilà, c'est tout!"* as if it were little enough and there were even something clumsy in her having brought them so far for nothing, and in their all sitting there waiting and looking at each other till it was time for her to change her dress. But to Miriam it was occupation enough to note what she did and said: these things and her whole person and carriage struck our young woman as exquisite in their adaptation to the particular occasion. She had had an idea that foreign actresses were rather of the *cabotin* order, but her hostess suggested to her much more a princess than a *cabotine*. She would do things as she liked and do them straight off: Miriam couldn't fancy her in the gropings and humiliations of rehearsal. Everything in her had been sifted and formed, her tone was perfect, her amiability complete, and she might have been the charming young wife of a secretary of state receiving a pair of strangers of distinction. The girl observed all her movements. And then, as Sherringham had said, she was particularly lovely. But she suddenly told this gentleman that she must put him *à la porte*—she wanted to change her dress. He retired and returned to the foyer, where Miriam was to rejoin him after remaining the few minutes more with Mademoiselle Voisin and coming down with her. He waited for his companion, walking up and down and making up his mind; and when she presently came in he said to her:

"Please don't go back for the rest of the play. Stay here." They now had the foyer virtually to themselves.

"I want to stay here. I like it better," She moved back to the chimney-piece, from above which the cold portrait of Rachel looked down, and as he accompanied her he went on:

"I meant what I said just now."

"What you said to Voisin?"

"No, no; to you. Give it up and live with *me.*"

"Give it up?" She turned her stage face on him.

"Give it up and I'll marry you to-morrow."

"This is a happy time to ask it!" she said with superior amusement. "And this is a good place!"

"Very good indeed, and that's why I speak: it's a place to make one choose—it puts it all before one."

"To make *you* choose, you mean. I'm much obliged, but that's not my choice," laughed Miriam.

"You shall be anything you like except this."

"Except what I most want to be? I *am* much obliged."

"Don't you care for me? Haven't you any gratitude?" Sherringham insisted.

"Gratitude for kindly removing the blest cup from my lips? I want to be what *she* is—I want it more than ever."

"Ah what she is—!" He took it impatiently.

"Do you mean I can't? Well see if I can't. Tell me more about her—tell me everything."

"Haven't you seen for yourself and, knowing things as you do, can't you judge?"

"She's strange, she's mysterious," Miriam allowed, looking at the fire. "She showed us nothing—nothing of her real self."

"So much the better, all things considered."

"Are there all sorts of other things in her life? That's what I believe," the girl went on, raising her eyes to him.

"I can't tell you what there is in the life of such a woman."

"Imagine—when she's so perfect!" she exclaimed thoughtfully. "Ah she kept me off—she kept me off! Her charming manner is in itself a kind of contempt. It's an abyss—it's the wall of China. She has a hard polish, an inimitable surface, like some wonderful porcelain that costs more than you'd think."

"Do you want to become like that?" Sherringham asked.

"If I could I should be enchanted. One can always try."

"You must act better than she," he went on.

"Better? I thought you wanted me to give it up."

"Ah I don't know what I want," he cried, "and you torment me and turn me inside out! What I want is you yourself."

"Oh don't worry," said Miriam—now all kindly. Then she added that Mademoiselle Voisin had invited her to "call"; to which Sherringham replied with a certain dryness that she would probably not find that necessary. This made the girl stare and she asked: "Do you mean it won't do on account of mamma's prejudices?"

"Say this time on account of mine."

"Do you mean because she has lovers?"

"Her lovers are none of our business."

"None of mine, I see. So you've been one of them?"

"No such luck!"

"What a pity!" she richly wailed. "I should have liked to see that. One must see everything—to be able to do everything." And as he pressed for what in particular she had wished to see she replied: "The way a woman like that receives one of the old ones."

Peter gave a groan at this, which was at the same time partly a laugh, and, turning away to drop on a bench, ejaculated: "You'll do—you'll do!"

He sat there some minutes with his elbows on his knees and his face in his hands. His friend remained looking at the portrait of Rachel, after which she put to him: "Doesn't such a woman as that receive—receive every one?"

"Every one who goes to see her, no doubt."

"And who goes?"

"Lots of men—clever men, eminent men."

"Ah what a charming life! Then doesn't she go out?"

"Not what we Philistines mean by that—not into society, never. She never enters a lady's drawing-room."

"How strange, when one's as distinguished as that; except that she must escape a lot of stupidities and *corvées*. Then where does she learn such manners?"

"She teaches manners, *à ses heures*: she doesn't need to learn them."

"Oh she has given me ideas! But in London actresses go into society," Miriam continued.

"Oh into ours, such as it is. In London *nous mêlons les genres*."

"And shan't I go—I mean if I want?"

"You'll have every facility to bore yourself. Don't doubt it."

"And doesn't she feel excluded?" Miriam asked.

"Excluded from what? She has the fullest life."

"The fullest?"

"An intense artistic life. The cleverest men in Paris talk over her work with her; the principal authors of plays discuss with her subjects and characters and questions of treatment. She lives in the world of art."

"Ah the world of art—how I envy her! And you offer me Dashwood!"

Sherringham rose in his emotion. "I 'offer' you—?"

Miriam burst out laughing. "You look so droll! You offer me yourself, then, instead of all these things."

"My dear child, I also am a very clever man," he said, trying to sink his consciousness of having for a moment stood gaping.

"You are—you are; I delight in you. No ladies at all—no *femmes comme il faut?*" she began again.

"Ah what do *they* matter? Your business is the artistic life!" he broke out with inconsequence, irritated, moreover, at hearing her sound that trivial note again.

"You're a dear—your charming good sense comes back to you! What do you want of me, then?"

"I want you for myself—not for others; and now, in time, before anything's done."

"Why, then, did you bring me here? Everything's done—I feel it to-night."

"I know the way you should look at it—if you do look at it at all," Sherringham conceded.

"That's so easy! I thought you liked the stage so," Miriam artfully added.

"Don't you want me to be a great swell?"

"And don't you want *me* to be?"

"You *will* be—you'll share my glory."

"So will you share mine."

"The husband of an actress? Yes, I see myself that!" Peter cried with a frank ring of disgust.

"It's a silly position, no doubt. But if you're too good for it why talk about it? Don't you think I'm important?" she demanded. Her companion met her eyes and she suddenly said in a different tone: "Ah why should we quarrel when you've been so kind, so generous? Can't we always be friends—the truest friends?"

Her voice sank to the sweetest cadence and her eyes were grateful and good as they rested on him. She sometimes said things with such perfection that they seemed dishonest, but in this case he was stirred to an expressive response. Just as he was making it, however, he was moved to utter other words: "Take care, here's Dashwood!" Mrs. Rooth's tried attendant was in the doorway. He had come back to say that they really must relieve him.

BOOK FIFTH

XXII

Mrs. Dallow came up to London soon after the meeting of Parliament; she made no secret of the fact that she was fond of "town" and that in present conditions it would of course not have become less attractive to her. But she prepared to retreat again for the Easter vacation, not to go back to Harsh, but to pay a couple of country visits. She did not, however, depart with the crowd—she never did anything with the crowd—but waited till the Monday after Parliament rose; facing with composure, in Great Stanhope Street, the horrors, as she had been taught to consider them, of a Sunday out of the session. She had done what she could to mitigate them by asking a handful of "stray men" to dine with her that evening. Several members of this disconsolate class sought comfort in Great Stanhope Street in the afternoon, and them for the most part she also invited to return at eight o'clock. There were accordingly almost too many people at dinner; there were even a couple of wives. Nick Dormer was then present, though he had not been in the afternoon. Each of the other persons had said on coming in, "So you've not gone—I'm awfully glad." Mrs. Dallow had replied, "No, I've not gone," but she had in no case added that she was glad, nor had she offered an explanation. She never offered explanations; she always assumed that no one could invent them so well as those who had the florid taste to desire them.

And in this case she was right, since it is probable that few of her visitors failed to say to themselves that her not having gone would have had something to do with Dormer. That could pass for an explanation with many of Mrs. Dallow's friends, who as a general thing were not morbidly analytic; especially with those who met Nick as a matter of course at dinner. His figuring at this lady's entertainments, being in her house whenever a candle was lighted, was taken as a sign that there was something rather particular between them. Nick had said to her more than once that people would wonder why they didn't marry; but he was wrong in this, inasmuch as there were many of their friends to whom it wouldn't have occurred that his position could be improved. That they were cousins was a fact not so evident to others as to themselves, in consequence of which they appeared remarkably intimate. The person seeing clearest in the matter was Mrs. Gresham, who lived so much in the world that being left now and then to one's own company had become her idea of true sociability. She knew very well that if she had been privately engaged to a young man as amiable as Nick Dormer she would have managed that publicity shouldn't play such a part in their intercourse; and she had her secret scorn for the stupidity of people whose conception of Nick's relation to Julia rested on the fact that he was always included in her parties. "If he never was there they might talk," she said to herself. But Mrs. Gresham was supersubtle. To her it would have appeared natural that her friend should celebrate the parliamentary recess by going down to Harsh and securing the young man's presence there for a fortnight; she recognised Mrs. Dallow's actual plan as a comparatively poor substitute—the project of spending the holidays in other people's houses, to which Nick had also promised to come. Mrs. Gresham was romantic; she wondered what was the good of mere snippets and snatches, the chances that any one might have, when large, still days *à deux* were open to you—chances of which half the sanctity was in what they excluded. However, there were more unsettled matters between Mrs. Dallow and her queer kinsman than even Mrs. Gresham's fine insight could embrace. She was not on the Sunday evening before Easter among the guests in Great Stanhope Street; but if she had been Julia's singular indifference to observation would have stopped short of encouraging her to remain in the drawing-room, along with Nick, after the others had gone. I may add that Mrs. Gresham's extreme curiosity would have emboldened her as little to do so. She would have taken for granted that the pair wished to be alone together, though she would have regarded this only as a snippet. The company had at all events stayed late, and it was nearly twelve o'clock when the last of them, standing before the fire in the room they had quitted, broke out to his companion:

"See here, Julia, how long do you really expect me to endure this kind of thing?" Julia made him no answer; she only leaned back in her chair with her eyes upon his. He met her gaze a moment; then he turned round to the fire and for another moment looked into it. After this he faced his hostess again with the exclamation: "It's so foolish—it's so damnably foolish!"

She still said nothing, but at the end of a minute she spoke without answering him. "I shall expect you on Tuesday, and I hope you'll come by a decent train."

"What do you mean by a decent train?"

"I mean I hope you'll not leave it till the last thing before dinner, so that we can have a little walk or something."

"What's a little walk or something? Why, if you make such a point of my coming to Griffin, do you want me to come at all?"

She hesitated an instant; then she returned; "I knew you hated it!"

"You provoke me so," said Nick. "You try to, I think."

"And Severals is still worse. You'll get out of that if you can," Mrs. Dallow went on.

"If I can? What's to prevent me?"

"You promised Lady Whiteroy. But of course that's nothing."

"I don't care a straw for Lady Whiteroy."

"And you promised me. But that's less still."

"It *is* foolish—it's quite idiotic," said Nick with his hands in his pockets and his eyes on the ceiling.

There was another silence, at the end of which Julia remarked: "You might have answered Mr. Macgeorge when he spoke to you."

"Mr. Macgeorge—what has he to do with it?"

"He has to do with your getting on a little. If you think that's the way—!"

Nick broke into a laugh. "I like lessons in getting on—in other words I suppose you mean in urbanity—from you, Julia!"

"Why not from me?"

"Because you can do nothing base. You're incapable of putting on a flattering manner to get something by it: therefore why should you expect me to? You're unflattering—that is, you're austere—in proportion as there may be something to be got."

She sprang from her chair, coming toward him. "There's only one thing I want in the world—you know very well."

"Yes, you want it so much that you won't even take it when it's pressed on you. How long do you seriously expect me to bear it?" Nick repeated.

"I never asked you to do anything base," she said as she stood in front of him. "If I'm not clever about throwing myself into things it's all the more reason you should be."

"If you're not clever, my dear Julia—?" Nick, close to her, placed his hands on her shoulders and shook her with a mixture of tenderness and passion. "You're clever enough to make me furious, sometimes!"

She opened and closed her fan looking down at it while she submitted to his mild violence. "All I want is that when a man like Mr. Macgeorge talks to you you shouldn't appear bored to death. You used to be so charming under those inflictions. Now you appear to take no interest in anything. At dinner to-night you scarcely opened your lips; you treated them all as if you only wished they'd go."

"I did wish they'd go. Haven't I told you a hundred times what I think of your salon?"

"How then do you want me to live?" she asked. "Am I not to have a creature in the house?"

"As many creatures as you like. Your freedom's complete and, as far as I'm concerned, always will be. Only when you challenge me and overhaul me—not justly, I think—I must confess the simple truth, that there are many of your friends I don't delight in."

"Oh *your* idea of pleasant people!" Julia lamented. "I should like once for all to know what it really is."

"I can tell you what it really isn't: it isn't Mr. Macgeorge. He's a being almost grotesquely limited."

"He'll be where you'll never be—unless you change."

"To be where Mr. Macgeorge is not would be very much my desire. Therefore why should I change?" Nick demanded. "However, I hadn't the least intention of being rude to him, and I don't think I was," he went on. "To the best of my ability I assume a virtue if I haven't it; but apparently I'm not enough of a comedian."

"If you haven't it?" she echoed. "It's when you say things like that that you're so dreadfully tiresome. As if there were anything that you haven't or mightn't have!"

Nick turned away from her; he took a few impatient steps in the room, looking at the carpet, his hands always in his pockets. Then he came back to the fire with the observation: "It's rather hard to be found so wanting when one has tried to play one's part so beautifully." He paused with his eyes on her own and then went on with a vibration in his voice: "I've imperilled my immortal soul, or at least bemuddled my intelligence, by all the things I don't care for that I've tried to do, and all the things I detest that I've tried to be, and all the things I never can be that I've tried to look as if I were—all the appearances and imitations, the pretences and hypocrisies in which I've steeped myself to the eyes; and at the end of it (it serves me right!) my reward is simply to learn that I'm still not half humbug enough!"

Julia looked away from him as soon as he had spoken these words; she attached her eyes to the clock behind him and observed irrelevantly: "I'm very sorry, but I think you had better go. I don't like you to stay after midnight."

"Ah what you like and what you don't like, and where one begins and the other ends—all that's an impenetrable mystery!" the young man declared. But he took no further notice of her allusion to his departure, adding in a different tone: "'A man like Mr. Macgeorge'! When you say a thing of that sort in a certain, particular way I should rather like to suffer you to perish."

Mrs. Dallow stared; it might have seemed for an instant that she was trying to look stupid. "How can I help it if a few years hence he's certain to be at the head of any Liberal Government?"

"We can't help it of course, but we can help talking about it," Nick smiled. "If we don't mention it, it mayn't be noticed."

"You're trying to make me angry. You're in one of your vicious moods," she returned, blowing out on the chimney-piece a guttering candle.

"That I'm exasperated I've already had the honour very positively to inform you. All the same I maintain that I was irreproachable at dinner. I don't want you to think I shall always be as good as that."

"You looked so out of it; you were as gloomy as if every earthly hope had left you, and you didn't make a single contribution to any discussion that took place. Don't you think I observe you?" she asked with an irony tempered by a tenderness unsuccessfully concealed.

"Ah my darling, what you observe—!" Nick cried with a certain bitterness of amusement. But he added the next moment more seriously, as if his tone had been disrespectful: "You probe me to the bottom, no doubt."

"You needn't come either to Griffin or to Severals if you don't want to."

"Give them up yourself; stay here with me!"

She coloured quickly as he said this, and broke out: "Lord, how you hate political houses!"

"How can you say that when from February to August I spend every blessed night in one?"

"Yes, and hate that worst of all."

"So do half the people who are in it. You, my dear, must have so many things, so many people, so much *mise-en-scène* and such a perpetual spectacle to live," Nick went on. "Perpetual motion, perpetual visits, perpetual crowds! If you go into the country you'll see forty people every day and be mixed up with them all day. The idea of a quiet fortnight in town, when by a happy if

303

idiotic superstition everybody goes out of it, disconcerts and frightens you. It's the very time, it's the very place, to do a little work and possess one's soul."

This vehement allocution found her evidently somewhat unprepared; but she was sagacious enough, instead of attempting for the moment a general rejoinder, to seize on a single phrase and say: "Work? What work can you do in London at such a moment as this?"

Nick considered. "I might tell you I want to get up a lot of subjects, to sit at home and read blue-books; but that wouldn't be quite what I mean."

"Do you mean you want to paint?"

"Yes, that's it, since you gouge it out of me."

"Why do you make such a mystery about it? You're at perfect liberty," Julia said.

She put out her hand to rest it on the mantel-shelf, but her companion took it on the way and held it in both his own. "You're delightful, Julia, when you speak in that tone—then I know why it is I love you. But I can't do anything if I go to Griffin, if I go to Severals."

"I see—I see," she answered thoughtfully and kindly.

"I've scarcely been inside of my studio for months, and I feel quite homesick for it. The idea of putting in a few quiet days there has taken hold of me: I rather cling to it."

"It seems so odd your having a studio!" Julia dropped, speaking so quickly that the words were almost incomprehensible.

"Doesn't it sound absurd, for all the good it does me, or I do *in* it? Of course one can produce nothing but rubbish on such terms—without continuity or persistence, with just a few days here and there. I ought to be ashamed of myself, no doubt; but even my rubbish interests me. '*Guenille si l'on veut, ma guenille m'est chère.*' But I'll go down to Harsh with you in a moment, Julia," Nick pursued: "that would do as well if we could be quiet there, without people, without a creature; and I should really be perfectly content. You'd beautifully sit for me; it would be the occasion we've so often wanted and never found."

She shook her head slowly and with a smile that had a meaning for him. "Thank you, my dear; nothing would induce me to go to Harsh with you."

He looked at her hard. "What's the matter whenever it's a question of anything of that sort? Are you afraid of me?" She pulled her hand from him quickly, turning away; but he went on: "Stay with me here then, when everything's so right for it. We shall do beautifully—have the whole place, have the whole day, to ourselves. Hang your engagements! Telegraph you won't come. We'll live at the studio—you'll sit to me every day. Now or never's our chance—when shall we have so good a one? Think how charming it will be! I'll make you wish awfully that I may do something."

"I can't get out of Griffin—it's impossible," Julia said, moving further away and with her back presented to him.

"Then you *are* afraid of me—simply!"

She turned straight round, very pale. "Of course I am. You're welcome to know it."

He went toward her, and for a moment she seemed to make another slight movement of retreat. This, however, was scarcely perceptible, and there was nothing to alarm in the tone of reasonable entreaty in which he spoke as he stood there. "Put an end, Julia, to our absurd situation—it really can't go on. You've no right to expect a man to be happy or comfortable in so false a position. We're spoken of odiously—of that we may be sure; and yet what good have we of it?"

"Spoken of? Do I care for that?"

"Do you mean you're indifferent because there are no grounds? That's just why I hate it."

"I don't know what you're talking about!" she returned with sharp disdain.

"Be my wife to-morrow—be my wife next week. Let us have done with this fantastic probation and be happy."

"Leave me now—come back to-morrow. I'll write to you." She had the air of pleading with him at present, pleading as he pleaded.

"You can't resign yourself to the idea of one's looking 'out of it'!" Nick laughed.

"Come to-morrow, before lunch," she went on.

"To be told I must wait six months more and then be sent about my business? Ah, Julia, Julia!" the young man groaned.

Something in this simple lament—it sounded natural and perfectly unstudied—seemed straightway to make a great impression on her. "You shall wait no longer," she said after a short silence.

"What do you mean by no longer?"

"Give me about five weeks—say till the Whitsuntide recess."

"Five weeks are a great deal," smiled Nick.

"There are things to be done—you ought to understand."

"I only understand how I love you."

She let herself go—"Dearest Nick!"—and he caught her and kept her in his arms.

"I've your promise then for five weeks hence to a day?" he demanded as she at last released herself.

"We'll settle that—the exact day; there are things to consider and to arrange. Come to luncheon to-morrow."

"I'll come early—I'll come at one," he said; and for a moment they stood all deeply and intimately taking each other in.

"Do you think I *want* to wait, any more than you?" she asked in congruity with this.

"I don't feel so much out of it now!" he declared by way of answer. "You'll stay of course now—you'll give up your visits?"

She had hold of the lappet of his coat; she had kept it in her hand even while she detached herself from his embrace. There was a white flower in his buttonhole that she looked at and played with a moment before she said; "I've a better idea—you needn't come to Griffin. Stay in your studio—do as you like—paint dozens of pictures."

"Dozens? Barbarian!" Nick wailed.

The epithet apparently had an endearing suggestion for her; it at any rate led her to let him possess himself of her head and, so holding it, kiss her—led her to say: "What on earth do I want but that you should do absolutely as you please and be as happy as you can?"

He kissed her in another place at this; but he put it to her; "What dreadful proposition is coming now?"

"I'll go off and do up my visits and come back."

"And leave me alone?"

"Don't be affected! You know you'll work much better without me. You'll live in your studio—I shall be well out of the way."

"That's not what one wants of a sitter. How can I paint you?"

"You can paint me all the rest of your life. I shall be a perpetual sitter."

"I believe I could paint you without looking at you"—and his lighted face shone down on her. "You do excuse me then from those dreary places?"

"How can I insist after what you said about the pleasure of keeping these days?" she admirably—it was so all sincerely—asked.

"You're the best woman on earth—though it does seem odd you should rush away as soon as our little business is settled."

"We shall make it up. I know what I'm about. And now go!" She ended by almost pushing him out of the room.

XXIII

It was certainly singular, in the light of other matters, that on sitting down in his studio after she had left town Nick should not, as regards the effort to project plastically some beautiful form, have felt more chilled by the absence of a friend who was such an embodiment of beauty. She was away and he missed her and longed for her, and yet without her the place was more filled with what he wanted to find in it. He turned into it with confused feelings, the strongest of which was a sense of release and recreation. It looked blighted and lonely and dusty, and his old studies, as he rummaged them out, struck him even as less inspired than the last time he had ventured to face them. But amid this neglected litter, in the colourless and obstructed light of a high north window which needed washing, he came nearer tasting the possibility of positive happiness: it appeared to him that, as he had said to Julia, he was more in possession of his soul. It was frivolity and folly, it was puerility, to spend valuable hours pottering over the vain implements of an art he had relinquished; and a certain shame that he had felt in presenting his plea to Julia that Sunday night arose from the sense not of what he clung to, but of what he had given up. He had turned his back on serious work, so that pottering was now all he could aspire to. It couldn't be fruitful, it couldn't be anything but ridiculous, almost ignoble; but it soothed his nerves, it was in the nature of a secret dissipation. He had never suspected he should some day have nerves on his own part to count with; but this possibility had been revealed to him on the day it became clear that he was letting something precious go. He was glad he had not to justify himself to the critical, for this might have been a delicate business. The critical were mostly absent; and besides, shut up all day in his studio, how should he ever meet them? It was the place in the world where he felt furthest away from his constituents. That was a part of the pleasure—the consciousness that for the hour the coast was clear and his mind independent. His mother and his sister had gone to Broadwood: Lady Agnes—the phrase sounds brutal but represents his state of mind—was well out of the way. He had written to her as soon as Julia left town—he had apprised her of the fact that his wedding-day was fixed: a relief for poor Lady Agnes to a period of intolerable mystification, of dark, dumb wondering and watching. She had said her say the day of the poll at Harsh; she was too proud to ask and too discreet to "nag"; so she could only wait for something that didn't come. The unconditioned loan of Broadwood had of course been something of a bribe to patience: she had at first felt that on the day she should take possession of that capital house Julia would indeed seem to have entered the family. But the gift had confirmed expectations just enough to make disappointment more bitter; and the discomfort was greater in proportion as she failed to discover what was the matter. Her daughter Grace was much occupied with this question, and brought it up for discussion in a manner irritating to her ladyship, who had a high theory of being silent about it, but who, however, in the long run, was more unhappy when, in consequence of a reprimand, the girl suggested no reasons at all than when she suggested stupid ones. It eased Lady Agnes a little to advert to the mystery when she could have the air of not having begun.

The letter Nick received from her the first day of Passion Week in reply to his important communication was the only one he read at that moment; not counting of course the several notes Mrs. Dallow addressed to him from Griffin. There were letters piled up, as he knew, in Calcutta Gardens, which his servant had strict orders not to bring to the studio. Nick slept now in the bedroom attached to this retreat; got things, as he wanted them, from Calcutta Gardens; and dined at his club, where a stray surviving friend or two, seeing him prowl about the library in the evening, was free to impute to such eccentricity some subtly political basis. When he thought of his neglected letters he remembered Mr. Carteret's convictions on the subject of not "getting behind"; they made him laugh, in the slightly sonorous painting-room, as he bent over one of the old canvases that he had ventured to turn to the light. He was fully determined, however, to master his correspondence before going down, the last thing before Parliament should reassemble, to spend another day at Beauclere. Mastering his correspondence meant, in Nick's mind, breaking open envelopes; writing answers was scarcely involved in the idea. But Mr. Carteret would never guess that. Nick was not moved even to write to him that the affair with Julia was on the point of taking the form he had been so good as to desire: he reserved the pleasure of this announcement for a personal interview.

The day before Good Friday, in the morning, his stillness was broken by a rat-tat-tat on the outer door of his studio, administered apparently by the knob of a walking-stick. His servant was out and he went to the door, wondering who his visitor could be at such a time, especially of the rather presuming class. The class was indicated by the visitor's failure to look for the bell—since there *was* a bell, though it required a little research. In a moment the mystery was solved: the gentleman who stood smiling at him from the threshold could only be Gabriel Nash. Nick had not seen this whimsical personage for several months, and had had no news of him beyond a general intimation that he was following his fancy in foreign parts. His old friend had sufficiently prepared him, at the time of their reunion in Paris, for the idea of the fitful in intercourse; and he had not been ignorant, on his return from Paris, that he should have had an opportunity to miss him if he had not been too busy to take advantage of it. In London, after the episode at Harsh, Gabriel had not reappeared: he had redeemed none of the pledges given the night they walked together to Notre Dame and conversed on important matters. He was to have interposed in Nick's destiny, but he had not interposed; he was to have pulled him hard and in the opposite sense from Julia, but there had been no pulling; he was to have saved him, as he called it, and yet Nick was lost. This circumstance indeed formed his excuse: the member for Harsh had rushed so wantonly to perdition. Nick had for the hour seriously wished to keep hold of him: he valued him as a salutary influence. Yet on coming to his senses after his election our young man had recognised that Nash might very well have reflected on the thanklessness of such a slippery subject—might have held himself released from his vows. Of course it had been particularly in the event of a Liberal triumph that he had threatened to make himself felt; the effect of a brand plucked from the burning would be so much greater if the flames were already high. Yet Nick had not kept him to the letter of this pledge, and had so fully admitted the right of a thorough connoisseur, let alone a faithful friend, to lose patience with him that he was now far from greeting his visitor with a reproach. He felt much more thrown on his defence.

Gabriel, however, forbore at first to attack him. He brought in only blandness and benevolence and a great content at having obeyed the mystic voice—it was really a remarkable case of second sight—which had whispered him that the recreant comrade of his prime was in town. He had just come back from Sicily after a southern winter, according to a custom frequent with him, and had been moved by a miraculous prescience, unfavourable as the moment might seem, to go and ask for Nick in Calcutta Gardens, where he had extracted from his friend's servant an address not known to all the world. He showed Nick what a mistake it had been to fear a dull arraignment, and how he habitually ignored all lapses and kept up the standard only by taking a hundred fine things for granted. He also abounded more than ever in his own sense, reminding his relieved listener how no recollection of him, no evocation of him in absence, could ever do him justice. You couldn't recall him without seeming to exaggerate him, and then acknowledged, when you saw him, that your exaggeration had fallen short. He emerged out of vagueness—his Sicily might have been the Sicily of *A Winter's Tale*—and would evidently be reabsorbed in it; but his presence was positive and pervasive enough. He was duly "intense" while he lasted. His connexions were with beauty, urbanity and conversation, as usual, but they made up a circle you couldn't find in the Court Guide. Nick had a sense that he knew "a lot of esthetic people," but he dealt in ideas much more than in names and addresses. He was genial and jocose, sunburnt and romantically allusive. It was to be gathered that he had been living for many days in a Saracenic tower where his principal occupation was to watch for the flushing of the west. He had retained all the serenity of his opinions and made light, with a candour of which the only defect was apparently that it was not quite enough a conscious virtue, of many of the objects of common esteem. When Nick asked him what he had been doing he replied, "Oh living, you know"; and the tone of the words offered them as the story of a great deed. He made a long visit, staying to luncheon and after luncheon, so that the little studio heard all at once a greater quantity of brave talk than in the several previous years of its history. With much of our tale left to tell it is a pity that so little of this colloquy may be reported here; since, as affairs took their course, it marked really—if the question be of noting the exact point—a turn of the tide in Nick Dormer's personal situation. He was destined to remember the accent with which Nash exclaimed, on his drawing forth sundry specimens of amateurish earnestness:

"I say—I say—I say!"

He glanced round with a heightened colour. "They're pretty bad, eh?"

"Oh you're a deep one," Nash went on.

"What's the matter?"

"Do you call your conduct that of a man of honour?"

"Scarcely perhaps. But when no one has seen them—!"

"That's your villainy. *C'est de l'exquis, du pur exquis.* Come, my dear fellow, this is very serious—it's a bad business," said Gabriel Nash. Then he added almost with austerity: "You'll be so good as to place before me every patch of paint, every sketch and scrap, that this room contains."

Nick complied in great good humour. He turned out his boxes and drawers, shovelled forth the contents of bulging portfolios, mounted on chairs to unhook old canvases that had been severely "skied." He was modest and docile and patient and amused, above all he was quite thrilled—thrilled with the idea of eliciting a note of appreciation so late in the day. It was the oddest thing how he at present in fact found himself imputing value to his visitor—attributing to him, among attributions more confused, the dignity of judgement, the authority of knowledge. Nash was an ambiguous character but an excellent touchstone. The two said very little for a while, and they had almost half an hour's silence, during which, after our young man had hastily improvised an exhibition, there was only a puffing of cigarettes. Gabriel walked about, looking at this and that, taking up rough studies and laying them down, asking a question of fact, fishing with his umbrella, on the floor, amid a pile of unarranged sketches. Nick accepted jocosely the attitude of suspense, but there was even more of it in his heart than in his face. So few people had seen his young work—almost no one who really counted. He had been ashamed of it, never showing it to bring on a conclusion, since a conclusion was precisely what he feared. He whistled now while he let his companion take time. He rubbed old panels with his sleeve and dabbed wet sponges on surfaces that had sunk. It was a long time since he had felt so gay, strange as such an assertion sounds in regard to a young man whose bridal-day had at his urgent solicitation lately been fixed. He had stayed in town to be alone with his imagination, and suddenly, paradoxically, the sense of that result had arrived with poor Nash.

"Nicholas Dormer," this personage remarked at last, "for grossness of immorality I think I've never seen your equal."

"That sounds so well," Nick returned, "that I hesitate to risk spoiling it by wishing it explained."

"Don't you recognise in *any* degree the grand idea of duty?"

"If I don't grasp it with a certain firmness I'm a deadly failure, for I was quite brought up on it," Nick said.

"Then you're indeed the wretchedest failure I know. Life is ugly, after all."

"Do I gather that you yourself recognise obligations of the order you allude to?"

"Do you 'gather'?" Nash stared. "Why, aren't they the very flame of my faith, the burden of my song?"

"My dear fellow, duty is doing, and I've inferred that you think rather poorly of doing—that it spoils one's style."

"Doing wrong, assuredly."

"But what do you call right? What's your canon of certainty there?" Nick asked.

"The conscience that's in us—that charming, conversible, infinite thing, the intensest thing we know. But you must treat the oracle civilly if you wish to make it speak. You mustn't stride into the temple in muddy jack-boots and with your hat on your head, as the Puritan troopers tramped into the dear old abbeys. One must do one's best to find out the right, and your criminality appears to be that you've not taken the commonest trouble."

"I hadn't you to ask," smiled Nick. "But duty strikes me as doing something in particular. If you're too afraid it may be the wrong thing you may let everything go."

"Being is doing, and if doing is duty being is duty. Do you follow?"

"At a very great distance."

"To be what one *may* be, really and efficaciously," Nash went on, "to feel it and understand it, to accept it, adopt it, embrace it—that's conduct, that's life."

"And suppose one's a brute or an ass, where's the efficacy?"

"In one's very want of intelligence. In such cases one's out of it—the question doesn't exist; one simply becomes a part of the duty of others. The brute, the ass," Nick's visitor developed, "neither feels nor understands, nor accepts nor adopts. Those fine processes in themselves classify us. They educate, they exalt, they preserve; so that to profit by them we must be as perceptive as we can. We must recognise our particular form, the instrument that each of us—each of us who carries anything—carries in his being. Mastering this instrument, learning to play it in perfection—that's what I call duty, what I call conduct, what I call success."

Nick listened with friendly attention and the air of general assent was in his face as he said: "Every one has it then, this individual pipe?"

"'Every one,' my dear fellow, is too much to say, for the world's full of the crudest *remplissage*. The book of life's padded, ah but padded—a deplorable want of editing! I speak of every one who's any one. Of course there are pipes and pipes—little quavering flutes for the concerted movements and big *cornets-à-piston* for the great solos."

"I see, I see. And what might your instrument be?"

Nash hesitated not a moment; his answer was radiantly there. "To speak to people just as I'm speaking to you. To prevent for instance a great wrong being done."

"A great wrong—?"

"Yes—to the human race. I talk—I talk; I say the things other people don't, the things they can't the things they won't," Gabriel went on with his inimitable candour.

"If it's a question of mastery and perfection you certainly have them," his companion replied.

"And you haven't, alas; that's the pity of it, that's the scandal. That's the wrong I want to set right before it becomes too public a shame. If I called you just now grossly immoral it's on account of the spectacle you present—a spectacle to be hidden from the eye of ingenuous youth: that of a man neglecting his own fiddle to blunder away on that of one of his fellows. We can't afford such mistakes, we can't tolerate such licence."

"You think then I *have* a fiddle?"—and our young man, in spite of himself, attached to the question a quaver of suspense finer, doubtless, than any that had ever passed his lips.

"A regular Stradivarius! All these things you've shown me are remarkably interesting. You've a talent of a wonderfully pure strain."

"I say—I say—I say!" Nick exclaimed, hovering there with his hands in his pockets and a blush on his lighted face, while he repeated with a change of accent Nash's exclamation of half an hour before.

"I like it, your talent; I measure it, I appreciate it, I insist upon it," that critic went on between the whiffs of his cigarette. "I have to be awfully wise and good to do so, but fortunately I am. In such a case that's my duty. I shall make you my business for a while. Therefore," he added piously; "don't say I'm unconscious of the moral law."

"A Stradivarius?" said Nick interrogatively and with his eyes wide open. The thought in his mind was of how different this seemed from his having gone to Griffin.

XXIV

His counsellor had plenty of further opportunity to develop this and other figurative remarks, for he not only spent several of the middle hours of the day at the studio, but came back in the evening—the pair had dined together at a little foreign pothouse in Soho, revealed to Nick on this occasion—and discussed the great question far into the night. The great question was whether, on the showing of those examples of his ability with which the scene of their discourse was now densely bestrewn, Nick Dormer would be justified in "really going in" for the practice of pictorial art. This may strike many readers of his history as a limited and even trivial inquiry, with little of the heroic or the romantic in it; but it was none the less carried to the finest point by our impassioned young men. Nick suspected Nash of exaggerating his encouragement in order to play a malign trick on the political world at whose expense it was his fond fancy to divert himself—without indeed making that organisation perceptibly totter—and reminded him that his present accusation of immorality was strangely inconsistent with the wanton hope expressed by him in Paris, the hope that the Liberal candidate at Harsh would be returned. Nash replied, first, "Oh I hadn't been in this place then!" but he defended himself later and more effectually by saying that it was not of Nick's having got elected he complained: it was of his visible hesitancy to throw up his seat. Nick begged that he wouldn't mention this, and his gallantry failed to render him incapable of saying: "The fact is I haven't the nerve for it." They talked then for a while of what he *could* do, not of what he couldn't; of the mysteries and miracles of reproduction and representation; of the strong, sane joys of the artistic life. Nick made afresh, with more fulness, his great confession, that his private ideal of happiness was the life of a great painter of portraits. He uttered his thought on that head so copiously and lucidly that Nash's own abundance was stilled and he listened almost as if he had been listening to something new—difficult as it was to conceive a point of view for such a matter with which he was unacquainted.

"There it is," said Nick at last—"there's the naked, preposterous truth: that if I were to do exactly as I liked I should spend my years reproducing the more or less vacuous countenances of my fellow-mortals. I should find peace and pleasure and wisdom and worth, I should find fascination and a measure of success in it—out of the din and the dust and the scramble, the world of party labels, party cries, party bargains and party treacheries: of humbuggery, hypocrisy and cant. The cleanness and quietness of it, the independent effort to do something, to leave something which shall give joy to man long after the howling has died away to the last ghost of an echo—such a vision solicits me in the watches of night with an almost irresistible force."

As he dropped these remarks he lolled on a big divan with one of his long legs folded up, while his visitor stopped in front of him after moving about the room vaguely and softly, almost on tiptoe, so as not to interrupt him. "You speak," Nash said, "with the special and dreadful eloquence that rises to a man's lips when he has practically, whatever his theory may be, renounced the right and dropped hideously into the wrong. Then his regret for the right, a certain exquisite appreciation of it, puts on an accent I know well how to recognise."

Nick looked up at him a moment. "You've hit it if you mean by that that I haven't resigned my seat and that I don't intend to."

"I thought you took it only to give it up. Don't you remember our talk in Paris?"

"I like to be a part of the spectacle that amuses you," Nick returned, "but I could scarcely have taken so much trouble as that for it."

"Isn't it then an absurd comedy, the life you lead?"

"Comedy or tragedy—I don't know which; whatever it is I appear to be capable of it to please two or three people."

"Then you *can* take trouble?" said Nash.

"Yes, for the woman I'm to marry."

"Oh you're to marry?"

"That's what has come on since we met in Paris," Nick explained, "and it makes just the difference."

"Ah my poor friend," smiled Gabriel, much arrested, "no wonder you've an eloquence, an accent!"

"It's a pity I have them in the wrong place. I'm expected to have them in the House of Commons."

"You will when you make your farewell speech there—to announce that you chuck it up. And may I venture to ask who's to be your wife?" the visitor pursued.

"Mrs. Dallow has kindly consented to accept that yoke. I think you saw her in Paris."

"Ah yes: you spoke of her to me, and I remember asking you even then if you were in love with her."

"I wasn't then," said Nick.

Nash had a grave pause. "And are you now?"

"Oh dear, yes."

"That would be better—if it wasn't worse."

"Nothing could be better," Nick declared. "It's the best thing that can happen to me."

"Well," his friend continued, "you must let me very respectfully approach this lady. You must let me bring her round."

"Bring her round to what?"

"To everything. Talk her over."

"Talk her under!" Nick laughed—but making his joke a little as to gain time. He remembered the effect this adviser had produced on Julia—an effect that scantly ministered to the idea of another meeting. Julia had had no occasion to allude again to Nick's imperturbable friend; he had passed out of her life at once and for ever; but there flickered up a quick memory of the contempt he had led her to express, together with a sense of how odd she would think it her intended should have thrown over two pleasant visits to cultivate such company.

"Over to a proper pride in what you may do," Nash returned—"what you may do above all if she'll help you."

"I scarcely see how she can help me," said Nick with an air of thinking.

"She's extremely handsome as I remember her. You could do great things with *her*."

"Ah, there's the rub," Nick went on. "I wanted her to sit for me this week, but she wouldn't hear of it."

"*Elle a bien tort*. You should attack some fine strong type. Is Mrs. Dallow in London?" Nash inquired.

"For what do you take her? She's paying visits."

"Then I've a model for you."

"Then *you* have—?" Nick stared. "What has that to do with Mrs. Dallow's being away?"

"Doesn't it give you more time?"

"Oh the time flies!" sighed Nick with a spontaneity that made his companion again laugh out—a demonstration in which for a moment he himself rather ruefully joined.

"Does she like you to paint?" that personage asked with one of his candid intonations.

"So she says."

"Well, do something fine to show her."

"I'd rather show it to you," Nick confessed.

"My dear fellow, I see it from here—if you do your duty. Do you remember the Tragic Muse?" Nash added for explanation.

"The Tragic Muse?"

"That girl in Paris, whom we heard at the old actress's and afterwards met at the charming entertainment given by your cousin—isn't he?—the secretary of embassy."

"Oh Peter's girl! Of course I remember her."

"Don't call her Peter's; call her rather mine," Nash said with easy rectification. "I invented her. I introduced her. I revealed her."

"I thought you on the contrary ridiculed and repudiated her."

"As a fine, handsome young woman surely not—I seem to myself to have been all the while rendering her services. I said I disliked tea-party ranters, and so I do; but if my estimate of her powers was below the mark she has more than punished me."

"What has she done?" Nick asked.

"She has become interesting, as I suppose you know."

"How should I know?"

"Well, you must see her, you must paint her," Nash returned. "She tells me something was said about it that day at Madame Carré's."

"Oh I remember—said by Peter."

"Then it will please Mr. Sherringham—you'll be glad to do that. I suppose you know all he has done for Miriam?" Gabriel pursued.

"Not a bit, I know nothing about Peter's affairs," Nick said, "unless it be in general that he goes in for mountebanks and mimes and that it occurs to me I've heard one of my sisters mention—the rumour had come to her—that he has been backing Miss Rooth."

"Miss Rooth delights to talk of his kindness; she's charming when she speaks of it. It's to his good offices that she owes her appearance here."

"Here?" Nick's interest rose. "Is she in London?"

"*D'où tombez-vous?* I thought you people read the papers."

"What should I read, when I sit—sometimes—through the stuff they put into them?"

"Of course I see that—that your engagement at your own variety-show, with its interminable 'turns,' keeps you from going to the others. Learn then," said Gabriel Nash, "that you've a great competitor and that you're distinctly not, much as you may suppose it, *the* rising comedian. The Tragic Muse is the great modern personage. Haven't you heard people speak of her, haven't you been taken to see her?"

Nick bethought himself. "I daresay I've heard of her, but with a good many other things on my mind I had forgotten it."

"Certainly I can imagine what has been on your mind. She remembers you at any rate; she repays neglect with sympathy. She wants," said Nash, "to come and see you."

"'See' me?" It was all for Nick now a wonder.

"To be seen by you—it comes to the same thing. She's really worth seeing; you must let me bring her; you'll find her very suggestive. That idea that you should paint her—she appears to consider it a sort of bargain."

"A bargain?" Our young man entered, as he believed, into the humour of the thing. "What will she give me?"

"A splendid model. She *is* splendid."

"Oh then bring her," said Nick.

XXV

Nash brought her, the great modern personage, as he had described her, the very next day, and it took his friend no long time to test his assurance that Miriam Rooth was now splendid. She had made an impression on him

321

ten months before, but it had haunted him only a day, soon overlaid as it had been with other images. Yet after Nash had talked of her a while he recalled her better; some of her attitudes, some of her looks and tones began to hover before him. He was charmed in advance with the notion of painting her. When she stood there in fact, however, it seemed to him he had remembered her wrong; the brave, free, rather grand creature who instantly filled his studio with such an unexampled presence had so shaken off her clumsiness, the rudeness and crudeness that had made him pity her, a whole provincial and "second-rate" side. Miss Rooth was light and bright and direct to-day—direct without being stiff and bright without being garish. To Nick's perhaps inadequately sophisticated mind the model, the actress were figures of a vulgar setting; but it would have been impossible to show that taint less than this extremely natural yet extremely distinguished aspirant to distinction. She was more natural even than Gabriel Nash—"nature" was still Nick's formula for his amusing old friend—and beside her he appeared almost commonplace.

Nash recognised her superiority with a frankness honourable to both of them—testifying in this manner to his sense that they were all three serious beings, worthy to deal with fine realities. She attracted crowds to her theatre, but to his appreciation of such a fact as that, important doubtless in its way, there were the limits he had already expressed. What he now felt bound in all integrity to register was his perception that she had, in general and quite apart from the question of the box-office, a remarkable, a very remarkable, artistic nature. He allowed that she had surprised him here; knowing of her in other days mainly that she was hungry to adopt an overrated profession he had not imputed to her the normal measure of intelligence. Now he saw—he had had some talks with her—that she was capable almost of a violent play of mind; so much so that he was sorry for the embarrassment it would be to her. Nick could imagine the discomfort of having anything in the nature of a mind to arrange for in such conditions. "She's a woman of the best intentions, really of the best," Nash explained kindly and lucidly, almost paternally, "and the quite rare head you can see for yourself."

Miriam, smiling as she sat on an old Venetian chair, held aloft, with the noblest effect, that quarter of her person to which this patronage was extended, remarking to her host that, strange as it might appear, she had got quite to like poor Mr. Nash: she could make him go about with her—it was a relief to her mother.

"When I take him she has perfect peace," the girl said; "then she can stay at home and see the interviewers. She delights in that and I hate it, so our friend here is a great comfort. Of course a *femme de théâtre* is supposed to be able to go out alone, but there's a kind of 'smartness,' an added *chic*, in having some one. People think he's my 'companion '; I'm sure they fancy I pay him. I'd pay him, if he'd take it—and perhaps he will yet!—rather than give him up, for it doesn't matter that he's not a lady. He *is* one in tact and sympathy, as you see. And base as he thinks the sort of thing I do he can't keep away from the theatre. When you're celebrated people will look at you who could never before find out for themselves why they should."

"When you're celebrated you grow handsomer; at least that's what has happened to you, though you were pretty too of old," Gabriel placidly argued. "I go to the theatre to look at your head; it gives me the greatest pleasure. I take up anything of that sort as soon as I find it. One never knows how long it may last."

"Are you attributing that uncertainty to my appearance?" Miriam beautifully asked.

"Dear no, to my own pleasure, the first precious bloom of it," Nash went on. "Dormer at least, let me tell you in justice to him, hasn't waited till you were celebrated to want to see you again—he stands there open-eyed—for the simple reason that he hadn't the least idea of your renown. I had to announce it to him."

"Haven't you seen me act?" Miriam put, without reproach, to her host.

"I'll go to-night," he handsomely declared.

"You have your terrible House, haven't you? What do they call it—the demands of public life?" Miriam continued: in answer to which Gabriel explained that he had the demands of private life as well, inasmuch as he was in love—he was on the point of being married. She listened to this with participation; then she said: "Ah then do bring your—what do they call her in English? I'm always afraid of saying something improper—your *future*. I'll send you a box, under the circumstances; you'll like that better." She added that if he were to paint her he would have to see her often on the stage, wouldn't he? to profit by the *optique de la scène*—what did they call *that* in English?—studying her and fixing his impression. But before he had time to meet this proposition she asked him if it disgusted him to hear her speak like that, as if she were always posing and thinking about herself, living only to be looked at, thrusting forward her person. She already often got sick of doing so, but *à la guerre comme à la guerre.*

"That's the fine artistic nature, you see—a sort of divine disgust breaking out in her," Nash expounded.

"If you want to paint me 'at all at all' of course. I'm struck with the way I'm taking that for granted," the girl decently continued. "When Mr. Nash spoke of it to me I jumped at the idea. I remembered our meeting in Paris and the kind things you said to me. But no doubt one oughtn't to jump at ideas when they represent serious sacrifices on the part of others."

"Doesn't she speak well?" Nash demanded of Nick. "Oh she'll go far!"

"It's a great privilege to me to paint you: what title in the world have I to pretend to such a model?" Nick replied to Miriam. "The sacrifice is yours—a sacrifice of time and good nature and credulity. You come, in your bright beauty and your genius, to this shabby place where I've nothing worth speaking of to show, not a guarantee to offer you; and I wonder what I've done to deserve such a gift of the gods."

"Doesn't *he* speak well?"—and Nash appealed with radiance to their companion.

She took no notice of him, only repeating to Nick that she hadn't forgotten his friendly attitude in Paris; and when he answered that he surely had done very little she broke out, first resting her eyes on him with a deep, reasonable smile and then springing up quickly; "Ah well, if I must justify myself I liked you!"

"Fancy my appearing to challenge you!" laughed Nick in deprecation. "To see you again is to want tremendously to try something. But you must have an infinite patience, because I'm an awful duffer."

She looked round the walls. "I see what you've done—*bien des choses*."

"She understands—she understands," Gabriel dropped. And he added to their visitor: "Imagine, when he might do something, his choosing a life of shams! At bottom he's like you—a wonderful artistic nature."

"I'll have patience," said the girl, smiling at Nick.

"Then, my children, I leave you—the peace of the Lord be with you." With which words Nash took his departure.

The others chose a position for the young woman's sitting after she had placed herself in many different attitudes and different lights; but an hour had elapsed before Nick got to work—began, on a large canvas, to "knock her in," as he called it. He was hindered even by the fine element of agitation, the emotion of finding himself, out of a clear sky, confronted with such a subject and launched in such a task. What could the situation be but incongruous just after he had formally renounced all manner of "art"?—the renunciation taking effect not a bit the less from the whim he had all consciously treated himself to *as* a whim (the last he should ever descend to!) the freak of a fortnight's relapse into a fingering of old sketches for the purpose, as he might have said, of burning them up, of clearing out his studio and terminating his lease. There were both embarrassment and inspiration in the strange chance of snatching back for an hour a relinquished joy: the jump with which he found he could still rise to such an occasion took away his breath a little, at the same time that the idea—the idea of what one might make of such material—touched him with an irresistible wand. On the spot, to his inner vision, Miriam became a rich result, drawing a hundred formative forces out of their troubled sleep, defying him where he privately felt strongest and imposing herself triumphantly in her own strength. He had the good fortune, without striking matches, to see her, as a subject, in a vivid light, and his quick attempt was as exciting as a sudden gallop—he might have been astride, in a boundless field, of a runaway horse.

She was in her way so fine that he could only think how to "do" her: that hard calculation soon flattened out the consciousness, lively in him at first, that she was a beautiful woman who had sought him out of his retirement. At the end of their first sitting her having done so appeared the most natural thing in the world: he had a perfect right to entertain her there—explanations and complications were engulfed in the productive mood. The business of "knocking her in" held up a lamp to her beauty, showed him how much there was of it and that she was infinitely interesting. He didn't want to fall in love with her—that *would* be a sell, he said to himself—and she promptly became much too interesting for it. Nick might have reflected, for simplification's sake, as his cousin Peter had done, but with more validity, that he was engaged with Miss Rooth in an undertaking which didn't in the least refer to themselves, that they were working together seriously and that decent work quite gainsaid sensibility—the humbugging sorts alone had to help themselves out with it. But after her first sitting—she came, poor girl, but twice—the need of such exorcisms passed from his spirit: he had so thoroughly, so practically taken her up. As to whether his visitor had the same bright and still sense of co-operation to a definite end, the sense of the distinctively technical nature of the answer to every question to which the occasion might give birth, that mystery would be lighted only were it open to us to regard this young lady through some other medium than the mind of her friends. We have chosen, as it happens, for some of the great advantages it carries with it, the indirect vision; and it fails as yet to tell us—what Nick of course wondered about before he ceased to care, as indeed he intimated to her—why a budding celebrity should have dreamed of there being something for her in so blighted a spot. She should have gone to one of the regular people, the great people: they would have welcomed her with open arms. When Nick asked her if some of the R.A.'s hadn't expressed a wish for a crack at her she replied: "Oh dear no, only the tiresome photographers; and fancy *them* in the future. If mamma could only do *that* for me!" And she added with the charming fellowship for which she was conspicuous at these hours: "You know I don't think any one yet has been quite so much struck with me as you."

"Not even Peter Sherringham?" her host jested while he stepped back to judge of the effect of a line.

"Oh Mr. Sherringham's different. You're an artist."

"For pity's sake don't say that!" he cried. "And as regards *your* art I thought Peter knew more than any one."

"Ah you're severe," said Miriam.

"Severe—?"

"Because that's what the poor dear thinks. But he does know a lot—he has been a providence to me."

"Then why hasn't he come over to see you act?"

She had a pause. "How do you know he hasn't come?"

"Because I take for granted he'd have called on me if he had."

"Does he like you very much?" the girl asked.

"I don't know. I like *him*."

"He's a gentleman—*pour cela*," she said.

"Oh yes, for that!" Nick went on absently, labouring hard.

"But he's afraid of me—afraid to see me."

"Doesn't he think you good enough?"

"On the contrary—he believes I shall carry him away and he's in a terror of my doing it."

"He ought to like that," said Nick with conscious folly.

"That's what I mean when I say he's not an artist. However, he declares he does like it, only it appears to be not the right thing for him. Oh the right thing—he's ravenous for that. But it's not for me to blame him, since I am too. He's coming some night, however. Then," she added almost grimly, "he shall have a dose."

"Poor Peter!" Nick returned with a compassion none the less real because it was mirthful: the girl's tone was so expressive of easy unscrupulous power.

327

"He's such a curious mixture," she luxuriously went on; "sometimes I quite lose patience with him. It isn't exactly trying to serve both God and Mammon, but it's muddling up the stage and the world. The world be hanged! The stage, or anything of that sort—I mean one's artistic conscience, one's true faith—comes first."

"Brava, brava! you do me good," Nick murmured, still amused, beguiled, and at work. "But it's very kind of you, when I was in this absurd state of ignorance, to impute to me the honour of having been more struck with you than any one else," he continued after a moment.

"Yes, I confess I don't quite see—when the shops were full of my photographs."

"Oh I'm so poor—I don't go into shops," he explained.

"Are you very poor?"

"I live on alms."

"And don't they pay you—the government, the ministry?"

"Dear young lady, for what?—for shutting myself up with beautiful women?"

"Ah you've others then?" she extravagantly groaned.

"They're not so kind as you, I confess."

"I'll buy it from you—what you're doing: I'll pay you well when it's done," said the girl. "I've got money now. I make it, you know—a good lot of it. It's too delightful after scraping and starving. Try it and you'll see. Give up the base, bad world."

"But isn't it supposed to be the base, bad world that pays?"

"Precisely; make it pay without mercy—knock it silly, squeeze it dry. That's what it's meant for—to pay for art. Ah if it wasn't for that! I'll bring you a quantity of photographs to-morrow—you must let me come back to-morrow: it's so amusing to have them, by the hundred, all for nothing, to give away. That's what takes mamma most: she can't get over it. That's luxury and glory; even at Castle Nugent they didn't do that. People used to sketch me, but not so much as mamma *veut bien le dire*; and in all my life I never had but one poor little carte-de-visite, when I was sixteen, in a plaid frock, with the banks of a river, at three francs the dozen."

XXVI

It was success, the member for Harsh felt, that had made her finer— the full possession of her talent and the sense of the recognition of it. There was an intimation in her presence (if he had given his mind to it) that for him too the same cause would produce the same effect—that is would show him how being launched in the practice of an art makes strange and prompt revelations. Nick felt clumsy beside a person who manifestly, now, had such an extraordinary familiarity with the esthetic point of view. He remembered too the clumsiness that had been in his visitor—something silly and shabby, pert rather than proper, and of quite another value than her actual smartness, as London people would call it, her well-appointedness and her evident command of more than one manner. Handsome as she had been the year before, she had suggested sordid lodgings, bread and butter, heavy tragedy and tears; and if then she was an ill-dressed girl with thick hair who wanted to be an actress, she was already in these few weeks a performer who could even produce an impression of not performing. She showed what a light hand she could have, forbore to startle and looked as well, for unprofessional life, as Julia: which was only the perfection of her professional character.

This function came out much in her talk, for there were many little bursts of confidence as well as many familiar pauses as she sat there; and she was ready to tell Nick the whole history of her *début*—the chance that had suddenly turned up and that she had caught, with a fierce leap, as it passed. He missed some of the details in his attention to his own task, and some of them he failed to understand, attached as they were to the name of Mr. Basil Dashwood, which he heard for the first time. It was through Mr. Dashwood's extraordinary exertions that a hearing—a morning performance at a London theatre—had been obtained for her. That had been the great step, for it had led to the putting on at night of the play, at the same theatre, in place of a wretched thing they were trying (it was no use) to keep on its feet, and to her engagement for the principal part. She had made a hit in it—she couldn't pretend not to know that; but she was already tired of it, there were so many other things she wanted to do; and when she thought it would probably run a month or two more she fell to cursing the odious conditions of artistic production in such an age. The play was a more or less idiotised version of a new French piece, a thing that had taken in Paris at a third-rate theatre and was now proving itself in London good enough for houses mainly made up of ten-shilling stalls. It was Dashwood who had said it would go if they could get the rights and a fellow to make some changes: he had discovered it at a nasty little place she had never been to, over the Seine. They had got the rights, and the fellow who had made the changes was practically Dashwood himself; there was another man in London, Mr. Gushmore—Miriam didn't know if Nick had heard of him (Nick hadn't) who had done some of it. It had been awfully chopped down, to a mere bone, with the meat all gone; but that was what people in London seemed to like. They were very innocent—thousands of little dogs amusing themselves with a bone. At any rate she had made something, she had made a figure, of the woman—a dreadful stick, with what Dashwood had muddled her into; and Miriam added in the complacency of her young expansion: "Oh give me fifty words any time and the ghost of a situation, and I'll set you up somebody. Besides, I mustn't abuse poor Yolande—she has saved us," she said.

"'Yolande'—?"

"Our ridiculous play. That's the name of the impossible woman. She has put bread into our mouths and she's a loaf on the shelf for the future. The rights are mine."

"You're lucky to have them," said Nick a little vaguely, troubled about his sitter's nose, which was somehow Jewish without the convex arch.

"Indeed I am. He gave them to me. Wasn't it charming?"

"'He' gave them—Mr. Dashwood?"

"Dear me, no—where should poor Dashwood have got them? He hasn't a penny in the world. Besides, if he had got them he'd have kept them. I mean your blessed cousin."

"I see—they're a present from Peter."

"Like many other things. Isn't he a dear? If it hadn't been for him the shelf would have remained bare. He bought the play for this country and America for four hundred pounds, and on the chance: fancy! There was no rush for it, and how could he tell? And then he gracefully pressed it on me. So I've my little capital. Isn't he a duck? You've nice cousins."

Nick assented to the proposition, only inserting an amendment to the effect that surely Peter had nice cousins too, and making, as he went on with his work, a tacit, preoccupied reflexion or two; such as that it must be pleasant to render little services like that to youth, beauty and genius—he rather wondered how Peter could afford them—and that, "duck" as he was, Miss Rooth's benefactor was rather taken for granted. *Sic vos non vobis* softly sounded in his brain. This community of interests, or at least of relations, quickened the flight of time, so that he was still fresh when the sitting came to an end. It was settled Miriam should come back on the morrow, to enable her artist to make the most of the few days of the parliamentary recess; and just before she left him she asked:

"Then you *will* come to-night?"

"Without fail. I hate to lose an hour of you."

"Then I'll place you. It will be my affair."

"You're very kind"—he quite rose to it. "Isn't it a simple matter for me to take a stall? This week I suppose they're to be had."

"I'll send you a box," said Miriam. "You shall do it well. There are plenty now."

"Why should I be lost, all alone, in the grandeur of a box?"

"Can't you bring your friend?"

"My friend?"

"The lady you're engaged to."

"Unfortunately she's out of town."

Miriam looked at him in the grand manner. "Does she leave you alone like that?"

"She thought I should like it—I should be more free to paint. You see I am."

"Yes, perhaps it's good for *me*. Have you got her portrait?" Miriam asked.

"She doesn't like me to paint her."

"Really? Perhaps then she won't like you to paint me."

"That's why I want to be quick!" laughed Nick.

"Before she knows it?"

"Shell know it to-morrow. I shall write to her."

The girl faced him again portentously. "I see you're afraid of her." But she added: "Mention my name; they'll give you the box at the office."

Whether or no Nick were afraid of Mrs. Dallow he still waved away this bounty, protesting that he would rather take a stall according to his wont and pay for it. Which led his guest to declare with a sudden flicker of passion that if he didn't do as she wished she would never sit to him again.

"Ah then you have me," he had to reply. "Only I *don't* see why you should give me so many things."

"What in the world have I given you?"

"Why an idea." And Nick looked at his picture rather ruefully. "I don't mean to say though that I haven't let it fall and smashed it."

"Ah an idea—that *is* a great thing for people in our line. But you'll see me much better from the box and I'll send you Gabriel Nash." She got into the hansom her host's servant had fetched for her, and as Nick turned back into his studio after watching her drive away he laughed at the conception that they were in the same "line."

He did share, in the event, his box at the theatre with Nash, who talked during the *entr'actes* not in the least about the performance or the performer, but about the possible greatness of the art of the portraitist—its reach, its range, its fascination, the magnificent examples it had left us in the past: windows open into history, into psychology, things that were among the most precious possessions of the human race. He insisted above all on the interest, the importance of this great peculiarity of it, that unlike most other forms it was a revelation of two realities, the man whom it was the artist's conscious effort to reveal and the man—the interpreter—expressed in the very quality and temper of that effort. It offered a double vision, the strongest dose of life that art could give, the strongest dose of art that life could give. Nick Dormer had already become aware of having two states of mind when listening to this philosopher; one in which he laughed, doubted, sometimes even reprobated, failed to follow or accept, and another in which his old friend seemed to take the words out of his mouth, to utter for him, better and more completely, the very things he was on the point of saying. Gabriel's saying them at such moments appeared to make them true, to set them up in the world, and to-night he said a good many, especially as to the happiness of cultivating one's own garden, growing there, in stillness and freedom, certain strong, pure flowers that would bloom for ever, bloom long after the rank weeds of the hour were withered and blown away.

It was to keep Miriam Rooth in his eye for his current work that Nick had come to the play; and she dwelt there all the evening, being constantly on the stage. He was so occupied in watching her face—for he now saw pretty clearly what he should attempt to make of it—that he was conscious only in a secondary degree of the story she illustrated, and had in regard to her acting a surprised sense that she was extraordinarily quiet. He remembered her loudness, her violence in Paris, at Peter Sherringham's, her wild wails, the first time, at Madame Carré's; compared with which her present manner was eminently temperate and modern. Nick Dormer was not critical at the theatre; he believed what he saw and had a pleasant sense of the inevitable; therefore he wouldn't have guessed what Gabriel Nash had to tell him—that for this young woman, with her tragic cast and her peculiar attributes, her present performance, full of actuality, of light fine indications and at moments of pointed touches of comedy, was a rare *tour de force*. It went on altogether in a register he hadn't supposed her to possess and in which, as he said, she didn't touch her capital, doing it all with her wonderful little savings. It conveyed to him that she was capable of almost anything.

In one of the intervals they went round to see her; but for Nick this purpose was partly defeated by the extravagant transports, as they struck him, of Mrs. Rooth, whom they found sitting with her daughter and who attacked him with a hundred questions about his dear mother and his charming sisters. She had volumes to say about the day in Paris when they had shown her the kindness she should never forget. She abounded also in admiration of the portrait he had so cleverly begun, declaring she was so eager to see it, however little he might as yet have accomplished, that she should do herself the honour to wait upon him in the morning when Miriam came to sit.

"I'm acting for you to-night," the girl more effectively said before he returned to his place.

"No, that's exactly what you're not doing," Nash interposed with one of his happy sagacities. "You've stopped acting, you've reduced it to the least that will do, you simply are—you're just the visible image, the picture on the wall. It keeps you wonderfully in focus. I've never seen you so beautiful."

Miriam stared at this; then it could be seen that she coloured. "What a luxury in life to have everything explained! He's the great explainer," she herself explained to Nick.

He shook hands with her for good-night. "Well then, we must give him lots to do."

334

She came to his studio in the morning, but unaccompanied by her mother, in allusion to whom she simply said, "Mamma wished to come but I wouldn't let her." They proceeded promptly to business. The girl divested herself of her hat and coat, taking the position already determined. After they had worked more than an hour with much less talk than the day before, Nick being extremely absorbed and Miriam wearing in silence an air of noble compunction for the burden imposed on him, at the end of this period of patience, pervaded by a holy calm, our young lady suddenly got up and exclaimed, "I say, I must see it!"—with which, quickly, she stepped down from her place and came round to the canvas. She had at Nick's request not looked at his work the day before. He fell back, glad to rest, and put down his palette and brushes.

"*Ah bien, c'est tapé!*" she cried as she stood before the easel. Nick was pleased with her ejaculation, he was even pleased with what he had done; he had had a long, happy spurt and felt excited and sanctioned. Miriam, retreating also a little, sank into a high-backed, old-fashioned chair that stood two or three yards from the picture and reclined in it, her head on one side, looking at the rough resemblance. She made a remark or two about it, to which Nick replied, standing behind her and after a moment leaning on the top of the chair. He was away from his work and his eyes searched it with a shy fondness of hope. They rose, however, as he presently became conscious that the door of the large room opposite him had opened without making a sound and that some one stood upon the threshold. The person on the threshold was Julia Dallow.

As soon as he was aware Nick wished he had posted a letter to her the night before. He had written only that morning. There was nevertheless genuine joy in the words with which he bounded toward her—"Ah my dear Julia, what a jolly surprise!"—for her unannounced descent spoke to him above all of an irresistible desire to see him again sooner than they had arranged. She had taken a step forward, but she had done no more, stopping short at the sight of the strange woman, so divested of visiting-gear that she looked half-undressed, who lounged familiarly in the middle of the room and over whom Nick had been still more familiarly hanging. Julia's eyes rested on this embodied unexpectedness, and as they did so she grew pale—so pale that Nick, observing it, instinctively looked back to see what Miriam had done to produce such an effect. She had done nothing at all, which was precisely what was embarrassing; she only stared at the intruder, motionless and superb. She seemed somehow in easy possession of the place, and even at that instant Nick noted how handsome she looked; so that he said to himself inaudibly, in some deeper depth of consciousness, "How I should like to paint her that way!" Mrs. Dallow's eyes moved for a single moment to her friend's; then they turned away—away from Miriam, ranging over the room.

"I've got a sitter, but you mustn't mind that; we're taking a rest. I'm delighted to see you"—he was all cordiality. He closed the door of the studio behind her; his servant was still at the outer door, which was open and through which he saw Julia's carriage drawn up. This made her advance a little further, but still she said nothing; she dropped no answer even when Nick went on with a sense of awkwardness: "When did you come back? I hope nothing has gone wrong. You come at a very interesting moment," he continued, aware as soon as he had spoken of something in his words that might have made her laugh. She was far from laughing, however; she only managed to look neither at him nor at Miriam and to say, after a little, when he had repeated his question about her return:

"I came back this morning—I came straight here."

"And nothing's wrong, I hope?"

"Oh no—everything's all right," she returned very quickly and without expression. She vouchsafed no explanation of her premature descent and took no notice of the seat Nick offered her; neither did she appear to hear him when he begged her not to look yet at the work on the easel—it was in such a dreadful state. He was conscious, as he phrased it, that this request gave to Miriam's position, directly in front of his canvas, an air of privilege which her neglect to recognise in any way Mrs. Dallow's entrance or her importance did nothing to correct. But that mattered less if the appeal failed to reach Julia's intelligence, as he judged, seeing presently how deeply she was agitated. Nothing mattered in face of the sense of danger taking possession of him after she had been in the room a few moments. He wanted to say, "What's the difficulty? Has anything happened?" but he felt how little she would like him to utter words so intimate in presence of the person she had been rudely startled to find between them. He pronounced Miriam's name to her and her own to Miriam, but Julia's recognition of the ceremony was so slight as to be scarcely perceptible. Miriam had the air of waiting for something more before she herself made a sign; and as nothing more came she continued to say nothing and not to budge. Nick added a remark to the effect that Julia would remember to have had the pleasure of meeting her the year before—in Paris, that day at old Peter's; to which Mrs. Dallow made answer, "Ah yes," without any qualification, while she looked down at some rather rusty studies on panels ranged along the floor and resting against the base of the wall. Her discomposure was a clear pain to herself; she had had a shock of extreme violence, and Nick saw that as Miriam showed no symptom of offering to give up her sitting her stay would be of the briefest. He wished that young woman would do something—say she would go, get up, move about; as it was she had the appearance of watching from her point of vantage the other's upset. He made a series of inquiries about Julia's doings in the country, to two or three of which she gave answers monosyllabic and scarcely comprehensible, only turning her eyes round and round the room as in search of something she couldn't find—of an escape, of something that was not Miriam. At last she said—it was at the end of a very few minutes:

"I didn't come to stay—when you're so busy. I only looked in to see if you were here. Good-bye."

"It's charming of you to have come. I'm so glad you've seen for yourself how well I'm occupied," Nick replied, not unconscious of how red he was. This made Mrs. Dallow look at him while Miriam considered them both. Julia's eyes had a strange light he had never seen before—a flash of fear by which he was himself frightened. "Of course I'll see you later," he added in awkward, in really misplaced gaiety while she reached the door, which she opened herself, getting out with no further attention to Miriam. "I wrote to you this morning—you've missed my letter," he repeated behind her, having already given her this information. The door of the studio was very near that of the house, but before she had reached the street the visitors' bell was set ringing. The passage was narrow and she kept in advance of Nick, anticipating his motion to open the street-door. The bell was tinkling still when, by the action of her own hand, a gentleman on the step stood revealed.

"Ah my dear, don't go!" Nick heard pronounced in quick, soft dissuasion and in the now familiar accents of Gabriel Nash. The rectification followed more quickly still, if that were a rectification which so little improved the matter: "I beg a thousand pardons—I thought you were Miriam."

Gabriel gave way and Julia the more sharply pursued her retreat. Her carriage, a victoria with a pair of precious heated horses, had taken a turn up the street, but the coachman had already seen his mistress and was rapidly coming back. He drew near; not so fast, however, but that Gabriel Nash had time to accompany Mrs. Dallow to the edge of the pavement with an apology for the freedom into which he had blundered. Nick was at her other hand, waiting to put her into the carriage and freshly disconcerted by the encounter with Nash, who somehow, as he stood making Julia an explanation that she didn't listen to, looked less eminent than usual, though not more conscious of difficulties. Our young man coloured deeper and watched the footman spring down as the victoria drove up; he heard Nash say something about the honour of having met Mrs. Dallow in Paris. Nick wanted him to go into the house; he damned inwardly his lack of delicacy. He desired a word with Julia alone—as much alone as the two annoying servants would allow. But Nash was not too much discouraged to say: "You came for a glimpse of the great model? Doesn't she sit? That's what I wanted too, this morning—just a look, for a blessing on the day. Ah but you, madam—"

Julia had sprung into her corner while he was still speaking and had flashed out to the coachman a "Home!" which of itself set the horses in motion. The carriage went a few yards, but while Gabriel, with an undiscouraged bow, turned away, Nick Dormer, his hand on the edge of the hood, moved with it.

"You don't like it, but I'll explain," he tried to say for its occupant alone.

"Explain what?" she asked, still very pale and grave, but in a voice that showed nothing. She was thinking of the servants—she could think of them even then.

"Oh it's all right. I'll come in at five," Nick returned, gallantly jocular, while she was whirled away.

Gabriel had gone into the studio and Nick found him standing in admiration before Miriam, who had resumed the position in which she was sitting. "Lord, she's good to-day! Isn't she good to-day?" he broke out, seizing their host by the arm to give him a particular view. Miriam looked indeed still handsomer than before, and she had taken up her attitude again with a splendid, sphinx-like air of being capable of keeping it for ever. Nick said nothing, but went back to work with a tingle of confusion, which began to act after he had resumed his palette as a sharp, a delightful stimulus. Miriam spoke never a word, but she was doubly grand, and for more than an hour, till Nick, exhausted, declared he must stop, the industrious silence was broken only by the desultory discourse of their friend.

XXVII

Nick went to Great Stanhope Street at five o'clock and learned, rather to his surprise, that Julia was not at home—to his surprise because he had told her he would come at that hour, and he attributed to her, with a certain simplicity, an eager state of mind in regard to his explanation. Apparently she was not eager; the eagerness was his own—he was eager to explain. He recognised, not without a certain consciousness of magnanimity in doing so, that there had been some reason for her quick withdrawal from his studio or at any rate for her extreme discomposure there. He had a few days before put in a plea for a snatch of worship in that sanctuary and she had accepted and approved it; but the worship, when the curtain happened to blow back, showed for that of a magnificent young woman, an actress with disordered hair, who wore in a singular degree the appearance of a person settled for many hours. The explanation was easy: it dwelt in the simple truth that when one was painting, even very badly and only for a moment, one had to have models. Nick was impatient to give it with frank, affectionate lips and a full, pleasant admission that it was natural Julia should have been startled; and he was the more impatient that, though he would not in the least have expected her to like finding a strange woman intimately installed with him, she had disliked it even more than would have seemed probable or natural. That was because, not having heard from him about the matter, the impression was for the moment irresistible with her that a trick had been played her. But three minutes with him alone would make the difference.

They would indeed have a considerable difference to make, Nick reflected, as minutes much more numerous elapsed without bringing Mrs. Dallow home. For he had said to the butler that he would come in and wait—though it was odd she should not have left a message for him: she would doubtless return from one moment to the other. He had of course full licence to wait anywhere he preferred; and he was ushered into Julia's particular sitting-room and supplied with tea and the evening papers. After a quarter of an hour, however, he gave little attention to these beguilements, thanks to his feeling still more acutely that since she definitely knew he was coming she might have taken the trouble to be at home. He walked up and down and looked out of the window, took up her books and dropped them again, and then, as half an hour had elapsed, became aware he was really sore. What could she be about when, with London a thankless void, she was of course not paying visits? A footman came in to attend to the fire, whereupon Nick questioned him as to the manner in which she was possibly engaged. The man disclosed the fact that his mistress had gone out but a quarter of an hour before Nick's arrival, and, as if appreciating the opportunity for a little decorous conversation, gave him still more information than he invited. From this it appeared that, as Nick knew, or could surmise, she had the evening before, from the country, wired for the victoria to meet her in the morning at Paddington and then gone straight from the station to the studio, while her maid, with her luggage, proceeded in a cab to Great Stanhope Street. On leaving the studio, however, she had not come directly home; she had chosen this unusual season for an hour's drive in the Park. She had finally re-entered her house, but had remained upstairs all day, seeing no one and not coming down to luncheon. At four o'clock she had ordered the brougham for four forty-five, and had got into it punctually, saying, "To the Park!" as she did so.

Nick, after the footman had left him, made what he could of Julia's sudden passion for the banks of the Serpentine, forsaken and foggy now, inasmuch as the afternoon had come on grey and the light was waning. She usually hated the Park and hated a closed carriage. He had a gruesome vision of her, shrunken into a corner of her brougham and veiled as if in consequence of tears, revolving round the solitude of the Drive. She had of course been deeply displeased and was not herself; the motion of the carriage soothed her, had an effect on her nerves. Nick remembered that in the morning, at his door, she had appeared to be going home; so she had plunged into the drearier resort on second thoughts and as she noted herself near it. He lingered another half-hour, walked up and down the room many times and thought of many things. Had she misunderstood him when he said he would come at five? Couldn't she be sure, even if she had, that he would come early rather than late, and mightn't she have left a message for him on the chance? Going out that way a few minutes before he was to come had even a little the air of a thing done on purpose to offend him; as if she had been so displeased that she had taken the nearest occasion of giving him a sign she meant to break with him. But were these the things Julia did and was that the way she did them—his fine, proud, delicate, generous Julia?

When six o'clock came poor Nick felt distinctly resentful; but he stayed ten minutes longer on the possibility that she would in the morning have understood him to mention that hour. The April dusk began to gather and the unsociability of her behaviour, especially if she were still rumbling round the Park, became absurd. Anecdotes came back to him, vaguely remembered, heard he couldn't have said when or where, of poor artists for whom life had been rendered difficult by wives who wouldn't allow them the use of the living female model and who made scenes if they encountered on the staircase such sources of inspiration. These ladies struck him as vulgar and odious persons, with whom it seemed grotesque that Julia should have anything in common. Of course she was not his wife yet, and of course if she were he should have washed his hands of every form of activity requiring the services of the sitter; but even these qualifications left him with a power to wince at the way in which the woman he was so sure he loved just escaped ranking herself with the Philistines.

At a quarter past six he rang a bell and told the servant who answered it that he was going and that Mrs. Dallow was to be informed as soon as she came in that he had expected to find her and had waited an hour and a quarter. But he had just reached the doorstep of departure when her brougham, emerging from the evening mist, stopped in front of the house. Nick stood there hanging back till she got out, allowing the servants only to help her. She saw him—she was less veiled than his mental vision of her; but this didn't prevent her pausing to give an order to the coachman, a matter apparently requiring some discussion. When she came to the door her visitor remarked that he had been waiting an eternity; to which she replied that he must make no grievance of that—she was too unwell to do him justice. He immediately professed regret and sympathy, adding, however, that in that case she had much better not have gone out. She made no answer to this—there were three servants in the hall who looked as if they might understand at least what was not said to them; only when he followed her in she asked if his idea had been to stay longer.

"Certainly, if you're not too ill to see me."

"Come in then," Julia said, turning back after having gone to the foot of the stairs.

This struck him immediately as a further restriction of his visit: she wouldn't readmit him to the drawing-room or to her boudoir; she would receive him in the impersonal apartment downstairs where she saw people on business. What did she want to do to him? He was prepared by this time for a scene of jealousy, since he was sure he had learned to read her character justly in feeling that if she had the appearance of a cold woman a forked flame in her was liable on occasion to break out. She was very still, but from time to time she would fire off a pistol. As soon as he had closed the door she said without sitting down:

"I daresay you saw I didn't like that at all."

"My having a sitter in that professional way? I was very much annoyed at it myself," Nick answered.

"Why were *you* annoyed? She's very handsome," Mrs. Dallow perversely said.

"I didn't know you had looked at her!" Nick laughed.

Julia had a pause. "Was I very rude?"

"Oh it was all right; it was only awkward for me because you didn't know," he replied.

"I did know; that's why I came."

"How do you mean? My letter couldn't have reached you."

"I don't know anything about your letter," Julia cast about her for a chair and then seated herself on the edge of a sofa with her eyes on the floor.

"She sat to me yesterday; she was there all the morning; but I didn't write to tell you. I went at her with great energy and, absurd as it may seem to you, found myself very tired afterwards. Besides, in the evening I went to see her act."

"Does she act?" asked Mrs. Dallow.

"She's an actress: it's her profession. Don't you remember her that day at Peter's in Paris? She's already a celebrity; she has great talent; she's engaged at a theatre here and is making a sensation. As I tell you, I saw her last night."

"You needn't tell me," Julia returned, looking up at him with a face of which the intense, the tragic sadness startled him.

He had been standing before her, but at this he instantly sat down close, taking her passive hand. "I want to, please; otherwise it must seem so odd to you. I knew she was coming when I wrote to you the day before yesterday. But I didn't tell you then because I didn't know how it would turn out, and I didn't want to exult in advance over a poor little attempt that might come to nothing. Moreover, it was no use speaking of the matter at all unless I told you exactly how it had come about," Nick went on, explaining kindly and copiously. "It was the result of a visit unexpectedly paid me by Gabriel Nash."

"That man—the man who spoke to me?" Her memory of him shuddered into life.

"He did what he thought would please you, but I daresay it didn't. You met him in Paris and didn't like him; so I judged best to hold my tongue about him."

"Do *you* like him?"

"Very much."

"Great heaven!" Julia ejaculated, almost under her breath.

"The reason I was annoyed was because, somehow, when you came in, I suddenly had the air of having got out of those visits and shut myself up in town to do something that I had kept from you. And I have been very unhappy till I could explain."

"You don't explain—you can't explain," Mrs Dallow declared, turning on her companion eyes which, in spite of her studied stillness, expressed deep excitement. "I knew it—I knew everything; that's why I came."

"It was a sort of second-sight—what they call a brainwave," Nick smiled.

"I felt uneasy, I felt a kind of call; it came suddenly, yesterday. It was irresistible; nothing could have kept me this morning."

"That's very serious, but it's still more delightful. You mustn't go away again," said Nick. "We must stick together—forever and ever."

He put his arm round her, but she detached herself as soon as she felt its pressure. She rose quickly, moving away, while, mystified, he sat looking up at her as she had looked a few moments before at him. "I've thought it all over; I've been thinking of it all day," she began. "That's why I didn't come in."

"Don't think of it too much; it isn't worth it."

"You like it more than anything else. You do—you can't deny it," she went on.

"My dear child, what are you talking about?" Nick asked, gently...

"That's what you like—doing what you were this morning; with women lolling, with their things off, to be painted, and people like that man."

Nick slowly got up, hesitating. "My dear Julia, apart from the surprise this morning, do you object to the living model?"

"Not a bit, for you."

"What's the inconvenience then, since in my studio they're only for me?"

"You love it, you revel in it; that's what you want—the only thing you want!" Julia broke out.

"To have models, lolling undressed women, do you mean?"

"That's what I felt, what I knew," she went on—"what came over me and haunted me yesterday so that I couldn't throw it off. It seemed to me that if I could see it with my eyes and have the perfect proof I should feel better, I should be quiet. And now I *am* quiet—after a struggle of some hours, I confess. I *have* seen; the whole thing's before me and I'm satisfied."

"I'm not—to me neither the whole thing nor half of it is before me. What exactly are you talking about?" Nick demanded.

"About what you were doing this morning. That's your innermost preference, that's your secret passion."

"A feeble scratch at something serious? Yes, it was almost serious," he said. "But it was an accident, this morning and yesterday: I got on less wretchedly than I intended."

"I'm sure you've immense talent," Julia returned with a dreariness that was almost droll.

"No, no, I might have had. I've plucked it up: it's too late for it to flower. My dear Julia, I'm perfectly incompetent and perfectly resigned."

"Yes, you looked so this morning, when you hung over her. Oh she'll bring back your talent!"

"She's an obliging and even an intelligent creature, and I've no doubt she would if she could," Nick conceded. "But I've received from you all the help any woman's destined to give me. No one can do for me again what you've done."

"I shouldn't try it again; I acted in ignorance. Oh I've thought it all out!" Julia declared. And then with a strange face of anguish resting on his own: "Before it's too late—before it's too late!"

"Too late for what?"

"For you to be free—for you to be free. And for me—for me to be free too. You hate everything I like!" she flashed out. "Don't pretend, don't pretend!" she went on as a sound of protest broke from him.

"I thought you so awfully *wanted* me to paint," he gasped, flushed and staring.

"I do—I do. That's why you must be free, why we must part?"

"Why we must part—?"

"Oh I've turned it well over. I've faced the hard truth. It wouldn't do at all!" Julia rang out.

"I like the way you talk of it—as if it were a trimming for your dress!" Nick retorted with bitterness. "Won't it do for you to be loved and cherished as well as any woman in England?"

She turned away from him, closing her eyes as not to see something dangerous. "You mustn't give anything up for me. I should feel it all the while and I should hate it. I'm not afraid of the truth, but you are."

"The truth, dear Julia? I only want to know it," Nick insisted. "It seems to me in fact just what I've got hold of. When two persons are united by the tenderest affection and are sane and generous and just, no difficulties that occur in the union their life makes for them are insurmountable, no problems are insoluble."

She appeared for a moment to reflect upon this: it was spoken in a tone that might have touched her. Yet at the end of the moment, lifting her eyes, she brought out: "I hate art, as you call it. I thought I did, I knew I did; but till this morning I didn't know how much."

"Bless your dear soul, *that* wasn't art," Nick pleaded. "The real thing will be a thousand miles away from us; it will never come into the house, *soyez tranquille*. It knows where to look in and where to flee shrieking. Why then should you worry?"

"Because I want to understand, I want to know what I'm doing. You're an artist: you are, you are!" Julia cried, accusing him passionately.

"My poor Julia, it isn't so easy as that, nor a character one can take on from one day to the other. There are all sorts of things; one must be caught young and put through the mill—one must see things as they are. There are very few professions that goes with. There would be sacrifices I never can make."

"Well then, there are sacrifices for both of us, and I can't make them either. I daresay it's all right for you, but for me it would be a terrible mistake. When I think I'm doing a certain thing I mustn't do just the opposite," she kept on as for true lucidity. "There are things I've thought of, the things I like best; and they're not what you mean. It would be a great deception, and it's not the way I see my life, and it would be misery if we don't understand."

He looked at her with eyes not lighted by her words. "If we don't understand what?"

"That we're utterly different—that you're doing it all for *me*."

"And is that an objection to me—what I do for you?" he asked.

"You do too much. You're awfully good, you're generous, you're a dear, oh yes—a dear. But that doesn't make me believe in it. I didn't at bottom, from the first—that's why I made you wait, why I gave you your freedom. Oh I've suspected you," Julia continued, "I had my ideas. It's all right for you, but it won't do for me: I'm different altogether. Why should it always be put upon me when I hate it? What have I done? I was drenched with it before." These last words, as they broke forth, were attended with a quick blush; so that Nick could as quickly discern in them the uncalculated betrayal of an old irritation, an old shame almost—her late husband's flat, inglorious taste for pretty things, his indifference to every chance to play a public part. This had been the humiliation of her youth, and it was indeed a perversity of fate that a new alliance should contain for her even an oblique demand for the same spirit of accommodation, impose on her the secret bitterness of the same concessions. As Nick stood there before her, struggling sincerely with the force that he now felt to be strong in her, the intense resolution to break with him, a force matured in a few hours, he read a riddle that hitherto had baffled him, saw a great mystery become simple. A personal passion for him had all but thrown her into his arms (the sort of thing that even a vain man—and Nick was not especially vain—might hesitate to recognise the strength of); held in check at moments, with a strain of the cord that he could still feel vibrate, by her deep, her rare ambition, and arrested at the last only just in time to save her calculations. His present glimpse of the immense extent of these calculations didn't make him think her cold or poor; there was in fact a positive strange heat in them and they struck him rather as grand and high. The fact that she could drop him even while she longed for him—drop him because it was now fixed in her mind that he wouldn't after all serve her resolve to be associated, so far as a woman could, with great affairs; that she could postpone, and postpone to an uncertainty, the satisfaction of an aching tenderness and plan for the long run—this exhibition of will and courage, of the larger scheme that possessed her, commanded his admiration on the spot. He paid the heavy price of the man of imagination; he was capable of far excursions of the spirit, disloyalties to habit and even to faith, he was open to rare communications. He ached, on his side, for the moment, to convince her that he would achieve what he wouldn't, for the vision of his future she had tried to entertain shone before him as a bribe and a challenge. It struck him there was nothing he couldn't work for enough with her to be so worked with by her. Presently he said:

"You want to be sure the man you marry will be prime minister of England. But how can you be really sure with any one?"

"I can be really sure some men won't!" Julia returned.

"The only safe thing perhaps would be to-marry Mr. Macgeorge," he suggested.

"Possibly not even him."

"You're a prime minister yourself," Nick made answer. "To hold fast to you as I hold, to be determined to be of your party—isn't that political enough, since you're the incarnation of politics?"

"Ah how you hate them!" she wailed again. "I saw that when I saw you this morning. The whole place reeked of your aversion."

"My dear child, the greatest statesmen have had their distractions. What do you make of my hereditary talent? That's a tremendous force."

"It wouldn't carry you far." Then she terribly added, "You must be a great artist." He tossed his head at the involuntary contempt of this, but she went on: "It's beautiful of you to want to give up anything, and I like you for it. I shall always like you. We shall be friends, and I shall always take an interest—!"

But he stopped her there, made a movement which interrupted her phrase, and she suffered him to hold her hand as if she were not afraid of him now. "It isn't only for you," he argued gently; "you're a great deal, but you're not everything. Innumerable vows and pledges repose upon my head. I'm inextricably committed and dedicated. I was brought up in the temple like an infant Samuel; my father was a high-priest and I'm a child of the Lord. And then the life itself—when *you* speak of it I feel stirred to my depths; it's like a herald's trumpet. Fight *with* me, Julia—not against me! Be on my side and we shall do everything. It is uplifting to be a great man before the people— to be loved by them, to be followed by them. An artist isn't—never, never. Why *should* he be? Don't forget how clever I am."

"Oh if it wasn't for that!" she panted, pale with the effort to resist his tone. Then she put it to him: "Do you pretend that if I were to die to-morrow you'd stay in the House?"

"If you were to die? God knows! But you do singularly little justice to my incentives," he pursued. "My political career's everything to my mother."

This but made her say after a moment: "Are you afraid of your mother?"

"Yes, immensely; for she represents ever so many possibilities of disappointment and distress. She represents all my father's as well as all her own, and in them my father tragically lives again. On the other hand I see him in bliss, as I see my mother, over our marriage and our life of common aspirations—though of course that's not a consideration that I can expect to have power with you."

She shook her head slowly, even smiling with her recovered calmness and lucidity. "You'll never hold high office."

"But why not take me as I am?"

"Because I'm abominably keen about that sort of thing—I must recognise my keenness. I must face the ugly truth. I've been through the worst; it's all settled."

"The worst, I suppose, was when you found me this morning."

"Oh that was all right—for you."

"You're magnanimous, Julia; but evidently what's good enough for me isn't good enough for you," Nick spoke with bitterness.

"I don't like you enough—that's the obstacle," she held herself in hand to say.

"You did a year ago; you confessed to it."

"Well, a year ago was a year ago. Things are changed to-day."

"You're very fortunate—to be able to throw away a real devotion," Nick returned.

She had her pocket-handkerchief in her hand, and at this she quickly pressed it to her lips as to check an exclamation. Then for an instant she appeared to be listening to some sound from outside. He interpreted her movement as an honourable impulse to repress the "Do you mean the devotion I was witness of this morning?" But immediately afterwards she said something very different: "I thought I heard a ring. I've telegraphed for Mrs. Gresham."

He wondered. "Why did you do that?"

"Oh I want her."

He walked to the window, where the curtains had not been drawn, and saw in the dusk a cab at the door. When he turned back he went on: "Why won't you trust me to make you like me, as you call it, better? If I make you like me as well as I like you it will be about enough, I think."

"Oh I like you enough for *your* happiness. And I don't throw away a devotion," Mrs. Dallow continued. "I shall be constantly kind to you. I shall be beautiful to you."

"You'll make me lose a fortune," Nick after a moment said.

It brought a slight convulsion, instantly repressed, into her face. "Ah you may have all the money you want!"

"I don't mean yours," he answered with plenty of expression of his own. He had determined on the instant, since it might serve, to tell her what he had never breathed to her before. "Mr. Carteret last year promised me a pot of money on the day we should be man and wife. He has thoroughly set his heart on it."

"I'm sorry to disappoint Mr. Carteret," said Julia. "I'll go and see him. I'll make it all right," she went on. "Then your work, you know, will bring you an income. The great men get a thousand just for a head."

"I'm only joking," Nick returned with sombre eyes that contradicted this profession. "But what things you deserve I should do!"

"Do you mean striking likenesses?"

He watched her a moment. "You do hate it! Pushed to that point, it's curious," he audibly mused.

351

"Do you mean you're joking about Mr. Carteret's promise?"

"No—the promise is real, but I don't seriously offer it as a reason."

"I shall go to Beauclere," Julia said. "You're an hour late," she added in a different tone; for at that moment the door of the room was thrown open and Mrs. Gresham, the butler pronouncing her name, ushered in.

"Ah don't impugn my punctuality—it's my character!" the useful lady protested, putting a sixpence from the cabman into her purse. Nick went off at this with a simplified farewell—went off foreseeing exactly what he found the next day, that the useful lady would have received orders not to budge from her hostess's side. He called on the morrow, late in the afternoon, and Julia saw him liberally, in the spirit of her assurance that she would be "beautiful" to him, that she had not thrown away his devotion; but Mrs. Gresham remained, with whatever delicacies of deprecation, a spectator of her liberality. Julia looked at him kindly, but her companion was more benignant still; so that what Nick did with his own eyes was not to appeal to her to see him a moment alone, but to solicit, in the name of this luxury, the second occupant of the drawing-room. Mrs. Gresham seemed to say, while Julia said so little, "I understand, my poor friend, I know everything—she has told me only *her* side, but I'm so competent that I know yours too—and I enter into the whole thing deeply. But it would be as much as my place is worth to accommodate you." Still, she didn't go so far as to give him an inkling of what he learned on the third day and what he had not gone so far as to suspect—that the two ladies had made rapid arrangements for a scheme of foreign travel. These arrangements had already been carried out when, at the door of the house in Great Stanhope Street, the announcement was made him that the subtle creatures had started that morning for Paris.

XXVIII

They spent on their way to Florence several days in Paris, where Peter Sherringham had as much free talk with his sister as it often befell one member of their family to have with another. He enjoyed, that is, on two different occasions, half an hour's gossip with her in her sitting-room at the hotel. On one of these he took the liberty of asking her whether or no, decidedly, she meant to marry Nick Dormer. Julia expressed to him that she appreciated his curiosity, but that Nick and she were nothing more than relations and good friends. "He tremendously wants it," Peter none the less observed; to which she simply made answer, "Well then, he may want!"

After this, for a while, they sat as silent as if the subject had been quite threshed out between them. Peter felt no impulse to penetrate further, for it was not a habit of the Sherringhams to talk with each other of their love-affairs; and he was conscious of the particular deterrent that he and Julia entertained in general such different sentiments that they could never go far together in discussion. He liked her and was sorry for her, thought her life lonely and wondered she didn't make a "great" marriage. Moreover he pitied her for being without the interests and consolations he himself had found substantial: those of the intellectual, the studious order he considered these to be, not knowing how much she supposed she reflected and studied and what an education she had found in her political aspirations, viewed by him as scarce more a personal part of her than the livery of her servants or the jewels George Dallow's money had bought. Her relations with Nick struck him as queer, but were fortunately none of his business. No business of Julia's was sufficiently his to justify him in an attempt to understand it. That there should have been a question of her marrying Nick was the funny thing rather than that the question should have been dropped. He liked his clever cousin very well as he was—enough for a vague sense that he might be spoiled by alteration to a brother-in-law. Moreover, though not perhaps distinctly conscious of this, Peter pressed lightly on Julia's doings from a tacit understanding that in this case she would let him off as easily. He couldn't have said exactly what it was he judged it pertinent to be let off from: perhaps from irritating inquiry as to whether he had given any more tea-parties for gross young women connected with the theatre.

Peter's forbearance, however, brought him not quite all the security he prefigured. After an interval he indeed went so far as to ask Julia if Nick had been wanting in respect to her; but this was an appeal intended for sympathy, not for other intervention. She answered: "Dear no—though he's very provoking." Thus Peter guessed that they had had a quarrel in which it didn't concern him to meddle: he added her epithet and her flight from England together, and they made up to his perception one of the little magnified embroilments which do duty for the real in superficial lives. It was worse to provoke Julia than not, and Peter thought Nick's doing so not particularly characteristic of his versatility for good. He might wonder why she didn't marry the member for Harsh if the subject had pressingly come up between them; but he wondered still more why Nick didn't marry that gentleman's great backer. Julia said nothing again, as if to give him a chance to address her some challenge that would save her from gushing; but as his impulse appeared to be to change the subject, and as he changed it only by silence, she was reduced to resuming presently:

"I should have thought you'd have come over to see your friend the actress."

"Which of my friends? I know so many actresses," Peter pleaded.

"The woman you inflicted on us in this place a year ago—the one who's in London now."

"Oh Miriam Rooth? I should have liked to come over, but I've been tied fast. Have you seen her there?"

"Yes, I've seen her."

"Do you like her?"

"Not at all."

"She has a lovely voice," Peter hazarded after a moment.

"I don't know anything about her voice—I haven't heard it."

"But she doesn't act in pantomime, does she?"

"I don't know anything about her acting. I saw her in private—at Nick Dormer's studio."

"At Nick's—?" He was interested now.

"What was she doing there?"

"She was sprawling over the room and—rather insolently—staring at me."

If Mrs. Dallow had wished to "draw" her brother she must at this point have suspected she succeeded, in spite of his care to divest his tone of all emotion. "Why, does he know her so well? I didn't know."

"She's sitting to him for her portrait—at least she was then."

"Oh yes, I remember—I put him up to that. I'm greatly interested. Is the portrait good?"

"I haven't the least idea—I didn't look at it. I daresay it's like," Julia threw off.

"But how in the world"—and Peter's interest grew franker—"does Nick find time to paint?"

"I don't know. That horrid man brought her."

"Which horrid man?"—he spoke as if they had their choice.

"The one Nick thinks so clever—the vulgar little man who was at your place that day and tried to talk to me. I remember he abused theatrical people to me—as if I cared anything about them. But he has apparently something to do with your girl."

"Oh I recollect him—I had a discussion with him," Peter patiently said.

"How could you? I must go and dress," his sister went on more importantly.

"He *was* clever, remarkably. Miss Rooth and her mother were old friends of his, and he was the first person to speak of them to me."

"What a distinction! I thought him disgusting!" cried Julia, who was pressed for time and who had now got up.

"Oh you're severe," said Peter, still bland; but when they separated she had given him something to think of.

That Nick was painting a beautiful actress was no doubt in part at least the reason why he was provoking and why his most intimate female friend had come abroad. The fact didn't render him provoking to his kinsman: Peter had on the contrary been quite sincere when he qualified it as interesting. It became indeed on reflexion so interesting that it had perhaps almost as much to do with Sherringham's now prompt rush over to London as it had to do with Julia's coming away. Reflexion taught him further that the matter was altogether a delicate one and suggested that it was odd he should be mixed up with it in fact when, as Julia's own affair, he had but wished to keep out of it. It might after all be his affair a little as well—there was somehow a still more pointed implication of that in his sister's saying to him the next day that she wished immensely he would take a fancy to Biddy Dormer. She said more: she said there had been a time when she believed he *had* done so—believed too that the poor child herself had believed the same. Biddy was far away the nicest girl she knew—the dearest, sweetest, cleverest, *best*, and one of the prettiest creatures in England, which never spoiled anything. She would make as charming a wife as ever a man had, suited to any position, however high, and—Julia didn't mind mentioning it, since her brother would believe it whether she mentioned it or no—was so predisposed in his favour that he would have no trouble at all. In short she herself would see him through—she'd answer for it that he'd have but to speak. Biddy's life at home was horrid; she was very sorry for her—the child was worthy of a better fate. Peter wondered what constituted the horridness of Biddy's life, and gathered that it mainly arose from the fact of Julia's disliking Lady Agnes and Grace and of her profiting comfortably by that freedom to do so which was a fruit of her having given them a house she had perhaps not felt the want of till they were in possession of it. He knew she had always liked Biddy, but he asked himself—this was the rest of his wonder—why she had taken to liking her so extraordinarily just now. He liked her himself—he even liked to be talked to about her and could believe everything Julia said: the only thing that had mystified him was her motive for suddenly saying it. He had assured her he was perfectly sensible of her goodness in so plotting out his future, but was also sorry if he had put it into any one's head—most of all into the girl's own—that he had ever looked at Biddy with a covetous eye. He wasn't in the least sure she would make a good wife, but liked her quite too much to wish to put any such mystery to the test. She was certainly not offered them for cruel experiments. As it happened, really, he wasn't thinking of marrying any one—he had ever so many grounds for neglecting that. Of course one was never safe against accidents, but one could at least take precautions, and he didn't mind telling her that there were several he had taken.

"I don't know what you mean, but it seems to me quite the best precaution would be to care for a charming, steady girl like Biddy. Then you'd be quite in shelter, you'd know the worst that can happen to you, and it wouldn't be bad." The objection he had made to this plea is not important, especially as it was not quite candid; it need only be mentioned that before the pair parted Julia said to him, still in reference to their young friend: "Do go and see her and be nice to her; she'll save you disappointments."

These last words reverberated for him—there was a shade of the portentous in them and they seemed to proceed from a larger knowledge of the subject than he himself as yet possessed. They were not absent from his memory when, in the beginning of May, availing himself, to save time, of the night-service, he crossed from Paris to London. He arrived before the breakfast-hour and went to his sister's house in Great Stanhope Street, where he always found quarters, were she in town or not. When at home she welcomed him, and in her absence the relaxed servants hailed him for the chance he gave them to recover their "form." In either case his allowance of space was large and his independence complete. He had obtained permission this year to take in scattered snatches rather than as a single draught the quantum of holiday to which he was entitled; and there was, moreover, a question of his being transferred to another capital—in which event he believed he might count on a month or two in England before proceeding to his new post.

He waited, after breakfast, but a very few minutes before jumping into a hansom and rattling away to the north. A part of his waiting indeed consisted of a fidgety walk up Bond Street, during which he looked at his watch three or four times while he paused at shop windows for fear of being a little early.

In the cab, as he rolled along, after having given an address—Balaklava Place, Saint John's Wood—the fear he might be too early took curiously at moments the form of a fear that he should be too late: a symbol of the inconsistencies of which his spirit at present was full. Peter Sherringham was nervously formed, too nervously for a diplomatist, and haunted with inclinations and indeed with designs which contradicted each other. He wanted to be out of it and yet dreaded not to be in it, and on this particular occasion the sense of exclusion was an ache. At the same time he was not unconscious of the impulse to stop his cab and make it turn round and drive due south. He saw himself launched in the breezy fact while morally speaking he was hauled up on the hot sand of the principle, and he could easily note how little these two faces of the same idea had in common. However, as the consciousness of going helped him to reflect, a principle was a poor affair if it merely became a fact. Yet from the hour it did turn to action the action *had* to be the particular one in which he was engaged; so that he was in the absurd position of thinking his conduct wiser for the reason that it was directly opposed to his intentions.

He had kept away from London ever since Miriam Rooth came over; resisting curiosity, sympathy, importunate haunting passion, and considering that his resistance, founded, to be salutary, on a general scheme of life, was the greatest success he had yet achieved. He was deeply occupied with plucking up the feeling that attached him to her, and he had already, by various little ingenuities, loosened some of its roots. He had suffered her to make her first appearance on any stage without the comfort of his voice or the applause of his hand; saying to himself that the man who could do the more could do the less and that such an act of fortitude was a proof he should keep straight. It was not exactly keeping straight to run over to London three months later and, the hour he arrived, scramble off to Balaklava Place; but after all he pretended only to be human and aimed in behaviour only at the heroic, never at the monstrous. The highest heroism was obviously three parts tact. He had not written to his young friend that he was coming to England and would call upon her at eleven o'clock in the morning, because it was his secret pride that he had ceased to correspond with her. Sherringham took his prudence where he could find it, and in doing so was rather like a drunkard who should flatter himself he had forsworn liquor since he didn't touch lemonade.

It is a sign of how far he was drawn in different directions at once that when, on reaching Balaklava Place and alighting at the door of a small detached villa of the type of the "retreat," he learned that Miss Rooth had but a quarter of an hour before quitted the spot with her mother—they had gone to the theatre, to rehearsal, said the maid who answered the bell he had set tinkling behind a stuccoed garden-wall: when at the end of his pilgrimage he was greeted by a disappointment he suddenly found himself relieved and for the moment even saved. Providence was after all taking care of him and he submitted to Providence. He would still be watched over doubtless, even should he follow the two ladies to the theatre, send in his card and obtain admission to the scene of their experiments. All his keen taste for these matters flamed up again, and he wondered what the girl was studying, was rehearsing, what she was to do next. He got back into his hansom and drove down the Edgware Road. By the time he reached the Marble Arch he had changed his mind again, had determined to let Miriam alone for that day. It would be over at eight in the evening—he hardly played fair—and then he should consider himself free. Instead of pursuing his friends he directed himself upon a shop in Bond Street to take a place for their performance. On first coming out he had tried, at one of those establishments strangely denominated "libraries," to get a stall, but the people to whom he applied were unable to accommodate him—they hadn't a single seat left. His actual attempt, at another library, was more successful: there was no question of obtaining a stall, but he might by a miracle still have a box. There was a wantonness in paying for a box at a play on which he had already expended four hundred pounds; but while he was mentally measuring this abyss an idea came into his head which flushed the extravagance with the hue of persuasion.

Peter came out of the shop with the voucher for the box in his pocket, turned into Piccadilly, noted that the day was growing warm and fine, felt glad that this time he had no other strict business than to leave a card or two on official people, and asked himself where he should go if he didn't go after Miriam. Then it was that he found himself attaching a lively desire and imputing a high importance to the possible view of Nick Dormer's portrait of her. He wondered which would be the natural place at that hour of the day to look for the artist. The House of Commons was perhaps the nearest one, but

Nick, inconsequent and incalculable though so many of his steps, probably didn't keep the picture there; and, moreover, it was not generally characteristic of him to be in the natural place. The end of Peter's debate was that he again entered a hansom and drove to Calcutta Gardens. The hour was early for calling, but cousins with whom one's intercourse was mainly a conversational scuffle would accept it as a practical illustration of that method. And if Julia wanted him to be nice to Biddy—which was exactly, even if with a different view, what he wanted himself—how could he better testify than by a visit to Lady Agnes—he would have in decency to go to see her some time—at a friendly, fraternising hour when they would all be likely to be at home?

Unfortunately, as it turned out, they were none of them at home, so that he had to fall back on neutrality and the butler, who was, however, more luckily, an old friend. Her ladyship and Miss Dormer were absent from town, paying a visit; and Mr. Dormer was also away, or was on the point of going away for the day. Miss Bridget was in London, but was out; Peter's informant mentioned with earnest vagueness that he thought she had gone somewhere to take a lesson. On Peter's asking what sort of lesson he meant he replied: "Oh I think—a—the a-sculpture, you know, sir." Peter knew, but Biddy's lesson in "a-sculpture"—it sounded on the butler's lips like a fashionable new art—struck him a little as a mockery of the helpful spirit in which he had come to look her up. The man had an air of participating respectfully in his disappointment and, to make up for it, added that he might perhaps find Mr. Dormer at his other address. He had gone out early and had directed his servant to come to Rosedale Road in an hour or two with a portmanteau: he was going down to Beauclere in the course of the day, Mr. Carteret being ill—perhaps Mr. Sherringham didn't know it. Perhaps too Mr. Sherringham would catch him in Rosedale Road before he took his train—he was to have been busy there for an hour. This was worth trying, and Peter immediately drove to Rosedale Road; where in answer to his ring the door was opened to him by Biddy Dormer.

XXIX

When that young woman saw him her cheek exhibited the prettiest, pleased, surprised red he had ever observed there, though far from unacquainted with its living tides, and she stood smiling at him with the outer dazzle in her eyes, still making him no motion to enter. She only said, "Oh Peter!" and then, "I'm all alone."

"So much the better, dear Biddy. Is that any reason I shouldn't come in?"

"Dear no—do come in. You've just missed Nick; he has gone to the country—half an hour ago." She had on a large apron and in her hand carried a small stick, besmeared, as his quick eye saw, with modelling-clay. She dropped the door and fled back before him into the studio, where, when he followed her, she was in the act of flinging a damp cloth over a rough head, in clay, which, in the middle of the room, was supported on a high wooden stand. The effort to hide what she had been doing before he caught a glimpse of it made her redder still and led to her smiling more, to her laughing with a confusion of shyness and gladness that charmed him. She rubbed her hands on her apron, she pulled it off, she looked delightfully awkward, not meeting Peter's eye, and she said: "I'm just scraping here a little—you mustn't mind me. What I do is awful, you know. *Please*, Peter, don't look, I've been coming here lately to make my little mess, because mamma doesn't particularly like it at home. I've had a lesson or two from a lady who exhibits, but you wouldn't suppose it to see what I do. Nick's so kind; he lets me come here; he uses the studio so little; I do what I want, or rather what I can. What a pity he's gone—he'd have been so glad. I'm really alone—I hope you don't mind. Peter, *please* don't look."

Peter was not bent on looking; his eyes had occupation enough in Biddy's own agreeable aspect, which was full of a rare element of domestication and responsibility. Though she had, stretching her bravery, taken possession of her brother's quarters, she struck her visitor as more at home and more herself than he had ever seen her. It was the first time she had been, to his notice, so separate from her mother and sister. She seemed to know this herself and to be a little frightened by it—just enough to make him wish to be reassuring. At the same time Peter also, on this occasion, found himself touched with diffidence, especially after he had gone back and closed the door and settled down to a regular call; for he became acutely conscious of what Julia had said to him in Paris and was unable to rid himself of the suspicion that it had been said with Biddy's knowledge. It wasn't that he supposed his sister had told the girl she meant to do what she could to make him propose to her: that would have been cruel to her—if she liked him enough to consent—in Julia's perfect uncertainty. But Biddy participated by imagination, by divination, by a clever girl's secret, tremulous instincts, in her good friend's views about her, and this probability constituted for Sherringham a sort of embarrassing publicity. He had impressions, possibly gross and unjust, in regard to the way women move constantly together amid such considerations and subtly intercommunicate, when they don't still more subtly dissemble, the hopes or fears of which persons of the opposite sex form the subject. Therefore poor Biddy would know that if she failed to strike him in the right light it wouldn't be for want of an attention definitely called to her claims. She would have been tacitly rejected, virtually condemned. He couldn't without an impulse of fatuity endeavour to make up for this to her by consoling kindness; he was aware that if any one knew it a man would be ridiculous who should take so much as that for granted. But no one would know it: he oddly enough in this calculation of security left Biddy herself out. It didn't occur to him that she might have a secret, small irony to spare for his ingenious and magnanimous effort to show her how much he liked her in reparation to her for not liking her more. This high charity coloured at any rate the whole of his visit to Rosedale Road, the whole of the pleasant, prolonged chat that kept him there more than an hour. He begged the girl to go on with her work, not to let him interrupt it; and she obliged him at last, taking the cloth off the lump of clay and giving him a chance to be delightful by guessing that the shapeless mass was intended, or would be intended after a while, for Nick. He saw she was more comfortable when she began again to smooth it and scrape it with her little stick, to manipulate it with an ineffectual air of knowing how; for this gave her something to do, relieved her nervousness and permitted her to turn away from him when she talked.

He walked about the room and sat down; got up and looked at Nick's things; watched her at moments in silence—which made her always say in a minute that he was not to pass judgement or she could do nothing; observed how her position before her high stand, her lifted arms, her turns of the head, considering her work this way and that, all helped her to be pretty. She repeated again and again that it was an immense pity about Nick, till he was obliged to say he didn't care a straw for Nick and was perfectly content with the company he found. This was not the sort of tone he thought it right, given the conditions, to take; but then even the circumstances didn't require him to pretend he liked her less than he did. After all she was his cousin; she would cease to be so if she should become his wife; but one advantage of her not entering into that relation was precisely that she would remain his cousin. It was very pleasant to find a young, bright, slim, rose-coloured kinswoman all ready to recognise consanguinity when one came back from cousinless foreign lands. Peter talked about family matters; he didn't know, in his exile, where no one took an interest in them, what a fund of latent curiosity about them he treasured. It drew him on to gossip accordingly and to feel how he had with Biddy indefeasible properties in common—ever so many things as to which they'd always understand each other *à demi-mot*. He smoked a cigarette because she begged him—people always smoked in studios and it made her feel so much more an artist. She apologised for the badness of her work on the ground that Nick was so busy he could scarcely ever give her a sitting; so that she had to do the head from photographs and occasional glimpses. They had hoped to be able to put in an hour that morning, but news had suddenly come that Mr. Carteret was worse, and Nick had hurried down to Beauclere. Mr. Carteret was very ill, poor old dear, and Nick and he were immense friends. Nick had always been charming to him. Peter and Biddy took the concerns of the houses of Dormer and Sherringham in order, and the young man felt after a little as if they were as wise as a French *conseil de famille* and settling what was best for every one. He heard all about Lady Agnes; he showed an interest in the detail of her existence that he had not supposed himself to possess, though indeed Biddy threw out intimations which excited his curiosity, presenting her mother in a light that might call on his sympathy.

"I don't think she has been very happy or very pleased of late," the girl said. "I think she has had some disappointments, poor dear mamma; and Grace has made her go out of town for three or four days in the hope of a little change. They've gone down to see an old lady, Lady St. Dunstans, who never comes to London now and who, you know—she's tremendously old—was papa's godmother. It's not very lively for Grace, but Grace is such a dear she'll do anything for mamma. Mamma will go anywhere, no matter at what risk of discomfort, to see people she can talk with about papa."

Biddy added in reply to a further question that what her mother was disappointed about was—well, themselves, her children and all their affairs; and she explained that Lady Agnes wanted all kinds of things for them that didn't come, that they didn't get or seem likely to get, so that their life appeared altogether a failure. She wanted a great deal, Biddy admitted; she really wanted everything, for she had thought in her happier days that everything was to be hers. She loved them all so much and was so proud too: she couldn't get over the thought of their not being successful. Peter was unwilling to press at this point, for he suspected one of the things Lady Agnes wanted; but Biddy relieved him a little by describing her as eager above all that Grace should get married.

"That's too unselfish of her," he pronounced, not caring at all for Grace. "Cousin Agnes ought to keep her near her always, if Grace is so obliging and devoted."

"Oh mamma would give up anything of that sort for our good; she wouldn't sacrifice us that way!" Biddy protested. "Besides, I'm the one to stay with mamma; not that I can manage and look after her and do everything so well as Grace. But, you know, I *want* to," said Biddy with a liquid note in her voice—and giving her lump of clay a little stab for mendacious emphasis.

"But doesn't your mother want the rest of you to get married—Percival and Nick and you?" Peter asked.

"Oh she has given up Percy. I don't suppose she thinks it would do. Dear Nick of course—that's just what she does want."

He had a pause. "And you, Biddy?"

"Oh I daresay. But that doesn't signify—I never shall."

Peter got up at this; the tone of it set him in motion and he took a turn round the room. He threw off something cheap about her being too proud; to which she replied that that was the only thing for a girl to be to get on.

"What do you mean by getting on?"—and he stopped with his hands in his pockets on the other side of the studio.

"I mean crying one's eyes out!" Biddy unexpectedly exclaimed; but she drowned the effect of this pathetic paradox in a laugh of clear irrelevance and in the quick declaration: "Of course it's about Nick that she's really broken-hearted."

"What's the matter with Nick?" he went on with all his diplomacy.

"Oh Peter, what's the matter with Julia?" Biddy quavered softly back to him, her eyes suddenly frank and mournful. "I daresay you know what we all hoped, what we all supposed from what they told us. And now they won't!" said the girl.

"Yes, Biddy, I know. I had the brightest prospect of becoming your brother-in-law: wouldn't that have been it—or something like that? But it's indeed visibly clouded. What's the matter with them? May I have another cigarette?" Peter came back to the wide, cushioned bench where he had previously lounged: this was the way they took up the subject he wanted most to look into. "Don't they know how to love?" he speculated as he seated himself again.

"It seems a kind of fatality!" Biddy sighed.

He said nothing for some moments, at the end of which he asked if his companion were to be quite alone during her mother's absence. She replied that this parent was very droll about that: would never leave her alone and always thought something dreadful would happen to her. She had therefore arranged that Florence Tressilian should come and stay in Calcutta Gardens for the next few days—to look after her and see she did no wrong. Peter inquired with fulness into Florence Tressilian's identity: he greatly hoped that for the success of Lady Agnes's precautions she wasn't a flighty young genius like Biddy. She was described to him as tremendously nice and tremendously clever, but also tremendously old and tremendously safe; with the addition that Biddy was tremendously fond of her and that while she remained in Calcutta Gardens they expected to enjoy themselves tremendously. She was to come that afternoon before dinner.

"And are you to dine at home?" said Peter.

"Certainly; where else?"

"And just you two alone? Do you call that enjoying yourselves tremendously?"

"It will do for me. No doubt I oughtn't in modesty to speak for poor Florence."

"It isn't fair to her; you ought to invite some one to meet her."

"Do you mean you, Peter?" the girl asked, turning to him quickly and with a look that vanished the instant he caught it.

"Try me. I'll come like a shot."

"That's kind," said Biddy, dropping her hands and now resting her eyes on him gratefully. She remained in this position as if under a charm; then she jerked herself back to her work with the remark: "Florence will like that immensely."

"I'm delighted to please Florence—your description of her's so attractive!" Sherringham laughed. And when his companion asked him if he minded there not being a great feast, because when her mother went away she allowed her a fixed amount for that sort of thing and, as he might imagine, it wasn't millions—when Biddy, with the frankness of their pleasant kinship, touched anxiously on this economic point (illustrating, as Peter saw, the lucidity with which Lady Agnes had had in her old age to learn to recognise the occasions when she could be conveniently frugal) he answered that the shortest dinners were the best, especially when one was going to the theatre. That was his case to-night, and did Biddy think he might look to Miss Tressilian to go with them? They'd have to dine early—he wanted not to miss a moment.

"The theatre—Miss Tressilian?" she stared, interrupted and in suspense again.

"Would it incommode you very much to dine say at 7.15 and accept a place in my box? The finger of Providence was in it when I took a box an hour ago. I particularly like your being free to go—if you are free."

She began almost to rave with pleasure. "Dear Peter, how good you are! They'll have it at any hour. Florence will be so glad."

"And has Florence seen Miss Rooth?"

"Miss Rooth?" the girl repeated, redder than before. He felt on the spot that she had heard of the expenditure of his time and attention on that young lady. It was as if she were conscious of how conscious he would himself be in speaking of her, and there was a sweetness in her allowance for him on that score. But Biddy was more confused for him than he was for himself. He guessed in a moment how much she had thought over what she had heard; this was indicated by her saying vaguely, "No, no, I've not seen her." Then she knew she was answering a question he hadn't asked her, and she went on: "We shall be too delighted. I saw her—perhaps you remember—in your rooms in Paris. I thought her so wonderful then! Every one's talking of her here. But we don't go to the theatre much, you know: we don't have boxes offered us except when *you* come. Poor Nick's too much taken up in the evening. I've wanted awfully to see her. They say she's magnificent."

"I don't know," Peter was glad to be able honestly to answer. "I haven't seen her."

"You haven't seen her?"

"Never, Biddy. I mean on the stage. In private often—yes," he conscientiously added.

"Oh!" Biddy exclaimed, bending her face on Nick's bust again. She asked him no question about the new star, and he offered her no further information. There were things in his mind pulling him different ways, so that for some minutes silence was the result of the conflict. At last he said, after an hesitation caused by the possibility that she was ignorant of the fact he had lately elicited from Julia, though it was more probable she might have learned it from the same source:

"Am I perhaps indiscreet in alluding to the circumstance that Nick has been painting Miss Rooth's portrait?"

"You're not indiscreet in alluding to it to me, because I know it."

"Then there's no secret nor mystery about it?"

Biddy just considered. "I don't think mamma knows it."

"You mean you've been keeping it from her because she wouldn't like it?"

"We're afraid she may think papa wouldn't have liked it."

This was said with an absence of humour at which Peter could but show amusement, though he quickly recovered himself, repenting of any apparent failure of respect to the high memory of his late celebrated relative. He threw off rather vaguely: "Ah yes, I remember that great man's ideas," and then went on: "May I ask if you know it, the fact we're talking of, through Julia or through Nick?"

"I know it from both of them."

"Then if you're in their confidence may I further ask if this undertaking of Nick's is the reason why things seem to be at an end between them?"

"Oh I don't think she likes it," Biddy had to say.

"Isn't it good?"

"Oh I don't mean the picture—she hasn't seen it. But his having done it."

"Does she dislike it so much that that's why she won't marry him?"

368

Biddy gave up her work, moving away from it to look at it. She came and sat down on the long bench on which Sherringham had placed himself. Then she broke out: "Oh Peter, it's a great trouble—it's a very great trouble; and I can't tell you, for I don't understand it."

"If I ask you," he said, "it's not to pry into what doesn't concern me; but Julia's my sister, and I can't after all help taking some interest in her life. She tells me herself so little. She doesn't think me worthy."

"Ah poor Julia!" Biddy wailed defensively. Her tone recalled to him that Julia had at least thought him worthy to unite himself to Bridget Dormer, and inevitably betrayed that the girl was thinking of that also. While they both thought of it they sat looking into each other's eyes.

"Nick, I'm sure, doesn't treat *you* that way; I'm sure he confides in you; he talks to you about his occupations, his ambitions," Peter continued. "And you understand him, you enter into them, you're nice to him, you help him."

"Oh Nick's life—it's very dear to me," Biddy granted.

"That must be jolly for him."

"It makes *me* very happy."

Peter uttered a low, ambiguous groan; then he cried with irritation; "What the deuce is the matter with them then? Why can't they hit it off together and be quiet and rational and do what every one wants them to?"

"Oh Peter, it's awfully complicated!" the girl sighed with sagacity.

"Do you mean that Nick's in love with her?"

"In love with Julia?"

"No, no, with Miriam Rooth."

She shook her head slowly, then with a smile which struck him as one of the sweetest things he had ever seen—it conveyed, at the expense of her own prospects, such a shy, generous little mercy of reassurance—"He isn't, Peter," she brought out. "Julia thinks it trifling—all that sort of thing," she added, "She wants him to go in for different honours."

"Julia's the oddest woman. I mean I thought she loved him," Peter explained. "And when you love a person—!" He continued to make it out, leaving his sentence impatiently unfinished, while Biddy, with lowered eyes, sat waiting—it so interested her—to learn what you did when you loved a person. "I can't conceive her giving him up. He has great ability, besides being such a good fellow."

"It's for his happiness, Peter—that's the way she reasons," Biddy set forth. "She does it for an idea; she has told me a great deal about it, and I see the way she feels."

"You try to, Biddy, because you're such a dear good-natured girl, but I don't believe you do in the least," he took the liberty of replying. "It's too little the way you yourself would feel. Julia's idea, as you call it, must be curious."

"Well, it is, Peter," Biddy mournfully admitted. "She won't risk not coming out at the top."

"At the top of what?"

"Oh of everything." Her tone showed a trace of awe of such high views.

"Surely one's at the top of everything when one's in love."

"I don't know," said the girl.

"Do you doubt it?" Peter asked.

"I've never been in love and I never shall be."

"You're as perverse, in your way, as Julia," he returned to this. "But I confess I don't understand Nick's attitude any better. He seems to me, if I may say so, neither fish nor flesh."

"Oh his attitude's very noble, Peter; his state of mind's wonderfully interesting," Biddy pleaded. "Surely *you* must be in favour of art," she beautifully said.

It made him look at her a moment. "Dear Biddy, your little digs are as soft as zephyrs."

She coloured, but she protested. "My little digs? What do you mean? Aren't you in favour of art?"

"The question's delightfully simple. I don't know what you're talking about. Everything has its place. A parliamentary life," he opined, "scarce seems to me the situation for portrait-painting."

"That's just what Nick says."

"You talk of it together a great deal?"

"Yes, Nick's very good to me."

"Clever Nick! And what do you advise him?"

"Oh to *do* something."

"That's valuable," Peter laughed. "Not to give up his sweetheart for the sake of a paint-pot, I hope?"

"Never, never, Peter! It's not a question of his giving up," Biddy pursued, "for Julia has herself shaken free. I think she never really felt safe—she loved him, but was afraid of him. Now she's only afraid—she has lost the confidence she tried to have. Nick has tried to hold her, but she has wrested herself away. Do you know what she said to me? She said, 'My confidence has gone for ever.'"

"I didn't know she was such a prig!" Julia's brother commented. "They're queer people, verily, with water in their veins instead of blood. You and I wouldn't be like that, should we?—though you *have* taken up such a discouraging position about caring for a fellow."

"I care for art," poor Biddy returned.

"You do, to some purpose"—and Peter glanced at the bust.

"To that of making you laugh at me."

But this he didn't heed. "Would you give a good man up for 'art'?"

"A good man? What man?"

"Well, say me—if I wanted to marry you."

She had the briefest of pauses. "Of course I would—in a moment. At any rate I'd give up the House of Commons," she amended. "That's what Nick's going to do now—only you mustn't tell any one."

Peter wondered. "He's going to chuck up his seat?"

"I think his mind is made up to it. He has talked me over—we've had some deep discussions. Yes, I'm on the side of art!" she ardently said.

"Do you mean in order to paint—to paint that girl?" Peter went on.

"To paint every one—that's what he wants. By keeping his seat he hasn't kept Julia, and she was the thing he cared for most in public life. When he has got out of the whole thing his attitude, as he says, will be at least clear. He's tremendously interesting about it, Peter," Biddy declared; "has talked to me wonderfully—has won me over. Mamma's heart-broken; telling *her* will be the hardest part."

"If she doesn't know," he asked, "why then is she heart-broken?"

"Oh at the hitch about their marriage—she knows that. Their marriage has been so what she wanted. She thought it perfection. She blames Nick fearfully. She thinks he held the whole thing in his hand and that he has thrown away a magnificent opportunity."

"And what does Nick say to her?"

"He says, 'Dear old mummy!'"

"That's good," Peter pronounced.

"I don't know what will become of her when this other blow arrives," Biddy went on. "Poor Nick wants to please her—he does, he does. But, as he says, you can't please every one and you must before you die please yourself a little."

Nick's kinsman, whose brother-in-law he was to have been, sat looking at the floor; the colour had risen to his face while he listened. Then he sprang up and took another turn about the room. His companion's artless but vivid recital had set his blood in motion. He had taken Nick's political prospects very much for granted, thought of them as definite and almost dazzling. To learn there was something for which he was ready to renounce such honours, and to recognise the nature of that bribe, affected our young man powerfully and strangely. He felt as if he had heard the sudden blare of a trumpet, yet felt at the same time as if he had received a sudden slap in the face. Nick's bribe was "art"—the strange temptress with whom he himself had been wrestling and over whom he had finally ventured to believe that wisdom and training had won a victory. There was something in the conduct of his old friend and playfellow that made all his reasonings small. So unexpected, so courageous a choice moved him as a reproach and a challenge. He felt ashamed of having placed himself so unromantically on his guard, and rapidly said to himself that if Nick could afford to allow so much for "art" he might surely exhibit some of the same confidence. There had never been the least avowed competition between the cousins—their lines lay too far apart for that; but they nevertheless rode their course in sight of each other, and Peter had now the impression of suddenly seeing Nick Dormer give his horse the spur, bound forward and fly over a wall. He was put on his mettle and hadn't to look long to spy an obstacle he too might ride at. High rose his curiosity to see what warrant his kinsman might have for such risks—how he was mounted for such exploits. He really knew little about Nick's talent—so little as to feel no right to exclaim "What an ass!" when Biddy mentioned the fact which the existence of real talent alone could redeem from absurdity. All his eagerness to see what Nick had been able to make of such a subject as Miriam Rooth came back to him: though it was what mainly had brought him to Rosedale Road he had forgotten it in the happy accident of his encounter with the girl. He was conscious that if the surprise of a revelation of power were in store for him Nick would be justified more than he himself would feel reinstated in self-respect; since the courage of renouncing the forum for the studio hovered before him as greater than the courage of marrying an actress whom one was in love with: the reward was in the latter case so much more immediate. Peter at any rate asked Biddy what Nick had done with his portrait of Miriam. He hadn't seen it anywhere in rummaging about the room.

"I think it's here somewhere, but I don't know," she replied, getting up to look vaguely round her.

"Haven't you seen it? Hasn't he shown it to you?"

She rested her eyes on him strangely a moment, then turned them away with a mechanical air of still searching. "I think it's in the room, put away with its face to the wall."

"One of those dozen canvases with their backs to us?"

"One of those perhaps."

"Haven't you tried to see?"

"I haven't touched them"—and Biddy had a colour.

"Hasn't Nick had it out to show you?"

"He says it's in too bad a state—it isn't finished—it won't do."

"And haven't you had the curiosity to turn it round for yourself?"

The embarrassed look in her face deepened under his insistence and it seemed to him that her eyes pleaded with him a moment almost to tears. "I've had an idea he wouldn't like it."

Her visitor's own desire, however, had become too sharp for easy forbearance. He laid his hand on two or three canvases which proved, as he extricated them, to be either blank or covered with rudimentary forms. "Dear Biddy, have you such intense delicacy?" he asked, pulling out something else.

The inquiry was meant in familiar kindness, for Peter was struck even to admiration with her having a sense of honour that all girls haven't. She must in this particular case have longed for a sight of Nick's work—the work that had brought about such a crisis in his life. But she had passed hours in his studio alone without permitting herself a stolen peep; she was capable of that if she believed it would please him. Peter liked a charming girl's being capable of that—he had known charming girls who wouldn't in the least have been—and his question was really a form of homage. Biddy, however, apparently discovered some light mockery in it, and she broke out incongruously:

"I haven't wanted so much to see it! I don't care for her so much as that!"

"So much as what?" He couldn't but wonder.

"I don't care for his actress—for that vulgar creature. I don't like her!" said Biddy almost startlingly.

Peter stared. "I thought you hadn't seen her."

"I saw her in Paris—twice. She was wonderfully clever, but she didn't charm me."

He quickly considered, saying then all kindly: "I won't inflict the thing on you in that case—we'll leave it alone for the present." Biddy made no reply to this at first, but after a moment went straight over to the row of stacked canvases and exposed several of them to the light. "Why did you say you wished to go to the theatre to-night?" her companion continued.

Still she was silent; after which, with her back turned to him and a little tremor in her voice while she drew forth successively her brother's studies, she made answer: "For the sake of your company, Peter! Here it is, I think," she added, moving a large canvas with some effort. "No, no, I'll hold it for you. Is that the light?"

She wouldn't let him take it; she bade him stand off and allow her to place it in the right position. In this position she carefully presented it, supporting it at the proper angle from behind and showing her head and shoulders above it. From the moment his eyes rested on the picture Peter accepted this service without protest. Unfinished, simplified and in some portions merely suggested, it was strong, vivid and assured, it had already the look of life and the promise of power. Peter felt all this and was startled, was strangely affected—he had no idea Nick moved with that stride. Miriam, seated, was represented in three-quarters, almost to her feet. She leaned forward with one of her legs crossed over the other, her arms extended and foreshortened, her hands locked together round her knee. Her beautiful head was bent a little, broodingly, and her splendid face seemed to look down at life. She had a grand appearance of being raised aloft, with a wide regard, a survey from a height of intelligence, for the great field of the artist, all the figures and passions he may represent. Peter asked himself where his kinsman had learned to paint like that. He almost gasped at the composition of the thing and at the drawing of the difficult arms. Biddy abstained from looking round the corner of the canvas as she held it; she only watched, in Peter's eyes, for this gentleman's impression of it. That she easily caught, and he measured her impression—her impression of *his* impression—when he went after a few minutes to relieve her. She let him lift the thing out of her grasp; he moved it and rested it, so that they could still see it, against the high back of a chair. "It's tremendously good," he then handsomely pronounced.

"Dear, dear Nick," Biddy murmured, looking at it now.

"Poor, poor Julia!" Peter was prompted to exclaim in a different tone. His companion made no rejoinder to this, and they stood another minute or two side by side and in silence, gazing at the portrait. At last he took up his hat—he had no more time, he must go. "Will you come to-night all the same?" he asked with a laugh that was somewhat awkward and an offer of a hand-shake.

"All the same?" Biddy seemed to wonder.

"Why you say she's a terrible creature," Peter completed with his eyes on the painted face.

"Oh anything for art!" Biddy smiled.

"Well, at seven o'clock then." And Sherringham departed, leaving the girl alone with the Tragic Muse and feeling with a quickened rush the beauty of that young woman as well as, all freshly, the peculiar possibilities of Nick.

XXX

It was not till after the noon of the next day that he was to see Miriam Rooth. He wrote her a note that evening, to be delivered to her at the theatre, and during the performance she sent round to him a card with "All right, come to luncheon to-morrow" scrawled on it in pencil.

376

When he presented himself at Balaklava Place he learned that the two ladies had not come in—they had gone again early to rehearsal; but they had left word that he was to be pleased to wait, they would appear from one moment to the other. It was further mentioned to him, as he was ushered into the drawing-room, that Mr. Dashwood was in possession of that ground. This circumstance, however, Peter barely noted: he had been soaring so high for the past twelve hours that he had almost lost consciousness of the minor differences of earthly things. He had taken Biddy Dormer and her friend Miss Tressilian home from the play and after leaving them had walked about the streets, had roamed back to his sister's house, in a state of exaltation the intenser from his having for the previous time contained himself, thinking it more decorous and considerate, less invidious and less blatant, not to "rave." Sitting there in the shade of the box with his companions he had watched Miriam in attentive but inexpressive silence, glowing and vibrating inwardly, yet for these fine, deep reasons not committing himself to the spoken rapture. Delicacy, it appeared to him, should rule the hour; and indeed he had never had a pleasure less alloyed than this little period of still observation and repressed ecstasy. Miriam's art lost nothing by it, and Biddy's mild nearness only gained. This young lady was virtually mute as well—wonderingly, dauntedly, as if she too associated with the performer various other questions than that of her mastery of her art. To this mastery Biddy's attitude was a candid and liberal tribute: the poor girl sat quenched and pale, as if in the blinding light of a comparison by which it would be presumptuous even to be annihilated. Her subjection, however, was a gratified, a charmed subjection: there was beneficence in such beauty—the beauty of the figure that moved before the footlights and spoke in music—even if it deprived one of hope. Peter didn't say to her in vulgar elation and in reference to her whimsical profession of dislike at the studio, "Well, do you find our friend so disagreeable now?" and she was grateful to him for his forbearance, for the tacit kindness of which the idea seemed to be: "My poor child, I'd prefer you if I could; but—judge for yourself—how can I? Expect of me only the possible. Expect that certainly, but only that." In the same degree Peter liked Biddy's sweet, hushed air of judging for herself, of recognising his discretion and letting him off while she was lost in the illusion, in the convincing picture of the stage. Miss Tressilian did most of the criticism: she broke out cheerfully and sonorously from time to time, in reference to the actress, "Most striking certainly," or "She *is* clever, isn't she?" She uttered a series of propositions to which her companions found it impossible to respond. Miss Tressilian was disappointed in nothing but their enjoyment: they didn't seem to think the exhibition as amusing as she.

Walking away through the ordered void of Lady Agnes's quarter, with the four acts of the play glowing again before him in the smokeless London night, Peter found the liveliest thing in his impression the certitude that if he had never seen Miriam before and she had had for him none of the advantages of association, he would still have recognised in her performance the richest interest the theatre had ever offered him. He floated in the felicity of it, in the general encouragement of a sense of the perfectly *done*, in the almost aggressive bravery of still larger claims for an art which could so triumphantly, so exquisitely render life. "Render it?" he said to himself. "Create it and reveal it, rather; give us something new and large and of the first order!" He had *seen* Miriam now; he had never seen her before; he had never seen her till he saw her in her conditions. Oh her conditions—there were many things to be said about them; they were paltry enough as yet, inferior, inadequate, obstructive, as compared with the right, full, finished setting of such a talent; but the essence of them was now, irremovably, in our young man's eyes, the vision of how the uplifted stage and the listening house transformed her. That idea of her having no character of her own came back to him with a force that made him laugh in the empty street: this was a disadvantage she reduced so to nothing that obviously he hadn't known her till to-night. Her character was simply to hold you by the particular spell; any other—the good nature of home, the relation to her mother, her friends, her lovers, her debts, the practice of virtues or industries or vices—was not worth speaking of. These things were the fictions and shadows; the representation was the deep substance.

Peter had as he went an intense vision—he had often had it before—of the conditions still absent, the great and complete ones, those which would give the girl's talent a superior, a discussable stage. More than ever he desired them, mentally invoked them, filled them out in imagination, cheated himself with the idea that they were possible. He saw them in a momentary illusion and confusion: a great academic, artistic theatre, subsidised and unburdened with money-getting, rich in its repertory, rich in the high quality and the wide array of its servants, rich above all in the authority of an impossible administrator—a manager personally disinterested, not an actor with an eye to the main chance; pouring forth a continuity of tradition, striving for perfection, laying a splendid literature under contribution. He saw the heroine of a hundred "situations," variously dramatic and vividly real; he saw comedy and drama and passion and character and English life; he saw all humanity and history and poetry, and then perpetually, in the midst of them, shining out in the high relief of some great moment, an image as fresh as an unveiled statue. He was not unconscious that he was taking all sorts of impossibilities and miracles for granted; but he was under the conviction, for the time, that the woman he had been watching three hours, the incarnation of the serious drama, would be a new and vivifying force. The world was just then so bright to him that even Basil Dashwood struck him at first as a conceivable agent of his dream.

It must be added that before Miriam arrived the breeze that filled Sherringham's sail began to sink a little. He passed out of the eminently "let" drawing-room, where twenty large photographs of the young actress bloomed in the desert; he went into the garden by a glass door that stood open, and found Mr. Dashwood lolling on a bench and smoking cigarettes. This young man's conversation was a different music—it took him down, as he felt; showed him, very sensibly and intelligibly, it must be confessed, the actual theatre, the one they were all concerned with, the one they would have to make the miserable best of. It was fortunate that he kept his intoxication mainly to himself: the Englishman's habit of not being effusive still prevailed with him after his years of exposure to the foreign infection. Nothing could have been less exclamatory than the meeting of the two men, with its question or two, its remark or two, about the new visitor's arrival in London; its off-hand "I noticed you last night, I was glad you turned up at last" on one side and its attenuated "Oh yes, it was the first time; I was very much interested" on the other. Basil Dashwood played a part in Yolande and Peter had not failed to take with some comfort the measure of his aptitude. He judged it to be of the small order, as indeed the part, which was neither that of the virtuous nor that of the villainous hero, restricted him to two or three inconspicuous effects and three or four changes of dress. He represented an ardent but respectful young lover whom the distracted heroine found time to pity a little and even to rail at; but it was impressed upon his critic that he scarcely represented young love. He looked very well, but Peter had heard him already in a hundred contemporary pieces; he never got out of rehearsal. He uttered sentiments and breathed vows with a nice voice, with a shy, boyish tremor, but as if he were afraid of being chaffed for it afterwards; giving the spectator in the stalls the sense of holding the prompt-book and listening to a recitation. He made one think of country-houses and lawn-tennis and private theatricals; than which there couldn't be, to Peter's mind, a range of association more disconnected from the actor's art.

Dashwood knew all about the new thing, the piece in rehearsal; he knew all about everything—receipts and salaries and expenses and newspaper articles, and what old Baskerville said and what Mrs. Ruffler thought: matters of superficial concern to his fellow-guest, who wondered, before they had sight of Miriam, if she talked with her "walking-gentleman" about them by the hour, deep in them and finding them not vulgar and boring but the natural air of her life and the essence of her profession. Of course she did— she naturally would; it was all in the day's work and he might feel sure she wouldn't turn up her nose at the shop. He had to remind himself that he didn't care if she didn't, that he would really think worse of her if she should. She certainly was in deep with her bland playmate, talking shop by the hour: he could see this from the fellow's ease of attitude, the air of a man at home and doing the honours. He divined a great intimacy between the two young artists, but asked himself at the same time what he, Peter Sherringham, had to say about it. He didn't pretend to control Miriam's intimacies, it was to be supposed; and if he had encouraged her to adopt a profession rich in opportunities for comradeship it was not for him to cry out because she had taken to it kindly. He had already descried a fund of utility in Mrs. Lovick's light brother; but it irritated him, all the same, after a while, to hear the youth represent himself as almost indispensable. He was practical—there was no doubt of that; and this idea added to Peter's paradoxical sense that as regards the matters actually in question he himself had not this virtue. Dashwood had got Mrs. Rooth the house; it happened by a lucky chance that Laura Lumley, to whom it belonged—Sherringham would know Laura Lumley?— wanted to get rid, for a mere song, of the remainder of the lease. She was going to Australia with a troupe of her own. They just stepped into it; it was good air—the best sort of London air to live in, to sleep in, for people of their trade. Peter came back to his wonder at what Miriam's personal relations with this deucedly knowing gentleman might be, and was again able to assure himself that they might be anything in the world she liked, for any stake he, the familiar of the Foreign Office, had in them. Dashwood told him of all the smart people who had tried to take up the new star—the way the London world had already held out its hand; and perhaps it was Sherringham's irritation, the crushed sentiment I just mentioned, that gave a little heave in the exclamation, "Oh that—that's all rubbish: the less of that the better!" At this Mr. Dashwood sniffed a little, rather resentful; he had expected Peter to be pleased with the names of the eager ladies who had "called"—which proved how low a view he took of his art. Our friend explained—it is to be hoped not pedantically—that this art was serious work and that society was humbug and imbecility; also that of old the great comedians wouldn't have known such people. Garrick had essentially his own circle.

"No, I suppose they didn't 'call' in the old narrow-minded time," said Basil Dashwood.

"Your profession didn't call. They had better company—that of the romantic gallant characters they represented. They lived with *them*, so it was better all round." And Peter asked himself—for that clearly struck the young man as a dreary period—if *he* only, for Miriam, in her new life and among the futilities of those who tried to lionise her, expressed the artistic idea. This at least, Sherringham reflected, was a situation that could be improved.

He learned from his companion that the new play, the thing they were rehearsing, was an old play, a romantic drama of thirty years before, very frequently revived and threadbare with honourable service. Dashwood had a part in it, but there was an act in which he didn't appear, and this was the act they were doing that morning. Yolande had done all Yolande could do;

the visitor was mistaken if he supposed Yolande such a tremendous hit. It had done very well, it had run three months, but they were by no means coining money with it. It wouldn't take them to the end of the season; they had seen for a month past that they would have to put on something else. Miss Rooth, moreover, wanted a new part; she was above all impatient to show her big range. She had grand ideas; she thought herself very good-natured to repeat the same stuff for three months. The young man lighted another cigarette and described to his listener some of Miss Rooth's ideas. He abounded in information about her—about her character, her temper, her peculiarities, her little ways, her manner of producing some of her effects. He spoke with familiarity and confidence, as if knowing more about her than any one else— as if he had invented or discovered her, were in a sense her proprietor or guarantor. It was the talk of the shop, both with a native sharpness and a touching young candour; the expansion of the commercial spirit when it relaxes and generalises, is conscious of safety with another member of the guild.

Peter at any rate couldn't help protesting against the lame old war-horse it was proposed to bring into action, who had been ridden to death and had saved a thousand desperate fields; and he exclaimed on the strange passion of the good British public for sitting again and again through expected situations, watching for speeches they had heard and surprises that struck the hour. Dashwood defended the taste of London, praised it as loyal, constant, faithful; to which his interlocutor retorted with some vivacity that it was faithful to sad trash. He justified this sally by declaring the play in rehearsal sad trash, clumsy mediocrity with all its convenience gone, and that the fault was the want of life in the critical sense of the public, which was ignobly docile, opening its mouth for its dose like the pupils of Dotheboys Hall; not insisting on something different, on a fresh brew altogether. Dashwood asked him if he then wished their friend to go on playing for ever a part she had repeated more than eighty nights on end: he thought the modern "run" was just what he had heard him denounce in Paris as the disease the theatre was dying of. This imputation Peter quite denied, wanting to know if she couldn't change to something less stale than the greatest staleness of all. Dashwood opined that Miss Rooth must have a strong part and that there happened to be one for her in the before-mentioned venerable novelty. She had to take what she could get—she wasn't a person to cry for the moon. This was a stop-gap—she would try other things later; she would have to look round her; you couldn't have a new piece, one that would do, left at your door every day with the milk. On one point Sherringham's mind might be at rest: Miss Rooth was a woman who would do every blessed thing there was to do. Give her time and she would walk straight through the repertory. She was a woman who would do this—she was a woman who would do that: her spokesman employed this phrase so often that Peter, nervous, got up and threw an unsmoked cigarette away. Of course she was a woman; there was no need of his saying it a hundred times.

As for the repertory, the young man went on, the most beautiful girl in the world could give but what she had. He explained, after their visitor sat down again, that the noise made by Miss Rooth was not exactly what this admirer appeared to suppose. Sherringham had seen the house the night before and would recognise that, though good, it was very far from great. She had done very well, it was all right, but she had never gone above a point which Dashwood expressed in pounds sterling, to the edification of his companion, who vaguely thought the figure high. Peter remembered that he had been unable to get a stall, but Dashwood insisted that "Miriam" had not leaped into commanding fame: that was a thing that never happened in fact—it happened only in grotesque works of fiction. She had attracted notice, unusual notice for a woman whose name, the day before, had never been heard of: she was recognised as having, for a novice, extraordinary cleverness and confidence—in addition to her looks, of course, which were the thing that had really fetched the crowd. But she hadn't been the talk of London; she had only been the talk of Gabriel Nash. He wasn't London, more was the pity. He knew the esthetic people—the worldly, semi-smart ones, not the frumpy, sickly lot who wore dirty drapery; and the esthetic people had run after her. Mr. Dashwood sketchily instructed the pilgrim from Paris as to the different sects in the great religion of beauty, and was able to give him the particular "note" of the critical clique to which Miriam had begun so quickly to owe it that she had a vogue. The information made our friend feel very ignorant of the world, very uninitiated and buried in his little professional hole. Dashwood warned him that it would be a long time before the general public would wake up to Miss Rooth, even after she had waked up to herself; she would have to do some really big thing first. *They* knew it was in her, the big thing—Peter and he and even poor Nash—because they had seen her as no one else had; but London never took any one on trust—it had to be cash down. It would take their young lady two or three years to pay out her cash and get her equivalent. But of course the equivalent would be simply a gold-mine. Within its limits, however, certainly, the mark she had made was already quite a fairy-tale: there was magic in the way she had concealed from the first her want of experience. She absolutely made you think she had a lot of it, more than any one else. Mr. Dashwood repeated several times that she was a cool hand—a deucedly cool hand, and that he watched her himself, saw ideas come to her, saw her have different notions, and more or less put them to the test, on different nights. She was always alive—she liked it herself. She gave him ideas, long as he had been on the stage. Naturally she had a great deal to learn, no end even of quite basic things; a cosmopolite like Sherringham would understand that a girl of that age, who had never had a friend but her mother—her mother was greater fun than ever now— naturally *would* have. Sherringham winced at being dubbed a "cosmopolite" by his young entertainer, just as he had winced a moment before at hearing himself lumped in esoteric knowledge with Dashwood and Gabriel Nash; but the former of these gentlemen took no account of his sensibility while he enumerated a few of the elements of the "basic." He was a mixture of acuteness and innocent fatuity; and Peter had to recognise in him a rudiment or two of criticism when he said that the wonderful thing in the girl was that she learned so fast—learned something every night, learned from the same old piece a lot more than any one else would have learned from twenty. "That's what it is to be a genius," Peter concurred. "Genius is only the art of getting your experience fast, of stealing it, as it were; and in this sense Miss Rooth's a regular brigand." Dashwood condoned the subtlety and added less analytically, "Oh she'll do!" It was exactly in these simple words, addressed to her, that her other admirer had phrased the same truth; yet he didn't enjoy hearing them on his neighbour's lips: they had a profane, patronising sound and suggested displeasing equalities.

The two men sat in silence for some minutes, watching a fat robin hop about on the little seedy lawn; at the end of which they heard a vehicle stop on the other side of the garden-wall and the voices of occupants alighting. "Here they come, the dear creatures," said Basil Dashwood without moving; and from where they sat Peter saw the small door in the wall pushed open. The dear creatures were three in number, for a gentleman had added himself to Mrs. Rooth and her daughter. As soon as Miriam's eyes took in her Parisian friend she fell into a large, droll, theatrical attitude and, seizing her mother's arm, exclaimed passionately: "Look where he sits, the author of all my woes— cold, cynical, cruel!" She was evidently in the highest spirits; of which Mrs. Rooth partook as she cried indulgently, giving her a slap, "Oh get along, you gypsy!"

"She's always up to something," Dashwood laughed as Miriam, radiant and with a conscious stage tread, glided toward Sherringham as if she were coming to the footlights. He rose slowly from his seat, looking at her and struck with her beauty: he had been impatient to see her, yet in the act his impatience had had a disconcerting check.

He had had time to note that the man who had come in with her was Gabriel Nash, and this recognition brought a low sigh to his lips as he held out his hand to her—a sigh expressive of the sudden sense that his interest in her now could only be a gross community. Of course that didn't matter, since he had set it, at the most, such rigid limits; but he none the less felt vividly reminded that it would be public and notorious, that inferior people would be inveterately mixed up with it, that she had crossed the line and sold herself to the vulgar, making him indeed only one of an equalised multitude. The way Nash turned up there just when he didn't want to see him proved how complicated a thing it was to have a friendship with a young woman so clearly booked for renown. He quite forgot that the intruder had had this object of interest long before his own first view of it and had been present at that passage, which he had in a measure brought about. Had Sherringham not been so cut out to make trouble of this particular joy he might have found some adequate assurance that their young hostess distinguished him in the way in which, taking his hand in both of hers, she looked up at him and murmured, "Dear old master!" Then as if this were not acknowledgment enough she raised her head still higher and, whimsically, gratefully, charmingly, almost nobly, kissed him on the lips before the other men, before the good mother whose "Oh you honest creature!" made everything regular.

XXXI

If he was ruffled by some of her conditions there was thus comfort and consolation to be drawn from others, beside the essential fascination—so small the doubt of that now—of the young lady's own society. He spent the afternoon, they all spent the afternoon, and the occasion reminded him of pages in *Wilhelm Meister*. He himself could pass for Wilhelm, and if Mrs. Rooth had little resemblance to Mignon, Miriam was remarkably like Philina. The movable feast awaiting them—luncheon, tea, dinner?—was delayed two or three hours; but the interval was a source of gaiety, for they all smoked cigarettes in the garden and Miriam gave striking illustrations of the parts she was studying. Peter was in the state of a man whose toothache has suddenly stopped—he was exhilarated by the cessation of pain. The pain had been the effort to remain in Paris after the creature in the world in whom he was most interested had gone to London, and the balm of seeing her now was the measure of the previous soreness.

Gabriel Nash had, as usual, plenty to say, and he talked of Nick's picture so long that Peter wondered if he did it on purpose to vex him. They went in and out of the house; they made excursions to see what form the vague meal was taking; and Sherringham got half an hour alone, or virtually alone, with the mistress of his unsanctioned passion—drawing her publicly away from the others and making her sit with him in the most sequestered part of the little gravelled grounds. There was summer enough for the trees to shut out the adjacent villas, and Basil Dashwood and Gabriel Nash lounged together at a convenient distance while Nick's whimsical friend dropped polished pebbles, sometimes audibly splashing, into the deep well of the histrionic simplicity. Miriam confessed that like all comedians they ate at queer hours;

she sent Dashwood in for biscuits and sherry—she proposed sending him round to the grocer's in the Circus Road for superior wine. Peter judged him the factotum of the little household: he knew where the biscuits were kept and the state of the grocer's account. When he himself congratulated her on having so useful an inmate she said genially, but as if the words disposed of him, "Oh he's awfully handy." To this she added, "You're not, you know"; resting the kindest, most pitying eyes on him. The sensation they gave him was as sweet as if she had stroked his cheek, and her manner was responsive even to tenderness. She called him "Dear master" again and again, and still often "*Cher maître,*" and appeared to express gratitude and reverence by every intonation.

"You're doing the humble dependent now," he said: "you do it beautifully, as you do everything." She replied that she didn't make it humble enough— she couldn't; she was too proud, too insolent in her triumph. She liked that, the triumph, too much, and she didn't mind telling him she was perfectly happy. Of course as yet the triumph was very limited; but success was success, whatever its quantity; the dish was a small one but had the right taste. Her imagination had already bounded beyond the first phase unexpectedly great as this had been: her position struck her as modest compared with the probably future now vivid to her. Peter had never seen her so soft and sympathetic; she had insisted in Paris that her personal character was that of the good girl—she used the term in a fine loose way—and it was impossible to be a better girl than she showed herself this pleasant afternoon. She was full of gossip and anecdote and drollery; she had exactly the air he would have wished her to have—that of thinking of no end of things to tell him. It was as if she had just returned from a long journey and had had strange adventures and made wonderful discoveries. She began to speak of this and that, then broke off to speak of something else; she talked of the theatre, of the "critics," and above all of London, of the people she had met and the extraordinary things they said to her, of the parts she was going to take up, of lots of new ideas that had come to her about the art of comedy. She wanted to do comedy now—to do the comedy of London life. She was delighted to find that seeing more of the world suggested things to her; they came straight from the fact, from nature, if you could call it nature; she was thus convinced more than ever that the artist ought to *live* so as to get on with his business, gathering ideas and lights from experience—ought to welcome any experience that would give him lights. But work of course *was* experience, and everything in one's life that was good was work. That was the jolly thing in the actor's trade—it made up for other elements that were odious: if you only kept your eyes open nothing could happen to you that wouldn't be food for observation and grist to your mill, showing you how people looked and moved and spoke, cried and grimaced, writhed and dissimulated, in given situations. She saw all round her things she wanted to "do"—London bristled with them if you had eyes to see. She was fierce to know why people didn't take them up, put them into plays and parts, give one a chance with them; she expressed her sharp impatience of the general literary *bétise*. She had never been chary of this particular displeasure, and there were moments—it was an old story and a subject of frank raillery to Sherringham—when to hear her you might have thought there was no cleverness anywhere but in her own splendid impatience. She wanted tremendous things done that she might use them, but she didn't pretend to say exactly what they were to be, nor even approximately how they were to be handled: her ground was rather that if *she* only had a pen—it was exasperating to have to explain! She mainly contented herself with the view that nothing had really been touched: she felt that more and more as she saw more of people's goings-on.

Peter went to her theatre again that evening and indeed made no scruple of going every night for a week. Rather perhaps I should say he made a scruple, but a high part of the pleasure of his life during these arbitrary days was to overcome it. The only way to prove he could overcome it was to go; and he was satisfied, after he had been seven times, not only with the spectacle on the stage but with his perfect independence. He knew no satiety, however, with the spectacle on the stage, which induced for him but a further curiosity. Miriam's performance was a thing alive, with a power to change, to grow, to develop, to beget new forms of the same life. Peter contributed to it in his amateurish way and watched with solicitude the effect of his care and the fortune of his hints. He talked it over in Balaklava Place, suggested modifications and variations worth trying. She professed herself thankful for any refreshment that could be administered to her interest in *Yolande*, and with an energy that showed large resource touched up her part and drew several new airs from it. Peter's liberties bore on her way of uttering certain speeches, the intonations that would have more beauty or make the words mean more. She had her ideas, or rather she had her instincts, which she defended and illustrated, with a vividness superior to argument, by a happy pictorial phrase or a snatch of mimicry; but she was always for trying; she liked experiments and caught at them, and she was especially thankful when some one gave her a showy reason, a plausible formula, in a case where she only stood on an intuition. She pretended to despise reasons and to like and dislike at her sovereign pleasure; but she always honoured the exotic gift, so that Sherringham was amused with the liberal way she produced it, as if she had been a naked islander rejoicing in a present of crimson cloth.

Day after day he spent most of his time in her society, and Miss Laura Lumley's recent habitation became the place in London to which his thoughts and his steps were most attached. He was highly conscious of his not now carrying out that principle of abstention he had brought to such maturity before leaving Paris; but he contented himself with a much cruder justification of this lapse than he would have thought adequate in advance. It consisted simply in the idea that to be identified with the first fresh exploits of a young genius was a delightful experience. What was the harm of it when the genius was real? His main security was thus that his relations with Miriam had been placed under the protection of that idea of approved extravagance. In this department they made a very creditable figure and required much less watching and pruning than when it had been his effort to adjust them to a worldly plan. He had in fine a sense of real wisdom when he pronounced it surely enough that this momentary intellectual participation in the girl's dawning fame was a charming thing. Charming things were not frequent enough in a busy man's life to be kicked out of the way. Balaklava Place, looked at in this philosophic way, became almost idyllic: it gave Peter the pleasantest impression he had ever had of London.

The season happened to be remarkably fine; the temperature was high, but not so high as to keep people from the theatre. Miriam's "business" visibly increased, so that the question of putting on the second play underwent some revision. The girl persisted, showing in her persistence a temper of which Peter had already caught some sharp gleams. It was plain that through her career she would expect to carry things with a high hand. Her managers and agents wouldn't find her an easy victim or a calculable force; but the public would adore her, surround her with the popularity that attaches to a good-natured and free-spoken princess, and her comrades would have a kindness for her because she wouldn't be selfish. They too would, besides representing her body-guard, form in a manner a portion of her affectionate public. This was the way her friend read the signs, liking her whimsical tolerance of some of her vulgar playfellows almost well enough to forgive their presence in Balaklava Place, where they were a sore trial to her mother, who wanted her to multiply her points of contact only with the higher orders. There were hours when Peter seemed to make out that her principal relation to the proper world would be to have within two or three years a grand battle with it resulting in its taking her, should she let it have her at all, absolutely on her own terms: a picture which led our young man to ask himself with a helplessness that was not exempt, as he perfectly knew, from absurdity, what part *he* should find himself playing in such a contest and if it would be reserved to him to be the more ridiculous as a peacemaker or as a heavy backer.

"She might know any one she would, and the only person she appears to take any pleasure in is that dreadful Miss Rover," Mrs. Rooth whimpered to him more than once—leading him thus to recognise in the young lady so designated the principal complication of Balaklava Place. Miss Rover was a little actress who played at Miriam's theatre, combining with an unusual aptitude for delicate comedy a less exceptional absence of rigour in private life. She was pretty and quick and brave, and had a fineness that Miriam professed herself already in a position to estimate as rare. She had no control of her inclinations, yet sometimes they were wholly laudable, like the devotion she had formed for her beautiful colleague, whom she admired not only as an ornament of the profession but as a being altogether of a more fortunate essence. She had had an idea that real ladies were "nasty," but Miriam was not nasty, and who could gainsay that Miriam was a real lady? The girl justified herself to her patron from Paris, who had found no fault with her; she knew how much her mother feared the proper world wouldn't come in if they knew that the improper, in the person of pretty Miss Rover, was on the ground. What did she care who came and who didn't, and what was to be gained by receiving half the snobs in London? People would have to take her exactly as they found her—that they would have to learn; and they would be much mistaken if they thought her capable of turning snob too for the sake of their sweet company. She didn't pretend to be anything but what she meant to be, the best general actress of her time; and what had that to do with her seeing or not seeing a poor ignorant girl who had loved—well, she needn't say what Fanny had done. They had met in the way of business; she didn't say she would have run after her. She had liked her because she wasn't a slick, and when Fanny Rover had asked her quite wistfully if she mightn't come and see her and like her she hadn't bristled with scandalised virtue. Miss Rover wasn't a bit more stupid or more ill-natured than any one else; it would be time enough to shut the door when she should become so.

Peter commended even to extravagance the liberality of such comradeship; said that of course a woman didn't go into that profession to see how little she could swallow. She was right to live with the others so long as they were at all possible, and it was for her and only for her to judge how long that might be. This was rather heroic on his part, for his assumed detachment from the girl's personal life still left him a margin for some forms of uneasiness. It would have made in his spirit a great difference for the worse that the woman he loved, and for whom he wished no baser lover than himself, should have embraced the prospect of consorting only with the cheaper kind. It was all very well, but Fanny Rover was simply a rank *cabotine*, and that sort of association was an odd training for a young woman who was to have been good enough—he couldn't forget that, but kept remembering it as if it might still have a future use—to be his admired wife. Certainly he ought to have thought of such things before he permitted himself to become so interested in a theatrical nature. His heroism did him service, however, for the hour; it helped him by the end of the week to feel quite broken in to Miriam's little circle. What helped him most indeed was to reflect that she would get tired of a good many of its members herself in time; for if it was not that they were shocking—very few of them shone with that intense light—they could yet be thoroughly trusted in the long run to bore you.

There was a lovely Sunday in particular, spent by him almost all in Balaklava Place—he arrived so early—when, in the afternoon, every sort of odd person dropped in. Miriam held a reception in the little garden and insisted on all the company's staying to supper. Her mother shed tears to Peter, in the desecrated house, because they had accepted, Miriam and she, an invitation—and in Cromwell Road too—for the evening. Miriam had now decreed they shouldn't go—they would have so much better fun with their good friends at home. She was sending off a message—it was a terrible distance—by a cabman, and Peter had the privilege of paying the messenger. Basil Dashwood, in another vehicle, proceeded to an hotel known to him, a mile away, for supplementary provisions, and came back with a cold ham and a dozen of champagne. It was all very Bohemian and dishevelled and delightful, very supposedly droll and enviable to outsiders; and Miriam told anecdotes and gave imitations of the people she would have met if she had gone out, so that no one had a sense of loss—the two occasions were fantastically united. Mrs. Rooth drank champagne for consolation, though the consolation was imperfect when she remembered she might have drunk it, though not quite so much perhaps, in Cromwell Road.

Taken in connection with the evening before, the day formed for our friend the most complete exhibition of his young woman he had yet enjoyed. He had been at the theatre, to which the Saturday night happened to have brought the very fullest house she had played to, and he came early to Balaklava Place, to tell her once again—he had told her half-a-dozen times the evening before—that with the excitement of her biggest audience she had surpassed herself, acted with remarkable intensity. It pleased her to hear this, and the spirit with which she interpreted the signs of the future and, during an hour he spent alone with her, Mrs. Rooth being upstairs and Basil Dashwood luckily absent, treated him to twenty specimens of feigned passion and character, was beyond any natural abundance he had yet seen in a woman. The impression could scarcely have been other if she had been playing wild snatches to him at the piano: the bright up-darting flame of her talk rose and fell like an improvisation on the keys. Later, the rest of the day, he could as little miss the good grace with which she fraternised with her visitors, finding always the fair word for each—the key to a common ease, the right turn to keep vanity quiet and make humility brave. It was a wonderful expenditure of generous, nervous life. But what he read in it above all was the sense of success in youth, with the future loose and big, and the action of that charm on the faculties. Miriam's limited past had yet pinched her enough to make emancipation sweet, and the emancipation had come at last in an hour. She had stepped into her magic shoes, divined and appropriated everything they could help her to, become in a day a really original contemporary. He was of course not less conscious of that than Nick Dormer had been when in the cold light of his studio this more detached observer saw too how she had altered.

But the great thing to his mind, and during these first days the irresistible seduction of the theatre, was that she was a rare revelation of beauty. Beauty was the principle of everything she did and of the way she unerringly did it—an exquisite harmony of line and motion and attitude and tone, what was at once most general and most special in her performance. Accidents and instincts played together to this end and constituted something that was independent of her talent or of her merit in a given case, and which as a value to Peter's imagination was far superior to any merit and any talent. He could but call it a felicity and an importance incalculable, and but know that it connected itself with universal values. To see this force in operation, to sit within its radius and feel it shift and revolve and change and never fail, was a corrective to the depression, the humiliation, the bewilderment of life. It transported our troubled friend from the vulgar hour and the ugly fact; drew him to something that had no warrant but its sweetness, no name nor place save as the pure, the remote, the antique. It was what most made him say to himself "Oh hang it, what does it matter?" when he reflected that an *homme sérieux*, as they said in Paris, rather gave himself away, as they said in America, by going every night to the same sordid stall at which all the world might stare. It was what kept him from doing anything but hover round Miriam—kept him from paying any other visits, from attending to any business, from going back to Calcutta Gardens. It was a spell he shrank intensely from breaking and the cause of a hundred postponements, confusions, and absurdities. It put him in a false position altogether, but it made of the crooked little stucco villa in Saint John's Wood a place in the upper air, commanding the prospect;

393

a nest of winged liberties and ironies far aloft above the huddled town. One should live at altitudes when one could—they braced and simplified; and for a happy interval he never touched the earth.

It was not that there were no influences tending at moments to drag him down—an abasement from which he escaped only because he was up so high. We have seen that Basil Dashwood could affect him at times as a chunk of wood tied to his ankle—this through the circumstance that he made Miriam's famous conditions, those of the public exhibition of her genius, seem small and prosaic; so that Peter had to remind himself how much this smallness was perhaps involved in their being at all. She carried his imagination off into infinite spaces, whereas she carried Dashwood's only into the box-office and the revival of plays that were barbarously bad. The worst was its being so open to him to see that a sharp young man really in the business might know better than he. Another vessel of superior knowledge— he talked, that is, as if he knew better than any one—was Gabriel Nash, who lacked no leisure for hatefully haunting Balaklava Place, or in other words appeared to enjoy the same command of his time as Peter Sherringham. The pilgrim from Paris regarded him with mingled feelings, for he had not forgotten the contentious character of their first meeting or the degree to which he had been moved to urge upon Nick Dormer's consideration that his talkative friend was probably one of the most eminent of asses. This personage turned up now as an admirer of the charming creature he had scoffed at, and there was much to exasperate in the smooth gloss of his inconsistency, at which he never cast an embarrassed glance. He practised indeed such loose license of regard to every question that it was difficult, in vulgar parlance, to "have" him; his sympathies hummed about like bees in a garden, with no visible plan, no economy in their flight. He thought meanly of the modern theatre and yet had discovered a fund of satisfaction in the most promising of its exponents; and Peter could more than once but say to him that he should really, to keep his opinions at all in hand, attach more value to the stage or less to the interesting a tress. Miriam took her perfect ease at his expense and treated him as the most abject of her slaves: all of which was worth seeing as an exhibition, on Nash's part, of the beautifully imperturbable. When Peter all too grossly pronounced him "damned" impudent he always felt guilty later

394

on of an injustice—Nash had so little the air of a man with something to gain. He was aware nevertheless of a certain itching in his boot-toe when his fellow-visitor brought out, and for the most part to Miriam herself, in answer to any charge of tergiversation, "Oh it's all right; it's the voice, you know—the enchanting voice!" Nash meant by this, as indeed he more fully set forth, that he came to the theatre or to the villa simply to treat his ear to the sound—the richest then to be heard on earth, as he maintained—issuing from Miriam's lips. Its richness was quite independent of the words she might pronounce or the poor fable they might subserve, and if the pleasure of hearing her in public was the greater by reason of the larger volume of her utterance it was still highly agreeable to see her at home, for it was there the strictly mimetic gift he freely conceded to her came out most. He spoke as if she had been formed by the bounty of nature to be his particular recreation, and as if, being an expert in innocent joys, he took his pleasure wherever he found it.

He was perpetually in the field, sociable, amiable, communicative, inverately contradicted but never confounded, ready to talk to any one about anything and making disagreement—of which he left the responsibility wholly to others—a basis of harmony. Every one knew what he thought of the theatrical profession, and yet who could say he didn't regard, its members as embodiments of comedy when he touched with such a hand the spring of their foibles?—touched it with an art that made even Peter laugh, notwithstanding his attitude of reserve where this interloper was concerned. At any rate, though he had committed himself as to their general fatuity he put up with their company, for the sake of Miriam's vocal vibrations, with a practical philosophy that was all his own. And she frankly took him for her supreme, her incorrigible adorer, masquerading as a critic to save his vanity and tolerated for his secret constancy in spite of being a bore. He was meanwhile really not a bore to Peter, who failed of the luxury of being able to regard him as one. He had seen too many strange countries and curious things, observed and explored too much, to be void of illustration. Peter had a sense that if he himself was in the *grandes espaces* Gabriel had probably, as a finer critic, a still wider range. If among Miriam's associates Mr. Dashwood dragged him down, the other main sharer of his privilege challenged him rather to higher and more fantastic flights. If he saw the girl in larger relations than the young actor, who mainly saw her in ill-written parts, Nash went a step further and regarded her, irresponsibly and sublimely, as a priestess of harmony, a figure with which the vulgar ideas of success and failure had nothing to do. He laughed at her "parts," holding that without them she would still be great. Peter envied him his power to content himself with the pleasures he could get; Peter had a shrewd impression that contentment wouldn't be the final sweetener of his own repast.

Above all Nash held his attention by a constant element of easy reference to Nick Dormer, who, as we know, had suddenly become much more interesting to his kinsman. Peter found food for observation, and in some measure for perplexity, in the relations of all these clever people with each other. He knew why his sister, who had a personal impatience of unapplied ideas, had not been agreeably affected by Miriam's prime patron and had not felt happy about the attribution of value to "such people" by the man she was to marry. This was a side on which he had no desire to resemble Julia, for he needed no teaching to divine that Nash must have found her accessible to no light—none even about himself. He, Peter, would have been sorry to have to confess he couldn't more or less understand him. He understood furthermore that Miriam, in Nick's studio, might very well have appeared to Julia a formidable force. She was younger and would have "seen nothing," but she had quite as much her own resources and was beautiful enough to have made Nick compare her with the lady of Harsh even if he had been in love with that benefactress—a pretension as to which her brother, as we know, entertained doubts.

Peter at all events saw for many days nothing of his cousin, though it might have been said that Nick participated by implication at least in the life of Balaklava Place. Had he given Julia tangible grounds and was his unexpectedly fine rendering of Miriam an act of virtual infidelity? In that case to what degree was the girl to be regarded as an accomplice in his defection, and what was the real nature of Miriam's esteem for her new and (as he might be called) distinguished ally? These questions would have given Peter still more to think about had he not flattered himself he had made up his mind that they concerned Nick and his sitter herself infinitely more than they concerned any one else. That young lady meanwhile was personally before him, so that he had no need to consult for his pleasure his fresh recollection of the portrait. But he thought of this striking production each time he thought of his so good-looking kinsman's variety of range. And that happened often, for in his hearing Miriam often discussed the happy artist and his possibilities with Gabriel Nash, and Nash broke out about them to all who might hear. Her own tone on the subject was uniform: she kept it on record to a degree slightly irritating that Mr. Dormer had been unforgettably—Peter particularly noted "unforgettably"—kind to her. She never mentioned Julia's irruption to Julia's brother; she only referred to the portrait, with inscrutable amenity, as a direct consequence of this gentleman's fortunate suggestion that first day at Madame Carré's. Nash showed, however, such a disposition to dwell sociably and luminously on the peculiarly interesting character of what he called Dormer's predicament and on the fine suspense it was fitted to kindle in the breast of the truly discerning, that Peter wondered, as I have already hinted, if this insistence were not a subtle perversity, a devilish little invention to torment a man whose jealousy was presumable. Yet his fellow-pilgrim struck him as on the whole but scantly devilish and as still less occupied with the prefigurement of so plain a man's emotions. Indeed he threw a glamour of romance over Nick; tossed off toward him such illuminating yet mystifying references that they operated quite as a bait to curiosity, invested with amusement the view of the possible, any wish to follow out the chain of events. He learned from Gabriel that Nick was still away, and he then felt he could almost submit to instruction, to initiation. The loose charm of these days was troubled, however—it ceased to be idyllic—when late on the evening of the second Sunday he walked away with Nash southward from Saint John's Wood. For then something came out.

BOOK SIX

XXXII

It mattered not so much what the doctors thought—and Sir Matthew Hope, the greatest of them all, had been down twice in one week—as that Mr. Chayter, the omniscient butler, declared with all the authority of his position and his experience that Mr. Carteret was very bad indeed. Nick Dormer had a long talk with him—it lasted six minutes—the day he hurried to Beauclere in response to a telegram. It was Mr. Chayter who had taken upon himself to telegraph in spite of the presence in the house of Mr. Carteret's nearest relation and only surviving sister, Mrs. Lendon. This lady, a large, mild, healthy woman with a heavy tread, a person who preferred early breakfasts, uncomfortable chairs and the advertisement-sheet of the *Times*, had arrived the week before and was awaiting the turn of events. She was a widow and occupied in Cornwall a house nine miles from a station, which had, to make up for this inconvenience as she had once told Nick, a fine old herbaceous garden. She was extremely fond of an herbaceous garden—her main consciousness was of herbaceous possibilities. Nick had often seen her—she had always come to Beauclere once or twice a year. Her sojourn there made no great difference; she was only an "Urania dear" for Mr. Carteret to look across the table at when, on the close of dinner, it was time for her to retire. She went out of the room always as if it were after some one else; and on the gentlemen's "joining" her later—the junction was not very close—she received them with an air of gratified surprise.

Chayter honoured Nick with a regard which approached, though not improperly competing with it, the affection his master had placed on the same young head, and Chayter knew a good many things. Among them he knew his place; but it was wonderful how little that knowledge had rendered him inaccessible to other kinds. He took upon himself to send for Nick without speaking to Mrs. Lendon, whose influence was now a good deal like that of some large occasional piece of furniture introduced on a contingency. She was one of the solid conveniences that a comfortable house would have, but you couldn't talk with a mahogany sofa or a folding screen. Chayter knew how much she had "had" from her brother, and how much her two daughters had each received on marriage; and he was of the opinion that it was quite enough, especially considering the society in which they—you could scarcely call it—moved. He knew beyond this that they would all have more, and that was why he hesitated little about communicating with Nick. If Mrs. Lendon should be ruffled at the intrusion of a young man who neither was the child of a cousin nor had been formally adopted, Chayter was parliamentary enough to see that the forms of debate were observed. He had indeed a slightly compassionate sense that Mrs. Lendon was not easily ruffled. She was always down an extraordinary time before breakfast—Chayter refused to take it as in the least admonitory—but usually went straight into the garden as if to see that none of the plants had been stolen in the night, and had in the end to be looked for by the footman in some out-of-the-way spot behind the shrubbery, where, plumped upon the ground, she was mostly doing something "rum" to a flower.

Mr. Carteret himself had expressed no wishes. He slept most of the time—his failure at the last had been sudden, but he was rheumatic and seventy-seven—and the situation was in Chayter's hands. Sir Matthew Hope had opined even on a second visit that he would rally and go on, in rudimentary comfort, some time longer; but Chayter took a different and a still more intimate view. Nick was embarrassed: he scarcely knew what he was there for from the moment he could give his good old friend no conscious satisfaction. The doctors, the nurses, the servants, Mrs. Lendon, and above all the settled equilibrium of the square thick house, where an immutable order appeared to slant through the polished windows and tinkle in the quieter bells, all these things represented best the kind of supreme solace to which the master was most accessible.

It was judged best that for the first day Nick should not be introduced into the darkened room. This was the decision of the two decorous nurses, of whom the visitor had had a glimpse and who, with their black uniforms and fresh faces of business, suggested the barmaid emulating the nun. He was depressed and restless, felt himself in a false position, and thought it lucky Mrs. Lendon had powers of placid acceptance. They were old acquaintances: she treated him formally, anxiously, but it was not the rigour of mistrust. It was much more an expression of remote Cornish respect for young abilities and distinguished connexions, inasmuch as she asked him rather yearningly about Lady Agnes and about Lady Flora and Lady Elizabeth. He knew she was kind and ungrudging, and his main regret was for his meagre knowledge and poor responses in regard to his large blank aunts. He sat in the garden with newspapers and looked at the lowered blinds in Mr. Carteret's windows; he wandered round the abbey with cigarettes and lightened his tread and felt grave, wishing everything might be over. He would have liked much to see Mr. Carteret again, but had no desire that Mr. Carteret should see him. In the evening he dined with Mrs. Lendon, and she talked to him at his request and as much as she could about her brother's early years, his beginnings of life. She was so much younger that they appeared to have been rather a tradition of her own youth; but her talk made Nick feel how tremendously different Mr. Carteret had been at that period from what he, Nick, was to-day. He had published at the age of thirty a little volume, thought at the time wonderfully clever, called *The Incidence of Rates*; but Nick had not yet collected the material for any such treatise. After dinner Mrs. Lendon, who was in merciless full dress, retired to the drawing-room, where at the end of ten minutes she was followed by Nick, who had remained behind only because he thought Chayter would expect it. Mrs. Lendon almost shook hands with him again and then Chayter brought in coffee. Almost in no time afterwards he brought in tea, and the occupants of the drawing-room sat for a slow half-hour, during which the lady looked round at the apartment with a sigh and said: "Don't you think poor Charles had exquisite taste?"

Fortunately the "local man" was at this moment ushered in. He had been upstairs and he smiled himself in with the remark: "It's quite wonderful, quite wonderful." What was wonderful was a marked improvement in the breathing, a distinct indication of revival. The doctor had some tea and chatted for a quarter of an hour in a way that showed what a "good" manner and how large an experience a local man could have. When he retired Nick walked out with him. The doctor's house was near by and he had come on foot. He left the visitor with the assurance that in all probability Mr. Carteret, who was certainly picking up, would be able to see him on the morrow. Our young man turned his steps again to the abbey and took a stroll about it in the starlight. It never looked so huge as when it reared itself into the night, and Nick had never felt more fond of it than on this occasion, more comforted and confirmed by its beauty. When he came back he was readmitted by Chayter, who surveyed him in respectful deprecation of the frivolity which had led him to attempt to help himself through such an evening in such a way.

He went to bed early and slept badly, which was unusual with him; but it was a pleasure to him to be told almost as soon as he appeared that Mr. Carteret had asked for him. He went in to see him and was struck with the change in his appearance. He had, however, spent a day with him just after the New Year and another at the beginning of March, and had then noted in him the menace of the final weakness. A week after Julia Dallow's departure for the Continent he had again devoted several hours to the place and to the intention of telling his old friend how the happy event had been brought to naught—the advantage he had been so good as to desire for him and to make the condition of a splendid gift. Before this, for a few days, he had been keeping back, to announce it personally, the good news that Julia had at last set their situation in order: he wanted to enjoy the old man's pleasure—so sore a trial had her arbitrary behaviour been for a year. If she had offered Mr. Carteret a conciliatory visit before Christmas, had come down from London one day to lunch with him, this had but contributed to make him subsequently exhibit to poor Nick, as the victim of her elegant perversity, a great deal of earnest commiseration in a jocose form. Upon his honour, as he said, she was as clever and "specious" a woman—this was his odd expression—as he had ever seen in his life. The merit of her behaviour on that occasion, as Nick knew, was that she had not been specious at her lover's expense: she had breathed no doubt of his public purpose and had had the strange grace to say that in truth she was older than he, so that it was only fair to give his affections time to mature. But when Nick saw their hopeful host after the rupture at which we have been present he found him in no state to deal with worries: he was seriously ailing, it was the beginning of worse things and not a time to put his attention to the stretch. After this excursion Nick had gone back to town saddened by his patient's now unmistakably settled decline, but rather relieved that he had had himself to make no confession. It had even occurred to him that the need for making one at all might never come up. Certainly it wouldn't if the ebb of Mr. Carteret's strength should continue unchecked. He might pass away in the persuasion that everything would happen as he wished it, though indeed without enriching Nick on his wedding-day to the tune he had promised. Very likely he had made legal arrangements in virtue of which his bounty would take effect in case of the right event and in that case alone. At present Nick had a bigger, an uglier truth to tell—the last three days had made the difference; but, oddly enough, though his responsibility had increased his reluctance to speak had vanished: he was positively eager to clear up a situation over which it was not consistent with his honour to leave a shade.

The doctor had been right on coming in after dinner; it was clear in the morning that they had not seen the last of Mr. Carteret's power of picking up. Chayter, who had waited on him, refused austerely to change his opinion with every change in his master's temperature; but the nurses took the cheering view that it would do their charge good for Mr. Dormer to sit with him a little. One of them remained in the room in the deep window-seat, and Nick spent twenty minutes by the bedside. It was not a case for much conversation, but his helpless host seemed still to like to look at him. There was life in his kind old eyes, a stir of something that would express itself yet in some further wise provision. He laid his liberal hand on Nick's with a confidence that showed how little it was really disabled. He said very little, and the nurse had recommended that the visitor himself should not overflow in speech; but from time to time he murmured with a faint smile: "To-night's division, you know—you mustn't miss it." There was probably to be no division that night, as happened, but even Mr. Carteret's aberrations were parliamentary. Before Nick withdrew he had been able to assure him he was rapidly getting better and that such valuable hours, the young man's own, mustn't be wasted. "Come back on Friday if they come to the second reading." These were the words with which Nick was dismissed, and at noon the doctor said the invalid was doing very well, but that Nick had better leave him quiet for that day. Our young man accordingly determined to go up to town for the night, and even, should he receive no summons, for the next day. He arranged with Chayter that he should be telegraphed to if Mr. Carteret were either better or worse.

"Oh he can't very well be worse, sir," Chayter replied inexorably; but he relaxed so far as to remark that of course it wouldn't do for Nick to neglect the House.

"Oh the House!"—Nick was ambiguous and avoided the butler's eye. It would be easy enough to tell Mr. Carteret, but nothing would have sustained him in the effort to make a clean breast to Chayter.

He might equivocate about the House, but he had the sense of things to be done awaiting him in London. He telegraphed to his servant and spent that night in Rosedale Road. The things to be done were apparently to be done in his studio: his servant met him there with a large bundle of letters. He failed that evening to stray within two miles of Westminster, and the legislature of his country reassembled without his support. The next morning he received a telegram from Chayter, to whom he had given Rosedale Road as an address. This missive simply informed him that Mr. Carteret wished to see him; it seemed a sign that he was better, though Chayter wouldn't say so. Nick again accordingly took his place in the train to Beauclere. He had been there very often, but it was present to him that now, after a little, he should go only once more—for a particular dismal occasion. All that was over, everything that belonged to it was over. He learned on his arrival—he saw Mrs. Lendon immediately—that his old friend had continued to pick up. He had expressed a strong and a perfectly rational desire to talk with his expected visitor, and the doctor had said that if it was about anything important they should forbear to oppose him. "He says it's about something very important," Mrs. Lendon remarked, resting shy eyes on him while she added that she herself was now sitting with her dear brother. She had sent those wonderful young ladies out to see the abbey. Nick paused with her outside Mr. Carteret's door. He wanted to say something rather intimate and all soothing to her in return for her homely charity—give her a hint, for which she was far from looking, that practically he had now no interest in her brother's estate. This was of course impossible; her lack of irony, of play of mind, gave him no pretext, and such a reference would be an insult to her simple discretion. She was either not thinking of his interest at all, or was thinking of it with the tolerance of a nature trained to a hundred decent submissions. Nick looked a little into her mild, uninvestigating eyes, and it came over him supremely that the goodness of these people was singularly pure: they were a part of what was cleanest and sanest and dullest in humanity. There had been just a little mocking inflexion in Mrs. Lendon's pleasant voice; but it was dedicated to the young ladies in the black uniforms—she could perhaps be humorous about *them*—and not to the theory of the "importance" of Nick's interview with her brother. His arrested desire to let her know he was not greedy translated itself into a vague friendliness and into the abrupt, rather bewildering words: "I can't tell you half the good I think of you." As he passed into Mr. Carteret's room it occurred to him that she would perhaps interpret this speech as an acknowledgment of obligation—of her good nature in not keeping him away from the rich old man.

XXXIII

The rich old man was propped up on pillows, and in this attitude, beneath the high, spare canopy of his bed, presented himself to Nick's picture-seeking vision as a figure in a clever composition or a "story." He had gathered strength, though this strength was not much in his voice; it was mainly in his brighter eyes and his air of being pleased with himself. He put out his hand and said, "I daresay you know why I sent for you"; on which Nick sank into the seat he had occupied the day before, replying that he had been delighted to come, whatever the reason. Mr. Carteret said nothing more about the division or the second reading; he only murmured that they were keeping the newspapers for him. "I'm rather behind—I'm rather behind," he went on; "but two or three quiet mornings will make it all right. You can go back to-night, you know—you can easily go back." This was the only thing not quite straight that Nick found in him—his making light of his young friend's flying to and fro. The young friend sat looking at him with a sense that was half compunction and half the idea of the rare beauty of his face, to which, strangely, the waste of illness now seemed to have restored something of its youth. Mr. Carteret was evidently conscious that this morning he shouldn't be able to go on long, so that he must be practical and concise. "I daresay you know—you've only to remember," he continued.

"I needn't tell you what a pleasure it is to me to see you—there can be no better reason than that," was what Nick could say.

"Hasn't the year come round—the year of that foolish arrangement?"

Nick thought a little, asking himself if it were really necessary to disturb his companion's earnest faith. Then the consciousness of the falsity of his own position surged over him again and he replied: "Do you mean the period for which Mrs. Dallow insisted on keeping me dangling? Oh *that's* over!" he almost gaily brought out.

"And are you married—has it come off?" the old man asked eagerly. "How long have I been ill?"

"We're uncomfortable, unreasonable people, not deserving of your interest. We're not married," Nick said.

"Then I haven't been ill so long?" his host quavered with vague relief.

"Not very long—but things *are* different," he went on.

The old man's eyes rested on his—he noted how much larger they appeared. "You mean the arrangements are made—the day's at hand?"

"There are no arrangements," Nick smiled. "But why should it trouble you?"

"What then will you do—without arrangements?" The inquiry was plaintive and childlike.

"We shall do nothing—there's nothing to be done. We're not to be married—it's all off," said poor Nick. Then he added: "Mrs. Dallow has gone abroad."

The old man, motionless among his pillows, gave a long groan. "Ah I don't like that."

"No more do I, sir."

"What's the matter? It was so good—so good."

"It wasn't good enough for Julia," Nick declared.

"For Julia? Is Julia so great as that? She told me she had the greatest regard for you. You're good enough for the best, my dear boy," Mr. Carteret pursued.

"You don't know me: I *am* disappointing. She had, I believe, a great regard for me, but I've forfeited her good opinion."

The old man stared at this cynical announcement: he searched his visitor's face for some attenuation of the words. But Nick apparently struck him as unashamed, and a faint colour coming into his withered cheek indicated his mystification and alarm. "Have you been unfaithful to her?" he still considerately asked.

"She thinks so—it comes to the same thing. As I told you a year ago, she doesn't believe in me."

"You ought to have made her—you ought to have made her," said Mr. Carteret. Nick was about to plead some reason when he continued: "Do you remember what I told you I'd give you if you did? Do you remember what I told you I'd give you on your wedding-day?"

"You expressed the most generous intentions; and I remember them as much as a man may do who has no wish to remind you of them."

"The money's there—I've put it aside."

"I haven't earned it—I haven't earned a penny of it. Give it to those who deserve it more," said Nick.

"I don't understand, I don't understand," Mr. Carteret whimpered, the tears of weakness in his eyes. His face flushed and he added: "I'm not good for much discussion; I'm very much disappointed."

"I think I may say it's not my fault—I've done what I can," Nick declared.

"But when people are in love they do more than that."

"Oh it's all over!" said our young man; not caring much now, for the moment, how disconcerted his companion might be, so long as he disabused him of the idea that they were partners to a bargain. "We've tormented each other and we've tormented you—and that's all that has come of it."

His companion's eyes seemed to stare at strange things. "Don't you care for what I'd have done for you—shouldn't you have liked it?"

"Of course one likes kindness—one likes money. But it's all over," Nick repeated. Then he added: "I fatigue you, I knock you up, with telling you these troubles. I only do so because it seems to me right you should know. But don't be worried—everything's for the best."

He patted the pale hand reassuringly, inclined himself affectionately, but Mr. Carteret was not easily soothed. He had practised lucidity all his life, had expected it of others and had never given his assent to an indistinct proposition. He was weak, yet not too weak to recognise that he had formed a calculation now vitiated by a wrong factor—put his name to a contract of which the other side had not been carried out. More than fifty years of conscious success pressed him to try to understand; he had never muddled his affairs and he couldn't muddle them now. At the same time he was aware of the necessity of economising his effort, and he would gather that inward force, patiently and almost cunningly, for the right question and the right induction. He was still able to make his agitation reflective, and it could still consort with his high hopes of Nick that he should find himself regarding mere vague, verbal comfort, words in the air, as an inadequate guarantee. So after he had attached his dim vision to his young friend's face a moment he brought out: "Have you done anything bad?"

"Nothing worse than usual," Nick laughed.

"Ah everything should have been better than usual."

"Well, it hasn't been that—that I must say."

"Do you sometimes think of your father?" Mr. Carteret continued.

Nick had a decent pause. "*You* make me think of him—you've always that pleasant effect."

"His name would have lived—it mustn't be lost."

"Yes, but the competition to-day is terrible," Nick returned.

His host considered this as if he found a serious flaw in it; after which he began again: "I never supposed you a trifler."

"I'm determined not to be."

"I thought her charming. Don't you love Mrs. Dallow?" Mr. Carteret profoundly asked.

"Don't put it to me so to-day, for I feel sore and injured. I don't think she has treated me well."

"You should have held her—you shouldn't have let her go," the old man returned with unexpected fire.

His visitor flushed at this, so strange was it to receive a lesson in energy from a dying octogenarian. Yet after an instant Nick answered with due modesty: "I haven't been clever enough, no doubt."

"Don't say that, don't say that—!" Mr. Carteret shrunk from the thought. "Don't think I can allow you any easing-off of that sort. I know how well you've done. You're taking your place. Several gentlemen have told me. Hasn't she felt a scruple, knowing my settlement on you to depend——?" he pursued.

"Oh she hasn't known—hasn't known anything about it."

"I don't understand; though I think you explained somewhat a year ago"—the poor gentleman gave it up. "I think she wanted to speak to me—of any intentions I might have in regard to you—the day she was here. Very nicely, very properly she'd have done it, I'm sure. I think her idea was that I ought to make any settlement quite independent of your marrying her or not marrying her. But I tried to convey to her—I don't know whether she understood me—that I liked her too much for that, I wanted too much to make sure of her."

"To make sure of me, you mean," said Nick. "And now after all you see you haven't."

"Well, perhaps it was that," sighed the old man confusedly.

"All this is very bad for you—we'll talk again," Nick urged.

"No, no—let us finish it now. I like to know what I'm doing. I shall rest better when I do know. There are great things to be done; the future will be full—the future will be fine," Mr. Carteret wandered.

"Let me be distinct about this for Julia: that if we hadn't been sundered her generosity to me would have been complete—she'd have put her great fortune absolutely at my disposal," Nick said after a moment. "Her consciousness of all that naturally carries her over any particular distress in regard to what won't come to me now from another source."

"Ah don't lose it!" the old man painfully pleaded.

"It's in your hands, sir," Nick returned.

"I mean Mrs. Dallow's fortune. It will be of the highest utility. That was what your father missed."

"I shall miss more than my father did," said Nick.

"Shell come back to you—I can't look at you and doubt that."

Nick smiled with a slow headshake. "Never, never, never! You look at me, my grand old friend, but you don't see me. I'm not what you think."

"What is it—what is it? *Have* you been bad?" Mr. Carteret panted.

"No, no; I'm not bad. But I'm different."

"Different——?"

"Different from my father. Different from Mrs. Dallow. Different from you."

"Ah why do you perplex me?" the old man moaned. "You've done something."

"I don't want to perplex you, but I have done something," said Nick, getting up.

He had heard the door open softly behind him and Mrs. Lendon come forward with precautions. "What has he done—what has he done?" quavered Mr. Carteret to his sister. She, however, after a glance at the patient, motioned their young friend away and, bending over the bed, replied, in a voice expressive at that moment of an ample provision of vital comfort:

"He has only excited you, I'm afraid, a little more than is good for you. Isn't your dear old head a little too high?" Nick regarded himself as justly banished, and he quitted the room with a ready acquiescence in any power to carry on the scene of which Mrs. Lendon might find herself possessed. He felt distinctly brutal as he heard his host emit a weak exhalation of assent to some change of position. But he would have reproached himself more if he had wished less to guard against the acceptance of an equivalent for duties unperformed. Mr. Carteret had had in his mind, characteristically, the idea of a fine high contract, and there was something more to be said about that.

Nick went out of the house and stayed away for two or three hours, quite ready to regard the place as quieter and safer without him. He haunted the abbey as usual and sat a long time in its simplifying stillness, turning over many things. He came back again at the luncheon-hour, through the garden, and heard, somewhat to his surprise and greatly to his relief, that his host had composed himself promptly enough after their agitating interview. Mrs. Lendon talked at luncheon much as if she expected her brother to be, as she said, really quite fit again. She asked Nick no awkward question; which was uncommonly good of her, he thought, considering that she might have said, "What in the world were you trying to get out of him?" She only reported to our young man that the invalid had every hope of a short interview about half-past seven, a *very* short one: this gentle emphasis was Mrs. Lendon's single tribute to the critical spirit. Nick divined that Mr. Carteret's desire for further explanations was really strong and had been capable of sustaining him through a bad morning, capable even of helping him—it would have been a secret and wonderful momentary conquest of weakness—to pass it off for a good one. He wished he might make a sketch of him, from the life, as he had seen him after breakfast; he had a conviction he could make a strong one, which would be a precious memento. But he shrank from proposing this—the dear man might think it unparliamentary. The doctor had called while Nick was out, and he came again at five o'clock without that inmate's seeing him. The latter was busy in his room at that hour: he wrote a short letter which took him a long time. But apparently there had been no veto on a resumption of talk, for at half-past seven his friend sent for him. The nurse at the door said, "Only a moment, I hope, sir?" but took him in and then withdrew.

The prolonged daylight was in the room and its occupant again established on his pile of pillows, but with his head a little lower. Nick sat down by him and expressed the hope of not having upset him in the morning; but the old man, with fixed, enlarged eyes, took up their conversation exactly where they had left it. "What have you done—what have you done? Have you associated yourself with some other woman?"

"No, no; I don't think she can accuse me of that."

"Well then she'll come back to you if you take the right way with her."

It might have been droll to hear the poor gentleman, in his situation, give his views on the right way with women; but Nick was not moved to enjoy that diversion. "I've taken the wrong way. I've done something that must spoil my prospects in that direction for ever. I've written a letter," the visitor went on; but his companion had already interrupted him.

"You've written a letter?"

"To my constituents, informing them of my determination to resign my seat."

"To resign your seat?"

"I've made up my mind, after no end of reflexion, dear Mr. Carteret, to work on quite other lines. I've a plan of becoming a painter. So I've given up the idea of a political life."

"A painter?" Mr. Carteret seemed to turn whiter. "I'm going in for the portrait in oils. It sounds absurd, I know, and I'm thus specific only to show you I don't in the least expect you to count on me." The invalid had continued to stare at first; then his eyes slowly closed and he lay motionless and blank. "Don't let it trouble you now; it's a long story and rather a poor one; when you get better I'll tell you all about it. Well talk it over amicably and I'll bring you to my view," Nick went on hypocritically. He had laid his hand again on the hand beside him; it felt cold, and as the old man remained silent he had a moment of exaggerated fear.

"This is dreadful news"—and Mr. Carteret opened his eyes.

"Certainly it must seem so to you, for I've always kept from you—I was ashamed, and my present confusion is a just chastisement—the great interest I have always taken in the——!" But Nick broke down with a gasp, to add presently, with an intention of the pleasant and a sense of the foolish: "In the pencil and the brush." He spoke of his current confusion, though his manner might have been thought to show it but little. He was himself surprised at his brazen assurance and had to recognise that at the point things had come to now he was profoundly obstinate and quiet.

"The pencil—the brush? They're not the weapons of a gentleman," Mr. Carteret pronounced.

"I was sure that would be your feeling. I repeat that I mention them only because you once said you intended to do something for me, as the phrase is, and I thought you oughtn't to do it in ignorance."

"My ignorance was better. Such knowledge isn't good for me."

"Forgive me, my dear old friend," Nick kept it bravely up. "When you're better you'll see it differently."

"I shall never be better now."

"Ah no," Nick insisted; "it will really do you good after a little. Think it over quietly and you'll be glad I've stopped humbugging."

"I loved you—I loved you as my son," the old man wailed.

He sank on his knee beside the bed and leaned over him tenderly. "Get better, get better, and I'll be your son for the rest of your life."

"Poor Dormer—poor Dormer!" Mr. Carteret continued to lament.

"I admit that if he had lived I probably shouldn't have done it," said Nick. "I daresay I should have deferred to his prejudices even though thinking them narrow."

"Do you turn against your father?" his host asked, making, to disengage his arm from the young man's touch, an effort betraying the irritation of conscious weakness. Nick got up at this and stood a moment looking down at him while he went on: "Do you give up your name, do you give up your country?"

"If I do something good my country may like it," Nick spoke as if he had thought that out.

"Do you regard them as equal, the two glories?"

"Here comes your nurse to blow me up and turn me out," said Nick.

The nurse had come in, but Mr. Carteret directed to her an audible dry, courteous "Be so good as to wait till I send for you," which arrested her in the large room at some distance from the bed and then had the effect of making her turn on her heel with a professional laugh. She clearly judged that an old gentleman with the fine manner of his prime might still be trusted to take care of himself. When she had gone that personage addressed to his visitor the question for which his deep displeasure lent him strength. "Do you pretend there's a nobler life than a high political career?"

"I think the noble life's doing one's work well. One can do it very ill and be very base and mean in what you call a high political career. I haven't been in the House so many months without finding that out. It contains some very small souls."

"You should stand against them—you should expose them!" stammered Mr. Carteret.

"Stand against them, against one's own party!"

The old man contended a moment with this and then broke out: "God forgive you, are you a Tory, are you a Tory?"

"How little you understand me!" laughed Nick with a ring of bitterness.

"Little enough—little enough, my boy. Have you sent your electors your dreadful letter?"

"Not yet; but it's all ready and I shan't change my mind."

"You will—you will. You'll think better of it. You'll see your duty," said the invalid almost coaxingly.

"That seems very improbable, for my determination, crudely and abruptly as, to my great regret, it comes to you here, is the fruit of a long and painful struggle. The difficulty is that I see my duty just in this other effort."

"An effort? Do you call it an effort to fall away, to sink far down, to give up every effort? What does your mother say, heaven help her?" Mr. Carteret went on before Nick could answer the other question.

"I haven't told her yet."

"You're ashamed, you're ashamed!" Nick only looked out of the west window now—he felt his ears turn hot. "Tell her it would have been sixty thousand. I had the money all ready."

"I shan't tell her that," said Nick, redder still.

"Poor woman—poor dear woman!" Mr. Carteret woefully cried.

"Yes indeed—she won't like it."

"Think it all over again; don't throw away a splendid future!" These words were uttered with a final flicker of passion—Nick had never heard such an accent on his old friend's lips. But he next began to murmur, "I'm tired—I'm very tired," and sank back with a groan and with closed lips. His guest gently assured him that he had but too much cause to be exhausted and that the worst was over now. He smoothed his pillows for him and said he must leave him, would send in the nurse. "Come back, come back," Mr. Carteret pleaded against that; "come back and tell me it's a horrible dream."

Nick did go back very late that evening; his host had sent a message to his room. But one of the nurses was on the ground this time and made good her opposition watch in hand. The sick-room was shrouded and darkened; the shaded candle left the bed in gloom. Nick's interview with his venerable friend was the affair of but a moment; the nurse interposed, impatient and not understanding. She heard Nick say that he had posted his letter now and their companion flash out with an acerbity still savouring of the sordid associations of a world he had not done with: "Then of course my settlement doesn't take effect!"

"Oh that's all right," Nick answered kindly; and he went off next morning by the early train—his injured host was still sleeping. Mrs. Lendon's habits made it easy for her to be present in matutinal bloom at the young man's hasty breakfast, and she sent a particular remembrance to Lady Agnes and (when he should see them) to the Ladies Flora and Elizabeth. Nick had a prevision of the spirit in which his mother at least would now receive hollow compliments from Beauclere.

The night before, as soon as he had quitted Mr. Carteret, the old man said to the nurse that he wished Mr. Chayter instructed to go and fetch Mr. Mitton the first thing in the morning. Mr. Mitton was the leading solicitor at Beauclere.

XXXIV

The really formidable thing for Nick had been to tell his mother: a truth of which he was so conscious that he had the matter out with her the very morning he returned from Beauclere. She and Grace had come back the afternoon before from their own enjoyment of rural hospitality, and, knowing this—she had written him her intention from the country—he drove straight from the station to Calcutta Gardens. There was a little room on the right of the house-door known as his own room; but in which of a morning, when he was not at home, Lady Agnes sometimes wrote her letters. These were always numerous, and when she heard our young man's cab she happened to be engaged with them at the big brass-mounted bureau that had belonged to his father, where, amid a margin of works of political reference, she seemed to herself to make public affairs feel the point of her elbow.

She came into the hall to meet her son and to hear about their benefactor, and Nick went straight back into the room with her and closed the door. It would be in the evening paper and she would see it, and he had no right to allow her to wait for that. It proved indeed a terrible hour; and when ten minutes later Grace, who had learned upstairs her brother's return, went down for further news of him she heard from the hall a sound of voices that made her first pause and then retrace her steps on tiptoe. She mounted to the drawing-room and crept about there, palpitating, looking at moments into the dull street and wondering what on earth had taken place. She had no one to express her wonder to, for Florence Tressilian had departed and Biddy after breakfast betaken herself, in accordance with a custom now inveterate, to Rosedale Road. Her mother was unmistakably and passionately crying—a fact tremendous in its significance, for Lady Agnes had not often been brought so low. Nick had seen her cry, but this almost awful spectacle had seldom been offered to Grace, and it now convinced her that some dreadful thing had happened.

That was of course in order, after Nick's mysterious quarrel with Julia, which had made his mother so ill and was at present followed up with new horrors. The row, as Grace mentally phrased it, had had something to do with the rupture of the lovers—some deeper depth of disappointment had begun to yawn. Grace asked herself if they were talking about Broadwood; if Nick had demanded that in the conditions so unpleasantly altered Lady Agnes should restore that awfully nice house to its owner. This was very possible, but why should he so suddenly have broken out about it? And, moreover, their mother, though sore to bleeding about the whole business—for Broadwood, in its fresh comfort, was too delightful—wouldn't have met this pretension with tears: hadn't she already so perversely declared that they couldn't decently continue to make use of the place? Julia had said that of course they must go on, but Lady Agnes was prepared with an effective rejoinder to that. It didn't consist of words—it was to be austerely practical, was to consist of letting Julia see, at the moment she should least expect it, that they quite wouldn't go on. Lady Agnes was ostensibly waiting for this moment—the moment when her renunciation would be most impressive.

Grace was conscious of how she had for many days been moving with her mother in darkness, deeply stricken by Nick's culpable—oh he was culpable!—loss of his prize, but feeling an obscure element in the matter they didn't grasp, an undiscovered explanation that would perhaps make it still worse, though it might make *them*, poor things, a little better. He had explained nothing, he had simply said, "Dear mother, we don't hit it off, after all; it's an awful bore, but we don't"—as if that were in the dire conditions an adequate balm for two aching hearts. From Julia naturally no flood of light was to be looked for—Julia *never* humoured curiosity—and, though she very often did the thing you wouldn't suppose, she was not unexpectedly apologetic in this case. Grace recognised that in such a position it would savour of apology for her to disclose to Lady Agnes her grounds for having let Nick off; and she wouldn't have liked to be the person to suggest to Julia that any one looked for anything from her. Neither of the disunited pair blamed the other or cast an aspersion, and it was all very magnanimous and superior and impenetrable and exasperating. With all this Grace had a suspicion that Biddy knew something more, that for Biddy the tormenting curtain had been lifted.

Biddy had come and gone in these days with a perceptible air of detachment from the tribulations of home. It had made her, fortunately, very pretty—still prettier than usual: it sometimes happened that at moments when Grace was most angry she had a faint sweet smile which might have been drawn from some source of occult consolation. It was perhaps in some degree connected with Peter Sherringham's visit, as to which the girl had not been superstitiously silent. When Grace asked her if she had secret information and if it pointed to the idea that everything would be all right in the end, she pretended to know nothing—What should she know? she asked with the loveliest arch of eyebrows over an unblinking candour—and begged her sister not to let Lady Agnes believe her better off than themselves. She contributed nothing to their gropings save a much better patience, but she went with noticeable regularity, on the pretext of her foolish modelling, to Rosedale Road. She was frankly on Nick's side; not going so far as to say he had been right, but saying distinctly how sure she was that, whatever had happened, he couldn't have helped it, not a mite. This was striking, because, as Grace knew, the younger of the sisters had been much favoured by Julia and wouldn't have sacrificed her easily. It associated itself in the irritated mind of the elder with Biddy's frequent visits to the studio and made Miss Dormer ask herself if the crisis in Nick's and Julia's business had not somehow been linked to that unnatural spot.

She had gone there two or three times while Biddy was working, gone to pick up any clue to the mystery that might peep out. But she had put her hand on nothing more—it wouldn't have occurred to her to say nothing less—than the so dreadfully pointed presence of Gabriel Nash. She once found that odd satellite, to her surprise, paying a visit to her sister—he had come for Nick, who was absent; she remembered how they had met in Paris and how little he had succeeded with them. When she had asked Biddy afterwards how she could receive him that way Biddy had replied that even she, Grace, would have some charity for him if she could hear how fond he was of poor Nick. He had talked to her only of Nick—of nothing else. Grace had observed how she spoke of Nick as injured, and had noted the implication that some one else, ceasing to be fond of him, was thereby condemned in Biddy's eyes. It seemed to Grace that some one else had at least a right not to like some of his friends. The studio struck her as mean and horrid; and so far from suggesting to her that it could have played a part in making Nick and Julia fall out she only felt how little its dusty want of consequence, could count, one way or the other, for Julia. Grace, who had no opinions on art, saw no merit whatever in those "impressions" on canvas from Nick's hand with which the place was bestrewn. She didn't at all wish her brother to have talent in that direction, yet it was secretly humiliating to her that he hadn't more.

Nick meanwhile felt a pang of almost horrified penitence, in the little room on the right of the hall, the moment after he had made his mother really understand he had thrown up his seat and that it would probably be in the evening papers. That she would take this very ill was an idea that had pressed upon him hard enough, but she took it even worse than he had feared. He measured, in the look she gave him when the full truth loomed upon her, the mortal cruelty of her distress; her face was like that of a passenger on a ship who sees the huge bows of another vessel towering close out of the fog. There are visions of dismay before which the best conscience recoils, and though Nick had made his choice on all the grounds there were a few minutes in which he would gladly have admitted that his wisdom was a dark mistake. His heart was in his throat, he had gone too far; he had been ready to disappoint his mother—he had not been ready to destroy her.

Lady Agnes, I hasten to add, was not destroyed; she made, after her first drowning gasp, a tremendous scene of opposition, in the face of which her son could only fall back on his intrenchments. She must know the worst, he had thought: so he told her everything, including the little story of the forfeiture of his "expectations" from Mr. Carteret. He showed her this time not only the face of the matter, but what lay below it; narrated briefly the incident in his studio which had led to Julia Dallow's deciding she couldn't after all put up with him. This was wholly new to Lady Agnes, she had had no clue to it, and he could instantly see how it made the event worse for her, adding a hideous positive to an abominable negative. He noted now that, distressed and distracted as she had been by his rupture with Julia, she had still held to the faith that their engagement would come on again; believing evidently that he had a personal empire over the mistress of Harsh which would bring her back. Lady Agnes was forced to recognise this empire as precarious, to forswear the hope of a blessed renewal from the moment the question was of base infatuations on his own part. Nick confessed to an infatuation, but did his best to show her it wasn't base; that it wasn't—since Julia had had faith in his loyalty—for the person of the young lady who had been discovered posturing to him and whom he had seen but half-a-dozen times in his life. He endeavoured to recall to his mother the identity of this young lady, he adverted to the occasion in Paris when they all had seen her

419

together. But Lady Agnes's mind and memory were a blank on the subject of Miss Miriam Rooth and she wanted to hear nothing whatever about her: it was enough that she was the cause of their ruin and a part of his pitiless folly. She needed to know nothing of her to allude to her as if it were superfluous to give a definite name to the class to which she belonged.

But she gave a name to the group in which Nick had now taken his place, and it made him feel after the lapse of years like a small, scolded, sorry boy again; for it was so far away he could scarcely remember it—besides there having been but a moment or two of that sort in his happy childhood—the time when this parent had slapped him and called him a little fool. He was a big fool now—hugely immeasurable; she repeated the term over and over with high-pitched passion. The most painful thing in this painful hour was perhaps his glimpse of the strange feminine cynicism that lurked in her fine sense of injury. Where there was such a complexity of revolt it would have been difficult to pick out particular wrongs; but Nick could see that, to his mother's imagination, he was most a fool for not having kept his relations with the actress, whatever they were, better from Julia's knowledge. He remained indeed freshly surprised at the ardour with which she had rested her hopes on Julia. Julia was certainly a combination—she was accomplished, she was a sort of leading woman and she was rich; but after all—putting aside what she might be to a man in love with her—she was not the keystone of the universe. Yet the form in which the consequences of his apostasy appeared most to come home to Lady Agnes was the loss for the Dormer family of the advantages attached to the possession of Mrs. Dallow. The larger mortification would round itself later; for the hour the damning thing was that Nick had made that lady the gift of an unforgivable grievance. He had clinched their separation by his letter to his electors—and that above all was the wickedness of the letter. Julia would have got over the other woman, but she would never get over his becoming a nobody.

Lady Agnes challenged him upon this low prospect exactly as if he had embraced it with the malignant purpose of making the return of his late intended impossible. She contradicted her premises and lost her way in her wrath. What had made him suddenly turn round if he had been in good faith

before? He had never been in good faith—never, never; he had had from
his earliest childhood the nastiest hankerings after a vulgar little daubing,
trash-talking life; they were not in him, the grander, nobler aspirations—they
never had been—and he had been anything but honest to lead her on, to
lead them all on, to think he would do something: the fall and the shame
would have been less for them if they had come earlier. Moreover, what need
under heaven had he to tell Charles Carteret of the cruel folly on his very
death-bed?—as if he mightn't have let it all alone and accepted the benefit
the old man was so delighted to confer. No wonder Mr. Carteret would keep
his money for his heirs if that was the way Nick proposed to repay him; but
where was the common sense, where was the common charity, where was the
common decency of tormenting him with such vile news in his last hours?
Was he trying what he could invent that would break her heart, that would
send her in sorrow down to her grave? Weren't they all miserable enough and
hadn't he a ray of pity for his wretched sisters?

The relation of effect and cause, in regard to his sisters' wretchedness, was
but dimly discernible to Nick, who, however, perceived his mother genuinely
to consider that his action had disconnected them all, still more than she
held they were already disconnected, from the good things of life. Julia was
money, Mr. Carteret was money—everything else was the absence of it. If
these precious people had been primarily money for Nick it after all flattered
the distributive impulse in him to have taken for granted that for the rest of
the family too the difference would have been so great. For days, for weeks
and months to come, the little room on the right of the hall was to vibrate for
our young man, as if the very walls and window-panes still suffered, with the
odious trial of his true temper.

XXXV

That evening—the evening of his return from Beauclere—he was
conscious of a keen desire to get away, to go abroad, to leave behind him the
little chatter his resignation would be sure to produce in an age of publicity

which never discriminated as to the quality of events. Then he felt it decidedly better to stay, to see the business through on the spot. Besides, he would have to meet his constituents—would a parcel of cheese-eating burgesses ever have been "met" on so queer an occasion?—and when that was over the incident would practically be closed. Nick had an idea he knew in advance how it would affect him to be pointed at as a person who had given up a considerable chance of eventual "office" to take likenesses at so much a head. He wouldn't attempt down at Harsh to touch on the question of motive; for, given the nature of the public mind of Harsh, that would be a strain on his faculty of exposition. But as regards the chaff of the political world and of society he had a hope he should find chaff enough for retorts. It was true that when his mother twitted him in her own effective way he had felt rather flattened out; but then one's mother might have a heavier hand than any one else. He had not thrown up the House of Commons to amuse himself; he had thrown it up to work, to sit quietly down and bend over his task. If he should go abroad his parent might think he had some weak-minded view of joining Julia and trying, with however little hope, to win her back—an illusion it would be singularly pernicious to encourage. His desire for Julia's society had succumbed for the present at any rate to a dire interruption—he had become more and more aware of their speaking a different language. Nick felt like a young man who has gone to the Rhineland to "get up" his German for an examination—committed to talk, to read, to dream only in the new idiom. Now that he had taken his jump everything was simplified, at the same time that everything was pitched in a higher and intenser key; and he wondered how in the absence of a common dialect he had conversed on the whole so happily with Mrs. Dallow. Then he had aftertastes of understandings tolerably independent of words. He was excited because every fresh responsibility is exciting, and there was no manner of doubt he had accepted one. No one knew what it was but himself—Gabriel Nash scarcely counted, his whole attitude on the question of responsibility being so fantastic—and he would have to ask his dearest friends to take him on trust. Rather indeed he would ask nothing of any one, but would cultivate independence, mulishness, and gaiety, and fix his thoughts on a bright if distant morrow. It was disagreeable to have to remember that his task would not be sweetened by a sense of heroism;

for if it might be heroic to give up the muses for the strife of great affairs, no romantic glamour worth speaking of would ever gather round an Englishman who in the prime of his strength had given up great or even small affairs for the muses. Such an original might himself privately and perversely regard certain phases of this inferior commerce as a great affair; but who would give him the benefit of that sort of confidence—except indeed a faithful, clever, exalted little sister Biddy, if he should have the good luck to have one? Biddy was in fact all ready for heroic flights and eager to think she might fight the battle of the beautiful by her brother's side; so that he had really to moderate her and remind her how little his actual job was a crusade with bugles and banners and how much a grey, sedentary grind, the charm of which was all at the core. You might have an emotion about it, and an emotion that would be a help, but this was not the sort of thing you could show—the end in view would seem so disproportionately small. Nick put it to her that one really couldn't talk to people about the "responsibility" of what she would see him pottering at in his studio.

He therefore didn't "run," as he would have said, to winged words any more than he was forced to, having, moreover, a sense that apologetic work (if apology it should be called to carry the war straight into the enemy's country) might be freely left to Gabriel Nash. He laid the weight of explanation on his commentators, meeting them all on the firm ground of his own amusement. He saw he should live for months in a thick cloud of irony, not the finest air of the season, and he adopted the weapon to which a person whose use of tobacco is only occasional resorts when every one else produces a cigar—he puffed the spasmodic, defensive cigarette. He accepted as to what he had done the postulate of the obscurely tortuous, abounding so in that sense that his critics were themselves bewildered. Some of them felt that they got, as the phrase is, little out of him—he rose in his good humour so much higher than the "rise" they had looked for—on his very first encounter with the world after his scrimmage with his mother. He went to a dinner-party—he had accepted the invitation many days before—having seen his resignation, in the form of a telegram from Harsh, announced in the evening papers. The people he found there had seen it as well, and the wittiest wanted to know what he was now going to do. Even the most embarrassed asked if it were true he had changed his politics. He gave different answers to different persons, but left most of them under the impression that he had strange scruples of conscience. This, however, was not a formidable occasion, for there had happened to be no one present he would have desired, on the old basis, especially to gratify. There were real good friends it would be less easy to meet—Nick was almost sorry for an hour that he had so many real good friends. If he had had more enemies the case would have been simpler, and he was fully aware that the hardest thing of all would be to be let off too easily. Then he would appear to himself to have been put, all round, on his generosity, and his deviation would thus wear its ugliest face.

When he left the place at which he had been dining he betook himself to Rosedale Road: he saw no reason why he should go down to the House, though he knew he had not done with that yet. He had a dread of behaving as if he supposed he should be expected to make a farewell speech, and was thankful his eminence was not of a nature to create on such an occasion a demand for his oratory. He had in fact nothing whatever to say in public— not a vain word, not a sorry syllable. Though the hour was late he found Gabriel Nash established in his studio, drawn thither by the fine exhilaration of having seen an evening paper. Trying it late, on the chance, he had been told by Nick's servant that Nick would sleep there that night, and he had come in to wait, he was so eager to congratulate him. Nick submitted with a good grace to his society—he was tired enough to go to bed, but was restless too— in spite of noting now, oddly enough, that Nash's congratulations could add little to his fortitude. He had felt a good deal, before, as if he were in this philosopher's hands; but since making his final choice he had begun to strike himself as all in his own. Gabriel might have been the angel of that name, but no angel could assist him much henceforth.

Nash indeed was as true as ever to his genius while he lolled on a divan and emitted a series of reflexions that were even more ingenious than opportune. Nick walked up and down the room, and it might have been supposed from his manner that he was impatient for his friend to withdraw. This idea would have been contradicted, however, by the fact that subsequently, after the latter had quitted him, he continued to perambulate. He had grown used to

Gabriel and must now have been possessed of all he had to say. That was one's penalty with persons whose main gift was for talk, however inspiring; talk engendered a sense of sameness much sooner than action. The things a man did were necessarily more different from each other than the things he said, even if he went in for surprising you. Nick felt Nash could never surprise him any more save by mere plain perpetration.

He talked of his host's future, talked of Miriam Rooth and of Peter Sherringham, whom he had seen at that young woman's and whom he described as in a predicament delightful to behold. Nick put a question about Peter's predicament and learned, rather to his disappointment, that it consisted only of the fact that he was in love with Miriam. He appealed to his visitor to do better than this, and Nash then added the touch that Sherringham wouldn't be able to have her. "Oh they've ideas!" he said when Nick asked him why.

"What ideas? So has he, I suppose."

"Yes, but they're not the same."

"Well, they'll nevertheless arrange something," Nick opined.

"You'll have to help them a bit. She's in love with another man," Nash went on.

"Do you mean with you?"

"Oh, I'm never another man—I'm always more the wrong one than the man himself. It's you she's after." And on his friend's asking him what he meant by this Nash added: "While you were engaged in transferring her image to the tablet of your genius you stamped your own on that of her heart."

Nick stopped in his walk, staring. "Ah, what a bore!"

"A bore? Don't you think her formed to please?"

Nick wondered, but didn't conclude. "I wanted to go on with her—now I can't."

Nash himself, however, jumped straight to what really mattered. "My dear fellow, it only makes her handsomer. I wondered what happy turn she had taken."

"Oh, that's twaddle," said Nick, turning away. "Besides, has she told you?"

"No, but her mother has."

"Has she told her mother?"

"Mrs. Rooth says not. But I've known Mrs. Rooth to say that which isn't."

"Apply that rule then to the information you speak of."

"Well, since you press me, I know more," Gabriel said. "Miriam knows you're engaged to a wonderful, rich lady; she told me as much, told me she had seen her here. That was enough to set her off—she likes forbidden fruit."

"I'm not engaged to any lady whatever. I was," Nick handsomely conceded, "but we've altered our minds."

"Ah, what a pity!" his friend wailed.

"Mephistopheles!"—and he stopped again with the point of this.

"Pray then whom do you call Margaret? May I ask if your failure of interest in the political situation is the cause of this change in your personal one?" Nash went on. Nick signified that he mightn't; whereupon he added: "I'm not in the least devilish—I only mean it's a pity you've altered your minds, since Miriam may in consequence alter hers. She goes from one thing to another. However, I won't tell her."

"I will then!" Nick declared between jest and earnest.

"Would that really be prudent?" his companion asked more completely in the frolic key.

"At any rate," he resumed, "nothing would induce me to interfere with Peter Sherringham. That sounds fatuous, but to you I don't mind appearing an ass."

"The thing would be to get Sherringham, out of spite," Nash threw off, "to entangle himself with another woman."

"What good would that do?"

"Ah, Miriam would then begin to think of him."

"Spite surely isn't a conceivable motive—for a healthy man."

The plea, however, found Gabriel ready. "Sherringham's just precisely not a healthy man. He's too much in love."

"Then he won't care for another woman."

"He would try to, and that would produce its effect—its effect on Miriam."

"You talk like an American novel. Let him try, and God keep us all straight." Nick adverted in extreme silence to his poor little Biddy and greatly hoped—he would have to see to it a little—that Peter wouldn't "try" on *her*. He changed the subject and before Nash withdrew took occasion to remark—the occasion was offered by some new allusion of the visitor's to the sport he hoped to extract from seeing Nick carry out everything to which he stood committed—that the comedy of the matter would fall flat and the incident pass unnoticed.

But Nash lost no heart. "Oh, if you'll simply do your part I'll take care of the rest."

"If you mean by doing my part minding my business and working like a beaver I shall easily satisfy you," Nick replied.

"Ah, you reprobate, you'll become another Sir Joshua, a mere P.R.A.!" his companion railed, getting up to go.

When he had gone Nick threw himself back on the cushions of the divan and, with his hands locked above his head, sat a long time lost in thought. He had sent his servant to bed; he was unmolested. He gazed before him into the gloom produced by the unheeded burning-out of the last candle. The vague outer light came in through the tall studio window and the painted images, ranged about, looked confused in the dusk. If his mother had seen him she might have thought he was staring at his father's ghost.

XXXVI

The night Peter Sherringham walked away from Balaklava Place with Gabriel Nash the talk of the two men directed itself, as was natural at the time, to the question of Miriam's future fame and the pace, as Nash called it, at which she would go. Critical spirits as they both were, and one of them as dissimulative in passion as the other was paradoxical in the absence of it, they yet took her career for granted as completely as the simple-minded, a pair of hot spectators in the pit, might have done, and exchanged observations on the assumption that the only uncertain element would be the pace. This was a proof of general subjugation. Peter wished not to show, yet wished to know, and in the restlessness of his anxiety was ready even to risk exposure, great as the sacrifice might be of the imperturbable, urbane scepticism most appropriate to a secretary of embassy. He couldn't rid himself of the sense that Nash had got up earlier than he, had had opportunities of contact in days already distant, the days of Mrs. Rooth's hungry foreign rambles. Something of authority and privilege stuck to him from this, and it made Sherringham still more uncomfortable when he was most conscious that, at the best, even the trained diplomatic mind would never get a grasp of Miriam as a whole. She was constructed to revolve like the terraqueous globe; some part or other of her was always out of sight or in shadow.

Peter talked to conceal his feelings, and, like many a man practising that indirectness, rather lost himself in the wood. They agreed that, putting strange accidents aside, the girl would go further than any one had gone in England within the memory of man; and that it was a pity, as regards marking the comparison, that for so long no one had gone any distance worth speaking of. They further agreed that it would naturally seem absurd to any one who didn't know, their prophesying such big things on such small evidence; and they agreed lastly that the absurdity quite vanished as soon as the prophets knew as *they* knew. Their knowledge—they quite recognised this—was simply confidence raised to a high point, the communication of their young friend's own confidence. The conditions were enormously to make, but it was of the very essence of Miriam's confidence that she would make them. The parts, the plays, the theatres, the "support," the audiences, the critics, the money were all to be found, but she cast a spell that prevented this from seeming a serious hitch. One mightn't see from one day to the other what she would do or how she would do it, but this wouldn't stay her steps—she would none the less go on. She would have to construct her own road, as it were, but at the worst there would only be delays in making it. These delays would depend on the hardness of the stones she had to break.

As Peter had noted, you never knew where to "have" Gabriel Nash; a truth exemplified in his unexpected delight at the prospect of Miriam's drawing forth the modernness of the age. You might have thought he would loathe that modernness; but he had a joyous, amused, amusing vision of it— saw it as something huge and fantastically vulgar. Its vulgarity would rise to the grand style, like that of a London railway station, and the publicity achieved by their charming charge be as big as the globe itself. All the machinery was ready, the platform laid; the facilities, the wires and bells and trumpets, the roaring, deafening newspaperism of the period—its most distinctive sign— were waiting for her, their predestined mistress, to press her foot on the spring and set them all in motion. Gabriel brushed in a large, bright picture of her progress through the time and round the world, round it and round it again, from continent to continent and clime to clime; with populations and deputations, reporters and photographers, placards and interviews and banquets, steamers, railways, dollars, diamonds, speeches and artistic ruin all jumbled into her train. Regardless of expense the spectacle would be and thrilling, though somewhat monotonous, the drama—a drama more bustling than any she would put on the stage and a spectacle that would beat everything for scenery. In the end her divine voice would crack, screaming to foreign ears and antipodal barbarians, and her clever manner would lose all quality, simplified to a few unmistakable knock-down dodges. Then she would be at the fine climax of life and glory, still young and insatiate, but already coarse, hard, and raddled, with nothing left to do and nothing left to do it with, the remaining years all before her and the *raison d'être* all behind. It would be splendid, dreadful, grotesque.

"Oh, she'll have some good years—they'll be worth having," Peter insisted as they went. "Besides, you see her too much as a humbug and too little as a real producer. She has ideas—great ones; she loves the thing for itself. That may keep a woman serious."

"Her greatest idea must always be to show herself, and fortunately she has a great quantity of that treasure to show. I think of her absolutely as a real producer, but as a producer whose production is her own person. No 'person,' even as fine a one as hers, will stand that for more than an hour, so that humbuggery has very soon to lend a hand. However," Nash continued, "if she's a fine humbug it will do as well, it will perfectly suit the time. We can all be saved by vulgarity; that's the solvent of all difficulties and the blessing of this delightful age. One doesn't die of it—save in soul and sense: one dies only of minding it. Therefore let no man despair—a new hope has dawned."

"She'll do her work like any other worker, with the advantage over many that her talent's rare," Peter obliquely answered. "Compared with the life of many women that's security and sanity of the highest order. Then she can't help her beauty. You can't vulgarise that."

"Oh, can't you?" Gabriel cried.

"It will abide with her till the day of her death. It isn't a mere superficial freshness. She's very noble."

"Yes, that's the pity of it," said Nash. "She's a big more or less directed force, and I quite admit that she'll do for a while a lot of good. She'll have brightened up the world for a great many people—have brought the ideal nearer to them and held it fast for an hour with its feet on earth and its great wings trembling. That's always something, for blest is he who has dropped even the smallest coin into the little iron box that contains the precious savings of mankind. Miriam will doubtless have dropped a big gold-piece. It will be found in the general scramble on the day the race goes bankrupt. And then for herself she'll have had a great go at life."

"Oh yes, she'll have got out of her hole—she won't have vegetated," Peter concurred. "That makes her touching to me—it adds to the many good reasons for which one may want to help her. She's tackling a big job, and tackling it by herself; throwing herself upon the world in good faith and dealing with it as she can; meeting alone, in her youth, her beauty, her generosity, all the embarrassments of notoriety and all the difficulties of a profession of which, if one half's what's called brilliant the other's frankly odious."

"She has great courage, but you speak of her as solitary with such a lot of us all round her?" Nash candidly inquired.

"She's a great thing for you and me, but we're a small thing for her."

"Well, a good many small things, if they but stick together, may make up a mass," Gabriel said. "There must always be the man, you see. He's the indispensable element in such a life, and he'll be the last thing she'll ever lack."

"What man are you talking about?" Peter asked with imperfect ease.

"The man of the hour, whoever he is. She'll inspire innumerable devotions."

"Of course she will, and they'll be precisely a part of the insufferable side of her life."

"Insufferable to whom?" Nash demanded. "Don't forget that the insufferable side of her life will be just the side she'll thrive on. You can't eat your cake and have it, and you can't make omelettes without breaking eggs. You can't at once sit by the fire and parade about the world, and you can't take all chances without having some adventures. You can't be a great actress without the luxury of nerves. Without a plentiful supply—or without the right ones—you'll only be second fiddle. If you've all the tense strings you may take life for your fiddlestick. Your nerves and your adventures, your eggs and your cake, are part of the cost of the most expensive of professions. You play with human passions, with exaltations and ecstasies and terrors, and if you trade on the fury of the elements you must know how to ride the storm."

Well, Peter thought it over. "Those are the fine old commonplaces about the artistic temperament, but I usually find the artist a very meek, decent, little person."

431

"You *never* find the artist—you only find his work, and that's all you need find. When the artist's a woman, and the woman's an actress, meekness and decency will doubtless be there in the right proportions," Nash went on. "Miriam will represent them for you, if you give her her cue, with the utmost charm."

"Of course she'll inspire devotions—*that's* all right," said Peter with a wild cheerfulness.

"And of course they'll inspire responses, and with that consequence—don't you see?—they'll mitigate her solitude, they'll even enliven it," Nash set forth.

"She'll probably box a good many ears: that'll be lively!" Peter returned with some grimness.

"Oh magnificent!—it will be a merry life. Yet with its tragic passages, its distracted or its pathetic hours," Gabriel insisted. "In short, a little of everything."

They walked on without further speech till at last Peter resumed: "The best thing for a woman in her situation is to marry some decent care-taking man."

"Oh I daresay she'll do that too!" Nash laughed; a remark as a result of which his companion lapsed afresh into silence. Gabriel left him a little to enjoy this; after which he added: "There's somebody she'd marry to-morrow."

Peter wondered. "Do you mean her friend Dashwood?"

"No, no, I mean Nick Dormer."

"She'd marry *him?*" Peter gasped.

"I mean her head's full of him. But she'll hardly get the chance."

Peter watched himself. "Does she like him as much as that?"

"I don't quite know how much you mean, but enough for all practical ends."

"Marrying a fashionable actress is hardly a practical end."

"Certainly not, but I'm not speaking from his point of view." Nash was perfectly lucid. "Moreover, I thought you just now said it would be such a good thing for her."

"To marry Nick Dormer?"

"You said a good decent man, and he's one of the very decentest."

"I wasn't thinking of the individual, but of the protection. It would fence her about, settle certain questions, or appear to; it would make things safe and comfortable for her and keep a lot of cads and blackguards away."

"She ought to marry the prompter or the box-keeper," said Nash. "Then it would be all right. I think indeed they generally do, don't they?"

Peter felt for a moment a strong disposition to drop his friend on the spot, to cross to the other side of the street and walk away without him. But there was a different impulse which struggled with this one and after a minute overcame it, the impulse that led to his saying presently: "Has she told you she's—a—she's in love with Nick?"

"No, no—that's not the way I know it."

"Has Nick told you then?"

"On the contrary, I've told *him*."

"You've rendered him a questionable service if you've no proof," Peter pronounced.

"My proof's only that I've seen her with him. She's charming, poor dear thing."

"But surely she isn't in love with every man she's charming to."

"I mean she's charming to *me*," Nash returned. "I see her that way. I see her interested—and what it does to her, with her, *for* her. But judge for yourself—the first time you get a chance."

"When shall I get a chance? Nick doesn't come near her."

"Oh he'll come, he'll come; his picture isn't finished."

"You mean *he'll* be the box-keeper, then?"

"My dear fellow, I shall never allow it," said Gabriel Nash. "It would be idiotic and quite unnecessary. He's beautifully arranged—in quite a different line. Fancy his taking that sort of job on his hands! Besides, she'd never expect it; she's not such a goose. They're very good friends—it will go on that way. She's an excellent person for him to know; she'll give him lots of ideas of the plastic kind. He would have been up there before this, but it has taken him time to play his delightful trick on his constituents. That of course is pure amusement; but when once his effect has been well produced he'll get back to business, and his business will be a very different matter from Miriam's. Imagine him writing her advertisements, living on her money, adding up her profits, having rows and recriminations with her agent, carrying her shawl, spending his days in her rouge-pot. The right man for that, if she must have one, will turn up. '*Pour le mariage, non.*' She isn't wholly an idiot; she really, for a woman, quite sees things as they are."

As Peter had not crossed the street and left Gabriel planted he now suffered the extremity of irritation. But descrying in the dim vista of the Edgware Road a vague and vigilant hansom he waved his stick with eagerness and with the abrupt declaration that, feeling tired, he must drive the rest of his way. He offered Nash, as he entered the vehicle, no seat, but this coldness was not reflected in the lucidity with which that master of every subject went on to affirm that there was of course a danger—the danger that in given circumstances Miriam would leave the stage.

"Leave it, you mean, for some man?"

"For the man we're talking about."

"For Nick Dormer?" Peter asked from his place in the cab, his paleness lighted by its lamps.

"If he should make it a condition. But why should he? why should he make *any* conditions? He's not an ass either. You see it would be a bore"—Nash kept it up while the hansom waited—"because if she were to do anything of that sort she'd make him pay for the sacrifice."

"Oh yes, she'd make him pay for the sacrifice," Peter blindly concurred.

"And then when he had paid she'd go back to her footlights," Gabriel developed from the curbstone as his companion closed the apron of the cab.

"I see—she'd go back—good-night," Peter returned. "*Please* go on!" he cried to the driver through the hole in the roof. And while the vehicle rolled away he growled to himself: "Of course she would—and quite right!"

XXXVII

"Judge for yourself when you get a chance," Nash had said to him; and as it turned out he was able to judge two days later, for he found his cousin in Balaklava Place on the Tuesday following his walk with their insufferable friend. He had not only stayed away from the theatre on the Monday evening—he regarded this as an achievement of some importance—but had not been near Miriam during the day. He had meant to absent himself from her company on Tuesday as well; a determination confirmed by the fact that the afternoon turned to rain. But when at ten minutes to five o'clock he jumped into a hansom and directed his course to Saint John's Wood it was precisely upon the weather that he shifted the responsibility of his behaviour.

Miriam had dined when he reached the villa, but she was lying down, unduly fatigued, before going to the theatre. Mrs. Rooth was, however, in the drawing-room with three gentlemen, in two of whom the fourth visitor was not startled to recognise Basil Dashwood and Gabriel Nash. Dashwood appeared to have become Miriam's brother-in-arms and a second child—a fonder one—to Mrs. Rooth; it had reached Peter on some late visit that the young actor had finally moved his lodgings into the quarter, making himself a near neighbour for all sorts of convenience. "Hang his convenience!"

Peter thought, perceiving that Mrs. Lovick's "Arty" was now altogether one of the family. Oh the family!—it was a queer one to be connected with: that consciousness was acute in Sherringham's breast to-day as he entered Mrs. Rooth's little circle. The place was filled with cigarette-smoke and there was a messy coffee-service on the piano, whose keys Basil Dashwood lightly touched for his own diversion. Nash, addressing the room of course, was at one end of a little sofa with his nose in the air, and Nick Dormer was at the other end, seated much at his ease and with a certain privileged appearance of having been there often before, though Sherringham knew he had not. He looked uncritical and very young, as rosy as a school-boy on a half-holiday. It was past five o'clock in the day, but Mrs. Rooth was not dressed; there was, however, no want of finish in her elegant attitude—the same relaxed grandeur (she seemed to let you understand) for which she used to be distinguished at Castle Nugent when the house was full. She toyed incongruously, in her unbuttoned wrapper, with a large tinsel fan which resembled a theatrical property.

It was one of the discomforts of Peter's position that many of those minor matters which are superficially at least most characteristic of the histrionic life had power to displease him, so that he was obliged constantly to overlook and condone and pretend. He disliked besmoked drawing-rooms and irregular meals and untidy arrangements; he could suffer from the vulgarity of Mrs. Rooth's apartments, the importunate photographs which gave on his nerves, the barbarous absence of signs of an orderly domestic life, the odd volumes from the circulating library (you could see what they were—the very covers told you—at a glance) tumbled about under smeary cups and glasses. He hadn't waited till now to feel it "rum" that fate should have let him in for such contacts; but as he stood before his hostess and her companions he wondered perhaps more than ever why he should. Her companions somehow, who were not responsible, didn't keep down his wonder; which was particularly odd, since they were not superficially in the least of Bohemian type. Almost the first thing that struck him, as happened, in coming into the room, was the fresh fact of the high good looks of his cousin, a gentleman, to one's taste and for one's faith, in a different enough degree from the stiff-collared, conversible Dashwood. Peter didn't hate Nick for being of so fine an English grain; he knew rather the brush of a new wave of annoyance at Julia's stupid failure to get on with him under that good omen.

It was his first encounter with the late member for Harsh since his arrival in London: they had been on one side and the other so much taken up with their affairs. Since their last meeting Nick had, as we know, to his kinsman's perception, really put on a new character: he had done the finest stroke of business in the quietest way. This had made him a presence to be counted with, and in just the sense in which poor Peter desired least to count. Poor Peter, after his somersault in the blue, had just lately been much troubled; he was ravaged by contending passions; he paid every hour in a torment of unrest for what was false in his position, the impossibility of keeping the presentable parts of his character together, the opposition of interest and desire. Nick, his junior and a lighter weight, had settled *his* problem and showed no wounds; there was something impertinent and mystifying in it. Yet he looked, into the bargain, too innocently young and happy, and too careless and modest and amateurish, to figure as a rival or even as the genius he was apparently going to try to be—the genius that the other day, in the studio there with Biddy, Peter had got a startled glimpse of his power to become. Julia's brother would have liked to be aware of grounds of resentment, to be able to hold she had been badly treated or that Nick was basely fatuous, for in that case he might have had the resource of taking offence. But where was the outrage of his merely being liked by a woman in respect to whom one had definitely denied one's self the luxury of pretensions, especially if, as the wrong-doer, he had taken no action in the matter? It could scarcely be called wrong-doing to call, casually, on an afternoon when the lady didn't seem to be there. Peter could at any rate rejoice that Miriam didn't; and he proposed to himself suggesting to Nick after a little that they should adjourn together—they had such interesting things to talk about. Meanwhile Nick greeted him with a friendly freedom in which he could read neither confusion nor defiance. Peter was reassured against a danger he believed he didn't recognise and puzzled by a mystery he flattered himself he hadn't heeded. And he was still more ashamed of being reassured than of being puzzled.

It must be recorded that Miriam's absence from the scene was not prolonged. Nick, as Sherringham gathered, had been about a quarter of an hour in the house, which would have given her, gratified by his presence, due time to array herself to come down to him. At all events she was in the room, prepared apparently to go to the theatre, very shortly after one of her guests had become sensible of how glad he was she was out of it. Familiarity had never yet cured him of a certain tremor of expectation, and even of suspense, in regard to her entrances; a flutter caused by the simple circumstance of her infinite variety. To say she was always acting would too much convey that she was often fatiguing; since her changing face affected this particular admirer at least not as a series of masks, but as a response to perceived differences, an intensity of that perception, or still more as something richly constructional, like the shifting of the scene in a play or like a room with many windows. The image she was to project was always incalculable, but if her present denied her past and declined responsibility for her future it made a good thing of the hour and kept the actual peculiarly fresh. This time the actual was a bright, gentle, graceful, smiling, young woman in a new dress, eager to go out, drawing on fresh gloves, who looked as if she were about to step into a carriage and—it was Gabriel Nash who thus formulated her physiognomy—do a lot of London things.

The young woman had time to spare, however, and she sat down and talked and laughed and presently gave, as seemed to Peter, a deeper glow to the tawdry little room, which could do for others if it had to do for her. She described herself as in a state of nervous muddle, exhausted, blinded, *abrutie*, with the rehearsals of the forthcoming piece—the first night was close at hand, and it was going to be of a vileness: they would all see!—but there was no correspondence between this account of the matter and her present bravery of mood. She sent her mother away—to "put on some clothes or something"—and, left alone with the visitors, went to a long glass between the windows, talking always to Nick Dormer, and revised and rearranged a little her own attire. She talked to Nick, over her shoulder, and to Nick only, as if he were the guest to recognise and the others didn't count. She broke out at once on his having thrown up his seat, wished to know if the strange story told her by Mr. Nash were true—that he had knocked all the hopes of his party into pie.

Nick took it any way she liked and gave a pleasant picture of his party's ruin, the critical condition of public affairs: he was as yet clearly closed to contrition or shame. The pilgrim from Paris, before Miriam's entrance, had not, in shaking hands with him, made even a roundabout allusion to his odd "game"; he felt he must somehow show good taste—so English people often feel—at the cost of good manners. But he winced on seeing how his scruples had been wasted, and was struck with the fine, jocose, direct turn of his kinsman's conversation with the young actress. It was a part of her unexpectedness that she took the heavy literal view of Nick's behaviour; declared frankly, though without ill nature, that she had no patience with his mistake. She was horribly disappointed—she had set her heart on his being a great statesman, one of the rulers of the people and the glories of England. What was so useful, what was so noble?—how it belittled everything else! She had expected him to wear a cordon and a star some day—acquiring them with the greatest promptitude—and then to come and see her in her *loge*: it would look so particularly well. She talked after the manner of a lovely Philistine, except perhaps when she expressed surprise at hearing—hearing from Gabriel Nash—that in England gentlemen accoutred with those emblems of their sovereign's esteem didn't so far forget themselves as to stray into the dressing-rooms of actresses. She admitted after a moment that they were quite right and the dressing-rooms of actresses nasty places; but she was sorry, for that was the sort of thing she had always figured in a corner—a distinguished man, slightly bald, in evening dress, with orders, admiring the smallness of a satin shoe and saying witty things. Nash was convulsed with hilarity at this—such a vision of the British political hero. Coming back from the glass and making that critic give her his place on the sofa, she seated herself near Nick and continued to express her regret at his perversity.

"They all say that—all the charming women, but I shouldn't have looked for it from you," Nick replied. "I've given you such an example of what I can do in another line."

"Do you mean my portrait? Oh I've got it, with your name and 'M.P.' in the corner, and that's precisely why I'm content. 'M.P.' in the corner of a picture is delightful, but I want to break the mould: I don't in the least insist on your giving specimens to others. And the artistic life, when you can lead another—if you've any alternative, however modest—is a very poor business. It comes last in dignity—after everything else. Ain't I up to my eyes in it and don't I truly know?"

"You talk like my broken-hearted mother," said Nick.

"Does she hate it so intensely?"

"She has the darkest ideas about it—the wildest theories. I can't imagine where she gets them; partly I think from a general conviction that the 'esthetic'—a horrible insidious foreign disease—is eating the healthy core out of English life (dear old English life!) and partly from the charming pictures in *Punch* and the clever satirical articles, pointing at mysterious depths of contamination, in the other weekly papers. She believes there's a dreadful coterie of uncannily artful and desperately refined people who wear a kind of loose faded uniform and worship only beauty—which is a fearful thing; that Gabriel has introduced me to it; that I now spend all my time in it, and that for its sweet sake I've broken the most sacred vows. Poor Gabriel, who, so far as I can make out, isn't in any sort of society, however bad!"

"But I'm uncannily artful," Nash objected, "and though I can't afford the uniform—I believe you get it best somewhere in South Audley Street—I do worship beauty. I really think it's me the weekly papers mean."

"Oh I've read the articles—I know the sort!" said Basil Dashwood.

Miriam looked at him. "Go and see if the brougham's there—I ordered it early."

Dashwood, without moving, consulted his watch. "It isn't time yet—I know more about the brougham than you. I've made a ripping good arrangement for her stable—it really costs her nothing," the young actor continued confidentially to Peter, near whom he had placed himself.

"Your mother's quite right to be broken-hearted," Miriam declared, "and I can imagine exactly what she has been through. I should like to talk with her—I should like to see her." Nick showed on this easy amusement, reminding her she had talked to him while she sat for her portrait in quite the opposite sense, most helpfully and inspiringly; and Nash explained that she was studying the part of a political duchess and wished to take observations for it, to work herself into the character. The girl might in fact have been a political duchess as she sat, her head erect and her gloved hands folded, smiling with aristocratic dimness at Nick. She shook her head with stately sadness; she might have been trying some effect for Mary Stuart in Schiller's play. "I've changed since that. I want you to be the grandest thing there is—the counsellor of kings."

Peter wondered if it possibly weren't since she had met his sister in Nick's studio that she had changed, if perhaps she hadn't seen how it might give Julia the sense of being more effectually routed to know that the woman who had thrown the bomb was one who also tried to keep Nick in the straight path. This indeed would involve an assumption that Julia might know, whereas it was perfectly possible she mightn't and more than possible that if she should she wouldn't care. Miriam's essential fondness for trying different ways was always there as an adequate reason for any particular way; a truth which, however, sometimes only half-prevented the particular way from being vexatious to a particular observer.

"Yet after all who's more esthetic than you and who goes in more for the beautiful?" Nick asked. "You're never so beautiful as when you pitch into it."

"Oh, I'm an inferior creature, of an inferior sex, and I've to earn my bread as I can. I'd give it all up in a moment, my odious trade—for an inducement."

"And pray what do you mean by an inducement?" Nick demanded.

"My dear fellow, she means you—if you'll give her a permanent engagement to sit for you!" Gabriel volunteered. "What singularly crude questions you ask!"

"I like the way she talks," Mr. Dashwood derisively said, "when I gave up the most brilliant prospects, of very much the same kind as Mr. Dormer's, expressly to go on the stage."

"You're an inferior creature too," Miriam promptly pronounced.

"Miss Rooth's very hard to satisfy," Peter observed at this. "A man of distinction, slightly bald, in evening dress, with orders, in the corner of her *loge*—she has such a personage ready made to her hand and she doesn't so much as look at him. Am *I* not an inducement? Haven't I offered you a permanent engagement?"

"Your orders—where are your orders?" she returned with a sweet smile, getting up.

"I shall be a minister next year and an ambassador before you know it. Then I shall stick on everything that can be had."

"And they call *us* mountebanks!" cried the girl. "I've been so glad to see you again—do you want another sitting?" she went on to Nick as if to take leave of him.

"As many as you'll give me—I shall be grateful for all," he made answer. "I should like to do you as you are at present. You're totally different from the woman I painted—you're wonderful."

"The Comic Muse!" she laughed. "Well, you must wait till our first nights are over—I'm *sur les dents* till then. There's everything to do and I've to do it all. That fellow's good for nothing, for nothing but domestic life"—and she glanced at Basil Dashwood. "He hasn't an idea—not one you'd willingly tell of him, though he's rather useful for the stables. We've got stables now—or we try to look as if we had: Dashwood's ideas are *de cette force*. In ten days I shall have more time."

"The Comic Muse? Never, never," Peter protested. "You're not to go smirking through the age and down to posterity—I'd rather see you as Medusa crowned with serpents. That's what you look like when you look best."

"That's consoling—when I've just bought a lovely new bonnet, all red roses and bows. I forgot to tell you just now that when you're an ambassador you may propose anything you like," Miriam went on. "But forgive me if I make that condition. Seriously speaking, come to me glittering with orders and I shall probably succumb. I can't resist stars and garters. Only you must, as you say, have them all. I *don't* like to hear Mr. Dormer talk the slang of the studio—like that phrase just now: it *is* a fall to a lower state. However, when one's low one must crawl, and I'm crawling down to the Strand. Dashwood, see if mamma's ready. If she isn't I decline to wait; you must bring her in a hansom. I'll take Mr. Dormer in the brougham; I want to talk with Mr. Dormer; he must drive with me to the theatre. His situation's full of interest." Miriam led the way out of the room as she continued to chatter, and when she reached the house-door with the four men in her train the carriage had just drawn up at the garden-gate. It appeared that Mrs. Rooth was not ready, and the girl, in spite of a remonstrance from Nick, who had a sense of usurping the old lady's place, repeated her injunction that she should be brought on in a cab. Miriam's gentlemen hung about her at the gate, and she insisted on Nick's taking his seat in the brougham and taking it first. Before she entered she put her hand out to Peter and, looking up at him, held his own kindly. "Dear old master, aren't you coming to-night? I miss you when you're not there."

"Don't go—don't go—it's too much," Nash freely declared.

"She is wonderful," said Mr. Dashwood, all expert admiration; "she *has* gone into the rehearsals tooth and nail. But nothing takes it out of her."

"Nothing puts it into you, my dear!" Miriam returned. Then she pursued to Peter: "You're the faithful one—you're the one I count on." He was not looking at her; his eyes travelled into the carriage, where they rested on Nick Dormer, established on the farther seat with his face turned toward the farther window. He was the one, faithful or no, counted on or no, whom a charming woman had preferred to carry off, and there was clear triumph for him in that fact. Yet it pleased, it somewhat relieved, his kinsman to see his passivity as not a little foolish. Miriam noted something of this in Peter's eyes, for she exclaimed abruptly, "Don't kill him—he doesn't care for me!" With which she passed into the carriage and let it roll away.

Peter stood watching it till he heard Dashwood again beside him. "You wouldn't believe what I make him do the whole thing for—a little rascal I know."

"Good-bye; take good care of Mrs. Rooth," said Gabriel Nash, waving a bland farewell to the young actor. He gave a smiling survey of the heavens and remarked to Sherringham that the rain had stopped. Was he walking, was he driving, should they be going in the same direction? Peter cared little about his direction and had little account of it to give; he simply moved away in silence and with Gabriel at his side. This converser was partly an affliction to him; indeed the fact that he couldn't only make light of him added to the oppression. It was just to him nevertheless to note that he could hold his peace occasionally: he had for instance this afternoon taken little part in the talk at Balaklava Place. Peter greatly disliked to speak to him of Miriam, but he liked Nash himself to make free with her, and even liked him to say such things as might be a little viciously and unguardedly contradicted. He was not, however, moved to gainsay something dropped by his companion, disconnectedly, at the end of a few minutes; a word to the effect that she was after all the best-natured soul alive. All the same, Nash added, it wouldn't do for her to take possession of a nice life like Nick's; and he repeated that for his part he would never allow it. It would be on his conscience to interfere. To which Peter returned disingenuously that they might all do as they liked—it didn't matter a button to *him*. And with an effort to carry off that comedy he changed the subject.

XXXVIII

He wouldn't for a moment have admitted that he was jealous of his old comrade, but would almost have liked to be accused of it: for this would have given him a chance he rather lacked and missed, the right occasion to declare with plausibility that motives he couldn't avow had no application to his case. How could a man be jealous when he was not a suitor? how could he pretend to guard a property which was neither his own nor destined to become his own? There could be no question of loss when one had nothing at stake, and no question of envy when the responsibility of possession was exactly what one prayed to be delivered from. The measure of one's susceptibility was one's pretensions, and Peter was not only ready to declare over and over again that, thank God, he had none: his spiritual detachment was still more complete—he literally suffered from the fact that nobody appeared to care to hear him say it. He connected an idea of virtue and honour with his attitude, since surely it was a high case of conduct to have quenched a personal passion for the good of the public service. He had gone over the whole question at odd, irrepressible hours; he had returned, spiritually speaking, the buffet administered to him all at once, that day in Rosedale Road, by the spectacle of the *crânerie* with which Nick could let worldly glories slide. Resolution for resolution he preferred after all another sort, and his own *crânerie* would be shown in the way he should stick to his profession and stand up for British interests. If Nick had leaped over a wall he would leap over a river. The course of his river was already traced and his loins were already girded. Thus he was justified in holding that the measure of a man's susceptibility was a man's attitude: that was the only thing he was bound to give an account of.

He was perpetually giving an account of it to his own soul in default of other listeners. He was quite angry at having tasted a sweetness in Miriam's assurance at the carriage—door, bestowed indeed with very little solemnity, that Nick didn't care for her. Wherein did it concern him that Nick cared for her or that Nick didn't? Wherein did it signify to him that Gabriel Nash should have taken upon himself to disapprove of a union between the young actress and the young painter and to frustrate an accident that might perhaps prove fortunate? For those had also been cooling words at the hour, though Peter blushed on the morrow to think that he felt in them anything but Nash's personal sublimity. He was ashamed of having been refreshed, and refreshed by so sickly a draught—it being all his theory that he was not in a fever. As for keeping an eye on Nick, it would soon become clear to that young man and that young man's charming friend that he had quite other uses for his eyes. The pair, with Nash to help, might straighten out their complications according to their light. He would never speak to Nick of Miriam; he felt indeed just now as if he should never speak to Nick of anything. He had traced the course of his river, as I say, and the real proof would be in the way he should, clearing the air, land on the opposite bank. It was a case for action—for vigorous, unmistakable action. He had done very little since his arrival in London but moon round a *fille de théâtre* who was taken up partly, though she bluffed it off, with another man, and partly with arranging new petticoats for a beastly old "poetic drama"; but this little waste of time should instantly be made up. He had given himself a definite rope, and he had danced to the end of his rope, and now he would dance back. That was all right—so right that Peter could only express to himself how right it was by whistling with extravagance.

He whistled as he went to dine with a great personage the day after his meeting with Nick in Balaklava Place; a great personage to whom he had originally paid his respects—it was high time—the day before that meeting, the previous Monday. The sense of omissions to repair, of a superior line to take, perhaps made him study with more zeal to please the personage, who gave him ten minutes and asked him five questions. A great many doors were successively opened before any palpitating pilgrim who was about to enter the presence of this distinguished man; but they were discreetly closed again behind Sherringham, and I must ask the reader to pause with me at the nearer end of the momentary vista. This particular pilgrim fortunately felt he could count on recognition not only as a faithful if obscure official in the great hierarchy, but as a clever young man who happened to be connected by blood with people his lordship had intimately known. No doubt it was simply as the clever young man that Peter received the next morning, from the dispenser of his lordship's hospitality, a note asking him to dine on the morrow. Such cards had come to him before, and he had always obeyed their call; he did so at present, however, with a sense of unusual intention. In due course his intention was translated into words; before the gentlemen left the dining-room he respectfully asked his noble host for some further brief and benevolent hearing.

"What is it you want? Tell me now," the master of his fate replied, motioning to the rest of the company to pass out and detaining him where they stood.

Peter's excellent training covered every contingency: he could always be as concise or as diffuse as the occasion required. Even he himself, however, was surprised at the quick felicity of the terms in which he was conscious of conveying that, were it compatible with higher conveniences, he should extremely like to be transferred to duties in a more distant quarter of the globe. Indeed, fond as he was of thinking himself a man of emotions controlled by civility, it is not impossible that a greater candour than he knew glimmered through Peter's expression and trembled through his tone as he presented this petition. He had aimed at a good manner in presenting it, but perhaps the best of the effect produced for his interlocutor was just where it failed, where it confessed a secret that the highest diplomacy would have guarded. Sherringham remarked to the minister that he didn't care in the least where the place might be, nor how little coveted a post; the further away the better, and the climate didn't matter. He would only prefer of course that there should be really something to do, though he would make the best of it even if there were not. He stopped in time, or at least thought he did, not to betray his covertly seeking relief from minding his having been jilted in a flight to latitudes unfavourable to human life. His august patron gave him a sharp look which for a moment seemed the precursor of a sharper question; but the moment elapsed and the question failed to come. This considerate omission, characteristic of a true man of the world and representing quick guesses and still quicker indifferences, made our gentleman from that moment his lordship's ardent partisan. What did come was a good-natured laugh and the exclamation: "You know there are plenty of swamps and jungles, if you want that sort of thing," Peter replied that it was very much that sort of thing he did want; whereupon his chief continued: "I'll see—I'll see. If anything turns up you shall hear."

Something turned up the very next day: our young man, taken at his word, found himself indebted to the postman for a note of concise intimation that the high position of minister to the smallest of Central American republics would be apportioned him. The republic, though small, was big enough to be "shaky," and the position, though high, not so exalted that there were not much greater altitudes above it to which it was a stepping-stone. Peter, quite ready to take one thing with another, rejoiced at his easy triumph, reflected that he must have been even more noticed at headquarters than he had hoped, and, on the spot, consulting nobody and waiting for nothing, signified his unqualified acceptance of the place. Nobody with a grain of sense would have advised him to do anything else. It made him happier than he had supposed he should ever be again; it made him feel professionally in the train, as they said in Paris; it was serious, it was interesting, it was exciting, and his imagination, letting itself loose into the future, began once more to scale the crowning eminence. It was very simple to hold one's course if one really tried, and he blessed the variety of peoples. Further communications passed, the last enjoining on him to return to Paris for a short interval a week later, after which he would be advised of the date for his proceeding to his remoter duties.

XXXIX

The next thing he meanwhile did was to call with his news on Lady Agnes Dormer; it is not unworthy of note that he took on the other hand no step to make his promotion known to Miriam Rooth. To render it probable he should find his aunt he went at the luncheon-hour; and she was indeed on the point of sitting down to that repast with Grace. Biddy was not at home—Biddy was never at home now, her mother said: she was always at Nick's place, she spent her life there, she ate and drank there, she almost slept there. What she contrived to do there for so many hours and what was the irresistible spell Lady Agnes couldn't pretend she had succeeded in discovering. She spoke of this baleful resort only as "Nick's place," and spoke of it at first as little as possible. She judged highly probable, however, that Biddy would come in early that afternoon: there was something or other, some common social duty, she had condescended to promise she would perform with Grace. Poor Lady Agnes, whom Peter found somehow at once grim and very prostrate—she assured her nephew her nerves were all gone—almost abused her younger daughter for two minutes, having evidently a deep-seated need of abusing some one. I must yet add that she didn't wait to meet Grace's eye before recovering, by a rapid gyration, her view of the possibilities of things—those possibilities from which she still might squeeze, as a parent almost in despair, the drop that would sweeten her cup. "Dear child," she had the presence of mind to subjoin, "her only fault is after all that she adores her brother. She has a capacity for adoration and must always take her gospel from some one."

Grace declared to Peter that her sister would have stayed at home if she had dreamed he was coming, and Lady Agnes let him know that she had heard all about the hour he had spent with the poor child at Nick's place and about his extraordinary good nature in taking the two girls to the play. Peter lunched in Calcutta Gardens, spending an hour there which proved at first unexpectedly and, as seemed to him, unfairly dismal. He knew from his own general perceptions, from what Biddy had told him and from what he had heard Nick say in Balaklava Place, that his aunt would have been wounded by her son's apostasy; but it was not till he saw her that he appreciated the dark difference this young man's behaviour had made in the outlook of his family. Evidently that behaviour had sprung a dreadful leak in the great vessel of their hopes. These were things no outsider could measure, and they were none of an outsider's business; it was enough that Lady Agnes struck him really as a woman who had received her death-blow. She looked ten years older; she was white and haggard and tragic. Her eyes burned with a strange fitful fire that prompted one to conclude her children had better look out for her. When not filled with this unnatural flame they were suffused with comfortless tears; and altogether the afflicted lady was, as he viewed her, very bad, a case for anxiety. It was because he had known she would be very bad that he had, in his kindness, called on her exactly in this manner; but he recognised that to undertake to be kind to her in proportion to her need might carry one very far. He was glad he had not himself a wronged mad mother, and he wondered how Nick could bear the burden of the home he had ruined. Apparently he didn't bear it very far, but had taken final, convenient refuge in Rosedale Road.

Peter's judgement of his perverse cousin was considerably confused, and not the less so for the consciousness that he was perhaps just now not in the best state of mind for judging him at all. At the same time, though he held in general that a man of sense has always warrant enough in his sense for doing the particular thing he prefers, he could scarcely help asking himself whether, in the exercise of a virile freedom, it had been absolutely indispensable Nick should work such domestic woe. He admitted indeed that that was an anomalous figure for Nick, the worker of domestic woe. Then he saw that his aunt's grievance—there came a moment, later, when she asserted as much—was not quite what her recreant child, in Balaklava Place, had represented it—with questionable taste perhaps—to a mocking actress; was not a mere shocked quarrel with his adoption of a "low" career, or a horror, the old-fashioned horror, of the *louches* licences taken by artists under pretext of being conscientious: the day for this was past, and English society thought the brush and the fiddle as good as anything else—with two or three exceptions. It was not what he had taken up but what he had put down that made the sorry difference, and the tragedy would have been equally great if he had become a wine-merchant or a horse-dealer. Peter had gathered at first that Lady Agnes wouldn't trust herself to speak directly of her trouble, and he had obeyed what he supposed the best discretion in making no allusion to it. But a few minutes before they rose from table she broke out, and when he attempted to utter a word of mitigation there was something that went to his heart in the way she returned: "Oh you don't know—you don't know!" He felt Grace's eyes fixed on him at this instant in a mystery of supplication, and was uncertain as to what she wanted—that he should say something more to console her mother or should hurry away from the subject. Grace looked old and plain and—he had thought on coming in—rather cross, but she evidently wanted something. "You don't know," Lady Agnes repeated with a trembling voice, "you don't know." She had pushed her chair a little away from her place; she held her pocket-handkerchief pressed hard to her mouth, almost stuffed into it, and her eyes were fixed on the floor. She made him aware he did virtually know—know what towering piles of confidence and hope had been dashed to the earth. Then she finished her sentence unexpectedly—"You don't know what my life with my great husband was." Here on the other hand Peter was slightly at fault—he didn't exactly see what her life with her great husband had to do with it. What was clear to him, however, was that they literally had looked for things all in the very key of that greatness from Nick. It was not quite easy to see why this had been the case—it had not been precisely Peter's own prefigurement. Nick appeared to have had the faculty of planting that sort of flattering faith in women; he had originally given Julia a tremendous dose of it, though she had since shaken off the effects.

"Do you really think he would have done such great things, politically speaking?" Peter risked. "Do you consider that the root of the matter was so essentially in him?"

His hostess had a pause, looking at him rather hard. "I only think what all his friends—all his father's friends—have thought. He was his father's son after all. No young man ever had a finer training, and he gave from the first repeated proof of the highest ability, the highest ambition. See how he got in everywhere. Look at his first seat—look at his second," Lady Agnes continued. "Look at what every one says at this moment."

"Look at all the papers!" said Grace. "Did you ever hear him speak?" she asked. And when Peter reminded her how he had spent his life in foreign lands, shut out from such pleasures, she went on: "Well, you lost something."

"It was very charming," said Lady Agnes quietly and poignantly.

"Of course he's charming, whatever he does," Peter returned. "He'll be a charming artist."

"Oh God help us!" the poor lady groaned, rising quickly.

"He won't—that's the worst," Grace amended. "It isn't as if he'd do things people would like, I've been to his place, and I never saw such a horrid lot of things—not at all clever or pretty."

Yet her mother, at this, turned upon her with sudden asperity. "You know nothing whatever about the matter!" Then she added for Peter that, as it happened, her children did have a good deal of artistic taste: Grace was the only one who was totally deficient in it. Biddy was very clever—Biddy really might learn to do pretty things. And anything the poor child could learn was now no more than her duty—there was so little knowing what the future had in store for them all.

"You think too much of the future—you take terribly gloomy views," said Peter, looking for his hat.

"What other views can one take when one's son has deliberately thrown away a fortune?"

"Thrown one away? Do you mean through not marrying——?"

"I mean through killing by his perversity the best friend he ever had."

Peter stared a moment; then with laughter: "Ah but Julia isn't dead of it!"

451

"I'm not talking of Julia," said his aunt with a good deal of majesty. "Nick isn't mercenary, and I'm not complaining of that."

"She means Mr. Carteret," Grace explained with all her competence. "He'd have done anything if Nick had stayed in the House."

"But he's not dead?"

"Charles Carteret's dying," said Lady Agnes—"his end's dreadfully near. He has been a sort of providence to us—he was Sir Nicholas's second self. But he won't put up with such insanity, such wickedness, and that chapter's closed."

"You mean he has dropped Nick out of his will?"

"Cut him off utterly. He has given him notice."

"The old scoundrel!"—Peter couldn't keep this back. "But Nick will work the better for that—he'll depend on himself."

"Yes, and whom shall we depend on?" Grace spoke up.

"Don't be vulgar, for God's sake!" her mother ejaculated with a certain inconsequence.

"Oh leave Nick alone—he'll make a lot of money," Peter declared cheerfully, following his two companions into the hall.

"I don't in the least care if he does or not," said Lady Agnes. "You must come upstairs again—I've lots to say to you yet," she went on, seeing him make for his hat. "You must arrange to come and dine with us immediately; it's only because I've been so steeped in misery that I didn't write to you the other day—directly after you had called. We don't give parties, as you may imagine, but if you'll come just as we are, for old acquaintance' sake—"

"Just with Nick—if Nick will come—and dear Biddy," Grace interposed.

"Nick must certainly come, as well as dear Biddy, whom I hoped so much to find," Peter pronounced. "Because I'm going away—I don't know when I, shall see them again."

"Wait with mamma. Biddy will come in now at any moment," Grace urged.

"You're going away?" said Lady Agnes, pausing at the foot of the stairs and turning her white face upon him. Something in her voice showed she had been struck by his own tone.

"I've had promotion and you must congratulate me. They're sending me out as minister to a little hot hole in Central America—six thousand miles away. I shall have to go rather soon."

"Oh I'm so glad!" Lady Agnes breathed. Still she paused at the foot of the stair and still she gazed.

"How very delightful—it will lead straight off to all sorts of other good things!" Grace a little coarsely commented.

"Oh I'm crawling up—I'm an excellency," Peter laughed.

"Then if you dine with us your excellency must have great people to meet you."

"Nick and Biddy—they're great enough."

"Come upstairs—come upstairs," said Lady Agnes, turning quickly and beginning to ascend.

"Wait for Biddy—I'm going out," Grace continued, extending her hand to her kinsman. "I shall see you again—not that you care; but good-bye now. Wait for Biddy," the girl repeated in a lower tone, fastening her eyes on his with the same urgent mystifying gleam he thought he had noted at luncheon.

"Oh I'll go and see her in Rosedale Road," he threw off.

"Do you mean to-day—now?"

"I don't know about to-day, but before I leave England."

"Well, she'll be in immediately," said Grace. "Good-bye to your excellency."

"Come up, Peter—*please* come up," called Lady Agnes from the top of the stairs.

He mounted and when he found himself in the drawing-room with her and the door closed she expressed her great interest in his fine prospects and position, which she wished to hear all about. She rang for coffee and indicated the seat he would find most comfortable: it shone before him for a moment that she would tell him he might if he wished light a cigar. For Peter had suddenly become restless—too restless to occupy a comfortable chair; he seated himself in it only to jump up again, and he went to the window, while he imparted to his hostess the very little he knew about his post, on hearing a vehicle drive up to the door. A strong light had just been thrown into his mind, and it grew stronger when, looking out, he saw Grace Dormer issue from the house in a hat and a jacket which had all the air of having been assumed with extraordinary speed. Her jacket was unbuttoned and her gloves still dangling from the hands with which she was settling her hat. The vehicle into which she hastily sprang was a hansom-cab which had been summoned by the butler from the doorstep and which rolled away with her after she had given an address.

"Where's Grace going in such a hurry?" he asked of Lady Agnes; to which she replied that she hadn't the least idea—her children, at the pass they had all come to, knocked about as they liked.

Well, he sat down again; he stayed a quarter of an hour and then he stayed longer, and during this time his appreciation of what she had in her mind gathered force. She showed him that precious quantity clearly enough, though she showed it by no clumsy, no voluntary arts. It looked out of her sombre, conscious eyes and quavered in her preoccupied, perfunctory tones. She took an extravagant interest in his future proceedings, the probable succession of events in his career, the different honours he would be likely to come in for, the salary attached to his actual appointment, the salary attached to the appointments that would follow—they would be sure to, wouldn't they?—and what he might reasonably expect to save. Oh he must save—Lady Agnes was an advocate of saving; and he must take tremendous pains and get on and be clever and fiercely ambitious: he must make himself indispensable and rise to the top. She was urgent and suggestive and sympathetic; she threw herself into the vision of his achievements and emoluments as if to appease a little the sore hunger with which Nick's treachery had left her. This was touching to her nephew, who didn't remain unmoved even at those more importunate moments when, as she fell into silence, fidgeting feverishly with a morsel of fancy-work she had plucked from a table, her whole presence became an intense, repressed appeal to him. What that appeal would have been had it been uttered was: "Oh Peter, take little Biddy; oh my dear young friend, understand your interests at the same time that you understand mine; be kind and reasonable and clever; save me all further anxiety and tribulation and accept my lovely, faultless child from my hands."

That was what Lady Agnes had always meant, more or less, that was what Grace had meant, and they meant it with singular lucidity on the present occasion, Lady Agnes meant it so much that from one moment to another he scarce knew what she might do; and Grace meant it so much that she had rushed away in a hansom to fetch her sister from the studio. Grace, however, was a fool, for Biddy certainly wouldn't come. The news of his promotion had started them off, adding point to their idea of his being an excellent match; bringing home to them sharply the sense that if he were going away to strange countries he must take Biddy with him—that something at all events must be settled about Biddy before he went. They had suddenly begun to throb, poor things, with alarm at the ebbing hours.

Strangely enough the perception of all this hadn't the effect of throwing him on the defensive and still less that of making him wish to bolt. When once he had made sure what was in the air he recognised a propriety, a real felicity in it; couldn't deny that he was in certain ways a good match, since it was quite probable he would go far; and was even generous enough—as he had no fear of being materially dragged to the altar—to enter into the conception that he might offer some balm to a mother who had had a horrid disappointment. The feasibility of marrying Biddy was not exactly augmented by the idea that his doing so would be a great offset to what Nick had made Lady Agnes suffer; but at least Peter didn't dislike his strenuous aunt so much as to wish to punish her for her nature. He was not afraid of her, whatever she might do; and though unable to grasp the practical relevancy of Biddy's being produced on the instant was willing to linger half an hour on the chance of successful production.

There was meanwhile, moreover, a certain contagion in Lady Agnes's appeal—it made him appeal sensibly to himself, since indeed, as it is time to say, the glass of our young man's spirit had been polished for that reflexion. It was only at this moment really that he became inwardly candid. While making up his mind that his only safety was in flight and taking the strong measure of a request for help toward it, he was yet very conscious that another and probably still more effectual safeguard—especially if the two should be conjoined—lay in the hollow of his hand. His sister's words in Paris had come back to him and had seemed still wiser than when uttered: "She'll save you disappointments; you'd know the worst that can happen to you, and it wouldn't be bad." Julia had put it into a nutshell—Biddy would probably save him disappointments. And then she was—well, she was Biddy. Peter knew better what that was since the hour he had spent with her in Rosedale Road. But he had brushed away the sense of it, though aware that in doing so he took only half-measures and was even guilty of a sort of fraud upon himself. If he was sincere in wishing to put a gulf between his future and that sad expanse of his past and present over which Miriam had cast her shadow there was a very simple way to do so. He had dodged this way, dishonestly fixing on another which, taken alone, was far from being so good; but Lady Agnes brought him back to it. She held him in well-nigh confused contemplation of it, during which the safety, as Julia had called it, of the remedy wrought upon him as he wouldn't have believed beforehand, and not least to the effect of sweetening, of prettily colouring, the pill. It would be simple and it would deal with all his problems; it would put an end to all alternatives, which, as alternatives were otherwise putting an end to him, would be an excellent thing. It would settle the whole question of his future, and it was high time this should be settled.

Peter took two cups of coffee while he made out his future with Lady Agnes, but though he drank them slowly he had finished them before Biddy turned up. He stayed three-quarters of an hour, saying to himself she wouldn't come—why should she come? Lady Agnes stooped to no avowal; she really stooped, so far as bald words went, to no part of the business; but she made him fix the next day save one for coming to dinner, and her repeated declaration that there would be no one else, not another creature but themselves, had almost the force of the supplied form for a promise to pay. In giving his word that he would come without fail, and not write the next day to throw them over for some function he should choose to dub obligatory, he felt quite as if he were putting his name to such a document. He went away at half-past three; Biddy of course hadn't come, and he had been sure she wouldn't. He couldn't imagine what Grace's idea had been, nor what pretext she had put forward to her sister. Whatever these things Biddy had seen through them and hated them. Peter could but like her the more for that.

XL

Lady Agnes would doubtless have done better, in her own interest or in that of her child, to have secured his company for the very next evening. This she had indeed attempted, but her application of her thought had miscarried, Peter bethinking himself that he was importantly engaged. Her ladyship, moreover, couldn't presume to answer for Nick, since after all they must of course *have* Nick, though, to tell the truth, the hideous truth, she and her son were scarcely on terms. Peter insisted on Nick, wished particularly to see him, and gave his hostess notice that he would make each of them forgive everything to the other. She returned that all her son had to forgive was her loving him more than her life, and she would have challenged Peter, had he allowed it, on the general ground of the comparative dignity of the two arts of painting portraits and governing nations. Our friend declined the challenge: the most he did was to intimate that he perhaps saw Nick more vividly as a painter than as a governor. Later he remembered vaguely something his aunt had said about their being a governing family.

He was going, by what he could ascertain, to a very queer climate and had many preparations to make. He gave his best attention to these, and for a couple of hours after leaving Lady Agnes rummaged London for books from which he might extract information about his new habitat. It made apparently no great figure in literature, and Peter could reflect that he was perhaps destined to find a salutary distraction in himself filling the void with a volume of impressions. After he had resigned himself to necessary ignorance he went into the Park. He treated himself to an afternoon or two there when he happened to drop upon London in summer—it refreshed his sense of the British interests he would have to stand up for. Moreover, he had been hiding more or less, and now all that was changed and this was the simplest way not to hide. He met a host of friends, made his situation as public as possible and accepted on the spot a great many invitations; all subject, however, to the mental reservation that he should allow none of them to interfere with his being present the first night of Miriam's new venture. He was going to the equator to get away from her, but to repudiate the past with some decency of form he must show an affected interest, if he could muster none other, in an occasion that meant so much for her. The least intimate of her associates would do that, and Peter remembered how, at the expense of good manners, he had stayed away from her first appearance on any stage at all. He would have been shocked had he found himself obliged to go back to Paris without giving her at the imminent crisis the personal countenance she had so good a right to expect.

It was nearly eight o'clock when he went to Great Stanhope Street to dress for dinner and learn that a note awaiting him on the hall-table and which bore the marks of hasty despatch had come three or four hours before. It exhibited the signature of Miriam Rooth and let him know that she positively expected him at the theatre by eleven o'clock the next morning, for which hour a dress-rehearsal of the revived play had been hurriedly projected, the first night being now definitely fixed for the impending Saturday. She counted on his attendance at both ceremonies, but with particular reasons for wishing to see him in the morning. "I want you to see and judge and tell me," she said, "for my mind's like a flogged horse—it won't give another kick." It was for the Saturday he had made Lady Agnes his promise; he had thought of the possibility of the play in doing so, but had rested in the faith that, from valid symptoms, this complication would not occur till the following week.

He decided nothing on the spot as to the conflict of occupations—it was enough to send Miriam three words to the effect that he would sooner perish than fail her on the morrow.

He went to the theatre in the morning, and the episode proved curious and instructive. Though there were twenty people in the stalls it bore little resemblance to those *répétitions générales* to which, in Paris, his love of the drama had often attracted him and which, taking place at night, in the theatre closed to the public, are virtually first performances with invited spectators. They were to his sense always settled and stately, rehearsals of the *première* even more than rehearsals of the play. The present occasion was less august; it was not so much a concert as a confusion of sounds, and it took audible and at times disputatious counsel with itself. It was rough and frank and spasmodic, but was lively and vivid and, in spite of the serious character of the piece, often exceedingly droll: while it gave Sherringham, oddly enough, a more present sense than ever of bending over the hissing, smoking, sputtering caldron in which a palatable performance is stewed. He looked into the gross darkness that may result from excess of light; that is, he understood how knocked up, on the eve of production, every one concerned in the preparation of a piece might be, with nerves overstretched and glasses blurred, awaiting the test and the response, the echo to be given back by the big, receptive, artless, stupid, delightful public. Peter's interest had been great in advance, and as Miriam since his arrival had taken him much into her confidence he knew what she intended to do and had discussed a hundred points with her. They had differed about some of them and she had always said: "Ah but wait till you see how I shall do it at the time!" That was usually her principal reason and her most convincing argument. She had made some changes at the last hour—she was going to do several things in another way. But she wanted a touchstone, wanted a fresh ear, and, as she told Sherringham when he went behind after the first act, that was why she had insisted on this private trial, to which a few fresh ears were to be admitted. They didn't want to allow it her, the theatre people, they were such a parcel of donkeys; but as to what she meant in general to insist on she had given them a hint she flattered herself they wouldn't soon forget.

She spoke as if she had had a great battle with her fellow-workers and had routed them utterly. It was not the first time he had heard her talk as if such a life as hers could only be a fighting life and of her frank measure of the fine uses of a faculty for making a row. She rejoiced she possessed this faculty, for she knew what to do with it; and though there might be a certain swagger in taking such a stand in advance when one had done the infinitely little she had yet done, she nevertheless trusted to the future to show how right she should have been in believing a pack of idiots would never hold out against her and would know they couldn't afford to. Her assumption of course was that she fought for the light and the right, for the good way and the thorough, for doing a thing properly if one did it at all. What she had really wanted was the theatre closed for a night and the dress-rehearsal, put on for a few people, given instead of *Yolande.* That she had not got, but she would have it the next time. She spoke as if her triumphs behind the scenes as well as before would go by leaps and bounds, and he could perfectly see, for the time, that she would drive her coadjutors in front of her like sheep. Her tone was the sort of thing that would have struck one as preposterous if one hadn't believed in her; but if one did so believe it only seemed thrown in with the other gifts. How was she going to act that night and what could be said for such a hateful way of doing things? She thrust on poor Peter questions he was all unable to answer; she abounded in superlatives and tremendously strong objections. He had a sharper vision than usual of the queer fate, for a peaceable man, of being involved in a life of so violent a rhythm: one might as well be hooked to a Catharine-wheel and whiz round in flame and smoke.

It had only been for five minutes, in the wing, amid jostling and shuffling and shoving, that they held this conference. Miriam, splendid in a brocaded anachronism, a false dress of the beginning of the century, and excited and appealing, imperious, reckless and good-humoured, full of exaggerated propositions, supreme determinations and comic irrelevancies, showed as radiant a young head as the stage had ever seen. Other people quickly surrounded her, and Peter saw that though, she wanted, as she said, a fresh ear and a fresh eye she was liable to rap out to those who possessed these advantages that they didn't know what they were talking about. It was rather hard for her victims—Basil Dashwood let him into this, wonderfully painted and in a dress even more beautiful than Miriam's, that of a young dandy under Charles the Second: if you were not in the business you were one kind of donkey and if you *were* in the business you were another kind. Peter noted with a certain chagrin that Gabriel Nash had failed; he preferred to base his annoyance on that ground when the girl, after the remark just quoted from Dashwood, laughing and saying that at any rate the thing would do because it would just have to do, thrust vindictively but familiarly into the young actor's face a magnificent feather fan. "Isn't he too lovely," she asked, "and doesn't he know how to do it?" Dashwood had the sense of costume even more than Peter had inferred or supposed he minded, inasmuch as it now appeared he had gone profoundly into the question of what the leading lady was to wear. He had drawn patterns and hunted up stuffs, had helped her to try on her clothes, had bristled with ideas and pins. It would not have been quite clear, Peter's ground for resenting Nash's cynical absence; it may even be thought singular he should have missed him. At any rate he flushed a little when their young woman, of whom he inquired whether she hadn't invited her oldest and dearest friend, made answer: "Oh he says he doesn't like the kitchen-fire—he only wants the pudding!" It would have taken the kitchen-fire to account at that point for the red of Sherringham's cheek; and he was indeed uncomfortably heated by helping to handle, as he phrased it, the saucepans.

This he felt so much after he had returned to his seat, which he forbore to quit again till the curtain had fallen on the last act, that in spite of the high beauty of that part of the performance of which Miriam carried the weight there were moments when his relief overflowed into gasps, as if he had been scrambling up the bank of a torrent after an immersion. The girl herself, out in the open of her field to win, was of the incorruptible faith: she had been saturated to good purpose with the great spirit of Madame Carré. That was conspicuous while the play went on and she guarded the whole march with fagged piety and passion. Sherringham had never liked the piece itself; he held that as barbarous in form and false in feeling it did little honour to the British theatre; he despised many of the speeches, pitied Miriam for having to utter them, and considered that, lighted by that sort of candle, the path of fame might very well lead nowhere.

461

When the ordeal was over he went behind again, where in the rose-coloured satin of the silly issue the heroine of the occasion said to him: "Fancy my having to drag through that other stuff to-night—the brutes!" He was vague about the persons designated in this allusion, but he let it pass: he had at the moment a kind of detached foreboding of the way any gentleman familiarly connected with her in the future would probably form the habit of letting objurgations and some other things pass. This had become indeed now a frequent state of mind with him; the instant he was before her, near her, next her, he found himself a helpless subject of the spell which, so far at least as he was concerned, she put forth by contact and of which the potency was punctual and absolute: the fit came on, as he said, exactly as some esteemed express-train on a great line bangs at a given moment into the station. At a distance he partly recovered himself—that was the encouragement for going to the shaky republic; but as soon as he entered her presence his life struck him as a thing disconnected from his will. It was as if he himself had been one thing and his behaviour another; he had shining views of this difference, drawn as they might be from the coming years—little illustrative scenes in which he saw himself in strange attitudes of resignation, always rather sad and still and with a slightly bent head. Such images should not have been inspiring, but it is a fact that they were something to go upon. The gentleman with the bent head had evidently given up something that was dear to him, but it was exactly because he had got his price that he was there. "Come and see me three or four hours hence," Miriam said—"come, that is, about six. I shall rest till then, but I want particularly to talk with you. There will be no one else—not the tip of any tiresome nose. You'll do me good." So of course he drove up at six.

XLI

"I don't know; I haven't the least idea; I don't care; don't ask me!"—it was so he met some immediate appeal of her artistic egotism, some challenge of his impression of her at this and that moment. Hadn't she frankly better give up such and such a point and return to their first idea, the one they had talked over so much? Peter replied to this that he disowned all ideas; that at any rate he should never have another as long as he lived, and that, so help him heaven, they had worried that hard bone more than enough.

"You're tired of me—yes, already," she said sadly and kindly. They were alone, her mother had not peeped out and she had prepared herself to return to the Strand. "However, it doesn't matter and of course your head's full of other things. You must think me ravenously selfish—perpetually chattering about my vulgar shop. What will you have when one's a vulgar shop-girl? You used to like it, but then you weren't an ambassador."

"What do you know about my being a minister?" he asked, leaning back in his chair and showing sombre eyes. Sometimes he held her handsomer on the stage than off, and sometimes he reversed that judgement. The former of these convictions had held his mind in the morning, and it was now punctually followed by the other. As soon as she stepped on the boards a great and special alteration usually took place in her—she was in focus and in her frame; yet there were hours too in which she wore her world's face before the audience, just as there were hours when she wore her stage face in the world. She took up either mask as it suited her humour. To-day he was seeing each in its order and feeling each the best. "I should know very little if I waited for you to tell me—that's very certain," Miriam returned. "It's in the papers that you've got a high appointment, but I don't read the papers unless there's something in them about myself. Next week I shall devour them and think them, no doubt, inane. It was Basil told me this afternoon of your promotion—he had seen it announced somewhere, I'm delighted if it gives you more money and more advantages, but don't expect me to be glad that you're going away to some distant, disgusting country."

"The matter has only just been settled and we've each been busy with our own affairs. But even if you hadn't given me these opportunities," Peter went on, "I should have tried to see you to-day, to tell you my news and take leave of you."

"Take leave? Aren't you coming to-morrow?"

"Oh yes, I shall see you through that. But I shall rush away the very moment it's over."

"I shall be much better then—really I shall," the girl said.

"The better you are the worse you are."

She returned his frown with a beautiful charity. "If it would do you any good I'd be bad."

"The worse you are the better you are!" Peter laughed. "You're a devouring demon."

"Not a bit! It's you."

"It's I? I like that."

"It's you who make trouble, who are sore and suspicious and supersubtle, not taking things as they come and for what they are, but twisting them into misery and falsity. Oh I've watched you enough, my dear friend, and I've been sorry for you—and sorry as well for myself; for I'm not so taken up with myself, in the low greedy sense, as you think. I'm not such a base creature. I'm capable of gratitude, I'm capable of affection. One may live in paint and tinsel, but one isn't absolutely without a soul. Yes, I've got one," the girl went on, "though I do smear my face and grin at myself in the glass and practise my intonations. If what you're going to do is good for you I'm very glad. If it leads to good things, to honour and fortune and greatness, I'm enchanted. If it means your being away always, for ever and ever, of course that's serious. You know it—I needn't tell you—I regard you as I really don't regard any one else. I've a confidence in you—ah it's a luxury! You're a gentleman, *mon bon*— ah you're a gentleman! It's just that. And then you see, you understand, and that's a luxury too. You're a luxury altogether, dear clever Mr. Sherringham. Your being where I shall never see you isn't a thing I shall enjoy; I know that from the separation of these last months—after our beautiful life in Paris, the best thing that ever happened to me or that ever will. But if it's your career, if it's your happiness—well, I can miss you and hold my tongue. I *can* be disinterested—I can!"

"What did you want me to come for?" he asked, all attentive and motionless. The same impression, the old impression, was with him again; the sense that if she was sincere it was sincerity of execution, if she was genuine it was the genuineness of doing it well. She did it so well now that this very fact was charming and touching. In claiming from him at the theatre this hour of the afternoon she had wanted honestly (the more as she had not seen him at home for several days) to go over with him once again, on the eve of the great night—it would be for her second creation the critics would lie so in wait; the first success might have been a fluke—some of her recurrent doubts: knowing from experience of what good counsel he often was, how he could give a worrying question its "settler" at the last. Then she had heard from Dashwood of the change in his situation, and that had really from one moment to the other made her think sympathetically of his preoccupations—led her open-handedly to drop her own. She was sorry to lose him and eager to let him know how good a friend she was conscious he had been to her. But the expression of this was already, at the end of a minute, a strange bedevilment: she began to listen to herself, to speak dramatically, to represent. She uttered the things she felt as if they were snatches of old play-books, and really felt them the more because they sounded so well. This, however, didn't prevent their really being as good feelings as those of anybody else, and at the moment her friend, to still a rising emotion—which he knew he shouldn't still—articulated the challenge I have just recorded, she had for his sensibility, at any rate, the truth of gentleness and generosity.

"There's something the matter with you, my dear—you're jealous," Miriam said. "You're jealous of poor Mr. Dormer. That's an example of the way you tangle everything up. Lord, he won't hurt you, nor me either!"

"He can't hurt me, certainly," Peter returned, "and neither can you; for I've a nice little heart of stone and a smart new breastplate of iron. The interest I take in you is something quite extraordinary; but the most extraordinary thing in it is that it's perfectly prepared to tolerate the interest of others."

"The interest of others needn't trouble it much!" Miriam declared. "If Mr. Dormer has broken off his marriage to such an awfully fine woman—for she's that, your swell of a sister—it isn't for a ranting wretch like me. He's kind to me because that's his nature and he notices me because that's his business; but he's away up in the clouds—a thousand miles over my head. He has got something 'on,' as they say; he's in love with an idea. I think it's a shocking bad one, but that's his own affair. He's quite *exalté*; living on nectar and ambrosia—what he has to spare for us poor crawling things on earth is only a few dry crumbs. I didn't even ask him to come to rehearsal. Besides, he thinks you're in love with me and that it wouldn't be honourable to cut in. He's capable of that—isn't it charming?"

"If he were to relent and give up his scruples would you marry him?" Peter asked.

"Mercy, how you chatter about 'marrying'!" the girl laughed. "*C'est la maladie anglaise*—you've all got it on the brain."

"Why I put it that way to please you," he explained. "You complained to me last year precisely that this was not what seemed generally wanted."

"Oh last year!"—she made nothing of that. Then differently, "Yes, it's very tiresome!" she conceded.

"You told me, moreover, in Paris more than once that you wouldn't listen to anything but that."

"Well," she declared, "I won't, but I shall wait till I find a husband who's charming enough and bad enough. One who'll beat me and swindle me and spend my money on other women—that's the sort of man for me. Mr. Dormer, delightful as he is, doesn't come up to that."

"You'll marry Basil Dashwood." He spoke it with conviction.

"Oh 'marry'?—call it marry if you like. That's what poor mother threatens me with—she lives in dread of it."

"To this hour," he mentioned, "I haven't managed to make out what your mother wants. She has so many ideas, as Madame Carré said."

"She wants me to be some sort of tremendous creature—all her ideas are reducible to that. What makes the muddle is that she isn't clear about the creature she wants most. A great actress or a great lady—sometimes she inclines for one and sometimes for the other, but on the whole persuading herself that a great actress, if she'll cultivate the right people, may *be* a great lady. When I tell her that won't do and that a great actress can never be anything but a great vagabond, then the dear old thing has tantrums, and we have scenes—the most grotesque: they'd make the fortune, for a subject, of some play-writing rascal, if he had the wit to guess them; which, luckily for us perhaps, he never will. She usually winds up by protesting—*devinez un peu quoi!*" Miriam added. And as her companion professed his complete inability to divine: "By declaring that rather than take it that way I must marry *you*."

"She's shrewder than I thought," Peter returned. "It's the last of vanities to talk about, but I may state in passing that if you'd marry me you should be the greatest of all possible ladies."

She had a beautiful, comical gape. "Lord o' mercy, my dear fellow, what natural capacity have I for that?"

"You're artist enough for anything. I shall be a great diplomatist: my resolution's firmly taken, I'm infinitely cleverer than you have the least idea of, and you shall be," he went on, "a great diplomatist's wife."

"And the demon, the devil, the devourer and destroyer, that you are so fond of talking about: what, in such a position, do you do with that element of my nature? *Où le fourrez-vous?*" she cried as with a real anxiety.

"I'll look after it, I'll keep it under. Rather perhaps I should say I'll bribe it and amuse it; I'll gorge it with earthly grandeurs."

"That's better," said Miriam; "for a demon that's kept under is a shabby little demon. Don't let's be shabby." Then she added: "Do you really go away the beginning of next week?"

"Monday night if possible."

"Ah that's but to Paris. Before you go to your new post they must give you an interval here."

"I shan't take it—I'm so tremendously keen for my duties. I shall insist on going sooner. Oh," he went on, "I shall be concentrated now."

"I'll come and act there." She met it all—she was amused and amusing. "I've already forgotten what it was I wanted to discuss with you," she said—"it was some trumpery stuff. What I want to say now is only one thing: that it's not in the least true that because my life pitches me in every direction and mixes me up with all sorts of people—or rather with one sort mainly, poor dears!—I haven't a decent character, I haven't common honesty. Your sympathy, your generosity, your patience, your precious suggestions, our dear sweet days last summer in Paris, I shall never forget. You're the best—you're different from all the others. Think of me as you please and make profane jokes about my mating with a disguised 'Arty'—I shall think of *you* only in one way. I've a great respect for you. With all my heart I hope you'll be a great diplomatist. God bless you, dear clever man."

She got up as she spoke and in so doing glanced at the clock—a movement that somehow only added to the noble gravity of her discourse: she was considering his time so much more than her own. Sherringham, at this, rising too, took out his watch and stood a moment with his eyes bent upon it, though without in the least seeing what the needles marked. "You'll have to go, to reach the theatre at your usual hour, won't you? Let me not keep you. That is, let me keep you only long enough just to say this, once for all, as I shall never speak of it again. I'm going away to save myself," he frankly said, planted before her and seeking her eyes with his own. "I ought to go, no doubt, in silence, in decorum, in virtuous submission to hard necessity—without asking for credit or sympathy, without provoking any sort of scene or calling attention to my fortitude. But I can't—upon my soul I can't. I can go, I can see it through, but I can't hold my tongue. I want you to know all about it, so that over there, when I'm bored to death, I shall at least have the exasperatingly vain consolation of feeling that you do know—and that it does neither you nor me any good!"

He paused a moment; on which, as quite vague, she appealed. "That I 'do know' what?"

"That I've a consuming passion for you and that it's impossible."

"Oh impossible, my friend!" she sighed, but with a quickness in her assent.

"Very good; it interferes, the gratification of it would interfere fatally, with the ambition of each of us. Our ambitions are inferior and odious, but we're tied fast to them."

"Ah why ain't we simple?" she quavered as if all touched by it. "Why ain't we of the people—*comme tout le monde*—just a man and a girl liking each other?"

He waited a little—she was so tenderly mocking, so sweetly ambiguous. "Because we're precious asses! However, I'm simple enough, after all, to care for you as I've never cared for any human creature. You have, as it happens, a personal charm for me that no one has ever approached, and from the top of your splendid head to the sole of your theatrical shoe (I could go down on my face—there, abjectly—and kiss it!) every inch of you is dear and delightful to me. Therefore good-bye."

She took this in with wider eyes: he had put the matter in a way that struck her. For a moment, all the same, he was afraid she would reply as on the confessed experience of so many such tributes, handsome as this one was. But she was too much moved—the pure colour that had risen to her face showed it—to have recourse to this particular facility. She was moved even to the glimmer of tears, though she gave him her hand with a smile. "I'm so glad you've said all that, for from you I know what it means. Certainly it's better for you to go away. Of course it's all wrong, isn't it?—but that's the only thing it can be: therefore it's all right, isn't it? Some day when we're both great people we'll talk these things over; then we shall be quiet, we shall be rich, we shall be at peace—let us hope so at least—and better friends than others about us will know." She paused, smiling still, and then said while he held her hand: "Don't, *don't* come to-morrow night."

With this she attempted to draw her hand away, as if everything were settled and over; but the effect of her movement was that, as he held her tight, he was simply drawn toward her and close to her. The effect of this, in turn, was that, releasing her only to possess her the more completely, he seized her in his arms and, breathing deeply "I love you, you know," clasped her in a long embrace. His demonstration and her conscious sufferance, almost equally liberal, so sustained themselves that the door of the room had time to open slowly before either had taken notice. Mrs. Rooth, who had not peeped in before, peeped in now, becoming in this manner witness of an incident she could scarce have counted on. The unexpected indeed had for Mrs. Rooth never been an insuperable element in things; it was her position in general to be too acquainted with all the passions for any crude surprise. As the others turned round they saw her stand there and smile, and heard her ejaculate with wise indulgence: "Oh you extravagant children!"

Miriam brushed off her tears, quickly but unconfusedly. "He's going away, the wretch; he's bidding us farewell."

Peter—it was perhaps a result of his acute agitation—laughed out at the "us" (he had already laughed at the charge of puerility), and Mrs. Rooth went on: "Going away? Ah then I must have one too!" She held out both her hands, and Sherringham, stepping forward to take them, kissed her respectfully on each cheek, in the foreign manner, while she continued: "Our dear old friend—our kind, gallant gentleman!"

"The gallant gentleman has been promoted to a great post—the proper reward of his gallantry," Miriam said. "He's going out as minister to some impossible place—where is it?"

"As minister—how very charming! We *are* getting on." And their companion languished up at him with a world of approval.

"Oh well enough. One must take what one can get," he answered.

"You'll get everything now, I'm sure, shan't you?" Mrs. Rooth asked with an inflexion that called back to him comically—the source of the sound was so different—the very vibrations he had heard the day before from Lady Agnes.

"He's going to glory and he'll forget all about us—forget he has ever known such low people. So we shall never see him again, and it's better so. Good-bye, good-bye," Miriam repeated; "the brougham must be there, but I won't take you. I want to talk to mother about you, and we shall say things not fit for you to hear. Oh I'll let you know what we lose—don't be afraid," she added to Mrs. Rooth. "He's the rising star of diplomacy."

"I knew it from the first—I know how things turn out for such people as you!" cried the old woman, gazing fondly at Sherringham. "But you don't mean to say you're not coming to-morrow night?"

"Don't—don't; it's great folly," Miriam interposed; "and it's quite needless, since you saw me to-day."

Peter turned from the mother to the daughter, the former of whom broke out to the latter: "Oh you dear rogue, to say one has *seen* you yet! You know how you'll come up to it—you'll be beyond everything."

"Yes, I shall be there—certainly," Peter said, at the door, to Mrs. Rooth.

"Oh you dreadful goose!" Miriam called after him. But he went out without looking round at her.

BOOK SEVENTH

XLII

Nick Dormer had for the hour quite taken up his abode at his studio, where Biddy usually arrived after breakfast to give him news of the state of affairs in Calcutta Gardens and where many letters and telegrams were now addressed him. Among such missives, on the morning of the Saturday on which Peter Sherringham had promised to dine at the other house, was a note from Miriam Rooth, informing Nick that if he shouldn't telegraph to put her off she would turn up about half-past eleven, probably with her mother, for just one more sitting. She added that it was a nervous day for her and that she couldn't keep still, so that it would really be very kind to let her come to him as a refuge. She wished to stay away from the theatre, where everything was now settled—or so much the worse for the others if it wasn't—till the evening; in spite of which she should if left to herself be sure to go there. It would keep her quiet and soothe her to sit—he could keep her quiet (he was such a blessing that way!) at any time. Therefore she would give him two or three hours—or rather she would herself ask for them—if he didn't positively turn her from the door.

It had not been definite to Nick that he wanted another sitting at all for the slight work, as he held it to be, that Miriam had already helped him to achieve. He regarded this work as a mere light wind-fall of the shaken tree: he had made what he could of it and would have been embarrassed to make more. If it was not finished this was because it was not finishable; at any rate he had said all he had to say in that particular phrase. The young man, in truth, was not just now in the highest spirits; his imagination had within two or three days become conscious of a check that he tried to explain by the idea of a natural reaction. Any decision or violent turn, any need of a new sharp choice in one's career, was upsetting, and, exaggerate that importance and one's own as little as one would, a deal of flurry couldn't help attending, especially in the face of so much scandal, the horrid act, odious to one's modesty at the best, of changing one's clothes in the marketplace. That made life not at all positively pleasant, yet decidedly thrilling, for the hour; and it was well enough till the thrill abated. When this occurred, as it inevitably would, the romance and the glow of the adventure were exchanged for the chill and the prose. It was to these latter elements he had waked up pretty wide on this particular morning; and the prospect was not appreciably fresher from the fact that he had warned himself in advance it would be dull. He had in fact known how dull it would be, but now he would have time to learn even better. A reaction was a reaction, but it was not after all a catastrophe. It would be a feature of his very freedom that he should ask himself if he hadn't made a great mistake; this privilege would doubtless even remain within the limits of its nature in exposing him to hours of intimate conviction of his madness. But he would live to retract his retractions—this was the first thing to bear in mind.

He was absorbed, even while he dressed, in the effort to achieve intelligibly to himself some such revolution when, by the first post, Miriam's note arrived. At first it did little to help his agility—it made him, seeing her esthetic faith as so much stronger and simpler than his own, wonder how he should keep with her at her high level. Ambition, in her, was always on the rush, and she was not a person to conceive that others might in bad moments listen for the trumpet in vain. It would never have occurred to her that only the day before he had spent a part of the afternoon quite at the bottom of the hill. He had in fact turned into the National Gallery and had wandered about there for more than an hour, and it was just while he did so that the immitigable recoil had begun perversely to make itself felt. The perversity was all the greater from the fact that if the experience was depressing this was not because he had been discouraged beyond measure by the sight of the grand things that had been done—things so much grander than any that would ever bear his signature. That variation he was duly acquainted with and should know in abundance again. What had happened to him, as he passed on this occasion from Titian to Rubens and from Gainsborough to Rembrandt, was that he found himself calling the whole exhibited art into question. What was it after all at the best and why had people given it so high a place? Its weakness, its limits broke upon him; tacitly blaspheming he looked with a lustreless eye at the palpable, polished, "toned" objects designed for suspension on hooks. That is, he blasphemed if it were blasphemy to feel that as bearing on the energies of man they were a poor and secondary show. The human force producing them was so far from one of the greatest; their place was a small place and their connexion with the heroic life casual and slight. They represented so little great ideas, and it was great ideas that kept the world from chaos. He had incontestably been in much closer relation with them a few months before than he was to-day: it made up a great deal for what was false and hollow, what was merely personal, in "politics" that, were the idea greater or smaller, they could at their best so directly deal with it. The love of it had really been much of the time at the bottom of his impulse to follow them up; though this was not what he had most talked of with his political friends or even with Julia. No, political as Julia was, he had not conferred with her much about the idea. However, this might have been his own fault quite as much as hers, and she in fact took such things, such enthusiasms, for granted—there was an immense deal in every way that she took for granted. On the other hand, he had often put forward this brighter side of the care for the public weal in his discussions with Gabriel Nash, to the end, it is true, of making that worthy scoff aloud at what he was pleased to term his hypocrisy. Gabriel maintained precisely that there were more ideas, more of those that man lived by, in a single room of the National Gallery than in all the statutes of Parliament. Nick had replied to this more than once that the determination of what man did live by was required; to which Nash had retorted (and it was very rarely that he quoted Scripture) that it was at any rate not by bread and beans alone. The statutes of Parliament gave him bread and beans *tout au plus*.

Nick had at present no pretension of trying this question over again: he reminded himself that his ambiguity was subjective, as the philosophers said; the result of a mood which in due course would be at the mercy of another mood. It made him curse, and cursing, as a finality, lacked firmness—one had to drive in posts somewhere under. The greatest time to do one's work was when it didn't seem worth doing, for then one gave it a brilliant chance, that of resisting the stiffest test of all—the test of striking one as too bad. To do the most when there would be the least to be got by it was to be most in the spirit of high production. One thing at any rate was certain, Nick reflected: nothing on earth would induce him to change back again—not even if this twilight of the soul should last for the rest of his days. He hardened himself in his posture with a good conscience which, had they had a glimpse of it, would have made him still more diverting to those who already thought him so; and now, by a happy chance, Miriam suddenly supplied the bridge correcting the gap in his continuity. If he had made his sketch it was a proof he had done her, and that he had done her flashed upon him as a sign that she would be still more feasible. Art was *doing*—it came back to that—which politics in most cases weren't. He thus, to pursue our image, planted his supports in the dimness beneath all cursing, and on the platform so improvised was able, in his relief, to dance. He sent out a telegram to Balaklava Place requesting his beautiful sitter by no manner of means to fail him. When his servant came back it was to usher into the studio Peter Sherringham, whom the man had apparently found at the door.

The hour was so early for general commerce that Nick immediately guessed his visitor had come on some rare errand; but this inference yielded to the reflexion that Peter might after all only wish to make up by present zeal for not having been near him before. He forgot that, as he had subsequently learned from Biddy, their foreign, or all but foreign, cousin had spent an hour in Rosedale Road, missing him there but pulling out Miriam's portrait, the day of his own last visit to Beauclere. These young men were not on a ceremonious footing and it was not in Nick's nature to keep a record of civilities rendered or omitted; nevertheless he had been vaguely conscious that during a stay in London elastic enough on Peter's part he and his kinsman had foregathered less than of yore. It was indeed an absorbing moment in the career of each, but even while recognising such a truth Nick judged it not impossible that Julia's brother might have taken upon himself to resent some suppositious failure of consideration for that lady; though this indeed would have been stupid and the newly appointed minister (to he had forgotten where) didn't often make mistakes. Nick held that as he had treated Julia with studious generosity she had nothing whatever to visit on him—wherefore Peter had still less. It was at any rate none of that gentleman's business. There were only two abatements to disposing in a few frank words of all this: one of them Nick's general hatred of talking of his private affairs (a reluctance in which he and Peter were well matched); and the other a truth involving more of a confession—the subtle truth that the most definite and even most soothing result of the collapse of his engagement was, as happened, an unprecedented consciousness of freedom. Nick's observation was of a different sort from his cousin's; he noted much less the signs of the hour and kept throughout a looser register of life; nevertheless, just as one of our young men had during these days in London found the air peopled with personal influences, the concussion of human atoms, so the other, though only asking to live without too many questions and work without too many rubs, to be glad and sorry in short on easy terms, had become aware of a certain social tightness, of the fact that life is crowded and passion restless, accident and community inevitable. Everybody with whom one had relations had other relations too, and even indifference was a mixture and detachment a compromise. The only wisdom was to consent to the loss, if necessary, of everything but one's temper and to the ruin, if necessary, of everything but one's work. It must be added that Peter's relative took precautions against irritation perhaps in excess of the danger, as departing travellers about to whiz through foreign countries mouth in phrase-books combinations of words they will never use. He was at home in clear air and disliked to struggle either for breath or for light. He had a dim sense that Peter felt some discomfort from him and might have come now to tell him so; in which case he should be sorry for the sufferer in various ways. But as soon as that aspirant began to speak suspicion reverted to mere ancient kindness, and this in spite of the fact that his speech had a slightly exaggerated promptitude, like the promptitude of business, which might have denoted self-consciousness. To Nick it quickly appeared better to be glad than to be sorry: this simple argument was more than sufficient to make him glad Peter was there.

"My dear fellow, it's an unpardonable hour, isn't it? I wasn't even sure you'd be up, yet had to risk it, because my hours are numbered. I'm going away to-morrow," Peter went on; "I've a thousand things to do. I've had no talk with you this time such as we used to have of old (it's an irreparable loss, but it's your fault, you know), and as I've got to rush about all day I thought I'd just catch you before any one else does."

"Some one has already caught me, but there's plenty of time," Nick returned.

Peter all but asked a question—it fell short. "I see, I see. I'm sorry to say I've only a few minutes at best."

"Man of crushing responsibilities, you've come to humiliate me!" his companion cried. "I know all about it."

"It's more than I do then. That's not what I've come for, but I shall be delighted if I humiliate you a little by the way. I've two things in mind, and I'll mention the most difficult first. I came here the other day—the day after my arrival in town."

"Ah yes, so you did; it was very good of you"—Nick remembered. "I ought to have returned your visit or left a card or written my name—to have done something in Great Stanhope Street, oughtn't I? You hadn't got this new thing then, or I'd have 'called.'"

Peter eyed him a moment. "I say, what's the matter with you? Am I really unforgivable for having taken that liberty?"

"What liberty?" Nick looked now quite innocent of care, and indeed his visitor's allusion was not promptly clear. He was thinking for the instant all of Biddy, of whom and whose secret inclinations Grace had insisted on talking to him. They were none of his business, and if he wouldn't for the world have let the girl herself suspect he had violent lights on what was most screened and curtained in her, much less would he have made Peter a clumsy present of this knowledge. Grace had a queer theory that Peter treated Biddy badly—treated them all somehow badly; but Grace's zeal (she had plenty of it, though she affected all sorts of fine indifference) almost always took the form of her being unusually wrong. Nick wanted to do only what Biddy would thank him for, and he knew very well what she wouldn't. She wished him and Peter to be great friends, and the only obstacle to this was that Peter was too much of a diplomatist. Peter made him for an instant think of her and of the hour

477

they had lately spent together in the studio in his absence—an hour of which Biddy had given him a history full of items and omissions; and this in turn brought Nick's imagination back to his visitor's own side of the matter. That general human complexity of which the sense had lately increased with him, and to which it was owing that any thread one might take hold of would probably be the extremely wrong end of something, was illustrated by the fact that while poor Biddy was thinking of Peter it was ten to one poor Peter was thinking of Miriam Rooth. All of which danced before Nick's intellectual vision for a space briefer than my too numerous words.

"I pitched into your treasures—I rummaged among your canvases," Peter said. "Biddy had nothing whatever to do with it—she maintained an attitude of irreproachable reserve. It has been on my conscience all these days and I ought to have done penance before. I've been putting it off partly because I'm so ashamed of my indiscretion. *Que voulez-vous*, my dear chap? My provocation was great. I heard you had been painting Miss Rooth, so that I couldn't restrain my curiosity. I simply went into that corner and struck out there—a trifle wildly no doubt. I dragged the young lady to the light—your sister turned pale as she saw me. It was a good deal like breaking open one of your letters, wasn't it? However, I assure you it's all right, for I congratulate you both on your style and on your correspondent."

"You're as clever, as witty, as humorous as ever, old boy," Nick pronounced, going himself into the corner designated by his companion and laying his hands on the same canvas. "Your curiosity's the highest possible tribute to my little attempt and your sympathy sets me right with myself. There she is again," Nick went on, thrusting the picture into an empty frame; "you shall see her whether you wish to or not."

"Right with yourself? You don't mean to say you've been wrong!" Peter returned, standing opposite the portrait.

"Oh I don't know. I've been kicking up such a row. Anything's better than a row."

"She's awfully good—she's awfully true," said Peter. "You've done more to her since the other day. You've put in several things."

"Yes, but I've worked distractedly. I've not altogether conformed to the good rule about being off with the old love."

"With the old love?"—and the visitor looked hard at the picture.

"Before you're on with the new!" Nick had no sooner uttered these words than he coloured: it occurred to him his friend would probably infer an allusion to Julia. He therefore added quickly: "It isn't so easy to cease to represent an affectionate constituency. Really most of my time for a fortnight has been given to letter-writing. They've all been unexpectedly charming. I should have thought they'd have loathed and despised me. But not a bit of it; they cling to me fondly—they struggle with me tenderly. I've been down to talk with them about it, and we've passed the most sociable, delightful hours. I've designated my successor; I've felt a good deal like the Emperor Charles the Fifth when about to retire to the monastery of Yuste. The more I've seen of them in this way the more I've liked them, and they declare it has been the same with themselves about me. We spend our time assuring each other we hadn't begun to know each other till now. In short it's all wonderfully jolly, but it isn't business. *C'est magnifique, mais ce n'est pas la guerre.*"

"They're not so charming as they might be if they don't offer to keep you and let you paint."

"They do, almost—it's fantastic," said Nick. "Remember they haven't yet seen a daub of my brush."

"Well, I'm sorry for you; we live in too enlightened an age," Peter returned. "You can't suffer for art—that grand romance is over. Your experience is interesting; it seems to show that at the tremendous pitch of civilisation we've reached you can't suffer from anything but hunger."

"I shall doubtless," Nick allowed, "do that enough to make up for the rest."

"Never, never, when you paint so well as this."

"Oh come, you're too good to be true," Nick said. "But where did you learn that one's larder's full in proportion as one's work's fine?"

Peter waived this curious point—he only continued to look at the picture; after which he roundly brought out: "I'll give you your price for it on the spot."

"Ah you're so magnanimous that you shall have it for nothing!" And Nick, touched to gratitude, passed his arm into his visitor's.

Peter had a pause. "Why do you call me magnanimous?"

"Oh bless my soul, it's hers—I forgot!" laughed Nick, failing in his turn to answer the other's inquiry. "But you shall have another."

"Another? Are you going to do another?"

"This very morning. That is, I shall begin it. I've heard from her; she's coming to sit—a short time hence."

Peter turned away a little at this, releasing himself, and, as if the movement had been an effect of his host's words, looked at his watch earnestly to dissipate that appearance. He fell back to consider the work from further off. "The more you do her the better—she has all the qualities of a great model. From that point of view it's a pity she has another trade: she might make so good a thing of this one. But how shall you do her again?" he asked ingenuously.

"Oh I can scarcely say; we'll arrange something; we'll talk it over. It's extraordinary how well she enters into what one wants: she knows more than one does one's self. She isn't, as you Frenchmen say, the first comer. However, you know all about that, since you invented her, didn't you? That's what she says; she's awfully sweet on you," Nick kindly pursued. "What I ought to do is to try something as different as possible from that thing; not the sibyl, the muse, the tremendous creature, but the charming woman, the person one knows, differently arranged as she appears *en ville*, she calls it. I'll do something really serious and send it to you out there with my respects. It will remind you of home and perhaps a little even of me. If she knows it's for you she'll throw herself into it in the right spirit. Leave it to us, my dear fellow; we'll turn out something splendid."

480

"It's jolly to hear you, but I shall send you a cheque," said Peter very stoutly.

"I suppose it's all right in your position, but you're too proud," his kinsman answered.

"What do you mean by my position?"

"Your exaltation, your high connexion with the country, your treating with sovereign powers as the representative of a sovereign power. Isn't that what they call 'em?"

Peter, who had turned round again, listened to this with his eyes fixed on Nick's face while he once more drew forth his watch. "Brute!" he exclaimed familiarly, at the same time dropping his eyes on the watch. "When did you say you expect your sitter?"

"Oh we've plenty of time; don't be afraid of letting me see you agitated by her presence."

"Brute!" Peter again ejaculated.

This friendly personal note cleared the air, made their communication closer. "Stay with me and talk to me," said Nick; "I daresay it's good for me. It may be the last time I shall see you without having before anything else to koo-too."

"Beast!" his kinsman once more, and a little helplessly, threw off; though next going on: "Haven't you something more to show me then—some other fruit of your genius?"

"Must I bribe you by setting my sign-boards in a row? You know what I've done; by which I mean of course you know what I haven't. My genius, as you're so good as to call it, has hitherto been dreadfully sterile. I've had no time, no opportunity, no continuity. I must go and sit down in a corner and learn my alphabet. That thing isn't good; what I shall do for you won't be good. Don't protest, my dear fellow; nothing will be fit to look at for a long time." After which poor Nick wound up: "And think of my ridiculous age! As the good people say (or don't they say it?), it's a rum go. It won't be amusing."

"Ah you're so clever you'll get on fast," Peter returned, trying to think how he could most richly defy the injunction not to protest.

"I mean it won't be amusing for others," said Nick, unperturbed by this levity. "They want results, and small blame to them."

"Well, whatever you do, don't talk like Mr. Gabriel Nash," Peter went on. "Sometimes I think you're just going to."

Nick stared a moment. "Ah he never would have said *that* 'They want results, the damned asses'—that would have been more in his key."

"It's the difference of a *nuance*! And are you extraordinarily happy?" Peter added as his host now obliged him by arranging half-a-dozen canvases so that he could look at them.

"Not so much so, doubtless, as the artistic life ought to make one: because all one's people are not so infatuated as one's electors. But little by little I'm learning the charm of pig-headedness."

"Your mother's very bad," Peter allowed—"I lunched with her day before yesterday."

"Yes, I know, I know"—Nick had such reason to know; "but it's too late, too late. I must just peg away here and not mind. I've after all a great advantage in my life."

His companion waited impartially to hear. "And that would be—?"

"Well, knowing what I want to do. That's everything, you know."

"It's an advantage, however, that you've only just come in for, isn't it?"

"Yes, but the delay and the probation only make me prize it the more. I've got it now; and it makes up for the absence of some other things."

Again Peter had a pause. "That sounds a little flat," he remarked at last.

"It depends on what you compare it with. It has more point than I sometimes found in the House of Commons."

"Oh I never thought I should like that!"

There was another drop during which Nick moved about the room turning up old sketches to see if he had anything more to show, while his visitor continued to look at the unfinished and in some cases, as seemed, unpromising productions already exposed. They were far less interesting than the portrait of Miriam Rooth and, it would have appeared, less significant of ability. For that particular effort Nick's talent had taken an inspired flight. So much Peter thought, as he had thought it intensely before; but the words he presently uttered had no visible connexion with it. They only consisted of the abrupt inquiry; "Have you heard anything from Julia?"

"Not a syllable. Have you?"

"Dear no; she never writes to me."

"But won't she on the occasion of your promotion?"

"I daresay not," said Peter; and this was the only reference to Mrs. Dallow that passed between her brother and her late intended. It left a slight stir of the air which Peter proceeded to allay by an allusion comparatively speaking more relevant. He expressed disappointment that Biddy shouldn't have come in, having had an idea she was always in Rosedale Road of a morning. That was the other branch of his present errand—the wish to see her and give her a message for Lady Agnes, upon whom, at so early an hour, he had not presumed to intrude in Calcutta Gardens. Nick replied that Biddy did in point of fact almost always turn up, and for the most part early: she came to wish him good-morning and start him for the day. She was a devoted Electra, laying a cool, healing hand on a distracted, perspiring Orestes. He reminded Peter, however, that he would have a chance of seeing her that evening, and of seeing Lady Agnes; for wasn't he to do them the honour of dining in Calcutta Gardens? Biddy, the day before, had arrived full of that excitement. Peter explained that this was exactly the sad subject of his actual *démarche*: the project of the dinner in Calcutta Gardens had, to his exceeding regret, fallen to pieces. The fact was (didn't Nick know it?) the night had been suddenly and perversely fixed for Miriam's première, and he was under a definite engagement with her not to stay away from it. To add to the bore of the thing he was obliged to return to Paris the very next morning. He was quite awfully sorry, for he had promised Lady Agnes: he didn't understand then about Miriam's affair, in regard to which he had given a previous pledge. He was more grieved than he could say, but he could never fail Miss Rooth: he had professed from the first an interest in her which he must live up to a little more. This was his last chance—he hadn't been near her at the trying time of her first braving of the public. And the second night of the play wouldn't do—it must be the first or nothing. Besides, he couldn't wait over till Monday.

While Peter recited all his hindrance Nick was occupied in rubbing with a cloth a palette he had just scraped. "I see what you mean—I'm very sorry too. I'm sorry you can't give my mother this joy—I give her so little."

"My dear fellow, you might give her a little more!" it came to Peter to say. "It's rather too much to expect *me* to make up for your omissions!"

Nick looked at him with a moment's fixedness while he polished the palette; and for that moment he felt the temptation to reply: "There's a way you could do that, to a considerable extent—I think you guess it—which wouldn't be intrinsically disagreeable." But the impulse passed without expressing itself in speech, and he simply brought out; "You can make this all clear to Biddy when she comes, and she'll make it clear to my mother."

"Poor little Biddy!" Peter mentally sighed, thinking of the girl with that job before her; but what he articulated was that this was exactly why he had come to the studio. He had inflicted his company on Lady Agnes the previous Thursday and had partaken of a meal with her, but had not seen Biddy though he had waited for her, had hoped immensely she'd come in. Now he'd wait again—dear Bid was thoroughly worth it.

"Patience, patience then—you've always me!" said Nick; to which he subjoined: "If it's a question of going to the play I scarcely see why you shouldn't dine at my mother's all the same. People go to the play after dinner."

"Yes, but it wouldn't be fair, it wouldn't be decent: it's a case when I must be in my seat from the rise of the curtain." Peter, about this, was thoroughly lucid. "I should force your mother to dine an hour earlier than usual and then in return for her courtesy should go off to my entertainment at eight o'clock, leaving her and Grace and Biddy languishing there. I wish I had proposed in time that they should go with me," he continued not very ingenuously.

"You might do that still," Nick suggested.

"Oh at this time of day it would be impossible to get a box."

"I'll speak to Miss Rooth about it if you like when she comes," smiled Nick.

"No, it wouldn't do," said Peter, turning away and looking once more at his watch. He made tacitly the addition that still less than asking Lady Agnes for his convenience to dine early would *this* be decent, would it be thinkable. His taking Biddy the night he dined with her and with Miss Tressilian had been something very like a violation of those proprieties. He couldn't say that, however, to the girl's brother, who remarked in a moment that it was all right, since Peter's action left him his own freedom.

"Your own freedom?"—and Peter's question made him turn.

"Why you see now I can go to the theatre myself."

"Certainly; I hadn't thought of that. You'd naturally have been going."

"I gave it up for the prospect of your company at home."

"Upon my word you're too good—I don't deserve such sacrifices," said Peter, who read in his kinsman's face that this was not a figure of speech but the absolute truth. "Didn't it, however, occur to you that, as it would turn out, I might—I even naturally *would*—myself be going?" he put forth.

Nick broke into a laugh. "It would have occurred to me if I understood a little better—!" But he paused, as still too amused.

"If you understood a little better what?"

"Your situation, simply."

Peter looked at him a moment. "Dine with me to-night by ourselves and at a club. We'll go to the theatre together and then you'll understand it."

"With pleasure, with pleasure: we'll have a jolly evening," said Nick.

"Call it jolly if you like. When did you say she was coming?" Peter asked.

"Biddy? Oh probably, as I tell you, at any moment."

"I mean the great Miriam," Peter amended.

"The great Miriam, if she's punctual, will be here in about forty minutes."

"And will she be likely to find your sister?"

"That will depend, my dear fellow, on whether my sister remains to see her."

"Exactly; but the point's whether you'll allow her to remain, isn't it?"

Nick looked slightly mystified. "Why shouldn't she do as she likes?"

"In that case she'll probably go."

"Yes, unless she stays."

"Don't let her," Peter dropped; "send her away." And to explain this he added: "It doesn't seem exactly the right sort of thing, fresh young creatures like Bid meeting *des femmes de théâtre*." His explanation, in turn, struck him as requiring another clause; so he went on: "At least it isn't thought the right sort of thing abroad, and even in England my foreign ideas stick to me."

Even with this amplification, however, his plea evidently still had for his companion a flaw; which, after he had considered it a moment, Nick exposed in the simple words: "Why, you originally introduced them in Paris, Biddy and Miss Rooth. Didn't they meet at your rooms and fraternise, and wasn't that much more 'abroad' than this?"

"So they did, but my hand had been forced and she didn't like it," Peter answered, suspecting that for a diplomatist he looked foolish.

"Miss Rooth didn't like it?" Nick persisted.

"That I confess I've forgotten. Besides, she wasn't an actress then. What I mean is that Biddy wasn't particularly pleased with her."

"Why she thought her wonderful—praised her to the sides. I remember that."

"She didn't like her as a woman; she praised her as an actress."

"I thought you said she wasn't an actress then," Nick returned.

Peter had a pause. "Oh Biddy thought so. She has seen her since, moreover. I took her the other night, and her curiosity's satisfied."

"It's not of any consequence, and if there's a reason for it I'll bundle her off directly," Nick made haste to say. "But the great Miriam seems such a kind, good person."

"So she is, charming, charming,"—and his visitor looked hard at him.

"Here comes Biddy now," Nick went on. "I hear her at the door: you can warn her yourself."

"It isn't a question of 'warning'—that's not in the least my idea. But I'll take Biddy away," said Peter.

"That will be still more energetic."

"No, it will be simply more selfish—I like her company." Peter had turned as if to go to the door and meet the girl; but he quickly checked himself, lingering in the middle of the room, and the next instant Biddy had come in. When she saw him there she also stopped.

XLIII

"Come on boldly, my dear," said Nick. "Peter's bored to death waiting for you."

"Ah he's come to say he won't dine with us to-night!" Biddy stood with her hand on the latch.

"I leave town to-morrow: I've everything to do; I'm broken-hearted; it's impossible"—Peter made of it again such a case as he could. "Please make my peace with your mother—I'm ashamed of not having written to her last night."

She closed the door and came in while her brother said to her, "How in the world did you guess it?"

"I saw it in the *Morning Post*." And she kept her eyes on their kinsman.

"In the *Morning Post*?" he vaguely echoed.

"I saw there's to be a first night at that theatre, the one you took us to. So I said, 'Oh he'll go there.'"

"Yes, I've got to do that too," Peter admitted.

"She's going to sit to me again this morning, his wonderful actress—she has made an appointment: so you see I'm getting on," Nick pursued to his sister.

"Oh I'm so glad—she's so splendid!" The girl looked away from her cousin now, but not, though it seemed to fill the place, at the triumphant portrait of Miriam Rooth.

"I'm delighted you've come in. I *have* waited for you," Peter hastened to declare to her, though conscious that this was in the conditions meagre.

"Aren't you coming to see us again?"

"I'm in despair, but I shall really not have time. Therefore it's a blessing not to have missed you here."

"I'm very glad," said Biddy. Then she added: "And you're going to America—to stay a long time?"

"Till I'm sent to some better place."

"And will that better place be as far away?"

"Oh Biddy, it wouldn't be better then," said Peter.

"Do you mean they'll give you something to do at home?"

"Hardly that. But I've a tremendous lot to do at home to-day." For the twentieth time Peter referred to his watch.

She turned to her brother, who had admonished her that she might bid him good-morning. She kissed him and he asked what the news would be in Calcutta Gardens; to which she made answer: "The only news is of course the great preparations they're making, poor dears, for Peter. Mamma thinks you must have had such a nasty dinner the other day," the girl continued to the guest of that romantic occasion.

"Faithless Peter!" said Nick, beginning to whistle and to arrange a canvas in anticipation of Miriam's arrival.

"Dear Biddy, thank your stars you're not in my horrid profession," protested the personage so designated. "One's bowled about like a cricket-ball, unable to answer for one's freedom or one's comfort from one moment to another."

"Oh ours is the true profession—Biddy's and mine," Nick broke out, setting up his canvas; "the career of liberty and peace, of charming long mornings spent in a still north light and in the contemplation, I may even say in the company, of the amiable and the beautiful."

"That certainty's the case when Biddy comes to see you," Peter returned.

Biddy smiled at him. "I come every day. Anch'io son pittore! I encourage Nick awfully."

"It's a pity I'm not a martyr—she'd bravely perish with me," Nick said.

"You are—you're a martyr—when people say such odious things!" the girl cried. "They do say them. I've heard many more than I've repeated to you."

"It's you yourself then, indignant and loyal, who are the martyr," observed Peter, who wanted greatly to be kind to her.

"Oh I don't care!"—but she threw herself, flushed and charming, into a straight appeal to him. "Don't you think one can do as much good by painting great works of art as by—as by what papa used to do? Don't you think art's necessary to the happiness, to the greatness of a people? Don't you think it's manly and honourable? Do you think a passion for it's a thing to be ashamed of? Don't you think the artist—the conscientious, the serious one—is as distinguished a member of society as any one else?"

Peter and Nick looked at each other and laughed at the way she had got up her subject, and Nick asked their kinsman if she didn't express it all in perfection. "I delight in general in artists, but I delight still more in their defenders," Peter made reply, perhaps a little meagrely, to Biddy.

"Ah don't attack me if you're wise!" Nick said.

"One's tempted to when it makes Biddy so fine."

"Well, that's the way she encourages me: it's meat and drink to me," Nick went on. "At the same time I'm bound to say there's a little whistling in the dark in it."

"In the dark?" his sister demanded.

"The obscurity, my dear child, of your own aspirations, your mysterious ambitions and esthetic views. Aren't there some heavyish shadows there?"

"Why I never cared for politics."

"No, but you cared for life, you cared for society, and you've chosen the path of solitude and concentration."

"You horrid boy!" said Biddy.

"Give it up, that arduous steep—give it up and come out with me," Peter interposed.

"Come out with you?"

"Let us walk a little or even drive a little. Let us at any rate talk a little."

"I thought you had so much to do," Biddy candidly objected.

"So I have, but why shouldn't you do a part of it with me? Would there be any harm? I'm going to some tiresome shops—you'll cheer the frugal hour."

The girl hesitated, then turned to Nick. "Would there be any harm?"

"Oh it's none of *his* business!" Peter protested.

"He had better take you home to your mother."

"I'm going home—I shan't stay here to-day," Biddy went on. Then to Peter: "I came in a hansom, but I shall walk back. Come that way with me."

"With pleasure. But I shall not be able to go in," Peter added.

"Oh that's no matter," said the girl. "Good-bye, Nick."

"You understand then that we dine together—at seven sharp. Wouldn't a club, as I say, be best?" Peter, before going, inquired of Nick. He suggested further which club it should be; and his words led Biddy, who had directed her steps toward the door, to turn a moment as with a reproachful question—whether it was for this Peter had given up Calcutta Gardens. But her impulse, if impulse it was, had no sequel save so far as it was a sequel that Peter freely explained to her, after Nick had assented to his conditions, that her brother too had a desire to go to Miss Rooth's first night and had already promised to accompany him.

"Oh that's perfect; it will be so good for him—won't it?—if he's going to paint her again," Biddy responded.

"I think there's nothing so good for him as that he happens to have such a sister as you," Peter declared as they went out. He heard at the same time the sound of a carriage stopping, and before Biddy, who was in front of him, opened the door of the house had been able to say to himself, "What a bore—there's Miriam!" The opened door showed him that truth—this young lady in the act of alighting from the brougham provided by Basil Dashwood's thrifty zeal. Her mother followed her, and both the new visitors exclaimed and rejoiced, in their demonstrative way, as their eyes fell on their valued friend. The door had closed behind Peter, but he instantly and violently rang, so that they should be admitted with as little delay as possible, while he stood disconcerted, and fearing he showed it, by the prompt occurrence of an encounter he had particularly sought to avert. It ministered, moreover, a little to this sensibility that Miriam appeared to have come somewhat before her time. The incident promised, however, to pass off in a fine florid way. Before he knew it both the ladies had taken possession of Biddy, who looked at them with comparative coldness, tempered indeed by a faint glow of apprehension, and Miriam had broken out:

"We know you, we know you; we saw you in Paris, and you came to my theatre a short time ago with Mr. Sherringham!"

"We know your mother, Lady Agnes Dormer. I hope her ladyship's very well," said Mrs. Rooth, who had never struck Peter as a more objectionable old woman.

"You offered to do a head of me or something or other: didn't you tell me you work in clay? I daresay you've forgotten all about it, but I should be delighted," Miriam pursued with the richest urbanity. Peter was not concerned with her mother's pervasiveness, though he didn't like Biddy to see even that; but he hoped his companion would take the overcharged benevolence of the young actress in the spirit in which, rather to his surprise, it evidently was offered. "I've sat to your clever brother many times," said Miriam; "I'm going to sit again. I daresay you've seen what we've done—he's too delightful. *Si vous saviez comme cela me repose!*" she added, turning for a moment to Peter. Then she continued, smiling at Biddy; "Only he oughtn't to have thrown up such prospects, you know. I've an idea I wasn't nice to you that day in Paris—I was nervous and scared and perverse. I remember perfectly; I *was* odious. But I'm better now—you'd see if you were to know me. I'm not a bad sort—really I'm not. But you must have your own friends. Happy they—you look so charming! Immensely like Mr. Dormer, especially about the eyes; isn't she, mamma?"

"She comes of a beautiful Norman race—the finest, purest strain," the old woman simpered. "Mr. Dormer's sometimes so good as to come and see us—we're always at home on Sunday; and if some day you found courage to come with him you might perhaps find it pleasant, though very different of course from the circle in which you habitually move."

Biddy murmured a vague recognition of these wonderful civilities, and Miriam commented: "Different, yes; but we're all right, you know. Do come," she added. Then turning to Sherringham: "Remember what I told you—I don't expect you to-night."

"Oh I understand; I shall come,"—and Peter knew he grew red.

"It will be idiotic. Keep him, keep him away—don't let him," Miriam insisted to Biddy; with which, as Nick's portals now were gaping, she drew her mother away.

Peter, at this, walked off briskly with Biddy, dropping as he did so: "She's too fantastic!"

"Yes, but so tremendously good-looking. I shall ask Nick to take me there," the girl said after a moment.

"Well, she'll do you no harm. They're all right, as she says. It's the world of art—you were standing up so for art just now."

"Oh I wasn't thinking so much of that kind," she demurred.

"There's only one kind—it's all the same thing. If one sort's good the other is."

Biddy walked along a moment. "Is she serious? Is she conscientious?"

"She has the makings of a great artist," Peter opined.

"I'm glad to hear you think a woman can be one."

"In that line there has never been any doubt about it."

"And only in that line?"

"I mean on the stage in general, dramatic or lyric. It's as the actress that the woman produces the most complete and satisfactory artistic results."

"And only as the actress?"

He weighed it. "Yes, there's another art in which she's not bad."

493

"Which one do you mean?" asked Biddy.

"That of being charming and good, that of being indispensable to man."

"Oh that isn't an art."

"Then you leave her only the stage. Take it if you like in the widest sense."

Biddy appeared to reflect a moment, as to judge what sense this might be. But she found none that was wide enough, for she cried the next minute: "Do you mean to say there's nothing for a woman but to be an actress?"

"Never in my life. I only say that that's the best thing for a woman to be who finds herself irresistibly carried into the practice of the arts; for there her capacity for them has most application and her incapacity for them least. But at the same time I strongly recommend her not to be an artist if she can possibly help it. It's a devil of a life."

"Oh I know; men want women not to be anything."

"It's a poor little refuge they try to take from the overwhelming consciousness that you're in very fact everything."

"Everything?" And the girl gave a toss. "That's the kind of thing you say to keep us quiet."

"Dear Biddy, you see how well we succeed!" laughed Peter.

To which she replied by asking irrelevantly: "Why is it so necessary for you to go to the theatre to-night if Miss Rooth doesn't want you to?"

"My dear child, she does want me to. But that has nothing to do with it."

"Why then did she say that she doesn't?"

"Oh because she meant just the contrary."

"Is she so false then—is she so vulgar?"

"She speaks a special language; practically it isn't false, because it renders her thought and those who know her understand it."

"But she doesn't use it only to those who know her," Biddy returned, "since she asked me, who have so little the honour of her acquaintance, to keep you away to-night. How am I to know that she meant by that that I'm to urge you on to go?"

He was on the point of replying, "Because you've my word for it"; but he shrank in fact from giving his word—he had some fine scruples—and sought to relieve his embarrassment by a general tribute. "Dear Biddy, you're delightfully acute: you're quite as clever as Miss Rooth." He felt, however, that this was scarcely adequate and he continued: "The truth is that its being important for me to go is a matter quite independent of that young lady's wishing it or not wishing it. There happens to be a definite intrinsic propriety in it which determines the thing and which it would take me long to explain."

"I see. But fancy your 'explaining' to me: you make me feel so indiscreet!" the girl cried quickly—an exclamation which touched him because he was not aware that, quick as it had been, she had still had time to be struck first—though she wouldn't for the world have expressed it—with the oddity of such a duty at such a season. In fact that oddity, during a silence of some minutes, came back to Peter himself: the note had been forced—it sounded almost ignobly frivolous from a man on the eve of proceeding to a high diplomatic post. The effect of this, none the less, was not to make him break out with "Hang it, I *will* keep my engagement to your mother!" but to fill him with the wish to shorten his present strain by taking Biddy the rest of the way in a cab. He was uncomfortable, and there were hansoms about that he looked at wistfully. While he was so occupied his companion took up the talk by an abrupt appeal.

"Why did she say that Nick oughtn't to have resigned his seat?"

"Oh I don't know. It struck her so. It doesn't matter much."

But Biddy kept it up. "If she's an artist herself why doesn't she like people to go in for art, especially when Nick has given his time to painting her so beautifully? Why does she come there so often if she disapproves of what he has done?"

"Oh Miriam's disapproval—it doesn't count; it's a manner of speaking."

"Of speaking untruths, do you mean? Does she think just the reverse—is that the way she talks about everything?"

"We always admire most what we can do least," Peter brought forth; "and Miriam of course isn't political. She ranks painters more or less with her own profession, about which already, new as she is to it, she has no illusions. They're all artists; it's the same general sort of thing. She prefers men of the world—men of action."

"Is that the reason she likes you?" Biddy mildly mocked.

"Ah she doesn't like me—couldn't you see it?"

The girl at first said nothing; then she asked: "Is that why she lets you call her 'Miriam'?"

"Oh I don't, to her face."

"Ah only to mine!" laughed Biddy.

"One says that as one says 'Rachel' of her great predecessor."

"Except that she isn't so great, quite yet, is she?"

"Far from it; she's the freshest of novices—she has scarcely been four months on the stage. But no novice has ever been such an adept. She'll go very fast," Peter pursued, "and I daresay that before long she'll be magnificent."

"What a pity you'll not see that!" Biddy sighed after a pause.

"Not see it?"

"If you're thousands of miles away."

"It is a pity," Peter said; "and since you mention it I don't mind frankly telling you—throwing myself on your mercy, as it were—that that's why I make such a point of a rare occasion like to-night. I've a weakness for the drama that, as you perhaps know, I've never concealed, and this impression will probably have to last me in some barren spot for many, many years."

496

"I understand—I understand. I hope therefore it will be charming." And the girl walked faster.

"Just as some other charming impressions will have to last," Peter added, conscious of keeping up with her by some effort. She seemed almost to be running away from him, an impression that led him to suggest, after they had proceeded a little further without more words, that if she were in a hurry they had perhaps better take a cab. Her face was strange and touching to him as she turned it to make answer:

"Oh I'm not in the least in a hurry and I really think I had better walk."

"We'll walk then by all means!" Peter said with slightly exaggerated gaiety; in pursuance of which they went on a hundred yards. Biddy kept the same pace; yet it was scarcely a surprise to him that she should suddenly stop with the exclamation:

"After all, though I'm not in a hurry I'm tired! I had better have a cab; please call that one," she added, looking about her.

They were in a straight, blank, ugly street, where the small, cheap, grey-faced houses had no expression save that of a rueful, unconsoled acknowledgment of the universal want of identity. They would have constituted a "terrace" if they could, but they had dolefully given it up. Even a hansom that loitered across the end of the vista turned a sceptical back upon it, so that Sherringham had to lift his voice in a loud appeal. He stood with Biddy watching the cab approach them. "This is one of the charming things you'll remember," she said, turning her eyes to the general dreariness from the particular figure of the vehicle, which was antiquated and clumsy. Before he could reply she had lightly stepped into the cab; but as he answered, "Most assuredly it is," and prepared to follow her she quickly closed the apron.

"I must go alone; you've lots of things to do—it's all right"; and through the aperture in the roof she gave the driver her address. She had spoken with decision, and Peter fully felt now that she wished to get away from him. Her eyes betrayed it, as well as her voice, in a look, a strange, wandering ray that as he stood there with his hand on the cab he had time to take from her. "Good-bye, Peter," she smiled; and as the thing began to rumble away he uttered the same tepid, ridiculous farewell.

XLIV

At the entrance of Miriam and her mother Nick, in the studio, had stopped whistling, but he was still gay enough to receive them with every appearance of warmth. He thought it a poor place, ungarnished, untapestried, a bare, almost grim workshop, with all its revelations and honours still to come. But his visitors smiled on it a good deal in the same way in which they had smiled on Bridget Dormer when they met her at the door: Mrs. Rooth because vague, prudent approbation was the habit of her foolish face—it was ever the least danger; and Miriam because, as seemed, she was genuinely glad to find herself within the walls of which she spoke now as her asylum. She broke out in this strain to her host almost as soon as she had crossed the threshold, commending his circumstances, his conditions of work, as infinitely happier than her own. He was quiet, independent, absolute, free to do what he liked as he liked it, shut up in his little temple with his altar and his divinity; not hustled about in a mob of people, having to posture and grin to pit and gallery, to square himself at every step with insufferable conventions and with the ignorance and vanity of others. He was blissfully alone.

"Mercy, how you do abuse your fine profession! I'm sure I never urged you to adopt it!" Mrs. Rooth cried, in real bewilderment, to her daughter.

"She was abusing mine still more the other day," joked Nick—"telling me I ought to be ashamed of it and of myself."

"Oh I never know from one moment to the other—I live with my heart in my mouth," sighed the old woman.

"Aren't you quiet about the great thing—about my personal behaviour?" Miriam smiled. "My improprieties are all of the mind."

"I don't know what you *call* your personal behaviour," her mother objected.

"You would very soon if it were not what it is."

"And I don't know why you should wish to have it thought you've a wicked mind," Mrs. Rooth agreeably grumbled.

"Yes, but I don't see very well how I can make you understand that. At any rate," Miriam pursued with her grand eyes on Nick, "I retract what I said the other day about Mr. Dormer. I've no wish to quarrel with him on the way he has determined to dispose of his life, because after all it does suit me very well. It rests me, this little devoted corner; oh it rests me! It's out of the row and the dust, it's deliciously still and they can't get at me. Ah when art's like this, *à la bonne heure!*" And she looked round on such a presentment of "art" in a splendid way that produced amusement on the young man's part at its contrast with the humble fact. Miriam shone upon him as if she liked to be the cause of his mirth and went on appealing to him: "You'll always let me come here for an hour, won't you, to take breath—to let the whirlwind pass? You needn't trouble yourself about me; I don't mean to impose on you in the least the necessity of painting me, though if that's a manner of helping you to get on you may be sure it will always be open to you. Do what you like with me in that respect; only let me sit here on a high stool, keeping well out of your way, and see what you happen to be doing. I'll tell you my own adventures when you want to hear them."

"The fewer adventures you have to tell the better, my dear," said Mrs. Rooth; "and if Mr. Dormer keeps you quiet he'll add ten years to my life."

"It all makes an interesting comment on Mr. Dormer's own quietness, on his independence and sweet solitude," Nick observed. "Miss Rooth has to work with others, which is after all only what Mr. Dormer has to do when he works with Miss Rooth. What do you make of the inevitable sitter?"

"Oh," answered Miriam, "you can say to the inevitable sitter, 'Hold your tongue, you brute!'"

"Isn't it a good deal in that manner that I've heard you address your comrades at the theatre?" Mrs. Rooth inquired. "That's why my heart's in my mouth."

"Yes, but they hit me back; they reply to me—*comme de raison*—as I should never think of replying to Mr. Dormer. It's a great advantage to him that when he's peremptory with his model it only makes her better, adds to her expression of gloomy grandeur."

"We did the gloomy grandeur in the other picture: suppose therefore we try something different in this," Nick threw off.

"It *is* serious, it *is* grand," murmured Mrs. Rooth, who had taken up a rapt attitude before the portrait of her daughter. "It makes one wonder what she's thinking of. Beautiful, commendable things—that's what it seems to say."

"What can I be thinking of but the tremendous wisdom of my mother?" Miriam returned. "I brought her this morning to see that thing—she had only seen it in its earliest stage—and not to presume to advise you about anything else you may be so good as to embark on. She wanted, or professed she wanted, terribly to know what you had finally arrived at. She was too impatient to wait till you should send it home."

"Ah send it home—send it home; let us have it always with us!" Mrs. Rooth engagingly said. "It will keep us up, up, and up on the heights, near the stars—be always for us a symbol and a reminder!"

"You see I was right," Miriam went on; "for she appreciates thoroughly, in her own way, and almost understands. But if she worries or distracts you I'll send her directly home—I've kept the carriage there on purpose. I must add that I don't feel quite safe to-day in letting her out of my sight. She's liable to make dashes at the theatre and play unconscionable tricks there. I shall never again accuse mamma of a want of interest in my profession. Her interest to-day exceeds even my own. She's all over the place and she has ideas—ah but ideas! She's capable of turning up at the theatre at five o'clock this afternoon to demand the repainting of the set in the third act. For myself I've not a word more to say on the subject—I've accepted every danger, I've swallowed my fate. Everything's no doubt wrong, but nothing can possibly be right. Let us eat and drink, for to-night we die. If you say so mamma shall go and sit in the carriage, and as there's no means of fastening the doors (is there?) your servant shall keep guard over her."

"Just as you are now—be so good as to remain so; sitting just that way—leaning back with a smile in your eyes and one hand on the sofa beside you and supporting you a little. I shall stick a flower into the other hand—let it lie in your lap just as it is. Keep that thing on your head—it's admirably uncovered: do you call such an unconsidered trifle a bonnet?—and let your head fall back a little. There it is—it's found. This time I shall really do something, and it will be as different as you like from that other crazy job. Here we go!" It was in these irrelevant but earnest words that Nick responded to his sitter's uttered vagaries, of which her charming tone and countenance diminished the superficial acerbity. He held up his hands a moment, to fix her in her limits, and in a few minutes had a happy sense of having begun to work.

"The smile in her eyes—don't forget the smile in her eyes!" Mrs. Rooth softly chanted, turning away and creeping about the room. "That will make it so different from the other picture and show the two sides of her genius, the wonderful range between them. They'll be splendid mates, and though I daresay I shall strike you as greedy you must let me hope you'll send this one home too."

She explored the place discreetly and on tiptoe, talking twaddle as she went and bending her head and her eyeglass over various objects with an air of imperfect comprehension that didn't prevent Nick's private recall of the story of her underhand, commercial habits told by Gabriel Nash at the exhibition in Paris the first time her name had fallen on his ear. A queer old woman from whom, if you approached her in the right way, you could buy old pots—it was in this character that she had originally been introduced to him. He had lost sight of it afterwards, but it revived again as his observant eyes, at the same time that they followed his active hand, became aware of her instinctive, appraising gestures. There was a moment when he frankly laughed out—there was so little in his poor studio to appraise. Mrs. Rooth's wandering eyeglass and vague, polite, disappointed, bent back and head made a subject for a sketch on the instant: they gave such a sudden pictorial glimpse of the element of race. He found himself seeing the immemorial Jewess in her hold up a candle in a crammed back shop. There was no candle indeed and his studio was not crammed, and it had never occurred to him before that she was a grand-daughter of Israel save on the general theory, so stoutly held by several clever people, that few of us are not under suspicion. The late Rudolf Roth had at least been, and his daughter was visibly her father's child; so that, flanked by such a pair, good Semitic presumptions sufficiently crowned the mother. Receiving Miriam's sharp, satiric shower without shaking her shoulders she might at any rate have been the descendant of a tribe long persecuted. Her blandness was beyond all baiting; she professed she could be as still as a mouse. Miriam, on the other side of the room, in the tranquil beauty of her attitude—"found" indeed, as Nick had said—watched her a little and then declared she had best have been locked up at home. Putting aside her free account of the dangers to which her mother exposed her, it wasn't whimsical to imagine that within the limits of that repose from which the Neville-Nugents never wholly departed the elder lady might indeed be a trifle fidgety and have something her mind. Nick presently mentioned that it wouldn't be possible for him to "send home" his second performance; and he added, in the exuberance of having already got a little into relation with his work, that perhaps this didn't matter, inasmuch as—if Miriam would give him his time, to say nothing of her own—a third and a fourth masterpiece might also some day very well struggle into the light. His model rose to this without conditions, assuring him he might count upon her till she grew too old and too ugly and that nothing would make her so happy as that he should paint her as often as Romney had painted the celebrated Lady Hamilton. "Ah Lady Hamilton!" deprecated Mrs. Rooth; while Miriam, who had on occasion the candour of a fine acquisitiveness, wished to know what particular reason there might be for his not letting them have the picture he was now beginning.

"Why I've promised it to Peter Sherringham—he has offered me money for it," Nick replied. "However, he's welcome to it for nothing, poor chap, and I shall be delighted to do the best I can for him."

Mrs. Rooth, still prowling, stopped in the middle of the room at this, while her daughter echoed: "He offered you money—just as we came in?"

"You met him then at the door with my sister? I supposed you had—he's taking her home," Nick explained.

"Your sister's a lovely girl—such an aristocratic type!" breathed Mrs. Rooth. Then she added: "I've a tremendous confession to make to you."

"Mamma's confessions have to be tremendous to correspond with her crimes," said Miriam. "She asked Miss Dormer to come and see us, suggested even that you might bring her some Sunday. I don't like the way mamma does such things—too much humility, too many *simagrées*, after all; but I also said what I could to be nice to her. Your sister *is* charming—awfully pretty and modest. If you were to press me I should tell you frankly that it seems to me rather a social muddle, this rubbing shoulders of 'nice girls' and *filles de théâtre*: I shouldn't think it would do your poor young things much good. However, it's their own affair, and no doubt there's no more need of their thinking we're worse than we are than of their thinking we're better. The people they live with don't seem to know the difference—I sometimes make my reflexions about the public one works for."

"Ah if you go in for the public's knowing differences you're far too particular," Nick laughed. "*D'où tombez-vous?* as you affected French people say. If you've anything at stake on that you had simply better not play."

"Dear Mr. Dormer, don't encourage her to be so dreadful; for it *is* dreadful, the way she talks," Mrs. Rooth broke in. "One would think we weren't respectable—one would think I had never known what I've known and been what I've been."

"What one would think, beloved mother, is that you're a still greater humbug than you are. It's you, on the contrary, who go down on your knees, who pour forth apologies about our being vagabonds."

"Vagabonds—listen to her!—after the education I've given her and our magnificent prospects!" wailed Mrs. Rooth, sinking with clasped hands upon the nearest ottoman.

"Not after our prospects, if prospects they be: a good deal before them. Yes, you've taught me tongues and I'm greatly obliged to you—they no doubt give variety as well as incoherency to my conversation; and that of people in our line is for the most part notoriously monotonous and shoppy. The gift of tongues is in general the sign of your true adventurer. Dear mamma, I've no low standard—that's the last thing," Miriam went on. "My weakness is my exalted conception of respectability. Ah *parlez-moi de ça* and of the way I understand it! If I were to go in for being respectable you'd see something fine. I'm awfully conservative and I know what respectability is, even when I meet people of society on the accidental middle ground of either glowering or smirking. I know also what it isn't—it isn't the sweet union of well-bred little girls ('carefully-nurtured,' don't they call them?) and painted she-mummers. I should carry it much further than any of these people: I should never look at the likes of us! Every hour I live I see that the wisdom of the ages was in the experience of dear old Madame Carré—was in a hundred things she told me. She's founded on a rock. After that," Miriam went on to her host, "I can assure you that if you were so good as to bring Miss Dormer to see us we should be angelically careful of her and surround her with every attention and precaution."

"The likes of us—the likes of us!" Mrs. Rooth repeated plaintively and with a resentment as vain as a failure to sneeze. "I don't know what you're talking about and I decline to be turned upside down, I've my ideas as well as you, and I repudiate the charge of false humility. I've been through too many troubles to be proud, and a pleasant, polite manner was the rule of my life even in the days when, God knows, I had everything. I've never changed and if with God's help I had a civil tongue then, I've a civil tongue now. It's more than you always have, my poor, perverse, passionate child. Once a lady always a lady—all the footlights in the world, turn them up as high as you will, make no difference there. And I think people know it, people who know anything—if I may use such an expression—and it's because they know it that I'm not afraid to address them in a pleasant way. So I must say—and I call Mr. Dormer to witness, for if he could reason with you a bit about it he might render several people a service—your conduct to Mr. Sherringham simply breaks my heart," Mrs. Rooth concluded, taking a jump of several steps in the fine modern avenue of her argument.

Nick was appealed to, but he hung back, drawing with a free hand, and while he forbore Miriam took it up. "Mother's good—mother's very good;

but it's only little by little that you discover how good she is." This seemed to leave him at ease to ask their companion, with the preliminary intimation that what she had just said was very striking, what she meant by her daughter's conduct to old Peter. Before Mrs. Rooth could answer this question, however, Miriam broke across with one of her own. "Do you mind telling me if you made your sister go off with Mr. Sherringham because you knew it was about time for me to turn up? Poor Mr. Dormer, I get you into trouble, don't I?" she added quite with tenderness.

"Into trouble?" echoed Nick, looking at her head but not at her eyes.

"Well, we won't talk about that!" she returned with a rich laugh.

He now hastened to say that he had nothing to do with his sister's leaving the studio—she had only come, as it happened, for a moment. She had walked away with Peter Sherringham because they were cousins and old friends: he was to leave England immediately, for a long time, and he had offered her his company going home. Mrs. Rooth shook her head very knowingly over the "long time" Mr. Sherringham would be absent—she plainly had her ideas about that; and she conscientiously related that in the course of the short conversation they had all had at the door of the house her daughter had reminded Miss Dormer of something that had passed between them in Paris on the question of the charming young lady's modelling her head.

"I did it to make the idea of our meeting less absurd—to put it on the footing of our both being artists. I don't ask you if she has talent," said Miriam.

"Then I needn't tell you," laughed Nick.

"I'm sure she has talent and a very refined inspiration. I see something in that corner, covered with a mysterious veil," Mrs. Rooth insinuated; which led Miriam to go on immediately:

"Has she been trying her hand at Mr. Sherringham?"

"When should she try her hand, poor dear young lady? He's always sitting with us," said Mrs. Rooth.

"Dear mamma, you exaggerate. He has his moments—when he seems to say his prayers to me; but we've had some success in cutting them down. *Il s'est bien détaché ces jours-ci*, and I'm very happy for him. Of course it's an impertinent allusion for me to make; but I should be so delighted if I could think of him as a little in love with Miss Dormer," the girl pursued, addressing Nick.

"He is, I think, just a little—just a tiny bit," her artist allowed, working away; while Mrs. Rooth ejaculated to her daughter simultaneously:

"How can you ask such fantastic questions when you know he's dying for *you?*"

"Oh dying!—he's dying very hard!" cried Miriam. "Mr. Sherringham's a man of whom I can't speak with too much esteem and affection and who may be destined to perish by some horrid fever (which God forbid!) in the unpleasant country he's going to. But he won't have caught his fever from your humble servant."

"You may kill him even while you remain in perfect health yourself," said Nick; "and since we're talking of the matter I don't see the harm of my confessing that he strikes me as far gone—oh as very bad indeed."

"And yet he's in love with your sister?—*je n'y suis plus.*"

"He tries to be, for he sees that as regards you there are difficulties. He'd like to put his hand on some nice girl who'd be an antidote to his poison."

"Difficulties are a mild name for them; poison even is a mild name for the ill he suffers from. The principal difficulty is that he doesn't know what the devil he wants. The next is that I don't either—or what the devil I want myself. I only know what I don't want," Miriam kept on brightly and as if uttering some happy, beneficent truth. "I don't want a person who takes things even less simply than I do myself. Mr. Sherringham, poor man, must be very uncomfortable, for one side of him's in a perpetual row with the other side. He's trying to serve God and Mammon, and I don't know how God will come off. What I like in you is that you've definitely let Mammon go—it's the only decent way. That's my earnest conviction, and yet they call us people light.

506

Dear Mr. Sherringham has tremendous ambitions—tremendous *riguardi*, as we used to say in Italy. He wants to enjoy every comfort and to save every appearance, and all without making a scrap of a sacrifice. He expects others—me, for instance—to make all the sacrifices. *Merci*, much as I esteem him and much as I owe him! I don't know how he ever came to stray at all into our bold, bad, downright Bohemia: it was a cruel trick for fortune to play him. He can't keep out of it, he's perpetually making dashes across the border, and yet as soon as he gets here he's on pins and needles. There's another in whose position—if I were in it—I wouldn't look at the likes of us!"

"I don't know much about the matter," Nick brought out after some intent smudging, "but I've an idea Peter thinks he has made or at least is making sacrifices."

"So much the better—you must encourage him, you must help him."

"I don't know what my daughter's talking about," Mrs. Rooth contributed—"she's much too paradoxical for my plain mind. But there's one way to encourage Mr. Sherringham—there's one way to help him; and perhaps it won't be a worse way for a gentleman of your good nature that it will help me at the same time. Can't I look to you, dear Mr. Dormer, to see that he does come to the theatre to-night—that he doesn't feel himself obliged to stay away?"

"What danger is there of his staying away?" Nick asked.

"If he's bent on sacrifices that's a very good one to begin with," Miriam observed.

"That's the mad, bad way she talks to him—she has forbidden the dear unhappy gentleman the house!" her mother cried. "She brought it up to him just now at the door—before Miss Dormer: such very odd form! She pretends to impose her commands upon him."

"Oh he'll be there—we're going to dine together," said Nick. And when Miriam asked him what that had to do with it he went on: "Why we've arranged it; I'm going, and he won't let me go alone."

"You're going? I sent you no places," his sitter objected.

"Yes, but I've got one. Why didn't you, after all I've done for you?"

She beautifully thought of it. "Because I'm so good. No matter," she added, "if Mr. Sherringham comes I won't act."

"Won't you act for me?"

"She'll act like an angel," Mrs. Rooth protested. "She might do, she might be, anything in all the world; but she won't take common pains."

"Of one thing there's no doubt," said Miriam: "that compared with the rest of us—poor passionless creatures—mamma does know what she wants."

"And what's that?" Nick inquired, chalking on.

"She wants everything."

"Never, never—I'm much more humble," retorted the old woman; upon which her daughter requested her to give then to Mr. Dormer, who was a reasonable man and an excellent judge, a general idea of the scope of her desires.

As, however, Mrs. Rooth, sighing and deprecating, was not quick to acquit herself, the girl tried a short cut to the truth with the abrupt demand: "Do you believe for a single moment he'd marry me?"

"Why he has proposed to you—you've told me yourself—a dozen times."

"Proposed what to me?" Miriam rang out. "I've told you *that* neither a dozen times nor once, because I've never understood. He has made wonderful speeches, but has never been serious."

"You told me he had been in the seventh heaven of devotion, especially that night we went to the foyer of the Français," Mrs. Rooth insisted.

"Do you call the seventh heaven of devotion serious? He's in love with me, *je le veux bien*; he's so poisoned—Mr. Dormer vividly puts it—as to require a strong antidote; but he has never spoken to me as if he really expected me to listen to him, and he's the more of a gentleman from that fact. He knows we haven't a square foot of common ground—that a grasshopper can't set up a house with a fish. So he has taken care to say to me only more than he can possibly mean. That makes it stand just for nothing."

"Did he say more than he can possibly mean when he took formal leave of you yesterday—for ever and ever?" the old woman cried.

On which Nick re-enforced her. "And don't you call that—his taking formal leave—a sacrifice?"

"Oh he took it all back, his sacrifice, before he left the house."

"Then has that no meaning?" demanded Mrs. Rooth.

"None that I can make out," said her daughter.

"Ah I've no patience with you: you can be stupid when you will—you can be even that too!" the poor lady groaned.

"What mamma wishes me to understand and to practise is the particular way to be artful with Mr. Sherringham," said Miriam. "There are doubtless depths of wisdom and virtue in it. But I see only one art—that of being perfectly honest."

"I like to hear you talk—it makes you live, brings you out," Nick contentedly dropped. "And you sit beautifully still. All I want to say is please continue to do so: remain exactly as you are—it's rather important—for the next ten minutes."

"We're washing our dirty linen before you, but it's all right," the girl returned, "because it shows you what sort of people we are, and that's what you need to know. Don't make me vague and arranged and fine in this new view," she continued: "make me characteristic and real; make life, with all its horrid facts and truths, stick out of me. I wish you could put mother in too; make us live there side by side and tell our little story. 'The wonderful actress and her still more wonderful mamma'—don't you think that's an awfully good subject?"

Mrs. Rooth, at this, cried shame on her daughter's wanton humour, professing that she herself would never accept so much from Nick's good nature, and Miriam settled it that at any rate he was some day and in some way to do her mother, *really* do her, and so make her, as one of the funniest persons that ever was, live on through the ages.

"She doesn't believe Mr. Sherringham wants to marry me any more than you do," the girl, taking up her dispute again after a moment, represented to Nick; "but she believes—how indeed can I tell you what she believes?—that I can work it so well, if you understand, that in the fulness of time I shall hold him in a vice. I'm to keep him along for the present, but not to listen to him, for if I listen to him I shall lose him. It's ingenious, it's complicated; but I daresay you follow me."

"Don't move—don't move," said Nick. "Pardon a poor clumsy beginner."

"No, I shall explain quietly. Somehow—here it's *very* complicated and you mustn't lose the thread—I shall be an actress and make a tremendous lot of money, and somehow too (I suppose a little later) I shall become an ambassadress and be the favourite of courts. So you see it will all be delightful. Only I shall have to go very straight. Mamma reminds me of a story I once heard about the mother of a young lady who was in receipt of much civility from the pretender to a crown, which indeed he, and the young lady too, afterwards more or less wore. The old countess watched the course of events and gave her daughter the cleverest advice: '*Tiens bon, ma fille*, and you shall sit upon a throne.' Mamma wishes me to *tenir bon*—she apparently thinks there's a danger I mayn't—so that if I don't sit upon a throne I shall at least parade at the foot of one. And if before that, for ten years, I pile up the money, they'll forgive me the way I've made it. I should hope so, if I've *tenu bon*! Only ten years is a good while to hold out, isn't it? If it isn't Mr. Sherringham it will be some one else. Mr. Sherringham has the great merit of being a bird in the hand. I'm to keep him along, I'm to be still more diplomatic than even he can be."

Mrs. Rooth listened to her daughter with an air of assumed reprobation which melted, before the girl had done, into a diverted, complacent smile—

the gratification of finding herself the proprietress of so much wit and irony and grace. Miriam's account of her mother's views was a scene of comedy, and there was instinctive art in the way she added touch to touch and made point upon point. She was so quiet, to oblige her painter, that only her fine lips moved—all her expression was in their charming utterance. Mrs. Rooth, after the first flutter of a less cynical spirit, consented to be sacrificed to an effect of the really high order she had now been educated to recognise; so that she scarce hesitated, when Miriam had ceased speaking, before she tittered out with the fondest indulgence: '*Comédienne!*' And she seemed to appeal to their companion. "Ain't she fascinating? That's the way she does for you!"

"It's rather cruel, isn't it," said Miriam, "to deprive people of the luxury of calling one an actress as they'd call one a liar? I represent, but I represent truly."

"Mr. Sherringham would marry you to-morrow—there's no question of ten years!" cried Mrs. Rooth with a comicality of plainness.

Miriam smiled at Nick, deprecating his horror of such talk. "Isn't it droll, the way she can't get it out of her head?" Then turning almost coaxingly to the old woman: "*Voyons*, look about you: they don't marry us like that."

"But they do—*cela se voit tous les jours*. Ask Mr. Dormer."

"Oh never! It would be as if I asked him to give us a practical proof."

"I shall never prove anything by marrying any one," Nick said. "For me that question's over."

Miriam rested kind eyes on him. "Dear me, how you must hate me!" And before he had time to reply she went on to her mother: "People marry them to make them leave the stage; which proves exactly what I say."

"Ah they offer them the finest positions," reasoned Mrs. Rooth.

"Do you want me to leave it then?"

"Oh you can manage if you will!"

"The only managing I know anything about is to do my work. If I manage that decently I shall pull through."

"But, dearest, may our work not be of many sorts?"

"I only know one," said Miriam.

At this her mother got up with a sigh. "I see you do wish to drive me into the street."

"Mamma's bewildered—there are so many paths she wants to follow, there are so many bundles of hay. As I told you, she wishes to gobble them all," the girl pursued. Then she added: "Yes, go and take the carriage; take a turn round the Park—you always delight in that—and come back for me in an hour."

"I'm too vexed with you; the air will do me good," said Mrs. Rooth. But before she went she addressed Nick: "I've your assurance that you'll bring him then to-night?"

"Bring Peter? I don't think I shall have to drag him," Nick returned. "But you must do me the justice to remember that if I should resort to force I should do something that's not particularly in my interest—I should be magnanimous."

"We must always be that, mustn't we?" moralised Mrs. Rooth.

"How could it affect your interest?" Miriam asked less abstractedly.

"Yes, as you say," her mother mused at their host, "the question of marriage has ceased to exist for you."

"Mamma goes straight at it!" laughed the girl, getting up while Nick rubbed his canvas before answering. Miriam went to mamma and settled her bonnet and mantle in preparation for her drive, then stood a moment with a filial arm about her and as if waiting for their friend's explanation. This, however, when it came halted visibly.

"Why you said a while ago that if Peter was there you wouldn't act."

"I'll act for *him*," smiled Miriam, inconsequently caressing her mother.

"It doesn't matter whom it's for!" Mrs. Rooth declared sagaciously.

"Take your drive and relax your mind," said the girl, kissing her. "Come for me in an hour; not later—but not sooner." She went with her to the door, bundled her out, closed it behind her and came back to the position she had quitted. "*This* is the peace I want!" she gratefully cried as she settled into it.

<u>XLV</u>

Peter Sherringham said so little during the performance that his companion was struck by his dumbness, especially as Miriam's acting seemed to Nick magnificent. He held his breath while she was on the stage—she gave the whole thing, including the spectator's emotion, such a lift. She had not carried out her fantastic menace of not exerting herself, and, as Mrs. Rooth had said, it little mattered for whom she acted. Nick was conscious in watching her that she went through it all for herself, for the idea that possessed her and that she rendered with extraordinary breadth. She couldn't open the door a part of the way to it and let it simply peep in; if it entered at all it must enter in full procession and occupy the premises in state.

This was what had happened on an occasion which, as the less tormented of our young men felt in his stall, grew larger with each throb of the responsive house; till by the time the play was half over it appeared to stretch out wide arms to the future. Nick had often heard more applause, but had never heard more attention, since they were all charmed and hushed together and success seemed to be sitting down with them. There had been of course plenty of announcement—the newspapers had abounded and the arts of the manager had taken the freest license; but it was easy to feel a fine, universal consensus and to recognise everywhere the light spring of hope. People snatched their eyes from the stage an instant to look at each other, all eager to hand on the torch passed to them by the actress over the footlights. It was a part of the impression that she was now only showing to the full, for this time she had verse to deal with and she made it unexpectedly exquisite. She was beauty, melody, truth; she was passion and persuasion and tenderness. She caught up the obstreperous play in soothing, entwining arms and, seeming to tread the air in the flutter of her robe, carried it into the high places of poetry, of art, of style. And she had such tones of nature, such concealments of art, such effusions of life, that the whole scene glowed with the colour she communicated, and the house, pervaded with rosy fire, glowed back at the scene. Nick looked round in the intervals; he felt excited and flushed—the night had turned to a feast of fraternity and he expected to see people embrace each other. The crowd, the agitation, the triumph, the surprise, the signals and rumours, the heated air, his associates, near him, pointing out other figures who presumably were celebrated but whom he had never heard of, all amused him and banished every impulse to question or to compare. Miriam was as happy as some right sensation—she would have fed the memory with deep draughts.

One of the things that amused him or at least helped to fill his attention was Peter's attitude, which apparently didn't exclude criticism—rather indeed mainly implied it. This admirer never took his eyes off the actress, but he made no remark about her and never stirred out of his chair. Nick had had from the first a plan of going round to speak to her, but as his companion evidently meant not to move he scrupled at being more forward. During their brief dinner together—they were determined not to be late—Peter had been silent, quite recklessly grave, but also, his kinsman judged, full of the wish to make it clear he was calm. In his seat he was calmer than ever and had an air even of trying to suggest that his attendance, preoccupied as he was with deeper solemnities, was more or less mechanical, the result of a conception of duty, a habit of courtesy. When during a scene in the second act—a scene from which Miriam was absent—Nick observed to him that one might judge from his reserve that he wasn't pleased he replied after a moment: "I've been looking for her mistakes." And when Nick made answer to this that he certainly wouldn't find them he said again in an odd tone: "No, I shan't find them—I shan't find them." It might have seemed that since the girl's performance was a dazzling success he regarded his evening as rather a failure.

After the third act Nick said candidly: "My dear fellow, how can you sit here? Aren't you going to speak to her?"

To which Peter replied inscrutably: "Lord, no, never again. I bade her good-bye yesterday. She knows what I think of her form. It's very good, but she carries it a little too far. Besides, she didn't want me to come, and it's therefore more discreet to keep away from her."

"Surely it isn't an hour for discretion!" Nick cried. "Excuse me at any rate for five minutes."

He went behind and reappeared only as the curtain was rising on the fourth act; and in the interval between the fourth and the fifth he went again for a shorter time. Peter was personally detached, but he consented to listen to his companion's vivid account of the state of things on the stage, where the elation of victory had lighted up the place. The strain was over, the ship in port—they were all wiping their faces and grinning. Miriam—yes, positively—was grinning too, and she hadn't asked a question about Peter nor sent him a message. They were kissing all round and dancing for joy. They were on the eve, worse luck, of a tremendous run. Peter groaned irrepressibly for this; it was, save for a slight sign a moment later, the only vibration caused in him by his cousin's report. There was but one voice of regret that they hadn't put on the piece earlier, as the end of the season would interrupt the run. There was but one voice too about the fourth act—it was believed all London would rush to see the fourth act. The crowd about her was a dozen deep and Miriam in the midst of it all charming; she was receiving in the ugly place after the fashion of royalty, almost as hedged with the famous "divinity," yet with a smile and a word for each. She was really like a young queen on her accession. When she saw him, Nick, she had kissed her hand to him over the heads of the courtiers. Nick's artless comment on this was that she had such pretty manners. It made Peter laugh—apparently at his friend's conception of the manners of a young queen. Mrs. Rooth, with a dozen shawls on her arm, was as red as the kitchen-fire, but you couldn't tell if Miriam were red or pale: she was so cleverly, finely made up—perhaps a little too much. Dashwood of course was greatly to the fore, but you hadn't to mention his own performance to him: he took it all handsomely and wouldn't hear of anything but that *her* fortune was made. He didn't say much indeed, but evidently had ideas about her fortune; he nodded significant things and whistled inimitable sounds—"Heuh, heuh!" He was perfectly satisfied; moreover, he looked further ahead than any one.

It was on coming back to his place after the fourth act that Nick put in, for his companion's benefit, most of these touches in his sketch of the situation. If Peter had continued to look for Miriam's mistakes he hadn't yet found them: the fourth act, bristling with dangers, putting a premium on every sort of cheap effect, had rounded itself without a flaw. Sitting there alone while Nick was away he had leisure to meditate on the wonder of this— on the art with which the girl had separated passion from violence, filling the whole place and never screaming; for it had often seemed to him in London of old that the yell of theatrical emotion rang through the shrinking night like the voice of the Sunday newsboy. Miriam had never been more present to him than at this hour; but she was inextricably transmuted—present essentially as the romantic heroine she represented. His state of mind was of the strangest and he was conscious of its strangeness, just as he was conscious in his very person of a lapse of resistance which likened itself absurdly to liberation. He felt weak at the same time that he felt inspired, and he felt inspired at the same time that he knew, or believed he knew, that his face was a blank. He saw things as a shining confusion, and yet somehow something monstrously definite kept surging out of them. Miriam was a beautiful, actual, fictive, impossible young woman of a past age, an undiscoverable country, who spoke in blank verse and overflowed with metaphor, who was exalted and heroic beyond all human convenience and who yet was irresistibly real and related to one's own affairs. But that reality was a part of her spectator's joy, and she was not changed back to the common by his perception of the magnificent trick of art with which it was connected. Before his kinsman rejoined him Peter, taking a visiting-card from his pocket, had written on it in pencil a few words in a foreign tongue; but as at that moment he saw Nick coming in he immediately put it out of view.

The last thing before the curtain rose on the fifth act that young man mentioned his having brought a message from Basil Dashwood, who hoped they both, on leaving the theatre, would come to supper with him in company with Miriam and her mother and several others: he had prepared a little informal banquet in honour of so famous a night. At this, while the curtain was about to rise, Peter immediately took out his card again and added something—he wrote the finest small hand you could see. Nick asked him what he was doing, and he waited but an instant. "It's a word to say I can't come."

"To Dashwood? Oh I shall go," said Nick.

"Well, I hope you'll enjoy it!" his companion replied in a tone which came back to him afterwards.

When the curtain fell on the last act the people stayed, standing up in their places for acclamation. The applause shook the house—the recall became a clamour, the relief from a long tension. This was in any performance a moment Peter detested, but he stood for an instant beside Nick, who clapped, to his cousin's diplomatic sense, after the fashion of a school-boy at the pantomime. There was a veritable roar while the curtain drew back at the side most removed from our pair. Peter could see Basil Dashwood holding it, making a passage for the male "juvenile lead," who had Miriam in tow. Nick redoubled his efforts; heard the plaudits swell; saw the bows of the leading gentleman, who was hot and fat; saw Miriam, personally conducted and closer to the footlights, grow brighter and bigger and more swaying; and then became aware that his own comrade had with extreme agility slipped out of the stalls. Nick had already lost sight of him—he had apparently taken but a minute to escape from the house; and wondered at his quitting him without a farewell if he was to leave England on the morrow and they were not to meet at the hospitable Dashwood's. He wondered even what Peter was "up to," since, as he had assured him, there was no question of his going round to Miriam. He waited to see this young lady reappear three times, dragging Dashwood behind her at the second with a friendly arm, to whom, in turn, was hooked Miss Fanny Rover, the actress entrusted in the piece with the inevitable comic relief. He went out slowly with the crowd and at the door looked again for Peter, who struck him as deficient for once in finish. He couldn't know that in another direction and while he was helping the house to "rise" at its heroine, his kinsman had been particularly explicit.

On reaching the lobby Peter had pounced on a small boy in buttons, who seemed superfluously connected with a desolate refreshment-room and, from the tips of his toes, was peeping at the stage through the glazed hole in the door of a box. Into one of the child's hands he thrust the card he had drawn again from his waistcoat and into the other the largest silver coin he could find in the same receptacle, while he bent over him with words of adjuration—words the little page tried to help himself to apprehend by instantly attempting to peruse the other words written on the card.

"That's no use—it's Italian," said Peter; "only carry it round to Miss Rooth without a minute's delay. Place it in her hand and she'll give you some object—a bracelet, a glove, or a flower—to bring me back as a sign that she has received it. I shall be outside; bring me there what she gives you and you shall have another shilling—only fly!"

His small messenger sounded him a moment with the sharp face of London wage-earning, and still more of London tip-earning, infancy, and vanished as swiftly as a slave of the Arabian Nights. While he waited in the lobby the audience began to pour out, and before the urchin had come back to him he was clapped on the shoulder by Nick.

"I'm glad I haven't lost you, but why didn't you stay to give her a hand?"

"Give her a hand? I hated it."

"My dear man, I don't follow you," Nick said. "If you won't come to Dashwood's supper I fear our ways don't lie together."

"Thank him very much; say I've to get up at an unnatural hour." To this Peter added: "I think I ought to tell you she may not be there."

"Miss Rooth? Why it's all *for* her."

"I'm waiting for a word from her—she may change her mind."

Nick showed his interest. "For you? What then have you proposed?"

"I've proposed marriage," said Peter in a strange voice.

"I say—!" Nick broke out; and at the same moment Peter's messenger squeezed through the press and stood before him.

"She has given me nothing, sir," the boy announced; "but she says I'm to say 'All right!'"

Nick's stare widened. "You've proposed through *him*?"

"Aye, and she accepts. Good-night!"—on which, turning away, Peter bounded into a hansom. He said something to the driver through the roof, and Nick's eyes followed the cab as it started off. This young man was mystified, was even amused; especially when the youth in buttons, planted there and wondering too, brought forth:

"Please sir, he told me he'd give me a shilling and he've forgot it."

"Oh I can't pay you for *that*!" Nick laughed. But he fished out a dole, though he was vexed at the injury to the supper.

XLVI

Peter meanwhile rolled away through the summer night to Saint John's Wood. He had put the pressure of strong words on his young friend, entreating her to drive home immediately, return there without any one, without even her mother. He wished to see her alone and for a purpose he would fully and satisfactorily explain—couldn't she trust him? He besought her to remember his own situation and throw over her supper, throw over everything. He would wait for her with unspeakable impatience in Balaklava Place.

He did so, when he got there, but it had taken half an hour. Interminable seemed his lonely vigil in Miss Lumley's drawing-room, where the character of the original proprietress came out to him more than ever before in a kind of afterglow of old sociabilities, a vulgar, ghostly reference. The numerous candles had been lighted for him, and Mrs. Rooth's familiar fictions lay about; but his nerves forbade him the solace of a chair and a book. He walked up and down, thinking and listening, and as the long window, the balmy air permitting, stood open to the garden, he passed several times in and out. A carriage appeared to stop at the gate—then there was nothing; he heard the rare rattle of wheels and the far-off hum of London. His impatience was overwrought, and though he knew this it persisted; it would have been no easy matter for Miriam to break away from the flock of her felicitators. Still less simple was it doubtless for her to leave poor Dashwood with his supper on his hands. Perhaps she would bring Dashwood with her, bring him to time her; she was capable of playing him—that is, of playing Her Majesty's new representative to the small far-off State, or even of playing them both—that trick. Perhaps the little wretch in buttons—Peter remembered now the neglected shilling—only pretending to go round with his card, had come back with an invented answer. But how could he know, since presumably he couldn't read Italian, that his answer would fit the message? Peter was sorry now that he himself had not gone round, not snatched Miriam bodily away, made sure of her and of what he wanted of her.

When forty minutes had elapsed he regarded it as proved that she wouldn't come, and, asking himself what he should do, determined to drive off again and seize her at her comrade's feast. Then he remembered how Nick had mentioned that this entertainment was not to be held at the young actor's lodgings but at some tavern or restaurant the name of which he had not heeded. Suddenly, however, Peter became aware with joy that this name didn't matter, for there was something at the garden door at last. He rushed out before she had had time to ring, and saw as she stepped from the carriage that she was alone. Now that she was there, that he had this evidence she had listened to him and trusted him, all his impatience and bitterness gave way and a flood of pleading tenderness took their place in the first words he spoke to her. It was far "dearer" of her than he had any right to dream, but she was the best and kindest creature—this showed it—as well as the most wonderful. He was really not off his head with his contradictory ways; no, before heaven he wasn't, and he would explain, he would make everything clear. Everything was changed.

She stopped short in the little dusky garden, looking at him in the light of the open window. Then she called back to the coachman—they had left the garden door open—"Wait for me, mind; I shall want you again."

"What's the matter—won't you stay?" Peter asked. "Are you going out again at this absurd hour? I won't hurt you," he gently urged. And he went back and closed the garden door. He wanted to say to the coachman, "It's no matter—please drive away." At the same time he wouldn't for the world have done anything offensive to her.

"I've come because I thought it better to-night, as things have turned out, to do the thing you ask me, whatever it may be," she had already begun. "That's probably what you calculated I would think, eh? What this evening has been you've seen, and I must allow that your hand's in it. That you know for yourself—that you doubtless felt as you sat there. But I confess I don't imagine what you want of me here now," she added. She had remained standing in the path.

Peter felt the irony of her "now" and how it made a fool of him, but he had been prepared for this and for much worse. He had begged her not to think him a fool, but in truth at present he cared little if she did. Very likely he was—in spite of his plea that everything was changed: he cared little even himself. However, he spoke in the tone of intense reason and of the fullest disposition to satisfy her. This lucidity only took still more from the dignity of his change of front: his separation from her the day before had had such pretensions to being lucid. But the explanation and the justification were in the very fact, the fact that had complete possession of him. He named it when he replied to her: "I've simply overrated my strength."

"Oh I knew—I knew! That's why I entreated you not to come!" Miriam groaned. She turned away lamenting, and for a moment he thought she would retreat to her carriage. But he passed his hand into her arm, to draw her forward, and after an instant felt her yield.

"The fact is we must have this thing out," he said. Then he added as he made her go into the house, bending over her, "The failure of my strength— that was just the reason of my coming."

She broke into her laugh at these words, as she entered the drawing-room, and it made them sound pompous in their false wisdom. She flung off, as a good-natured tribute to the image of their having the thing out, a white shawl that had been wrapped round her. She was still painted and bedizened, in the splendid dress of her climax, so that she seemed protected and alienated by the character she had been acting. "Whatever it is you want—when I understand—you'll be very brief, won't you? Do you know I've given up a charming supper for you? Mamma has gone there. I've promised to go back to them."

"You're an angel not to have let her come with you. I'm sure she wanted to," Peter made reply.

"Oh she's all right, but she's nervous." Then the girl added: "Couldn't she keep you away after all?"

"Whom are you talking about?" Biddy Dormer was as absent from his mind as if she had never existed.

"The charming thing you were with this morning. Is she so afraid of obliging me? Oh she'd be so good for you!"

"Don't speak of that," Peter gravely said. "I was in perfect good faith yesterday when I took leave of you. I was—I was. But I can't—I can't: you're too unutterably dear to me."

"Oh don't—*please* don't!" Miriam wailed at this. She stood before the fireless chimney-piece with one of her hands on it. "If it's only to say that, don't you know, what's the use?"

"It isn't only to say that. I've a plan, a perfect plan: the whole thing lies clear before me."

"And what's the whole thing?"

He had to make an effort. "You say your mother's nervous. Ah if you knew how nervous I am!"

"Well, I'm not. Go on."

"Give it up—give it up!" Peter stammered.

"Give it up?" She fixed him like a mild Medusa.

"I'll marry you to-morrow if you'll renounce; and in return for the sacrifice you make for me I'll do more for you than ever was done for a woman before."

"Renounce after to-night? Do you call that a plan?" she asked. "Those are old words and very foolish ones—you wanted something of that sort a year ago."

"Oh I fluttered round the idea at that time; we were talking in the air. I didn't really believe I could make you see it then, and certainly you didn't see it. My own future, moreover, wasn't definite to me. I didn't know what I could offer you. But these last months have made a difference—I do know now. Now what I say is deliberate—It's deeply meditated. I simply can't live without you, and I hold that together we may do great things."

She seemed to wonder. "What sort of things?"

"The things of my profession, of my life, the things one does for one's country, the responsibility and the honour of great affairs; deeply fascinating when one's immersed in them, and more exciting really—put them even at that—than the excitements of the theatre. Care for me only a little and you'll see what they are, they'll take hold of you. Believe me, believe me," Peter pleaded; "every fibre of my being trembles in what I say to you."

"You admitted yesterday it wouldn't do," she made answer. "Where were the fibres of your being then?"

"They throbbed in me even more than now, and I was trying, like an ass, not to feel them. Where was this evening yesterday—where were the maddening hours I've just spent? Ah you're the perfection of perfections, and as I sat there to-night you taught me what I really want."

"The perfection of perfections?" the girl echoed with the strangest smile.

"I needn't try to tell you: you must have felt to-night with such rapture what you are, what you can do. How can I give that up?" he piteously went on.

"How can *I*, my poor friend? I like your plans and your responsibilities and your great affairs, as you call them. *Voyons*, they're infantile. I've just shown that I'm a perfection of perfections: therefore it's just the moment to 'renounce,' as you gracefully say? Oh I was sure, I was sure!" And Miriam paused, resting eyes at once lighted and troubled on him as in the effort to think of some arrangement that would help him out of his absurdity. "I was sure, I mean, that if you did come your poor, dear, doting brain would be quite confused," she presently pursued. "I can't be a muff in public just for you, *pourtant*. Dear me, why do you like us so much?"

"Like you? I loathe you!"

"*Je le vois parbleu bien!*" she lightly returned. "I mean why do you feel us, judge us, understand us so well? I please you because you see, because you know; and then for that very reason of my pleasing you must adapt me to your convenience, you must take me over, as they say. You admire me as an artist and therefore want to put me into a box in which the artist will breathe her last. Ah be reasonable; you must let her live!"

"Let her live? As if I could prevent her living!" Peter cried with unmistakable conviction. "Even if I did wish how could I prevent a spirit like yours from expressing itself? Don't talk about my putting you in a box, for, dearest child, I'm taking you out of one," he all persuasively explained. "The artist is irrepressible, eternal; she'll be in everything you are and in everything you do, and you'll go about with her triumphantly exerting your powers, charming the world, carrying everything before you."

Miriam's colour rose, through all her artificial surfaces, at this all but convincing appeal, and she asked whimsically: "Shall you like that?"

"Like my wife to be the most brilliant woman in Europe? I think I can do with it."

"Aren't you afraid of me?"

"Not a bit."

"Bravely said. How little you know me after all!" sighed the girl.

"I tell the truth," Peter ardently went on; "and you must do me the justice to admit that I've taken the time to dig deep into my feelings. I'm not an infatuated boy; I've lived, I've had experience, I've observed; in short I know what I mean and what I want. It isn't a thing to reason about; it's simply a need that consumes me. I've put it on starvation diet, but that's no use—really, it's no use, Miriam," the young man declared with a ring that spoke enough of his sincerity. "It is no question of my trusting you; it's simply a question of your trusting me. You're all right, as I've heard you say yourself; you're frank, spontaneous, generous; you're a magnificent creature. Just quietly marry me and I'll manage you."

"'Manage' me?" The girl's inflexion was droll; it made him change colour.

"I mean I'll give you a larger life than the largest you can get in any other way. The stage is great, no doubt, but the world's greater. It's a bigger theatre than any of those places in the Strand. We'll go in for realities instead of fables, and you'll do them far better than you do the fables."

Miriam had listened attentively, but her face that could so show things showed her despair at his perverted ingenuity. "Pardon my saying it after your delightful tributes to my worth," she returned in a moment, "but I've never listened to anything quite so grandly unreal. You think so well of me that humility itself ought to keep me silent; nevertheless I *must* utter a few shabby words of sense. I'm a magnificent creature on the stage—well and good; it's what I want to be and it's charming to see such evidence that I succeed. But off the stage, woe betide us both, I should lose all my advantages. The fact's so patent that it seems to me I'm very good-natured even to discuss it with you."

"Are you on the stage now, pray? Ah Miriam, if it weren't for the respect I owe you!" her companion wailed.

"If it weren't for that I shouldn't have come here to meet you. My gift is the thing that takes you: could there be a better proof than that it's to-night's display of it that has brought you to this unreason? It's indeed a misfortune that you're so sensitive to our poor arts, since they play such tricks with your power to see things as they are. Without my share of them I should be a dull, empty, third-rate woman, and yet that's the fate you ask me to face and insanely pretend you're ready to face yourself."

"Without it—without it?" Sherringham cried. "Your own sophistry's infinitely worse than mine. I should like to see you without it for the fiftieth part of a second. What I ask you to give up is the dusty boards of the play-house and the flaring footlights, but not the very essence of your being. Your 'gift,' your genius, is yourself, and it's because it's yourself that I yearn for you. If it had been a thing you could leave behind by the easy dodge of stepping off the stage I would never have looked at you a second time. Don't talk to me as if I were a simpleton—with your own false simplifications! You were made to charm and console, to represent beauty and harmony and variety to miserable human beings; and the daily life of man is the theatre for that—not a vulgar shop with a turnstile that's open only once in the twenty-four hours. 'Without it,' verily!" Peter proceeded with a still, deep heat that kept down in a manner his rising scorn and exasperated passion. "Please let me know the first time you're without your face, without your voice, your step, your exquisite spirit, the turn of your head and the wonder of your look!"

Miriam at this moved away from him with a port that resembled what she sometimes showed on the stage when she turned her young back upon the footlights and then after a few steps grandly swept round again. This evolution she performed—it was over in an instant—on the present occasion; even to stopping short with her eyes upon him and her head admirably erect. "Surely it's strange," she said, "the way the other solution never occurs to you."

"The other solution?"

"That *you* should stay on the stage."

"I don't understand you," her friend gloomed.

"Stay on *my* stage. Come off your own."

For a little he said nothing; then: "You mean that if I'll do that you'll have me?"

"I mean that if it were to occur to you to offer me a little sacrifice on your own side it might place the matter in a slightly more attractive light."

"Continue to let you act—as my wife?" he appealed. "Is it a real condition? Am I to understand that those are your terms?"

"I may say so without fear, because you'll never accept them."

"Would you accept them *from* me?" he demanded; "accept the manly, the professional sacrifice, see me throw up my work, my prospects—of course I should have to do that—and simply become your appendage?"

She raised her arms for a prodigious fall. "My dear fellow, you invite me with the best conscience in the world to become yours."

"The cases are not equal. You'd make of me the husband of an actress. I should make of you the wife of an ambassador."

"The husband of an actress, *c'est bientôt dit*, in that tone of scorn! If you're consistent," said Miriam, all lucid and hard, "it ought to be a proud position for you."

"What do you mean, if I'm consistent?"

"Haven't you always insisted on the beauty and interest of our art and the greatness of our mission? Haven't you almost come to blows with poor Gabriel Nash about it? What did all that mean if you won't face the first consequences of your theory? Either it was an enlightened conviction or it was an empty pretence. If you were only talking against time I'm glad to know it," she rolled out with a darkening eye. "The better the cause, it seems to me, the better the deed; and if the theatre *is* important to the 'human spirit,' as you used to say so charmingly, and if into the bargain you've the pull of being so fond of me, I don't see why it should be monstrous of you to give us your services in an intelligent, indirect way. Of course if you're not serious we needn't talk at all; but if you are, with your conception of what the actor can do, why is it so base to come to the actor's aid, taking one devotion with another? If I'm so fine I'm worth looking after a bit, and the place where I'm finest is the place to look after me!"

He had a long pause again, taking her in as it seemed to him he had never done. "You were never finer than at this minute, in the deepest domesticity

527

of private life. I've no conception whatever of what the actor can do, and no theory whatever about the importance of the theatre. Any infatuation of that sort has completely dropped from me, and for all I care the theatre may go to the dogs—which I judge it altogether probably will!"

"You're dishonest, you're ungrateful, you're false!" Miriam flashed. "It was the theatre brought you here—if it hadn't been for the theatre I never would have looked at you. It was in the name of the theatre you first made love to me; it's to the theatre you owe every advantage that, so far as I'm concerned, you possess."

"I seem to possess a great many!" poor Peter derisively groaned.

"You might avail yourself better of those you have! You make me angry, but I want to be fair," said the shining creature, "and I can't be unless you are. You're not fair, nor candid, nor honourable, when you swallow your words and abjure your faith, when you throw over old friends and old memories for a selfish purpose."

"'Selfish purpose' is, in your own convenient idiom, *bientôt dit*," Peter promptly answered. "I suppose you consider that if I truly esteemed you I should be ashamed to deprive the world of the light of your genius. Perhaps my esteem isn't of the right quality—there are different kinds, aren't there? At any rate I've explained to you that I propose to deprive the world of nothing at all. You shall be celebrated, *allez!*"

"Vain words, vain words, my dear!" and she turned off again in her impatience. "I know of course," she added quickly, "that to befool yourself with such twaddle you must be pretty bad."

"Yes, I'm pretty bad," he admitted, looking at her dismally. "What do you do with the declaration you made me the other day—the day I found my cousin here—that you'd take me if I should come to you as one who had risen high?"

Miriam thought of it. "I remember—the chaff about the honours, the orders, the stars and garters. My poor foolish friend, don't be so painfully literal. Don't you know a joke when you see it? It was to worry your cousin, wasn't it? But it didn't in the least succeed."

"Why should you wish to worry my cousin?"

"Because he's so provoking!" she instantly answered; after which she laughed as if for her falling too simply into the trap he had laid. "Surely, at all events, I had my freedom no less than I have it now. Pray what explanations should I have owed you and in what fear of you should I have gone? However, that has nothing to do with it. Say I did tell you that we might arrange it on the day you should come to me covered with glory in the shape of little tinkling medals: why should you anticipate that transaction by so many years and knock me down such a long time in advance? Where's the glory, please, and where are the medals?"

"Dearest girl, am I not going to strange parts—a capital promotion—next month," he insistently demanded, "and can't you trust me enough to believe I speak with a real appreciation of the facts (that I'm not lying to you in short) when I tell you I've my foot in the stirrup? The glory's dawning. I'm all right too."

"What you propose to me, then, is to accompany you *tout bonnement* to your new post. What you propose to me is to pack up and start?"

"You put it in a nutshell." But Peter's smile was strained.

"You're touching—it has its charm. But you can't get anything in any of the Americas, you know. I'm assured there are no medals to be picked up in those parts—which are therefore 'strange' indeed. That's why the diplomatic body hate them all."

"They're on the way, they're on the way!"—he could only feverishly hammer. "The people here don't keep us long in disagreeable places unless we want to stay. There's one thing you can get anywhere if you've ability, and nowhere if you've not, and in the disagreeable places generally more than in the others; and that—since it's the element of the question we're discussing—is simply success. It's odious to be put on one's swagger, but I protest against being treated as if I had nothing to offer—to offer a person who has such glories of her own. I'm not a little presumptuous ass; I'm a man accomplished and determined, and the omens are on my side." Peter faltered a moment and then with a queer expression went on: "Remember, after all, that, strictly speaking, your glories are also still in the future." An exclamation at these words burst from Miriam's lips, but her companion resumed quickly: "Ask my official superiors, ask any of my colleagues, if they consider I've nothing to offer."

He had an idea as he ceased speaking that she was on the point of breaking out with some strong word of resentment at his allusion to the contingent nature of her prospects. But it only deepened his wound to hear her say with extraordinary mildness: "It's perfectly true that my glories are still to come, that I may fizzle out and that my little success of to-day is perhaps a mere flash in the pan. Stranger things have been—something of that sort happens every day. But don't we talk too much of that part of it?" she asked with a weary patience that was noble in its effect. "Surely it's vulgar to think only of the noise one's going to make—especially when one remembers how utterly *bêtes* most of the people will be among whom one makes it. It isn't to my possible glories I cling; it's simply to my idea, even if it's destined to betray me and sink me. I like it better than anything else—a thousand times better (I'm sorry to have to put it in such a way) than tossing up my head as the fine lady of a little coterie."

"A little coterie? I don't know what you're talking about!"—for this at least Peter could fight.

"A big coterie, then! It's only that at the best. A nasty, prim, 'official' woman who's perched on her little local pedestal and thinks she's a queen for ever because she's ridiculous for an hour! Oh you needn't tell me, I've seen them abroad—the dreariest females—and could imitate them here. I could do one for you on the spot if I weren't so tired. It's scarcely worth mentioning perhaps all this while—but I'm ready to drop." She picked up the white mantle she had tossed off, flinging it round her with her usual amplitude of gesture. "They're waiting for me and I confess I'm hungry. If I don't hurry they'll eat up all the nice things. Don't say I haven't been obliging, and come back when you're better. Good-night."

530

"I quite agree with you that we've talked too much about the vulgar side of our question," Peter returned, walking round to get between her and the French window by which she apparently had a view of leaving the room. "That's because I've wanted to bribe you. Bribery's almost always vulgar."

"Yes, you should do better. *Merci*! There's a cab: some of them have come for me. I must go," she added, listening for a sound that reached her from the road.

Peter listened too, making out no cab. "Believe me, it isn't wise to turn your back on such an affection as mine and on such a confidence," he broke out again, speaking almost in a warning tone—there was a touch of superior sternness in it, as of a rebuke for real folly, but it was meant to be tender—and stopping her within a few feet of the window. "Such things are the most precious that life has to give us," he added all but didactically.

She had listened once more for a little; then she appeared to give up the idea of the cab. The reader need hardly be told that at this stage of her youthful history the right way for her lover to take her wouldn't have been to picture himself as acting for her highest good. "I like your calling the feeling with which I inspire you confidence," she presently said; and the deep note of the few words had something of the distant mutter of thunder.

"What is it, then, when I offer you everything I have, everything I am, everything I shall ever be?"

She seemed to measure him as for the possible success of an attempt to pass him. But she remained where she was. "I'm sorry for you, yes, but I'm also rather ashamed."

"Ashamed of *me*?"

"A brave offer to see me through—that's what I should call confidence. You say to-day that you hate the theatre—and do you know what has made you do it? The fact that it has too large a place in your mind to let you disown it and throw it over with a good conscience. It has a deep fascination for you, and yet you're not strong enough to do so enlightened and public a thing as take up with it in my person. You're ashamed of yourself for that, as all your constant high claims for it are on record; so you blaspheme against it to try and cover your retreat and your treachery and straighten out your personal situation. But it won't do, dear Mr. Sherringham—it won't do at all," Miriam proceeded with a triumphant, almost judicial lucidity which made her companion stare; "you haven't the smallest excuse of stupidity, and your perversity is no excuse whatever. Leave her alone altogether—a poor girl who's making her way—or else come frankly to help her, to give her the benefit of your wisdom. Don't lock her up for life under the pretence of doing her good. What does one most good is to see a little honesty. You're the best judge, the best critic, the best observer, the best *believer*, that I've ever come across: you're committed to it by everything you've said to me for a twelvemonth, by the whole turn of your mind, by the way you've followed us up, all of us, from far back. If an art's noble and beneficent one shouldn't be afraid to offer it one's arm. Your cousin isn't: he can make sacrifices."

"My cousin?" Peter amazedly echoed. "Why, wasn't it only the other day you were throwing his sacrifices in his teeth?"

Under this imputation on her straightness Miriam flinched but for an instant. "I did that to worry *you*," she smiled.

"Why should you wish to worry me if you care so little about me?"

"Care little about you? Haven't I told you often, didn't I tell you yesterday, how much I care? Ain't I showing it now by spending half the night here with you—giving myself away to all those cynics—taking all this trouble to persuade you to hold up your head and have the courage of your opinions?"

"You invent my opinions for your convenience," said Peter all undaunted. "As long ago as the night I introduced you, in Paris, to Mademoiselle Voisin, you accused me of looking down on those who practise your art. I remember how you came down on me because I didn't take your friend Dashwood seriously enough. Perhaps I didn't; but if already at that time I was so wide of the mark you can scarcely accuse me of treachery now."

"I don't remember, but I daresay you're right," Miriam coldly meditated. "What I accused you of then was probably simply what I reproach you with now—the germ at least of your deplorable weakness. You consider that we do awfully valuable work, and yet you wouldn't for the world let people suppose you really take our side. If your position was even at that time so false, so much the worse for you, that's all. Oh it's refreshing," his formidable friend exclaimed after a pause during which Peter seemed to himself to taste the full bitterness of despair, so baffled and cheapened he intimately felt—"oh it's refreshing to see a man burn his ships in a cause that appeals to him, give up something precious for it and break with horrid timidities and snobberies! It's the most beautiful sight in the world."

Poor Peter, sore as he was, and with the cold breath of failure in his face, nevertheless burst out laughing at this fine irony. "You're magnificent, you give me at this moment the finest possible illustration of what you mean by burning one's ships. Verily, verily there's no one like you: talk of timidity, talk of refreshment! If I had any talent for it I'd go on the stage to-morrow, so as to spend my life with you the better."

"If you'll do that I'll be your wife the day after your first appearance. That would be really respectable," Miriam said.

"Unfortunately I've no talent."

"That would only make it the more respectable."

"You're just like poor Nick," Peter returned—"you've taken to imitating Gabriel Nash. Don't you see that it's only if it were a question of my going on the stage myself that there would be a certain fitness in your contrasting me invidiously with Nick and in my giving up one career for another? But simply to stand in the wing and hold your shawl and your smelling-bottle—!" he concluded mournfully, as if he had ceased to debate.

"Holding my shawl and my smelling-bottle is a mere detail, representing a very small part of the whole precious service, the protection and encouragement, for which a woman in my position might be indebted to a man interested in her work and as accomplished and determined as you very justly describe yourself."

"And would it be your idea that such a man should live on the money earned by an exhibition of the person of his still more accomplished and still more determined wife?"

"Why not if they work together—if there's something of his spirit and his support in everything she does?" Miriam demanded. "*Je vous attendais* with the famous 'person'; of course that's the great stick they beat us with. Yes, we show it for money, those of us who have anything decent to show, and some no doubt who haven't, which is the real scandal. What will you have? It's only the envelope of the idea, it's only our machinery, which ought to be conceded to us; and in proportion as the idea takes hold of us do we become unconscious of the clumsy body. Poor old 'person'—if you knew what *we* think of it! If you don't forget it that's your own affair: it shows you're dense before the idea."

"That *I'm* dense?"—and Peter appealed to their lamplit solitude, the favouring, intimate night that only witnessed his defeat, as if this outrage had been all that was wanting.

"I mean the public is—the public who pays us. After all, they expect us to look at *them* too, who are not half so well worth it. If you should see some of the creatures who have the face to plant themselves there in the stalls before one for three mortal hours! I daresay it would be simpler to have no bodies, but we're all in the same box, and it would be a great injustice to the idea, and we're all showing ourselves all the while; only some of us are not worth paying."

"You're extraordinarily droll, but somehow I can't laugh at you," he said, his handsome face drawn by his pain to a contraction sufficiently attesting the fact. "Do you remember the second time I ever saw you—the day you recited at my place?" he abruptly asked; a good deal as if he were taking from his quiver an arrow which, if it was the last, was also one of the sharpest.

"Perfectly, and what an idiot I was, though it was only yesterday!"

"You expressed to me then a deep detestation of the sort of self-exposure to which the profession you were taking up would commit you. If you compared yourself to a contortionist at a country fair I'm only taking my cue from you."

534

"I don't know what I may have said then," replied Miriam, whose steady flight was not arrested by this ineffectual bolt; "I was no doubt already wonderful for talking of things I know nothing about. I was only on the brink of the stream and I perhaps thought the water colder than it is. One warms it a bit one's self when once one's in. Of course I'm a contortionist and of course there's a hateful side, but don't you see how that very fact puts a price on every compensation, on the help of those who are ready to insist on the *other* side, the grand one, and especially on the sympathy of the person who's ready to insist most and to keep before us the great thing, the element that makes up for everything?"

"The element—?" Peter questioned with a vagueness that was pardonably exaggerated. "Do you mean your success?"

"I mean what you've so often been eloquent about," she returned with an indulgent shrug—"the way we simply stir people's souls. Ah there's where life can help us," she broke out with a change of tone, "there's where human relations and affections can help us; love and faith and joy and suffering and experience—I don't know what to call 'em! They suggest things, they light them up and sanctify them, as you may say; they make them appear worth doing." She became radiant a while, as if with a splendid vision; then melting into still another accent, which seemed all nature and harmony and charity, she proceeded: "I must tell you that in the matter of what we can do for each other I have a tremendously high ideal. I go in for closeness of union, for identity of interest. A true marriage, as they call it, must do one a lot of good!"

He stood there looking at her for a time during which her eyes sustained his penetration without a relenting gleam, some lapse of cruelty or of paradox. But with a passionate, inarticulate sound he turned away, to remain, on the edge of the window, his hands in his pockets, gazing defeatedly, doggedly, into the featureless night, into the little black garden which had nothing to give him but a familiar smell of damp. The warm darkness had no relief for him, and Miriam's histrionic hardness flung him back against a fifth-rate world, against a bedimmed, star-punctured nature which had no consolation—the bleared, irresponsive eyes of the London firmament. For the brief space of his glaring at these things he dumbly and helplessly raged. What he wanted was something that was not in *that* thick prospect. What was the meaning of this sudden, offensive importunity of "art," this senseless, mocking catch, like some irritating chorus of conspirators in a bad opera, in which her voice was so incongruously conjoined with Nick's and in which Biddy's sweet little pipe had not scrupled still more bewilderingly to mingle? Art might yield to damnation: what commission after all had he ever given it to better him or bother him? If the pointless groan in which Peter exhaled a part of his humiliation had been translated into words, these words would have been as heavily charged with a genuine British mistrust of the uncanny principle as if the poor fellow speaking them had never quitted his island. Several acquired perceptions had struck a deep root in him, but an immemorial, compact formation lay deeper still. He tried at the present hour to rest on it spiritually, but found it inelastic; and at the very moment when most conscious of this absence of the rebound or of any tolerable ease he felt his vision solicited by an object which, as he immediately guessed, could only add to the complication of things.

An undefined shape hovered before him in the garden, halfway between the gate and the house; it remained outside of the broad shaft of lamplight projected from the window. It wavered for a moment after it had become aware of his observation and then whisked round the corner of the lodge. This characteristic movement so effectually dispelled the mystery—it could only be Mrs. Rooth who resorted to such conspicuous secrecies—that, to feel the game up and his interview over, he had no need to see the figure reappear on second thoughts and dodge about in the dusk with a sportive, vexatious vagueness. Evidently Miriam's warning of a few minutes before had been founded: a cab had deposited her anxious mother at the garden door. Mrs. Rooth had entered with precautions; she had approached the house and retreated; she had effaced herself—had peered and waited and listened. Maternal solicitude and muddled calculations had drawn her from a feast as yet too imperfectly commemorative. The heroine of the occasion of course had been intolerably missed, so that the old woman had both obliged the company and quieted her own nerves by jumping insistently into a hansom and rattling up to Saint John's Wood to reclaim the absentee. But if she had wished to be in time she had also desired not to be impertinent, and would have been still more embarrassed to say what she aspired to promote than to phrase what she had proposed to hinder. She wanted to abstain tastefully, to interfere felicitously, and, more generally and justifiably—the small hours having come—to see what her young charges were "up to." She would probably have gathered that they were quarrelling, and she appeared now to be motioning to Peter to know if it were over. He took no notice of her signals, if signals they were; he only felt that before he made way for the poor, odious lady there was one small spark he might strike from Miriam's flint.

Without letting her guess that her mother was on the premises he turned again to his companion, half-expecting she would have taken her chance to regard their discussion as more than terminated and by the other egress flit away from him in silence. But she was still there; she was in the act of approaching him with a manifest intention of kindness, and she looked indeed, to his surprise, like an angel of mercy.

"Don't let us part so harshly," she said—"with your trying to make me feel as if I were merely disobliging. It's no use talking—we only hurt each other. Let us hold our tongues like decent people and go about our business. It isn't as if you hadn't any cure—when you've such a capital one. Try it, try it, my dear friend—you'll see! I wish you the highest promotion and the quickest—every success and every reward. When you've got them all, some day, and I've become a great swell too, we'll meet on that solid basis and you'll be glad I've been dreadful now."

"Surely before I leave you I've a right to ask you this," he answered, holding fast in both his own the cool hand of farewell she had chosen finally to torment him with. "Are you ready to follow up by a definite promise your implied assurance that I've a remedy?"

"A definite promise?" Miriam benignly gazed—it was the perfection of indirectness. "I don't 'imply' that you've a remedy. I declare it on the house-tops. That delightful girl—"

"I'm not talking of any delightful girl but you!" he broke in with a voice that, as he afterwards learned, struck Mrs. Rooth's ears in the garden with affright. "I simply hold you, under pain of being convicted of the grossest prevarication, to the strict sense of what you said ten minutes ago."

"Ah I've said so many things! One has to do that to get rid of you. You rather hurt my hand," she added—and jerked it away in a manner showing that if she was an angel of mercy her mercy was partly for herself.

"As I understand you, then, I may have some hope if I do renounce my profession?" Peter pursued. "If I break with everything, my prospects, my studies, my training, my emoluments, my past and my future, the service of my country and the ambition of my life, and engage to take up instead the business of watching your interests so far as I may learn how and ministering to your triumphs so far as may in me lie—if after further reflexion I decide to go through these preliminaries, have I your word that I may definitely look to you to reward me with your precious hand?"

"I don't think you've any right to put the question to me now," she returned with a promptitude partly produced perhaps by the clear-cut form his solemn speech had given—there was a charm in the sound of it—to each item of his enumeration. "The case is so very contingent, so dependent on what you ingeniously call your further reflexion. While you really reserve everything you ask me to commit myself. If it's a question of further reflexion why did you drag me up here? And then," she added, "I'm so far from wishing you to take any such monstrous step."

"Monstrous you call it? Just now you said it would be sublime."

"Sublime if it's done with spontaneity, with passion; ridiculous if it's done 'after further reflexion.' As you said, perfectly, a while ago, it isn't a thing to reason about."

"Ah what a help you'd be to me in diplomacy!" Peter yearningly cried. "Will you give me a year to consider?"

"Would you trust *me* for a year?"

"Why not, if I'm ready to trust you for life?"

"Oh I shouldn't be free then, worse luck. And how much you seem to take for granted one must like you!"

"Remember," he could immediately say, "that you've made a great point of your liking me. Wouldn't you do so still more if I were heroic?"

She showed him, for all her high impatience now, the interest of a long look. "I think I should pity you in such a cause. Give it all to *her*, don't throw away a real happiness!"

"Ah you can't back out of your position with a few vague and even rather impertinent words!" Peter protested. "You accuse me of swallowing my opinions, but you swallow your pledges. You've painted in heavenly colours the sacrifice I'm talking of, and now you must take the consequences."

"The consequences?"

"Why my coming back in a year to square you."

"Ah you're a bore!"—she let him have it at last. "Come back when you like. I don't wonder you've grown desperate, but fancy *me* then!" she added as she looked past him at a new interlocutor.

"Yes, but if he'll square you!" Peter heard Mrs. Rooth's voice respond all persuasively behind him. She had stolen up to the window now, had passed the threshold, was in the room, but her daughter had not been startled. "What is it he wants to do, dear?" she continued to Miriam.

"To induce me to marry him if he'll go upon the stage. He'll practise over there—where he's going—and then come back and appear. Isn't it too dreadful? Talk him out of it, stay with him, soothe him!" the girl hurried on. "You'll find some drinks and some biscuits in the cupboard—keep him with you, pacify him, give him *his* little supper. Meanwhile I'll go to mine; I'll take the brougham; don't follow!"

With which words Miriam bounded into the garden, her white drapery shining for an instant in the darkness before she disappeared. Peter looked about him to pick up his hat, but while he did so heard the bang of the gate and the quick carriage get into motion. Mrs. Rooth appeared to sway violently and in opposed directions: that of the impulse to rush after Miriam and that of the extraordinary possibility to which the young lady had alluded. She was in doubt, yet at a venture, detaining him with a maternal touch, she twinkled up at their visitor like an insinuating glow-worm. "I'm so glad you came."

"I'm not. I've got nothing by it," Peter said as he found his hat.

"Oh it was so beautiful!" she declared.

"The play—yes, wonderful. I'm afraid it's too late for me to avail myself of the privilege your daughter offers me. Good-night."

"Ah it's a pity; won't you take *anything*?" asked Mrs. Rooth. "When I heard your voice so high I was scared and hung back." But before he could reply she added: "Are you really thinking of the stage?"

"It comes to the same thing."

"Do you mean you've proposed?"

"Oh unmistakably."

"And what does she say?"

"Why you heard: she says I'm an ass."

"Ah the little wretch!" laughed Mrs. Rooth. "Leave her to me. I'll help you. But you are mad. Give up nothing—least of all your advantages."

"I won't give up your daughter," said Peter, reflecting that if this was cheap it was at any rate good enough for Mrs. Rooth. He mended it a little indeed by adding darkly: "But you can't make her take me."

"I can prevent her taking any one else."

"Oh *can* you?" Peter cried with more scepticism than ceremony.

"You'll see—you'll see." He passed into the garden, but, after she had blown out the candles and drawn the window to, Mrs. Rooth went with him. "All you've got to do is to be yourself—to be true to your fine position," she explained as they proceeded. "Trust me with the rest—trust me and be quiet."

"How can one be quiet after this magnificent evening?"

"Yes, but it's just that!" panted the eager old woman. "It has launched her so on this sea of dangers that to make up for the loss of the old security (don't you know?) we must take a still firmer hold."

"Aye, of what?" Peter asked as Mrs. Rooth's comfort became vague while she stopped with him at the garden door.

"Ah you know: of the *real* life, of the true anchor!" Her hansom was waiting for her and she added: "I kept it, you see; but a little extravagance on the night one's fortune has come!—"

Peter stared. Yes, there were people whose fortune had come; but he managed to stammer: "Are you following her again?"

"For you—for you!" And she clambered into the vehicle. From the seat, enticingly, she offered him the place beside her. "Won't you come too? I know he invited you." Peter declined with a quick gesture and as he turned away he heard her call after him, to cheer him on his lonely walk: "I shall keep this up; I shall never lose sight of her!"

BOOK EIGHTH

XLVII

When Mrs. Dallow returned to London just before London broke up the fact was immediately known in Calcutta Gardens and was promptly communicated to Nick Dormer by his sister Bridget. He had learnt it in no other way—he had had no correspondence with Julia during her absence. He gathered that his mother and sisters were not ignorant of her whereabouts— he never mentioned her name to them—but as to this he was not sure if the source of their information had been the *Morning Post* or a casual letter received by the inscrutable Biddy. He knew Biddy had some epistolary commerce with Julia; he had an impression Grace occasionally exchanged letters with Mrs. Gresham. Biddy, however, who, as he was also well aware, was always studying what he would like, forbore to talk to him about the absent mistress of Harsh beyond once dropping the remark that she had gone from Florence to Venice and was enjoying gondolas and sunsets too much to leave them. Nick's comment on this was that she was a happy woman to have such a go at Titian and Tintoret: as he spoke, and for some time afterwards, the sense of how he himself should enjoy a like "go" made him ache with ineffectual longing.

He had forbidden himself at the present to think of absence, not only because it would be inconvenient and expensive, but because it would be a kind of retreat from the enemy, a concession to difficulty. The enemy was no particular person and no particular body of persons: not his mother; not Mr. Carteret, who, as he heard from the doctor at Beauclere, lingered on, sinking and sinking till his vitality appeared to have the vertical depth of a gold-mine; not his pacified constituents, who had found a healthy diversion in returning another Liberal wholly without Mrs. Dallow's aid (she had not participated even to the extent of a responsive telegram in the election); not his late colleagues in the House, nor the biting satirists of the newspapers, nor the brilliant women he took down at dinner-parties—there was only one sense in which he ever took them down; not in short his friends, his foes, his private thoughts, the periodical phantom of his shocked father: the enemy was simply the general awkwardness of his situation. This awkwardness was connected with the sense of responsibility so greatly deprecated by Gabriel Nash, Gabriel who had ceased to roam of late on purpose to miss as few scenes as possible of the drama, rapidly growing dull alas, of his friend's destiny; but that compromising relation scarcely drew the soreness from it. The public flurry produced by his collapse had only been large enough to mark the flatness of our young man's position when it was over. To have had a few jokes cracked audibly at your expense wasn't an ordeal worth talking of; the hardest thing about it was merely that there had not been enough of them to yield a proportion of good ones. Nick had felt in fine the benefit of living in an age and in a society where number and pressure have, for the individual figure, especially when it's a zero, compensations almost equal to their cruelties.

No, the pinch for his conscience after a few weeks had passed was simply an acute mistrust of the superficiality of performance into which the desire to justify himself might hurry him. That desire was passionate as regards Julia Dallow; it was ardent also as regards his mother; and, to make it absolutely uncomfortable, it was complicated with the conviction that neither of them would know his justification even when she should see it. They probably couldn't know it if they would, and very certainly wouldn't if they could. He assured himself, however, that this limitation wouldn't matter; it was their affair—his own was simply to have the right sort of thing to show. The work he was now attempting wasn't the right sort of thing, though doubtless Julia, for instance, would dislike it almost as much as if it were. The two portraits of Miriam, after the first exhilaration of his finding himself at large, filled him with no private glee; they were not in the direction in which he wished for the present really to move. There were moments when he felt almost angry, though of course he held his tongue, when by the few persons who saw them they were pronounced wonderfully clever. That they were wonderfully clever was just the detestable thing in them, so active had that cleverness been in making them seem better than they were. There were people to whom he would have been ashamed to show them, and these were the people whom it would give him most pleasure some day to please. Not only had he many an hour of disgust at his actual work, but he thought he saw as in an ugly revelation that nature had cursed him with an odious facility and that the lesson of his life, the sternest and wholesomest, would be to keep out of the trap it had laid for him. He had fallen into this trap on the threshold and had only scrambled out with his honour. He had a talent for appearance, and that was the fatal thing; he had a damnable suppleness and a gift of immediate response, a readiness to oblige, that made him seem to take up causes which he really left lying, enabled him to learn enough about them in an hour to have all the air of having converted them to his use. Many people used them—that was the only thing to be said—who had taken them in much less. He was at all events too clever by half, since this pernicious overflow had wrecked most of his attempts. He had assumed a virtue and enjoyed assuming it, and the assumption had cheated his father and his mother and his affianced wife and his rich benefactor and the candid burgesses of Harsh and the cynical reporters of the newspapers. His enthusiasms had been but young curiosity, his speeches had been young agility, his professions and adhesions had been like postage-stamps without glue: the head was all right, but they wouldn't stick. He stood ready now to wring the neck of the irrepressible vice that certainly would tend to nothing so much as to get him into further trouble. His only real justification would be to turn patience—his own of course—inside out; yet if there should be a way to misread that recipe his humbugging genius could be trusted infallibly to discover it. Cheap and easy results would dangle before him, little amateurish conspicuities at exhibitions helped by his history; putting it in his power to triumph with a quick "What do you say to that?" over those he had wounded. The fear of this danger was corrosive; it poisoned even lawful joys. If he should have a striking picture at the Academy next year it wouldn't be a crime; yet he couldn't help suspecting any conditions that would enable him to be striking so soon. In this way he felt quite enough how Gabriel Nash had "had" him whenever railing at his fever for proof, and how inferior as a productive force the desire to win over the ill-disposed might be to the principle of quiet growth. Nash had a foreign manner of lifting up his finger and waving it before him, as if to put an end to everything, whenever it became, in conversation or discussion, to any extent a question whether any one would "like" anything.

It was presumably in some degree at least a due respect for the principle of quiet growth that kept Nick on the spot at present, made him stick fast to Rosedale Road and Calcutta Gardens and deny himself the simplifications of absence. Do what he would he couldn't despoil himself of the impression that the disagreeable was somehow connected with the salutary, and the "quiet" with the disagreeable, when stubbornly borne; so he resisted a hundred impulses to run away to Paris or to Florence, coarse forms of the temptation to persuade himself by material motion that he was launched. He stayed in London because it seemed to him he was there more conscious of what he had undertaken, and he had a horror of shirking the consciousness. One element in it indeed was his noting how little convenience he could have found in a foreign journey even had his judgement approved such a subterfuge. The stoppage of his supplies from Beauclere had now become an historic fact, with something of the majesty of its class about it: he had had time to see what a difference this would make in his life. His means were small and he had several old debts, the number of which, as he believed, loomed large to his mother's imagination. He could never tell her she exaggerated, because he told her nothing of that sort in these days: they had no intimate talk, for an impenetrable partition, a tall, bristling hedge of untrimmed misconceptions, had sprung up between them. Poor Biddy had made a hole in it through which she squeezed from side to side, to keep up communications, at the cost of many rents and scratches; but Lady Agnes walked straight and stiff, never turning her head, never stopping to pluck the least little daisy of consolation. It was in this manner she wished to signify that she had accepted her wrongs. She draped herself in them as in a Roman mantle and had never looked so proud and wasted and handsome as now that her eyes rested only on ruins.

Nick was extremely sorry for her, though he marked as a dreadful want of grace her never setting a foot in Rosedale Road—she mentioned his studio no more than if it had been a private gambling-house or something worse; sorry because he was well aware that for the hour everything must appear to her to have crumbled. The luxury of Broadwood would have to crumble: his mind was very clear about that. Biddy's prospects had withered to the finest, dreariest dust, and Biddy indeed, taking a lesson from her brother's perversities, seemed little disposed to better a bad business. She professed the most peace-making sentiments, but when it came really to doing something to brighten up the scene she showed herself portentously corrupt. After Peter Sherringham's heartless flight she had wantonly slighted an excellent opportunity to repair her misfortune. Lady Agnes had reason to infer, about the end of June, that young Mr. Grindon, the only son—the other children being girls—of an immensely rich industrial and political baronet in the north, was literally waiting for the faintest sign. This reason she promptly imparted to her younger daughter, whose intelligence had to take it in but who had shown it no other consideration. Biddy had set her charming face as a stone; she would have nothing to do with signs, and she, practically speaking, wilfully, wickedly refused a magnificent offer, so that the young man carried his high expectations elsewhere. How much in earnest he had been was proved by the fact that before Goodwood had come and gone he was captured by Lady Muriel Macpherson. It was superfluous to insist on the frantic determination to get married written on such an accident as that. Nick knew of this episode only through Grace, and he deplored its having occurred in the midst of other disasters.

He knew or he suspected something more as well—something about his brother Percival which, should it come to light, no phase of their common history would be genial enough to gloss over. It had usually been supposed that Percy's store of comfort against the ills of life was confined to the infallibility of his rifle. He was not sensitive, and his use of that weapon represented a resource against which common visitations might have spent themselves. It had suddenly come to Nick's ears, however, that he cultivated a concurrent support in the person of a robust countrywoman, housed in an ivied corner of Warwickshire, in whom he had long been interested and whom, without any flourish of magnanimity, he had ended by making his wife. The situation of the latest born of the pledges of this affection, a blooming boy—there had been two or three previously—was therefore perfectly regular and of a nature to make a difference in the worldly position, as the phrase ran, of his moneyless uncle. If there be degrees in the absolute and Percy had an heir—others, moreover, supposedly following—Nick would have to regard himself as still more moneyless than before. His brother's last step was doubtless, given the case, to be commended; but such discoveries were enlivening only when made in other families, and Lady Agnes would scarcely enjoy learning to what tune she had become a grandmother.

Nick forbore from delicacy to intimate to Biddy that he thought it a pity she couldn't care for Mr. Grindon; but he had a private sense that if she had been capable of such a feat it would have lightened a little the weight he himself had to carry. He bore her a slight grudge, which lasted till Julia Dallow came back; when the circumstance of the girl's being summoned immediately down to Harsh created a diversion that was perhaps after all only fanciful. Biddy, as we know, entertained a theory, which Nick had found occasion to combat, that Mrs. Dallow had not treated him perfectly well; therefore in going to Harsh the very first time that relative held out a hand to her so jealous a little sister must have recognised a special inducement. The inducement might have been that the relative had comfort for her, that she was acting by her cousin's direct advice, that they were still in close communion on the question of the offers Biddy was not to accept, that in short Peter's sister had taken upon herself to see that their young friend should remain free for the day of the fugitive's inevitable return. Once or twice indeed Nick wondered if Julia had herself been visited, in a larger sense, by the thought of retracing her steps—if she wished to draw out her young friend's opinion as to how she might do that gracefully. During the few days she was in town Nick had seen her twice in Great Stanhope Street, but neither time alone. She had said to him on one of these occasions in her odd, explosive way: "I should have thought you'd have gone away somewhere—it must be such a bore." Of course she firmly believed he was staying for Miriam, which he really was not; and probably she had written this false impression off to Peter, who, still more probably, would prefer to regard it as just. Nick was staying for Miriam only in the sense that he should very glad of the money he might receive for the portrait he was engaged in painting. That money would be a great convenience to him in spite of the obstructive ground Miriam had taken in pretending—she had blown half a gale about it—that he had had no right to dispose of such a production without her consent. His answer to this was simply that the purchaser was so little of a stranger that it didn't go, so to speak, out of the family, out of hers. It didn't matter, Miriam's retort that if Mr. Sherringham had formerly been no stranger he was utterly one now, so that nothing would ever less delight him than to see her hated image on his wall. He would back out of the bargain and Nick be left with the picture on his hands. Nick jeered at this shallow theory and when she came to sit the question served as well as another to sprinkle their familiar silences with chaff. He already knew something, as we have seen, of the conditions in which his distracted kinsman had left England; and this connected itself, in casual meditation, with some of the calculations imputable to Julia and to Biddy. There had naturally been a sequel to the queer behaviour perceptible in Peter, at the theatre, on the eve of his departure—a sequel lighted by a word of Miriam's in the course of her first sitting to Nick after her great night. "Fancy"—so this observation ran—"fancy the dear man finding time in the press of all his last duties to ask me to marry him!"

"He told me you had found time in the press of all yours to say you would," Nick replied. And this was pretty much all that had passed on the subject between them—save of course her immediately making clear that Peter had grossly misinformed him. What had happened was that she had said she would do nothing of the sort. She professed a desire not to be confronted again with this obnoxious theme, and Nick easily fell in with it—quite from his own settled inclination not to handle that kind of subject with her. If Julia had false ideas about him, and if Peter had them too, his part of the business was to take the simplest course to establish the falsity. There were difficulties indeed attached even to the simplest course, but there would be a difficulty the less if one should forbear to meddle in promiscuous talk with the general, suggestive topic of intimate unions. It is certain that in these days Nick cultivated the practice of forbearances for which he didn't receive, for which perhaps he never would receive, due credit.

He had been convinced for some time that one of the next things he should hear would be that Julia Dallow had arranged to marry either Mr. Macgeorge or some other master of multitudes. He could think of that now, he found—think of it with resignation even when Julia, before his eyes, looked so handsomely forgetful that her appearance had to be taken as referring still more to their original intimacy than to his comparatively superficial offence. What made this accomplishment of his own remarkable was that there was something else he thought of quite as much—the fact that he had only to see her again to feel by how great a charm she had in the old days taken possession of him. This charm operated apparently in a very direct, primitive way: her presence diffused it and fully established it, but her absence left comparatively little of it behind. It dwelt in the very facts of her person— it was something she happened physically to be; yet—considering that the question was of something very like loveliness—its envelope of associations, of memories and recurrences, had no great destiny. She packed it up and took it away with her quite as if she had been a woman who had come to sell a set of laces. The laces were as wonderful as ever when taken out of the box, but to admire again their rarity you had to send for the woman. What was above all remarkable for our young man was that Miriam Rooth fetched a fellow, vulgarly speaking, very much less than Julia at the times when, being on the spot, Julia did fetch. He could paint Miriam day after day without any agitating blur of vision; in fact the more he saw of her the clearer grew the atmosphere through which she blazed, the more her richness became one with that of the flowering work. There are reciprocities and special sympathies in such a relation; mysterious affinities they used to be called, divinations of private congruity. Nick had an unexpressed conviction that if, according to his defeated desire, he had embarked with Mrs. Dallow in this particular quest of a great prize, disaster would have overtaken them on the deep waters. Even with the limited risk indeed disaster had come; but it was of a different kind and it had the advantage for him that now she couldn't reproach and denounce him as the cause of it—couldn't do so at least on any ground he was obliged to recognise. She would never know how much he had cared for her, how much he cared for her still; inasmuch as the conclusive proof for himself was his conscious reluctance to care for another woman—evidence she positively misread. Some day he would doubtless try to do that; but such a day seemed as yet far off, and he had meanwhile no spite, no vindictive impulse, to help him. The soreness that mingled with his liberation, the sense of indignity even, as of a full cup suddenly dashed by a blundering hand from his lips, demanded certainly a balm; but it found the balm, for the time, in another passion, not in a rancorous exercise of the same—a passion strong enough to make him forget what a pity it was he was not so formed as to care for two women at once.

As soon as Julia returned to England he broke ground to his mother on the subject of her making the mistress of Broadwood understand that she and the girls now regarded their occupancy of that estate as absolutely over. He had already, several weeks before, picked a little at the arid tract of that indicated surrender, but in the interval the soil appeared to have formed again to a considerable thickness. It was disagreeable to him to call his parent's attention to the becoming course, and especially disagreeable to have to emphasise it and discuss it and perhaps clamour for it. He would have liked the whole business to be tacit—a little triumph of silent delicacy. But he found reasons to suspect that what in fact would be most tacit was Julia's certain endurance of any chance failure of that charm. Lady Agnes had a theory that they had virtually—"practically" as she said—given up the place, so that there was no need of making a splash about it; but Nick discovered in the course of an exploration of Biddy's view more rigorous perhaps than any to which he had ever subjected her, that none of their property had been removed from the delightful house—none of the things (there were ever so many things) heavily planted there when their mother took possession. Lady Agnes was the proprietor of innumerable articles of furniture, relics and survivals of her former greatness, and moved about the world with a train of heterogeneous baggage; so that her quiet overflow into the spaciousness of Broadwood had had all the luxury of a final subsidence. What Nick had to propose to her now was a dreadful combination, a relapse into the conditions she most hated—seaside lodgings, bald storehouses in the Marylebone Road, little London rooms crammed with objects that caught the dirt and made them stuffy. He was afraid he should really finish her, and he himself was surprised in a degree at his insistence. He wouldn't have supposed he should have cared so much, but he found he did care intensely. He cared enough—it says everything—to explain to his mother that her retention of Broadwood would show "practically" (since that was her great word) for the violation of an agreement. Julia had given them the place on the understanding that he was to marry her, and once he was definitely not to marry her they had no right to keep the place. "Yes, you make the mess and *we* pay the penalty!" the poor lady flashed out; but this was the only overt protest she made—except indeed to contend that their withdrawal would be an act ungracious and offensive to Julia. She looked as she had looked during the months that succeeded his father's death, but she gave a general, a final grim assent to the proposition that, let their kinswoman take it as she would, their own duty was unmistakably clear.

It was Grace who was principal representative of the idea that Julia would be outraged by such a step; she never ceased to repeat that she had never heard of anything so "nasty." Nick would have expected this of Grace, but he felt rather bereft and betrayed when Biddy murmured to him that *she* knew—that there was really no need of their sacrificing their mother's comfort to an extravagant scruple. She intimated that if Nick would only consent to their going on with Broadwood as if nothing had happened—or rather as if everything had happened—she would answer for the feelings of the owner. For almost the first time in his life Nick disliked what Biddy said to him, and he gave her a sharp rejoinder, a taste of the general opinion that they all had enough to do to answer for themselves. He remembered afterwards the way she looked at him—startled, even frightened and with rising tears—before turning away. He held that they should judge better how Julia would take it after they had thrown up the place; and he made it his duty to arrange that his mother should formally advise her, by letter, of their intending to depart at once. Julia could then protest to her heart's content. Nick was aware that for the most part he didn't pass for practical; he could imagine why, from his early years, people should have joked him about it. But this time he was determined to rest on a rigid view of things as they were. He didn't see his mother's letter, but he knew that it went. He felt she would have been more loyal if she had shown it to him, though of course there could be but little question of loyalty now. That it had really been written, however, very much on the lines he dictated was clear to him from the subsequent surprise which Lady Agnes's blankness didn't prevent his divining.

Julia acknowledged the offered news, but in unexpected terms: she had apparently neither resisted nor protested; she had simply been very glad to get her house back again and had not accused any of them of nastiness. Nick saw no more of her letter than he had seen of his mother's, but he was able to say to Grace—to their parent he was studiously mute—"My poor child, you see after all that we haven't kicked up such a row." Grace shook her head and looked gloomy and deeply wise, replying that he had no cause to triumph—they were so far from having seen the end of it yet. Thus he guessed that his mother had complied with his wish on the calculation that it would be a mere form, that Julia would entreat them not to be so fantastic and that he himself would then, in the presence of her wounded surprise, consent to a quiet continuance, so much in the interest—the air of Broadwood had a purity!—of the health of all of them. But since Julia jumped at their sacrifice he had no chance to be mollified: he had all grossly to persist in having been right.

At bottom probably he was a little surprised at Julia's so prompt assent. Literally speaking, it was not perfectly graceful. He was sorry his mother had been so deceived, but was sorrier still for Biddy's mistake—it showed she might be mistaken about other things. Nothing was left now but for Lady Agnes to say, as she did substantially whenever she saw him: "We're to prepare to spend the autumn at Worthing then or some other horrible place? I don't know their names: it's the only thing we can afford." There was an implication in this that if he expected her to drag her girls about to country-houses in a continuance of the fidgety effort to work them off he must understand at once that she was now too weary and too sad and too sick. She had done her best for them and it had all been vain and cruel—now therefore the poor creatures must look out for themselves. To the grossness of Biddy's misconduct she needn't refer, nor to the golden opportunity that young woman had forfeited by her odious treatment of Mr. Grindon. It was clear that this time Lady Agnes was incurably discouraged; so much so as to fail to glean the dimmest light from the fact that the girl was really making a long stay at Harsh. Biddy went to and fro two or three times and then in August fairly settled there; and what her mother mainly saw in her absence was the desire to keep out of the way of household reminders of her depravity. In fact, as turned out, Lady

Agnes and Grace gathered themselves together in the first days of that month for another visit to the very old lady who had been Sir Nicholas's godmother; after which they went somewhere else—so that the question of Worthing had not immediately to be faced.

Nick stayed on in London with the obsession of work humming in his ears; he was joyfully conscious that for three or four months, in the empty Babylon, he would have ample stores of time. But toward the end of August he got a letter from Grace in which she spoke of her situation and of her mother's in a manner that seemed to impose on him the doing of something tactful. They were paying a third visit—he knew that in Calcutta Gardens lady's-maids had been to and fro with boxes, replenishments of wardrobes— and yet somehow the outlook for the autumn was dark. Grace didn't say it in so many words, but what he read between the lines was that they had no more invitations. What, therefore, in pity's name was to become of them? People liked them well enough when Biddy was with them, but they didn't care for her mother and her, that prospect *tout pur*, and Biddy was cooped up indefinitely with Julia. This was not the manner in which Grace had anciently alluded to her sister's happy visits at Harsh, and the change of tone made Nick wince with a sense of all that had collapsed. Biddy was a little fish worth landing in short, scantly as she seemed disposed to bite, and Grace's rude probity could admit that she herself was not.

Nick had an inspiration: by way of doing something tactful he went down to Brighton and took lodgings, for several weeks, in the general interest, the very quietest and sunniest he could find. This he intended as a kindly surprise, a reminder of how he had his mother's and sisters' comfort at heart, how he could exert himself and save them trouble. But he had no sooner concluded his bargain—it was a more costly one than he had at first calculated—than he was bewildered and befogged to learn that the persons on whose behalf he had so exerted himself were to pass the autumn at Broadwood with Julia. That daughter of privilege had taken the place into familiar use again and was now correcting their former surprise at her crude indifference—this was infinitely characteristic of Julia—by inviting them to share it with her. Nick wondered vaguely what she was "up to"; but when his mother treated herself to the line irony of addressing him an elaborately humble request for his consent to their accepting the merciful refuge—she repeated this expression three times—he replied that she might do exactly as she liked: he would only mention that he shouldn't feel himself at liberty to come and see her there. This condition proved apparently to Lady Agnes's mind no hindrance, and she and her daughters were presently reinstated in the very apartments they had learned so to love. This time in fact it was even better than before—they had still fewer expenses. The expenses were Nick's: he had to pay a forfeit to the landlady at Brighton for backing out of his contract. He said nothing to his mother about that bungled business—he was literally afraid; but a sad event just then reminded him afresh how little it was the moment for squandering money. Mr. Carteret drew his last breath; quite painlessly it seemed, as the closing scene was described at Beauclere when the young man went down to the funeral. Two or three weeks later the contents of his will were made public in the *Illustrated London News*, where it definitely appeared that he left a very large fortune, not a penny of which was to go to Nick. The provision for Mr. Chayter's declining years was remarkably handsome.

XLVIII

Miriam had mounted at a bound, in her new part, several steps in the ladder of fame, and at the climax of the London season this fact was brought home to her from hour to hour. It produced a thousand solicitations and entanglements, and she rapidly learned that to be celebrated takes up almost as much of one's own time as of other people's. Even though, as she boasted, she had reduced to a science the practice of "working" her mother—she made use of the good lady socially to the utmost, pushing her perpetually into the breach—there was many a juncture at which it was clear that she couldn't too much disoblige without hurting her cause. She made almost an income out of the photographers—their appreciation of her as a subject knew no bounds—and she supplied the newspapers with columns of characteristic copy. To the gentlemen who sought speech of her on behalf of these organs she poured forth, vindictively, floods of unscrupulous romance; she told them all different tales, and, as her mother told them others more marvellous yet, publicity was cleverly caught by rival versions, which surpassed each other in authenticity. The whole case was remarkable, was unique; for if the girl was advertised by the bewilderment of her readers she seemed to every sceptic, on his going to see her, as fine as if he had discovered her for himself. She was still accommodating enough, however, from time to time, to find an hour to come and sit to Nick Dormer, and he helped himself further by going to her theatre whenever he could. He was conscious Julia Dallow would probably hear of this and triumph with a fresh sense of how right she had been; but the reflexion only made him sigh resignedly, so true it struck him as being that there are some things explanation can never better, can never touch.

Miriam brought Basil Dashwood once to see her portrait, and Basil, who commended it in general, directed his criticism mainly to two points— its not yet being finished and its not having gone into that year's Academy. The young actor audibly panted; he felt the short breath of Miriam's rapidity, the quick beat of her success, and, looking at everything now from the standpoint of that speculation, could scarcely contain his impatience at the painter's clumsy slowness. He thought the latter's second attempt much better than his first, but somehow it ought by that time to be shining in the eye of the public. He put it to their friend with an air of acuteness—he had those felicities—that in every great crisis there is nothing like striking while the iron is hot. He even betrayed the conviction that by putting on a spurt Nick might wind up the job and still get the Academy people to take him in. Basil knew some of them; he all but offered to speak to them—the case was so exceptional; he had no doubt he could get something done. Against the appropriation of the work by Peter Sherringham he explicitly and loudly protested, in spite of the homeliest recommendations of silence from Miriam; and it was indeed easy to guess how such an arrangement would interfere with his own conception of the eventual right place for the two portraits— the vestibule of the theatre, where every one going in and out would see them suspended face to face and surrounded by photographs, artistically disposed, of the young actress in a variety of characters. Dashwood showed superiority in his jump to the contention that so exhibited the pictures would really help to draw. Considering the virtue he attributed to Miriam the idea was exempt from narrow prejudice.

Moreover, though a trifle feverish, he was really genial; he repeated more than once, "Yes, my dear sir, you've done it this time." This was a favourite formula with him; when some allusion was made to the girl's success he greeted it also with a comfortable "This time she *has* done it." There was ever a hint of fine judgement and far calculation in his tone. It appeared before he went that this time even he himself had done it—he had taken up something that would really answer. He told Nick more about Miriam, more certainly about her outlook at that moment, than she herself had communicated, contributing strongly to our young man's impression that one by one every gage of a great career was being dropped into her cup. Nick himself tasted of success vicariously for the hour. Miriam let her comrade talk only to contradict him, and contradicted him only to show how indifferently she could do it. She treated him as if she had nothing more to learn about his folly, but as if it had taken intimate friendship to reveal to her the full extent of it. Nick didn't mind her intimate friendships, but he ended by disliking Dashwood, who gave on his nerves—a circumstance poor Julia, had it come to her knowledge, would doubtless have found deplorably significant. Miriam was more pleased with herself than ever: she now made no scruple of admitting that she enjoyed all her advantages. She had a fuller vision of how successful success could be; she took everything as it came—dined out every Sunday and even went into the country till the Monday morning; kept a hundred distinguished names on her lips and abounded in strange tales of the people who were making up to her. She struck Nick as less strenuous than she had been hitherto, as making even an aggressive show of inevitable laxities; but he was conscious of no obligation to rebuke her for it—the less as he had a dim vision that some effect of that sort, some irritation of his curiosity, was what she desired to produce. She would perhaps have liked, for reasons best known to herself, to look as if she were throwing herself away, not being able to do anything else. He couldn't talk to her as if he took a deep interest in her career, because in fact he didn't; she remained to him primarily and essentially a pictorial object, with the nature of whose vicissitudes he was concerned—putting common charity and his personal good nature of course aside—only so far as they had something to say in her face. How could he know in advance what turn of her experience, twist of her life, would say most?—so possible was it even that complete failure or some incalculable perversion (innumerable were the queer traps that might be set for her) would only make her for his particular purpose more precious.

When she had left him at any rate, the day she came with Basil Dashwood, and still more on a later occasion, that of his turning back to his work after putting her into her carriage, and otherwise bare-headedly manifesting, the last time, for that year apparently, that he was to see her—when she had left him it occurred to him in the light of her quick distinction that there were deep differences in the famous artistic life. Miriam was already in a glow of glory—which, moreover, was probably but a faint spark in relation to the blaze to come; and as he closed the door on her and took up his palette to rub it with a dirty cloth the little room in which his own battle was practically to be fought looked woefully cold and grey and mean. It was lonely and yet at the same time was peopled with unfriendly shadows—so thick he foresaw them gather in winter twilights to come—the duller conditions, the longer patiences, the less immediate and less personal joys. His late beginning was there and his wasted youth, the mistakes that would still bring forth children after their image, the sedentary solitude, the grey mediocrity, the poor explanations, the effect of foolishness he dreaded even from afar of in having to ask people to wait, and wait longer, and wait again, for a fruition which to their sense at least might well prove a grotesque anti-climax. He yearned enough over it, however it should figure, to feel that this possible pertinacity might enter into comparison even with such a productive force as Miriam's. That was after all in his bare studio the most collective dim presence, the one that kept him company best as he sat there and that made it the right place, however wrong—the sense that it was to the thing in itself he was attached. This was Miriam's case too, but the sharp contrast, which she showed him she also felt, was in the number of other things she got with the thing in itself.

I hasten to add that our young man had hours when this last mystic value struck him as requiring for its full operation no adjunct whatever—as being in its own splendour a summary of all adjuncts and apologies. I have related that the great collections, the National Gallery and the Museum, were sometimes rather a series of dead surfaces to him; but the sketch I have attempted of him will have been inadequate if it fails to suggest that there were other days when, as he strolled through them, he plucked right and left perfect nosegays of reassurance. Bent as he was on working in the modern, which spoke to him with a thousand voices, he judged it better for long periods not to haunt the earlier masters, whose conditions had been so different—later he came to see that it didn't matter much, especially if one kept away; but he was liable to accidental deflexions from this theory, liable in particular to feel the sanctity of the great portraits of the past. These were the things the most inspiring, in the sense that while generations, while worlds had come and gone, they seemed far most to prevail and survive and testify. As he stood before them the perfection of their survival often struck him as the supreme eloquence, the virtue that included all others, thanks to the language of art, the richest and most universal. Empires and systems and conquests had rolled over the globe and every kind of greatness had risen and passed away, but the beauty of the great pictures had known nothing of death or change, and the tragic centuries had only sweetened their freshness. The same faces, the same figures looked out at different worlds, knowing so many secrets the particular world didn't, and when they joined hands they made the indestructible thread on which the pearls of history were strung.

Miriam notified her artist that her theatre was to close on the tenth of August, immediately after which she was to start, with the company, on a tremendous tour of the provinces. They were to make a lot of money, but they were to have no holiday, and she didn't want one; she only wanted to keep at it and make the most of her limited opportunities for practice; inasmuch as at that rate, playing but two parts a year—and such parts: she despised them!—she shouldn't have mastered the rudiments of her trade before decrepitude would compel her to lay it by. The first time she came to the studio after her visit with Dashwood she sprang up abruptly at the end of half an hour, saying she could sit no more—she had had enough and to spare of it. She was visibly restless and preoccupied, and though Nick had not waited till now to note that she had more moods in her list than he had tints on his palette he had never yet seen her sensibility at this particular pitch. It struck him rather as a waste of passion, but he was ready to let her go. She looked round the place as if suddenly tired of it and then said mechanically, in a heartless London way, while she smoothed down her gloves, "So you're just going to stay on?" After he had confessed that this was his dark purpose she continued in the same casual, talk-making manner: "I daresay it's the best thing for you. You're just going to grind, eh?"

"I see before me an eternity of grinding."

"All alone by yourself in this dull little hole? You *will* be conscientious, you *will* be virtuous."

"Oh my solitude will be mitigated—I shall have models and people."

"What people—what models?" Miriam asked as she arranged her hat before the glass.

"Well, no one so good as you."

"That's a prospect!" the girl laughed—"for all the good you've got out of me!"

"You're no judge of that quantity," said Nick, "and even I can't measure it just yet. Have I been rather a bore and a brute? I can easily believe it; I haven't talked to you—I haven't amused you as I might. The truth is that taking people's likenesses is a very absorbing, inhuman occupation. You can't do much to them besides."

"Yes, it's a cruel honour to pay them."

"Cruel—that's too much," he objected.

"I mean it's one you shouldn't confer on those you like, for when it's over it's over: it kills your interest in them. After you've finished them you don't like them any more at all."

"Surely I like *you*," Nick returned, sitting tilted back before his picture with his hands in his pockets.

"We've done very well: it's something not to have quarrelled"—and she smiled at him now, seeming more "in" it. "I wouldn't have had you slight your work—I wouldn't have had you do it badly. But there's no fear of that for you," she went on. "You're the real thing and the rare bird. I haven't lived with you this way without seeing that: you're the sincere artist so much more than I. No, no, don't protest," she added with one of her sudden, fine transitions to a deeper tone. "You'll do things that will hand on your name when my screeching is happily over. Only you do seem to me, I confess, rather high and dry here—I speak from the point of view of your comfort and of my personal interest in you. You strike me as kind of lonely, as the Americans say—rather cut off and isolated in your grandeur. Haven't you any confrères—fellow-artists and people of that sort? Don't they come near you?"

"I don't know them much," Nick humbly confessed. "I've always been afraid of them, and how can they take me seriously?"

"Well, *I've* got confrères, and sometimes I wish I hadn't! But does your sister never come near you any more," she asked, "or is it only the fear of meeting me?"

He was aware of his mother's theory that Biddy was constantly bundled home from Rosedale Road at the approach of improper persons: she was as angry at this as if she wouldn't have been more so had her child suffered exposure; but the explanation he gave his present visitor was nearer the truth. He reminded her that he had already told her—he had been careful to do this, so as not to let it appear she was avoided—that his sister was now most of the time in the country, staying with an hospitable relation.

"Oh yes," the girl rejoined to this, "with Mr. Sherringham's sister, Mrs.—what's her name? I always forget." And when he had pronounced the word with a reluctance he doubtless failed sufficiently to conceal—he hated to talk of Julia by any name and didn't know what business Miriam had with her—she went on: "That's the one—the beauty, the wonderful beauty. I shall never forget how handsome she looked the day she found me here. I don't in the least resemble her, but I should like to have a try at that type some day in a comedy of manners. But who the devil will write me a comedy of manners? There it is! The danger would be, no doubt, that I should push her *à la charge*."

560

Nick listened to these remarks in silence, saying to himself that if she should have the bad taste—which she seemed trembling on the brink of—to make an allusion to what had passed between the lady in question and himself he should dislike her beyond remedy. It would show him she was a coarse creature after all. Her good genius interposed, however, as against this hard penalty, and she quickly, for the moment at least, whisked away from the topic, demanding, since they spoke of comrades and visitors, what had become of Gabriel Nash, whom she hadn't heard of for so many days.

"I think he's tired of me," said Nick; "he hasn't been near me either. But after all it's natural—he has seen me through."

"Seen you through? Do you mean," she laughed, "seen through you? Why you've only just begun."

"Precisely, and at bottom he doesn't like to see me begin. He's afraid I shall do something."

She wondered—as with the interest of that. "Do you mean he's jealous?"

"Not in the least, for from the moment one does anything one ceases to compete with him. It leaves him the field more clear. But that's just the discomfort for him—he feels, as you said just now, kind of lonely: he feels rather abandoned and even, I think, a little betrayed. So far from being jealous he yearns for me and regrets me. The only thing he really takes seriously is to speculate and understand, to talk about the reasons and the essence of things: the people who do that are the highest. The applications, the consequences, the vulgar little effects, belong to a lower plane, for which one must doubtless be tolerant and indulgent, but which is after all an affair of comparative accidents and trifles. Indeed he'll probably tell me frankly the next time I see him that he can't but feel that to come down to small questions of action—to the small prudences and compromises and simplifications of practice—is for the superior person really a fatal descent. One may be inoffensive and even commendable after it, but one can scarcely pretend to be interesting. 'Il en faut comme ça,' but one doesn't haunt them. He'll do his best for me; he'll come back again, but he'll come back sad, and finally he'll fade away altogether. He'll go off to Granada or somewhere."

"The simplifications of practice?" cried Miriam. "Why they're just precisely the most blessed things on earth. What should we do without them?"

"What indeed?" Nick echoed. "But if we need them it's because we're not superior persons. We're awful Philistines."

"I'll be one with *you*," the girl smiled. "Poor Nash isn't worth talking about. What was it but a small question of action when he preached to you, as I know he did, to give up your seat?"

"Yes, he has a weakness for giving up—he'll go with you as far as that. But I'm not giving up any more, you see. I'm pegging away, and that's gross."

"He's an idiot—*n'en parlons plus!*" she dropped, gathering up her parasol but lingering.

"Ah I stick to him," Nick said. "He helped me at a difficult time."

"You ought to be ashamed to confess it."

"Oh you *are* a Philistine!" Nick returned.

"Certainly I am," she declared, going toward the door—"if it makes me one to be sorry, awfully sorry and even rather angry, that I haven't before me a period of the same sort of unsociable pegging away that you have. For want of it I shall never really be good. However, if you don't tell people I've said so they'll never know. Your conditions are far better than mine and far more respectable: you can do as many things as you like in patient obscurity while I'm pitchforked into the *mêlée* and into the most improbable fame—all on the back of a solitary *cheval de bataille*, a poor broken-winded screw. I read it clear that I shall be condemned for the greater part of the rest of my days— do you see that?—to play the stuff I'm acting now. I'm studying Juliet and I want awfully to do her, but really I'm mortally afraid lest, making a success of her, I should find myself in such a box. Perhaps the brutes would want Juliet for ever instead of my present part. You see amid what delightful alternatives one moves. What I long for most I never shall have had—five quiet years of hard all-round work in a perfect company, with a manager more perfect still, playing five hundred things and never being heard of at all. I may be too particular, but that's what I should have liked. I think I'm disgusting with my successful crudities. It's discouraging; it makes one not care much what happens. What's the use, in such an age, of being good?"

"Good? Your haughty claim," Nick laughed, "is that you're bad."

"I mean *good*, you know—there are other ways. Don't be stupid." And Miriam tapped him—he was near her at the door—with her parasol.

"I scarcely know what to say to you," he logically pleaded, "for certainly it's your fault if you get on so fast."

"I'm too clever—I'm a humbug."

"That's the way I used to be," said Nick.

She rested her brave eyes on him, then turned them over the room slowly; after which she attached them again, kindly, musingly—rather as if he had been a fine view or an interesting object—to his face. "Ah, the pride of that—the sense of purification! He 'used' to be forsooth! Poor me! Of course you'll say, 'Look at the sort of thing I've undertaken to produce compared with the rot you have.' So it's all right. Become great in the proper way and don't expose me." She glanced back once more at the studio as if to leave it for ever, and gave another last look at the unfinished canvas on the easel. She shook her head sadly, "Poor Mr. Sherringham—with *that!*" she wailed.

"Oh I'll finish it—it will be very decent," Nick said.

"Finish it by yourself?"

"Not necessarily. You'll come back and sit when you return to London."

"Never, never, never again."

He wondered. "Why you've made me the most profuse offers and promises."

"Yes, but they were made in ignorance and I've backed out of them. I'm capricious too—*faites la part de ça.* I see it wouldn't do—I didn't know it then. We're too far apart—I *am*, as you say, a Philistine." And as he protested with vehemence against this unscrupulous bad faith she added: "You'll find other models. Paint Gabriel Nash."

"Gabriel Nash—as a substitute for you?"

"It will be a good way to get rid of him. Paint Mrs. Dallow too," Miriam went on as she passed out of the door he had opened for her—"paint Mrs. Dallow if you wish to eradicate the last possibility of a throb."

It was strange that, since only a moment before he had been in a state of mind to which the superfluity of this reference would have been the clearest thing about it, he should now have been moved to receive it quickly, naturally, irreflectively, receive it with the question: "The last possibility? Do you mean in her or in me?"

"Oh in you. I don't know anything about 'her.'"

"But that wouldn't be the effect," he argued with the same supervening candour. "I believe that if she were to sit to me the usual law would be reversed."

"The usual law?"

"Which you cited a while since and of which I recognised the general truth. In the case you speak of," he said, "I should probably make a shocking picture."

"And fall in love with her again? Then for God's sake risk the daub!" Miriam laughed out as she floated away to her victoria.

XLIX

She had guessed happily in saying to him that to offer to paint Gabriel Nash would be the way to get rid of that visitant. It was with no such invidious purpose indeed that our young man proposed to his intermittent friend to sit; rather, as August was dusty in the London streets, he had too little hope that Nash would remain in town at such a time to oblige him. Nick had no wish to get rid of his private philosopher; he liked his philosophy, and though of course premeditated paradox was the light to read him by he yet had frequently and incidentally an inspired unexpectedness. He remained in Rosedale Road the man who most produced by his presence the effect of company. All the other men of Nick's acquaintance, all his political friends, represented, often very communicatively, their own affairs, their own affairs alone; which when they did it well was the most their host could ask of them. But Nash had the rare distinction that he seemed somehow to figure *his* affairs, the said host's, and to show an interest in them unaffected by the ordinary social limitations of capacity. This relegated him to the class of high luxuries, and Nick was well aware that we hold our luxuries by a fitful and precarious tenure. If a friend without personal eagerness was one of the greatest of these it would be evident to the simplest mind that by the law of distribution of earthly boons such a convenience should be expected to forfeit in duration what it displayed in intensity. He had never been without a suspicion that Nash was too good to last, though for that matter nothing had yet confirmed a vague apprehension that his particular manner of breaking up or breaking down would be by his wishing to put so fresh a recruit in relation with other disciples.

That would practically amount to a catastrophe, Nick felt; for it was odd that one could both have a great kindness for him and not in the least, when it came to the point, yearn for a view of his personal extensions. His originality had always been that he appeared to have none; and if in the first instance he had introduced his bright, young, political prodigy to Miriam and her mother, that was an exception for which Peter Sherringham's interference had been mainly responsible. All the same, however, it was some time before Nick ceased to view it as perhaps on the awkward books that, to complete his education as it were, Gabriel would wish him to converse a little with spirits formed by a like tonic discipline. Nick had an instinct, in which there was no consciousness of detriment to Nash, that the pupils, possibly even the imitators, of such a genius would be, as he mentally phrased it, something awful. He could be sure, even Gabriel himself could be sure, of his own reservations, but how could either of them be sure of those of others? Imitation is a fortunate homage only in proportion as it rests on measurements, and there was an indefinable something in Nash's doctrine that would have been discredited by exaggeration or by zeal. Providence happily appeared to have spared it this ordeal; so that Nick had after months still to remind himself how his friend had never pressed on his attention the least little group of fellow-mystics, never offered to produce them for his edification. It scarcely mattered now that he was just the man to whom the superficial would attribute that sort of tail: it would probably have been hard, for example, to persuade Lady Agnes or Julia Dallow or Peter Sherringham that he was not most at home in some dusky, untidy, dimly-imagined suburb of "culture," a region peopled by unpleasant phrasemongers who thought him a gentleman and who had no human use but to be held up in the comic press—which was, moreover, probably restrained by decorum from touching upon the worst of their aberrations.

Nick at any rate never ran his academy to earth nor so much as skirted the suburb in question; never caught from the impenetrable background of his life the least reverberation of flitting or of flirting, the fainting esthetic ululation. There had been moments when he was even moved to anxiety by the silence that poor Gabriel's own faculty of sound made all about him— when at least it reduced to plainer elements (the mere bald terms of lonely singleness and thrift, of the lean philosophic life) the mystery he could never wholly dissociate from him, the air as of the transient and occasional, the likeness to curling vapour or murmuring wind or shifting light. It was, for instance, a symbol of this unclassified state, the lack of all position as a name in cited lists, that Nick in point of fact had no idea where he lived, would not have known how to go and see him or send him a doctor if he had heard he was ill. He had never walked with him to any door of Gabriel's own, even to pause at the threshold, though indeed Nash had a club, the Anonymous, in some improbable square, of which he might be suspected of being the only member—one had never heard of another—where it was vaguely understood letters would some day or other find him. Fortunately he pressed with no sharpness the spring of pity—his whole "form" was so easy a grasp of the helm of consciousness, which he would never let go. He would never consent to any deformity, but would steer his course straight through the eventual narrow pass and simply go down over the horizon.

He in any case turned up Rosedale Road one day after Miriam had left London; he had just come back from a fortnight in Brittany, where he had drawn refreshment from the tragic sweetness of—well, of everything. He was on his way somewhere else—was going abroad for the autumn but was not particular what he did, professing that he had come back just to get Nick utterly off his mind. "It's very nice, it's very nice; yes, yes, I see," he remarked, giving a little, general, assenting sigh as his eyes wandered over the simple scene—a sigh which for a suspicious ear would have testified to an insidious reaction.

Nick's ear, as we know, was already suspicious; a fact accounting for the expectant smile—it indicated the pleasant apprehension of a theory confirmed—with which he returned: "Do you mean my pictures are nice?"

"Yes, yes, your pictures and the whole thing."

"The whole thing?"

"Your existence in this little, remote, independent corner of the great city. The disinterestedness of your attitude, the persistence of your effort, the piety, the beauty, in short the edification, of the whole spectacle."

Nick laughed a little ruefully. "How near to having had enough of me you must be when you speak of me as edifying!" Nash changed colour slightly at this; it was the first time in his friend's remembrance that he had given a sign of embarrassment. "*Vous allez me lâcher*, I see it coming; and who can blame you?—for I've ceased to be in the least spectacular. I had my little hour; it was a great deal, for some people don't even have that. I've given you your curious case and I've been generous; I made the drama last for you as long as I could. You'll 'slope,' my dear fellow—you'll quietly slope; and it will be all right and inevitable, though I shall miss you greatly at first. Who knows whether without you I shouldn't still have been 'representing' Harsh, heaven help me? You rescued me; you converted me from a representative into an example—that's a shade better. But don't I know where you must be when you're reduced to praising my piety?"

"Don't turn me away," said Nash plaintively; "give me a cigarette."

"I shall never dream of turning you away; I shall cherish you till the latest possible hour. I'm only trying to keep myself in tune with the logic of things. The proof of how I cling is that precisely I want you to sit to me."

"To sit to you?" With which Nick could fancy his visitor a little blank.

"Certainly, for after all it isn't much to ask. Here we are and the hour's peculiarly propitious—long light days with no one coming near me, so that I've plenty of time. I had a hope I should have some orders: my younger sister, whom you know and who's a great optimist, plied me with that vision. In fact we invented together a charming little sordid theory that there might be rather a 'run' on me from the chatter (such as it was) produced by my taking up this line. My sister struck out the idea that a good many of the pretty ladies would think me interesting and would want to be done. Perhaps they do, but they've controlled themselves, for I can't say the run has commenced. They haven't even come to look, but I daresay they don't yet quite take it in. Of course it's a bad time—with every one out of town; though you know they might send for me to come and do them at home. Perhaps they will when they settle down. A portrait-tour of a dozen country-houses for the autumn and winter—what do you say to that for the ardent life? I know I excruciate you," Nick added, "but don't you see how it's in my interest to try how much you'll still stand?"

Gabriel puffed his cigarette with a serenity so perfect that it might have been assumed to falsify these words. "Mrs. Dallow will send for you—*vous allez voir ça*," he said in a moment, brushing aside all vagueness.

"She'll send for me?"

"To paint her portrait; she'll recapture you on that basis. She'll get you down to one of the country-houses, and it will all go off as charmingly—with sketching in the morning, on days you can't hunt, and anything you like in the afternoon, and fifteen courses in the evening; there'll be bishops and ambassadors staying—as if you were a 'well-known,' awfully clever amateur. Take care, take care, for, fickle as you may think me, I can read the future: don't imagine you've come to the end of me yet. Mrs. Dallow and your sister, of both of whom I speak with the greatest respect, are capable of hatching together the most conscientious, delightful plan for you. Your differences with the beautiful lady will be patched up and you'll each come round a little and meet the other halfway. The beautiful lady will swallow your profession if you'll swallow hers. She'll put up with the palette if you'll put up with the country-house. It will be a very unusual one in which you won't find a good north room where you can paint. You'll go about with her and do all her friends, all the bishops and ambassadors, and you'll eat your cake and have it, and every one, beginning with your wife, will forget there's anything queer about you, and everything will be for the best in the best of worlds; so that, together—you and she—you'll become a great social institution and every one will think she has a delightful husband; to say nothing of course of your having a delightful wife. Ah my dear fellow, you turn pale, and with reason!" Nash went lucidly on: "that's to pay you for having tried to make me let you have it. You have it then there! I may be a bore"—the emphasis of this, though a mere shade, testified to the first personal resentment Nick had ever heard his visitor express—"I may be a bore, but once in a while I strike a light, I make things out. Then I venture to repeat, 'Take care, take care.' If, as I say, I respect *ces dames* infinitely it's because they will be acting according to the highest wisdom of their sex. That's the sort of thing women do for a man—the sort of thing they invent when they're exceptionally good and clever. When they're not they don't do so well; but it's not for want of trying. There's only one thing in the world better than their incomparable charm: it's their abysmal conscience. Deep calleth unto deep—the one's indeed a part of the other. And when they club together, when they earnestly consider, as in the case we're supposing," Nash continued, "then the whole thing takes a lift; for it's no longer the virtue of the individual, it's that of the wondrous sex."

"You're so remarkable that, more than ever, I must paint you," Nick returned, "though I'm so agitated by your prophetic words that my hand trembles and I shall doubtless scarcely be able to hold my brush. Look how I rattle my easel trying to put it into position. I see it all there just as you show it. Yes, it will be a droll day, and more modern than anything yet, when the conscience of women makes out good reasons for men's not being in love with them. You talk of their goodness and cleverness, and it's certainly much to the point. I don't know what else they themselves might do with those graces, but I don't see what man can do with them but be fond of them where he finds them."

"Oh you'll do it—you'll do it!" cried Nash, brightly jubilant.

"What is it I shall do?"

"Exactly what I just said; if not next year then the year after, or the year after that. You'll go halfway to meet her and she'll drag you about and pass you off. You'll paint the bishops and become a social institution. That is, you'll do it if you don't take great care."

"I shall, no doubt, and that's why I cling to you. You must still look after me," Nick went on. "Don't melt away into a mere improbable reminiscence, a delightful, symbolic fable—don't if you can possibly help it. The trouble is, you see, that you can't really keep hold very tight, because at bottom it will amuse you much more to see me in another pickle than to find me simply jogging down the vista of the years on the straight course. Let me at any rate have some sort of sketch of you as a kind of feather from the angel's wing or a photograph of the ghost—to prove to me in the future that you were once a solid sociable fact, that I didn't invent you, didn't launch you as a deadly hoax. Of course I shall be able to say to myself that you can't have been a fable—otherwise you'd have a moral; but that won't be enough, because I'm not sure you won't have had one. Some day you'll peep in here languidly and find me in such an attitude of piety—presenting my bent back to you as I niggle over some interminable botch—that I shall give cruelly on your nerves and you'll just draw away, closing the door softly. You'll be gentle and considerate about it and spare me, you won't even make me look round. You'll steal off on tiptoe, never, never to return."

Gabriel consented to sit; he professed he should enjoy it and be glad to give up for it his immediate foreign commerce, so vague to Nick, so definite apparently to himself; and he came back three times for the purpose. Nick promised himself a deal of interest from this experiment, for with the first hour of it he began to feel that really as yet, given the conditions under which he now studied him, he had never at all thoroughly explored his friend. His impression had been that Nash had a head quite fine enough to be a challenge, and that as he sat there day by day all sorts of pleasant and paintable things would come out in his face. This impression was not gainsaid, but the whole tangle grew denser. It struck our young man that he had never *seen* his subject before, and yet somehow this revelation was not produced by the sense of actually seeing it. What was revealed was the difficulty—what he saw was not the measurable mask but the ambiguous meaning. He had taken things for granted which literally were not there, and he found things there—except that he couldn't catch them—which he had not hitherto counted in or presumed to handle. This baffling effect, eminently in the line of the mystifying, so familiar to Nash, might have been the result of his whimsical volition, had it not appeared to our artist, after a few hours of the job, that his sitter was not the one who enjoyed it most. He was uncomfortable, at first vaguely and then definitely so—silent, restless, gloomy, dim, as if on the test the homage of a director attention than he had ever had gave him less pleasure than he would have supposed. He had been willing to judge of this in good faith; but frankly he rather suffered. He wasn't cross, but was clearly unhappy, and Nick had never before felt him contract instead of expanding.

It was all accordingly as if a trap had been laid for him, and our young man asked himself if it were really fair. At the same time there was something richly rare in such a relation between the subject and the artist, and Nick was disposed to go on till he should have to stop for pity or for shame. He caught eventually a glimmer of the truth underlying the strangeness, guessed that what upset his friend was simply the reversal, in such a combination, of his usual terms of intercourse. He was so accustomed to living upon irony and the interpretation of things that it was new to him to be himself interpreted and—as a gentleman who sits for his portrait is always liable to be—interpreted all ironically. From being outside of the universe he was suddenly brought into it, and from the position of a free commentator and critic, an easy amateurish editor of the whole affair, reduced to that of humble ingredient and contributor. It occurred afterwards to Nick that he had perhaps brought on a catastrophe by having happened to throw off as they gossiped or languished, and not alone without a cruel intention, but with an impulse of genuine solicitude: "But, my dear fellow, what will you do when you're old?"

"Old? What do you call old?" Nash had replied bravely enough, but with another perceptible tinge of irritation. "Must I really remind you at this time of day that that term has no application to such a condition as mine? It only belongs to you wretched people who have the incurable superstition of 'doing'; it's the ignoble collapse you prepare for yourselves when you cease to be able to do. For me there'll be no collapse, no transition, no clumsy readjustment of attitude; for I shall only *be*, more and more, with all the accumulations of experience, the longer I live."

"Oh I'm not particular about the term," said Nick. "If you don't call it old, the ultimate state, call it weary—call it final. The accumulations of experience are practically accumulations of fatigue."

"I don't know anything about weariness. I live freshly—it doesn't fatigue me."

"Then you need never die," Nick declared.

"Certainly; I daresay I'm indestructible, immortal."

Nick laughed out at this—it would be such fine news to some people. But it was uttered with perfect gravity, and it might very well have been in the spirit of that gravity that Nash failed to observe his agreement to sit again the next day. The next and the next and the next passed, but he never came back.

True enough, punctuality was not important for a man who felt that he had the command of all time. Nevertheless his disappearance "without a trace," that of a personage in a fairy-tale or a melodrama, made a considerable impression on his friend as the months went on; so that, though he had never before had the least difficulty about entering into the play of Gabriel's humour, Nick now recalled with a certain fanciful awe the special accent with which he had ranked himself among imperishable things. He wondered a little if he hadn't at last, balancing always on the stretched tight-rope of his wit, fallen over on the wrong side. He had never before, of a truth, been so nearly witless, and would have to have gone mad in short to become so singularly simple. Perhaps indeed he was acting only more than usual in his customary spirit—thoughtfully contributing, for Nick's enlivement, a purple rim of mystery to an horizon now so dreadfully let down. The mystery at any rate remained; another shade of purple in fact was virtually added to it. Nick had the prospect, for the future, of waiting to see, all curiously, when Nash would turn up, if ever, and the further diversion—it almost consoled him for the annoyance of being left with a second unfinished thing on his hands—of imagining in the portrait he had begun an odd tendency to fade gradually from the canvas. He couldn't catch it in the act, but he could have ever a suspicion on glancing at it that the hand of time was rubbing it away little by little—for all the world as in some delicate Hawthorne tale—and making the surface indistinct and bare of all resemblance to the model. Of course the moral of the Hawthorne tale would be that his personage would come back in quaint confidence on the day his last projected shadow should have vanished.

L

One day toward the end of March of the following year, in other words more than six months after Mr. Nash's disappearance, Bridget Dormer came into her brother's studio and greeted him with the effusion that accompanies a return from an absence. She had been staying at Broadwood—she had been staying at Harsh. She had various things to tell him about these episodes, about his mother, about Grace, about her small subterraneous self, and about Percy's having come, just before, over to Broadwood for two days; the longest visit with which, almost since they could remember, the head of the family had honoured their common parent. Nick noted indeed that this demonstration had apparently been taken as a great favour, and Biddy loyally testified to the fact that her elder brother was awfully jolly and that his presence had been a pretext for tremendous fun. Nick accordingly asked her what had passed about his marriage—what their mother had said to him.

"Oh nothing," she replied; and Percy had said nothing to Lady Agnes and not a word to herself. This partly explained, for his junior, the consequent beatitude—none but cheerful topics had been produced; but he questioned the girl further—to a point which led her to say: "Oh I daresay that before long she'll write to her."

"Who'll write to whom?"

"Mamma'll write to Percy's wife. I'm sure he'd like it. Of course we shall end by going to see her. He was awfully disappointed at what he found in Spain—he didn't find anything."

Biddy spoke of his disappointment almost with commiseration, for she was evidently inclined this morning to a fresh and kindly view of things. Nick could share her feeling but so far as was permitted by a recognition merely general of what his brother must have looked for. It might have been snipe and it might have been bristling boars. Biddy was indeed brief at first about everything, in spite of all the weeks that had gone since their last meeting; for he quickly enough saw she had something behind—something that made her gay and that she wanted to come to quickly. He was vaguely vexed at her being, fresh from Broadwood, so gay as that; for—it was impossible to shut one's eyes to the fact—what had practically come to pass in regard to that rural retreat was exactly what he had desired to avert. All winter, while it had been taken for granted his mother and sisters were doing what he wished, they had been doing precisely what he hated. He held Biddy perhaps least responsible, and there was no one he could exclusively blame. He washed his hands of the matter and succeeded fairly well, for the most part, in forgetting he was not pleased. Julia herself in truth appeared to have been the most active member of the little group united to make light of his decencies. There had been a formal restitution of Broadwood, but the three ladies were there more than ever, with the slight difference that they were mainly there with its mistress. Mahomet had declined to go any more to the mountain, so the mountain had virtually come to Mahomet.

After their long visit in the autumn Lady Agnes and her girls had come back to town; but they had gone down again for Christmas and Julia had taken this occasion to write to Nick that she hoped very much he wouldn't refuse them all his own company for just a little scrap of the supremely sociable time. Nick, after reflexion, judged it best not to refuse, so that he passed, in the event, four days under his cousin's roof. The "all" proved a great many people, for she had taken care to fill the house. She took the largest view of hospitality and Nick had never seen her so splendid, so free-handed, so gracefully active. She was a perfect mistress of the revels; she had arranged some ancient bravery for every day and for every night. The Dormers were so much in it, as the phrase was, that after all their discomfiture their fortune seemed in an hour to have come back. There had been a moment when, in extemporised charades, Lady Agnes, an elderly figure being required, appeared on the point of undertaking the part of the housekeeper at a castle, who, dropping her *h*'s, showed sheeplike tourists about; but she waived the opportunity in favour of her daughter Grace. Even Grace had a great success; Grace dropped her *h*'s as with the crash of empires. Nick of course was in the charades and in everything, but Julia was not; she only invented, directed, led the applause. When nothing else was forward Nick "sketched" the whole company: they followed him about, they waylaid him on staircases, clamouring to be allowed to sit. He obliged them so far as he could, all save Julia, who didn't clamour; and, growing rather red, he thought of Gabriel Nash while he bent over the paper. Early in the new year he went abroad for six weeks, but only as far as Paris. It was a new Paris for him then; a Paris of the Rue Bonaparte and three or four professional friends—he had more of these there than in London; a Paris of studios and studies and models, of researches and revelations, comparisons and contrasts, of strong impressions and long discussions and rather uncomfortable economies, small cafés, bad fires and the general sense of being twenty again.

While he was away his mother and sisters—Lady Agnes now sometimes wrote to him—returned to London for a month, and before he was again established in Rosedale Road they went back for a third course of Broadwood. After they had been there five days—and this was the salt of the whole feast— Julia took herself off to Harsh, leaving them in undisturbed possession. They had remained so—they wouldn't come up to town till after Easter. The trick was played, and Biddy, as I have mentioned, was now very content. Her brother presently learned, however, that the reason of this was not wholly the success of the trick; unless indeed her further ground were only a continuation of it. She was not in London as a forerunner of her mother; she was not even as yet in Calcutta Gardens. She had come to spend a week with Florry Tressilian, who had lately taken the dearest little flat in a charming new place, just put up, on the other side of the Park, with all kinds of lifts and tubes and electricities. Florry had been awfully nice to her—had been with them ever so long at Broadwood while the flat was being painted and prepared—and mamma had then let her, let Biddy, promise to come to her, when everything was ready, so that they might have a happy old maids' (for they *were*, old maids now!) house-warming together. If Florry could by this time do without a chaperon—she had two latchkeys and went alone on the top of omnibuses, and her name was in the Red Book—she was enough of a duenna for another girl. Biddy referred with sweet cynical eyes to the fine happy stride she had thus taken in the direction of enlightened spinsterhood; and Nick hung his head, immensely abashed and humiliated, for, modern as he had fatuously supposed himself, there were evidently currents more modern yet.

It so happened that on this particular morning he had drawn out of a corner his interrupted study of Gabriel Nash; on no further curiosity—he had only been looking round the room in a rummaging spirit—than to see how much or how little of it remained. It had become to his view so dim an adumbration—he was sure of this, and it pressed some spring of melancholy mirth—that it didn't seem worth putting away, and he left it leaning against a table as if it had been a blank canvas or a "preparation" to be painted over. In this posture it attracted Biddy's attention, for on a second glance it showed distinguishable features. She had not seen it before and now asked whom it might represent, remarking also that she could almost guess, yet not quite: she had known the original but couldn't name him.

"Six months ago, for a few days, it represented Gabriel Nash," Nick replied. "But it isn't anybody or anything now."

"Six months ago? What's the matter with it and why don't you go on?"

"What's the matter with it is more than I can tell you. But I can't go on because I've lost my model."

She had an almost hopeful stare. "Is he beautifully dead?"

Her brother laughed out at the candid cheerfulness, hopefulness almost, with which this inquiry broke from her. "He's only dead to me. He has gone away."

"Where has he gone?"

"I haven't the least idea."

"Why, have you quarrelled?"—Biddy shone again.

"Quarrelled? For what do you take us? Docs the nightingale quarrel with the moon?"

"I needn't ask which of you is the moon," she said.

"Of course I'm the nightingale. But, more literally," Nick continued, "Nash has melted back into the elements—he's part of the great air of the world." And then as even with this lucidity he saw the girl still mystified: "I've a notion he has gone to India and at the present moment is reclining on a bank of flowers in the vale of Cashmere."

Biddy had a pause, after which she dropped: "Julia will be glad—she dislikes him so."

"If she dislikes him why should she be glad he's so enviably placed?"

"I mean about his going away. She'll be glad of that."

"My poor incorrigible child," Nick cried, "what has Julia to do with it?"

"She has more to do with things than you think," Biddy returned with all her bravery. Yet she had no sooner uttered the words than she perceptibly blushed. Hereupon, to attenuate the foolishness of her blush—only it had the opposite effect—she added: "She thinks he has been a bad element in your life."

Nick emitted a long strange sound. "She thinks perhaps, but she doesn't think enough; otherwise she'd arrive at this better thought—that she knows nothing whatever about my life."

"Ah brother," the girl pleaded with solemn eyes, "you don't imagine what an interest she takes in it. She has told me many times—she has talked lots to me about it." Biddy paused and then went on, an anxious little smile shining through her gravity as if from a cautious wonder as to how much he would take: "She has a conviction it was Mr. Nash who made trouble between you."

"Best of little sisters," Nick pronounced, "those are thoroughly second-rate ideas, the result of a perfectly superficial view. Excuse my possibly priggish tone, but they really attribute to my dear detached friend a part he's quite incapable of playing. He can neither make trouble nor take trouble; no trouble could ever either have come out of him or have got into him. Moreover," our young man continued, "if Julia has talked to you so much about the matter there's no harm in my talking to you a little. When she threw me over in an hour it was on a perfectly definite occasion. That occasion was the presence in my studio of a dishevelled, an abandoned actress."

"Oh Nick, she has not thrown you over!" Biddy protested. "She has not—I've proof."

He felt at this direct denial a certain stir of indignation and looked at the girl with momentary sternness. "Has she sent you here to tell me this? What do you mean by proof?"

Biddy's eyes, at these questions, met her brother's with a strange expression, and for a few seconds, while she looked entreatingly into them, she wavered there with parted lips and vaguely stretched out her hands. The next minute she had burst into tears—she was sobbing on his breast. He said "Hallo!" and soothed her; but it was very quickly over. Then she told him what she meant by her proof and what she had had on her mind ever since her present arrival. It was a message from Julia, but not to say—not to say what he had questioned her about just before; though indeed, more familiar now that he had his arm round her, she boldly expressed the hope it might in the end come to the same thing. Julia simply wanted to know—- she had instructed her to sound him discreetly—if Nick would undertake her portrait; and she wound up this experiment in "sounding" by the statement that their beautiful kinswoman was dying to sit.

"Dying to sit?" echoed Nick, whose turn it was this time to feel his colour rise.

"At any moment you like after Easter, when she comes up. She wants a full-length and your very best, your most splendid work."

Nick stared, not caring that he had blushed. "Is she serious?"

"Ah Nick—serious!" Biddy reasoned tenderly. She came nearer again and he thought her again about to weep. He took her by the shoulders, looking into her eyes.

"It's all right if she knows *I* am. But why doesn't she come like any one else? I don't refuse people!"

"Nick, dearest Nick!" she went on, her eyes conscious and pleading. He looked into them intently—as well as she could he play at sounding—and for a moment, between these young persons, the air was lighted by the glimmer of mutual searchings and suppressed confessions. Nick read deep and then, suddenly releasing his sister, turned away. She didn't see his face in that movement, but an observer to whom it had been presented might have fancied it denoted a foreboding that was not exactly a dread, yet was not exclusively a joy.

The first thing he made out in the room, when he could distinguish, was Gabriel Nash's portrait, which suddenly filled him with an unreasoning rancour. He seized it and turned it about, jammed it back into its corner with its face against the wall. This small diversion might have served to carry off the embarrassment with which he had finally averted himself from Biddy. The embarrassment, however, was all his own; none of it was reflected in the way she resumed, after a silence in which she had followed his disposal of the picture:

"If she's so eager to come here—for it's here she wants to sit, not in Great Stanhope Street, never!—how can she prove better that she doesn't care a bit if she meets Miss Rooth?"

"She won't meet Miss Rooth," Nick replied rather dryly.

"Oh I'm sorry!" said Biddy. She was as frank as if she had achieved a virtual victory, and seemed to regret the loss of a chance for Julia to show an equal mildness. Her tone made her brother laugh, but she went on with confidence: "She thought it was Mr. Nash who made Miss Rooth come."

"So he did, by the way," said Nick.

"Well then, wasn't that making trouble?"

"I thought you admitted there was no harm in her being here."

"Yes, but *he* hoped there'd be."

"Poor Nash's hopes!" Nick laughed. "My dear child, it would take a cleverer head than you or me, or even Julia, who must have invented that wise theory, to say what they were. However, let us agree that even if they were perfectly fiendish my good sense has been a match for them."

"Oh Nick, that's delightful!" chanted Biddy. Then she added: "Do you mean she doesn't come any more?"

"The dishevelled actress? She hasn't been near me for months."

"But she's in London—she's always acting? I've been away so much I've scarcely observed," Biddy explained with a slight change of note.

"The same silly part, poor creature, for nearly a year. It appears that that's 'success'—in her profession. I saw her in the character several times last summer, but haven't set foot in her theatre since."

Biddy took this in; then she suggested; "Peter wouldn't have liked that."

"Oh Peter's likes—!" Nick at his easel, beginning to work, conveniently sighed.

"I mean her acting the same part for a year."

"I'm sure I don't know; he has never written me a word."

"Nor me either," Biddy returned.

There was another short silence, during which Nick brushed at a panel. It ended in his presently saying: "There's one thing certainly Peter *would* like—that is simply to be here to-night. It's a great night—another great night—for the abandoned one. She's to act Juliet for the first time."

"Ah how I should like to see her!" the girl cried.

Nick glanced at her; she sat watching him. "She has sent me a stall; I wish she had sent me two. I should have been delighted to take you."

"Don't you think you could get another?" Biddy quavered.

"They must be in tremendous demand. But who knows after all?" Nick added, at the same moment looking round. "Here's a chance—here's quite an extraordinary chance!"

His servant had opened the door and was ushering in a lady whose identity was indeed justly reflected in those words. "Miss Rooth!" the man announced; but he was caught up by a gentleman who came next and who exclaimed, laughing and with a gesture gracefully corrective: "No, no—no longer Miss Rooth!"

Miriam entered the place with her charming familiar grandeur—entered very much as she might have appeared, as she appeared every night, early in her first act, at the back of the stage, by the immemorial middle door. She might exactly now have been presenting herself to the house, taking easy possession, repeating old movements, looking from one to the other of the actors before the footlights. The rich "Good-morning" she threw into the air, holding out her right hand to Biddy and then giving her left to Nick—as she might have given it to her own brother—had nothing to tell of intervals or alienations. She struck Biddy as still more terrible in her splendid practice than when she had seen her before—the practice and the splendour had now something almost royal. The girl had had occasion to make her curtsey to majesties and highnesses, but the flutter those effigies produced was nothing to the way in which at the approach of this young lady the agitated air seemed to recognise something supreme. So the deep mild eyes she bent on Biddy were not soothing, though for that matter evidently intended to soothe. Biddy wondered Nick could have got so used to her—he joked at her as she loomed—and later in the day, still under the great impression of this incident, she even wondered that Peter could have full an impunity. It was true that Peter apparently didn't quite feel one.

"You never came—you never came," Miriam said to her kindly and sadly; and Biddy, recognising the allusion, the invitation to visit the actress at

581

home, had to explain how much she had been absent from London and then even that her brother hadn't proposed to take her.

"Very true—he hasn't come himself. What's he doing now?" asked Miss Rooth, standing near her young friend but looking at Nick, who had immediately engaged in conversation with his other visitor, a gentleman whose face came back to the girl. She had seen this gentleman on the stage with the great performer—that was it, the night Peter took her to the theatre with Florry Tressilian. Oh that Nick would only do something of that sort now! This desire, quickened by the presence of the strange, expressive woman, by the way she scattered sweet syllables as if she were touching the piano-keys, combined with other things to make our young lady's head swim—other things too mingled to name, admiration and fear and dim divination and purposeless pride and curiosity and resistance, the impulse to go away and the determination to (as she would have liked fondly to fancy it) "hold her ground." The actress courted her with a wondrous voice—what was the matter with the actress and what did she want?—and Biddy tried in return to give an idea of what Nick was doing. Not succeeding very well she was about to appeal to her brother, but Miriam stopped her with the remark that it didn't signify; besides, Dashwood was telling Nick something—something they wanted him to know. "We're in a great excitement—he has taken a theatre," Miriam added.

"Taken a theatre?" Biddy was vague.

"We're going to set up for ourselves. He's going to do for me altogether. It has all been arranged only within a day or two. It remains to be seen how it will answer," Miriam smiled. Biddy murmured some friendly hope, and the shining presence went on: "Do you know why I've broken in here to-day after a long absence—interrupting your poor brother so basely, taking up his precious time? It's because I'm so nervous."

"About your first night?" Biddy risked.

"Do you know about that—are you coming?" Miriam had caught at it.

"No, I'm not coming—I haven't a place."

"Will you come if I send you one?"

"Oh but really it's too beautiful of you!" breathed the girl.

"You shall have a box; your brother shall bring you. They can't squeeze in a pin, I'm told; but I've kept a box, I'll manage it. Only if I do, you know, mind you positively come!" She sounded it as the highest of favours, resting her hand on Biddy's.

"Don't be afraid. And may I bring a friend—the friend with whom I'm staying?"

Miriam now just gloomed. "Do you mean Mrs. Dallow?"

"No, no—Miss Tressilian. She puts me up, she has got a flat. Did you ever see a flat?" asked Biddy expansively. "My cousin's not in London." Miriam replied that she might bring whom she liked and Biddy broke out to her brother: "Fancy what kindness, Nick: we're to have a box to-night and you're to take me!"

Nick turned to her a face of levity which struck her even at the time as too cynically free, but which she understood when the finer sense of it subsequently recurred to her. Mr. Dashwood interposed with the remark that it was all very well to talk about boxes, but that he didn't see how at that time of day the miracle was to be worked.

"You haven't kept one as I told you?" Miriam demanded.

"As you told me, my dear? Tell the lamb to keep its tenderest mutton from the wolves!"

"You shall have one: we'll arrange it," Miriam went on to Biddy.

"Let me qualify that statement a little, Miss Dormer," said Basil Dashwood. "We'll arrange it if it's humanly possible."

"We'll arrange it even if it's inhumanly *im*possible—that's just the point," Miriam declared to the girl. "Don't talk about trouble—what's he meant for but to take it? *Cela s'annonce bien*, you see," she continued to Nick: "doesn't it look as if we should pull beautifully together?" And as he answered that

583

he heartily congratulated her—he was immensely interested in what he had been told—she exclaimed after resting her eyes on him a moment: "What will you have? It seemed simpler! It was clear there had to be some one." She explained further to Nick what had led her to come in at that moment, while Dashwood approached Biddy with a civil assurance that they would see, they would leave no stone unturned, though he would not have taken upon himself to promise.

Miriam reminded Nick of the blessing he had been to her nearly a year before, on her other first night, when she was all impatient and on edge; how he had let her come and sit there for hours—helped her to possess her soul till the evening and to keep out of harm's way. The case was the same at present, with the aggravation indeed that he would understand—Dashwood's nerves as well as her own: Dashwood's were a great deal worse than hers. Everything was ready for Juliet; they had been rehearsing for five months—it had kept her from going mad from the treadmill of the other piece—and he, Nick, had occurred to her again, in the last intolerable hours, as the friend in need, the salutary stop-gap, no matter how much she worried him. She shouldn't be turned out? Biddy broke away from Basil Dashwood: she must go, she must hurry off to Miss Tressilian with her news. Florry might make some other stupid engagement for the evening: she must be warned in time. The girl took a flushed, excited leave after having received a renewal of Miriam's pledge and even heard her say to Nick that he must now give back the seat already sent him—they should be sure to have another use for it.

LI

That night at the theatre and in the box—the miracle had been wrought, the treasure found—Nick Dormer pointed out to his two companions the stall he had relinquished, which was close in front; noting how oddly it remained during the whole of the first act vacant. The house was beyond everything, the actress beyond any one; though to describe again so famous an occasion—it has been described repeatedly by other reporters—is not in the compass of the closing words of a history already too sustained. It is enough to say that these great hours marked an era in contemporary art and that for those who had a spectator's share in them the words "revelation," "incarnation," "acclamation," "demonstration," "ovation"—to name only a few, and all accompanied by the word "extraordinary"—acquired a new force. Miriam's Juliet was an exquisite image of young passion and young despair, expressed in the truest, divinest music that had ever poured from tragic lips. The great childish audience, gaping at her points, expanded there before her like a lap to catch flowers.

During the first interval our three friends in the box had plenty to talk about, and they were so occupied with it that for some time they failed to observe a gentleman who had at last come into the empty stall near the front. This discovery was presently formulated by Miss Tressilian in the cheerful exclamation: "Only fancy—there's Mr. Sherringham!" This of course immediately became a high wonder—a wonder for Nick and Biddy, who had not heard of his return; and the prodigy was quickened by the fact that he gave no sign of looking for them or even at them. Having taken possession of his place he sat very still in it, staring straight before him at the curtain. His abrupt reappearance held the seeds of anxiety both for Biddy and for Nick, so that it was mainly Miss Tressilian who had freedom of mind to throw off the theory that he had come back that very hour—had arrived from a long journey. Couldn't they see how strange he was and how brown, how burnt and how red, how tired and how worn? They all inspected him, though Biddy declined Miss Tressilian's glass; but he was evidently indifferent to notice and finally Biddy, leaning back in her chair, dropped the fantastic words:

"He has come home to marry Juliet!"

Nick glanced at her and then replied: "What a disaster—to make such a journey as that and to be late for the fair!"

"Late for the fair?"

"Why she's married—these three days. They did it very quietly; Miriam says because her mother hated it and hopes it won't be much known! All the same she's Basil Dashwood's wedded wife—he has come in just in time to take the receipts for Juliet. It's a good thing, no doubt, for there are at least two fortunes to be made out of her, and he'll give up the stage." Nick explained to Miss Tressilian, who had inquired, that the gentleman in question was the actor who was playing Mercutio, and he asked Biddy if she hadn't known that this was what they were telling him in Rosedale Road that morning. She replied that she had understood nothing but that she was to be where she was, and she sank considerably behind the drapery of the box. From this cover she was able to launch, creditably enough, the exclamation:

"Poor, poor Peter!"

Nick got up and stood looking at poor, poor Peter. "He ought to come round and speak to us, but if he doesn't see us I suppose he doesn't." He quitted the box as to go to the restored exile, and I may add that as soon as he had done so Florence Tressilian bounded over to the dusk in which Biddy had nestled. What passed immediately between these young ladies needn't concern us: it is sufficient to mention that two minutes later Miss Tressilian broke out:

"Look at him, dearest; he's turning his head this way!"

"Thank you, I don't care to watch his turns," said Biddy; and she doubtless demeaned herself in the high spirit of these words. It nevertheless happened that directly afterwards she had certain knowledge of his having glanced at his watch as if to judge how soon the curtain would rise again, as well as of his having then jumped up and passed quickly out of his place. The curtain had risen again without his reappearing and without Nick's returning. Indeed by the time Nick slipped in a good deal of the third act was over; and even then, even when the curtain descended, Peter had not come back. Nick sat down in silence to watch the stage, to which the breathless attention of his companions seemed attached, though Biddy after a moment threw round at him a single quick look. At the end of the act they were all occupied with the recalls, the applause and the responsive loveliness of Juliet as she was led out—Mercutio had to give her up to Romeo—and even for a few minutes after the deafening roar had subsided nothing was said among the three. At last Nick began:

"It's quite true he has just arrived; he's in Great Stanhope Street. They've given him several weeks, to make up for the uncomfortable way they bundled him off—to get there in time for some special business that had suddenly to be gone into—when he first went out: he tells me they even then promised that. He got into Southampton only a few hours ago, rushed up by the first train he could catch and came off here without any dinner."

"Fancy!" said Miss Tressilian; while Biddy more generally asked if Peter might be in good health and appeared to have been happy. Nick replied that he described his post as beastly but didn't seem to have suffered from it. He was to be in England probably a month, he was awfully brown, he sent his love to Biddy. Miss Tressilian looked at his empty stall and was of the opinion that it would be more to the point if he were to come in to see her.

"Oh he'll turn up; we had a goodish talk in the lobby where he met me. I think he went out somewhere."

"How odd to come so many thousand miles for this and then not to stay!" Biddy fluted.

"Did he come on purpose for this?" Miss Tressilian asked.

"Perhaps he's gone out to get his dinner!" joked Biddy.

Her friend suggested that he might be behind the scenes, but Nick cast doubts; whereupon Biddy asked if he himself were not going round. At this moment the curtain rose; Nick said he would go in the next interval. As soon as it came he quitted the box, remaining absent while it lasted.

All this time, in the house, there was no sign of Peter. Nick reappeared only as the fourth act was beginning and uttered no word to his companions till it was over. Then, after a further delay produced by renewed vociferous proofs of the personal victory won, he depicted his visit to the stage and the wonderful sight of Miriam on the field of battle. Miss Tressilian inquired if he had found Mr. Sherringham with her; to which he replied that, save across the footlights, she had not been in touch with him. At this a soft exclamation broke from Biddy. "Poor Peter! Where is he, then?"

Nick seemed to falter. "He's walking the streets."

"Walking the streets?"

"I don't know—I give it up!" our young man replied; and his tone, for some minutes, reduced his companions to silence. But a little later Biddy said:

"Was it for him this morning she wanted that place—when she asked you to give yours back?"

"For him exactly. It's very odd she had just managed to keep it—for all the good use he makes of it! She told me just now that she heard from him, at his post, a short time ago, to the effect that he had seen in a newspaper a statement she was going to do Juliet and that he firmly intended, though the ways and means were not clear to him—his leave of absence hadn't yet come out and he couldn't be sure when it would come—to be present on her first night; whereby she must do him the service to provide him a place. She thought this a speech rather in the air, so that in the midst of all her cares she took no particular pains about the matter. She had an idea she had really done with him for a long time. But this afternoon what does he do but telegraph to her from Southampton that he keeps his appointment and counts on her for a stall? Unless she had got back mine she wouldn't have been able to help him. When she was in Rosedale Road this morning she hadn't received his telegram; but his promise, his threat, whatever it was, came back to her: she had a vague foreboding and thought that on the chance she had better hold something ready. When she got home she found his telegram, and she told me he was the first person she saw in the house, through her fright when she came on in the second act. It appears she was terrified this time, and it lasted half through the play."

"She must be rather annoyed at his having gone away," Miss Tressilian observed.

"Annoyed? I'm not so sure!" laughed Nick.

"Ah here he comes back!" cried Biddy, behind her fan, while the absentee edged into his seat in time for the fifth act. He stood there a moment, first looking round the theatre; then he turned his eyes to the box occupied by his relatives, smiling and waving his hand.

"After that he'll surely come and see you," said Miss Tressilian.

"We shall see him as we go out," Biddy returned: "he must lose no more time."

Nick looked at him with a glass, then exclaiming: "Well, I'm glad he has pulled himself together!"

"Why what's the matter with him—if he wasn't disappointed of his seat?" Miss Tressilian demanded.

"The matter with him is that a couple of hours ago he had a great shock."

"A great shock?"

"I may as well mention it at last," Nick went on. "I had to say something to him in the lobby there when we met—something I was pretty sure he couldn't like. I let him have it full in the face—it seemed to me better and wiser. I let him know that Juliet's married."

"Didn't he know it?" asked Biddy, who, with her face raised, had listened in deep stillness to every word that fell from her brother.

"How should he have known it? It has only just taken place, and they've been so clever, for reasons of their own—those people move among a lot of considerations that are absolutely foreign to us—about keeping it out of the papers. They put in a lot of lies and they leave out the real things."

"You don't mean to say Mr. Sherringham wanted to *marry* her!" Miss Tressilian gasped.

"Don't ask me what he wanted—I daresay we shall never know. One thing's very certain—that he didn't like my news, dear old Peter, and that I shan't soon forget the look in his face as he turned away from me and slipped out into the street. He was too much upset—he couldn't trust himself to come back; he had to walk about—he tried to walk it off."

"Let us hope, then, he *has* walked it off!"

"Ah poor fellow—he couldn't hold out to the end; he has had to come back and look at her once more. He knows she'll be sublime in these last scenes."

"Is he so much in love with her as that? What difference does it make for an actress if she *is* mar—?" But in this rash inquiry Miss Tressilian suddenly checked herself.

"We shall probably never know how much he has been in love with her, nor what difference it makes. We shall never know exactly what he came back for, nor why he couldn't stand it out there any longer without relief, nor why he scrambled down here all but straight from the station, nor why after all, for the last two hours, he has been roaming the streets. And it doesn't matter, for it's none of our business. But I'm sorry for him—she is going to be sublime," Nick added. The curtain was rising on the tragic climax of the play.

Miriam Rooth was sublime; yet it may be confided to the reader that during these supreme scenes Bridget Dormer directed her eyes less to the inspired actress than to a figure in the stalls who sat with his own gaze fastened to the stage. It may further be intimated that Peter Sherringham, though he saw but a fragment of the performance, read clear, at the last, in the intense light of genius with which this fragment was charged, that even so after all he had been rewarded for his formidable journey. The great trouble of his infatuation subsided, leaving behind it something appreciably deep and pure. This pacification was far from taking place at once, but it was helped on, unexpectedly to him—it began to work at least—the very next night he saw the play, through the whole of which he then sat. He felt somehow recalled to the real by the very felicity of this experience, the supreme exhibition itself. He began to come back as from a far-off province of his history where miserable madness had reigned. He had been baffled, he had got his answer; it must last him—that was plain. He didn't fully accept it the first week or the second; but he accepted it sooner than he could have supposed had he known what it was to be when he paced at night, under the southern stars, the deck of the ship bearing him to England.

It had been, as we know, Miss Tressilian's view, and even Biddy's, that evening, that Peter Sherringham would join them as they left the theatre. This view, however, was not confirmed by the event, for our troubled gentleman vanished utterly—disappointingly crude behaviour on the part of a young diplomatist who had distinguished himself—before any one could put a hand on him. And he failed to make up for his crudity by coming to see any one the next day, or even the next. Indeed many days elapsed and very little would have been known about him had it not been that, in the country, Mrs. Dallow knew. What Mrs. Dallow knew was eventually known to Biddy Dormer; and in this way it could be established in his favour that he had remained some extraordinarily small number of days in London, had almost directly gone over to Paris to see his old chief. He came back from Paris—Biddy learnt this not from Julia, but in a much more immediate way: she knew it by his pressing the little electric button at the door of Florence Tressilian's flat one day when the good Florence was out and she herself was at home. He made on this occasion a very long visit. The good Florence knew it not much later, you may be sure—and how he had got their address from Nick—and she took an extravagant pleasure in it. Mr. Sherringham had never been to see *her*—the like of her—in his life: therefore it was clear what had made him begin. When he had once begun he kept it up, and Miss Tressilian's pleasure grew.

Good as she was, she could remember without the slightest relenting what Nick Dormer had repeated to them at the theatre about the dreary side of Peter's present post. However, she was not bound to make a stand at this if persons more nearly concerned, Lady Agnes and the girl herself, didn't mind it. How little *they* minded it, and Grace and Julia Dallow and even Nick, was proved in the course of a meeting that took place at Harsh during the Easter holidays. The mistress of that seat had a small and intimate party to celebrate her brother's betrothal. The two ladies came over from Broadwood; even Nick, for two days, went back to his old hunting-ground, and Miss Tressilian relinquished for as long a time the delights of her newly arranged flat. Peter Sherringham obtained an extension of leave, so that he might go back to his legation with a wife. Fortunately, as it turned out, Biddy's ordeal, in the more or less torrid zone, was not cruelly prolonged, for the pair have already received a superior appointment. It is Lady Agnes's proud opinion that her daughter is even now shaping their destiny. I say "even now," for these facts bring me very close to contemporary history. During those two days at Harsh Nick arranged with the former mistress of his fate the conditions, as they might be called, under which she should sit to him; and every one will remember in how recent an exhibition general attention was attracted, as the newspapers said in describing the private view, to the noble portrait of a lady which was the final outcome of that arrangement. Gabriel Nash had been at many a private view, but he was not at that one.

These matters are highly recent, however, as I say; so that in glancing about the little circle of the interests I have tried to evoke I am suddenly warned by a sharp sense of modernness. This renders it difficult to me, for instance, in taking leave of our wonderful Miriam, to do much more than allude to the general impression that her remarkable career is even yet only in its early prime. Basil Dashwood has got his theatre, and his wife—people know now she *is* his wife—has added three or four new parts to her repertory; but every one is agreed that both in public and in private she has a great deal more to show. This is equally true of Nick Dormer, in regard to whom I may finally say that his friend Nash's predictions about his reunion with Mrs. Dallow have not up to this time been justified. On the other hand, I must not omit to add, this lady has not, at the latest accounts, married Mr. Macgeorge. It is very true there has been a rumour that Mr. Macgeorge is worried about her—has even ceased at all fondly to believe in her.

THE TURN OF THE SCREW

THE TURN OF THE SCREW

The story had held us, round the fire, sufficiently breathless, but except the obvious remark that it was gruesome, as, on Christmas Eve in an old house, a strange tale should essentially be, I remember no comment uttered till somebody happened to say that it was the only case he had met in which such a visitation had fallen on a child. The case, I may mention, was that of an apparition in just such an old house as had gathered us for the occasion—an appearance, of a dreadful kind, to a little boy sleeping in the room with his mother and waking her up in the terror of it; waking her not to dissipate his dread and soothe him to sleep again, but to encounter also, herself, before she had succeeded in doing so, the same sight that had shaken him. It was this observation that drew from Douglas—not immediately, but later in the evening—a reply that had the interesting consequence to which I call attention. Someone else told a story not particularly effective, which I saw he was not following. This I took for a sign that he had himself something to produce and that we should only have to wait. We waited in fact till two nights later; but that same evening, before we scattered, he brought out what was in his mind.

"I quite agree—in regard to Griffin's ghost, or whatever it was—that its appearing first to the little boy, at so tender an age, adds a particular touch. But it's not the first occurrence of its charming kind that I know to have involved a child. If the child gives the effect another turn of the screw, what do you say to *two* children—?"

"We say, of course," somebody exclaimed, "that they give two turns! Also that we want to hear about them."

I can see Douglas there before the fire, to which he had got up to present his back, looking down at his interlocutor with his hands in his pockets. "Nobody but me, till now, has ever heard. It's quite too horrible." This, naturally, was declared by several voices to give the thing the utmost price, and our friend, with quiet art, prepared his triumph by turning his eyes over the rest of us and going on: "It's beyond everything. Nothing at all that I know touches it."

"For sheer terror?" I remember asking.

He seemed to say it was not so simple as that; to be really at a loss how to qualify it. He passed his hand over his eyes, made a little wincing grimace. "For dreadful—dreadfulness!"

"Oh, how delicious!" cried one of the women.

He took no notice of her; he looked at me, but as if, instead of me, he saw what he spoke of. "For general uncanny ugliness and horror and pain."

"Well then," I said, "just sit right down and begin."

He turned round to the fire, gave a kick to a log, watched it an instant. Then as he faced us again: "I can't begin. I shall have to send to town." There was a unanimous groan at this, and much reproach; after which, in his preoccupied way, he explained. "The story's written. It's in a locked drawer— it has not been out for years. I could write to my man and enclose the key; he could send down the packet as he finds it." It was to me in particular that he appeared to propound this—appeared almost to appeal for aid not to hesitate. He had broken a thickness of ice, the formation of many a winter; had had his reasons for a long silence. The others resented postponement, but it was just his scruples that charmed me. I adjured him to write by the first post and to agree with us for an early hearing; then I asked him if the experience in question had been his own. To this his answer was prompt. "Oh, thank God, no!"

"And is the record yours? You took the thing down?"

"Nothing but the impression. I took that *here*"—he tapped his heart. "I've never lost it."

"Then your manuscript—?"

"Is in old, faded ink, and in the most beautiful hand." He hung fire again. "A woman's. She has been dead these twenty years. She sent me the pages in question before she died." They were all listening now, and of course there was somebody to be arch, or at any rate to draw the inference. But if he put the inference by without a smile it was also without irritation. "She was a most charming person, but she was ten years older than I. She was my sister's governess," he quietly said. "She was the most agreeable woman I've ever known in her position; she would have been worthy of any whatever. It was long ago, and this episode was long before. I was at Trinity, and I found her at home on my coming down the second summer. I was much there that year—it was a beautiful one; and we had, in her off-hours, some strolls and talks in the garden—talks in which she struck me as awfully clever and nice. Oh yes; don't grin: I liked her extremely and am glad to this day to think she liked me, too. If she hadn't she wouldn't have told me. She had never told anyone. It wasn't simply that she said so, but that I knew she hadn't. I was sure; I could see. You'll easily judge why when you hear."

"Because the thing had been such a scare?"

He continued to fix me. "You'll easily judge," he repeated: *"you will."*

I fixed him, too. "I see. She was in love."

He laughed for the first time. "You *are* acute. Yes, she was in love. That is, she had been. That came out—she couldn't tell her story without its coming out. I saw it, and she saw I saw it; but neither of us spoke of it. I remember the time and the place—the corner of the lawn, the shade of the great beeches and the long, hot summer afternoon. It wasn't a scene for a shudder; but oh—!" He quitted the fire and dropped back into his chair.

"You'll receive the packet Thursday morning?" I inquired.

"Probably not till the second post."

"Well then; after dinner—"

"You'll all meet me here?" He looked us round again. "Isn't anybody going?" It was almost the tone of hope.

"Everybody will stay!"

"*I* will"—and "*I* will!" cried the ladies whose departure had been fixed. Mrs. Griffin, however, expressed the need for a little more light. "Who was it she was in love with?"

"The story will tell," I took upon myself to reply.

"Oh, I can't wait for the story!"

"The story *won't* tell," said Douglas; "not in any literal, vulgar way."

"More's the pity, then. That's the only way I ever understand."

"Won't *you* tell, Douglas?" somebody else inquired.

He sprang to his feet again. "Yes—tomorrow. Now I must go to bed. Good night." And quickly catching up a candlestick, he left us slightly bewildered. From our end of the great brown hall we heard his step on the stair; whereupon Mrs. Griffin spoke. "Well, if I don't know who she was in love with, I know who *he* was."

"She was ten years older," said her husband.

"*Raison de plus*—at that age! But it's rather nice, his long reticence."

"Forty years!" Griffin put in.

"With this outbreak at last."

"The outbreak," I returned, "will make a tremendous occasion of Thursday night;" and everyone so agreed with me that, in the light of it, we lost all attention for everything else. The last story, however incomplete and like the mere opening of a serial, had been told; we handshook and "candlestuck," as somebody said, and went to bed.

I knew the next day that a letter containing the key had, by the first post, gone off to his London apartments; but in spite of—or perhaps just on account of—the eventual diffusion of this knowledge we quite let him alone till after dinner, till such an hour of the evening, in fact, as might best accord with the kind of emotion on which our hopes were fixed. Then he became as communicative as we could desire and indeed gave us his best reason for being so. We had it from him again before the fire in the hall, as we had had our mild wonders of the previous night. It appeared that the narrative he had promised to read us really required for a proper intelligence a few words of prologue. Let me say here distinctly, to have done with it, that this narrative, from an exact transcript of my own made much later, is what I shall presently give. Poor Douglas, before his death—when it was in sight—committed to me the manuscript that reached him on the third of these days and that, on the same spot, with immense effect, he began to read to our hushed little circle on the night of the fourth. The departing ladies who had said they would stay didn't, of course, thank heaven, stay: they departed, in consequence of arrangements made, in a rage of curiosity, as they professed, produced by the touches with which he had already worked us up. But that only made his little final auditory more compact and select, kept it, round the hearth, subject to a common thrill.

The first of these touches conveyed that the written statement took up the tale at a point after it had, in a manner, begun. The fact to be in possession of was therefore that his old friend, the youngest of several daughters of a poor country parson, had, at the age of twenty, on taking service for the first time in the schoolroom, come up to London, in trepidation, to answer in person an advertisement that had already placed her in brief correspondence with the advertiser. This person proved, on her presenting herself, for judgment, at a house in Harley Street, that impressed her as vast and imposing—this prospective patron proved a gentleman, a bachelor in the prime of life, such a figure as had never risen, save in a dream or an old novel, before a fluttered, anxious girl out of a Hampshire vicarage. One could easily fix his type; it never, happily, dies out. He was handsome and bold and pleasant, off-hand and gay and kind. He struck her, inevitably, as gallant and splendid, but what took her most of all and gave her the courage she afterward showed was that he put the whole thing to her as a kind of favor, an obligation he should gratefully incur. She conceived him as rich, but as fearfully extravagant—saw him all in a glow of high fashion, of good looks, of expensive habits, of charming ways with women. He had for his own town residence a big house filled with the spoils of travel and the trophies of the chase; but it was to his country home, an old family place in Essex, that he wished her immediately to proceed.

He had been left, by the death of their parents in India, guardian to a small nephew and a small niece, children of a younger, a military brother, whom he had lost two years before. These children were, by the strangest of chances for a man in his position—a lone man without the right sort of experience or a grain of patience—very heavily on his hands. It had all been a great worry and, on his own part doubtless, a series of blunders, but he immensely pitied the poor chicks and had done all he could; had in particular sent them down to his other house, the proper place for them being of course the country, and kept them there, from the first, with the best people he could find to look after them, parting even with his own servants to wait on them and going down himself, whenever he might, to see how they were doing. The awkward thing was that they had practically no other relations and that his own affairs took up all his time. He had put them in possession of Bly, which was healthy and secure, and had placed at the head of their little establishment—but below stairs only—an excellent woman, Mrs. Grose, whom he was sure his visitor would like and who had formerly been maid to his mother. She was now housekeeper and was also acting for the time as superintendent to the little girl, of whom, without children of her own, she was, by good luck, extremely fond. There were plenty of people to help, but of course the young lady who should go down as governess would be in supreme authority. She would also have, in holidays, to look after the small boy, who had been for a term at school—young as he was to be sent, but what else could be done?—and who, as the holidays were about to begin, would be back from one day to the other. There had been for the two children at first a young lady whom they had had the misfortune to lose. She had done for them quite beautifully—she was a most respectable person—till her death, the great awkwardness of which had, precisely, left no alternative but the school for little Miles. Mrs. Grose, since then, in the way of manners and things, had done as she could for Flora; and there were, further, a cook, a housemaid, a dairywoman, an old pony, an old groom, and an old gardener, all likewise thoroughly respectable.

So far had Douglas presented his picture when someone put a question. "And what did the former governess die of?—of so much respectability?"

Our friend's answer was prompt. "That will come out. I don't anticipate."

"Excuse me—I thought that was just what you *are* doing."

"In her successor's place," I suggested, "I should have wished to learn if the office brought with it—"

"Necessary danger to life?" Douglas completed my thought. "She did wish to learn, and she did learn. You shall hear tomorrow what she learned. Meanwhile, of course, the prospect struck her as slightly grim. She was young, untried, nervous: it was a vision of serious duties and little company, of really great loneliness. She hesitated—took a couple of days to consult and consider. But the salary offered much exceeded her modest measure, and on a second interview she faced the music, she engaged." And Douglas, with this, made a pause that, for the benefit of the company, moved me to throw in—

"The moral of which was of course the seduction exercised by the splendid young man. She succumbed to it."

He got up and, as he had done the night before, went to the fire, gave a stir to a log with his foot, then stood a moment with his back to us. "She saw him only twice."

"Yes, but that's just the beauty of her passion."

A little to my surprise, on this, Douglas turned round to me. "It *was* the beauty of it. There were others," he went on, "who hadn't succumbed. He told her frankly all his difficulty—that for several applicants the conditions had been prohibitive. They were, somehow, simply afraid. It sounded dull—it sounded strange; and all the more so because of his main condition."

"Which was—?"

"That she should never trouble him—but never, never: neither appeal nor complain nor write about anything; only meet all questions herself, receive all moneys from his solicitor, take the whole thing over and let him alone. She promised to do this, and she mentioned to me that when, for a moment, disburdened, delighted, he held her hand, thanking her for the sacrifice, she already felt rewarded."

"But was that all her reward?" one of the ladies asked.

"She never saw him again."

"Oh!" said the lady; which, as our friend immediately left us again, was the only other word of importance contributed to the subject till, the next night, by the corner of the hearth, in the best chair, he opened the faded red cover of a thin old-fashioned gilt-edged album. The whole thing took indeed more nights than one, but on the first occasion the same lady put another question. "What is your title?"

"I haven't one."

"Oh, *I* have!" I said. But Douglas, without heeding me, had begun to read with a fine clearness that was like a rendering to the ear of the beauty of his author's hand.

I

I remember the whole beginning as a succession of flights and drops, a little seesaw of the right throbs and the wrong. After rising, in town, to meet his appeal, I had at all events a couple of very bad days—found myself doubtful again, felt indeed sure I had made a mistake. In this state of mind I spent the long hours of bumping, swinging coach that carried me to the stopping place at which I was to be met by a vehicle from the house. This convenience, I was told, had been ordered, and I found, toward the close of the June afternoon, a commodious fly in waiting for me. Driving at that hour, on a lovely day, through a country to which the summer sweetness seemed to offer me a friendly welcome, my fortitude mounted afresh and, as we turned into the avenue, encountered a reprieve that was probably but a proof of the point to which it had sunk. I suppose I had expected, or had dreaded, something so melancholy that what greeted me was a good surprise. I remember as a most pleasant impression the broad, clear front, its open windows and fresh curtains and the pair of maids looking out; I remember the lawn and the bright flowers and the crunch of my wheels on the gravel and the clustered treetops over which the rooks circled and cawed in the golden sky. The scene had a greatness that made it a different affair from my own scant home, and there immediately appeared at the door, with a little girl in her hand, a civil person who dropped me as decent a curtsy as if I had been the mistress or a distinguished visitor. I had received in Harley Street a narrower notion of the place, and that, as I recalled it, made me think the proprietor still more of a gentleman, suggested that what I was to enjoy might be something beyond his promise.

I had no drop again till the next day, for I was carried triumphantly through the following hours by my introduction to the younger of my pupils. The little girl who accompanied Mrs. Grose appeared to me on the spot a creature so charming as to make it a great fortune to have to do with her. She was the most beautiful child I had ever seen, and I afterward wondered that my employer had not told me more of her. I slept little that night—I was too much excited; and this astonished me, too, I recollect, remained with me, adding to my sense of the liberality with which I was treated. The large, impressive room, one of the best in the house, the great state bed, as I almost felt it, the full, figured draperies, the long glasses in which, for the first time, I could see myself from head to foot, all struck me—like the extraordinary charm of my small charge—as so many things thrown in. It was thrown in as well, from the first moment, that I should get on with Mrs. Grose in a relation over which, on my way, in the coach, I fear I had rather brooded. The only thing indeed that in this early outlook might have made me shrink again was the clear circumstance of her being so glad to see me. I perceived within half an hour that she was so glad—stout, simple, plain, clean, wholesome woman—as to be positively on her guard against showing it too much. I wondered even then a little why she should wish not to show it, and that, with reflection, with suspicion, might of course have made me uneasy.

But it was a comfort that there could be no uneasiness in a connection with anything so beatific as the radiant image of my little girl, the vision of whose angelic beauty had probably more than anything else to do with the restlessness that, before morning, made me several times rise and wander about my room to take in the whole picture and prospect; to watch, from my open window, the faint summer dawn, to look at such portions of the rest of the house as I could catch, and to listen, while, in the fading dusk, the first birds began to twitter, for the possible recurrence of a sound or two, less natural and not without, but within, that I had fancied I heard. There had been a moment when I believed I recognized, faint and far, the cry of a child; there had been another when I found myself just consciously starting as at the passage, before my door, of a light footstep. But these fancies were not marked enough not to be thrown off, and it is only in the light, or the gloom, I should rather say, of other and subsequent matters that they now come back to me. To watch, teach, "form" little Flora would too evidently be the making of a happy and useful life. It had been agreed between us downstairs that after this first occasion I should have her as a matter of course at night, her small white bed being already arranged, to that end, in my room. What I had undertaken was the whole care of her, and she had remained, just this last time, with Mrs. Grose only as an effect of our consideration for my inevitable strangeness and her natural timidity. In spite of this timidity—which the child herself, in the oddest way in the world, had been perfectly frank and brave about, allowing it, without a sign of uncomfortable consciousness, with the deep, sweet serenity indeed of one of Raphael's holy infants, to be discussed, to be imputed to her, and to determine us—I feel quite sure she would presently like me. It was part of what I already liked Mrs. Grose herself for, the pleasure I could see her feel in my admiration and wonder as I sat at supper with four tall candles and with my pupil, in a high chair and a bib, brightly facing me, between them, over bread and milk. There were naturally things that in Flora's presence could pass between us only as prodigious and gratified looks, obscure and roundabout allusions.

"And the little boy—does he look like her? Is he too so very remarkable?"

One wouldn't flatter a child. "Oh, miss, *most* remarkable. If you think well of this one!"—and she stood there with a plate in her hand, beaming at our companion, who looked from one of us to the other with placid heavenly eyes that contained nothing to check us.

"Yes; if I do—?"

"You *will* be carried away by the little gentleman!"

"Well, that, I think, is what I came for—to be carried away. I'm afraid, however," I remember feeling the impulse to add, "I'm rather easily carried away. I was carried away in London!"

I can still see Mrs. Grose's broad face as she took this in. "In Harley Street?"

"In Harley Street."

"Well, miss, you're not the first—and you won't be the last."

"Oh, I've no pretension," I could laugh, "to being the only one. My other pupil, at any rate, as I understand, comes back tomorrow?"

"Not tomorrow—Friday, miss. He arrives, as you did, by the coach, under care of the guard, and is to be met by the same carriage."

I forthwith expressed that the proper as well as the pleasant and friendly thing would be therefore that on the arrival of the public conveyance I should be in waiting for him with his little sister; an idea in which Mrs. Grose concurred so heartily that I somehow took her manner as a kind of comforting pledge—never falsified, thank heaven!—that we should on every question be quite at one. Oh, she was glad I was there!

What I felt the next day was, I suppose, nothing that could be fairly called a reaction from the cheer of my arrival; it was probably at the most only a slight oppression produced by a fuller measure of the scale, as I walked round them, gazed up at them, took them in, of my new circumstances. They had, as it were, an extent and mass for which I had not been prepared and in the presence of which I found myself, freshly, a little scared as well as a little proud. Lessons, in this agitation, certainly suffered some delay; I reflected that my first duty was, by the gentlest arts I could contrive, to win the child into the sense of knowing me. I spent the day with her out-of-doors; I arranged with her, to her great satisfaction, that it should be she, she only, who might show me the place. She showed it step by step and room by room and secret by secret, with droll, delightful, childish talk about it and with the result, in half an hour, of our becoming immense friends. Young as she was, I was struck, throughout our little tour, with her confidence and courage with the way, in empty chambers and dull corridors, on crooked staircases that made me pause and even on the summit of an old machicolated square tower that made me dizzy, her morning music, her disposition to tell me so many more things than she asked, rang out and led me on. I have not seen Bly since the day I left it, and I daresay that to my older and more informed eyes it would now appear sufficiently contracted. But as my little conductress, with her hair of gold and her frock of blue, danced before me round corners and pattered down passages, I had the view of a castle of romance inhabited by a rosy sprite, such a place as would somehow, for diversion of the young idea, take all color out of storybooks and fairytales. Wasn't it just a storybook over which I had fallen adoze and adream? No; it was a big, ugly, antique, but convenient house, embodying a few features of a building still older, half-replaced and half-utilized, in which I had the fancy of our being almost as lost as a handful of passengers in a great drifting ship. Well, I was, strangely, at the helm!

II

This came home to me when, two days later, I drove over with Flora
to meet, as Mrs. Grose said, the little gentleman; and all the more for an
incident that, presenting itself the second evening, had deeply disconcerted
me. The first day had been, on the whole, as I have expressed, reassuring; but
I was to see it wind up in keen apprehension. The postbag, that evening—it
came late—contained a letter for me, which, however, in the hand of my
employer, I found to be composed but of a few words enclosing another,
addressed to himself, with a seal still unbroken. "This, I recognize, is from
the headmaster, and the headmaster's an awful bore. Read him, please; deal
with him; but mind you don't report. Not a word. I'm off!" I broke the seal
with a great effort—so great a one that I was a long time coming to it; took
the unopened missive at last up to my room and only attacked it just before
going to bed. I had better have let it wait till morning, for it gave me a second
sleepless night. With no counsel to take, the next day, I was full of distress;
and it finally got so the better of me that I determined to open myself at least
to Mrs. Grose.

"What does it mean? The child's dismissed his school."

She gave me a look that I remarked at the moment; then, visibly, with a
quick blankness, seemed to try to take it back. "But aren't they all—?"

"Sent home—yes. But only for the holidays. Miles may never go back
at all."

Consciously, under my attention, she reddened. "They won't take him?"

"They absolutely decline."

At this she raised her eyes, which she had turned from me; I saw them
fill with good tears. "What has he done?"

I hesitated; then I judged best simply to hand her my letter—which,
however, had the effect of making her, without taking it, simply put her hands
behind her. She shook her head sadly. "Such things are not for me, miss."

My counselor couldn't read! I winced at my mistake, which I attenuated as I could, and opened my letter again to repeat it to her; then, faltering in the act and folding it up once more, I put it back in my pocket. "Is he really *bad?*"

The tears were still in her eyes. "Do the gentlemen say so?"

"They go into no particulars. They simply express their regret that it should be impossible to keep him. That can have only one meaning." Mrs. Grose listened with dumb emotion; she forbore to ask me what this meaning might be; so that, presently, to put the thing with some coherence and with the mere aid of her presence to my own mind, I went on: "That he's an injury to the others."

At this, with one of the quick turns of simple folk, she suddenly flamed up. "Master Miles! *him* an injury?"

There was such a flood of good faith in it that, though I had not yet seen the child, my very fears made me jump to the absurdity of the idea. I found myself, to meet my friend the better, offering it, on the spot, sarcastically. "To his poor little innocent mates!"

"It's too dreadful," cried Mrs. Grose, "to say such cruel things! Why, he's scarce ten years old."

"Yes, yes; it would be incredible."

She was evidently grateful for such a profession. "See him, miss, first. *Then* believe it!" I felt forthwith a new impatience to see him; it was the beginning of a curiosity that, for all the next hours, was to deepen almost to pain. Mrs. Grose was aware, I could judge, of what she had produced in me, and she followed it up with assurance. "You might as well believe it of the little lady. Bless her," she added the next moment—"*look* at her!"

I turned and saw that Flora, whom, ten minutes before, I had established in the schoolroom with a sheet of white paper, a pencil, and a copy of nice "round O's," now presented herself to view at the open door. She expressed in her little way an extraordinary detachment from disagreeable duties, looking to me, however, with a great childish light that seemed to offer it as a mere result of the affection she had conceived for my person, which had rendered necessary that she should follow me. I needed nothing more than this to feel the full force of Mrs. Grose's comparison, and, catching my pupil in my arms, covered her with kisses in which there was a sob of atonement.

Nonetheless, the rest of the day I watched for further occasion to approach my colleague, especially as, toward evening, I began to fancy she rather sought to avoid me. I overtook her, I remember, on the staircase; we went down together, and at the bottom I detained her, holding her there with a hand on her arm. "I take what you said to me at noon as a declaration that *you've* never known him to be bad."

She threw back her head; she had clearly, by this time, and very honestly, adopted an attitude. "Oh, never known him—I don't pretend *that!*"

I was upset again. "Then you *have* known him—?"

"Yes indeed, miss, thank God!"

On reflection I accepted this. "You mean that a boy who never is—?"

"Is no boy for *me!*"

I held her tighter. "You like them with the spirit to be naughty?" Then, keeping pace with her answer, "So do I!" I eagerly brought out. "But not to the degree to contaminate—"

"To contaminate?"—my big word left her at a loss. I explained it. "To corrupt."

She stared, taking my meaning in; but it produced in her an odd laugh. "Are you afraid he'll corrupt *you?*" She put the question with such a fine bold humor that, with a laugh, a little silly doubtless, to match her own, I gave way for the time to the apprehension of ridicule.

But the next day, as the hour for my drive approached, I cropped up in another place. "What was the lady who was here before?"

"The last governess? She was also young and pretty—almost as young and almost as pretty, miss, even as you."

"Ah, then, I hope her youth and her beauty helped her!" I recollect throwing off. "He seems to like us young and pretty!"

"Oh, he *did*," Mrs. Grose assented: "it was the way he liked everyone!" She had no sooner spoken indeed than she caught herself up. "I mean that's *his* way—the master's."

I was struck. "But of whom did you speak first?"

She looked blank, but she colored. "Why, of *him.*"

"Of the master?"

"Of who else?"

There was so obviously no one else that the next moment I had lost my impression of her having accidentally said more than she meant; and I merely asked what I wanted to know. "Did *she* see anything in the boy—?"

"That wasn't right? She never told me."

I had a scruple, but I overcame it. "Was she careful—particular?"

Mrs. Grose appeared to try to be conscientious. "About some things—yes."

"But not about all?"

Again she considered. "Well, miss—she's gone. I won't tell tales."

"I quite understand your feeling," I hastened to reply; but I thought it, after an instant, not opposed to this concession to pursue: "Did she die here?"

"No—she went off."

I don't know what there was in this brevity of Mrs. Grose's that struck me as ambiguous. "Went off to die?" Mrs. Grose looked straight out of the window, but I felt that, hypothetically, I had a right to know what young persons engaged for Bly were expected to do. "She was taken ill, you mean, and went home?"

"She was not taken ill, so far as appeared, in this house. She left it, at the end of the year, to go home, as she said, for a short holiday, to which the time she had put in had certainly given her a right. We had then a young woman—a nursemaid who had stayed on and who was a good girl and clever; and *she* took the children altogether for the interval. But our young lady never came back, and at the very moment I was expecting her I heard from the master that she was dead."

I turned this over. "But of what?"

"He never told me! But please, miss," said Mrs. Grose, "I must get to my work."

III

Her thus turning her back on me was fortunately not, for my just preoccupations, a snub that could check the growth of our mutual esteem. We met, after I had brought home little Miles, more intimately than ever on the ground of my stupefaction, my general emotion: so monstrous was I then ready to pronounce it that such a child as had now been revealed to me should be under an interdict. I was a little late on the scene, and I felt, as he stood wistfully looking out for me before the door of the inn at which the coach had put him down, that I had seen him, on the instant, without and within, in the great glow of freshness, the same positive fragrance of purity, in which I had, from the first moment, seen his little sister. He was incredibly beautiful, and Mrs. Grose had put her finger on it: everything but a sort of passion of tenderness for him was swept away by his presence. What I then and there took him to my heart for was something divine that I have never found to the same degree in any child—his indescribable little air of knowing nothing in the world but love. It would have been impossible to carry a bad name with a greater sweetness of innocence, and by the time I had got back to Bly with him I remained merely bewildered—so far, that is, as I was not outraged—by the sense of the horrible letter locked up in my room, in a drawer. As soon as I could compass a private word with Mrs. Grose I declared to her that it was grotesque.

She promptly understood me. "You mean the cruel charge—?"

"It doesn't live an instant. My dear woman, *look* at him!"

She smiled at my pretention to have discovered his charm. "I assure you, miss, I do nothing else! What will you say, then?" she immediately added.

"In answer to the letter?" I had made up my mind. "Nothing."

"And to his uncle?"

I was incisive. "Nothing."

"And to the boy himself?"

I was wonderful. "Nothing."

She gave with her apron a great wipe to her mouth. "Then I'll stand by you. We'll see it out."

"We'll see it out!" I ardently echoed, giving her my hand to make it a vow.

She held me there a moment, then whisked up her apron again with her detached hand. "Would you mind, miss, if I used the freedom—"

"To kiss me? No!" I took the good creature in my arms and, after we had embraced like sisters, felt still more fortified and indignant.

This, at all events, was for the time: a time so full that, as I recall the way it went, it reminds me of all the art I now need to make it a little distinct. What I look back at with amazement is the situation I accepted. I had undertaken, with my companion, to see it out, and I was under a charm, apparently, that could smooth away the extent and the far and difficult connections of such an effort. I was lifted aloft on a great wave of infatuation and pity. I found it simple, in my ignorance, my confusion, and perhaps my conceit, to assume that I could deal with a boy whose education for the world was all on the point of beginning. I am unable even to remember at this day what proposal I framed for the end of his holidays and the resumption of his studies. Lessons with me, indeed, that charming summer, we all had a theory that he was to have; but I now feel that, for weeks, the lessons must have been rather my own. I learned something—at first, certainly—that had not been one of the teachings of my small, smothered life; learned to be amused, and even amusing, and not to think for the morrow. It was the first time, in a manner, that I had known space and air and freedom, all the music of summer and all the mystery of nature. And then there was consideration—and consideration was sweet. Oh, it was a trap—not designed, but deep—to my imagination, to my delicacy, perhaps to my vanity; to whatever, in me, was most excitable. The best way to picture it all is to say that I was off my guard. They gave me so little trouble—they were of a gentleness so extraordinary. I used to speculate—but even this with a dim disconnectedness—as to how the rough future (for all futures are rough!) would handle them and might bruise them. They had the bloom of health and happiness; and yet, as if I had been in charge of a pair of little grandees, of princes of the blood, for whom everything, to be right, would have to be enclosed and protected, the only form that, in my fancy, the afteryears could take for them was that of a romantic, a really royal extension of the garden and the park. It may be, of course, above all, that what suddenly broke into this gives the previous time a charm of stillness—that hush in which something gathers or crouches. The change was actually like the spring of a beast.

In the first weeks the days were long; they often, at their finest, gave me what I used to call my own hour, the hour when, for my pupils, teatime and bedtime having come and gone, I had, before my final retirement, a small interval alone. Much as I liked my companions, this hour was the thing in the day I liked most; and I liked it best of all when, as the light faded—or rather, I should say, the day lingered and the last calls of the last birds sounded, in a flushed sky, from the old trees—I could take a turn into the grounds and enjoy, almost with a sense of property that amused and flattered me, the beauty and dignity of the place. It was a pleasure at these moments to feel myself tranquil and justified; doubtless, perhaps, also to reflect that by my discretion, my quiet good sense and general high propriety, I was giving pleasure—if he ever thought of it!—to the person to whose pressure I had responded. What I was doing was what he had earnestly hoped and directly asked of me, and that I *could*, after all, do it proved even a greater joy than I had expected. I daresay I fancied myself, in short, a remarkable young woman and took comfort in the faith that this would more publicly appear. Well, I needed to be remarkable to offer a front to the remarkable things that presently gave their first sign.

It was plump, one afternoon, in the middle of my very hour: the children were tucked away, and I had come out for my stroll. One of the thoughts that, as I don't in the least shrink now from noting, used to be with me in these wanderings was that it would be as charming as a charming story suddenly to meet someone. Someone would appear there at the turn of a path and would stand before me and smile and approve. I didn't ask more than that—I only asked that he should *know;* and the only way to be sure he knew would be to see it, and the kind light of it, in his handsome face. That was exactly present to me—by which I mean the face was—when, on the first of these occasions, at the end of a long June day, I stopped short on emerging from one of the plantations and coming into view of the house. What arrested me on the spot—and with a shock much greater than any vision had allowed for—was the sense that my imagination had, in a flash, turned real. He did stand there!—but high up, beyond the lawn and at the very top of the tower to which, on that first morning, little Flora had conducted me. This tower was one of a pair—square, incongruous, crenelated structures—that were distinguished, for some reason, though I could see little difference, as the new and the old. They flanked opposite ends of the house and were probably architectural absurdities, redeemed in a measure indeed by not being wholly disengaged nor of a height too pretentious, dating, in their gingerbread antiquity, from a romantic revival that was already a respectable past. I admired them, had fancies about them, for we could all profit in a degree, especially when they loomed through the dusk, by the grandeur of their actual battlements; yet it was not at such an elevation that the figure I had so often invoked seemed most in place.

It produced in me, this figure, in the clear twilight, I remember, two distinct gasps of emotion, which were, sharply, the shock of my first and that of my second surprise. My second was a violent perception of the mistake of my first: the man who met my eyes was not the person I had precipitately supposed. There came to me thus a bewilderment of vision of which, after these years, there is no living view that I can hope to give. An unknown man in a lonely place is a permitted object of fear to a young woman privately bred; and the figure that faced me was—a few more seconds assured me—as little anyone else I knew as it was the image that had been in my mind. I had not seen it in Harley Street—I had not seen it anywhere. The place, moreover, in the strangest way in the world, had, on the instant, and by the very fact of its appearance, become a solitude. To me at least, making my statement here with a deliberation with which I have never made it, the whole feeling of the moment returns. It was as if, while I took in—what I did take in—all the rest of the scene had been stricken with death. I can hear again, as I write, the intense hush in which the sounds of evening dropped. The rooks stopped cawing in the golden sky, and the friendly hour lost, for the minute, all its voice. But there was no other change in nature, unless indeed it were a change that I saw with a stranger sharpness. The gold was still in the sky, the clearness in the air, and the man who looked at me over the battlements was as definite as a picture in a frame. That's how I thought, with extraordinary quickness, of each person that he might have been and that he was not. We were confronted across our distance quite long enough for me to ask myself with intensity who then he was and to feel, as an effect of my inability to say, a wonder that in a few instants more became intense.

The great question, or one of these, is, afterward, I know, with regard to certain matters, the question of how long they have lasted. Well, this matter of mine, think what you will of it, lasted while I caught at a dozen possibilities, none of which made a difference for the better, that I could see, in there having been in the house—and for how long, above all?—a person of whom I was in ignorance. It lasted while I just bridled a little with the sense that my office demanded that there should be no such ignorance and no such person. It lasted while this visitant, at all events—and there was a touch of the strange freedom, as I remember, in the sign of familiarity of his wearing no hat—seemed to fix me, from his position, with just the question, just the scrutiny through the fading light, that his own presence provoked. We were too far apart to call to each other, but there was a moment at which, at shorter range, some challenge between us, breaking the hush, would have been the right result of our straight mutual stare. He was in one of the angles, the one away from the house, very erect, as it struck me, and with both hands on the ledge. So I saw him as I see the letters I form on this page; then, exactly, after a minute, as if to add to the spectacle, he slowly changed his place—passed, looking at me hard all the while, to the opposite corner of the platform. Yes, I had the sharpest sense that during this transit he never took his eyes from me, and I can see at this moment the way his hand, as he went, passed from one of the crenelations to the next. He stopped at the other corner, but less long, and even as he turned away still markedly fixed me. He turned away; that was all I knew.

IV

It was not that I didn't wait, on this occasion, for more, for I was rooted as deeply as I was shaken. Was there a "secret" at Bly—a mystery of Udolpho or an insane, an unmentionable relative kept in unsuspected confinement? I can't say how long I turned it over, or how long, in a confusion of curiosity and dread, I remained where I had had my collision; I only recall that when I re-entered the house darkness had quite closed in. Agitation, in the interval, certainly had held me and driven me, for I must, in circling about the place, have walked three miles; but I was to be, later on, so much more overwhelmed that this mere dawn of alarm was a comparatively human chill. The most singular part of it, in fact—singular as the rest had been—was the part I became, in the hall, aware of in meeting Mrs. Grose. This picture comes back to me in the general train—the impression, as I received it on my return, of the wide white panelled space, bright in the lamplight and with its portraits and red carpet, and of the good surprised look of my friend, which immediately told me she had missed me. It came to me straightway, under her contact, that, with plain heartiness, mere relieved anxiety at my appearance, she knew nothing whatever that could bear upon the incident I had there ready for her. I had not suspected in advance that her comfortable face would pull me up, and I somehow measured the importance of what I had seen by my thus finding myself hesitate to mention it. Scarce anything in the whole history seems to me so odd as this fact that my real beginning of fear was one, as I may say, with the instinct of sparing my companion. On the spot, accordingly, in the pleasant hall and with her eyes on me, I, for a reason that I couldn't then have phrased, achieved an inward resolution—offered a vague pretext for my lateness and, with the plea of the beauty of the night and of the heavy dew and wet feet, went as soon as possible to my room.

Here it was another affair; here, for many days after, it was a queer affair enough. There were hours, from day to day—or at least there were moments, snatched even from clear duties—when I had to shut myself up to think. It was not so much yet that I was more nervous than I could bear to be as that

I was remarkably afraid of becoming so; for the truth I had now to turn over was, simply and clearly, the truth that I could arrive at no account whatever of the visitor with whom I had been so inexplicably and yet, as it seemed to me, so intimately concerned. It took little time to see that I could sound without forms of inquiry and without exciting remark any domestic complications. The shock I had suffered must have sharpened all my senses; I felt sure, at the end of three days and as the result of mere closer attention, that I had not been practiced upon by the servants nor made the object of any "game." Of whatever it was that I knew, nothing was known around me. There was but one sane inference: someone had taken a liberty rather gross. That was what, repeatedly, I dipped into my room and locked the door to say to myself. We had been, collectively, subject to an intrusion; some unscrupulous traveler, curious in old houses, had made his way in unobserved, enjoyed the prospect from the best point of view, and then stolen out as he came. If he had given me such a bold hard stare, that was but a part of his indiscretion. The good thing, after all, was that we should surely see no more of him.

This was not so good a thing, I admit, as not to leave me to judge that what, essentially, made nothing else much signify was simply my charming work. My charming work was just my life with Miles and Flora, and through nothing could I so like it as through feeling that I could throw myself into it in trouble. The attraction of my small charges was a constant joy, leading me to wonder afresh at the vanity of my original fears, the distaste I had begun by entertaining for the probable gray prose of my office. There was to be no gray prose, it appeared, and no long grind; so how could work not be charming that presented itself as daily beauty? It was all the romance of the nursery and the poetry of the schoolroom. I don't mean by this, of course, that we studied only fiction and verse; I mean I can express no otherwise the sort of interest my companions inspired. How can I describe that except by saying that instead of growing used to them—and it's a marvel for a governess: I call the sisterhood to witness!—I made constant fresh discoveries. There was one direction, assuredly, in which these discoveries stopped: deep obscurity continued to cover the region of the boy's conduct at school. It had been promptly given me, I have noted, to face that mystery without a pang. Perhaps even it would be nearer the truth to say that—without a word—he himself had cleared it up. He had made the whole charge absurd. My conclusion bloomed there with the real rose flush of his innocence: he was only too fine and fair for the little horrid, unclean school-world, and he had paid a price for it. I reflected acutely that the sense of such differences, such superiorities of quality, always, on the part of the majority—which could include even stupid, sordid headmasters—turn infallibly to the vindictive.

Both the children had a gentleness (it was their only fault, and it never made Miles a muff) that kept them—how shall I express it?—almost impersonal and certainly quite unpunishable. They were like the cherubs of the anecdote, who had—morally, at any rate—nothing to whack! I remember feeling with Miles in especial as if he had had, as it were, no history. We expect of a small child a scant one, but there was in this beautiful little boy something extraordinarily sensitive, yet extraordinarily happy, that, more than in any creature of his age I have seen, struck me as beginning anew each day. He had never for a second suffered. I took this as a direct disproof of his having really been chastised. If he had been wicked he would have "caught" it, and I should have caught it by the rebound—I should have found the trace. I found nothing at all, and he was therefore an angel. He never spoke of his school, never mentioned a comrade or a master; and I, for my part, was quite too much disgusted to allude to them. Of course I was under the spell, and the wonderful part is that, even at the time, I perfectly knew I was. But I gave myself up to it; it was an antidote to any pain, and I had more pains than one. I was in receipt in these days of disturbing letters from home, where things were not going well. But with my children, what things in the world mattered? That was the question I used to put to my scrappy retirements. I was dazzled by their loveliness.

There was a Sunday—to get on—when it rained with such force and for so many hours that there could be no procession to church; in consequence of which, as the day declined, I had arranged with Mrs. Grose that, should the evening show improvement, we would attend together the late service. The rain happily stopped, and I prepared for our walk, which, through the park and by the good road to the village, would be a matter of twenty minutes. Coming downstairs to meet my colleague in the hall, I remembered a pair of gloves that had required three stitches and that had received them—with a publicity perhaps not edifying—while I sat with the children at their tea, served on Sundays, by exception, in that cold, clean temple of mahogany and brass, the "grown-up" dining room. The gloves had been dropped there, and I turned in to recover them. The day was gray enough, but the afternoon light still lingered, and it enabled me, on crossing the threshold, not only to recognize, on a chair near the wide window, then closed, the articles I wanted, but to become aware of a person on the other side of the window and looking straight in. One step into the room had sufficed; my vision was instantaneous; it was all there. The person looking straight in was the person who had already appeared to me. He appeared thus again with I won't say greater distinctness, for that was impossible, but with a nearness that represented a forward stride in our intercourse and made me, as I met him, catch my breath and turn cold. He was the same—he was the same, and seen, this time, as he had been seen before, from the waist up, the window, though the dining room was on the ground floor, not going down to the terrace on which he stood. His face was close to the glass, yet the effect of this better view was, strangely, only to show me how intense the former had been. He remained but a few seconds— long enough to convince me he also saw and recognized; but it was as if I had been looking at him for years and had known him always. Something, however, happened this time that had not happened before; his stare into my face, through the glass and across the room, was as deep and hard as then, but it quitted me for a moment during which I could still watch it, see it fix successively several other things. On the spot there came to me the added shock of a certitude that it was not for me he had come there. He had come for someone else.

The flash of this knowledge—for it was knowledge in the midst of dread—produced in me the most extraordinary effect, started as I stood there, a sudden vibration of duty and courage. I say courage because I was beyond all doubt already far gone. I bounded straight out of the door again, reached that of the house, got, in an instant, upon the drive, and, passing along the terrace as fast as I could rush, turned a corner and came full in sight. But it was in sight of nothing now—my visitor had vanished. I stopped, I almost dropped, with the real relief of this; but I took in the whole scene—I gave him time to reappear. I call it time, but how long was it? I can't speak to the purpose today of the duration of these things. That kind of measure must have left me: they couldn't have lasted as they actually appeared to me to last. The terrace and the whole place, the lawn and the garden beyond it, all I could see of the park, were empty with a great emptiness. There were shrubberies and big trees, but I remember the clear assurance I felt that none of them concealed him. He was there or was not there: not there if I didn't see him. I got hold of this; then, instinctively, instead of returning as I had come, went to the window. It was confusedly present to me that I ought to place myself where he had stood. I did so; I applied my face to the pane and looked, as he had looked, into the room. As if, at this moment, to show me exactly what his range had been, Mrs. Grose, as I had done for himself just before, came in from the hall. With this I had the full image of a repetition of what had already occurred. She saw me as I had seen my own visitant; she pulled up short as I had done; I gave her something of the shock that I had received. She turned white, and this made me ask myself if I had blanched as much. She stared, in short, and retreated on just *my* lines, and I knew she had then passed out and come round to me and that I should presently meet her. I remained where I was, and while I waited I thought of more things than one. But there's only one I take space to mention. I wondered why she should be scared.

V

Oh, she let me know as soon as, round the corner of the house, she loomed again into view. "What in the name of goodness is the matter—?" She was now flushed and out of breath.

I said nothing till she came quite near. "With me?" I must have made a wonderful face. "Do I show it?"

"You're as white as a sheet. You look awful."

I considered; I could meet on this, without scruple, any innocence. My need to respect the bloom of Mrs. Grose's had dropped, without a rustle, from my shoulders, and if I wavered for the instant it was not with what I kept back. I put out my hand to her and she took it; I held her hard a little, liking to feel her close to me. There was a kind of support in the shy heave of her surprise. "You came for me for church, of course, but I can't go."

"Has anything happened?"

"Yes. You must know now. Did I look very queer?"

"Through this window? Dreadful!"

"Well," I said, "I've been frightened." Mrs. Grose's eyes expressed plainly that *she* had no wish to be, yet also that she knew too well her place not to be ready to share with me any marked inconvenience. Oh, it was quite settled that she *must* share! "Just what you saw from the dining room a minute ago was the effect of that. What *I* saw—just before—was much worse."

Her hand tightened. "What was it?"

"An extraordinary man. Looking in."

"What extraordinary man?"

"I haven't the least idea."

Mrs. Grose gazed round us in vain. "Then where is he gone?"

"I know still less."

"Have you seen him before?"

"Yes—once. On the old tower."

She could only look at me harder. "Do you mean he's a stranger?"

"Oh, very much!"

"Yet you didn't tell me?"

"No—for reasons. But now that you've guessed—"

Mrs. Grose's round eyes encountered this charge. "Ah, I haven't guessed!" she said very simply. "How can I if *you* don't imagine?"

"I don't in the very least."

"You've seen him nowhere but on the tower?"

"And on this spot just now."

Mrs. Grose looked round again. "What was he doing on the tower?"

"Only standing there and looking down at me."

She thought a minute. "Was he a gentleman?"

I found I had no need to think. "No." She gazed in deeper wonder. "No."

"Then nobody about the place? Nobody from the village?"

"Nobody—nobody. I didn't tell you, but I made sure."

She breathed a vague relief: this was, oddly, so much to the good. It only went indeed a little way. "But if he isn't a gentleman—"

"What *is* he? He's a horror."

"A horror?"

"He's—God help me if I know *what* he is!"

Mrs. Grose looked round once more; she fixed her eyes on the duskier distance, then, pulling herself together, turned to me with abrupt inconsequence. "It's time we should be at church."

"Oh, I'm not fit for church!"

"Won't it do you good?"

"It won't do *them*!— I nodded at the house.

"The children?"

"I can't leave them now."

"You're afraid—?"

I spoke boldly. "I'm afraid of *him*."

Mrs. Grose's large face showed me, at this, for the first time, the faraway faint glimmer of a consciousness more acute: I somehow made out in it the delayed dawn of an idea I myself had not given her and that was as yet quite obscure to me. It comes back to me that I thought instantly of this as something I could get from her; and I felt it to be connected with the desire she presently showed to know more. "When was it—on the tower?"

"About the middle of the month. At this same hour."

"Almost at dark," said Mrs. Grose.

"Oh, no, not nearly. I saw him as I see you."

"Then how did he get in?"

"And how did he get out?" I laughed. "I had no opportunity to ask him! This evening, you see," I pursued, "he has not been able to get in."

"He only peeps?"

"I hope it will be confined to that!" She had now let go my hand; she turned away a little. I waited an instant; then I brought out: "Go to church. Goodbye. I must watch."

Slowly she faced me again. "Do you fear for them?"

We met in another long look. "Don't *you?*" Instead of answering she came nearer to the window and, for a minute, applied her face to the glass. "You see how he could see," I meanwhile went on.

She didn't move. "How long was he here?"

"Till I came out. I came to meet him."

Mrs. Grose at last turned round, and there was still more in her face. "*I* couldn't have come out."

"Neither could I!" I laughed again. "But I did come. I have my duty."

"So have I mine," she replied; after which she added: "What is he like?"

"I've been dying to tell you. But he's like nobody."

"Nobody?" she echoed.

"He has no hat." Then seeing in her face that she already, in this, with a deeper dismay, found a touch of picture, I quickly added stroke to stroke. "He has red hair, very red, close-curling, and a pale face, long in shape, with straight, good features and little, rather queer whiskers that are as red as his hair. His eyebrows are, somehow, darker; they look particularly arched and as if they might move a good deal. His eyes are sharp, strange—awfully; but I only know clearly that they're rather small and very fixed. His mouth's wide, and his lips are thin, and except for his little whiskers he's quite clean-shaven. He gives me a sort of sense of looking like an actor."

"An actor!" It was impossible to resemble one less, at least, than Mrs. Grose at that moment.

"I've never seen one, but so I suppose them. He's tall, active, erect," I continued, "but never—no, never!—a gentleman."

My companion's face had blanched as I went on; her round eyes started and her mild mouth gaped. "A gentleman?" she gasped, confounded, stupefied: "a gentleman *he?*"

627

"You know him then?"

She visibly tried to hold herself. "But he *is* handsome?"

I saw the way to help her. "Remarkably!"

"And dressed—?"

"In somebody's clothes." "They're smart, but they're not his own."

She broke into a breathless affirmative groan: "They're the master's!"

I caught it up. "You *do* know him?"

She faltered but a second. "Quint!" she cried.

"Quint?"

"Peter Quint—his own man, his valet, when he was here!"

"When the master was?"

Gaping still, but meeting me, she pieced it all together. "He never wore his hat, but he did wear—well, there were waistcoats missed. They were both here—last year. Then the master went, and Quint was alone."

I followed, but halting a little. "Alone?"

"Alone with *us.*" Then, as from a deeper depth, "In charge," she added.

"And what became of him?"

She hung fire so long that I was still more mystified. "He went, too," she brought out at last.

"Went where?"

Her expression, at this, became extraordinary. "God knows where! He died."

"Died?" I almost shrieked.

She seemed fairly to square herself, plant herself more firmly to utter the wonder of it. "Yes. Mr. Quint is dead."

VI

It took of course more than that particular passage to place us together in presence of what we had now to live with as we could—my dreadful liability to impressions of the order so vividly exemplified, and my companion's knowledge, henceforth—a knowledge half consternation and half compassion—of that liability. There had been, this evening, after the revelation left me, for an hour, so prostrate—there had been, for either of us, no attendance on any service but a little service of tears and vows, of prayers and promises, a climax to the series of mutual challenges and pledges that had straightway ensued on our retreating together to the schoolroom and shutting ourselves up there to have everything out. The result of our having everything out was simply to reduce our situation to the last rigor of its elements. She herself had seen nothing, not the shadow of a shadow, and nobody in the house but the governess was in the governess's plight; yet she accepted without directly impugning my sanity the truth as I gave it to her, and ended by showing me, on this ground, an awestricken tenderness, an expression of the sense of my more than questionable privilege, of which the very breath has remained with me as that of the sweetest of human charities.

What was settled between us, accordingly, that night, was that we thought we might bear things together; and I was not even sure that, in spite of her exemption, it was she who had the best of the burden. I knew at this hour, I think, as well as I knew later, what I was capable of meeting to shelter my pupils; but it took me some time to be wholly sure of what my honest ally was prepared for to keep terms with so compromising a contract. I was queer company enough—quite as queer as the company I received; but as I trace over what we went through I see how much common ground we must have found in the one idea that, by good fortune, *could* steady us. It was the idea, the second movement, that led me straight out, as I may say, of the inner chamber of my dread. I could take the air in the court, at least, and there Mrs. Grose could join me. Perfectly can I recall now the particular way strength came to me before we separated for the night. We had gone over and over every feature of what I had seen.

"He was looking for someone else, you say—someone who was not you?"

"He was looking for little Miles." A portentous clearness now possessed me. "*That's* whom he was looking for."

"But how do you know?"

"I know, I know, I know!" My exaltation grew. "And *you* know, my dear!"

She didn't deny this, but I required, I felt, not even so much telling as that. She resumed in a moment, at any rate: "What if *he* should see him?"

"Little Miles? That's what he wants!"

She looked immensely scared again. "The child?"

"Heaven forbid! The man. He wants to appear to *them*." That he might was an awful conception, and yet, somehow, I could keep it at bay; which, moreover, as we lingered there, was what I succeeded in practically proving. I had an absolute certainty that I should see again what I had already seen, but something within me said that by offering myself bravely as the sole subject of such experience, by accepting, by inviting, by surmounting it all, I should serve as an expiatory victim and guard the tranquility of my companions. The children, in especial, I should thus fence about and absolutely save. I recall one of the last things I said that night to Mrs. Grose.

"It does strike me that my pupils have never mentioned—"

She looked at me hard as I musingly pulled up. "His having been here and the time they were with him?"

"The time they were with him, and his name, his presence, his history, in any way."

"Oh, the little lady doesn't remember. She never heard or knew."

"The circumstances of his death?" I thought with some intensity. "Perhaps not. But Miles would remember—Miles would know."

"Ah, don't try him!" broke from Mrs. Grose.

I returned her the look she had given me. "Don't be afraid." I continued to think. "It is rather odd."

"That he has never spoken of him?"

"Never by the least allusion. And you tell me they were 'great friends'?"

"Oh, it wasn't him!" Mrs. Grose with emphasis declared. "It was Quint's own fancy. To play with him, I mean—to spoil him." She paused a moment; then she added: "Quint was much too free."

This gave me, straight from my vision of his face—such a face!—a sudden sickness of disgust. "Too free with my boy?"

"Too free with everyone!"

I forbore, for the moment, to analyze this description further than by the reflection that a part of it applied to several of the members of the household, of the half-dozen maids and men who were still of our small colony. But there was everything, for our apprehension, in the lucky fact that no discomfortable legend, no perturbation of scullions, had ever, within anyone's memory attached to the kind old place. It had neither bad name nor ill fame, and Mrs. Grose, most apparently, only desired to cling to me and to quake in silence. I even put her, the very last thing of all, to the test. It was when, at midnight, she had her hand on the schoolroom door to take leave. "I have it from you then—for it's of great importance—that he was definitely and admittedly bad?"

"Oh, not admittedly. I knew it—but the master didn't."

"And you never told him?"

"Well, he didn't like tale-bearing—he hated complaints. He was terribly short with anything of that kind, and if people were all right to him—"

"He wouldn't be bothered with more?" This squared well enough with my impressions of him: he was not a trouble-loving gentleman, nor so very particular perhaps about some of the company he kept. All the same, I pressed my interlocutress. "I promise you I would have told!"

631

She felt my discrimination. "I daresay I was wrong. But, really, I was afraid."

"Afraid of what?"

"Of things that man could do. Quint was so clever—he was so deep."

I took this in still more than, probably, I showed. "You weren't afraid of anything else? Not of his effect—?"

"His effect?" she repeated with a face of anguish and waiting while I faltered.

"On innocent little precious lives. They were in your charge."

"No, they were not in mine!" she roundly and distressfully returned. "The master believed in him and placed him here because he was supposed not to be well and the country air so good for him. So he had everything to say. Yes"—she let me have it—"even about *them*."

"Them—that creature?" I had to smother a kind of howl. "And you could bear it!"

"No. I couldn't—and I can't now!" And the poor woman burst into tears.

A rigid control, from the next day, was, as I have said, to follow them; yet how often and how passionately, for a week, we came back together to the subject! Much as we had discussed it that Sunday night, I was, in the immediate later hours in especial—for it may be imagined whether I slept—still haunted with the shadow of something she had not told me. I myself had kept back nothing, but there was a word Mrs. Grose had kept back. I was sure, moreover, by morning, that this was not from a failure of frankness, but because on every side there were fears. It seems to me indeed, in retrospect, that by the time the morrow's sun was high I had restlessly read into the fact before us almost all the meaning they were to receive from subsequent and more cruel occurrences. What they gave me above all was just the sinister figure of the living man—the dead one would keep awhile!—and of the months he had continuously passed at Bly, which, added up, made a formidable stretch.

632

The limit of this evil time had arrived only when, on the dawn of a winter's morning, Peter Quint was found, by a laborer going to early work, stone dead on the road from the village: a catastrophe explained—superficially at least—by a visible wound to his head; such a wound as might have been produced—and as, on the final evidence, *had been*—by a fatal slip, in the dark and after leaving the public house, on the steepish icy slope, a wrong path altogether, at the bottom of which he lay. The icy slope, the turn mistaken at night and in liquor, accounted for much—practically, in the end and after the inquest and boundless chatter, for everything; but there had been matters in his life—strange passages and perils, secret disorders, vices more than suspected—that would have accounted for a good deal more.

I scarce know how to put my story into words that shall be a credible picture of my state of mind; but I was in these days literally able to find a joy in the extraordinary flight of heroism the occasion demanded of me. I now saw that I had been asked for a service admirable and difficult; and there would be a greatness in letting it be seen—oh, in the right quarter!—that I could succeed where many another girl might have failed. It was an immense help to me—I confess I rather applaud myself as I look back!—that I saw my service so strongly and so simply. I was there to protect and defend the little creatures in the world the most bereaved and the most lovable, the appeal of whose helplessness had suddenly become only too explicit, a deep, constant ache of one's own committed heart. We were cut off, really, together; we were united in our danger. They had nothing but me, and I—well, I had *them*. It was in short a magnificent chance. This chance presented itself to me in an image richly material. I was a screen—I was to stand before them. The more I saw, the less they would. I began to watch them in a stifled suspense, a disguised excitement that might well, had it continued too long, have turned to something like madness. What saved me, as I now see, was that it turned to something else altogether. It didn't last as suspense—it was superseded by horrible proofs. Proofs, I say, yes—from the moment I really took hold.

This moment dated from an afternoon hour that I happened to spend in the grounds with the younger of my pupils alone. We had left Miles indoors, on the red cushion of a deep window seat; he had wished to finish a book, and

I had been glad to encourage a purpose so laudable in a young man whose only defect was an occasional excess of the restless. His sister, on the contrary, had been alert to come out, and I strolled with her half an hour, seeking the shade, for the sun was still high and the day exceptionally warm. I was aware afresh, with her, as we went, of how, like her brother, she contrived—it was the charming thing in both children—to let me alone without appearing to drop me and to accompany me without appearing to surround. They were never importunate and yet never listless. My attention to them all really went to seeing them amuse themselves immensely without me: this was a spectacle they seemed actively to prepare and that engaged me as an active admirer. I walked in a world of their invention—they had no occasion whatever to draw upon mine; so that my time was taken only with being, for them, some remarkable person or thing that the game of the moment required and that was merely, thanks to my superior, my exalted stamp, a happy and highly distinguished sinecure. I forget what I was on the present occasion; I only remember that I was something very important and very quiet and that Flora was playing very hard. We were on the edge of the lake, and, as we had lately begun geography, the lake was the Sea of Azof.

Suddenly, in these circumstances, I became aware that, on the other side of the Sea of Azof, we had an interested spectator. The way this knowledge gathered in me was the strangest thing in the world—the strangest, that is, except the very much stranger in which it quickly merged itself. I had sat down with a piece of work—for I was something or other that could sit—on the old stone bench which overlooked the pond; and in this position I began to take in with certitude, and yet without direct vision, the presence, at a distance, of a third person. The old trees, the thick shrubbery, made a great and pleasant shade, but it was all suffused with the brightness of the hot, still hour. There was no ambiguity in anything; none whatever, at least, in the conviction I from one moment to another found myself forming as to what I should see straight before me and across the lake as a consequence of raising my eyes. They were attached at this juncture to the stitching in which I was engaged, and I can feel once more the spasm of my effort not to move them till I should so have steadied myself as to be able to make up my mind what to do. There was an alien object in view—a figure whose right of presence I instantly, passionately questioned. I recollect counting over perfectly the possibilities, reminding myself that nothing was more natural, for instance, then the appearance of one of the men about the place, or even of a messenger, a postman, or a tradesman's boy, from the village. That reminder had as little effect on my practical certitude as I was conscious—still even without looking—of its having upon the character and attitude of our visitor. Nothing was more natural than that these things should be the other things that they absolutely were not.

Of the positive identity of the apparition I would assure myself as soon as the small clock of my courage should have ticked out the right second; meanwhile, with an effort that was already sharp enough, I transferred my eyes straight to little Flora, who, at the moment, was about ten yards away. My heart had stood still for an instant with the wonder and terror of the question whether she too would see; and I held my breath while I waited for what a cry from her, what some sudden innocent sign either of interest or of alarm, would tell me. I waited, but nothing came; then, in the first place—and there is something more dire in this, I feel, than in anything I have to relate—I was determined by a sense that, within a minute, all sounds from her had previously dropped; and, in the second, by the circumstance that, also within the minute, she had, in her play, turned her back to the water. This was her attitude when I at last looked at her—looked with the confirmed conviction that we were still, together, under direct personal notice. She had picked up a small flat piece of wood, which happened to have in it a little hole that had evidently suggested to her the idea of sticking in another fragment that might figure as a mast and make the thing a boat. This second morsel, as I watched her, she was very markedly and intently attempting to tighten in its place. My apprehension of what she was doing sustained me so that after some seconds I felt I was ready for more. Then I again shifted my eyes—I faced what I had to face.

VII

I got hold of Mrs. Grose as soon after this as I could; and I can give no intelligible account of how I fought out the interval. Yet I still hear myself cry as I fairly threw myself into her arms: "*They know*—it's too monstrous: they know, they know!"

"And what on earth—?" I felt her incredulity as she held me.

"Why, all that *we* know—and heaven knows what else besides!" Then, as she released me, I made it out to her, made it out perhaps only now with full coherency even to myself. "Two hours ago, in the garden"—I could scarce articulate—"Flora *saw!*"

Mrs. Grose took it as she might have taken a blow in the stomach. "She has told you?" she panted.

"Not a word—that's the horror. She kept it to herself! The child of eight, that child!" Unutterable still, for me, was the stupefaction of it.

Mrs. Grose, of course, could only gape the wider. "Then how do you know?"

"I was there—I saw with my eyes: saw that she was perfectly aware."

"Do you mean aware of *him*?"

"No—of *her*." I was conscious as I spoke that I looked prodigious things, for I got the slow reflection of them in my companion's face. "Another person—this time; but a figure of quite as unmistakable horror and evil: a woman in black, pale and dreadful—with such an air also, and such a face!—on the other side of the lake. I was there with the child—quiet for the hour; and in the midst of it she came."

"Came how—from where?"

"From where they come from! She just appeared and stood there—but not so near."

"And without coming nearer?"

"Oh, for the effect and the feeling, she might have been as close as you!"

My friend, with an odd impulse, fell back a step. "Was she someone you've never seen?"

"Yes. But someone the child has. Someone *you* have." Then, to show how I had thought it all out: "My predecessor—the one who died."

"Miss Jessel?"

"Miss Jessel. You don't believe me?" I pressed.

She turned right and left in her distress. "How can you be sure?"

This drew from me, in the state of my nerves, a flash of impatience. "Then ask Flora—*she's* sure!" But I had no sooner spoken than I caught myself up. "No, for God's sake, *don't*! She'll say she isn't—she'll lie!"

Mrs. Grose was not too bewildered instinctively to protest. "Ah, how *can* you?"

"Because I'm clear. Flora doesn't want me to know."

"It's only then to spare you."

"No, no—there are depths, depths! The more I go over it, the more I see in it, and the more I see in it, the more I fear. I don't know what I *don't* see—what I *don't* fear!"

Mrs. Grose tried to keep up with me. "You mean you're afraid of seeing her again?"

"Oh, no; that's nothing—now!" Then I explained. "It's of *not* seeing her."

But my companion only looked wan. "I don't understand you."

"Why, it's that the child may keep it up—and that the child assuredly *will*—without my knowing it."

At the image of this possibility Mrs. Grose for a moment collapsed, yet presently to pull herself together again, as if from the positive force of the sense of what, should we yield an inch, there would really be to give way to. "Dear, dear—we must keep our heads! And after all, if she doesn't mind it—!" She even tried a grim joke. "Perhaps she likes it!"

"Likes *such* things—a scrap of an infant!"

"Isn't it just a proof of her blessed innocence?" my friend bravely inquired.

She brought me, for the instant, almost round. "Oh, we must clutch at *that*—we must cling to it! If it isn't a proof of what you say, it's a proof of—God knows what! For the woman's a horror of horrors."

Mrs. Grose, at this, fixed her eyes a minute on the ground; then at last raising them, "Tell me how you know," she said.

"Then you admit it's what she was?" I cried.

"Tell me how you know," my friend simply repeated.

"Know? By seeing her! By the way she looked."

"At you, do you mean—so wickedly?"

"Dear me, no—I could have borne that. She gave me never a glance. She only fixed the child."

Mrs. Grose tried to see it. "Fixed her?"

"Ah, with such awful eyes!"

She stared at mine as if they might really have resembled them. "Do you mean of dislike?"

"God help us, no. Of something much worse."

"Worse than dislike?"—this left her indeed at a loss.

"With a determination—indescribable. With a kind of fury of intention."

I made her turn pale. "Intention?"

"To get hold of her." Mrs. Grose—her eyes just lingering on mine—gave a shudder and walked to the window; and while she stood there looking out I completed my statement. *"That's* what Flora knows."

After a little she turned round. "The person was in black, you say?"

"In mourning—rather poor, almost shabby. But—yes—with extraordinary beauty." I now recognized to what I had at last, stroke by stroke, brought the victim of my confidence, for she quite visibly weighed this. "Oh, handsome—very, very," I insisted; "wonderfully handsome. But infamous."

She slowly came back to me. "Miss Jessel—*was* infamous." She once more took my hand in both her own, holding it as tight as if to fortify me against the increase of alarm I might draw from this disclosure. "They were both infamous," she finally said.

So, for a little, we faced it once more together; and I found absolutely a degree of help in seeing it now so straight. "I appreciate," I said, "the great decency of your not having hitherto spoken; but the time has certainly come to give me the whole thing." She appeared to assent to this, but still only in silence; seeing which I went on: "I must have it now. Of what did she die? Come, there was something between them."

"There was everything."

"In spite of the difference—?"

"Oh, of their rank, their condition"—she brought it woefully out. *"She* was a lady."

I turned it over; I again saw. "Yes—she was a lady."

"And he so dreadfully below," said Mrs. Grose.

I felt that I doubtless needn't press too hard, in such company, on the place of a servant in the scale; but there was nothing to prevent an acceptance of my companion's own measure of my predecessor's abasement. There was a way to deal with that, and I dealt; the more readily for my full vision—on the evidence—of our employer's late clever, good-looking "own" man; impudent, assured, spoiled, depraved. "The fellow was a hound."

Mrs. Grose considered as if it were perhaps a little a case for a sense of shades. "I've never seen one like him. He did what he wished."

"With *her*?"

"With them all."

It was as if now in my friend's own eyes Miss Jessel had again appeared. I seemed at any rate, for an instant, to see their evocation of her as distinctly as I had seen her by the pond; and I brought out with decision: "It must have been also what *she* wished!"

Mrs. Grose's face signified that it had been indeed, but she said at the same time: "Poor woman—she paid for it!"

"Then you do know what she died of?" I asked.

"No—I know nothing. I wanted not to know; I was glad enough I didn't; and I thanked heaven she was well out of this!"

"Yet you had, then, your idea—"

"Of her real reason for leaving? Oh, yes—as to that. She couldn't have stayed. Fancy it here—for a governess! And afterward I imagined—and I still imagine. And what I imagine is dreadful."

"Not so dreadful as what *I* do," I replied; on which I must have shown her—as I was indeed but too conscious—a front of miserable defeat. It brought out again all her compassion for me, and at the renewed touch of her kindness my power to resist broke down. I burst, as I had, the other time, made her burst, into tears; she took me to her motherly breast, and my lamentation overflowed. "I don't do it!" I sobbed in despair; "I don't save or shield them! It's far worse than I dreamed—they're lost!"

VIII

What I had said to Mrs. Grose was true enough: there were in the matter I had put before her depths and possibilities that I lacked resolution to sound; so that when we met once more in the wonder of it we were of a common mind about the duty of resistance to extravagant fancies. We were to keep our heads if we should keep nothing else—difficult indeed as that might be in the face of what, in our prodigious experience, was least to be questioned. Late that night, while the house slept, we had another talk in my room, when she went all the way with me as to its being beyond doubt that I had seen exactly what I had seen. To hold her perfectly in the pinch of that, I found I had only to ask her how, if I had "made it up," I came to be able to give, of each of the persons appearing to me, a picture disclosing, to the last detail, their special marks—a portrait on the exhibition of which she had instantly recognized and named them. She wished of course—small blame to her!—to sink the whole subject; and I was quick to assure her that my own interest in it had now violently taken the form of a search for the way to escape from it. I encountered her on the ground of a probability that with recurrence—for recurrence we took for granted—I should get used to my danger, distinctly professing that my personal exposure had suddenly become the least of my discomforts. It was my new suspicion that was intolerable; and yet even to this complication the later hours of the day had brought a little ease.

On leaving her, after my first outbreak, I had of course returned to my pupils, associating the right remedy for my dismay with that sense of their charm which I had already found to be a thing I could positively cultivate and which had never failed me yet. I had simply, in other words, plunged afresh into Flora's special society and there become aware—it was almost a luxury!— that she could put her little conscious hand straight upon the spot that ached. She had looked at me in sweet speculation and then had accused me to my face of having "cried." I had supposed I had brushed away the ugly signs: but I could literally—for the time, at all events—rejoice, under this fathomless charity, that they had not entirely disappeared. To gaze into the depths of blue of the child's eyes and pronounce their loveliness a trick of premature cunning was to be guilty of a cynicism in preference to which I naturally preferred to abjure my judgment and, so far as might be, my agitation. I couldn't abjure for merely wanting to, but I could repeat to Mrs. Grose—as I did there, over and over, in the small hours—that with their voices in the air, their pressure on one's heart, and their fragrant faces against one's cheek, everything fell to the ground but their incapacity and their beauty. It was a pity that, somehow, to settle this once for all, I had equally to re-enumerate the signs of subtlety that, in the afternoon, by the lake had made a miracle of my show of self-possession. It was a pity to be obliged to reinvestigate the certitude of the moment itself and repeat how it had come to me as a revelation that the inconceivable communion I then surprised was a matter, for either party, of habit. It was a pity that I should have had to quaver out again the reasons for my not having, in my delusion, so much as questioned that the little girl saw our visitant even as I actually saw Mrs. Grose herself, and that she wanted, by just so much as she did thus see, to make me suppose she didn't, and at the same time, without showing anything, arrive at a guess as to whether I myself did! It was a pity that I needed once more to describe the portentous little activity by which she sought to divert my attention—the perceptible increase of movement, the greater intensity of play, the singing, the gabbling of nonsense, and the invitation to romp.

Yet if I had not indulged, to prove there was nothing in it, in this review, I should have missed the two or three dim elements of comfort that still remained to me. I should not for instance have been able to asseverate to my friend that I was certain—which was so much to the good—that I at least had not betrayed myself. I should not have been prompted, by stress of need, by desperation of mind—I scarce know what to call it—to invoke such further aid to intelligence as might spring from pushing my colleague fairly to the wall. She had told me, bit by bit, under pressure, a great deal; but a small shifty spot on the wrong side of it all still sometimes brushed my brow like the wing of a bat; and I remember how on this occasion—for the sleeping house and the concentration alike of our danger and our watch seemed to help—I felt the importance of giving the last jerk to the curtain. "I don't believe anything so horrible," I recollect saying; "no, let us put it definitely, my dear, that I don't. But if I did, you know, there's a thing I should require now, just without sparing you the least bit more—oh, not a scrap, come!—to get out of you. What was it you had in mind when, in our distress, before Miles came back, over the letter from his school, you said, under my insistence, that you didn't pretend for him that he had not literally *ever* been 'bad'? He has *not* literally 'ever,' in these weeks that I myself have lived with him and so closely watched him; he has been an imperturbable little prodigy of delightful, lovable goodness. Therefore you might perfectly have made the claim for him if you had not, as it happened, seen an exception to take. What was your exception, and to what passage in your personal observation of him did you refer?"

It was a dreadfully austere inquiry, but levity was not our note, and, at any rate, before the gray dawn admonished us to separate I had got my answer. What my friend had had in mind proved to be immensely to the purpose. It was neither more nor less than the circumstance that for a period of several months Quint and the boy had been perpetually together. It was in fact the very appropriate truth that she had ventured to criticize the propriety, to hint at the incongruity, of so close an alliance, and even to go so far on the subject as a frank overture to Miss Jessel. Miss Jessel had, with a most strange manner, requested her to mind her business, and the good woman had, on this, directly approached little Miles. What she had said to him, since I pressed, was that *she* liked to see young gentlemen not forget their station.

I pressed again, of course, at this. "You reminded him that Quint was only a base menial?"

"As you might say! And it was his answer, for one thing, that was bad."

"And for another thing?" I waited. "He repeated your words to Quint?"

"No, not that. It's just what he *wouldn't!*" she could still impress upon me. "I was sure, at any rate," she added, "that he didn't. But he denied certain occasions."

"What occasions?"

"When they had been about together quite as if Quint were his tutor—and a very grand one—and Miss Jessel only for the little lady. When he had gone off with the fellow, I mean, and spent hours with him."

"He then prevaricated about it—he said he hadn't?" Her assent was clear enough to cause me to add in a moment: "I see. He lied."

"Oh!" Mrs. Grose mumbled. This was a suggestion that it didn't matter; which indeed she backed up by a further remark. "You see, after all, Miss Jessel didn't mind. She didn't forbid him."

I considered. "Did he put that to you as a justification?"

At this she dropped again. "No, he never spoke of it."

"Never mentioned her in connection with Quint?"

She saw, visibly flushing, where I was coming out. "Well, he didn't show anything. He denied," she repeated; "he denied."

Lord, how I pressed her now! "So that you could see he knew what was between the two wretches?"

"I don't know—I don't know!" the poor woman groaned.

"You do know, you dear thing," I replied; "only you haven't my dreadful boldness of mind, and you keep back, out of timidity and modesty and delicacy, even the impression that, in the past, when you had, without my aid, to flounder about in silence, most of all made you miserable. But I shall get it out of you yet! There was something in the boy that suggested to you," I continued, "that he covered and concealed their relation."

"Oh, he couldn't prevent—"

"Your learning the truth? I daresay! But, heavens," I fell, with vehemence, athinking, "what it shows that they must, to that extent, have succeeded in making of him!"

"Ah, nothing that's not nice *now!*" Mrs. Grose lugubriously pleaded.

"I don't wonder you looked queer," I persisted, "when I mentioned to you the letter from his school!"

"I doubt if I looked as queer as you!" she retorted with homely force. "And if he was so bad then as that comes to, how is he such an angel now?"

"Yes, indeed—and if he was a fiend at school! How, how, how? Well," I said in my torment, "you must put it to me again, but I shall not be able to tell you for some days. Only, put it to me again!" I cried in a way that made my friend stare. "There are directions in which I must not for the present let myself go." Meanwhile I returned to her first example—the one to which she had just previously referred—of the boy's happy capacity for an occasional slip. "If Quint—on your remonstrance at the time you speak of—was a base menial, one of the things Miles said to you, I find myself guessing, was that you were another." Again her admission was so adequate that I continued: "And you forgave him that?"

"Wouldn't *you?*"

"Oh, yes!" And we exchanged there, in the stillness, a sound of the oddest amusement. Then I went on: "At all events, while he was with the man—"

"Miss Flora was with the woman. It suited them all!"

It suited me, too, I felt, only too well; by which I mean that it suited exactly the particularly deadly view I was in the very act of forbidding myself to entertain. But I so far succeeded in checking the expression of this view that I will throw, just here, no further light on it than may be offered by the mention of my final observation to Mrs. Grose. "His having lied and been impudent are, I confess, less engaging specimens than I had hoped to have from you of the outbreak in him of the little natural man. Still," I mused, "They must do, for they make me feel more than ever that I must watch."

It made me blush, the next minute, to see in my friend's face how much more unreservedly she had forgiven him than her anecdote struck me as presenting to my own tenderness an occasion for doing. This came out when, at the schoolroom door, she quitted me. "Surely you don't accuse *him*—"

"Of carrying on an intercourse that he conceals from me? Ah, remember that, until further evidence, I now accuse nobody." Then, before shutting her out to go, by another passage, to her own place, "I must just wait," I wound up.

IX

I waited and waited, and the days, as they elapsed, took something from my consternation. A very few of them, in fact, passing, in constant sight of my pupils, without a fresh incident, sufficed to give to grievous fancies and even to odious memories a kind of brush of the sponge. I have spoken of the surrender to their extraordinary childish grace as a thing I could actively cultivate, and it may be imagined if I neglected now to address myself to this source for whatever it would yield. Stranger than I can express, certainly, was the effort to struggle against my new lights; it would doubtless have been, however, a greater tension still had it not been so frequently successful. I used to wonder how my little charges could help guessing that I thought strange things about them; and the circumstances that these things only made them more interesting was not by itself a direct aid to keeping them in the dark. I trembled lest they should see that they *were* so immensely more interesting. Putting things at the worst, at all events, as in meditation I so often did, any clouding of their innocence could only be—blameless and foredoomed as they were—a reason the more for taking risks. There were moments when, by an irresistible impulse, I found myself catching them up and pressing them to my heart. As soon as I had done so I used to say to myself: "What will they think of that? Doesn't it betray too much?" It would have been easy to get into a sad, wild tangle about how much I might betray; but the real account, I feel, of the hours of peace that I could still enjoy was that the immediate charm of my companions was a beguilement still effective even under the shadow of the possibility that it was studied. For if it occurred to me that I might occasionally excite suspicion by the little outbreaks of my sharper passion for them, so too I remember wondering if I mightn't see a queerness in the traceable increase of their own demonstrations.

They were at this period extravagantly and preternaturally fond of me; which, after all, I could reflect, was no more than a graceful response in children perpetually bowed over and hugged. The homage of which they were so lavish succeeded, in truth, for my nerves, quite as well as if I never appeared to myself, as I may say, literally to catch them at a purpose in it. They had never, I think, wanted to do so many things for their poor protectress; I mean—though they got their lessons better and better, which was naturally what would please her most—in the way of diverting, entertaining, surprising her; reading her passages, telling her stories, acting her charades, pouncing out at her, in disguises, as animals and historical characters, and above all astonishing her by the "pieces" they had secretly got by heart and could interminably recite. I should never get to the bottom—were I to let myself go even now—of the prodigious private commentary, all under still more private correction, with which, in these days, I overscored their full hours. They had shown me from the first a facility for everything, a general faculty which, taking a fresh start, achieved remarkable flights. They got their little tasks as if they loved them, and indulged, from the mere exuberance of the gift, in the most unimposed little miracles of memory. They not only popped out at me as tigers and as Romans, but as Shakespeareans, astronomers, and navigators. This was so singularly the case that it had presumably much to do with the fact as to which, at the present day, I am at a loss for a different explanation: I allude to my unnatural composure on the subject of another school for Miles. What I remember is that I was content not, for the time, to open the question, and that contentment must have sprung from the sense of his perpetually striking show of cleverness. He was too clever for a bad governess, for a parson's daughter, to spoil; and the strangest if not the brightest thread in the pensive embroidery I just spoke of was the impression I might have got, if I had dared to work it out, that he was under some influence operating in his small intellectual life as a tremendous incitement.

If it was easy to reflect, however, that such a boy could postpone school, it was at least as marked that for such a boy to have been "kicked out" by a schoolmaster was a mystification without end. Let me add that in their company now—and I was careful almost never to be out of it—I could follow no scent very far. We lived in a cloud of music and love and success and private theatricals. The musical sense in each of the children was of the quickest, but the elder in especial had a marvelous knack of catching and repeating. The schoolroom piano broke into all gruesome fancies; and when that failed there were confabulations in corners, with a sequel of one of them going out in the highest spirits in order to "come in" as something new. I had had brothers myself, and it was no revelation to me that little girls could be slavish idolaters of little boys. What surpassed everything was that there was a little boy in the world who could have for the inferior age, sex, and intelligence so fine a consideration. They were extraordinarily at one, and to say that they never either quarreled or complained is to make the note of praise coarse for their quality of sweetness. Sometimes, indeed, when I dropped into coarseness, I perhaps came across traces of little understandings between them by which one of them should keep me occupied while the other slipped away. There is a *naïf* side, I suppose, in all diplomacy; but if my pupils practiced upon me, it was surely with the minimum of grossness. It was all in the other quarter that, after a lull, the grossness broke out.

I find that I really hang back; but I must take my plunge. In going on with the record of what was hideous at Bly, I not only challenge the most liberal faith—for which I little care; but—and this is another matter—I renew what I myself suffered, I again push my way through it to the end. There came suddenly an hour after which, as I look back, the affair seems to me to have been all pure suffering; but I have at least reached the heart of it, and the straightest road out is doubtless to advance. One evening—with nothing to lead up or to prepare it—I felt the cold touch of the impression that had breathed on me the night of my arrival and which, much lighter then, as I have mentioned, I should probably have made little of in memory had my subsequent sojourn been less agitated. I had not gone to bed; I sat reading by a couple of candles. There was a roomful of old books at Bly—last-century fiction, some of it, which, to the extent of a distinctly deprecated renown, but never to so much as that of a stray specimen, had reached the sequestered home and appealed to the unavowed curiosity of my youth. I remember that the book I had in my hand was Fielding's *Amelia*; also that I was wholly awake. I recall further both a general conviction that it was horribly late and a particular objection to looking at my watch. I figure, finally, that the white curtain draping, in the fashion of those days, the head of Flora's little bed, shrouded, as I had assured myself long before, the perfection of childish rest. I recollect in short that, though I was deeply interested in my author, I found myself, at the turn of a page and with his spell all scattered, looking straight up from him and hard at the door of my room. There was a moment during which I listened, reminded of the faint sense I had had, the first night, of there being something undefinably astir in the house, and noted the soft breath of the open casement just move the half-drawn blind. Then, with all the marks of a deliberation that must have seemed magnificent had there been anyone to admire it, I laid down my book, rose to my feet, and, taking a candle, went straight out of the room and, from the passage, on which my light made little impression, noiselessly closed and locked the door.

I can say now neither what determined nor what guided me, but I went straight along the lobby, holding my candle high, till I came within sight of the tall window that presided over the great turn of the staircase. At this point I precipitately found myself aware of three things. They were practically simultaneous, yet they had flashes of succession. My candle, under a bold flourish, went out, and I perceived, by the uncovered window, that the yielding dusk of earliest morning rendered it unnecessary. Without it, the next instant, I saw that there was someone on the stair. I speak of sequences, but I required no lapse of seconds to stiffen myself for a third encounter with Quint. The apparition had reached the landing halfway up and was therefore on the spot nearest the window, where at sight of me, it stopped short and fixed me exactly as it had fixed me from the tower and from the garden. He knew me as well as I knew him; and so, in the cold, faint twilight, with a glimmer in the high glass and another on the polish of the oak stair below, we faced each other in our common intensity. He was absolutely, on this occasion, a living, detestable, dangerous presence. But that was not the wonder of wonders; I reserve this distinction for quite another circumstance: the circumstance that dread had unmistakably quitted me and that there was nothing in me there that didn't meet and measure him.

I had plenty of anguish after that extraordinary moment, but I had, thank God, no terror. And he knew I had not—I found myself at the end of an instant magnificently aware of this. I felt, in a fierce rigor of confidence, that if I stood my ground a minute I should cease—for the time, at least—to have him to reckon with; and during the minute, accordingly, the thing was as human and hideous as a real interview: hideous just because it *was* human, as human as to have met alone, in the small hours, in a sleeping house, some enemy, some adventurer, some criminal. It was the dead silence of our long gaze at such close quarters that gave the whole horror, huge as it was, its only note of the unnatural. If I had met a murderer in such a place and at such an hour, we still at least would have spoken. Something would have passed, in life, between us; if nothing had passed, one of us would have moved. The moment was so prolonged that it would have taken but little more to make me doubt if even I were in life. I can't express what followed it save by saying that the silence itself—which was indeed in a manner an attestation of my strength—became the element into which I saw the figure disappear; in which I definitely saw it turn as I might have seen the low wretch to which it had once belonged turn on receipt of an order, and pass, with my eyes on the villainous back that no hunch could have more disfigured, straight down the staircase and into the darkness in which the next bend was lost.

X

I remained awhile at the top of the stair, but with the effect presently of understanding that when my visitor had gone, he had gone: then I returned to my room. The foremost thing I saw there by the light of the candle I had left burning was that Flora's little bed was empty; and on this I caught my breath with all the terror that, five minutes before, I had been able to resist. I dashed at the place in which I had left her lying and over which (for the small silk counterpane and the sheets were disarranged) the white curtains had been deceivingly pulled forward; then my step, to my unutterable relief, produced an answering sound: I perceived an agitation of the window blind, and the child, ducking down, emerged rosily from the other side of it. She stood there in so much of her candor and so little of her nightgown, with her pink bare feet and the golden glow of her curls. She looked intensely grave, and I had never had such a sense of losing an advantage acquired (the thrill of which had just been so prodigious) as on my consciousness that she addressed me with a reproach. "You naughty: where *have* you been?"—instead of challenging her own irregularity I found myself arraigned and explaining. She herself explained, for that matter, with the loveliest, eagerest simplicity. She had known suddenly, as she lay there, that I was out of the room, and had jumped up to see what had become of me. I had dropped, with the joy of her reappearance, back into my chair—feeling then, and then only, a little faint; and she had pattered straight over to me, thrown herself upon my knee, given herself to be held with the flame of the candle full in the wonderful little face that was still flushed with sleep. I remember closing my eyes an instant, yieldingly, consciously, as before the excess of something beautiful that shone out of the blue of her own. "You were looking for me out of the window?" I said. "You thought I might be walking in the grounds?"

"Well, you know, I thought someone was"—she never blanched as she smiled out that at me.

Oh, how I looked at her now! "And did you see anyone?"

"Ah, *no!*" she returned, almost with the full privilege of childish inconsequence, resentfully, though with a long sweetness in her little drawl of the negative.

At that moment, in the state of my nerves, I absolutely believed she lied; and if I once more closed my eyes it was before the dazzle of the three or four possible ways in which I might take this up. One of these, for a moment, tempted me with such singular intensity that, to withstand it, I must have gripped my little girl with a spasm that, wonderfully, she submitted to without a cry or a sign of fright. Why not break out at her on the spot and have it all over?—give it to her straight in her lovely little lighted face? "You see, you see, you *know* that you do and that you already quite suspect I believe it; therefore, why not frankly confess it to me, so that we may at least live with it together and learn perhaps, in the strangeness of our fate, where we are and what it means?" This solicitation dropped, alas, as it came: if I could immediately have succumbed to it I might have spared myself—well, you'll see what. Instead of succumbing I sprang again to my feet, looked at her bed, and took a helpless middle way. "Why did you pull the curtain over the place to make me think you were still there?"

Flora luminously considered; after which, with her little divine smile: "Because I don't like to frighten you!"

"But if I had, by your idea, gone out—?"

She absolutely declined to be puzzled; she turned her eyes to the flame of the candle as if the question were as irrelevant, or at any rate as impersonal, as Mrs. Marcet or nine-times-nine. "Oh, but you know," she quite adequately answered, "that you might come back, you dear, and that you *have!*" And after a little, when she had got into bed, I had, for a long time, by almost sitting on her to hold her hand, to prove that I recognized the pertinence of my return.

You may imagine the general complexion, from that moment, of my nights. I repeatedly sat up till I didn't know when; I selected moments when my roommate unmistakably slept, and, stealing out, took noiseless turns in the passage and even pushed as far as to where I had last met Quint. But I never met him there again; and I may as well say at once that I on no other occasion saw him in the house. I just missed, on the staircase, on the other hand, a different adventure. Looking down it from the top I once recognized the presence of a woman seated on one of the lower steps with her back presented to me, her body half-bowed and her head, in an attitude of woe, in her hands. I had been there but an instant, however, when she vanished without looking round at me. I knew, nonetheless, exactly what dreadful face she had to show; and I wondered whether, if instead of being above I had been below, I should have had, for going up, the same nerve I had lately shown Quint. Well, there continued to be plenty of chance for nerve. On the eleventh night after my latest encounter with that gentleman—they were all numbered now—I had an alarm that perilously skirted it and that indeed, from the particular quality of its unexpectedness, proved quite my sharpest shock. It was precisely the first night during this series that, weary with watching, I had felt that I might again without laxity lay myself down at my old hour. I slept immediately and, as I afterward knew, till about one o'clock; but when I woke it was to sit straight up, as completely roused as if a hand had shook me. I had left a light burning, but it was now out, and I felt an instant certainty that Flora had extinguished it. This brought me to my feet and straight, in the darkness, to her bed, which I found she had left. A glance at the window enlightened me further, and the striking of a match completed the picture.

The child had again got up—this time blowing out the taper, and had again, for some purpose of observation or response, squeezed in behind the blind and was peering out into the night. That she now saw—as she had not, I had satisfied myself, the previous time—was proved to me by the fact that she was disturbed neither by my reillumination nor by the haste I made to get into slippers and into a wrap. Hidden, protected, absorbed, she evidently rested on the sill—the casement opened forward—and gave herself up. There was a great still moon to help her, and this fact had counted in my quick decision. She was face to face with the apparition we had met at the lake, and could now communicate with it as she had not then been able to do. What I, on my side, had to care for was, without disturbing her, to reach, from the corridor, some other window in the same quarter. I got to the door without her hearing me; I got out of it, closed it, and listened, from the other side, for some sound from her. While I stood in the passage I had my eyes on her brother's door, which was but ten steps off and which, indescribably, produced in me a renewal of the strange impulse that I lately spoke of as my temptation. What if I should go straight in and march to his window?—what if, by risking to his boyish bewilderment a revelation of my motive, I should throw across the rest of the mystery the long halter of my boldness?

This thought held me sufficiently to make me cross to his threshold and pause again. I preternaturally listened; I figured to myself what might portentously be; I wondered if his bed were also empty and he too were secretly at watch. It was a deep, soundless minute, at the end of which my impulse failed. He was quiet; he might be innocent; the risk was hideous; I turned away. There was a figure in the grounds—a figure prowling for a sight, the visitor with whom Flora was engaged; but it was not the visitor most concerned with my boy. I hesitated afresh, but on other grounds and only for a few seconds; then I had made my choice. There were empty rooms at Bly, and it was only a question of choosing the right one. The right one suddenly presented itself to me as the lower one—though high above the gardens—in the solid corner of the house that I have spoken of as the old tower. This was a large, square chamber, arranged with some state as a bedroom, the extravagant size of which made it so inconvenient that it had not for years, though kept by Mrs. Grose in exemplary order, been occupied. I had often admired it and I knew my way about in it; I had only, after just faltering at the first chill gloom of its disuse, to pass across it and unbolt as quietly as I could one of the shutters. Achieving this transit, I uncovered the glass without a sound and, applying my face to the pane, was able, the darkness without being much less than within, to see that I commanded the right direction. Then I saw something more. The moon made the night extraordinarily penetrable and showed me on the lawn a person, diminished by distance, who stood there motionless and as if fascinated, looking up to where I had appeared—looking, that is, not so much straight at me as at something that was apparently above me. There was clearly another person above me—there was a person on the tower; but the presence on the lawn was not in the least what I had conceived and had confidently hurried to meet. The presence on the lawn—I felt sick as I made it out—was poor little Miles himself.

XI

It was not till late next day that I spoke to Mrs. Grose; the rigor with which I kept my pupils in sight making it often difficult to meet her privately, and the more as we each felt the importance of not provoking—on the part of the servants quite as much as on that of the children—any suspicion of a secret flurry or that of a discussion of mysteries. I drew a great security in this particular from her mere smooth aspect. There was nothing in her fresh face to pass on to others my horrible confidences. She believed me, I was sure, absolutely: if she hadn't I don't know what would have become of me, for I couldn't have borne the business alone. But she was a magnificent monument to the blessing of a want of imagination, and if she could see in our little charges nothing but their beauty and amiability, their happiness and cleverness, she had no direct communication with the sources of my trouble. If they had been at all visibly blighted or battered, she would doubtless have grown, on tracing it back, haggard enough to match them; as matters stood, however, I could feel her, when she surveyed them, with her large white arms folded and the habit of serenity in all her look, thank the Lord's mercy that if they were ruined the pieces would still serve. Flights of fancy gave place, in her mind, to a steady fireside glow, and I had already begun to perceive how, with the development of the conviction that—as time went on without a public accident—our young things could, after all, look out for themselves, she addressed her greatest solicitude to the sad case presented by their instructress. That, for myself, was a sound simplification: I could engage that, to the world, my face should tell no tales, but it would have been, in the conditions, an immense added strain to find myself anxious about hers.

At the hour I now speak of she had joined me, under pressure, on the terrace, where, with the lapse of the season, the afternoon sun was now agreeable; and we sat there together while, before us, at a distance, but within call if we wished, the children strolled to and fro in one of their most manageable moods. They moved slowly, in unison, below us, over the lawn, the boy, as they went, reading aloud from a storybook and passing his arm round his sister to keep her quite in touch. Mrs. Grose watched them with positive placidity; then I caught the suppressed intellectual creak with which she conscientiously turned to take from me a view of the back of the tapestry. I had made her a receptacle of lurid things, but there was an odd recognition of my superiority—my accomplishments and my function—in her patience under my pain. She offered her mind to my disclosures as, had I wished to mix a witch's broth and proposed it with assurance, she would have held out a large clean saucepan. This had become thoroughly her attitude by the time that, in my recital of the events of the night, I reached the point of what Miles had said to me when, after seeing him, at such a monstrous hour, almost on the very spot where he happened now to be, I had gone down to bring him in; choosing then, at the window, with a concentrated need of not alarming the house, rather that method than a signal more resonant. I had left her meanwhile in little doubt of my small hope of representing with success even to her actual sympathy my sense of the real splendor of the little inspiration with which, after I had got him into the house, the boy met my final articulate challenge. As soon as I appeared in the moonlight on the terrace, he had come to me as straight as possible; on which I had taken his hand without a word and led him, through the dark spaces, up the staircase where Quint had so hungrily hovered for him, along the lobby where I had listened and trembled, and so to his forsaken room.

Not a sound, on the way, had passed between us, and I had wondered—oh, *how* I had wondered!—if he were groping about in his little mind for something plausible and not too grotesque. It would tax his invention, certainly, and I felt, this time, over his real embarrassment, a curious thrill of triumph. It was a sharp trap for the inscrutable! He couldn't play any longer at innocence; so how the deuce would he get out of it? There beat in me indeed, with the passionate throb of this question an equal dumb appeal as to how the deuce *I* should. I was confronted at last, as never yet, with all the risk attached even now to sounding my own horrid note. I remember in fact that as we pushed into his little chamber, where the bed had not been slept in at all and the window, uncovered to the moonlight, made the place so clear that there was no need of striking a match—I remember how I suddenly dropped, sank upon the edge of the bed from the force of the idea that he must know how he really, as they say, "had" me. He could do what he liked, with all his cleverness to help him, so long as I should continue to defer to the old tradition of the criminality of those caretakers of the young who minister to superstitions and fears. He "had" me indeed, and in a cleft stick; for who would ever absolve me, who would consent that I should go unhung, if, by the faintest tremor of an overture, I were the first to introduce into our perfect intercourse an element so dire? No, no: it was useless to attempt to convey to Mrs. Grose, just as it is scarcely less so to attempt to suggest here, how, in our short, stiff brush in the dark, he fairly shook me with admiration. I was of course thoroughly kind and merciful; never, never yet had I placed on his little shoulders hands of such tenderness as those with which, while I rested against the bed, I held him there well under fire. I had no alternative but, in form at least, to put it to him.

"You must tell me now—and all the truth. What did you go out for? What were you doing there?"

I can still see his wonderful smile, the whites of his beautiful eyes, and the uncovering of his little teeth shine to me in the dusk. "If I tell you why, will you understand?" My heart, at this, leaped into my mouth. *Would* he tell me why? I found no sound on my lips to press it, and I was aware of replying only with a vague, repeated, grimacing nod. He was gentleness itself, and while I wagged my head at him he stood there more than ever a little fairy prince. It was his brightness indeed that gave me a respite. Would it be so great if he were really going to tell me? "Well," he said at last, "just exactly in order that you should do this."

"Do what?"

"Think me—for a change—*bad!*" I shall never forget the sweetness and gaiety with which he brought out the word, nor how, on top of it, he bent forward and kissed me. It was practically the end of everything. I met his kiss and I had to make, while I folded him for a minute in my arms, the most stupendous effort not to cry. He had given exactly the account of himself that permitted least of my going behind it, and it was only with the effect of confirming my acceptance of it that, as I presently glanced about the room, I could say—

"Then you didn't undress at all?"

He fairly glittered in the gloom. "Not at all. I sat up and read."

"And when did you go down?"

"At midnight. When I'm bad I am bad!"

"I see, I see—it's charming. But how could you be sure I would know it?"

"Oh, I arranged that with Flora." His answers rang out with a readiness! "She was to get up and look out."

"Which is what she did do." It was I who fell into the trap!

"So she disturbed you, and, to see what she was looking at, you also looked—you saw."

"While you," I concurred, "caught your death in the night air!"

He literally bloomed so from this exploit that he could afford radiantly to assent. "How otherwise should I have been bad enough?" he asked. Then, after another embrace, the incident and our interview closed on my recognition of all the reserves of goodness that, for his joke, he had been able to draw upon.

XII

The particular impression I had received proved in the morning light, I repeat, not quite successfully presentable to Mrs. Grose, though I reinforced it with the mention of still another remark that he had made before we separated. "It all lies in half a dozen words," I said to her, "words that really settle the matter. 'Think, you know, what I might do!' He threw that off to show me how good he is. He knows down to the ground what he 'might' do. That's what he gave them a taste of at school."

"Lord, you do change!" cried my friend.

"I don't change—I simply make it out. The four, depend upon it, perpetually meet. If on either of these last nights you had been with either child, you would clearly have understood. The more I've watched and waited the more I've felt that if there were nothing else to make it sure it would be made so by the systematic silence of each. Never, by a slip of the tongue, have they so much as alluded to either of their old friends, any more than Miles has alluded to his expulsion. Oh, yes, we may sit here and look at them, and they may show off to us there to their fill; but even while they pretend to be lost in their fairytale they're steeped in their vision of the dead restored. He's not reading to her," I declared; "they're talking of them—they're talking horrors! I go on, I know, as if I were crazy; and it's a wonder I'm not. What I've seen would have made you so; but it has only made me more lucid, made me get hold of still other things."

My lucidity must have seemed awful, but the charming creatures who were victims of it, passing and repassing in their interlocked sweetness, gave my colleague something to hold on by; and I felt how tight she held as, without stirring in the breath of my passion, she covered them still with her eyes. "Of what other things have you got hold?"

"Why, of the very things that have delighted, fascinated, and yet, at bottom, as I now so strangely see, mystified and troubled me. Their more than earthly beauty, their absolutely unnatural goodness. It's a game," I went on; "it's a policy and a fraud!"

"On the part of little darlings—?"

"As yet mere lovely babies? Yes, mad as that seems!" The very act of bringing it out really helped me to trace it—follow it all up and piece it all together. "They haven't been good—they've only been absent. It has been easy to live with them, because they're simply leading a life of their own. They're not mine—they're not ours. They're his and they're hers!"

"Quint's and that woman's?"

"Quint's and that woman's. They want to get to them."

Oh, how, at this, poor Mrs. Grose appeared to study them! "But for what?"

"For the love of all the evil that, in those dreadful days, the pair put into them. And to ply them with that evil still, to keep up the work of demons, is what brings the others back."

"Laws!" said my friend under her breath. The exclamation was homely, but it revealed a real acceptance of my further proof of what, in the bad time—for there had been a worse even than this!—must have occurred. There could have been no such justification for me as the plain assent of her experience to whatever depth of depravity I found credible in our brace of scoundrels. It was in obvious submission of memory that she brought out after a moment: "They were rascals! But what can they now do?" she pursued.

"Do?" I echoed so loud that Miles and Flora, as they passed at their distance, paused an instant in their walk and looked at us. "Don't they do enough?" I demanded in a lower tone, while the children, having smiled and nodded and kissed hands to us, resumed their exhibition. We were held by it a minute; then I answered: "They can destroy them!" At this my companion did turn, but the inquiry she launched was a silent one, the effect of which was to make me more explicit. "They don't know, as yet, quite how—but they're trying hard. They're seen only across, as it were, and beyond—in strange places and on high places, the top of towers, the roof of houses, the outside of windows, the further edge of pools; but there's a deep design, on either side, to shorten the distance and overcome the obstacle; and the success of the tempters is only a question of time. They've only to keep to their suggestions of danger."

"For the children to come?"

"And perish in the attempt!" Mrs. Grose slowly got up, and I scrupulously added: "Unless, of course, we can prevent!"

Standing there before me while I kept my seat, she visibly turned things over. "Their uncle must do the preventing. He must take them away."

"And who's to make him?"

She had been scanning the distance, but she now dropped on me a foolish face. "You, miss."

"By writing to him that his house is poisoned and his little nephew and niece mad?"

"But if they are, miss?"

"And if I am myself, you mean? That's charming news to be sent him by a governess whose prime undertaking was to give him no worry."

Mrs. Grose considered, following the children again. "Yes, he do hate worry. That was the great reason—"

"Why those fiends took him in so long? No doubt, though his indifference must have been awful. As I'm not a fiend, at any rate, I shouldn't take him in."

My companion, after an instant and for all answer, sat down again and grasped my arm. "Make him at any rate come to you."

I stared. "To *me*?" I had a sudden fear of what she might do. "'Him'?"

"He ought to *be* here—he ought to help."

I quickly rose, and I think I must have shown her a queerer face than ever yet. "You see me asking him for a visit?" No, with her eyes on my face she evidently couldn't. Instead of it even—as a woman reads another—she could see what I myself saw: his derision, his amusement, his contempt for the breakdown of my resignation at being left alone and for the fine machinery I had set in motion to attract his attention to my slighted charms. She didn't know—no one knew—how proud I had been to serve him and to stick to our terms; yet she nonetheless took the measure, I think, of the warning I now gave her. "If you should so lose your head as to appeal to him for me—"

She was really frightened. "Yes, miss?"

"I would leave, on the spot, both him and you."

XIII

It was all very well to join them, but speaking to them proved quite as much as ever an effort beyond my strength—offered, in close quarters, difficulties as insurmountable as before. This situation continued a month, and with new aggravations and particular notes, the note above all, sharper and sharper, of the small ironic consciousness on the part of my pupils. It was not, I am as sure today as I was sure then, my mere infernal imagination: it was absolutely traceable that they were aware of my predicament and that this strange relation made, in a manner, for a long time, the air in which we moved. I don't mean that they had their tongues in their cheeks or did anything vulgar, for that was not one of their dangers: I do mean, on the other hand, that the element of the unnamed and untouched became, between us, greater than any other, and that so much avoidance could not have been so successfully effected without a great deal of tacit arrangement. It was as if, at moments, we were perpetually coming into sight of subjects before which we must stop short, turning suddenly out of alleys that we perceived to be blind, closing with a little bang that made us look at each other—for, like all bangs, it was something louder than we had intended—the doors we had indiscreetly opened. All roads lead to Rome, and there were times when it might have struck us that almost every branch of study or subject of conversation skirted forbidden ground. Forbidden ground was the question of the return of the dead in general and of whatever, in especial, might survive, in memory, of the friends little children had lost. There were days when I could have sworn that one of them had, with a small invisible nudge, said to the other: "She thinks she'll do it this time—but she won't!" To "do it" would have been to indulge for instance—and for once in a way—in some direct reference to the lady who had prepared them for my discipline. They had a delightful endless appetite for passages in my own history, to which I had again and again treated them; they were in possession of everything that had ever happened to me, had had, with every circumstance the story of my smallest adventures and of those of my brothers and sisters and of the cat and the dog at home, as well as many particulars of the eccentric nature of my father, of the furniture and arrangement of our house, and of the conversation of the old women of our village. There were things enough, taking one with another, to chatter about, if one went very fast and knew by instinct when to go round. They pulled with an art of their own the strings of my invention and my memory; and nothing else perhaps, when I thought of such occasions afterward, gave me so the suspicion of being watched from under cover. It was in any case over my life, my past, and my friends alone that we could take anything like our ease—a state of affairs that led them sometimes without the least pertinence to break out into sociable reminders. I was invited—with no visible connection—to repeat afresh Goody Gosling's celebrated mot or to confirm the details already supplied as to the cleverness of the vicarage pony.

It was partly at such junctures as these and partly at quite different ones that, with the turn my matters had now taken, my predicament, as I have called it, grew most sensible. The fact that the days passed for me without another encounter ought, it would have appeared, to have done something toward soothing my nerves. Since the light brush, that second night on the upper landing, of the presence of a woman at the foot of the stair, I had seen nothing, whether in or out of the house, that one had better not have seen. There was many a corner round which I expected to come upon Quint, and many a situation that, in a merely sinister way, would have favored the appearance of Miss Jessel. The summer had turned, the summer had gone; the autumn had dropped upon Bly and had blown out half our lights. The place, with its gray sky and withered garlands, its bared spaces and scattered dead leaves, was like a theater after the performance—all strewn with crumpled playbills. There were exactly states of the air, conditions of sound and of stillness, unspeakable impressions of the kind of ministering moment, that brought back to me, long enough to catch it, the feeling of the medium in which, that June evening out of doors, I had had my first sight of Quint, and in which, too, at those other instants, I had, after seeing him through the window, looked for him in vain in the circle of shrubbery. I recognized the signs, the portents—I recognized the moment, the spot. But they remained unaccompanied and empty, and I continued unmolested; if unmolested one could call a young woman whose sensibility had, in the most extraordinary fashion, not declined but deepened. I had said in my talk with Mrs. Grose on that horrid scene of Flora's by the lake—and had perplexed her by so saying—that it would from that moment distress me much more to lose my power than to keep it. I had then expressed what was vividly in my mind: the truth that, whether the children really saw or not—since, that is, it was not yet definitely proved—I greatly preferred, as a safeguard, the fullness of my own exposure. I was ready to know the very worst that was to be known. What I had then had an ugly glimpse of was that my eyes might be sealed just while theirs were most opened. Well, my eyes were sealed, it appeared, at present—a consummation for which it seemed blasphemous not to thank God. There was, alas, a difficulty about that: I would have thanked him with all my soul had I not had in a proportionate measure this conviction of the secret of my pupils.

How can I retrace today the strange steps of my obsession? There were times of our being together when I would have been ready to swear that, literally, in my presence, but with my direct sense of it closed, they had visitors who were known and were welcome. Then it was that, had I not been deterred by the very chance that such an injury might prove greater than the injury to be averted, my exultation would have broken out. "They're here, they're here, you little wretches," I would have cried, "and you can't deny it now!" The little wretches denied it with all the added volume of their sociability and their tenderness, in just the crystal depths of which—like the flash of a fish in a stream—the mockery of their advantage peeped up. The shock, in truth, had sunk into me still deeper than I knew on the night when, looking out to see either Quint or Miss Jessel under the stars, I had beheld the boy over whose rest I watched and who had immediately brought in with him—had straightway, there, turned it on me—the lovely upward look with which, from the battlements above me, the hideous apparition of Quint had played. If it was a question of a scare, my discovery on this occasion had scared me more than any other, and it was in the condition of nerves produced by it that I made my actual inductions. They harassed me so that sometimes, at odd moments, I shut myself up audibly to rehearse—it was at once a fantastic relief and a renewed despair—the manner in which I might come to the point. I approached it from one side and the other while, in my room, I flung myself about, but I always broke down in the monstrous utterance of names. As they died away on my lips, I said to myself that I should indeed help them to represent something infamous, if, by pronouncing them, I should violate as rare a little case of instinctive delicacy as any schoolroom, probably, had ever known. When I said to myself: "They have the manners to be silent, and you, trusted as you are, the baseness to speak!" I felt myself crimson and I covered my face with my hands. After these secret scenes I chattered more than ever, going on volubly enough till one of our prodigious, palpable hushes occurred—I can call them nothing else—the strange, dizzy lift or swim (I try for terms!) into a stillness, a pause of all life, that had nothing to do with the more or less noise that at the moment we might be engaged in making and that I could hear through any deepened exhilaration or quickened recitation or louder strum of the piano. Then it was that the others, the outsiders, were there. Though they were not angels, they "passed," as the French say, causing me, while they stayed, to tremble with the fear of their addressing to their younger victims some yet more infernal message or more vivid image than they had thought good enough for myself.

What it was most impossible to get rid of was the cruel idea that, whatever I had seen, Miles and Flora saw more—things terrible and unguessable and that sprang from dreadful passages of intercourse in the past. Such things naturally left on the surface, for the time, a chill which we vociferously denied that we felt; and we had, all three, with repetition, got into such splendid training that we went, each time, almost automatically, to mark the close of the incident, through the very same movements. It was striking of the children, at all events, to kiss me inveterately with a kind of wild irrelevance and never to fail—one or the other—of the precious question that had helped us through many a peril. "When do you think he will come? Don't you think we ought to write?"—there was nothing like that inquiry, we found by experience, for carrying off an awkwardness. "He" of course was their uncle in Harley Street; and we lived in much profusion of theory that he might at any moment arrive to mingle in our circle. It was impossible to have given less encouragement than he had done to such a doctrine, but if we had not had the doctrine to fall back upon we should have deprived each other of some of our finest exhibitions. He never wrote to them—that may have been selfish, but it was a part of the flattery of his trust of me; for the way in which a man pays his highest tribute to a woman is apt to be but by the more festal celebration of one of the sacred laws of his comfort; and I held that I carried out the spirit of the pledge given not to appeal to him when I let my charges understand that their own letters were but charming literary exercises. They were too beautiful to be posted; I kept them myself; I have them all to this hour. This was a rule indeed which only added to the satiric effect of my being plied with the supposition that he might at any moment be among us. It was exactly as if my charges knew how almost more awkward than anything else that might be for me. There appears to me, moreover, as I look back, no note in all this more extraordinary than the mere fact that, in spite of my tension and of their triumph, I never lost patience with them. Adorable they must in truth have been, I now reflect, that I didn't in these days hate them! Would exasperation, however, if relief had longer been postponed, finally have betrayed me? It little matters, for relief arrived. I call it relief, though it was only the relief that a snap brings to a strain or the burst of a thunderstorm to a day of suffocation. It was at least change, and it came with a rush.

XIV

Walking to church a certain Sunday morning, I had little Miles at my side and his sister, in advance of us and at Mrs. Grose's, well in sight. It was a crisp, clear day, the first of its order for some time; the night had brought a touch of frost, and the autumn air, bright and sharp, made the church bells almost gay. It was an odd accident of thought that I should have happened at such a moment to be particularly and very gratefully struck with the obedience of my little charges. Why did they never resent my inexorable, my perpetual society? Something or other had brought nearer home to me that I had all but pinned the boy to my shawl and that, in the way our companions were marshaled before me, I might have appeared to provide against some danger of rebellion. I was like a gaoler with an eye to possible surprises and escapes. But all this belonged—I mean their magnificent little surrender— just to the special array of the facts that were most abysmal. Turned out for Sunday by his uncle's tailor, who had had a free hand and a notion of pretty waistcoats and of his grand little air, Miles's whole title to independence, the rights of his sex and situation, were so stamped upon him that if he had suddenly struck for freedom I should have had nothing to say. I was by the strangest of chances wondering how I should meet him when the revolution unmistakably occurred. I call it a revolution because I now see how, with the word he spoke, the curtain rose on the last act of my dreadful drama, and the catastrophe was precipitated. "Look here, my dear, you know," he charmingly said, "when in the world, please, am I going back to school?"

Transcribed here the speech sounds harmless enough, particularly as uttered in the sweet, high, casual pipe with which, at all interlocutors, but above all at his eternal governess, he threw off intonations as if he were tossing roses. There was something in them that always made one "catch," and I caught, at any rate, now so effectually that I stopped as short as if one of the trees of the park had fallen across the road. There was something new, on the spot, between us, and he was perfectly aware that I recognized it, though, to enable me to do so, he had no need to look a whit less candid and charming than usual. I could feel in him how he already, from my at first finding nothing to reply, perceived the advantage he had gained. I was so slow to find anything that he had plenty of time, after a minute, to continue with his suggestive but inconclusive smile: "You know, my dear, that for a fellow to be with a lady always—!" His "my dear" was constantly on his lips for me, and nothing could have expressed more the exact shade of the sentiment with which I desired to inspire my pupils than its fond familiarity. It was so respectfully easy.

But, oh, how I felt that at present I must pick my own phrases! I remember that, to gain time, I tried to laugh, and I seemed to see in the beautiful face with which he watched me how ugly and queer I looked. "And always with the same lady?" I returned.

He neither blanched nor winked. The whole thing was virtually out between us. "Ah, of course, she's a jolly, 'perfect' lady; but, after all, I'm a fellow, don't you see? that's—well, getting on."

I lingered there with him an instant ever so kindly. "Yes, you're getting on." Oh, but I felt helpless!

I have kept to this day the heartbreaking little idea of how he seemed to know that and to play with it. "And you can't say I've not been awfully good, can you?"

I laid my hand on his shoulder, for, though I felt how much better it would have been to walk on, I was not yet quite able. "No, I can't say that, Miles."

"Except just that one night, you know—!"

"That one night?" I couldn't look as straight as he.

"Why, when I went down—went out of the house."

"Oh, yes. But I forget what you did it for."

"You forget?"—he spoke with the sweet extravagance of childish reproach. "Why, it was to show you I could!"

"Oh, yes, you could."

"And I can again."

I felt that I might, perhaps, after all, succeed in keeping my wits about me. "Certainly. But you won't."

"No, not that again. It was nothing."

"It was nothing," I said. "But we must go on."

He resumed our walk with me, passing his hand into my arm. "Then when am I going back?"

I wore, in turning it over, my most responsible air. "Were you very happy at school?"

He just considered. "Oh, I'm happy enough anywhere!"

"Well, then," I quavered, "if you're just as happy here—!"

"Ah, but that isn't everything! Of course you know a lot—"

"But you hint that you know almost as much?" I risked as he paused.

"Not half I want to!" Miles honestly professed. "But it isn't so much that."

"What is it, then?"

"Well—I want to see more life."

"I see; I see." We had arrived within sight of the church and of various persons, including several of the household of Bly, on their way to it and clustered about the door to see us go in. I quickened our step; I wanted to get there before the question between us opened up much further; I reflected hungrily that, for more than an hour, he would have to be silent; and I thought with envy of the comparative dusk of the pew and of the almost spiritual help of the hassock on which I might bend my knees. I seemed literally to be running a race with some confusion to which he was about to reduce me, but I felt that he had got in first when, before we had even entered the churchyard, he threw out—

"I want my own sort!"

It literally made me bound forward. "There are not many of your own sort, Miles!" I laughed. "Unless perhaps dear little Flora!"

"You really compare me to a baby girl?"

This found me singularly weak. "Don't you, then, *love* our sweet Flora?"

"If I didn't—and you, too; if I didn't—!" he repeated as if retreating for a jump, yet leaving his thought so unfinished that, after we had come into the gate, another stop, which he imposed on me by the pressure of his arm, had become inevitable. Mrs. Grose and Flora had passed into the church, the other worshippers had followed, and we were, for the minute, alone among the old, thick graves. We had paused, on the path from the gate, by a low, oblong, tablelike tomb.

"Yes, if you didn't—?"

He looked, while I waited, at the graves. "Well, you know what!" But he didn't move, and he presently produced something that made me drop straight down on the stone slab, as if suddenly to rest. "Does my uncle think what *you* think?"

I markedly rested. "How do you know what I think?"

"Ah, well, of course I don't; for it strikes me you never tell me. But I mean does *he* know?"

"Know what, Miles?"

"Why, the way I'm going on."

I perceived quickly enough that I could make, to this inquiry, no answer that would not involve something of a sacrifice of my employer. Yet it appeared to me that we were all, at Bly, sufficiently sacrificed to make that venial. "I don't think your uncle much cares."

Miles, on this, stood looking at me. "Then don't you think he can be made to?"

"In what way?"

"Why, by his coming down."

"But who'll get him to come down?"

"*I* will!" the boy said with extraordinary brightness and emphasis. He gave me another look charged with that expression and then marched off alone into church.

XV

The business was practically settled from the moment I never followed him. It was a pitiful surrender to agitation, but my being aware of this had somehow no power to restore me. I only sat there on my tomb and read into what my little friend had said to me the fullness of its meaning; by the time I had grasped the whole of which I had also embraced, for absence, the pretext that I was ashamed to offer my pupils and the rest of the congregation such an example of delay. What I said to myself above all was that Miles had got something out of me and that the proof of it, for him, would be just this awkward collapse. He had got out of me that there was something I was much afraid of and that he should probably be able to make use of my fear to gain, for his own purpose, more freedom. My fear was of having to deal with the intolerable question of the grounds of his dismissal from school, for that was really but the question of the horrors gathered behind. That his uncle should arrive to treat with me of these things was a solution that, strictly speaking, I ought now to have desired to bring on; but I could so little face the ugliness and the pain of it that I simply procrastinated and lived from hand to mouth. The boy, to my deep discomposure, was immensely in the right, was in a position to say to me: "Either you clear up with my guardian the mystery of this interruption of my studies, or you cease to expect me to lead with you a life that's so unnatural for a boy." What was so unnatural for the particular boy I was concerned with was this sudden revelation of a consciousness and a plan.

That was what really overcame me, what prevented my going in. I walked round the church, hesitating, hovering; I reflected that I had already, with him, hurt myself beyond repair. Therefore I could patch up nothing, and it was too extreme an effort to squeeze beside him into the pew: he would be so much more sure than ever to pass his arm into mine and make me sit there for an hour in close, silent contact with his commentary on our talk. For the first minute since his arrival I wanted to get away from him. As I paused beneath the high east window and listened to the sounds of worship, I was taken with an impulse that might master me, I felt, completely should I give it the least encouragement. I might easily put an end to my predicament by getting away altogether. Here was my chance; there was no one to stop me; I could give the whole thing up—turn my back and retreat. It was only a question of hurrying again, for a few preparations, to the house which the attendance at church of so many of the servants would practically have left unoccupied. No one, in short, could blame me if I should just drive desperately off. What was it to get away if I got away only till dinner? That would be in a couple of hours, at the end of which—I had the acute prevision—my little pupils would play at innocent wonder about my nonappearance in their train.

"What *did* you do, you naughty, bad thing? Why in the world, to worry us so—and take our thoughts off, too, don't you know?—did you desert us at the very door?" I couldn't meet such questions nor, as they asked them, their false little lovely eyes; yet it was all so exactly what I should have to meet that, as the prospect grew sharp to me, I at last let myself go.

I got, so far as the immediate moment was concerned, away; I came straight out of the churchyard and, thinking hard, retraced my steps through the park. It seemed to me that by the time I reached the house I had made up my mind I would fly. The Sunday stillness both of the approaches and of the interior, in which I met no one, fairly excited me with a sense of opportunity. Were I to get off quickly, this way, I should get off without a scene, without a word. My quickness would have to be remarkable, however, and the question of a conveyance was the great one to settle. Tormented, in the hall, with difficulties and obstacles, I remember sinking down at the foot of the staircase—suddenly collapsing there on the lowest step and then, with a revulsion, recalling that it was exactly where more than a month before, in the darkness of night and just so bowed with evil things, I had seen the specter of the most horrible of women. At this I was able to straighten myself; I went the rest of the way up; I made, in my bewilderment, for the schoolroom, where there were objects belonging to me that I should have to take. But I opened the door to find again, in a flash, my eyes unsealed. In the presence of what I saw I reeled straight back upon my resistance.

Seated at my own table in clear noonday light I saw a person whom, without my previous experience, I should have taken at the first blush for some housemaid who might have stayed at home to look after the place and who, availing herself of rare relief from observation and of the schoolroom table and my pens, ink, and paper, had applied herself to the considerable effort of a letter to her sweetheart. There was an effort in the way that, while her arms rested on the table, her hands with evident weariness supported her head; but at the moment I took this in I had already become aware that, in spite of my entrance, her attitude strangely persisted. Then it was—with the very act of its announcing itself—that her identity flared up in a change of posture. She rose, not as if she had heard me, but with an indescribable grand melancholy of indifference and detachment, and, within a dozen feet of me, stood there as my vile predecessor. Dishonored and tragic, she was all before me; but even as I fixed and, for memory, secured it, the awful image passed away. Dark as midnight in her black dress, her haggard beauty and her unutterable woe, she had looked at me long enough to appear to say that her right to sit at my table was as good as mine to sit at hers. While these instants lasted, indeed, I had the extraordinary chill of feeling that it was I who was the intruder. It was as a wild protest against it that, actually addressing her— "You terrible, miserable woman!"—I heard myself break into a sound that, by the open door, rang through the long passage and the empty house. She looked at me as if she heard me, but I had recovered myself and cleared the air. There was nothing in the room the next minute but the sunshine and a sense that I must stay.

XVI

I had so perfectly expected that the return of my pupils would be marked by a demonstration that I was freshly upset at having to take into account that they were dumb about my absence. Instead of gaily denouncing and caressing me, they made no allusion to my having failed them, and I was left, for the time, on perceiving that she too said nothing, to study Mrs. Grose's odd face. I did this to such purpose that I made sure they had in some way bribed her to silence; a silence that, however, I would engage to break down on the first private opportunity. This opportunity came before tea: I secured five minutes with her in the housekeeper's room, where, in the twilight, amid a smell of lately baked bread, but with the place all swept and garnished, I found her sitting in pained placidity before the fire. So I see her still, so I see her best: facing the flame from her straight chair in the dusky, shining room, a large clean image of the "put away"—of drawers closed and locked and rest without a remedy.

"Oh, yes, they asked me to say nothing; and to please them—so long as they were there—of course I promised. But what had happened to you?"

"I only went with you for the walk," I said. "I had then to come back to meet a friend."

She showed her surprise. "A friend—you?"

"Oh, yes, I have a couple!" I laughed. "But did the children give you a reason?"

"For not alluding to your leaving us? Yes; they said you would like it better. Do you like it better?"

My face had made her rueful. "No, I like it worse!" But after an instant I added: "Did they say why I should like it better?"

"No; Master Miles only said, 'We must do nothing but what she likes!'"

"I wish indeed he would. And what did Flora say?"

"Miss Flora was too sweet. She said, 'Oh, of course, of course!'—and I said the same."

I thought a moment. "You were too sweet, too—I can hear you all. But nonetheless, between Miles and me, it's now all out."

"All out?" My companion stared. "But what, miss?"

"Everything. It doesn't matter. I've made up my mind. I came home, my dear," I went on, "for a talk with Miss Jessel."

I had by this time formed the habit of having Mrs. Grose literally well in hand in advance of my sounding that note; so that even now, as she bravely blinked under the signal of my word, I could keep her comparatively firm. "A talk! Do you mean she spoke?"

"It came to that. I found her, on my return, in the schoolroom."

"And what did she say?" I can hear the good woman still, and the candor of her stupefaction.

"That she suffers the torments—!"

It was this, of a truth, that made her, as she filled out my picture, gape. "Do you mean," she faltered, "—of the lost?"

"Of the lost. Of the damned. And that's why, to share them—" I faltered myself with the horror of it.

But my companion, with less imagination, kept me up. "To share them—?"

"She wants Flora." Mrs. Grose might, as I gave it to her, fairly have fallen away from me had I not been prepared. I still held her there, to show I was. "As I've told you, however, it doesn't matter."

"Because you've made up your mind? But to what?"

"To everything."

"And what do you call 'everything'?"

"Why, sending for their uncle."

"Oh, miss, in pity do," my friend broke out. "ah, but I will, I *will!* I see it's the only way. What's 'out,' as I told you, with Miles is that if he thinks I'm afraid to—and has ideas of what he gains by that—he shall see he's mistaken. Yes, yes; his uncle shall have it here from me on the spot (and before the boy himself, if necessary) that if I'm to be reproached with having done nothing again about more school—"

"Yes, miss—" my companion pressed me.

"Well, there's that awful reason."

There were now clearly so many of these for my poor colleague that she was excusable for being vague. "But—a—which?"

"Why, the letter from his old place."

"You'll show it to the master?"

"I ought to have done so on the instant."

"Oh, no!" said Mrs. Grose with decision.

"I'll put it before him," I went on inexorably, "that I can't undertake to work the question on behalf of a child who has been expelled—"

"For we've never in the least known what!" Mrs. Grose declared.

"For wickedness. For what else—when he's so clever and beautiful and perfect? Is he stupid? Is he untidy? Is he infirm? Is he ill-natured? He's exquisite—so it can be only *that;* and that would open up the whole thing. After all," I said, "it's their uncle's fault. If he left here such people—!"

"He didn't really in the least know them. The fault's mine." She had turned quite pale.

"Well, you shan't suffer," I answered.

"The children shan't!" she emphatically returned.

I was silent awhile; we looked at each other. "Then what am I to tell him?"

"You needn't tell him anything. *I'll* tell him."

I measured this. "Do you mean you'll write—?" Remembering she couldn't, I caught myself up. "How do you communicate?"

"I tell the bailiff. He writes."

"And should you like him to write our story?"

My question had a sarcastic force that I had not fully intended, and it made her, after a moment, inconsequently break down. The tears were again in her eyes. "Ah, miss, you write!"

"Well—tonight," I at last answered; and on this we separated.

XVII

I went so far, in the evening, as to make a beginning. The weather had changed back, a great wind was abroad, and beneath the lamp, in my room, with Flora at peace beside me, I sat for a long time before a blank sheet of paper and listened to the lash of the rain and the batter of the gusts. Finally I went out, taking a candle; I crossed the passage and listened a minute at Miles's door. What, under my endless obsession, I had been impelled to listen for was some betrayal of his not being at rest, and I presently caught one, but not in the form I had expected. His voice tinkled out. "I say, you there— come in." It was a gaiety in the gloom!

I went in with my light and found him, in bed, very wide awake, but very much at his ease. "Well, what are *you* up to?" he asked with a grace of sociability in which it occurred to me that Mrs. Grose, had she been present, might have looked in vain for proof that anything was "out."

I stood over him with my candle. "How did you know I was there?"

"Why, of course I heard you. Did you fancy you made no noise? You're like a troop of cavalry!" he beautifully laughed.

"Then you weren't asleep?"

"Not much! I lie awake and think."

I had put my candle, designedly, a short way off, and then, as he held out his friendly old hand to me, had sat down on the edge of his bed. "What is it," I asked, "that you think of?"

"What in the world, my dear, but *you?*"

"Ah, the pride I take in your appreciation doesn't insist on that! I had so far rather you slept."

"Well, I think also, you know, of this queer business of ours."

I marked the coolness of his firm little hand. "Of what queer business, Miles?"

"Why, the way you bring me up. And all the rest!"

I fairly held my breath a minute, and even from my glimmering taper there was light enough to show how he smiled up at me from his pillow. "What do you mean by all the rest?"

"Oh, you know, you know!"

I could say nothing for a minute, though I felt, as I held his hand and our eyes continued to meet, that my silence had all the air of admitting his charge and that nothing in the whole world of reality was perhaps at that moment so fabulous as our actual relation. "Certainly you shall go back to school," I said, "if it be that that troubles you. But not to the old place— we must find another, a better. How could I know it did trouble you, this question, when you never told me so, never spoke of it at all?" His clear, listening face, framed in its smooth whiteness, made him for the minute as appealing as some wistful patient in a children's hospital; and I would have given, as the resemblance came to me, all I possessed on earth really to be the nurse or the sister of charity who might have helped to cure him. Well, even as it was, I perhaps might help! "Do you know you've never said a word to me about your school—I mean the old one; never mentioned it in any way?"

He seemed to wonder; he smiled with the same loveliness. But he clearly gained time; he waited, he called for guidance. "Haven't I?" It wasn't for *me* to help him—it was for the thing I had met!

Something in his tone and the expression of his face, as I got this from him, set my heart aching with such a pang as it had never yet known; so unutterably touching was it to see his little brain puzzled and his little resources taxed to play, under the spell laid on him, a part of innocence and consistency. "No, never—from the hour you came back. You've never mentioned to me one of your masters, one of your comrades, nor the least little thing that ever happened to you at school. Never, little Miles—no, never—have you given me an inkling of anything that *may* have happened there. Therefore you can fancy how much I'm in the dark. Until you came out, that way, this morning, you had, since the first hour I saw you, scarce even made a reference to anything in your previous life. You seemed so perfectly to accept the present." It was extraordinary how my absolute conviction of his secret precocity (or whatever I might call the poison of an influence that I dared but half to phrase) made him, in spite of the faint breath of his inward trouble, appear as accessible as an older person—imposed him almost as an intellectual equal. "I thought you wanted to go on as you are."

It struck me that at this he just faintly colored. He gave, at any rate, like a convalescent slightly fatigued, a languid shake of his head. "I don't—I don't. I want to get away."

"You're tired of Bly?"

"Oh, no, I like Bly."

"Well, then—?"

"Oh, *you* know what a boy wants!"

I felt that I didn't know so well as Miles, and I took temporary refuge. "You want to go to your uncle?"

Again, at this, with his sweet ironic face, he made a movement on the pillow. "Ah, you can't get off with that!"

I was silent a little, and it was I, now, I think, who changed color. "My dear, I don't want to get off!"

"You can't, even if you do. You can't, you can't!"—he lay beautifully staring. "My uncle must come down, and you must completely settle things."

"If we do," I returned with some spirit, "you may be sure it will be to take you quite away."

"Well, don't you understand that that's exactly what I'm working for? You'll have to tell him—about the way you've let it all drop: you'll have to tell him a tremendous lot!"

The exultation with which he uttered this helped me somehow, for the instant, to meet him rather more. "And how much will *you*, Miles, have to tell him? There are things he'll ask you!"

He turned it over. "Very likely. But what things?"

"The things you've never told me. To make up his mind what to do with you. He can't send you back—"

"Oh, I don't want to go back!" he broke in. "I want a new field."

He said it with admirable serenity, with positive unimpeachable gaiety; and doubtless it was that very note that most evoked for me the poignancy, the unnatural childish tragedy, of his probable reappearance at the end of three months with all this bravado and still more dishonor. It overwhelmed me now that I should never be able to bear that, and it made me let myself go. I threw myself upon him and in the tenderness of my pity I embraced him. "Dear little Miles, dear little Miles—!"

My face was close to his, and he let me kiss him, simply taking it with indulgent good humor. "Well, old lady?"

"Is there nothing—nothing at all that you want to tell me?"

He turned off a little, facing round toward the wall and holding up his hand to look at as one had seen sick children look. "I've told you—I told you this morning."

Oh, I was sorry for him! "That you just want me not to worry you?"

He looked round at me now, as if in recognition of my understanding him; then ever so gently, "To let me alone," he replied.

There was even a singular little dignity in it, something that made me release him, yet, when I had slowly risen, linger beside him. God knows I never wished to harass him, but I felt that merely, at this, to turn my back on him was to abandon or, to put it more truly, to lose him. "I've just begun a letter to your uncle," I said.

"Well, then, finish it!"

I waited a minute. "What happened before?"

He gazed up at me again. "Before what?"

"Before you came back. And before you went away."

For some time he was silent, but he continued to meet my eyes. "What happened?"

It made me, the sound of the words, in which it seemed to me that I caught for the very first time a small faint quaver of consenting consciousness— it made me drop on my knees beside the bed and seize once more the chance of possessing him. "Dear little Miles, dear little Miles, if you *knew* how I want to help you! It's only that, it's nothing but that, and I'd rather die than give you a pain or do you a wrong—I'd rather die than hurt a hair of you. Dear little Miles"—oh, I brought it out now even if I *should* go too far—"I just want you to help me to save you!" But I knew in a moment after this that I had gone too far. The answer to my appeal was instantaneous, but it came in the form of an extraordinary blast and chill, a gust of frozen air, and a shake of the room as great as if, in the wild wind, the casement had crashed in. The boy gave a loud, high shriek, which, lost in the rest of the shock of sound, might have seemed, indistinctly, though I was so close to him, a note either of jubilation or of terror. I jumped to my feet again and was conscious of darkness. So for a moment we remained, while I stared about me and saw that the drawn curtains were unstirred and the window tight. "Why, the candle's out!" I then cried.

"It was I who blew it, dear!" said Miles.

XVIII

The next day, after lessons, Mrs. Grose found a moment to say to me quietly: "Have you written, miss?"

"Yes—I've written." But I didn't add—for the hour—that my letter, sealed and directed, was still in my pocket. There would be time enough to send it before the messenger should go to the village. Meanwhile there had been, on the part of my pupils, no more brilliant, more exemplary morning. It was exactly as if they had both had at heart to gloss over any recent little friction. They performed the dizziest feats of arithmetic, soaring quite out of *my* feeble range, and perpetrated, in higher spirits than ever, geographical and historical jokes. It was conspicuous of course in Miles in particular that he appeared to wish to show how easily he could let me down. This child, to my memory, really lives in a setting of beauty and misery that no words can translate; there was a distinction all his own in every impulse he revealed; never was a small natural creature, to the uninitiated eye all frankness and freedom, a more ingenious, a more extraordinary little gentleman. I had perpetually to guard against the wonder of contemplation into which my initiated view betrayed me; to check the irrelevant gaze and discouraged sigh in which I constantly both attacked and renounced the enigma of what such a little gentleman could have done that deserved a penalty. Say that, by the dark prodigy I knew, the imagination of all evil *had* been opened up to him: all the justice within me ached for the proof that it could ever have flowered into an act.

He had never, at any rate, been such a little gentleman as when, after our early dinner on this dreadful day, he came round to me and asked if I shouldn't like him, for half an hour, to play to me. David playing to Saul could never have shown a finer sense of the occasion. It was literally a charming exhibition of tact, of magnanimity, and quite tantamount to his saying outright: "The true knights we love to read about never push an advantage too far. I know what you mean now: you mean that—to be let alone yourself and not followed up—you'll cease to worry and spy upon me, won't keep me so close to you, will let me go and come. Well, I 'come,' you see—but I don't go! There'll be plenty of time for that. I do really delight in your society, and I only want to show you that I contended for a principle." It may be imagined whether I resisted this appeal or failed to accompany him again, hand in hand, to the schoolroom. He sat down at the old piano and played as he had never played; and if there are those who think he had better have been kicking a football I can only say that I wholly agree with them. For at the end of a time that under his influence I had quite ceased to measure, I started up with a strange sense of having literally slept at my post. It was after luncheon, and by the schoolroom fire, and yet I hadn't really, in the least, slept: I had only done something much worse—I had forgotten. Where, all this time, was Flora? When I put the question to Miles, he played on a minute before answering and then could only say: "Why, my dear, how do *I* know?"—breaking moreover into a happy laugh which, immediately after, as if it were a vocal accompaniment, he prolonged into incoherent, extravagant song.

I went straight to my room, but his sister was not there; then, before going downstairs, I looked into several others. As she was nowhere about she would surely be with Mrs. Grose, whom, in the comfort of that theory, I accordingly proceeded in quest of. I found her where I had found her the evening before, but she met my quick challenge with blank, scared ignorance. She had only supposed that, after the repast, I had carried off both the children; as to which she was quite in her right, for it was the very first time I had allowed the little girl out of my sight without some special provision. Of course now indeed she might be with the maids, so that the immediate thing was to look for her without an air of alarm. This we promptly arranged between us; but when, ten minutes later and in pursuance of our arrangement, we met in the hall, it was only to report on either side that after guarded inquiries we had altogether failed to trace her. For a minute there, apart from observation, we exchanged mute alarms, and I could feel with what high interest my friend returned me all those I had from the first given her.

"She'll be above," she presently said—"in one of the rooms you haven't searched."

"No; she's at a distance." I had made up my mind. "She has gone out."

Mrs. Grose stared. "Without a hat?"

I naturally also looked volumes. "Isn't that woman always without one?"

"She's with *her*?"

"She's with *her!*" I declared. "We must find them."

My hand was on my friend's arm, but she failed for the moment, confronted with such an account of the matter, to respond to my pressure. She communed, on the contrary, on the spot, with her uneasiness. "And where's Master Miles?"

"Oh, *he's* with Quint. They're in the schoolroom."

"Lord, miss!" My view, I was myself aware—and therefore I suppose my tone—had never yet reached so calm an assurance.

"The trick's played," I went on; "they've successfully worked their plan. He found the most divine little way to keep me quiet while she went off."

"'Divine'?" Mrs. Grose bewilderedly echoed.

"Infernal, then!" I almost cheerfully rejoined. "He has provided for himself as well. But come!"

She had helplessly gloomed at the upper regions. "You leave him—?"

"So long with Quint? Yes—I don't mind that now."

She always ended, at these moments, by getting possession of my hand, and in this manner she could at present still stay me. But after gasping an instant at my sudden resignation, "Because of your letter?" she eagerly brought out.

I quickly, by way of answer, felt for my letter, drew it forth, held it up, and then, freeing myself, went and laid it on the great hall table. "Luke will take it," I said as I came back. I reached the house door and opened it; I was already on the steps.

My companion still demurred: the storm of the night and the early morning had dropped, but the afternoon was damp and gray. I came down to the drive while she stood in the doorway. "You go with nothing on?"

"What do I care when the child has nothing? I can't wait to dress," I cried, "and if you must do so, I leave you. Try meanwhile, yourself, upstairs."

"With *them?*" Oh, on this, the poor woman promptly joined me!

XIX

We went straight to the lake, as it was called at Bly, and I daresay
rightly called, though I reflect that it may in fact have been a sheet of water
less remarkable than it appeared to my untraveled eyes. My acquaintance
with sheets of water was small, and the pool of Bly, at all events on the few
occasions of my consenting, under the protection of my pupils, to affront its
surface in the old flat-bottomed boat moored there for our use, had impressed
me both with its extent and its agitation. The usual place of embarkation was
half a mile from the house, but I had an intimate conviction that, wherever
Flora might be, she was not near home. She had not given me the slip for any
small adventure, and, since the day of the very great one that I had shared
with her by the pond, I had been aware, in our walks, of the quarter to which
she most inclined. This was why I had now given to Mrs. Grose's steps so
marked a direction—a direction that made her, when she perceived it, oppose
a resistance that showed me she was freshly mystified. "You're going to the
water, Miss?—you think she's *in*—?"

"She may be, though the depth is, I believe, nowhere very great. But
what I judge most likely is that she's on the spot from which, the other day,
we saw together what I told you."

"When she pretended not to see—?"

"With that astounding self-possession? I've always been sure she wanted
to go back alone. And now her brother has managed it for her."

Mrs. Grose still stood where she had stopped. "You suppose they
really *talk* of them?"

"I could meet this with a confidence! They say things that, if we heard
them, would simply appall us."

"And if she *is* there—"

"Yes?"

"Then Miss Jessel is?"

"Beyond a doubt. You shall see."

"Oh, thank you!" my friend cried, planted so firm that, taking it in, I went straight on without her. By the time I reached the pool, however, she was close behind me, and I knew that, whatever, to her apprehension, might befall me, the exposure of my society struck her as her least danger. She exhaled a moan of relief as we at last came in sight of the greater part of the water without a sight of the child. There was no trace of Flora on that nearer side of the bank where my observation of her had been most startling, and none on the opposite edge, where, save for a margin of some twenty yards, a thick copse came down to the water. The pond, oblong in shape, had a width so scant compared to its length that, with its ends out of view, it might have been taken for a scant river. We looked at the empty expanse, and then I felt the suggestion of my friend's eyes. I knew what she meant and I replied with a negative headshake.

"No, no; wait! She has taken the boat."

My companion stared at the vacant mooring place and then again across the lake. "Then where is it?"

"Our not seeing it is the strongest of proofs. She has used it to go over, and then has managed to hide it."

"All alone—that child?"

"She's not alone, and at such times she's not a child: she's an old, old woman." I scanned all the visible shore while Mrs. Grose took again, into the queer element I offered her, one of her plunges of submission; then I pointed out that the boat might perfectly be in a small refuge formed by one of the recesses of the pool, an indentation masked, for the hither side, by a projection of the bank and by a clump of trees growing close to the water.

"But if the boat's there, where on earth's *she*?" my colleague anxiously asked.

"That's exactly what we must learn." And I started to walk further.

"By going all the way round?"

"Certainly, far as it is. It will take us but ten minutes, but it's far enough to have made the child prefer not to walk. She went straight over."

"Laws!" cried my friend again; the chain of my logic was ever too much for her. It dragged her at my heels even now, and when we had got halfway round—a devious, tiresome process, on ground much broken and by a path choked with overgrowth—I paused to give her breath. I sustained her with a grateful arm, assuring her that she might hugely help me; and this started us afresh, so that in the course of but few minutes more we reached a point from which we found the boat to be where I had supposed it. It had been intentionally left as much as possible out of sight and was tied to one of the stakes of a fence that came, just there, down to the brink and that had been an assistance to disembarking. I recognized, as I looked at the pair of short, thick oars, quite safely drawn up, the prodigious character of the feat for a little girl; but I had lived, by this time, too long among wonders and had panted to too many livelier measures. There was a gate in the fence, through which we passed, and that brought us, after a trifling interval, more into the open. Then, "There she is!" we both exclaimed at once.

Flora, a short way off, stood before us on the grass and smiled as if her performance was now complete. The next thing she did, however, was to stoop straight down and pluck—quite as if it were all she was there for—a big, ugly spray of withered fern. I instantly became sure she had just come out of the copse. She waited for us, not herself taking a step, and I was conscious of the rare solemnity with which we presently approached her. She smiled and smiled, and we met; but it was all done in a silence by this time flagrantly ominous. Mrs. Grose was the first to break the spell: she threw herself on her knees and, drawing the child to her breast, clasped in a long embrace the little tender, yielding body. While this dumb convulsion lasted I could only watch it—which I did the more intently when I saw Flora's face peep at me over our companion's shoulder. It was serious now—the flicker had left it; but it strengthened the pang with which I at that moment envied Mrs. Grose the simplicity of her relation. Still, all this while, nothing more passed between us save that Flora had let her foolish fern again drop to the ground. What she and I had virtually said to each other was that pretexts were useless now. When Mrs. Grose finally got up she kept the child's hand, so that the two were still before me; and the singular reticence of our communion was even more marked in the frank look she launched me. "I'll be hanged," it said, "if *I'll* speak!"

It was Flora who, gazing all over me in candid wonder, was the first. She was struck with our bareheaded aspect. "Why, where are your things?"

"Where yours are, my dear!" I promptly returned.

She had already got back her gaiety, and appeared to take this as an answer quite sufficient. "And where's Miles?" she went on.

There was something in the small valor of it that quite finished me: these three words from her were, in a flash like the glitter of a drawn blade, the jostle of the cup that my hand, for weeks and weeks, had held high and full to the brim that now, even before speaking, I felt overflow in a deluge. "I'll tell you if you'll tell *me*—" I heard myself say, then heard the tremor in which it broke.

"Well, what?"

Mrs. Grose's suspense blazed at me, but it was too late now, and I brought the thing out handsomely. "Where, my pet, is Miss Jessel?"

XX

Just as in the churchyard with Miles, the whole thing was upon us. Much as I had made of the fact that this name had never once, between us, been sounded, the quick, smitten glare with which the child's face now received it fairly likened my breach of the silence to the smash of a pane of glass. It added to the interposing cry, as if to stay the blow, that Mrs. Grose, at the same instant, uttered over my violence—the shriek of a creature scared, or rather wounded, which, in turn, within a few seconds, was completed by a gasp of my own. I seized my colleague's arm. "She's there, she's there!"

Miss Jessel stood before us on the opposite bank exactly as she had stood the other time, and I remember, strangely, as the first feeling now produced in me, my thrill of joy at having brought on a proof. She was there, and I was justified; she was there, and I was neither cruel nor mad. She was there for poor scared Mrs. Grose, but she was there most for Flora; and no moment of my monstrous time was perhaps so extraordinary as that in which I consciously threw out to her—with the sense that, pale and ravenous demon as she was, she would catch and understand it—an inarticulate message of gratitude. She rose erect on the spot my friend and I had lately quitted, and there was not, in all the long reach of her desire, an inch of her evil that fell short. This first vividness of vision and emotion were things of a few seconds, during which Mrs. Grose's dazed blink across to where I pointed struck me as a sovereign sign that she too at last saw, just as it carried my own eyes precipitately to the child. The revelation then of the manner in which Flora was affected startled me, in truth, far more than it would have done to find her also merely agitated, for direct dismay was of course not what I had expected. Prepared and on her guard as our pursuit had actually made her, she would repress every betrayal; and I was therefore shaken, on the spot, by my first glimpse of the particular one for which I had not allowed. To see her, without a convulsion of her small pink face, not even feign to glance in the direction of the prodigy I announced, but only, instead of that, turn at *x* an expression of hard, still gravity, an expression absolutely new and unprecedented and that appeared to read and accuse and judge me—this was a stroke that somehow converted the little girl herself into the very presence that could make me quail. I quailed even though my certitude that she thoroughly saw was never greater than at that instant, and in the immediate need to defend myself I called it passionately to witness. "She's there, you little unhappy thing— there, there, *there*, and you see her as well as you see me!" I had said shortly before to Mrs. Grose that she was not at these times a child, but an old, old woman, and that description of her could not have been more strikingly confirmed than in the way in which, for all answer to this, she simply showed me, without a concession, an admission, of her eyes, a countenance of deeper and deeper, of indeed suddenly quite fixed, reprobation. I was by this time— if I can put the whole thing at all together—more appalled at what I may properly call her manner than at anything else, though it was simultaneously with this that I became aware of having Mrs. Grose also, and very formidably, to reckon with. My elder companion, the next moment, at any rate, blotted out everything but her own flushed face and her loud, shocked protest, a burst of high disapproval. "What a dreadful turn, to be sure, miss! Where on earth do you see anything?"

I could only grasp her more quickly yet, for even while she spoke the hideous plain presence stood undimmed and undaunted. It had already lasted a minute, and it lasted while I continued, seizing my colleague, quite thrusting her at it and presenting her to it, to insist with my pointing hand. "You don't see her exactly as *we* see?—you mean to say you don't now—*now?* She's as big as a blazing fire! Only look, dearest woman, *look—!*" She looked, even as I did, and gave me, with her deep groan of negation, repulsion, compassion— the mixture with her pity of her relief at her exemption—a sense, touching to me even then, that she would have backed me up if she could. I might well have needed that, for with this hard blow of the proof that her eyes were hopelessly sealed I felt my own situation horribly crumble, I felt—I saw—my livid predecessor press, from her position, on my defeat, and I was conscious, more than all, of what I should have from this instant to deal with in the astounding little attitude of Flora. Into this attitude Mrs. Grose immediately and violently entered, breaking, even while there pierced through my sense of ruin a prodigious private triumph, into breathless reassurance.

"She isn't there, little lady, and nobody's there—and you never see nothing, my sweet! How can poor Miss Jessel—when poor Miss Jessel's dead and buried? *We* know, don't we, love?"—and she appealed, blundering in, to the child. "It's all a mere mistake and a worry and a joke—and we'll go home as fast as we can!"

Our companion, on this, had responded with a strange, quick primness of propriety, and they were again, with Mrs. Grose on her feet, united, as it were, in pained opposition to me. Flora continued to fix me with her small mask of reprobation, and even at that minute I prayed God to forgive me for seeming to see that, as she stood there holding tight to our friend's dress, her incomparable childish beauty had suddenly failed, had quite vanished. I've said it already—she was literally, she was hideously, hard; she had turned common and almost ugly. "I don't know what you mean. I see nobody. I see nothing. I never *have*. I think you're cruel. I don't like you!" Then, after this deliverance, which might have been that of a vulgarly pert little girl in the street, she hugged Mrs. Grose more closely and buried in her skirts the dreadful little face. In this position she produced an almost furious wail. "Take me away, take me away—oh, take me away from *her!*"

"From *me?*" I panted.

"From you—from you!" she cried.

Even Mrs. Grose looked across at me dismayed, while I had nothing to do but communicate again with the figure that, on the opposite bank, without a movement, as rigidly still as if catching, beyond the interval, our voices, was as vividly there for my disaster as it was not there for my service. The wretched child had spoken exactly as if she had got from some outside source each of her stabbing little words, and I could therefore, in the full despair of all I had to accept, but sadly shake my head at her. "If I had ever doubted, all my doubt would at present have gone. I've been living with the miserable truth, and now it has only too much closed round me. Of course I've lost you: I've interfered, and you've seen—under *her* dictation"—with which I faced, over the pool again, our infernal witness—"the easy and perfect way to meet it. I've done my best, but I've lost you. Goodbye." For Mrs. Grose I had an imperative, an almost frantic "Go, go!" before which, in infinite distress, but mutely possessed of the little girl and clearly convinced, in spite of her blindness, that something awful had occurred and some collapse engulfed us, she retreated, by the way we had come, as fast as she could move.

Of what first happened when I was left alone I had no subsequent memory. I only knew that at the end of, I suppose, a quarter of an hour, an odorous dampness and roughness, chilling and piercing my trouble, had made me understand that I must have thrown myself, on my face, on the ground and given way to a wildness of grief. I must have lain there long and cried and sobbed, for when I raised my head the day was almost done. I got up and looked a moment, through the twilight, at the gray pool and its blank, haunted edge, and then I took, back to the house, my dreary and difficult course. When I reached the gate in the fence the boat, to my surprise, was gone, so that I had a fresh reflection to make on Flora's extraordinary command of the situation. She passed that night, by the most tacit, and I should add, were not the word so grotesque a false note, the happiest of arrangements, with Mrs. Grose. I saw neither of them on my return, but, on the other hand, as by an ambiguous compensation, I saw a great deal of Miles. I saw—I can use no other phrase—so much of him that it was as if it were more than it had ever been. No evening I had passed at Bly had the portentous quality of this one; in spite of which—and in spite also of the deeper depths of consternation that had opened beneath my feet— there was literally, in the ebbing actual, an extraordinarily sweet sadness. On reaching the house I had never so much as looked for the boy; I had simply gone straight to my room to change what I was wearing and to take in, at a glance, much material testimony to Flora's rupture. Her little belongings had all been removed. When later, by the schoolroom fire, I was served with tea by the usual maid, I indulged, on the article of my other pupil, in no inquiry whatever. He had his freedom now—he might have it to the end! Well, he did have it; and it consisted—in part at least—of his coming in at about eight o'clock and sitting down with me in silence. On the removal of the tea things I had blown out the candles and drawn my chair closer: I was conscious of a mortal coldness and felt as if I should never again be warm. So, when he appeared, I was sitting in the glow with my thoughts. He paused a moment by the door as if to look at me; then—as if to share them—came to the other side of the hearth and sank into a chair. We sat there in absolute stillness; yet he wanted, I felt, to be with me.

XXI

Before a new day, in my room, had fully broken, my eyes opened to Mrs. Grose, who had come to my bedside with worse news. Flora was so markedly feverish that an illness was perhaps at hand; she had passed a night of extreme unrest, a night agitated above all by fears that had for their subject not in the least her former, but wholly her present, governess. It was not against the possible re-entrance of Miss Jessel on the scene that she protested—it was conspicuously and passionately against mine. I was promptly on my feet of course, and with an immense deal to ask; the more that my friend had discernibly now girded her loins to meet me once more. This I felt as soon as I had put to her the question of her sense of the child's sincerity as against my own. "She persists in denying to you that she saw, or has ever seen, anything?"

My visitor's trouble, truly, was great. "Ah, miss, it isn't a matter on which I can push her! Yet it isn't either, I must say, as if I much needed to. It has made her, every inch of her, quite old."

"Oh, I see her perfectly from here. She resents, for all the world like some high little personage, the imputation on her truthfulness and, as it were, her respectability. 'Miss Jessel indeed—*she!* Ah, she's 'respectable,' the chit! The impression she gave me there yesterday was, I assure you, the very strangest of all; it was quite beyond any of the others. I *did* put my foot in it! She'll never speak to me again."

Hideous and obscure as it all was, it held Mrs. Grose briefly silent; then she granted my point with a frankness which, I made sure, had more behind it. "I think indeed, miss, she never will. She do have a grand manner about it!"

"And that manner"—I summed it up—"is practically what's the matter with her now!"

Oh, that manner, I could see in my visitor's face, and not a little else besides! "She asks me every three minutes if I think you're coming in."

"I see—I see." I, too, on my side, had so much more than worked it out. "Has she said to you since yesterday—except to repudiate her familiarity with anything so dreadful—a single other word about Miss Jessel?"

"Not one, miss. And of course you know," my friend added, "I took it from her, by the lake, that, just then and there at least, there *was* nobody."

"Rather! and, naturally, you take it from her still."

"I don't contradict her. What else can I do?"

"Nothing in the world! You've the cleverest little person to deal with. They've made them—their two friends, I mean—still cleverer even than nature did; for it was wondrous material to play on! Flora has now her grievance, and she'll work it to the end."

"Yes, miss; but to *what* end?"

"Why, that of dealing with me to her uncle. She'll make me out to him the lowest creature—!"

I winced at the fair show of the scene in Mrs. Grose's face; she looked for a minute as if she sharply saw them together. "And him who thinks so well of you!"

"He has an odd way—it comes over me now," I laughed, "—of proving it! But that doesn't matter. What Flora wants, of course, is to get rid of me."

My companion bravely concurred. "Never again to so much as look at you."

"So that what you've come to me now for," I asked, "is to speed me on my way?" Before she had time to reply, however, I had her in check. "I've a better idea—the result of my reflections. My going *would* seem the right thing, and on Sunday I was terribly near it. Yet that won't do. It's *you* who must go. You must take Flora."

My visitor, at this, did speculate. "But where in the world—?"

"Away from here. Away from *them*. Away, even most of all, now, from me. Straight to her uncle."

"Only to tell on you—?"

"No, not 'only'! To leave me, in addition, with my remedy."

She was still vague. "And what *is* your remedy?"

"Your loyalty, to begin with. And then Miles's."

She looked at me hard. "Do you think he—?"

"Won't, if he has the chance, turn on me? Yes, I venture still to think it. At all events, I want to try. Get off with his sister as soon as possible and leave me with him alone." I was amazed, myself, at the spirit I had still in reserve, and therefore perhaps a trifle the more disconcerted at the way in which, in spite of this fine example of it, she hesitated. "There's one thing, of course," I went on: "they mustn't, before she goes, see each other for three seconds." Then it came over me that, in spite of Flora's presumable sequestration from the instant of her return from the pool, it might already be too late. "Do you mean," I anxiously asked, "that they *have* met?"

At this she quite flushed. "Ah, miss, I'm not such a fool as that! If I've been obliged to leave her three or four times, it has been each time with one of the maids, and at present, though she's alone, she's locked in safe. And yet—and yet!" There were too many things.

"And yet what?"

"Well, are you so sure of the little gentleman?"

"I'm not sure of anything but *you*. But I have, since last evening, a new hope. I think he wants to give me an opening. I do believe that—poor little exquisite wretch!—he wants to speak. Last evening, in the firelight and the silence, he sat with me for two hours as if it were just coming."

Mrs. Grose looked hard, through the window, at the gray, gathering day. "And did it come?"

"No, though I waited and waited, I confess it didn't, and it was without a breach of the silence or so much as a faint allusion to his sister's condition and absence that we at last kissed for good night. All the same," I continued,

"I can't, if her uncle sees her, consent to his seeing her brother without my having given the boy—and most of all because things have got so bad—a little more time."

My friend appeared on this ground more reluctant than I could quite understand. "What do you mean by more time?"

"Well, a day or two—really to bring it out. He'll then be on *my* side—of which you see the importance. If nothing comes, I shall only fail, and you will, at the worst, have helped me by doing, on your arrival in town, whatever you may have found possible." So I put it before her, but she continued for a little so inscrutably embarrassed that I came again to her aid. "Unless, indeed," I wound up, "you really want *not* to go."

I could see it, in her face, at last clear itself; she put out her hand to me as a pledge. "I'll go—I'll go. I'll go this morning."

I wanted to be very just. "If you *should* wish still to wait, I would engage she shouldn't see me."

"No, no: it's the place itself. She must leave it." She held me a moment with heavy eyes, then brought out the rest. "Your idea's the right one. I myself, miss—"

"Well?"

"I can't stay."

The look she gave me with it made me jump at possibilities. "You mean that, since yesterday, you *have* seen—?"

She shook her head with dignity. "I've *heard*—!"

"Heard?"

"From that child—horrors! There!" she sighed with tragic relief. "On my honor, miss, she says things—!" But at this evocation she broke down; she dropped, with a sudden sob, upon my sofa and, as I had seen her do before, gave way to all the grief of it.

It was quite in another manner that I, for my part, let myself go. "Oh, thank God!"

She sprang up again at this, drying her eyes with a groan. "'Thank God'?"

"It so justifies me!"

"It does that, miss!"

I couldn't have desired more emphasis, but I just hesitated. "She's so horrible?"

I saw my colleague scarce knew how to put it. "Really shocking."

"And about me?"

"About you, miss—since you must have it. It's beyond everything, for a young lady; and I can't think wherever she must have picked up—"

"The appalling language she applied to me? I can, then!" I broke in with a laugh that was doubtless significant enough.

It only, in truth, left my friend still more grave. "Well, perhaps I ought to also—since I've heard some of it before! Yet I can't bear it," the poor woman went on while, with the same movement, she glanced, on my dressing table, at the face of my watch. "But I must go back."

I kept her, however. "Ah, if you can't bear it—!"

"How can I stop with her, you mean? Why, just *for* that: to get her away. Far from this," she pursued, "far from *them*—"

"She may be different? She may be free?" I seized her almost with joy. "Then, in spite of yesterday, you *believe*—"

"In such doings?" Her simple description of them required, in the light of her expression, to be carried no further, and she gave me the whole thing as she had never done. "I believe."

Yes, it was a joy, and we were still shoulder to shoulder: if I might continue sure of that I should care but little what else happened. My support in the presence of disaster would be the same as it had been in my early need of confidence, and if my friend would answer for my honesty, I would answer for all the rest. On the point of taking leave of her, nonetheless, I was to some extent embarrassed. "There's one thing, of course—it occurs to me—to remember. My letter, giving the alarm, will have reached town before you."

I now perceived still more how she had been beating about the bush and how weary at last it had made her. "Your letter won't have got there. Your letter never went."

"What then became of it?"

"Goodness knows! Master Miles—"

"Do you mean *he* took it?" I gasped.

She hung fire, but she overcame her reluctance. "I mean that I saw yesterday, when I came back with Miss Flora, that it wasn't where you had put it. Later in the evening I had the chance to question Luke, and he declared that he had neither noticed nor touched it." We could only exchange, on this, one of our deeper mutual soundings, and it was Mrs. Grose who first brought up the plumb with an almost elated "You see!"

"Yes, I see that if Miles took it instead he probably will have read it and destroyed it."

"And don't you see anything else?"

I faced her a moment with a sad smile. "It strikes me that by this time your eyes are open even wider than mine."

They proved to be so indeed, but she could still blush, almost, to show it. "I make out now what he must have done at school." And she gave, in her simple sharpness, an almost droll disillusioned nod. "He stole!"

I turned it over—I tried to be more judicial. "Well—perhaps."

She looked as if she found me unexpectedly calm. "He stole *letters!*"

She couldn't know my reasons for a calmness after all pretty shallow; so I showed them off as I might. "I hope then it was to more purpose than in this case! The note, at any rate, that I put on the table yesterday," I pursued, "will have given him so scant an advantage—for it contained only the bare demand for an interview—that he is already much ashamed of having gone so far for so little, and that what he had on his mind last evening was precisely the need of confession." I seemed to myself, for the instant, to have mastered it, to see it all. "Leave us, leave us"—I was already, at the door, hurrying her off. "I'll get it out of him. He'll meet me—he'll confess. If he confesses, he's saved. And if he's saved—"

"Then *you* are?" The dear woman kissed me on this, and I took her farewell. "I'll save you without him!" she cried as she went.

XXII

Yet it was when she had got off—and I missed her on the spot—that the great pinch really came. If I had counted on what it would give me to find myself alone with Miles, I speedily perceived, at least, that it would give me a measure. No hour of my stay in fact was so assailed with apprehensions as that of my coming down to learn that the carriage containing Mrs. Grose and my younger pupil had already rolled out of the gates. Now I *was*, I said to myself, face to face with the elements, and for much of the rest of the day, while I fought my weakness, I could consider that I had been supremely rash. It was a tighter place still than I had yet turned round in; all the more that, for the first time, I could see in the aspect of others a confused reflection of the crisis. What had happened naturally caused them all to stare; there was too little of the explained, throw out whatever we might, in the suddenness of my colleague's act. The maids and the men looked blank; the effect of which on my nerves was an aggravation until I saw the necessity of making it a positive aid. It was precisely, in short, by just clutching the helm that I avoided total wreck; and I dare say that, to bear up at all, I became, that morning, very grand and very dry. I welcomed the consciousness that I was charged with much to do, and I caused it to be known as well that, left thus to myself, I was quite remarkably firm. I wandered with that manner, for the next hour or two, all over the place and looked, I have no doubt, as if I were ready for any onset. So, for the benefit of whom it might concern, I paraded with a sick heart.

The person it appeared least to concern proved to be, till dinner, little Miles himself. My perambulations had given me, meanwhile, no glimpse of him, but they had tended to make more public the change taking place in our relation as a consequence of his having at the piano, the day before, kept me, in Flora's interest, so beguiled and befooled. The stamp of publicity had of course been fully given by her confinement and departure, and the change itself was now ushered in by our nonobservance of the regular custom of the schoolroom. He had already disappeared when, on my way down,

I pushed open his door, and I learned below that he had breakfasted—in the presence of a couple of the maids—with Mrs. Grose and his sister. He had then gone out, as he said, for a stroll; than which nothing, I reflected, could better have expressed his frank view of the abrupt transformation of my office. What he would not permit this office to consist of was yet to be settled: there was a queer relief, at all events—I mean for myself in especial—in the renouncement of one pretension. If so much had sprung to the surface, I scarce put it too strongly in saying that what had perhaps sprung highest was the absurdity of our prolonging the fiction that I had anything more to teach him. It sufficiently stuck out that, by tacit little tricks in which even more than myself he carried out the care for my dignity, I had had to appeal to him to let me off straining to meet him on the ground of his true capacity. He had at any rate his freedom now; I was never to touch it again; as I had amply shown, moreover, when, on his joining me in the schoolroom the previous night, I had uttered, on the subject of the interval just concluded, neither challenge nor hint. I had too much, from this moment, my other ideas. Yet when he at last arrived, the difficulty of applying them, the accumulations of my problem, were brought straight home to me by the beautiful little presence on which what had occurred had as yet, for the eye, dropped neither stain nor shadow.

To mark, for the house, the high state I cultivated I decreed that my meals with the boy should be served, as we called it, downstairs; so that I had been awaiting him in the ponderous pomp of the room outside of the window of which I had had from Mrs. Grose, that first scared Sunday, my flash of something it would scarce have done to call light. Here at present I felt afresh—for I had felt it again and again—how my equilibrium depended on the success of my rigid will, the will to shut my eyes as tight as possible to the truth that what I had to deal with was, revoltingly, against nature. I could only get on at all by taking "nature" into my confidence and my account, by treating my monstrous ordeal as a push in a direction unusual, of course, and unpleasant, but demanding, after all, for a fair front, only another turn of the screw of ordinary human virtue. No attempt, nonetheless, could well require more tact than just this attempt to supply, one's self, *all* the nature. How could I put even a little of that article into a suppression of reference to what had occurred? How, on the other hand, could I make reference without a new plunge into the hideous obscure? Well, a sort of answer, after a time, had come to me, and it was so far confirmed as that I was met, incontestably, by the quickened vision of what was rare in my little companion. It was indeed as if he had found even now—as he had so often found at lessons—still some other delicate way to ease me off. Wasn't there light in the fact which, as we shared our solitude, broke out with a specious glitter it had never yet quite worn?—the fact that (opportunity aiding, precious opportunity which had now come) it would be preposterous, with a child so endowed, to forego the help one might wrest from absolute intelligence? What had his intelligence been given him for but to save him? Mightn't one, to reach his mind, risk the stretch of an angular arm over his character? It was as if, when we were face to face in the dining room, he had literally shown me the way. The roast mutton was on the table, and I had dispensed with attendance. Miles, before he sat down, stood a moment with his hands in his pockets and looked at the joint, on which he seemed on the point of passing some humorous judgment. But what he presently produced was: "I say, my dear, is she really very awfully ill?"

"Little Flora? Not so bad but that she'll presently be better. London will set her up. Bly had ceased to agree with her. Come here and take your mutton."

He alertly obeyed me, carried the plate carefully to his seat, and, when he was established, went on. "Did Bly disagree with her so terribly suddenly?"

"Not so suddenly as you might think. One had seen it coming on."

"Then why didn't you get her off before?"

"Before what?"

"Before she became too ill to travel."

I found myself prompt. "She's *not* too ill to travel: she only might have become so if she had stayed. This was just the moment to seize. The journey will dissipate the influence"—oh, I was grand!—"and carry it off."

"I see, I see"—Miles, for that matter, was grand, too. He settled to his repast with the charming little "table manner" that, from the day of his arrival, had relieved me of all grossness of admonition. Whatever he had been driven from school for, it was not for ugly feeding. He was irreproachable, as always, today; but he was unmistakably more conscious. He was discernibly trying to take for granted more things than he found, without assistance, quite easy; and he dropped into peaceful silence while he felt his situation. Our meal was of the briefest—mine a vain pretense, and I had the things immediately removed. While this was done Miles stood again with his hands in his little pockets and his back to me—stood and looked out of the wide window through which, that other day, I had seen what pulled me up. We continued silent while the maid was with us—as silent, it whimsically occurred to me, as some young couple who, on their wedding journey, at the inn, feel shy in the presence of the waiter. He turned round only when the waiter had left us. "Well—so we're alone!"

"Oh, more or less." I fancy my smile was pale. "Not absolutely. We shouldn't like that!" I went on.

"No—I suppose we shouldn't. Of course we have the others."

"We have the others—we have indeed the others," I concurred.

"Yet even though we have them," he returned, still with his hands in his pockets and planted there in front of me, "they don't much count, do they?"

I made the best of it, but I felt wan. "It depends on what you call 'much'!"

"Yes"—with all accommodation—"everything depends!" On this, however, he faced to the window again and presently reached it with his vague, restless, cogitating step. He remained there awhile, with his forehead against the glass, in contemplation of the stupid shrubs I knew and the dull things of November. I had always my hypocrisy of "work," behind which, now, I gained the sofa. Steadying myself with it there as I had repeatedly done at those moments of torment that I have described as the moments of my knowing the children to be given to something from which I was barred, I sufficiently obeyed my habit of being prepared for the worst. But an extraordinary impression dropped on me as I extracted a meaning from the boy's embarrassed back—none other than the impression that I was not barred now. This inference grew in a few minutes to sharp intensity and seemed bound up with the direct perception that it was positively *he* who was. The frames and squares of the great window were a kind of image, for him, of a kind of failure. I felt that I saw him, at any rate, shut in or shut out. He was admirable, but not comfortable: I took it in with a throb of hope. Wasn't he looking, through the haunted pane, for something he couldn't see?—and wasn't it the first time in the whole business that he had known such a lapse? The first, the very first: I found it a splendid portent. It made him anxious, though he watched himself; he had been anxious all day and, even while in his usual sweet little manner he sat at table, had needed all his small strange genius to give it a gloss. When he at last turned round to meet me, it was almost as if this genius had succumbed. "Well, I think I'm glad Bly agrees with *me!*"

"You would certainly seem to have seen, these twenty-four hours, a good deal more of it than for some time before. I hope," I went on bravely, "that you've been enjoying yourself."

"Oh, yes, I've been ever so far; all round about—miles and miles away. I've never been so free."

He had really a manner of his own, and I could only try to keep up with him. "Well, do you like it?"

He stood there smiling; then at last he put into two words—"Do *you?*"— more discrimination than I had ever heard two words contain. Before I had time to deal with that, however, he continued as if with the sense that this was an impertinence to be softened. "Nothing could be more charming than the way you take it, for of course if we're alone together now it's you that are alone most. But I hope," he threw in, "you don't particularly mind!"

"Having to do with you?" I asked. "My dear child, how can I help minding? Though I've renounced all claim to your company—you're so beyond me—I at least greatly enjoy it. What else should I stay on for?"

He looked at me more directly, and the expression of his face, graver now, struck me as the most beautiful I had ever found in it. "You stay on just for *that?*"

"Certainly. I stay on as your friend and from the tremendous interest I take in you till something can be done for you that may be more worth your while. That needn't surprise you." My voice trembled so that I felt it impossible to suppress the shake. "Don't you remember how I told you, when I came and sat on your bed the night of the storm, that there was nothing in the world I wouldn't do for you?"

"Yes, yes!" He, on his side, more and more visibly nervous, had a tone to master; but he was so much more successful than I that, laughing out through his gravity, he could pretend we were pleasantly jesting. "Only that, I think, was to get me to do something for *you!*"

"It was partly to get you to do something," I conceded. "But, you know, you didn't do it."

"Oh, yes," he said with the brightest superficial eagerness, "you wanted me to tell you something."

"That's it. Out, straight out. What you have on your mind, you know."

"Ah, then, is *that* what you've stayed over for?"

He spoke with a gaiety through which I could still catch the finest little quiver of resentful passion; but I can't begin to express the effect upon me of an implication of surrender even so faint. It was as if what I had yearned for had come at last only to astonish me. "Well, yes—I may as well make a clean breast of it, it was precisely for that."

He waited so long that I supposed it for the purpose of repudiating the assumption on which my action had been founded; but what he finally said was: "Do you mean now—here?"

"There couldn't be a better place or time." He looked round him uneasily, and I had the rare—oh, the queer!—impression of the very first symptom I had seen in him of the approach of immediate fear. It was as if he were suddenly afraid of me—which struck me indeed as perhaps the best thing to make him. Yet in the very pang of the effort I felt it vain to try sternness, and I heard myself the next instant so gentle as to be almost grotesque. "You want so to go out again?"

"Awfully!" He smiled at me heroically, and the touching little bravery of it was enhanced by his actually flushing with pain. He had picked up his hat, which he had brought in, and stood twirling it in a way that gave me, even as I was just nearly reaching port, a perverse horror of what I was doing. To do it in *any* way was an act of violence, for what did it consist of but the obtrusion of the idea of grossness and guilt on a small helpless creature who had been for me a revelation of the possibilities of beautiful intercourse? Wasn't it base to create for a being so exquisite a mere alien awkwardness? I suppose I now read into our situation a clearness it couldn't have had at the time, for I seem to see our poor eyes already lighted with some spark of a prevision of the anguish that was to come. So we circled about, with terrors and scruples, like fighters not daring to close. But it was for each other we feared! That kept us a little longer suspended and unbruised. "I'll tell you everything," Miles said—"I mean I'll tell you anything you like. You'll stay on with me, and we shall both be all right, and I *will* tell you—I. But not now."

"Why not now?"

My insistence turned him from me and kept him once more at his window in a silence during which, between us, you might have heard a pin drop. Then he was before me again with the air of a person for whom, outside, someone who had frankly to be reckoned with was waiting. "I have to see Luke."

I had not yet reduced him to quite so vulgar a lie, and I felt proportionately ashamed. But, horrible as it was, his lies made up my truth. I achieved thoughtfully a few loops of my knitting. "Well, then, go to Luke, and I'll wait for what you promise. Only, in return for that, satisfy, before you leave me, one very much smaller request."

He looked as if he felt he had succeeded enough to be able still a little to bargain. "Very much smaller—?"

"Yes, a mere fraction of the whole. Tell me"—oh, my work preoccupied me, and I was offhand!—"if, yesterday afternoon, from the table in the hall, you took, you know, my letter."

XXIV

My sense of how he received this suffered for a minute from something that I can describe only as a fierce split of my attention—a stroke that at first, as I sprang straight up, reduced me to the mere blind movement of getting hold of him, drawing him close, and, while I just fell for support against the nearest piece of furniture, instinctively keeping him with his back to the window. The appearance was full upon us that I had already had to deal with here: Peter Quint had come into view like a sentinel before a prison. The next thing I saw was that, from outside, he had reached the window, and then I knew that, close to the glass and glaring in through it, he offered once more to the room his white face of damnation. It represents but grossly what took place within me at the sight to say that on the second my decision was made; yet I believe that no woman so overwhelmed ever in so short a time recovered her grasp of the *act*. It came to me in the very horror of the immediate presence that the act would be, seeing and facing what I saw and faced, to keep the boy himself unaware. The inspiration—I can call it by no other name—was that I felt how voluntarily, how transcendently, I *might*. It was like fighting with a demon for a human soul, and when I had fairly so appraised it I saw how the human soul—held out, in the tremor of my hands, at arm's length—had a perfect dew of sweat on a lovely childish forehead. The face that was close to mine was as white as the face against the glass, and out of it presently came a sound, not low nor weak, but as if from much further away, that I drank like a waft of fragrance.

"Yes—I took it."

At this, with a moan of joy, I enfolded, I drew him close; and while I held him to my breast, where I could feel in the sudden fever of his little body the tremendous pulse of his little heart, I kept my eyes on the thing at the window and saw it move and shift its posture. I have likened it to a sentinel, but its slow wheel, for a moment, was rather the prowl of a baffled beast. My present quickened courage, however, was such that, not too much to let it through, I had to shade, as it were, my flame. Meanwhile the glare of the face was again at the window, the scoundrel fixed as if to watch and wait. It was the very confidence that I might now defy him, as well as the positive certitude, by this time, of the child's unconsciousness, that made me go on. "What did you take it for?"

"To see what you said about me."

"You opened the letter?"

"I opened it."

My eyes were now, as I held him off a little again, on Miles's own face, in which the collapse of mockery showed me how complete was the ravage of uneasiness. What was prodigious was that at last, by my success, his sense was sealed and his communication stopped: he knew that he was in presence, but knew not of what, and knew still less that I also was and that I did know. And what did this strain of trouble matter when my eyes went back to the window only to see that the air was clear again and—by my personal triumph—the influence quenched? There was nothing there. I felt that the cause was mine and that I should surely get *all*. "And you found nothing!"—I let my elation out.

He gave the most mournful, thoughtful little headshake. "Nothing."

"Nothing, nothing!" I almost shouted in my joy.

"Nothing, nothing," he sadly repeated.

I kissed his forehead; it was drenched. "So what have you done with it?"

"I've burned it."

"Burned it?" It was now or never. "Is that what you did at school?"

Oh, what this brought up! "At school?"

"Did you take letters?—or other things?"

"Other things?" He appeared now to be thinking of something far off and that reached him only through the pressure of his anxiety. Yet it did reach him. "Did I *steal?*"

I felt myself redden to the roots of my hair as well as wonder if it were more strange to put to a gentleman such a question or to see him take it with allowances that gave the very distance of his fall in the world. "Was it for that you mightn't go back?"

The only thing he felt was rather a dreary little surprise. "Did you know I mightn't go back?"

"I know everything."

He gave me at this the longest and strangest look. "Everything?"

"Everything. Therefore *did* you—?" But I couldn't say it again.

Miles could, very simply. "No. I didn't steal."

My face must have shown him I believed him utterly; yet my hands— but it was for pure tenderness—shook him as if to ask him why, if it was all for nothing, he had condemned me to months of torment. "What then did you do?"

He looked in vague pain all round the top of the room and drew his breath, two or three times over, as if with difficulty. He might have been standing at the bottom of the sea and raising his eyes to some faint green twilight. "Well—I said things."

"Only that?"

"They thought it was enough!"

"To turn you out for?"

Never, truly, had a person "turned out" shown so little to explain it as this little person! He appeared to weigh my question, but in a manner quite detached and almost helpless. "Well, I suppose I oughtn't."

"But to whom did you say them?"

He evidently tried to remember, but it dropped—he had lost it. "I don't know!"

He almost smiled at me in the desolation of his surrender, which was indeed practically, by this time, so complete that I ought to have left it there. But I was infatuated—I was blind with victory, though even then the very effect that was to have brought him so much nearer was already that of added separation. "Was it to everyone?" I asked.

"No; it was only to—" But he gave a sick little headshake. "I don't remember their names."

"Were they then so many?"

"No—only a few. Those I liked."

Those he liked? I seemed to float not into clearness, but into a darker obscure, and within a minute there had come to me out of my very pity the appalling alarm of his being perhaps innocent. It was for the instant confounding and bottomless, for if he *were* innocent, what then on earth was *I*? Paralyzed, while it lasted, by the mere brush of the question, I let him go a little, so that, with a deep-drawn sigh, he turned away from me again; which, as he faced toward the clear window, I suffered, feeling that I had nothing now there to keep him from. "And did they repeat what you said?" I went on after a moment.

He was soon at some distance from me, still breathing hard and again with the air, though now without anger for it, of being confined against his will. Once more, as he had done before, he looked up at the dim day as if, of what had hitherto sustained him, nothing was left but an unspeakable anxiety. "Oh, yes," he nevertheless replied—"they must have repeated them. To *those* they liked," he added.

There was, somehow, less of it than I had expected; but I turned it over. "And these things came round—?"

"To the masters? Oh, yes!" he answered very simply. "But I didn't know they'd tell."

"The masters? They didn't—they've never told. That's why I ask you."

He turned to me again his little beautiful fevered face. "Yes, it was too bad."

"Too bad?"

"What I suppose I sometimes said. To write home."

I can't name the exquisite pathos of the contradiction given to such a speech by such a speaker; I only know that the next instant I heard myself throw off with homely force: "Stuff and nonsense!" But the next after that I must have sounded stern enough. "What *were* these things?"

My sternness was all for his judge, his executioner; yet it made him avert himself again, and that movement made *me,* with a single bound and an irrepressible cry, spring straight upon him. For there again, against the glass, as if to blight his confession and stay his answer, was the hideous author of our woe—the white face of damnation. I felt a sick swim at the drop of my victory and all the return of my battle, so that the wildness of my veritable leap only served as a great betrayal. I saw him, from the midst of my act, meet it with a divination, and on the perception that even now he only guessed, and that the window was still to his own eyes free, I let the impulse flame up to convert the climax of his dismay into the very proof of his liberation. "No more, no more, no more!" I shrieked, as I tried to press him against me, to my visitant.

"Is she *here?*" Miles panted as he caught with his sealed eyes the direction of my words. Then as his strange "she" staggered me and, with a gasp, I echoed it, "Miss Jessel, Miss Jessel!" he with a sudden fury gave me back.

I seized, stupefied, his supposition—some sequel to what we had done to Flora, but this made me only want to show him that it was better still than that. "It's not Miss Jessel! But it's at the window—straight before us. It's *there*—the coward horror, there for the last time!"

At this, after a second in which his head made the movement of a baffled dog's on a scent and then gave a frantic little shake for air and light, he was at me in a white rage, bewildered, glaring vainly over the place and missing wholly, though it now, to my sense, filled the room like the taste of poison, the wide, overwhelming presence. "It's *he?*"

I was so determined to have all my proof that I flashed into ice to challenge him. "Whom do you mean by 'he'?"

"Peter Quint—you devil!" His face gave again, round the room, its convulsed supplication. *"Where?"*

They are in my ears still, his supreme surrender of the name and his tribute to my devotion. "What does he matter now, my own?—what will he *ever* matter? *I* have you," I launched at the beast, "but he has lost you forever!" Then, for the demonstration of my work, "There, *there!*" I said to Miles.

But he had already jerked straight round, stared, glared again, and seen but the quiet day. With the stroke of the loss I was so proud of he uttered the cry of a creature hurled over an abyss, and the grasp with which I recovered him might have been that of catching him in his fall. I caught him, yes, I held him—it may be imagined with what a passion; but at the end of a minute I began to feel what it truly was that I held. We were alone with the quiet day, and his little heart, dispossessed, had stopped.

About Author

Henry James OM (15 April 1843 – 28 February 1916) was an American-British author regarded as a key transitional figure between literary realism and literary modernism, and is considered by many to be among the greatest novelists in the English language. He was the son of Henry James Sr. and the brother of renowned philosopher and psychologist William James and diarist Alice James.

He is best known for a number of novels dealing with the social and marital interplay between émigré Americans, English people, and continental Europeans. Examples of such novels include The Portrait of a Lady, The Ambassadors, and The Wings of the Dove. His later works were increasingly experimental. In describing the internal states of mind and social dynamics of his characters, James often made use of a style in which ambiguous or contradictory motives and impressions were overlaid or juxtaposed in the discussion of a character's psyche. For their unique ambiguity, as well as for other aspects of their composition, his late works have been compared to impressionist painting.

His novella The Turn of the Screw has garnered a reputation as the most analysed and ambiguous ghost story in the English language and remains his most widely adapted work in other media. He also wrote a number of other highly regarded ghost stories and is considered one of the greatest masters of the field.

James published articles and books of criticism, travel, biography, autobiography, and plays. Born in the United States, James largely relocated to Europe as a young man and eventually settled in England, becoming a British subject in 1915, one year before his death. James was nominated for the Nobel Prize in Literature in 1911, 1912 and 1916.

Life

Early years, 1843–1883

James was born at 2 Washington Place in New York City on 15 April 1843. His parents were Mary Walsh and Henry James Sr. His father was intelligent and steadfastly congenial. He was a lecturer and philosopher who had inherited independent means from his father, an Albany banker and investor. Mary came from a wealthy family long settled in New York City. Her sister Katherine lived with her adult family for an extended period of time. Henry Jr. had three brothers, William, who was one year his senior, and younger brothers Wilkinson (Wilkie) and Robertson. His younger sister was Alice. Both of his parents were of Irish and Scottish descent.

The family first lived in Albany, at 70 N. Pearl St., and then moved to Fourteenth Street in New York City when James was still a young boy. His education was calculated by his father to expose him to many influences, primarily scientific and philosophical; it was described by Percy Lubbock, the editor of his selected letters, as "extraordinarily haphazard and promiscuous." James did not share the usual education in Latin and Greek classics. Between 1855 and 1860, the James' household traveled to London, Paris, Geneva, Boulogne-sur-Mer and Newport, Rhode Island, according to the father's current interests and publishing ventures, retreating to the United States when funds were low. Henry studied primarily with tutors and briefly attended schools while the family traveled in Europe. Their longest stays were in France, where Henry began to feel at home and became fluent in French. He was afflicted with a stutter, which seems to have manifested itself only when he spoke English; in French, he did not stutter.

In 1860 the family returned to Newport. There Henry became a friend of the painter John La Farge, who introduced him to French literature, and in particular, to Balzac. James later called Balzac his "greatest master," and said that he had learned more about the craft of fiction from him than from anyone else.

In the autumn of 1861 Henry received an injury, probably to his back, while fighting a fire. This injury, which resurfaced at times throughout his life, made him unfit for military service in the American Civil War.

In 1864 the James family moved to Boston, Massachusetts to be near William, who had enrolled first in the Lawrence Scientific School at Harvard and then in the medical school. In 1862 Henry attended Harvard Law School, but realised that he was not interested in studying law. He pursued his interest in literature and associated with authors and critics William Dean Howells and Charles Eliot Norton in Boston and Cambridge, formed lifelong friendships with Oliver Wendell Holmes Jr., the future Supreme Court Justice, and with James and Annie Fields, his first professional mentors.

His first published work was a review of a stage performance, "Miss Maggie Mitchell in Fanchon the Cricket," published in 1863. About a year later, A Tragedy of Error, his first short story, was published anonymously. James's first payment was for an appreciation of Sir Walter Scott's novels, written for the North American Review. He wrote fiction and non-fiction pieces for The Nation and Atlantic Monthly, where Fields was editor. In 1871 he published his first novel, Watch and Ward, in serial form in the Atlantic Monthly. The novel was later published in book form in 1878.

During a 14-month trip through Europe in 1869–70 he met Ruskin, Dickens, Matthew Arnold, William Morris, and George Eliot. Rome impressed him profoundly. "Here I am then in the Eternal City," he wrote to his brother William. "At last—for the first time—I live!" He attempted to support himself as a freelance writer in Rome, then secured a position as Paris correspondent for the New York Tribune, through the influence of its editor John Hay. When these efforts failed he returned to New York City. During 1874 and 1875 he published Transatlantic Sketches, A Passionate Pilgrim, and Roderick Hudson. During this early period in his career he was influenced by Nathaniel Hawthorne.

In 1869 he settled in London. There he established relationships with Macmillan and other publishers, who paid for serial installments that they would later publish in book form. The audience for these serialized novels was largely made up of middle-class women, and James struggled to fashion serious literary work within the strictures imposed by editors' and publishers' notions of what was suitable for young women to read. He lived in rented rooms but was able to join gentlemen's clubs that had libraries and where he could entertain male friends. He was introduced to English society by Henry Adams and Charles Milnes Gaskell, the latter introducing him to the Travellers' and the Reform Clubs.

In the fall of 1875 he moved to the Latin Quarter of Paris. Aside from two trips to America, he spent the next three decades—the rest of his life—in Europe. In Paris he met Zola, Alphonse Daudet, Maupassant, Turgenev, and others. He stayed in Paris only a year before moving to London.

In England he met the leading figures of politics and culture. He continued to be a prolific writer, producing The American (1877), The Europeans (1878), a revision of Watch and Ward (1878), French Poets and Novelists (1878), Hawthorne (1879), and several shorter works of fiction. In 1878 Daisy Miller established his fame on both sides of the Atlantic. It drew notice perhaps mostly because it depicted a woman whose behavior is outside the social norms of Europe. He also began his first masterpiece, The Portrait of a Lady, which would appear in 1881.

In 1877 he first visited Wenlock Abbey in Shropshire, home of his friend Charles Milnes Gaskell whom he had met through Henry Adams. He was much inspired by the darkly romantic Abbey and the surrounding countryside, which features in his essay Abbeys and Castles. In particular the gloomy monastic fishponds behind the Abbey are said to have inspired the lake in The Turn of the Screw.

While living in London, James continued to follow the careers of the "French realists", Émile Zola in particular. Their stylistic methods influenced his own work in the years to come. Hawthorne's influence on him faded during this period, replaced by George Eliot and Ivan Turgenev. 1879–1882 saw the publication of The Europeans, Washington Square, Confidence, and The Portrait of a Lady. He visited America in 1882–1883, then returned to London.

The period from 1881 to 1883 was marked by several losses. His mother died in 1881, followed by his father a few months later, and then by his brother Wilkie. Emerson, an old family friend, died in 1882. His friend Turgenev died in 1883.

Middle years, 1884–1897

In 1884 James made another visit to Paris. There he met again with Zola, Daudet, and Goncourt. He had been following the careers of the French "realist" or "naturalist" writers, and was increasingly influenced by them. In 1886, he published The Bostonians and The Princess Casamassima, both influenced by the French writers he'd studied assiduously. Critical reaction and sales were poor. He wrote to Howells that the books had hurt his career rather than helped because they had "reduced the desire, and demand, for my productions to zero". During this time he became friends with Robert Louis Stevenson, John Singer Sargent, Edmund Gosse, George du Maurier, Paul Bourget, and Constance Fenimore Woolson. His third novel from the 1880s was The Tragic Muse. Although he was following the precepts of Zola in his novels of the '80s, their tone and attitude are closer to the fiction of Alphonse Daudet. The lack of critical and financial success for his novels during this period led him to try writing for the theatre. (His dramatic works and his experiences with theatre are discussed below.)

In the last quarter of 1889, he started translating "for pure and copious lucre" Port Tarascon, the third volume of Alphonse Daudet adventures of Tartarin de Tarascon. Serialized in Harper's Monthly Magazine from June 1890, this translation praised as "clever" by The Spectator was published in January 1891 by Sampson Low, Marston, Searle & Rivington.

After the stage failure of Guy Domville in 1895, James was near despair and thoughts of death plagued him. The years spent on dramatic works were not entirely a loss. As he moved into the last phase of his career he found ways to adapt dramatic techniques into the novel form.

In the late 1880s and throughout the 1890s James made several trips through Europe. He spent a long stay in Italy in 1887. In that year the short novel The Aspern Papers and The Reverberator were published.

Late years, 1898–1916

In 1897–1898 he moved to Rye, Sussex, and wrote The Turn of the Screw. 1899–1900 saw the publication of The Awkward Age and The Sacred

Fount. During 1902–1904 he wrote The Ambassadors, The Wings of the Dove, and The Golden Bowl.

In 1904 he revisited America and lectured on Balzac. In 1906–1910 he published The American Scene and edited the "New York Edition", a 24-volume collection of his works. In 1910 his brother William died; Henry had just joined William from an unsuccessful search for relief in Europe on what then turned out to be his (Henry's) last visit to the United States (from summer 1910 to July 1911), and was near him, according to a letter he wrote, when he died.

In 1913 he wrote his autobiographies, A Small Boy and Others, and Notes of a Son and Brother. After the outbreak of the First World War in 1914 he did war work. In 1915 he became a British subject and was awarded the Order of Merit the following year. He died on 28 February 1916, in Chelsea, London. As he requested, his ashes were buried in Cambridge Cemetery in Massachusetts.

Biographers

James regularly rejected suggestions that he should marry, and after settling in London proclaimed himself "a bachelor". F. W. Dupee, in several volumes on the James family, originated the theory that he had been in love with his cousin Mary ("Minnie") Temple, but that a neurotic fear of sex kept him from admitting such affections: "James's invalidism ... was itself the symptom of some fear of or scruple against sexual love on his part." Dupee used an episode from James's memoir A Small Boy and Others, recounting a dream of a Napoleonic image in the Louvre, to exemplify James's romanticism about Europe, a Napoleonic fantasy into which he fled.

Dupee had not had access to the James family papers and worked principally from James's published memoir of his older brother, William, and the limited collection of letters edited by Percy Lubbock, heavily weighted toward James's last years. His account therefore moved directly from James's childhood, when he trailed after his older brother, to elderly invalidism. As more material became available to scholars, including the diaries of contemporaries and hundreds of affectionate and sometimes erotic letters written by James to younger men, the picture of neurotic celibacy gave way to a portrait of a closeted homosexual.

Between 1953 and 1972, Leon Edel authored a major five-volume biography of James, which accessed unpublished letters and documents after Edel gained the permission of James's family. Edel's portrayal of James included the suggestion he was celibate. It was a view first propounded by critic Saul Rosenzweig in 1943. In 1996 Sheldon M. Novick published Henry James: The Young Master, followed by Henry James: The Mature Master (2007). The first book "caused something of an uproar in Jamesian circles" as it challenged the previous received notion of celibacy, a once-familiar paradigm in biographies of homosexuals when direct evidence was non-existent. Novick also criticised Edel for following the discounted Freudian interpretation of homosexuality "as a kind of failure." The difference of opinion erupted in a series of exchanges between Edel and Novick which were published by the online magazine Slate, with the latter arguing that even the suggestion of celibacy went against James's own injunction "live!"—not "fantasize!"

A letter James wrote in old age to Hugh Walpole has been cited as an explicit statement of this. Walpole confessed to him of indulging in "high jinks", and James wrote a reply endorsing it: "We must know, as much as possible, in our beautiful art, yours & mine, what we are talking about — & the only way to know it is to have lived & loved & cursed & floundered & enjoyed & suffered — I don't think I regret a single 'excess' of my responsive youth".

The interpretation of James as living a less austere emotional life has been subsequently explored by other scholars. The often intense politics of Jamesian scholarship has also been the subject of studies. Author Colm Tóibín has said that Eve Kosofsky Sedgwick's Epistemology of the Closet made a landmark difference to Jamesian scholarship by arguing that he be read as a homosexual writer whose desire to keep his sexuality a secret shaped his layered style and dramatic artistry. According to Tóibín such a reading "removed James from the realm of dead white males who wrote about posh people. He became our contemporary."

James's letters to expatriate American sculptor Hendrik Christian Andersen have attracted particular attention. James met the 27-year-old Andersen in Rome in 1899, when James was 56, and wrote letters to Andersen that are intensely emotional: "I hold you, dearest boy, in my innermost love, & count on your feeling me—in every throb of your soul". In a letter of 6 May 1904, to his brother William, James referred to himself as "always your hopelessly celibate even though sexagenarian Henry". How accurate that description might have been is the subject of contention among James's biographers,   but the letters to Andersen were occasionally quasi-erotic: "I put, my dear boy, my arm around you, & feel the pulsation, thereby, as it were, of our excellent future & your admirable endowment." To his homosexual friend Howard Sturgis, James could write: "I repeat, almost to indiscretion, that I could live with you. Meanwhile I can only try to live without you."

His numerous letters to the many young gay men among his close male friends are more forthcoming. In a letter to Howard Sturgis, following a long visit, James refers jocularly to their "happy little congress of two" and in letters to Hugh Walpole he pursues convoluted jokes and puns about their relationship, referring to himself as an elephant who "paws you oh so benevolently" and winds about Walpole his "well meaning old trunk". His letters to Walter Berry printed by the Black Sun Press have long been celebrated for their lightly veiled eroticism.

He corresponded in almost equally extravagant language with his many female friends, writing, for example, to fellow novelist Lucy Clifford: "Dearest Lucy! What shall I say? when I love you so very, very much, and see you nine times for once that I see Others! Therefore I think that—if you want it made clear to the meanest intelligence—I love you more than I love Others." To his New York friend Mary Cadwalader Jones: "Dearest Mary Cadwalader. I yearn over you, but I yearn in vain; & your long silence really breaks my heart, mystifies, depresses, almost alarms me, to the point even of making me wonder if poor unconscious & doting old Célimare [Jones's pet name for James] has 'done' anything, in some dark somnambulism of the spirit, which has ... given you a bad moment, or a wrong impression, or a 'colourable pretext' ... However these things may be, he loves you as tenderly as ever;

nothing, to the end of time, will ever detach him from you, & he remembers those Eleventh St. matutinal intimes hours, those telephonic matinées, as the most romantic of his life ..." His long friendship with American novelist Constance Fenimore Woolson, in whose house he lived for a number of weeks in Italy in 1887, and his shock and grief over her suicide in 1894, are discussed in detail in Edel's biography and play a central role in a study by Lyndall Gordon. (Edel conjectured that Woolson was in love with James and killed herself in part because of his coldness, but Woolson's biographers have objected to Edel's account.)

Works

Style and themes

James is one of the major figures of trans-Atlantic literature. His works frequently juxtapose characters from the Old World (Europe), embodying a feudal civilisation that is beautiful, often corrupt, and alluring, and from the New World (United States), where people are often brash, open, and assertive and embody the virtues—freedom and a more highly evolved moral character—of the new American society. James explores this clash of personalities and cultures, in stories of personal relationships in which power is exercised well or badly. His protagonists were often young American women facing oppression or abuse, and as his secretary Theodora Bosanquet remarked in her monograph Henry James at Work:

> When he walked out of the refuge of his study and into the world and looked around him, he saw a place of torment, where creatures of prey perpetually thrust their claws into the quivering flesh of doomed, defenseless children of light ... His novels are a repeated exposure of this wickedness, a reiterated and passionate plea for the fullest freedom of development, unimperiled by reckless and barbarous stupidity.

Critics have jokingly described three phases in the development of James's prose: "James I, James II, and The Old Pretender." He wrote short stories and plays. Finally, in his third and last period he returned to the long, serialised novel. Beginning in the second period, but most noticeably in the third, he increasingly abandoned direct statement in favour of frequent double negatives, and complex descriptive imagery. Single paragraphs began to run for page after page, in which an initial noun would be succeeded by pronouns surrounded by clouds of adjectives and prepositional clauses, far from their original referents, and verbs would be deferred and then preceded by a series of adverbs. The overall effect could be a vivid evocation of a scene as perceived by a sensitive observer. It has been debated whether this change of style was engendered by James's shifting from writing to dictating to a typist, a change made during the composition of What Maisie Knew.

In its intense focus on the consciousness of his major characters, James's later work foreshadows extensive developments in 20th century fiction. Indeed, he might have influenced stream-of-consciousness writers such as Virginia Woolf, who not only read some of his novels but also wrote essays about them. Both contemporary and modern readers have found the late style difficult and unnecessary; his friend Edith Wharton, who admired him greatly, said that there were passages in his work that were all but incomprehensible. James was harshly portrayed by H. G. Wells as a hippopotamus laboriously attempting to pick up a pea that had got into a corner of its cage. The "late James" style was ably parodied by Max Beerbohm in "The Mote in the Middle Distance".

More important for his work overall may have been his position as an expatriate, and in other ways an outsider, living in Europe. While he came from middle-class and provincial beginnings (seen from the perspective of European polite society) he worked very hard to gain access to all levels of society, and the settings of his fiction range from working class to aristocratic, and often describe the efforts of middle-class Americans to make their way in European capitals. He confessed he got some of his best story ideas from gossip at the dinner table or at country house weekends. He worked for a living, however, and lacked the experiences of select schools, university, and army service, the common bonds of masculine society. He was furthermore a man whose tastes and interests were, according to the prevailing standards of Victorian era Anglo-American culture, rather feminine, and who was shadowed by the cloud of prejudice that then and later accompanied suspicions of his homosexuality. Edmund Wilson famously compared James's objectivity to Shakespeare's:

One would be in a position to appreciate James better if one compared him with the dramatists of the seventeenth century—Racine and Molière, whom he resembles in form as well as in point of view, and even Shakespeare, when allowances are made for the most extreme differences in subject and form. These poets are not, like Dickens and Hardy, writers of melodrama—either humorous or pessimistic, nor secretaries of society like Balzac, nor prophets like Tolstoy: they are occupied simply with the presentation of conflicts of moral character, which they do not concern themselves about softening or averting. They do not indict society for these situations: they regard them as universal and inevitable. They do not even blame God for allowing them: they accept them as the conditions of life.

It is also possible to see many of James's stories as psychological thought-experiments. In his preface to the New York edition of The American he describes the development of the story in his mind as exactly such: the "situation" of an American, "some robust but insidiously beguiled and betrayed, some cruelly wronged, compatriot..." with the focus of the story being on the response of this wronged man. The Portrait of a Lady may be an experiment to see what happens when an idealistic young woman suddenly becomes very rich. In many of his tales, characters seem to exemplify alternative futures and possibilities, as most markedly in "The Jolly Corner", in which the protagonist and a ghost-doppelganger live alternative American and European lives; and in others, like The Ambassadors, an older James seems fondly to regard his own younger self facing a crucial moment.

Major novels

The first period of James's fiction, usually considered to have culminated in The Portrait of a Lady, concentrated on the contrast between Europe and America. The style of these novels is generally straightforward and, though personally characteristic, well within the norms of 19th-century fiction. Roderick Hudson (1875) is a Künstlerroman that traces the development of the title character, an extremely talented sculptor. Although the book shows some signs of immaturity—this was James's first serious attempt at

731

a full-length novel—it has attracted favourable comment due to the vivid realisation of the three major characters: Roderick Hudson, superbly gifted but unstable and unreliable; Rowland Mallet, Roderick's limited but much more mature friend and patron; and Christina Light, one of James's most enchanting and maddening femmes fatales. The pair of Hudson and Mallet has been seen as representing the two sides of James's own nature: the wildly imaginative artist and the brooding conscientious mentor.

In The Portrait of a Lady (1881) James concluded the first phase of his career with a novel that remains his most popular piece of long fiction. The story is of a spirited young American woman, Isabel Archer, who "affronts her destiny" and finds it overwhelming. She inherits a large amount of money and subsequently becomes the victim of Machiavellian scheming by two American expatriates. The narrative is set mainly in Europe, especially in England and Italy. Generally regarded as the masterpiece of his early phase, The Portrait of a Lady is described as a psychological novel, exploring the minds of his characters, and almost a work of social science, exploring the differences between Europeans and Americans, the old and the new worlds.

The second period of James's career, which extends from the publication of The Portrait of a Lady through the end of the nineteenth century, features less popular novels including The Princess Casamassima, published serially in The Atlantic Monthly in 1885–1886, and The Bostonians, published serially in The Century Magazine during the same period. This period also featured James's celebrated Gothic novella, The Turn of the Screw.

The third period of James's career reached its most significant achievement in three novels published just around the start of the 20th century: The Wings of the Dove (1902), The Ambassadors (1903), and The Golden Bowl (1904). Critic F. O. Matthiessen called this "trilogy" James's major phase, and these novels have certainly received intense critical study. It was the second-written of the books, The Wings of the Dove (1902) that was the first published because it attracted no serialization. This novel tells the story of Milly Theale, an American heiress stricken with a serious disease, and her impact on the people around her. Some of these people befriend Milly with honourable motives, while others are more self-interested. James stated in his autobiographical books that Milly was based on Minny Temple, his beloved cousin who died at an early age of tuberculosis. He said that he attempted in the novel to wrap her memory in the "beauty and dignity of art".

Shorter narratives

James was particularly interested in what he called the "beautiful and blest nouvelle", or the longer form of short narrative. Still, he produced a number of very short stories in which he achieved notable compression of sometimes complex subjects. The following narratives are representative of James's achievement in the shorter forms of fiction.

- "A Tragedy of Error" (1864), short story
- "The Story of a Year" (1865), short story
- A Passionate Pilgrim (1871), novella
- Madame de Mauves (1874), novella
- Daisy Miller (1878), novella
- The Aspern Papers (1888), novella
- The Lesson of the Master (1888), novella
- The Pupil (1891), short story
- "The Figure in the Carpet" (1896), short story
- The Beast in the Jungle (1903), novella
- An International Episode (1878)
- Picture and Text
- Four Meetings (1885)
- A London Life, and Other Tales (1889)
- The Spoils of Poynton (1896)

- Embarrassments (1896)

- The Two Magics: The Turn of the Screw, Covering End (1898)

- A Little Tour of France (1900)

- The Sacred Fount (1901)

- Views and Reviews (1908)

- The Wings of the Dove, Volume I (1902)

- The Wings of the Dove, Volume II (1909)

- The Finer Grain (1910)

- The Outcry (1911)

- Lady Barbarina: The Siege of London, An International Episode and Other Tales (1922)

- The Birthplace (1922)

Plays

At several points in his career James wrote plays, beginning with one-act plays written for periodicals in 1869 and 1871 and a dramatisation of his popular novella Daisy Miller in 1882. From 1890 to 1892, having received a bequest that freed him from magazine publication, he made a strenuous effort to succeed on the London stage, writing a half-dozen plays of which only one, a dramatisation of his novel The American, was produced. This play was performed for several years by a touring repertory company and had a respectable run in London, but did not earn very much money for James. His other plays written at this time were not produced.

In 1893, however, he responded to a request from actor-manager George Alexander for a serious play for the opening of his renovated St. James's Theatre, and wrote a long drama, Guy Domville, which Alexander produced. There was a noisy uproar on the opening night, 5 January 1895, with hissing from the gallery when James took his bow after the final curtain, and the author was upset. The play received moderately good reviews and had a modest run of four weeks before being taken off to make way for Oscar Wilde's The Importance of Being Earnest, which Alexander thought would have better prospects for the coming season.

After the stresses and disappointment of these efforts James insisted that he would write no more for the theatre, but within weeks had agreed to write a curtain-raiser for Ellen Terry. This became the one-act "Summersoft", which he later rewrote into a short story, "Covering End", and then expanded into a full-length play, The High Bid, which had a brief run in London in 1907, when James made another concerted effort to write for the stage. He wrote three new plays, two of which were in production when the death of Edward VII on 6 May 1910 plunged London into mourning and theatres closed. Discouraged by failing health and the stresses of theatrical work, James did not renew his efforts in the theatre, but recycled his plays as successful novels. The Outcry was a best-seller in the United States when it was published in 1911. During the years 1890–1893 when he was most engaged with the theatre, James wrote a good deal of theatrical criticism and assisted Elizabeth Robins and others in translating and producing Henrik Ibsen for the first time in London.

Leon Edel argued in his psychoanalytic biography that James was traumatised by the opening night uproar that greeted Guy Domville, and that it plunged him into a prolonged depression. The successful later novels, in Edel's view, were the result of a kind of self-analysis, expressed in fiction, which partly freed him from his fears. Other biographers and scholars have not accepted this account, however; the more common view being that of F.O. Matthiessen, who wrote: "Instead of being crushed by the collapse of his hopes [for the theatre]... he felt a resurgence of new energy."

Non-fiction

Beyond his fiction, James was one of the more important literary critics in the history of the novel. In his classic essay The Art of Fiction (1884), he argued against rigid prescriptions on the novelist's choice of subject and method of treatment. He maintained that the widest possible freedom in content and approach would help ensure narrative fiction's continued vitality.

James wrote many valuable critical articles on other novelists; typical is his book-length study of Nathaniel Hawthorne, which has been the subject of critical debate. Richard Brodhead has suggested that the study was emblematic of James's struggle with Hawthorne's influence, and constituted an effort to place the elder writer "at a disadvantage." Gordon Fraser, meanwhile, has suggested that the study was part of a more commercial effort by James to introduce himself to British readers as Hawthorne's natural successor.

When James assembled the New York Edition of his fiction in his final years, he wrote a series of prefaces that subjected his own work to searching, occasionally harsh criticism.

At 22 James wrote The Noble School of Fiction for The Nation's first issue in 1865. He would write, in all, over 200 essays and book, art, and theatre reviews for the magazine.

For most of his life James harboured ambitions for success as a playwright. He converted his novel The American into a play that enjoyed modest returns in the early 1890s. In all he wrote about a dozen plays, most of which went unproduced. His costume drama Guy Domville failed disastrously on its opening night in 1895. James then largely abandoned his efforts to conquer the stage and returned to his fiction. In his Notebooks he maintained that his theatrical experiment benefited his novels and tales by helping him dramatise his characters' thoughts and emotions. James produced a small but valuable amount of theatrical criticism, including perceptive appreciations of Henrik Ibsen.

With his wide-ranging artistic interests, James occasionally wrote on the visual arts. Perhaps his most valuable contribution was his favourable assessment of fellow expatriate John Singer Sargent, a painter whose critical status has improved markedly in recent decades. James also wrote sometimes charming, sometimes brooding articles about various places he visited and lived in. His most famous books of travel writing include Italian Hours (an example of the charming approach) and The American Scene (most definitely on the brooding side).

James was one of the great letter-writers of any era. More than ten thousand of his personal letters are extant, and over three thousand have been published in a large number of collections. A complete edition of James's letters began publication in 2006, edited by Pierre Walker and Greg Zacharias. As of 2014, eight volumes have been published, covering the period from 1855 to 1880. James's correspondents included celebrated contemporaries like Robert Louis Stevenson, Edith Wharton and Joseph Conrad, along with many others in his wide circle of friends and acquaintances. The letters range from the "mere twaddle of graciousness" to serious discussions of artistic, social and personal issues.

Very late in life James began a series of autobiographical works: A Small Boy and Others, Notes of a Son and Brother, and the unfinished The Middle Years. These books portray the development of a classic observer who was passionately interested in artistic creation but was somewhat reticent about participating fully in the life around him.

Reception

Criticism, biographies and fictional treatments

James's work has remained steadily popular with the limited audience of educated readers to whom he spoke during his lifetime, and has remained firmly in the canon, but, after his death, some American critics, such as Van Wyck Brooks, expressed hostility towards James for his long expatriation and eventual naturalisation as a British subject. Other critics such as E. M. Forster complained about what they saw as James's squeamishness in the treatment of sex and other possibly controversial material, or dismissed his late style as difficult and obscure, relying heavily on extremely long sentences and excessively latinate language. Similarly Oscar Wilde criticised him for writing "fiction as if it were a painful duty". Vernon Parrington, composing a canon of American literature, condemned James for having cut himself off from America. Jorge Luis Borges wrote about him, "Despite the scruples and delicate complexities of James, his work suffers from a major defect: the absence of life." And Virginia Woolf, writing to Lytton Strachey, asked, "Please tell me what you find in Henry James. ... we have his works here, and

I read, and I can't find anything but faintly tinged rose water, urbane and sleek, but vulgar and pale as Walter Lamb. Is there really any sense in it?" The novelist W. Somerset Maugham wrote, "He did not know the English as an Englishman instinctively knows them and so his English characters never to my mind quite ring true," and argued "The great novelists, even in seclusion, have lived life passionately. Henry James was content to observe it from a window." Maugham nevertheless wrote, "The fact remains that those last novels of his, notwithstanding their unreality, make all other novels, except the very best, unreadable." Colm Tóibín observed that James "never really wrote about the English very well. His English characters don't work for me."

Despite these criticisms, James is now valued for his psychological and moral realism, his masterful creation of character, his low-key but playful humour, and his assured command of the language. In his 1983 book, The Novels of Henry James, Edward Wagenknecht offers an assessment that echoes Theodora Bosanquet's:

> "To be completely great," Henry James wrote in an early review, "a work of art must lift up the heart," and his own novels do this to an outstanding degree ... More than sixty years after his death, the great novelist who sometimes professed to have no opinions stands foursquare in the great Christian humanistic and democratic tradition. The men and women who, at the height of World War II, raided the secondhand shops for his out-of-print books knew what they were about. For no writer ever raised a braver banner to which all who love freedom might adhere.

William Dean Howells saw James as a representative of a new realist school of literary art which broke with the English romantic tradition epitomised by the works of Charles Dickens and William Makepeace Thackeray. Howells wrote that realism found "its chief exemplar in Mr. James... A novelist he is not, after the old fashion, or after any fashion but his own." F.R. Leavis championed Henry James as a novelist of "established pre-eminence" in The Great Tradition (1948), asserting that The Portrait of a Lady and The Bostonians were "the two most brilliant novels in the language." James is now prized as a master of point of view who moved literary fiction forward by insisting in showing, not telling, his stories to the reader. (Source: Wikipedia)

NOTABLE WORKS

NOVELS

Watch and Ward (1871)

Roderick Hudson (1875)

The American (1877)

The Europeans (1878)

Confidence (1879)

Washington Square (1880)

The Portrait of a Lady (1881)

The Bostonians (1886)

The Princess Casamassima (1886)

The Reverberator (1888)

The Tragic Muse (1890)

The Other House (1896)

The Spoils of Poynton (1897)

What Maisie Knew (1897)

The Awkward Age (1899)

The Sacred Fount (1901)

The Wings of the Dove (1902)

The Ambassadors (1903)

The Golden Bowl (1904)

The Whole Family (collaborative novel with eleven other authors, 1908)

The Outcry (1911)

The Ivory Tower (unfinished, published posthumously 1917)

The Sense of the Past (unfinished, published posthumously 1917)

SHORT STORIES AND NOVELLAS

A Tragedy of Error (1864)

The Story of a Year (1865)

A Landscape Painter (1866)

A Day of Days (1866)

My Friend Bingham (1867)

Poor Richard (1867)

The Story of a Masterpiece (1868)

A Most Extraordinary Case (1868)

A Problem (1868)

De Grey: A Romance (1868)

Osborne's Revenge (1868)

The Romance of Certain Old Clothes (1868)

A Light Man (1869)

Gabrielle de Bergerac (1869)

Travelling Companions (1870)

A Passionate Pilgrim (1871)

At Isella (1871)

Master Eustace (1871)

Guest's Confession (1872)

The Madonna of the Future (1873)

The Sweetheart of M. Briseux (1873)

The Last of the Valerii (1874)

Madame de Mauves (1874)

Adina (1874)

Professor Fargo (1874)

Eugene Pickering (1874)

Benvolio (1875)

Crawford's Consistency (1876)

The Ghostly Rental (1876)

Four Meetings (1877)

Rose-Agathe (1878, as Théodolinde)

Daisy Miller (1878)

Longstaff's Marriage (1878)

An International Episode (1878)

The Pension Beaurepas (1879)

A Diary of a Man of Fifty (1879)

A Bundle of Letters (1879)

The Point of View (1882)

The Siege of London (1883)

Impressions of a Cousin (1883)

Lady Barberina (1884)

Pandora (1884)

The Author of Beltraffio (1884)

Georgina's Reasons (1884)

A New England Winter (1884)

The Path of Duty (1884)

Mrs. Temperly (1887)

Louisa Pallant (1888)

The Aspern Papers (1888)

The Liar (1888)

The Modern Warning (1888, originally published as The Two Countries)

A London Life (1888)

The Patagonia (1888)

The Lesson of the Master (1888)

The Solution (1888)

The Pupil (1891)

Brooksmith (1891)

The Marriages (1891)

The Chaperon (1891)

Sir Edmund Orme (1891)

Nona Vincent (1892)

The Real Thing (1892)

The Private Life (1892)

Lord Beaupré (1892)

The Visits (1892)

Sir Dominick Ferrand (1892)

Greville Fane (1892)

Collaboration (1892)

Owen Wingrave (1892)

The Wheel of Time (1892)

The Middle Years (1893)

The Death of the Lion (1894)

The Coxon Fund (1894)

The Next Time (1895)

Glasses (1896)

The Altar of the Dead (1895)

The Figure in the Carpet (1896)

The Way It Came (1896, also published as The Friends of the Friends)

The Turn of the Screw (1898)

Covering End (1898)

In the Cage (1898)

John Delavoy (1898)

The Given Case (1898)

Europe (1899)

The Great Condition (1899)

The Real Right Thing (1899)

Paste (1899)

The Great Good Place (1900)

Maud-Evelyn (1900)

Miss Gunton of Poughkeepsie (1900)

The Tree of Knowledge (1900)

The Abasement of the Northmores (1900)

The Third Person (1900)

The Special Type (1900)

The Tone of Time (1900)

Broken Wings (1900)

The Two Faces (1900)

Mrs. Medwin (1901)

The Beldonald Holbein (1901)

The Story in It (1902)

Flickerbridge (1902)

The Birthplace (1903)

The Beast in the Jungle (1903)

The Papers (1903)

Fordham Castle (1904)

Julia Bride (1908)

The Jolly Corner (1908)

The Velvet Glove (1909)

Mora Montravers (1909)

Crapy Cornelia (1909)

The Bench of Desolation (1909)

A Round of Visits (1910)

OTHER

Transatlantic Sketches (1875)

French Poets and Novelists (1878)

Hawthorne (1879)

Portraits of Places (1883)

A Little Tour in France (1884)

Partial Portraits (1888)

Essays in London and Elsewhere (1893)

Picture and Text (1893)

Terminations (1893)

Theatricals (1894)

Theatricals: Second Series (1895)

Guy Domville (1895)

The Soft Side (1900)

William Wetmore Story and His Friends (1903)

The Better Sort (1903)

English Hours (1905)

The Question of our Speech; The Lesson of Balzac. Two Lectures (1905)

The American Scene (1907)

Views and Reviews (1908)

Italian Hours (1909)

A Small Boy and Others (1913)

Notes on Novelists (1914)

Notes of a Son and Brother (1914)

Within the Rim (1918)

Travelling Companions (1919)

Notebooks (various, published posthumously)

The Middle Years (unfinished, published posthumously 1917)

A Most Unholy Trade (1925, published posthumously)

The Art of the Novel : Critical Prefaces (1934)